HOUSE OF
DARAKAI
THE HAIDREN LEGACY

HOUSE OF
DARAKAI
THE HAIDREN LEGACY

K.L. KOLARICH

ROGUE KITE
PUBLISHING

ISBN: 978-1-7354606-3-5 (eBook)
ISBN: 978-1-7354606-5-9 (Paperback)
ISBN: 978-1-7354606-4-2 (Hardcover)

Cover Art & Design: Fiona Jayde Media
Interior Book Design: Brent Spears

Printed by Rogue Kite Publishing, in the United States of America.

First printing edition 2021.

www.TheHaidrenLegacy.com

For Rory,
who believed in what only I could see.

Loyalty is forged not at the edge of a blade, but at its hilt.

And the seed of betrayal, within the heart of the one who wields it.

-Fallen Chief Warlord, Storm Age

SCAN ME

- Allöh'jomn'yeh -

Equip your journey out of the known and into the Other by enlisting
the regional glossary, hosted both online and after the epilogue.

For a more immersive reading experience, explore
the world of Orynthia outside the pages at
www.TheHaidrenLegacy.com
for instant access to a treasury of THL resources.

- Tredae'Aurynth -

PROLOGUE

The night was silent, deceptive and unassuming. Stooped on the banister of the narrow terrace, the figure strained his nostrils, splitting his newest scabs as he inhaled the purity of the heights.

A tremor rolled through his legs when he soundlessly slid off the stone, his gaze fixed on the telling crack between nearly closed doors where Alora waited on the other side. The figure held his breath, slipping his slender form between the glass panes and into the royal library, as if his unpolluted gulp might replace the shame coating his emaciated lungs. But his ebbing humanity knew better, hissing the truth like acid into his heart. Nothing could make him worthy of her closeness, not ever again.

He'd been unsurprised when her message had named this place, as none in Bastiion bothered with dusty books anymore. There wasn't a need for such devices when both court and courtesan squandered their age of peace on trivial diversion. His Alora, however, had always liked the quiet, the spaces unoccupied and since forgotten. It was a mutual preference, one that brought them together in sanctuaries such as this, long before he had committed the unfathomable and shattered her quietude forever.

And yet it was in the chaos of his transgression when Alora had become for him the very thing he'd stolen from her.

From behind the doors, the figure tugged at the hood of his battered cloak. He'd lost more hair in the three weeks that had passed, revealing another patch of irregular flesh surrounding his ear. Like the recent fingernail he'd shed, it would not return. Hiding his decay under the heavy fabric, the figure glided past the marble pillars, entering the cavern of shelves and disregarded literature.

He'd almost forgotten such smells, that incomparable musk of leather-bound knowledge and the sweetened tinge of aged lettering. With the thought, his cracked lips grinned, then sank. She'd chosen the library for him, a reminder of both the ghost she wished he could be and the man she'd lost.

At the center of a shelved dome, two winged-back chairs faced a double-sided fireplace, the crackling flames within it too inconsequential for the grandeur around it that reached toward the heavens. Like a flicker of starlight, an illuminated slice of platinum hair peaked over the chairback.

"Sit" was all she said when in the most graceful movement, her pale fingers gestured toward the accompanying seat.

An examination, he realized. Disclosing him in firelight, she was meaning to assess his rate of decline.

At his delay, a jingle emitted from her lap. Alora wordlessly set a velvet pouch on the small reading table between the two chairs. A vein in his neck leaped toward the set of vials, eager to taste her rescue. Swallowing the unwanted rush of saliva, the figure gingerly crept around the seating area. He swept the hem of his cloak and perched on the edge of the seat. Angling away from her, his gloved hand felt for the table and grabbed at the pouch.

A pressure fell upon his knuckles.

"It's impolite to ignore your host." Alora tut-tutted, patting his hand. "You'll have to face me if you are to accept my gift."

Gradually, the figure pivoted on his cushion and pointed his wiry knees at his mistress. When she removed her fingers, he hastily tucked the vials into his cloak, ashamed of his eagerness. He'd exhausted the last batch much too quickly. The ability to ration himself grew more difficult by the day.

"Tadöm, mistress," he murmured in gratitude. "I bring you news from Hagarh—"

"Pull back your hood," she stated, tersely interrupting.

The figure bent forward and abashedly drew back the material. The fire warmed the exposed areas of his scalp as she appraised the state of it. His ears, cursed by their enhancement, heard her suck in a breath. Staring into the flames, the figure continued his statement, aware her mind was flooding with new calculations for his remedy. Even for Boreal's most prominent healer, it was a futile endeavor.

"Tension at the border worsens," he reported, referring to his trek to the wetlands. "Pryde presence increases daily, but the Gulgons have started to respond more brashly. Demonstrations of their uprising were already brewing along the Mirajii Forest. However, a few weeks ago, something changed."

"How do you mean?" Alora inquired calmly.

From the corner of his eye, he saw her hands knit together. "Members of the Mirajii Pryde have begun to disappear. Whether kidnapped or murdered, I can't say. My Gulgou is not satisfactory enough to understand their motives either. There's a group wading through the northern marsh just past the border, but I only picked up fragments—none of it useful."

"Few learn to communicate effectively with the mudmen. You never had reason to." Alora traced the rim of her lip in consideration. "What is the pryde's reaction to their missing warriors?"

"A cloud of unease has settled over the men. Darakaians are super-stitious by nature, and losing their comrades doesn't bode well for their disposition. I expect their efforts to push the Gulgons out of the Mirajii and back into the wetlands, switching to the offensive—harsher, unbri-dled." The figure clenched his fingers to keep from scratching his neck in front of her, where it'd begun to peel. "But it isn't the pryde that should concern you mistress. It's Nyack."

He glowered at the sizzling logs and listened to Alora shift nervously on her chair. The figure was more than acquainted with her unease, for he shared it too.

"He has summoned Darakai's War Council. Not as commander of the Orynthian armies... but as their chief warlord."

"And the tribal chieftains, they attended his call?"

"All, mistress."

Alora stood abruptly and seized the ornate mantle in one hand. The other shielded her mouth. Her linsilk skirt, plain yet elegant, swished as she rotated toward the figure.

Tucking his chin, he tempted a glance. Alora pressed against molding and hotly shook her head as her voice lowered unforgivingly.

"He's taking advantage of Korbin's assassination. Luscia stated Dmitri suspects the Province of Agoston was involved in the poisoning. Dmitri's inexperience coupled with provincial unrest presents a perfect opportunity for someone so insatiable as Nyack Kasim. She always feared it, you know. I saw it, whenever she looked at her husband. Cyra knew what he was capable of, what he might do in his climb for power."

The figure remembered it too. The sudden black flood of Cyra's dilating pupils when he'd enter the room… Nyack's presence always snuffed out the brightness of her notoriously emboldened gaze. For a woman so revered by her own House, it had taken years before they'd understood the darkness lurking behind her expressions.

It was almost as if she had foreseen what would come to pass.

Had Korbin's Quadren been more united under his leadership, perhaps Cyra would have found confidence in Alora despite their opposition of House. Perhaps then, things would be different.

Another age for another lifetime, the figure chastised himself, keeping to the present.

"Why would Nyack push Orynthia to war with the Gulgons?" Surrendering to the itch, he rubbed the sore before she looked in his direction. Averting his eyes once more, he posed, "Hagarh's resources don't exceed our own. Even Korbin's son wouldn't agree to go to war without merit."

"There is an ocean of unknown about Nyack Kasim, one currently hosting a fleet of ships never recorded in Korbin's naval contract with Pilar. I doubt our new king knows of that either." Alora paced, her body intermittently blocking the light.

When she passed, the figure relaxed in the security of her shadow.

"How long did the chieftains stay in Faraji?"

"A single day. He went to great lengths to keep the council gathering discreet. Not one chieftain entered the fortress publicly. I made for Bastiion as soon as I saw Nyack depart Faraji, to attend the coming coronation... with an unnecessary number of warriors at his back."

Alora nodded repeatedly in his periphery and lifted her chin. "*Waedfrel.* He will return to the city after the Clann Darragh arrives. My scout relays Orien's party should be at the southern gate by sunset tomorrow. Nyack has never made Boreali entry a simple one."

"What will you have me do, mistress?"

"Trail behind the coronation tour. She will travel with the king while I transition to life as sil'haidren, exclusive to Boreal. Watch over Luscia. If your suspicions are correct about Nyack's plans, you may not be the only one doing so."

He spoke to the floor when her walking shade stalled in front of his tattered boots. "I am in your service, always."

And it was in that moment he recognized the pattern of the rug beneath them. After two decades, it was still the same.

With a rush of memories, the figure jerked on his hood, but at her touch, time suspended. Instantly his eyes welled, her warmth both cruel and damning. He sat immobilized on the plush cushion, a spasm going through his sunken chest. Embracing the anguish, he did not turn away. "The man you seek is gone."

After a troubled silence, Alora steadily lowered to her knees. Barely skimming his flesh with her fingertips, she leaned forward and skirted the fabric of his hood back, to cup his disfigured cheeks. His skin burned under the kiss of her fingertips. With the gentlest nudge, she angled his face into the firelight. Moisture scorched his senses at the familiarity of her posture. They'd lived this scene before.

When it had been him on his knees instead.

"Despite our likeness, I am able to see what you cannot. Or have you forgotten?"

He opened his eyes, and her Tiergan lineage shone in a luminescent kaleidoscope when she whispered his name, just inches away.

"I still see you." Alora's ancient eye sparkled. "I still see hope for redemption."

Clenching his jaw, he seized her gloved hands with his. He dragged them away, and his grasp shuddered uncontrollably. He was angry she'd brought him here. To this place.

The figure let go to return his hood where it belonged and butted his chair backward, separating them. Rising, he withdrew into the library's gloom and abandoned her kneeling on the rug, eager to erase the images of the night they'd spent together, intertwined upon it. As the picture of her bare body glimmered across his vision, the figure sprinted through the pillars, desperate to escape the wickedness that had come after that beautiful yet terrible, defining night.

Meeting the terrace, he stood between the doors and panted, though not for lack of air. Her vials hung burdensome inside the folds of his cloak.

"You may look for redemption," he declared within the lonely threshold, "but it does not wish to be found."

Climbing onto the banister, Amaranth soared over the dark expanse. At her call, the figure stepped off the ledge and into the welcomed emptiness, begging it to swallow him whole.

CHAPTER ONE
ZAETHAN

his was the last visit, Zaethan swore to the ceiling. The cracks in the plaster mocked his sentiments, as well as the arm slung over his chest. The fresh sheen of the night-caller's deep sienna-colored skin gleamed in the dwindling lamplight. He rotated his head on the pillow, careful not to disturb her well-earned slumber, and eyed the patinaed lantern. The oil was low. It'd been an eventful evening.

He ought to pay for that too.

Slithering out from under her embrace, Zaethan scooted off the mattress and ambled toward her dressing table, all but tripping over the garden of emptied glassware along the way. He cracked his naked spine, sorer than he'd like to admit, and balanced his hands on either side of the basin. Above it hung a small mirror, speckled with age. Zaethan barely recognized the man inside its blunt frame.

His bloodshot, wide-set eyes squinted back, their rims pinked from the long nights spent in the woman's clutches. Zaethan scratched his jaw, abrasive from days neglecting to shave. He would have to see to that before Dmitri's coronation later that afternoon. While his friend playacted readiness to wear Thoarne's crown, Zaethan felt its crushing weight each morning, like a boulder pressed against his ribcage. He scowled at the sunrise peeking through the gauzy curtains. Today was no different. With a palmful of lukewarm water, he splashed his face and glowered at the mirror. In a manner of weeks, Zaethan resembled the very yancies he so often abhorred.

"Shtàka," he grumbled, snagging the twin rings in his left brow on a dishtowel. He'd received the piercings the day before last, a doubly drunken decision, made inside an eager merchant's tent. He doubted the man's needle had been much cleaner than the towel Zaethan used to dab the punctures with now. After Salma, after forsaking his favorite *yaya* to the scorching sun of an unforgivable wasteland, he seemed to wake up daily only to discover he'd made one risky choice after another.

This was the last time, he reiterated and chucked the cloth into the cloudy water.

"Come back to bed, *Jaha.*"

He hated how much he welcomed Salma's nickname on the woman's lips. Most employed by The Veiled Lady had adopted it in their madam's absence—well, those of the more feminine disposition at least. Salma Nabhu's rumored treason collected dust in the corners of the well-known night den. Few here believed the infamous cross-caste had had any part in the assassination of a king. The only individuals who gave merit to her alleged crimes carried it in their pockets, pockets left emptied upon exiting the way they came.

Hitching into each pantleg, Zaethan glanced at the Darakaian woman sprawled across the lavish bed. Depths, she was beautiful. Dark and dangerous, her leg drew back and snaked over the thin sheet, nearly tempting him for another round. Instead, Zaethan latched his buckle and gruffly yanked on his shirt, emphasizing his decline.

"Kàchà kocho, Alpha Zà..." Her moistened lips simpered. "I'll see you tonight then, yeah?"

"Ano zà." Zaethan shook his head, resolved, and fastened his boots. "I won't return to warm your bed, Chenoa."

The night-caller chuckled smoothly. The sound was inviting and playful, like brooks flowing down the Andweles. "That's what you said two nights ago."

"For your family." Zaethan's fingertips sought the spare coin stuffed inside his leather breeches and smacked it onto her dressing table. "There's a ferry departing for Port Tadeas at sunset. Gather your siblings and build a better life with them, away from this bed."

Chenoa sat up against the band of cushions. The silky sheet barely veiled her bosom as she stared at the squat stack of dromas, no doubt counting it. Her eyes, like candied cacao, rounded and she twirled one of her curls in consideration. For a household of Southern breakaways, it was a decent amount—certainly enough to start over in Tadeas. "You won't return."

Zaethan smiled gently, stepping over the bottles and toward her bedside. "And neither should you, Chenoa," he said and pressed a kiss into her cheek, still flushed from the heat of his company. Moving to the door, he snatched his jacket off the back of a chair. "You did me a great service, more than you know." Twisting the knob, Zaethan pointed toward Owàa, rising in the skies outside the tavern. "You, my yaya, will never be forgotten."

Leaving her gawking, he quietly closed the door and entered the hallway. The distinct spice of byronia, one of their young king's cherished blossoms, flavored the air—their king who, ironically, would never dare enlist such services, nor imagine his childhood friend doing so. But there were many aspects of Zaethan's personal life he'd chosen to conceal from Dmitri, his newfound appreciation for a brothel just one of them.

Shared with Chenoa's sisters in the trade, the snug, dim corridor was lined with doorknobs, each a gateway to another fantasy. Gratefully, muffled moans from the bordering rooms were dulled as he neared the dense velvet tapestry, hung at the end of the hall. A division between the service menu and the peculiarities of their patrons. Zaethan welcomed the sleepy, drunken cheers from the other side, eager to reenter a more familiar world where the dirtiest deed was a lawless brawl or a fixed gamble.

When he was about to tow the heavy divider, an adjacent door creaked open and the floorboards drowned in a tide of yellow smoke as a nobleman stepped out, joining Zaethan in the hallway. Coughing, Zaethan tucked his face aside and fanned the air, feeling for the velvet in escape. A tackiness glazed his fingertips. Like a piss-fog, the acrid pipe marrow left an unpleasant film on everything it touched. Vapors disguised the yancy while he fumbled with the latch, and in what sounded like a confused shuffle, he somehow knocked Zaethan's face straight into the wall, earning him a clumsy throb through the bridge of his nose.

The wallpaper, he learned as he peeled away, was also tacky.

"Shtàka, my good fellow…"

Zaethan could've placed that annoyingly carefree lilt anywhere. As Dmitri's coronation neared, he'd been subjected to it daily. Smoke cleared and revealed a half-dressed haidren, scouting his feet from overtop his wadded bundle of fine clothing. "Whatever—" He hacked a puff of marrow. "Broke, consider it paid in full, courtesy of the Province of Wendylle."

Ira Hastings didn't trouble himself to look at Zaethan, who'd started to bleed, and searched for his pocketbook. A glossy robe dangled off his shoulder as he rummaged about in the low-wick candlelight. Zaethan grimaced at the flowery frock, uncertain if it belonged to Ira or his companion. Either was plausible, given Ira's preference for overpriced, flamboyant apparel. Shirtless, his lazy, untrained abdomen was on full display. It was a feat he had even managed to tie the front of his trousers, the lacing looking unpromisingly loose. Not waiting to find out, Zaethan angrily pushed off the film-coated wall as warmth dribbled from his bruised nostrils.

"Depths, Ira! Of all days!" Zaethan growled and skimmed the bone to assess the damage.

"Zaethan! When did you get here?"

"Thank the Fates it's not broken, or by Owàa, Ira, I'd have made that pretty face of yours look a lot worse."

"You know, that means a lot coming from you, Zaeth." Ira's brushed his own cheek, losing hold of his boot in the process. His weight shifted onto his shoed foot, haphazardly buckled at the ankle. "Who knew all it took was a neighboring romp to bring us together? We should coordinate visits. Next one is on me, my friend."

Ira's delicate features waggled at the room he'd exited. It was an unpalatable understanding, one Zaethan needed to strike from the record before word of his overnight stay reached the wrong ears, like those belonging to his father.

In his recent absence, Zaethan had taken advantage of his short-lived freedom. Though, were it for his betterment, that answer was best found at the bottom of his next shot of bwoloa. After Salma had been named in King Korbin's assassination, he'd left Bastiion for their fortress in Faraji, to consult with the tribes on the upcoming change in power. Having served on Korbin's Quadren for Zaethan's entire life, his father would not relinquish haidrenship that easily, Zaethan knew, but even Darakai's chief warlord could not thwart centuries of Orynthian tradition. As the regency passed to Korbin's heir, so Darakai's haidrenship passed to Zaethan. His titles threefold, Zaethan's father was still commander of the Orynthian armies—as long as the new king permitted—thus his control of the Unitarian forces remained intact. In the end, Nyack Kasim would be forced to surrender his seat at that pentagonal table to his son, however much it spurned him relinquish it.

Nyack Kasim's homecoming to the crown city had been delayed, for causes not communicated to his successor, and the first news to meet his ears should not be the way Zaethan had been spending his evenings. It was yet another reason to retire his fleeting patronage to The Veiled Lady.

Clutching the curtain, Zaethan scrutinized Bastiion's haidren when he scooped up his runaway boot and sardonically replied, "Not everything is as you imagine, Ira." He scanned the tavern through the opening, assessing its occupants. Being waking hours, the barstools were lightly littered, one man even snoring in his own drool. Scattered around the perimeter, bleary-eyed gamblers held their position at the playing tables, unwilling to give up on their wagers. "I merely drop in on Salma's girls sometimes, given their new management."

Ira's snicker came with a stale puff behind Zaethan's ear. "I also like to *drop in*, on occasion—"

Reaching back, Zaethan reeled the haidren into the main bar with a grunt. Ira hobbled on his uneven footwear, colliding with the chairs in passing. Wood clattered to the floor unceremoniously, garnering a few wayward glances from the couple of merchants entering the establishment, no doubt seeking refuge after their night of barters amid the bustling streets of Marketown. Even in the blackened hours, Àla*maia* reigned the skies. Bastiion's inhabitants flocked to the crowded booths, each packed with artisan goods from the farthest reaches of the realm. A warm glow trailed the merchants in the framing—Pilarese, by the crisscross manner their headscarves were fastened. Unsure of the time, Zaethan hastened his steps toward the door as he imagined the shadow of a teller's dial inching closer and closer to noon.

"Pick up the pace," Zaethan barked at Ira when he halted and fitfully patted his legs.

Flustered, Ira stooped to his knees. His ringed courtier fingers explored the baseboards, no doubt caked in grime from months of traffic. "Not today! Not today! Not—" Ira's head abruptly popped out from under the tabletop, and he glanced up at Zaethan, gulping. "Today."

His glassy, citrine eyes stretched with panic as his hands raked through his mussed hair and cupped the base of his neck. Then, with a relieved sigh, Ira patted the copper chain descending his chest and captured the cylindrical snuff canister hanging there. "Close call, that one!"

The yancy kissed the thing.

Zaethan snatched the other haidren's floral robe, thoroughly exasperated, and hauled Ira to his feet. "Can't go just one day without it,

Lord Bastiion?" He sarcastically enlisted Ira's Quadrennal address and navigated them around the empty chairs.

"We ought to keep the things most dear closest to the heart, Zaeth," Ira sputtered as he was dragged down the line of stools.

Zaethan slapped two crupas atop the bar. "Pour for the boss," he ordered the barkeep and jerked his chin toward the balcony. "On me."

Atop the landing, an imposing Darakaian cross-caste towered over the railing, coolly monitoring the activity from his late mistress's favored post. To Zaethan's knowledge, Ràoko hadn't learned of his or Kumo's involvement in Salma's sentencing to The Wastes. Courtly gossip assured it was only a matter of time. That in mind, it'd quickly become Zaethan's practice to buy management a drink upon his departure, hoping to win the man over before he did.

Dropping his regard, as no Southerner liked to be stared at for long, Zaethan pulled his attention to a flicker near the night-caller curtain, where a mirrored row of secreted pleasures awaited on the other side of the staircase. Following a raven-haired night-caller, a warrior ducked under the velvet as the tips of his witchiron blades hoisted the hem of the emerald cloak meant to disguise him. As he slinked after her into the dark, the cowl fell off his short golden plait, betraying him before the fabric swung closed.

Zaethan snickered dryly and angled Ira toward the door, wondering if the haughty haidren to Boreal knew of her shadowman's whereabouts. Apart from their mandated meetings in Quadrennal chambers, he'd given the highlander witch a wide berth in the wake of their last bargain and the spiraling aftermath that had accompanied it. As they prepared for Dmitri's formal ascent to the Orynthian throne, neither haidren seemed keen to discuss their deadly encounter with war-taint or the deceased lord who'd been its murderous host. Regardless, whichever of her Boreali twins graced the backrooms of The Veiled Lady the very morning of her ceremonial appointment to the Quadren, Zaethan doubted the Northern haidren would find the shadowman's celebration fitting.

Zaethan smirked to himself. The slap to the face of her piety made it delightfully fitting indeed.

Stepping off the tavern stoop, he released Ira into the busy street. "You better wash before I see you on that dais, Ira," Zaethan warned through terse lips. Mingled with the permeating odors from butcher row, Ira seemed to have ripened in a matter of minutes.

"Your wish, my command, Lord Darakai." Ira threw up his palms in mock surrender before a hurried washwoman, rather generous in figure, scuttled by and bounced the yancy into the crowded throng.

Zaethan shook out his arms, awakening to the day, and commenced down the street. Pausing at a fruit stand, he purchased a few apples with a bread loaf, excavating his breeches for the last of his coin. Another block over, he'd pass an alley teaming with underfed dirt-faced cubs, their parents either too poor, too unbothered, or too dead to feed them. Zaethan dropped his final crupas into the baker's coinbox and tied the makeshift meal inside a rag.

Leaving, he jumped when his beta appeared at his side.

"You still doing that, Ahoté?" Peering down, Kumo rubbed the overgrowth on his blocky chin as he laughed at his cousin—and alpha. "Rough night, yeah?" He wiggled his nose, eyeing Zaethan's, when Zaethan glared and gruffly sniffed back blood.

"Not as rough as that carpet you call a beard."

Kumo fluffed the bushy hairs he'd been stubbornly sporting. "Eh, those gutter rats always knew how to weasel into your wallet. *So hungry,*

Alpha Zà," he mocked and rubbed the broad belly of his belted tunic while they walked along.

"I'm hungry too, Alpha Zà." Takoda suddenly flanked them, swiping an apple from Zaethan's sack. "Need my strength. Recovering from this kakka-shtàka clawing takes a toll, ano? All I want to do is nap, but you won't let me."

Takoda broke into a cheeky grin and took a generous bite of the fruit, gesturing toward the healing gouge in his side, courtesy of the late Lord Ambrose. Zaethan had decided to not share details of the lord's demise with his pryde. Slaying a noble, even one war-tainted, was precarious enough. There was no need to endanger his men before the Ethnicam, should the Peerage of Nobility find out that Felix Ambrose had *not* fled Agoston, as Dmitri theorized, but in reality had been put down for his heinous crimes against Boreal's cross-caste children.

"Following me now, cousin?" Zaethan questioned tersely, evading Takoda's second jab at the food. "At least Zahra would have had the sense to be subtle about it."

"No need. You, uh, been a little predictable lately, ano?" Sheepishly, Kumo knocked his thumb backward, toward The Veiled Lady. "Wouldn't have rushed to interrupt either, but it couldn't wait." His beta's tone lowered as he sidestepped an overturned barrel. "The commander arrived at sunrise, just in time for the coronation."

Grinding his teeth, Zaethan asked the real question. "Wekesa?"

"Wasn't with him," Takoda happily answered, tossing the apple core.

"Dhalili reports the Valley Pryde returned to Fahime, yeah, but she hasn't spotted Wekesa among his warriors." Kumo continued, bending closer to Zaethan's ear. "Says he left his beta in charge."

Wekesa had openly departed Bastiion with his father's party to Faraji. If he hadn't returned to the Valley of Fahime with his pryde, then he was either based in their capital fortress or on special assignment. Neither scenario would benefit Zaethan or the militia, surely a move to further elevate his rival's prospects. In the past year, his father's favoritism was being displayed more publicly before the tribes. And now, allowing Wekesa to move about, independent of his pryde, spoke volumes to the men. Wekesa operated as if he were above pryde law and, ultimately, the law of their communal alpha zà.

"Assign Dhalili to track down his location. If Wekesa's in Faraji, I want to know why. Yeye qondai?"

"Uni zà, Alpha Zà," they uttered in unison, each man thumping the compass of his fist against his chest.

Crossing the mouth of the alley, Zaethan untied the cloth and ushered his men into the jungle of crude hammocks and stacked pallet bedding. Dirtied little cheeks could be seen around the corners of their discarded kingdom when the three Darakaians entered off the street. Kneeling, Zaethan ripped the loaf apart, nudging Takoda to go distribute the pieces.

"Eh, before I forget—the other reason I came." Kumo grabbed Zaethan's hand and pressed something cool into his palm. "She'd be proud to see you up there, Ahoté."

Seated in the mahogany creases of his fist was a handful of stout, gilded beads, engraved in Andwele runes.

"My mhàdda sent them from Holona, yeah?" Kumo pointed at the metal adornment. "Saved all these years, for this day. She says Cyra wore them to Korbin's coronation."

Guilt constricted Zaethan's throat for the bloodshot mess his mother would see claim Darakai's chair, were she alive to witness his Seating. When he and Kumo had been cubs, his aunt, Léola, would recite for him the story of the fearsome Cyra Shà. His father hated that story, how she'd braved the acid hail of the Zôueli tropics during the Shield Wars to rescue an ambitious Darakaian officer in the king's army from an enemy camp—her future husband, Nyack Kasim, who would later claim all she possessed and wash her name from the lips of every Darakaian who remembered it.

Zaethan frowned and considered Takoda handing out the last scraps of bread. Would she have seen herself in her son's pathetic charity within this alley, or her husband, through his actions outside it?

As he read her cuffs, each rune stung more than the first.

Courage. Strength. Victory. Honor.

"You must forgive yourself, Ahoté. It was the right call, when we sailed off The Wastes. And your mhàdda," Kumo whispered lowly, as if sensing his turmoil, "would have done the same. She watches on with pride."

Zaethan's gut tightened as he read the fifth rune and levelled with his beta. "Ano, cousin, I don't think she does."

Toying with it, Zaethan held the golden article toward the sun, presenting the last of her runes like an offering instead of a curse.

Heart.

Chapter Two
Luscia

The opening gong was struck, sending a hush over the diverse crowd of Orynthians. Luscia peered through the delicate loops of the brilliant floor-to-ceiling screen, a labyrinth of bronze-coated timber that segregated her from one identity and her next. The final division between the woman—the leader—she was intended to be, versus the one she would actually become.

Her lashes fluttered against the tiny eyelet as she watched the haidren to Bastiion lethargically drag his feet up the steps, the first to take his place on the grand dais inside the expansive Peerage chamber.

On the edge of the platform, Ira loosened his expertly tied plum cravat where he stood stationed before his countrymen. The design of the domed building erected an obvious separation between spectators native to Bastiion and those who had journeyed from outside its borders. Facing the company of councilmen, Ira troubled to keep still in his snug jacket of leafy brocade, perhaps discomforted by their visible and underwhelmed scrutiny. Bordering the much-more-distinguished, elevated benches reserved for members of the Peerage, rows rounded the main floor, crammed with every nobleman and courtier in the city. Each, undoubtedly, was unwilling to forfeit participation in the greatest spectacle of their generation.

The coronation of Dmitri Korbin Thoarne.

As if summoned by the very thought, Luscia heard the familiar clack of his walking cane draw close, though she did not pull away from the screen, too mesmerized by the restless throng seated on the other side. As the partitioned room pointed toward Darakai's balcony, her vantage prevented her from gazing upon the faces of her brethren above. Her father, Boreal's Clann Darragh, their *mighty oak*, surely sat among them. Luscia smiled feebly, the screen tickling her upper lip.

How she had missed him.

A tired tenor chimed. "Ravenous, the lot of them."

Rotating her cheek against the decorative loops, Luscia found her new king leaning toward the screen in the same manner, as he too assessed his expectant subjects.

"I see Lord Donnell of Galina managed to escort both his mistress and his wife here today."

Luscia followed the line of his fingertip, pointed toward a stout, perspiring yancy flanked by two rather perturbed courtiers.

"Alas, I suppose we should consider Lord Donnell's impending calamity a compliment to the crown. That misstep will certainly cost him later."

Chuckling, she was grateful for the distraction from the pestering flurry in her middle. "Wem. I expect he'll pay dearly for it," Luscia quipped, observing the lord in question nervously dab a kerchief against his forehead as each of his companions wielded their fans indignantly.

"Meanwhile," he muttered, still engrossed in the horde of nobles, "Lord and Lady Ambrose seem incapable to produce their missing son."

A flurry swam up her throat at the mention of the heir to Agoston. Their son would stay missing. Luscia had seen to that. "Aren't you supposed to be stowed away somewhere, Your Majesty?"

"Dmitri. Don't you dare start with that nonsense. These absurd robes weigh enough." He flippantly gestured toward the layered gold-and-indigo drapery tumbling off his normally thin shoulders, broadened by the superfluous padding of brass feathering and plush mink trim. "I beg we not add additional formality to what I already carry on my person."

"It's properly regal, at least." Luscia commented fondly, judging how very different he looked from the first night she'd entered Bastiion only a few months ago. Orynthia's gentle prince who favored the solace of his sofa, always employed it like a raft in his endless sea of ledgers. But that prince had disappeared after the stolen passing of his father, the great Stag King. Assuming his throne, Dmitri stood taller, determined yet saddened to his core.

Dmitri propped his cane against the screen and directed his gaze through the slits while he spoke. "You know why they layer it on me, don't you? Make it heavy enough, and I can't run away."

As Luscia pivoted toward him, the second gong sounded, pulling her attention back to the dais. With a more driven step than Ira, Darakai's haidren marched up the platform. The spread of his back stretched the limits of his sleek burgundy coat, cut to hug his form. In a bloodier hue than that threaded throughout Dmitri's waistcoat, Kasim's understated finery challenged the person she knew him to be—all his roughness buttoned into the tailored damask. Darakai's chieftains stared down their haidren from a daunting balcony of battle-scarred men and women. Luscia did not covet the harshness of their reception and for a moment empathized with her Southern counterpart.

The gong for Boreal would be next.

"Do you wish to?" Luscia quickly asked. "Run away, I mean."

Sluggishly, she tore her eye from Kasim when she felt Dmitri sweep his fingers up hers and cradle them carefully, like they were fragments of glass. Weary lines encircled his clear, melancholy gaze, and he brought her hand to his mouth. His Unitarian lips, lacking their warmth of color, barely brushed her skin in a reverential kiss.

"Not anymore it seems, my Lady Boreal."

Steadied by his kind candor, Luscia straightened her spine, conjuring the fortitude expected of the haidren to Boreal. Her young king took a profound breath, assumingly for both their sakes, but the finale gave way to a wheeze. Luscia's head quirked instantly, her Northern ears piquing. Focusing on an artery thumping behind the gilded edge of his embroidered lapel, she found the rhythm of his heartbeat to be terribly erratic.

"There's no need to ration," she stated, all but chiding him, "not when I'm by your side. I'll see the vials are delivered this evening, along with another sachet of Boreali tea leaves."

In the weeks following his father's assassination, the gravity of his loss wedded with the burden of an entire kingdom had only furthered Dmitri's reliance on his elixir. As Alora had disclosed, Luscia's blood—a mixture both ancient and *Other*—rescued the heirs of Thoarne from untimely expiration, be it from sickness or battlefield wounds. However, to their mutual perplexity, whatever consumption held Dmitri captive in his dying husk refused to heal. Unconceivably, no amount of lumin, from the earth or her veins, could rescue his weakening breaths.

Orynthia yearned for the peace only Dmitri Korbin Thoarne could sustain. His father's legacy—and the treaties it had forged—hinged on the stability of Dmitri's reign, a stability directly threatened by his hidden decline. Luscia, like her aunt, vowed to prolong the days he had left.

By whatever means necessary.

"Nerves dry the throat, as they say." He winked, but the waning gleam of his hazel irises said otherwise. Abruptly, the soothing color of soil and pine flashed widely, and he jumped under his sweeping robes. "*Shtàka*, one never does get used to that. A good afternoon to you too, Captaen Bailefore."

Luscia turned, for Marek had stepped away from his post, concealed in the shaded corner of the partitioned holding room. Only then did it strike her how disconcerting it was for their Unitarian king when the captaen of her najjani guard would make himself known, as she'd not bothered to expose his presence in the first place. Having spent a great deal of time with those whom the realm called *shadowmen*, her guard's continuous emergence from the darkness evolved into less of an imposition than a reassurance. Embarrassed for her lack of consideration, Luscia cleared her throat and took Marek's arm, wordlessly extended to escort her from their temporary solace.

"Perhaps only one of us could escape the inevitable, Sire." Luscia smirked inside the arched doorframe, glancing back at her sovereign. "Se'lah Aurynth, though I'm confident it will be much sooner."

She heard Dmitri softly repeat his name, correcting her once more. Luscia and Marek rounded the curved hall but stopped before the imposing entrance to the Peerage chamber. Sentries lined the doors, their squadron divided down either side of the windowed corridor. Neither man who'd met their gaze, the two nearest the threshold, could hold it for very long. Those who declined to acknowledge Luscia or her najjani captaen glared at the polished granite underfoot. This was the last building in all of Bastiion where Boreali presence was desired—the last place that Northern "y'siti," the *filthy ice-witches,* would ever be accepted.

Awaiting the third signal that would permit her to enter their dominion, the very edifice where legislation against her kinsman was inscribed, Luscia couldn't help but harden her grip on Marek's modest twill jacket engulfing her hand. With a slight shake, her fingertips crept to adjust the stiff, wide collar concealing the height of her scar. She elevated her chin, resolved and defiant, and looked up at Marek. The navy twill accentuated his smooth, crimson strands tucked behind his ear. At her side, the captaen stood out like a Northern torch, unapologetically ablaze before her pit of contenders.

Along his crisp jawline, a tendon skipped when the gong boomed through the thick slabs. The doors groaned apart, as if unwilling to open.

"Never lower your eyes for them, Ana'Sere," Marek murmured in a voice too muted for ordinary listeners.

Into the echo of hushed talk and displeased grumbles, Luscia entered their provincial domain with an unwavering fixation on the decorated risers ahead, occupied by the most powerful of the nobility. Thirty councilmen in total, the Peerage scowled at her approach, their arrangement resembling less a court of law and more an audience within the most grandiose theater in the city. Behind an empty row of extravagant chairs, nine luxuriously dressed men, awaiting their royal overseers no doubt, dominated the primary row, as their province, Wendylle, held the majority vote. Central to their line sat their minister and host of ceremony, Gregor Hastings.

Luscia's free hand joined its mate around Marek's arm as she counted the second line. Seven men from Agoston. The Agostons, equal to the Wendylleans in regalia but leading in dissatisfaction, objected either to the Boreali occupying their chamber or the coronation of their king—unclear given Agoston's unfavorable position toward Dmitri's taking the throne, per his recently shared insight into Peerage politics.

Third in prominence were five from Galina and behind them, their neighboring province. Although, the five Hildureans looked much less interested in Luscia nearing the dais than some private wager occurring behind their bench. Crowning the stack of delegates slumped three aged councilmen from Uriel, one of whom was already nodding off despite the room of witnesses.

Luscia's beaded upturned slipper greeted the first step, both Ira's and Kasim's back toward her ascent. From the opposite balcony, General Lateef broke an unrelenting assessment of his haidren and grated his harsh stare onto the Boreali pair. His band of chieftains followed suit. At the top of the dais, Luscia swiveled in place, catching a glimpse of the adjacent balcony above the chamber entrance. A hive of white and gray, the Shoto Collective awaited the haidren to Pilar, the fourth and final seat. Their anticipation cool and controlled, the gathered shotos and shoto primes silently surveyed the scene with unnerving acumen.

The entire Ethnicam had assembled. In one place. Because of the assassination of a king.

What could possibly go wrong? Luscia nervously mused and shifted toward her brethren, then realized her hand was still caught in the aid of Marek's grasp.

His lips moved as he spoke for her, alone. "You look like Aurynth touching earth today, Luscia." The apple of Marek's throat bobbed when he leaned forward and carried her hand toward his mouth, as Dmitri had done, though not nearly as delicately.

His eyes, cerulean beacons under stern brows, did not blink when the captaen let go and backed away from the dais. Stationing himself against the farthest wall, he raised his head, finding her once more. Luscia felt an unexpected flush scale her chest when she saw the tip of Marek's tongue absently sweep his bottom lip, as if tasting what lingered there.

She was grateful to Pilar for the first time in her life when the gong resounded, ushering its closing pronouncement.

While the chamber opened for Sayuri, Luscia instead searched the sparsely populated balcony hoisted above Marek's rather intimate posting, avoiding further looks from her captaen. Tilting her neck, a sobering calm anchored her feet to the platform. Under the byrnnzite cupola, her kinsmen sparkled, the afternoon sun glinting off each subtle movement of their ornate linsilk garbs, donned just for this moment in history. By his lonesome, their Clann Darragh inhabited the first row, the tallest and broadest among the Northern faces. Her father beamed, all but buried under his robust silvering beard laden with beading. It was the kind of expression that crinkled eyes as deep as the Drystan, which shimmered proudly at some emotion he tried to contain. Next to his wide occupation, an embroidered shawl was elegantly wrapped about an empty seat—the seat intended for his wife.

Seeing Luscia notice their tribute to her mother, he closed his eyes, but not before a tear escaped his composure. In a gesture both moving and surreal, her father folded his chin into his thick beard, bowing his head toward his daughter. Then, the half-dozen elders who'd made the voyage to Bastiion imitated their leader, bending forward in homage to welcome their young haidren. For what seemed like an age, they did not move but retained their posture of respect, one Luscia knew in her bones was undeserved. Only when a chiming caravan flooded the space did they return upright. Uninterested in the parade of priestesses rounding the room, her father nodded at Luscia confidently. It was time.

And in his regard, she was ready.

One of the priestesses mounted the steps, her bronze figure draped in the same pleated tunic ornamenting those who served in the temple where Lucia had once met Dmitri. Without warning, the woman chanted in an unfamiliar lyrical dialect and hitched a smoldering lantern above their heads. Strands of tiny bells jingled, chained at her ankles and wrists, as she initiated a strange and eerie dance. The priestess swayed, pouring tendrils of incense over Luscia, as her sisters did to the other haidrens on the dais. Luscia squeezed her lids shut. The musty aroma itched her tear ducts, causing her to wonder how long they had to endure the stench and how many washes it'd take to remove it later.

"Don't breathe it in." Alora's instruction pricked Luscia's Tiergan ears, her aunt's tone one the priestess would not detect. "It will soon pass."

Waiting to inhale, she heard Ira gasp and cough a few paces away, clearly having not received the same advice from his predecessor. In the blackness, Luscia listened as the priestess navigated her way down the platform, her bells fading like a melodic outro as her group departed the chamber.

Her aunt's voice returned. "Now."

Luscia lifted her lashes. Alora stood a step lower, her hands tucked neatly behind her traditional Boreali gown, the detailing more reserved than what she'd selected for Luscia's commissioned attire. Alora's dazzling train cascaded toward the base of the floor. Her aunt's serenity, no doubt contrived, did not waver before the Ethnicam. Her attention fell on her niece, as if they were the only beings present for the ceremonial exchange. Alora's ancestral eye, born of light and lumin, twinkled in a lustrous medley as she scanned Luscia, assessing the state of her. Her embellished garment had been crafted by Ödetha's master seamstress. Behind the column of leafed buttons, a knot unclenched inside Luscia when the corners of Alora's mouth twitched with the smallest approval.

For a fractured moment, it spurned Luscia that she wanted so badly to receive it.

In a percussion-filled chorus, Southern drummers encircled the platform, their rhythm full of promise and expectancy. Alora reached to where a gem-encrusted headdress haloed her whitening hair. Strings of starlight flowed from the headpiece down to her waist. Within each precious stone, lumin flickered at Alora's touch, resembling the brightest rain rolling off her head. Symbolizing Boreal's anointing over the bearer of insight both tempered and true, Alora removed the centuries old Eiide Corün, the Wreath of Wisdom, and suspended it between them.

With another drumming swell, her aunt exalted the headdress and settled it onto Luscia's untamable tresses. Poetically, their positioning emulated that of the Bestowing, on the night of Luscia's Ascension earlier that spring. Without pause, Alora uttered the same words she'd spoken when piercing the solrahs into Luscia's septum.

"*Meh'dajjeni Dönumn, weh'dajjeni Lux.* My strength in the Gift, our strength in the Light. May it never falter, Ana'Sere, and may you not forget from where it came."

Releasing the Eiide Corün, Alora bent in a curtsy, gathered her train, and disembarked the dais. Luscia blinked back tears, refusing to validate the sting. Her predecessor had not included the cautionary line the last time, and she begged the High One none of her brethren had heard it.

Repeating the stanza, the drummers set their mallets aside so that each musician could take a knee.

The luxiron solrahs heated Luscia's nose when Alora raised her voice, in unison with the other sil'haidrens, and powerfully proclaimed, "Turn, Haidren. Behold the Quadren of King Dmitri Korbin Thoarne."

Luscia's heart pounded in her chest as she rotated in place. Gradually, she lifted her chin, meeting Zaethan Kasim's gaze directly across the dais. Likely to intimidate her, he cracked his neck, rustling a cape of metal arrowheads he hadn't been wearing when she'd entered. Unlike his normally hostile expression, the haidren's features were solemn. His full mouth relaxed, and the usually puckered space between his brow flattened; a pair of gilded rings ornamented the hairs of his left. It posed an odd but admittedly arrestive addition to his overtly Unitarian ensemble. Beneath the set, his striking eyes, vivified by his claret jacket, trekked an unexpected exploration down her gown. Kasim's earthy appraisal unhurriedly trailed back up her body, causing Luscia to swallow disconcertingly. Yet when Kasim comprehended he was victim to her examination, her brow arched cynically, in question to the ugly bruise smattered across the swollen bridge of his nose.

Agitatedly, he scrunched said nose and sniffed aggressively, glancing downward. When he did, a spasm seized her temple. In partnership to its ache, an accompanying whisper hummed in her ears. Luscia clenched her fists, stifling her panic as the whispers increased their haunting advent, alarming and unwelcome.

The indiscernible voices hadn't returned since the eve of King Korbin's assassination, not since the night she'd ended Ambrose's life.

Shuddering her to her right, another pain shot down her spine.

After almost losing her balance on the dais, Luscia panted in place, fully expecting to hear some cruel response from the beautiful haidren to Pilar. But as she gaped at her neighbor, the whispers disappeared with a *snap*, abandoning Luscia when she discovered another frightening unknown.

Sayuri Naborū-Zuo was not there.

In her stead, someone even more nefarious crooked his head on its side and, with disturbing delay, stretched his marrow-stricken skin into a wicked grin.

CHAPTER THREE

ZAETHAN

Zaethan refused his lungs. Meanwhile, the entire Ethnicam listened to Ira dry-heave.

He loathed incense. It was pungent, and pointless, and clinging to him now, permeating the fibers of his fine Unitarian clothing like a brand. In front of the Peerage and their court of noble pets, Bastiion scented each haidren, marking them in servitude.

It was enough Zaethan had obliged to dress like them. Now he smelt like them too. Part of Zaethan hated that even more.

He felt the priestess ebb and flow as her skirts swatted his arms, relaxed at his sides. When her chanting finally ceased, he sensed her drawing away, leaving him to the hope of fresh air. With a puff, he cleared his nostrils, which had started to tingle from the vapored substance. Creaking his eyes apart, he instantly wished for the priestess to return.

His father's stare confronted him from less than a foot away. Like a pitiless tar pit, it trapped Zaethan, heaving him into the cold emptiness of his commander and chief warlord's appraisal. Nyack Kasim's notoriously pitted jaw was elevated, as even a step lower they were near level in standing. Strength filled out his father's formal cobalt tunic, his military might on show across his chest. Pinned in intimidating congress, whittled bone medals rivaled those of the bronze weighted beneath them. At his back, a glorious chainmail cape descended his squared shoulders, held erect despite the stress of it. The iconic fall of armor was far from ordinary. Metal links joined tiers of ancient rust-stained arrowheads, each tipped with the blood of their enemies. Most, it was said, tasted of Mworra.

While the mighty display was to be expected for such rites, Zaethan knew full well why his father wore every article that day, and it wasn't for celebration.

His father's eyes tapered. Disdain pinched his skin aggressively, transforming it into a sheet of charred hickory. At the rear, Zaethan hid his balled fists. He so often wanted to strike the man from whom he craved so much, especially when Bastiion provided an audience as hungry as this.

"I see Léola dug up the past." Nyack Kasim's nose buckled with scorn as it twitched toward the golden rune-engraved beads decorating Zaethan's locs. Breath hot, his father bent closer and whispered bitingly, "You always were your *mother's* son."

There was no compassion in the statement, no crack in his voice at the mention of her. Nyack Kasim didn't speak of his wife, not even to their son. Most days it was as if she never existed. Doing so now, in a moment forever forged into memory, was a tactic of cruelty—a twisted martial artform he'd mastered long ago. Acid raked Zaethan's throat as he forced his lips together, refusing his father the satisfaction of any weak, pained reply.

Silhouetting their leader, his kinsmen encircled the dais, beating the words into Zaethan's skull. The line of Darakaian drummers painted a formidable picture behind their chief warlord: his native position of power. Easing back, Nyack met Zaethan once more. A sneer tugged his father's pockmarked cheek as his hands, mirroring the scars atop his head, moved to unclasp the arrowhead cape.

Fierce. Victorious. Unrelenting. Aptly named, the mantle of the fallen exemplified centuries of Darakaian haidrenship and their crimson river of triumph, flowing from the right hand of the throne.

Leisurely, his father slid it off his shoulders to the bolstering tempo. The blemished arrowheads skated the marble with barbarous flourish. He was relishing it, this public exhibition of his glory before the entire Ethnicam.

As stated in the Accords, Orynthia's sword was a double-edged blade, balanced by Darakai's own. A blade wielded by the hand of Nyack Kasim. In dramatic demonstration, his Southern warriors over-powering the room, Orynthia's commander was warning the Houses what he could still do should they turn against him and how outnumbered any feeble rebellions would be. Zaethan saw it, the flickering threat deep inside the battered black trenches of his face.

But Zaethan's own lips curled. Today knocked down one pillar of his father's dominance. Regardless of his many titles, Nyack Kasim would never sit at that pentagonal table again.

Nyack hurled the iron cape around his successor. Zaethan stooped when his father dumped the load onto his shoulders from a height, making show of it for the spectators. As it dug through the costly silk over his skin, Zaethan's countrymen beat their drums with deafening fervor, the warriors in front of them loudest of all.

"Rhàana ne'Etswégo," his father announced with the mantle's abrupt transference. Rigidly, Zaethan's legs straightened under its startling heaviness. A lifetime of condescension dripped from his father's tongue. "Darakai's kwihila hangs off your back. My entire House looks on, waiting to see how long before you to crumble beneath it."

Zaethan bit his tongue until it hurt and watched his father trot down the steps to where the drummers hammered their anthem. Joining their line, he wiped imaginary grime off the leather gloves that encased his thick forearms.

Ano, Zaethan thought, *he wiped off his son*, an act the chieftains were surely devouring from above.

In a living ripple, the drumming stopped, and each performer bent a knee. A deep-rooted deference quieted each player's expression, stilling them into Andwele sculptures. At the voice of the sil'haidrens, Zaethan adjusted his footing and stared at a plaster medallion adorning the ceiling.

"Turn, Haidren."

He caught the gravel in his chief warlord's order, over the other predecessors.

"Behold the Quadren of King Dmitri Korbin Thoarne."

Guiding the cape, Zaethan twisted and found himself pitted

opposite Boreal. Taken by surprise, his jaw slackened. The young woman—rather, the witch he better acquainted with frayed sparring trousers and the tail of a whip—presented herself as another creature altogether. Her aunt's doing, no doubt. Zaethan flexed his shoulders, balancing the cape, and craned his neck. The elder Boreali's efforts were… annoyingly effective. Instead of the devious savage who'd vexed him on countless occasions, the haidren to Boreal resembled a specter of light. A peculiar headdress graced her unruly tawny hair. Like tears of the moon, strands of tiny stones glinted down the length of her abdomen, the twin curtains of her hair framing her severe cheeks where the palest strands toyed at her chin. Such radiance was out of place— out of character. Distracted by the deceptive curve of her hip where it melted under a tightly embroidered waist panel, his attention all but marched up each button toward her throat. A soft alabaster throat hid behind a distinctive collar piece that spread across her chest imperially. The sharp, scalloped edges were dulled, and Zaethan immediately recognized the prismatic metal.

Witchiron.

He couldn't help but smirk. She might conceal it with an iron shield, but Zaethan had once glimpsed what lay beneath. Darakaians bore their well-earned scars proudly, but apparently the Boreali considered them a dishonor. He'd use that to his advantage one day.

Brazenly, he greeted her inhuman eyes, but his smirk drooped when her dense brow arched mockingly and her mismatched gaze flicked to his puffy nose. Snorting dried blood, Zaethan huffed at his boots, imagining how enjoyable it would be to make hers match. Or how macabrely it might ruin her troublesome dress.

Such a dress didn't suit her. Which was why, Zaethan assured himself, he couldn't stop staring at it.

Glancing up again, he saw her arms shudder. Then, with alacrity, she shook her head to one side, as if to drain water from an ear. The gesture was both bizarre and familiar. Zaethan recalled her doing something similar the night on the docks, when they'd unknowingly hunted Ambrose through the slums. Unease pricked spindles along his Darakaian skin, suffocating inside his yancy waistcoat.

Suddenly the witch lost her footing, nearly tripping backward. Zaethan's boot sprung forward, a move to catch her, before remembering his father and the watchful balcony of Darakaian warlords. Zaethan reflexively slid his heel back in place. What the chieftains would interpret as concern for Boreal was sheer practicality. Depths, if she caused a disruption like the one from her own reception, they'd have to reprise the day's entire ritual, including that absurd vapor bath. Zaethan would rather spend a week subjected to Ira's whims than repeat this kakka-shtàka ceremony.

With a snap, the witch caught her balance. But in the process, her abnormal eyes narrowed assertively, anchored on Pilar's rim of the dais. Zaethan hadn't bothered to pay any mind to Sayuri. *Owàa* knew she didn't need any more attention than already showered from her admirers. The witch didn't move, and what little color had pinked her cheeks fled from sight.

The spindles returned under his jacket. Zaethan's neck turned to follow her gaze.

In his niece's place, Tetsu Naborū grinned at the haidren to Boreal, a demented humor spreading his reedy, chapped lips. His well-known keenness for pipe marrow intensified his jaundice. The angular jet slivers of facial hair sharpening the man's expression made him look more like a hornet-striped boa than the chancellor of the Shoto Collective—yet just as poisonous as those slithering through the bellies of

Hagarh. Zaethan gritted his teeth, for Sayuri was nowhere to be found. The fact didn't appear to concern her uncle in the least.

It was unnerving how Tetsu Naborū, now sil'haidren to Pilar, didn't flinch, utterly fixated on the witch. Drowning in the immaculate, frost-white robes of a shoto prime, he carried a garnet cushion between the bony notches of his knuckles. The contrast was a gory gut wound against his middle. In the center of the cushion, two golden wings crisscrossed, each welded to hooks the size and shape of the human ear—totems to Pilar that should have adorned Sayuri today.

At the sound of a rustle, Zaethan swiveled toward the other end of the dais, where Ira gaped, slack-jawed. A prominent livery collar of copper and bronze had been slung over his upper body. Bastiion's hungover haidren scratched his temple, clearly frazzled by the older diplomat. Ira blinked wildly as he fiddled with his eyelids. Statistically speaking, it probably wasn't the first time the yancy hallucinated that week.

"Depths, Ira." Zaethan growled. "*Don't you dare make a scene.*"

"You see him too? Thank the Fates." Ira exhaled, his volume barely quiet enough to be considered a whisper. "Starting to rethink last night's merrymaking…"

"Doru. Just shut your yancy trap—"

"Quiet, children." The oily snake tut-tutted softly. Sayuri's uncle broke his obsession with the haidren to Boreal, tipping his head the opposite way. "The adults are coming."

Before Zaethan could bite out a retort, Tetsu Naborū proved correct. The ornate doors screeched apart, welcoming in a flood of chittering chimes and twinkling bell tones, ringing in celebration for their king's approach. Zaethan's stomach recoiled. They'd brought more incense too.

A weak whine sounded from his right. With a sharp scowl, Zaethan threatened Ira to keep it together.

The women fanned out, crowding the main floor with synchronized dancing. The living percussion was accentuated by each spin and clap. Exalting a harmonized chant, the group of priestesses parted before the entrance of the chamber. Dancing, their bodies froze midstep. Within the threshold, Zaethan's best friend—his king—stood. Even from the distance he witnessed the thinly concealed sorrow riddling Dmitri's countenance.

Neither of them had ever pictured his coronation like this.

When Dmitri's cane struck the floor, the women resumed their dance, even livelier than before. In deference, they flounced away from his royal train, allowing an ample breadth for the Stag King's widow, Orynthia's queen mother. In line with her son, Queen Lourissa Thoarne glided serenely over the pattern of eight-pointed stars tiled into the marble. Her ladies-in-waiting, an exclusive syndicate of courtiers, dutifully fell in step behind her, many of whose husbands graced the Peerage benches. The duchess of Wendylle, Ira's mother, led their elite pack.

Concluding Dmitri's stately precession, the visiting queen of Razôuel, Bahira'zol'Jaell, and her accompanying children filed into the cavernous chamber. However now, it felt to be bursting at the joints. His pace unhurried, Dmitri skirted the dais while his royal party split off to occupy their seats, situated at the head of the room. Forgetting Tetsu Naborū, Zaethan tracked his friend's ascent up the platform. Even though Dmitri was buried under the robust ensemble—comical were it any other scenario—Zaethan's chest inflated with dignity. Immediately, he was struck with the understanding that all those years he'd not grown up with a prince. He'd been raised alongside a king.

Sage and solemn, the king would be written about for ages. He was the king Orynthia did not deserve.

Fur trim rippled each of Dmitri's steps as he came to the center of their Quadrennal quartet. As Dmitri turned to face the Peerage and his mother, Zaethan overheard him sigh, from either exhaustion or exasperation. While the whole event was ridiculously theatrical, he knew Dmitri hadn't been sleeping since his father's death. Evidence of those anxious nights plagued his eyes in a lavender plume. But when Gregor Hastings cleared his throat, silencing the chorus, the warmth above those lavender plumes swung toward Zaethan and winked.

In a shared look, seconds before their stations were separated further by Dmitri's crown, Zaethan felt his lips slide into a boyish grin and he nodded twice. His friend's shoulders raised as he inhaled deeply and turned away, but not before hiking his delicate chin just an inch higher.

Gregor Hastings, carrying a leather-bound lump, blew off the dust of an old page and recited monotonous legalities, the confines of which no one in that room cared to comprehend. Even Uriel's trio of crones snoozed in the top row of their Peerage risers.

As his reading finished, the temple's high priestess, equally as ancient from her creaking joints and profoundly pleated skin, joined them on the dais. Although, it did take her a while to get there. Escorting the matriarch, coupling priestesses swayed their steaming censers, suspended from thick chains. In tandem, they walked opposing circles about Dmitri, anointing him for their beloved Fates.

A third acolyte came to the top stair and in a worshipful bow, handed over a luxurious indigo pillow to the hunched elder, who wheezed at its retrieval. Zaethan could see it carried what drew them all to attendance. The bulbous spades surrounding King Korbin's crown, burrowed into the downy material, shone radiantly in the beam of sun as if calling for him from the skies. Zaethan felt a charge shoot through the audience, anticipating the moment it would inaugurate Thoarne's last living heir—a dangerous realization that had swept through Bastiion within the span of a few weeks.

In Zaethan's periphery, he glimpsed Felix Ambrose's father, the duke of Agoston, in the benches, mouthing something to another provincial councilmen.

Too dangerous.

As the high priestess removed the crown of Thoarne and lofted it above herself, the Darakaian drummers pounded to the chants of the convulsing women. Their rhythm gained speed and her warped spine curved before Dmitri, repeating a foreign stanza over and over. The verses were said to be discernible only to the Fates and their servants.

What's the point if we don't know what you're saying? Zaethan pondered derisively.

When his critique wandered from the Peerage to the onlooking royals, it appeared Bahira'Rasha shared similar thoughts. Her copper forehead crinkled under the cascade of emerald gems. She was obviously amused by the Orynthian practice. Evidently, the *Zôueli* didn't believe in the Fates either. Zaethan wondered if that had ever came up during their discussions of her and Dmitri's pending nuptials.

Dmitri clutched his cane and took to his knees, bowing his head toward the elderly priestess. In a blink, everything stopped. No instrument struck. No murmur of gossip tolled. Nothing but the creak and moan of her limbs echoed off the stately walls. As one, the Ethnicam held its breath. Inch by inch, the priestess's rickety arms trembled, hovering over Dmitri's umber waves until the seam of demarcation was sealed. Unfurling her frail fingers, she let go.

The crown of Thoarne was one with its next master.

Gradually, with his cane, Dmitri rose in place. The drummers, kneeling behind the temple servants, marched their mallets upon the hide of their kettledrums. Through the hollow sphere in the canopy, bright afternoon light bathed Dmitri in a sovereign glow. Brilliant and blinding, the historic crown reflected it over his gathered subjects, searing the truth of his birthright into their bones.

"Stand witness, House of Bastiion." Gregor Hastings boomed from his podium beside the Peerage bench. At his word, two attendants positioned a chair behind Ira. "Stand witness, House of Darakai," he stated.

Zaethan felt a nudge at his heels.

"Stand witness, House…" Gregor cleared his throat hesitantly. "Of Pilar." Sayuri's chair was brought to her uncle. Her absence must have been a shock to Gregor's generation as well then. "Stand witness," he said, less exuberantly. "House of Boreal."

Zaethan spied beyond Dmitri's fur collar and doggedly assessed the witch. Her opaline reception did not falter. Then, in an unusual exchange, her inhuman eye darted toward Pilar and back. She did it again, and Zaethan comprehended. She was questioning him amid Gregor's final statements. Curtly, Zaethan's chin tugged right to left, confirming he hadn't known about it. Without forethought, he subtly inclined toward Ira. If anyone had intel on Sayuri's whereabouts, it'd be him, the person most like her.

Dmitri's mother stood and, in an elegant gesture, graciously offered her hand to Bahira'Rasha. The Peerage, coming to their feet, scuffled within their benches, beckoning the Ethnicam to join them. With the aid of her maidens, the priestess tottered down the steps, leaving the wreathed platform to Dmitri and his fractured Quadren.

Gregor Hastings hammered a gavel four times and set it aside. Coming out from the podium, he smoothed his suitcoat, strained by its buttons, and directed the room beside the line of royals. "Stand witness, Houses of Orynthia, all we bound in accord, oath-sworn to the inheritance of Thoarne." As minister of the Peerage, he bowed, and in a tidal wave, so did the room. "By the authority of Fates and state, we recognize our true and rightful sovereign. Bound to the regency in service of council and ambassadorship, let our haidrens be seated at his arm."

The chair legs bumped Zaethan's calves, and in a swell, the four took their ceremonial seats.

"Son of Korbin, heir of Thoarne, we crown you, Dmitri Korbin Thoarne, king of Orynthia."

Cheers and applause resounded, masking any commentary within the throng of discontented councilmen. A sourness warped their smiles and the polite platitudes they extended past the bench toward their late king's widow. Unease primed Zaethan's instincts, sharpening his awareness of the masquerading vipers in their midst. Inside the cape of arrowheads, he skimmed the hilt of his kopar.

"Tonight, Zaeth, like old times!" Dmitri shouted to Zaethan over the racket, as attendants ushered him down to his *Zôueli* guests. Having prepared the sentries for the day's celebrations, Zaethan knew late evening would be one of few opportunities to see his friend at all.

But the promise of boyhood revelry couldn't dampen the disquieting fact that Dmitri's Quadren was far from whole, despite the smoke and declarations.

Lumbering off the dais, Zaethan lugged his armored cape, weaving *Rhàana ne'Etswégo* between the crowd and through the doors. Spotting the sleek lapel of Ira's plumage, he reeled the other haidren closer and wrenched him away from the nearest gambling house, back toward the palace main.

"My, you like it rough—"

"Haidrens are due elsewhere, Ira." Zaethan threw his arm around him aggressively. "And when we get there, you and I are going to have a little chat, *uni*?"

Chapter Four
Zaethan

Rivaling the proclamation of trumpets and unbridled cheers, Sayuri's totems demanded attention in a manner the woman herself never could. Her golden articles paraded the crowded streets of Bastiion between the arms of Boreal and Darakai, politically situated under the avian crest engraved into Pilar's vacant seat. Ribbons and banners twirled and spun as their float crept by, while each Orynthian in the street yelled louder than their neighbor.

The slow-moving spectacle was meant to gift the masses with an intimate introduction to their newly crowned king and his royal Quadren.

It was precisely the spectacle Sayuri Naborū-Zuo would never miss. Yet beside him, her chair was empty.

Zaethan's thoughts meandered from the delicate welded wings to the witch across the vacant seat. Her witchiron collar refracted the waning sunlight onto the crest stamped into her own chair. Its image was a wolf of sorts, possibly a *lycran*, like the war-tainted hound in her possession. Poised and controlled against the bump of each turn of the wheel, she sat forward, looking past Zaethan, awaiting Ira's answer. Beyond her ghostly form, a line of sentries separated the wide float from the banks of applause. Trapped upon their chairs, it was the perfect opportunity to interrogate a yancy.

The brow over her hueless eye flattened. It drooped even lower when Zaethan felt moisture splatter his trousers, and Ira cursed.

"Let's just dab that right up," he prattled as his hand appeared in Zaethan's lap. "Do the attendants just run alongside to refill—"

Smacking the yancy's fingers off, Zaethan ripped the goblet out of Ira's grasp and sloshed the rosy remnants off the side of the float onto the cobblestone street.

"But the wine!"

"Now that your distraction is removed…" Zaethan returned the empty goblet, shoving it against Ira's embellished lilac vest. "Answer the question."

"Well, I was about to tell you about my maid." Ira flipped the vessel upside down and shook out any last drops onto his tongue. "But then you had to go and waste that fine glass. That wine was from Galina, you know. And like my maid…" His expression went wistfully toward the sky. "Was remarkably full-bodied."

"Palace staff are to be respected." The witch interjected sternly, her mouth set. "Even you are to abide by that standard, Lord Bastiion."

"You needn't fret, my frigid dove." Ira leaned beyond Zaethan, hand to his chest. "I harbor the utmost respect for her... domestic faculties."

Curving in the uncomfortable, rigid seat, Zaethan blocked Ira's line of sight. "I'm not interested in your *kakka-shtàka* dalliances with the staff, Ira. I asked what you knew about Sayuri's whereabouts. I'm sure we all agree this isn't exactly the type of thing she'd willingly bow out of." He took hold of the haidren's shoulder, feigning friendship for the thousands of witnesses. Smiling, Zaethan flashed his teeth but tightened his grip. "As one who frequents Sayuri's circles, why don't you share what you've heard with the rest of the Quadren?"

Wincing under the bite of Zaethan's hold, Ira nervously tucked his hair behind his ear and reciprocated an impish grin. "That's what I keep saying, *Lord Darakai*. One of my maid's notable traits is her keenness for gossip—rather, the frequency in which she collects it."

He let go, releasing Ira's slender shoulder, and reclined against the lacquered wood. Crossing his legs, Zaethan waited for Ira to continue. "Well, get on with it."

"You really must work on your dreadful inability to woo, Zaeth. Positively impersonal. Behold..." Ira promptly stood and waved at the crowd, specifically at a pack of ladies and their bounty of multi-colored ribbons heralding overhead. "Greetings, beautiful creatures of the realm!" Cupping his hands, Ira yelled to them, "Yes, it is I, your haidren! Oh, hello, you..." He waggled his lapel and pointed at a jubilant woman in the throng. "Look at that, we match. You see, Zaeth, it's all about establishing a connection. Now you try—*oof!*"

Zaethan caught the tail of Ira's jacket and yanked him back onto the chair cushion. "For Fates' sake, if you don't answer the damn question, I'll feed you to every unpaid *connection* you owe your aurus."

Loosening the silk scarf tied at his neck, Ira cleared his throat, and he adjusted his jacket back into sorts. "Firstly, you don't believe in the Fates, so that threat is weaker than you think. Secondly…" His eyes widened, gathering the promise in Zaethan's. "Perhaps it's not. So, my maid. Lovely girl, longest legs you've ever—right. She's gotten pretty friendly with Sayuri's fleet of resident attendants, attendants who've not been permitted in her apartments for over a week."

As Sayuri was accustomed to a life managed by the lessors around her, Zaethan found that hard to believe. The thought of Sayuri tending to her quarters as well as her own lengthy list of demands seemed absurd. Everything the now-haidren to Pilar did was to garner more notoriety and social influence. Apart from the ever-present audience at her beck and call, there wasn't much else for which Sayuri could boast.

"Why would she quit the city just before Dmitri's coronation?" Zaethan pondered aloud, stroking the cleft in his chin.

"Oh, Sayuri didn't leave. She's still here, in that apartment." Ira inched closer, even though the nearest sentries were a fair distance off. "Her attendants deliver meals, to her door, in the middle of the night."

"But we just saw her, less than a fortnight ago at the Quadren's most recent assembly. She seemed fine."

Aside from her foul demeanor.

If anything, Sayuri had appeared more confident than usual, worsening her already rancid personality. Zaethan even recalled her grinning at the mention of *Bahira'*Rasha, a topic that habitually turned her face sour.

To his surprise, Ira started to snicker. "Apparently, Sayuri scheduled some exotic treatment or another in preparation for today. Always tweaking this or that… a weekly occurrence, I'm told. Well, word from her staff is that something went wrong. And now, she won't come out to play! Absolutely refuses!"

The yancy smacked his knee as he rolled with laughter. Zaethan's lips twitched at his theory. Amusing as it was, it did explain Dmitri's lack of shock that afternoon when he'd entered the Peerage chamber and Sayuri had not been on present on the dais—or how her uncle had stood in as proxy for Pilar. If Dmitri had been given prior notice of her absence, he'd not relayed it during yesterday's planning session regarding royal securities. Zaethan made note to mention it later, when they finally had the chance to discuss in private.

Ahead of the rows of fire dancers, a more majestic float couriered Orynthia's coronated king and his western guests through the city. Zaethan considered his friend, shaded by the ornate structure shielding their party from Owàa's intense glare. Dmitri wasn't accustomed to keeping secrets. But, as Zaethan was reminded by the outline of his outstretched hand interlocked with that of a certain coastal princess, things change.

Not always for the better.

When Ira resumed his post near the edge of the float, blowing a kiss to every woman in sight, Zaethan cricked his neck idly toward the quietest member of their inaugural trio.

"Nothing, Lady Boreal? No disapproving quip or haughty remark today?" he asked sarcastically. "I'm disappointed."

"I speak little to listen much," she stated flatly. "You ought to try it. So bolaeva, still that impetuous mouth so I might continue."

Turning toward her fully, he noticed a bead of perspiration trickle along the crisp of her cheek, though she made no attempt to wipe it away. Instead, her head cocked incrementally, and her glass-like irises tracked something toward the front of the parade on Ira's side of the gathered populace. Her spine straightened. She inched to the edge of her seat, as if to rise. Zaethan tracked the miniscule tells in her sweat-glistened face that betrayed her hawklike watch, which was entirely consumed on whatever lay ahead. Her porcelain skin twitched where her ears disappeared under her twisted tresses. Abruptly, her eyes widened, and her pale lips parted.

"Tell Ira to sit," she whispered urgently. "Kasim, get him down now."

He knew better than to doubt that look of dread. Zaethan again snatched Ira's waistcoat and thumped him back into place, to his audible dismay.

Which was when Zaethan saw the cause for her concern.

Breaking from the wall of people, two men charged the sentry barricade just as Dmitri's float passed by. Zaethan sprung upright and made to free his kopar from its scabbard, but a light touch against his thigh made him glance down. The young witch discreetly shook her head.

"Don't react," she warned, eyeing the rest of the crowd. "They will remember this."

Indiscernible animated shouts took form while the parade continued onward, as protocol dictated. It was best to move the royal party out of range should anything go awry.

As the haidrens rolled by the disturbance, the angry demonstration grew louder. Zaethan lowered himself but hovered readily and extended his arm partially across Ira. Their clothes shabby and torn, the two protesters screamed at the armed sentries. Their coal-streaked faces foretold their undesirable station, but it was the shape of their sharp features and deepened skins that declared their blended ancestry. Each man bore the dual image of Darakai and Pilar.

"Justice for the cross-caste!"

"Trial for the accused!"

Zaethan's stomach lurched at the reference to Salma's execution, out here in the open. Bile, mingled with regret, churned his insides.

Just as the guards doubled the line, Zaethan saw the first man, his outrage violently evident, stoop to the ground and disappear.

"For the children dead in the gutters!" the second screamed when his partner shot up and pummeled a stone straight into a sentry's skull.

Women shrieked as blood blasted off his head, and in a sentry's efficient swing, the attacker lost his own. Another sentry ran his sword through the second protestor when he lunged, enraged but unarmed.

Three deaths. In a matter of mere moments.

Contained by a dozen sentries, the bodies were dragged out of view, as if nothing had occurred. Trumpeters resumed their touting—if they'd ever paused at all. Adrenaline coursed through Zaethan's veins, and he spun toward the haidren to Boreal, though he did not know why.

The witch gulped. A shimmer of sadness brimmed her kohl-dusted lashes before she faced forward again, returning to stone.

"Well, I don't know about you." Ira's flustered commentary grated the hush. "But I think I'm ready for a trip after all."

A contemptuous rain spit against the darkening windows lining the walk to Dmitri's private residence. As if to rinse Bastiion of its golden façade, *Alámaia's* tears slid down the building's exterior as Zaethan walked by, eager to slip past her judgments. The storm had put an abrupt end to the afternoon's festivities, scattered the city's citizens as they'd stampeded toward cover. Zaethan shuttered the picture of the street, doused in preventable bloodshed now washing into the sewers. The crowd of yancies had stopped their parade for the weather.

But they could somehow ignore severed heads.

Acquainted with sentry protocol, he understood the need to

maintain appearances. Continuing in a calm procession was the safest manner to remove Dmitri's float from potential danger. Even still, the sounds of mothers screaming and the vehemence carved within those cross-castes' faces sat poorly on his mind, festering there. Zaethan gnawed the inside of his cheek, unsure why it bothered him so much more than any other unfortunate altercation in Marketown.

He grunted his curt greeting to the guards at his right. Stationed single file, they spanned the length of the entire corridor to their king's royal suite. With his crown, Dmitri had inherited the protection of Thoarne's Watchmen, the regency's elite guard. However, with Dmitri having opted to remain in his original apartments despite his coronation, the sentinels were instead posted outside the housing now intended for Dmitri's successor. As Zaethan passed the third man from the door, a shade of midnight pushed lithely off the stone wall, where his warrior had been waiting among the Unitarian line.

Zahra scanned the nearest sentinel and sniffed, unimpressed by his company. With a sharp whistle, she nudged her dark chin toward the rain-slicked windows. Obliging, Zaethan stepped aside as her unwavering, terra-cotta eyes leveled with him bluntly and she pinned her back toward the Watchmen, shirking potential lip-readers.

"You can pull Dhalili from assignment, Alpha Zà. I have the information you seek," Zahra muttered sharply, despite her deceptively relaxed stance. "My ear in the general's employ worked the stables today, collected General Lateef's horse after the parade dispersed. Said he'd been drinking, made his lips loose, yeah? Overhead him boasting to his footman…" Her mouth flattened, and she dipped her head. "Wekesa stays in Faraji, uni, to train with Lateef's brother."

Zaethan ran his tongue along his teeth, forcing his calm. It was only a matter of time. "The weapons master?" His fist shook when his third nodded. He directed flatly, "Send for Dhalili. Have her circle back and meet us at Rian."

"But, Alpha Zà… if Wekesa prepares to put forth his challenge during the tour—"

"That's exactly what he's planning to do. But he won't leave the House to do it. Ano," he said caustically. "Wekesa will want to make a bigger scene than I did. Probably on the same street."

"If he challenges upon your arrival—"

"I will be ready, Zahra," Zaethan snapped at his third. "Yeye qondai?"

"Uni zà." She held his stare. Zaethan hoped it was fear for Wekesa's welfare, not his own, wrinkling Zahra's forehead. "Shamàli, shall I task Jabari to ready for our travel then? Keep tabs on the y'siti while they do the same?"

Zaethan looked down and kicked a chunk of grime off his boot with the other.

"Don't call her that." He shifted and peered through the murky glass. "Not anymore. Not after what happened to Takoda." Memory of Takoda steeped in sweat, rasping for breath in the witch's bed, came to mind. It conflicted Zaethan's judgments about the haidren to Boreal. A creature who hid more than she revealed could not be trusted, no matter her charity.

In Zahra's silence, Zaethan arched a brow, registering her delay.

"Uni zà, Alpha Zà." She gingerly struck her chest. Backing away, she bid the moon watch him and, in the process, bared her teeth at a recently promoted member of the Watchmen.

Having thoroughly spooked him, her satisfied chuckle echoed off the vaulted canopy in her retreat. Zaethan should rescind the sentinel's assignment come morning; Zahra was the least of Dmitri's hazards. Though in fairness, she'd effectively spooked Zaethan on occasion too.

Gripping the stag handles, not bothering with the matching byrnnzite knocker, he welcomed himself into to Dmitri's apartments. Taken back to the simplicity of his youth, Zaethan snatched a candied date from a bowl of sweets in the foyer, eager to see his friend.

"Those were for His Majesty's guest…" An aged reproach croaked from behind a fat marble column. "Not his favorite freeloader." Eugenio tottered into view. His elderly hands balanced a tray of used glassware. "Regardless of our locale, Lord Haidren, you're still expected to knock."

"Regardless of your immortality, we expect you to be pleasant." Zaethan grinned, relishing the uncomplicated pleasure of riling the ancient valet. To Eugenio's audible *humph*, he stepped through the foyer, snatched a near-empty goblet off the tray, and brought it to his nose. "Still saving the good stuff for yourself. I respect that."

"Respect from pugnacious, despoiled territories…"

"To my *despoiled territory!*" Zaethan hailed and strutted straight into Dmitri's enormous receiving room.

Hot air dowsed his cheeks when he turned into the domed space. Ablaze at the end of the room, Dmitri's fireplace crackled and roared, reminding Zaethan of their shared adolescent lessons—and his longwinded Pilarese tutors. His friend had heated the room to new temperatures, even though it had not been long since the summer solstice.

Before the mantel, Dmitri lingered with a beautiful woman, cradling both her hands as he spoke quietly to her. Contrasting Dmitri's buttoned layers, the Zôueli princess's rusty skin melted into the flaming backdrop, her arms and shoulders both freely bared. Thin gauzy material floated around her figure, pinched the ankles. It was bizarre, her presence in this place—perhaps one of the most captivating women in the world occupying the rooms of a man who'd rather stare at an old book than her jewel-toned appearance.

Twin overstuffed armchairs had been dragged to the enormous hearth. They must have been sitting there a while. Good thing Bahira'Rasha was used to the blistering heat of the burgundy sands.

Zaethan cleared his throat, beginning to feel a bit awkward, an unfamiliar emotion he'd never known within these walls.

"Zaeth! Perfect timing!" Dmitri tiredly cheered and rotated his fiancée toward their guest.

Their guest. Zaethan soured at the thought. "Is it really though?" he questioned aloud, in search of his bar cart.

"Nonsense. Rasha, excuse Zaethan's Darakaian humor. You'll eventually find the charm in it," Dmitri said, patting her knuckles as he escorted her to the center of the room.

Nearing, Zaethan lamented the shadowy pits below the hazel sincerity of Dmitri's eyes. He knew the Zôueli princess, clearly a shrewd woman, saw it too. What she did with what she saw posed another question entirely.

"You've come just in time to say your good-byes, Zaeth. Rasha and her mother's party plan to quit Bastiion at first light."

"So much to prepare." Bahira'Rasha almost hummed. A melodic eagerness lilted her phrasing conspiratorially. "'No moment to waste,' as you say, wise Dmitri. But I cannot leave without visiting my highlander, Loo-Shah. Where is your shaky boy, to take me to her?"

A nervous chirp came from the rear, as Callister, Dmitri's young page, scuffled into the room.

"Ah, good. Shaky Boy, I'm ready to depart now." She flitted a finger for Callister to wait in the foyer and cupped Dmitri's face to kiss either side. "I will write to your designated seneschal while we travel. Our wedding demands much."

"No moment to waste." Zaethan pasted on a smile when she glided by, saying tersely, "Now that our king is crowned..."

The Zôueli princess stalled. Leaning in, she smoothed Zaethan's jacket front. "This rage you hide, Lord Haidren," she crooned. "It's delicious."

Whisking away, Bahira'Rasha tracked Callister out the foyer and onto her next victim, presumably the haidren to Boreal. With a huff, Zaethan cantered to the cart to pour himself a double shot of bwoloa—both sorely overdue.

"Well, she moves fast. It hasn't even been a day—"

"You know..." Dmitri interrupted, chortling. "The irony is that while you cannot stand her presence, she unquestionably is a fan of yours."

Zaethan shot an incredulous look over his shoulder, clutching the bottle of golden fluid. "And that doesn't concern you?"

"Hardly." Dmitri's voice waned amusedly as he again took residence near the fire. "Considering your palpable disdain for foreigners..."

Glass in hand, Zaethan leaned against the cart and raised it pointedly as he countered. "She decides to leave the day after your coronation to plan this wedding, and you don't think Razôuel is the least bit suspicious? Dmitri, the second that crown touched your head, she started plotting her place at your side. Probably has it embroidered on a cushion already."

Resting his wavy hairs against the back of the tufted chair, Dmitri sighed. "Not everything in life is part of some giant elaborate scheme,

Zaeth. Even after what happened this summer, we cannot suspect that of everyone we encounter. Razôuel is a fair distance, and there are elements of this engagement that must be planned from the Ilias coast, which is precisely why I suggested she return there."

Zaethan took a swig of his bwoloa, cherishing its bitter tang. "Then it seems you're the most duplicitous of all, Your Majesty."

"Me!" Dmitri scoffed. He snatched the fur off the back of his chair, wrapped it about himself, and folded his arms indignantly. "Preposterous. And I command you to never call me that in these apartments again. If I hear that name one more time today…"

"Eh, uni… *My Liege*! Invite me up here for darts and dice, just to ensnare me in some kakka-shtàka discussion about your impending matrimony to the most temperamental ally in history." Pouring another, Zaethan said, "It's your cruelest ruse to date, for the record."

Over the popping fire, he heard Dmitri's sluggish laughter, drawn-out and contented. "Come." His friend's tenor dropped soberly. "Sit with me."

Zaethan didn't like the sudden somberness in his friend's tone. But crossing the room, he angled the accompanying chair and sank into its plush folds. He'd always liked this chair. Zaethan propped his boots on the elevated hearth, glad Dmitri wasn't one to replace old comforts—himself included.

Their chairs not quite opposite each other, Zaethan rolled his neck and studied the lines in Dmitri's recently thinned face. Features elegant and refined, much like Lourissa's, now appeared sunken in the flicker of orange firelight. The woodsy enthusiasm that normally sparked Dmitri's eyes had faded, no doubt drained from the taxing harrows that haunted him still. Over the past weeks, Zaethan's and Dmitri's waking hours had been allocated apart, while Dmitri addressed issues of state and met with the Peerage daily—all while playing a doting host to his future bride and her fickle mother, the very blunt queen of Razôuel. Zaethan couldn't fathom when Dmitri could have possibly paused and grieved the death of his father amid his never-ending demands.

Dmitri lazily blinked back his exhaustion as Zaethan stared across the gap.

"You look terrible," he said.

Dmitri's brow vaulted as he elevated his head off the cushion. "You're one to talk. I mean… What is that?" His friend motioned toward the recent piercings in Zaethan's brow. "Decide to get reupholstered?"

"Don't change the subject," he sniped. "You must sleep eventually, Dmitri, be it here or in your proper chambers."

"When was the last time you slept in your own bed, instead of the one warmed for you at The Veiled Lady?"

Feeling like a cub caught in the kitchens, Zaethan scratched the skin beneath his silk collar uneasily, surprised Dmitri knew about his visits to Chenoa.

"I hear things too, Zaeth. That and you've begun to smell like Ira. What are you always calling that odor?" Dmitri's hand poked out of his furs, and he wafted the air theatrically. "*Yancy musk*, I believe it was."

"I promise, that's over—"

"I don't care how you govern your time, Zaeth," Dmitri stated, cutting him off, his seriousness suddenly fixated on the embers. "As long as it doesn't jeopardize your ability to serve our people. You're correct in suspecting we've other matters to review tonight. That horrifying display this afternoon only confirmed my reasons to commence the coronation tour as soon as the Quadren is able. The Ethnicam needs to see our unity. They need to see it ushered to their doorstep. And then…" Dmitri paused, nodding to himself. "They need to see an heir."

There was no secret in Zaethan's aversion to Dmitri's aggressive timetable, having never understood his king's decision to expedite their travel across the realm. It was Orynthian custom for the king's Quadren to embark on a joint voyage during the first year of a regent's reign, dedicating a liberal stay with each House and its appointed leaders. But Dmitri's absurd push for their immediate departure and subsequent rushed homecoming for his even more absurd wedding not only required they travel with limited resources and a smaller regiment but that they leave Bastiion unsettled in their wake.

Neither sat right with Zaethan, and were he to wager on the hard set of her mouth during their last Quadrennal session, even the witch would agree.

"The crown city is not stable enough for you to leave it unattended yet. Depths, Dmitri, you're not sleeping. You've barely eaten. Just wait a few months longer." Zaethan pleaded for his friend to hear sense. "Let your people heal. Let their angers subside… drowned in their cups and emptied of coin. Today was unrest exercised while you're here. What happens when you're not?"

Palming his forehead, Dmitri massaged it vigorously before speaking. Awaiting his response, Zaethan took another gulp of the Southern liquor. This was not the evening he'd had in mind. Perhaps those evenings of ease and brotherly banter would never return. A hollow sensation spread through Zaethan's middle.

He wasn't ready to let them go.

"My heir will stabilize the people," Dmitri reiterated, unshaken. "To have an heir, there must be a wedding. And before a wedding, there must be a tour. I hear you, Zaeth. I do. Which brings us to the more pressing issue of your appointment. I'd like to announce the change tomorrow or the day after—before we embark for Darakai."

Panicked, Zaethan scurried his feet off the hearth as he shot up in his chair. This is what happened to sleep-deprived kings. They stopped playing the long game. Dmitri, the most patient individual he knew, annoyingly so, just proposed his most hazardous strategy yet.

"*Ano zà.* Absolutely not, Dmitri." Zaethan set his glass on the stone and scooted his seat directly in front of his friend. He bent forward and pressed his palms together. "He just surrendered his haidrenship. And believe me, that is how he views it: a surrender. But his command of your armies? Dmitri." A very real fear cooled Zaethan's veins. "The Nyack Kasim I know will not relinquish such control without a fight. Especially…" He swallowed anxiously. "If he's to relinquish it to me."

"You said it yourself; our people need a show of goodwill." Head bobbing, Dmitri knit his fingers together. "A change of power is expected, Zaeth. You can't be surprised at my choosing you for Orynthia's next commander supreme. I thought…" Disappointment deflated his posture. "I guess I thought you'd be pleased by the appointment."

Zaethan propped his weight on each knee, searching the gaze of his friend and sovereign. "*Uni zà,* it is the utmost honor. But you have one chance to play this card. I'm just proposing you play the right candidate. At the right time. We cannot stroll into Darakai in open opposition to their chief warlord. My father's governance over the tribes will not change." Cradling his chin, Zaethan scrambled to offer Dmitri a wiser alternative before his entire House turned against their new king. "Demoting my father so soon, their elected leader, would be perceived as a grave insult. So when you do…" Zaethan locked eyes with Dmitri. "It must be *after* the tour's completion, and from the advantage of a packed throne room."

Tugging the mink blanket tighter, Dmitri bore his stare of consideration into the flames. A flutter of relief eased Zaethan against the cushion. Either his argumentative savvy had improved, or Dmitri was simply too weary to debate his counsel.

"If not you, then who?"

"Kumo and I share an uncle. Brother to our mothers." Zaethan carefully advised. "Yousif Shà, a beta warlord from Halona, seasoned from the late Shield Wars. His tactical experience would be an asset. Kumo knows him better than I, says he's a good man, respected by many. You'll need that in your next commander, should the change cause a divide. You can trust him."

His eyelids heavy, Dmitri yawned and peered at Zaethan. Then, he smiled emptily. "But I trust you more."

"Then trust me now."

Dmitri slid deeper into the chair, lying his head on a fur-wrapped fist beneath his opulent layers of stitched silk. "Okay," he replied, conceding, and let his lids close. As Zaethan reached around and added another log to the dying fire, for his friend's sake, Dmitri muttered faintly, "She would have been proud of you today. I know I was."

Stoking the embers to overtake the parched log, Zaethan brushed off his father's spiteful remarks about her on the dais. His mother. Cyra. The name he was unpermitted to speak. "You need to rest" was his only reply.

"Falling asleep is a terror all its own," Dmitri muffled into the blanket. "Send for Eugenio. My tea… Luscia's blend…"

"You're impossible." Zaethan stood and stretched, giddied at the chance to startle the old bat from his slumber.

Dmitri slanted more heavily atop his fist as Zaethan was hitching his leg over the armrest, causing him to pause and glance back. Dmitri's dense lashes fluttered over the violent bags beneath his eyes, and he mumbled incoherently. "Glad you're here... warmer now..."

Finally dozing, Dmitri released the heavy fur, revealing his wrist. The cuff of his regal jacket had tugged down where a frayed red string peeked out. The testament of their youth was still knotted about his right hand.

Brothers by choice. Not by blood.

"You can sleep now, My King," Zaethan said with promise to the crackling quiet. "I won't go anywhere."

CHAPTER FIVE
LUSCIA

L uscia stroked Aksel's muzzle, soothing the beast as his ears flattened, wary of the of the surrounding sentries. It was an unnecessary show of martial authority by General Lateef, who lingered in Bastiion, while his master, Commander Kasim, had left for Darakai ahead of the Quadren. The move was unexpected, given his chief responsibility was to safeguard their king, not his House. She imagined the elder Kasim now, whipping his scarred stallion in a furious race toward the Andweles.

She did not look forward to meeting him there.

Dressed in trim navy-and-bronze uniforms, a dozen sentries stood along the cedar stalls of the guest stable. Luscia ignored them, patterning her studied disregard for Bastiion's games, as she and her father voiced their good-byes. Boreal's Clann Darragh was not accustomed to ever-present disdain. On the contrary, the Boreali considered her father a modern-day hero for unifying the clans in his early tenure.

Staring up at their *mighty oak*, she recognized his anger furrowing the pleats about his mouth, nearly entombed by his graying beard. Luscia was no stranger to the subtle signs of his disapproval, rare as they were. His grimace compressed when a bead of sweat rolled down his temple.

He was also unaccustomed to the weather.

"It is just until the border, Clann Darragh," Alora assured, her voice even as she stood elbow-to-elbow with Luscia. "Once you cross the outer proper, the escort will withdraw."

The whites of her father's eye skirted aside when he looked side-long toward the mounted line of najjan and visiting elders awaiting his leave. "This is a mockery of our strength." The normal boom of his baritone dropped out of the sentries' range. "He insults the very order that shielded his ancestors for generations."

"Niit. This is not the king's doing, Fappa." Luscia's hand shot out, small atop his robust forearm. "Darakai's dominion is far greater than you remember. But with a new regime in place, House balance might be restored."

Teasing her periphery, she noticed Alora stiffen at the unintended slight. Luscia had meant Dmitri's regime, not King Korbin's, but to backtrack would worsen the matter. Her relationship with her aunt, while never particularly close, had strained during the months since Luscia's coming to Bastiion. Their dichotomy in perspective was palpable in their every conversation. Luscia had attempted to rise above her own "impetuousness," as Alora had labeled it, and bridge the chasm between them. She still needed her aunt's tutelage, especially now that

Dmitri was king. Though she disagreed with Alora on a multitude of certainties, there was one she could not contradict.

Her life was no longer her own. And it should never be wielded as such.

The heaviness of her father's enormous palms cupped Luscia's shoulders. A sound rattled from the base of his throat, lodged with feeling. Tightening his grip, he whispered, "I cannot bear to leave you here, lu'Lycran."

"And yet…" Luscia swallowed, refusing to parade her sadness before General Lateef's spectators. "It is here I belong, and here I must stay. Meh'dajjeni Dönumn, Fappa."

The beads in his beard bobbed when he nodded grimly, and his hand gently moved to her lace collar and straightened it higher. "Weh'dajjeni Lux," he said to finish, his worry evident by the hitch in his voice as he let go of the fabric covering her scar and outstretched a hand behind himself.

A sandy-haired najjan, the last on the ground, stepped forward to deposit a leather wrapping into the Clann Darragh's expectant palm. Then, he dipped his body in a quick, fluid bow, followed by a reverent "Ana'Sere."

It struck her moments later that he had bowed to only Luscia and not her aunt.

"From your brother, before I tear myself away from you both." Her father rumbled and placed the leatherbound casing tenderly in her grasp, then wrapped his fingers over hers. "Where you go, we cannot follow. But with Phalen's aid, Aniell will protect you day and night."

"Tadöm…" She lovingly skimmed the leather stay and started to unravel it.

"Niit. For later," her father swiftly instructed, leery of his unwanted escort. Adjusting the sheath across his belt, he lowered his upper body in a graceful bow. "The High One cover your step always, my Haidren. Ana'Mere," he added, then addressing Alora. "Se'lah Aurynth... to you both."

Without thought, Luscia abandoned her resolve and collided into her father, throwing her arms around his great frame. Pressing her eyes shut, she felt him chuckle inside her embrace.

In her ear, perhaps even beneath Alora's hearing, he murmured, "You are set apart, lu'Lycran. Don't lose yourself to this place."

Luscia cleared her throat, let go, and held her chin high, knowing the clan elders watched on. "Rul'Aniell, Clann Darragh." Glancing past him, she scanned the line of pale faces, some wrinkled, others smooth; all painted with a tinge of confliction, given the circumstances. "Tredae'Aurynth, meh Ana'Brödre."

A genuine smile twinkled her father's seafoam eyes before his grimace returned, remembering the sentry. He backed away and mounted for their journey home to Roüwen. He hiked his upturned boot into the stirrup and thumped into the saddle. Holding Luscia's gaze one last time, glistening from afar, he shook out his beaded beard gruffly, and with a forceful kick, he urged the bay gelding out of the stable. In his departure, the najjani brigade stampeded after him, no doubt eager to be rid of Bastiion's cancers.

She stared through the open gate well after their exit. She found herself replaying last night's unexpected visit, when Bahira'Rasha's late knock had startled the entire apartment, awaking Tallulah in a haphazard dash to receive the Zôueli princess. It surprised Luscia how expediently the western royals had left the crown city, nudging skepticism of their motives further into her consciousness. But her father's parting words, oddly like those of Bahira'Rasha's, cocooned Luscia's alert ears. It was as if through the contrast of their lips, they'd been spoken from the same mouth.

"We learn to play by their rules, Loo-Shah," the Zôueli princess had said *in the midnight threshold of the vacant foyer. She'd snatched Luscia's chin between her ringed fingers and elevated it endearingly. "So that one day, when we must break them"*—she'd winked with mischief—*"we can live by our own."*

Luscia wasn't sure how she could admire and mistrust a person so ardently at the same time, but were the conundrum to walk about the palace, it'd most certainly be wearing billowing pants and a sharpened Zôueli smirk.

"You will be reunited soon, Ana'Sere," Marek said, drawing close from his station beside the longstanding captaen of Alora's guard, Emiere.

Inches in front of him, Luscia felt his steady breath rustle the top of her hair. She was growing more aware of his proximity every day—the comfort in it, the fresh confidence of his stride whenever he minimized space between them.

Luscia had yet to decide how she felt about that awareness, and she habitually found it was never the occasion to figure it out.

"Not soon enough, Captaen. Boreal falls behind Darakai and Pilar on His Majesty's tour. It will be many months before we see my father again."

"Shall we, niece?" Alora started forward, assuming Luscia to follow.

Crossing the grounds, the four Boreali walked in silence, Luscia's highlander wolx trailing beside. Both generations remained acutely conscious of the eyes that watched them pass. Amassing on the vast green, squadrons of the king's regiment were being assessed and graded, likely in selection for their prolonged journey across the realm. A marshal of sorts seemed to be evaluating everything, from his soldiers to the horses they'd been assigned. But as their Boreali pod trekked along the mosaic stone path, the officer's interest in his task ceased, and his bleak, beady stare raced toward their grouping—an attempt at browbeating, Luscia supposed. Like his subordinates, the man did not appreciate protecting Northerners on this tour, and his undistracted glare ensured Luscia knew it. Intuition told she'd be saddled with such attempts for a season longer, as the squat marshal was bound to accompany the selected soldiers.

Once the man and his intrigue were at their backs, Alora dismissed their captaens. "Leave us to our thoughts."

At her subtle command, both Marek and Emiere withheld their step, falling back to grant discretion.

"That field marshal has ties to Lateef's purse strings. Be wary of his loyalties outside of the proper."

Luscia crinkled her forehead, then smoothed it as to give the impression they were merely speaking about last night's rainstorm. They'd embarked into the courtier gardens, which embellished the final stretch toward the palace main.

Luscia wanted to ask how Alora knew such things but stated instead, "The king's regiment ought to be his most loyal shield and shepherd. Were General Lateef to move against us, would not the regiment intervene?"

"Many things ought to be, yet many things are not so," Alora answered, always speaking in riddle. It infuriated Luscia as much as it perplexed her. "There should not be a secondary fleet of ships in the royal navy, yet they are berthed in Lempeii as we speak." A sourness piqued her words as she continued more quietly than before. "The snakes with whom you travel harbor their own agendas, Luscia. As haidren, it is your duty to unearth such things and judge the proper time to use that knowledge against them for the benefit of Boreal."

New-World masonry, laid centuries after the Forgotten Wars, lined the palace halls, the air tinkling with the chatter of hurried nobles and their resident attendants. Luscia risked a peek at her aunt. The picture of tranquility, Alora led them under a marble archway, her dainty features unemotive where they poked past her sheet of half-bound platinum hair.

"You mean for the benefit of the king," Luscia hushedly clarified.

Her aunt—and predecessor—did not reply in haste, letting Luscia wonder which Alora she was speaking to: the one who trained her in the Sight, who sat by her bedside after each painful episode, or the other, the woman who skirted questions by posing more yet somehow knew their answers all along.

Ever since her Ascension, Luscia had been starting to suspect that there were facets of her aunt's life that required Alora's agenda too.

"We serve for the benefit of our king *and* our people. To serve the first is to serve the second, Luscia." A chide laced Alora's retort as they met the corridor to the Boreali suites. "I pray your eyes open to accept the two as one before you carry Boreal's charge to the rest of the Ethnicam. As haidren, your perspective on these matters must broaden. Let us pray the travel grants you enough time for maturation."

At the rebuke, guilt caused Luscia to look down at Phalen's newest gift wrapped in her hands, which had slickened during the last minutes. His radials, sheathed in polished bone, gleamed up at her comfortingly. Luscia repressed her emotion and steered her face forward resolutely.

"Meh fyreon, Ana'Mere. I will heed the wisdom of my sil'haidren." Luscia submitted, hiding the sting behind her formality.

Her aunt paused outside the entrance to her apartments. Appeased,

Alora extended her arm in a rare gesture and resituated a messy cluster of Luscia's braids. "Tadöm. I do regret you are having to embark on this next path alone, Luscia. Being sil'haidren, my prompt return to Roüwen is vital to this transition." Alora's slender fingers tapped the braid, then fell to her side once more. "Tonight, Emiere will deliver a trunk. In it is a half-year supply of treatments to take with you. Ration the vials but do not neglect your taking them. We all saw you teeter on the dais yesterday. It cannot happen again, not in front of those wolves."

Referencing her near-episode, Alora hooked her gaze at Luscia, one thin brow climbing with surprising allegation.

"I've maintained your dosing and sched—" Luscia sprung to her own defense when the doors parted abruptly, and Declan's carroty topknot jutted through the opening.

"Ana'Mere, Ana'Sere." He nodded, pasting an awkward smile above his short beard. "Meh fyreon for interrupting, but you've got company waiting."

Dragging the door open on its hinges, he sheepishly stepped aside. Once his barrel-chested form was out of the way, Luscia saw the king of Orynthia putzing about her common room, an elongated wooden box under one arm. Beneath Noxolo's amused watch, Dmitri plucked a withered stem from an incense cannister and rolled it under his nose.

"Your Majesty!" Alora hailed her welcome, leading through Luscia's foyer. "To what do we owe this pleasure?"

Her aunt's countenance immediately warmed, driving Luscia's brow to climb.

Thoroughly startled, Dmitri dropped the stem to the floor from where he'd held it up to the light in examination. He bent to retrieve it before Aksel could, fumbling with the overlarge case, and shakily rose to stand, either because of his ailment or the competitive snap of her lycran's jaws.

"Might I ask what this is? Lovely fragrance."

"Nixberry," Luscia told him, circling the room under the cavernous byrnnzite dome toward her impulsive wolx. She clicked her tongue, commanding Aksel to her side, and caught a fistful of his scruff to keep him there.

"I'd like to bring some back from your homeland, to house in our royal garden." Dmitri brought the stem closer to his eye, disregarding the beast, and studied the barbs. "We've nothing like it."

Luscia ironed the front of her linsilk day dress, trying not to eavesdrop on Alora's rushed conversation with Tallulah in the washroom. The stout Boreali maid was flustered by the king's visit, which, for Tallulah, seemed to be her default reaction to every visit.

"Niit, it wouldn't take, I'm afraid. Nixberry roots are reborn in the winter," Luscia regrettably replied, acquainted with his love for exotic botanicals.

"Reborn in winter… There's profound poetry in that." He grinned slightly, carefully placing the fragile stem back into the incense burner. "Alas, I've come for much more important purposes. Shall we?"

He motioned at her expansive sofa and, taking residence, placed the box between them. Excitedly, Dmitri smiled not only to Luscia but to the three najjan dotting the room. He unlatched it and flipped open the top, as if he were a giddy boy who couldn't wait a moment longer.

"I brought you a gift, Lady Boreal. Although…" Her king beamed, his dimple on full display. "It's not really a gift when it's your own possession."

Lying across the snowy silk cushion was her father's kuerre. Spotless and unharmed, the sword's luxiron core gleamed, its subtle variegated light ricocheting off Dmitri's autumnal eyes. Luscia glanced away to compose herself. Her Northern ears pricked, hearing the communal exhale from her men. It was like welcoming home a long-lost relative.

"There are not enough words, in any language, to express my gratitude, Your Majesty…" She tried, but her voice cracked. Covering her mouth, she released Aksel and stroked the warm metal in the case.

"Take that back," he replied, jesting at her use of the title, then sobered. "It was wrong for us to take this from you—from *all* of you." In a bewildering move, their king dipped his head toward each najjan in apology, ending with her captaen. "After deliberating with the Peerage, it was decided not only this blade but every piece of luxiron brought to Bastiion is to be returned to najjani care. I've arranged for this restoration to occur before we depart for Darakai. As I reminded the councilmen…" He chuckled boyishly, swiping his waves out of his eyesight. "The Order of the Najjan is my secondary protection. Should Orynthia's most elite weaponry be barred from the king's disposal as well?'"

Luscia regretted having granted Creyvan the morning, wishing he could share in this historic news. His surly disposition could certainly use it of late. Lifting his spirits just one tenth of the others would be a prime improvement. It had been a month since Böwen left to transport Mila's family, on Luscia's order, and his twin had not forgiven her since.

Alora reappeared and wedged into the circle of furniture. "This is undeniably generous, Your Majesty."

"And diplomatically savvy," Luscia admitted truthfully.

She forgot Creyvan and found Marek across the divide, sharing her disguised elation. It puffed his chest and relaxed the hard set of his wide shoulders. He pinched his lips to keep himself from bursting as they each voiced thanks to their king. But defying his poise, it was Marek's aquamarine eyes that smiled unabashedly.

And they were smiling at her.

"Though I'd prefer to stay a while and rummage about your herbs, I fear I've kept the field marshal waiting long enough." Lifting off the luxurious sofa, Dmitri angled his lean neck, evaluating the skies through the window. "Quite a while, it appears. Forgive my haste, Lady Boreal, but I must be going now."

Escorting her regent into the foyer, Luscia wavered before speaking her curiosity. "Sayuri… She will be joining us, wem?"

Dmitri turned and lingered in the doorway. Disappointment dragged his expression downward when he vaguely replied, "A king must always have a contingency plan, Luscia. We'll find out together if I am to enact mine."

With that, Dmitri left her apartments a bit sadder than when she'd found him. Luscia reminded herself it was not curiosity to blame but the haidren to Pilar, for not emerging from her chambers—a selfish refusal that still did not make any sense.

"Noxolo?" Alora questioned the najjan when Luscia closed the door. "How long was His Majesty waiting for us?"

"About an hour," he mumbled dolefully.

"I told him, Ana'Mere. Told that oaf to go find yeh—"

Luscia raised her fingers, quelling Tallulah's scolding, and twirled them at Noxolo to elaborate.

"At the suggestion, King Dmitri ordered us not to shorten your final moments with your father."

"Wem, it's true, Ana'Sere," Declan said, chiming his confirmation.

Luscia picked up the latched box and held it close against her middle, indebted to Dmitri. Not only for the sword's return but for not wishing his loss would become hers.

Too gently for anyone to hear but her blade, she squeezed it tight and whispered, "Welcome home."

Flexing her grip, Luscia stretched the young hide where it crested her knuckles, just skimming the radials. Phalen was a mastermind, she conceded, marveling the devious way he'd secreted luxiron darts inside the boning of the fingerless leather gauntlets, which now sheathed the backs of her hands to her forearms. Reaching around the corner, marking the turnoff into the hall of Pilarese suites, Luscia was careful not to disturb the taut bands running the width of her palm, inventively affixed to the seams.

Like his radials, her brother had built a safety on the trigger, but Luscia wasn't eager to test its sensitivity, least of all on her opinionated captaen. He'd voiced his opposition to her plan the entire length of the west wing, and she'd finally started to enjoy the quiet.

"We shouldn't be here." Marek broke the fleeting silence and scowled, his back pressed against the cool stone. "You've more to lose than she does if we are seen, Luscia."

Gritting her jaw, Luscia mentally revisited the notion of using the handsome redhead for target practice and peered around the corner again. All clear, as she anticipated. In the commotion of current events, sentries wouldn't be wasted guarding the apartments of someone who refused to leave.

If Sayuri was, in fact, still in them.

A myriad of theories had taunted Luscia, ultimately inspiring her to investigate the haidren's whereabouts on her own. Perhaps a cosmetic treatment had gone awry, as Ira had asserted. Or there was another cause altogether. Sayuri had never hidden her dismay for Dmitri's engagement nor her salacious attempts to secure the match for herself. Luscia didn't put it past the western haidren to conjure some elaborate hoax to better impede his marital proceedings. Though to what end or practical application, Luscia couldn't say. It would be a foolhardy endeavor, for Dmitri was set on his course with Razôuel—not that the Ethnicam would ever allow a betrothal to Sayuri Naborū-Zuo or anyone else from the outer Houses.

"We're simply here to listen, Captaen," she said again, innocently. "So, bolaeva, let me do what I came to. Or next time I'll bring Declan and leave you in the apartment with Aksel."

Marek grunted. "Declan would not defy my command so easily…"

"On the contrary, he likes me much better than you," she countered, angling toward what she'd calculated to be Sayuri's replacement apartments, since Aksel's scent still dominated her primary housing. Luscia might have gone a little overboard back in the spring. It could be years before the stench faded.

"My men like me just fine," Marek declared in her ear and fidgeted uncomfortably. "Let's just hurry up and get this over with."

"Waedfrel," Luscia murmured and eased off the stone, gliding toward the door at the opposite end of the corridor. But after a few steps, she heard a faraway shuffle and suddenly propelled them behind the bend.

Her body retreated to against his abdomen, and a rush of heat prickled her skin beneath the sparring garb she'd adorned for their little mission, sending her back to the washroom where they'd kissed. Her glance twisted backward. Marek looked to have been transported there as well. A flush stained his cheeks as his pupils dilated.

"Ykah lö?" he asked hurriedly. "What did you see?"

"Not sure yet. Heh'ta," she instructed him, nudging his jacket front to stay put.

The shuffle grew louder from where the corridor intersected with another walkway. Soon enough, a pair of fine boots sounded through the hall, an oversized plant blocking the man's identity from view. Even so, Luscia knew him well, especially having met together prior that day.

Her king stooped to deposit potted shrubbery, an extravagantly floral-laden cluster, and brushed dirt off his trousers. He had come alone. His newly adopted Watchmen were nowhere to be found. More than anyone, Luscia could appreciate a desire for privacy.

Dmitri went to knock but faltered. It was then she spotted an existing pile of dirt at his feet, outside the doors. A trail of it littered the corridor from where he'd come. It was not his first visit to Sayuri.

After straightening his vest, he again lifted his fist and gave her door three gentlemanly knocks. "I was wondering if you'd be willing to see me today, Lady Pilar. It's rather beautiful out, and if you'd permit me a walk—"

An abrasive thud hit the wood from inside, causing Dmitri to lurch backward, followed by a shriek and a sob.

She was most definitely in there.

Defeat curved his spine, suggesting this was a pattern of theirs. Tidying his lapel, he came closer to the door and tried again. "We are leaving the day after tomorrow, Lady Pilar. I'm at an utter loss how to coax you from this room, and I'll not become a tyrant in the process. I had no choice but to call your brother to Bastiion last week, but this is *your* birthright, not Hachiro's." Dmitri rested his forehead against the wood, almost pleading. "Sayuri, please come out."

He stayed like that for a handful of minutes, unmoving and unrelenting. When his plea resulted in nothing but ongoing stillness, Dmitri toyed with a leaf of the plant sympathetically. "I will try again tomorrow, Lady Pilar" was all he said. Then he walked away.

Luscia's mind raced, wondering how many times he, a king, had begged at her door. She rotated away from the edge and flopped against the stone, reconsidering her previous theories.

"Do you know what any of this implies?" Marek probed earnestly, having witnessed the same abnormality.

No choice but to call your brother.

Astonishment heaped her contemplations. Then absolute dread.

"By the High One, there are two of them."

CHAPTER SIX
LUSCIA

Fiddling with the last gemstone, Luscia recited centuries-old stanzas as she prepared the mare for the road ahead, weaving and tying blessings into the horse's mane as she'd done to the rest. This duty was her first to her men, to the Order of the Najjan, before House ambassadorship or royal advisory. She was haidren to Boreal, the intended spiritual leader of a people, and despite her scarred spirit, Luscia intended to submit herself to that end entirely.

The mare stomped her back leg, again indicating her annoyance at Aksel's presence near the front of the stall. To lessen the animal's impending stress, Luscia had ordered the hybrid brute to keep watch. It was best to reacquaint the Boreali horses, boarded in the superior care of the haidren stables, with Aksel's presence before departing the next morning. While the animals had traveled to the crown city together in the spring, the lycran was still their natural predator, an instinctive detail the mare had not forgotten, given the alert swivel of her ears.

Conversely, Aksel's nearness calmed Luscia's brewing angst. Old habits, she supposed.

Humming the close of the melodic poem, she caressed the lilac stone to conclude her blessing but stumbled back when, alighted by her touch, subtle but startlingly, the petrified lumin flickered within the gem. At Luscia's separation, the intermittent twinkle deadened to its slumber. She'd experience a similar reaction just once, upon the inaugural use of her Sight, in a cliffside clearing outside the proper. But Luscia couldn't recall any physical responses to her aunt's handling of wildlife, having witnessed Alora's mastery in the apothic arts and lumin-enhanced botany firsthand.

A connection to nature should only exist behind the veil, if at all. Luscia's heart pounded; for here, she stood before it.

Alone in the stall, Luscia eyed her lycran. The russet fur streaking his white coat was unruffled and smooth; he had not felt the lumin awaken in the raw gem. Luscia listened for others but heard nothing but the sounds of the stable. Drawing a breath, she examined her fingertips as if to find something outside the ordinary. But there was only ivory, unmarked flesh.

Inquisition itched her spine. Luscia had not one but two sets of eyes. The second she'd not engaged since the night of Ambrose's demise.

Edging closer to the mare, Luscia cautiously let her lids fall, fearing the temporary darkness. She wrenched the surface of her mind ajar, like the sliding door of the stable in which she stood, and felt the for the mysterious tether that, as an out-of-place drawstring, tickled her consciousness. Mentally, Luscia tugged and parted the veil between worlds.

Cracking her eyelids apart, Luscia froze while her eyes gaped into the *Other*.

Threads of lumin radiated around the stall, peacefully wafting about with ease and grace. Clustered at various points around the dappled mare, the brightest threads danced together in the areas over which Luscia had prayed. In the horse's braided slate mane, the blessed stones glimmered, their vivid hues painting the drab wooden slats in watercolors. Luscia covered her mouth, speechless.

Not once had Alora described the Sight to be anything like this.

She heard a soft *pat pat* against the straw. Luscia pivoted as Aksel's voluminous tail thumped enthusiastically. His slitted pupils dilated, and the highlander wolx crooked his thick neck, fixing his icy gaze on something above. Luscia could have sworn a foxy grin puckered his muzzle before a prominent strand of lumin drifted between them, more brilliant than the rest.

A rush of cinder and chill unfurled along Luscia's skin as the strand floated in the middle of the air with authority, squaring at her.

The harbinger thread, as if it'd lingered in the *Other*, had been waiting for her return ever since that awful night.

She couldn't breathe. Her ears flooded with sound, whispers of all kinds mingled in an indiscernible onslaught, drowning her senses. An unwelcome pain seared Luscia's temples, and her legs began to buckle. She gave into the ache and collapsed to her knees. Throwing back her head in agony, a tear trickled down her cheek as she stared into the terrifying brilliance hovering before her face.

"Luscia..." The whispers loudened, and the harbinger thread convulsed.

On her hands, she thrashed through the straw for her aunt's remedy, desperate to make the chorused summoning end. Through quivering lashes, she watched the harbinger thread swirl around her hands where she struggled to open the vial.

"Luscia..."

Utterly frightened, Luscia shoved the glass to her lips and embraced the bitter fluid. As the tonic seeped down her throat, she felt a pop of pressure in her ears. The voices dissipated and vanished altogether.

She couldn't say how long she lay panting on the floorboards. It wasn't until the cold wet nudge of Aksel's insistent snout against her cheek did she gain the courage to look up. When she did, she was met by a framework of ordinary rafters.

"Thank the High One." Luscia moaned, rolling onto her elbows.

Gaining her balance, she knelt to her satchel and slipped the emptied vial inside, begrudging her residual trembles. Alora had already confirmed it; the threads did not speak. And if they did, it was madness that claimed to hear them. Luscia's mother had once made such claims. The haidren to Boreal should never fear the *Other* or its threads but commune with them ceaselessly. However, securing the satchel over her shoulder, Luscia wasn't sure how she could ever brave the veil again. If Eoine's fate was manifesting in her daughter, it was a slow ruin Luscia would be forced to hide, specifically from her aunt. She exited the stall, her head hung low, her dirty-blonde strands obstructing her vision in shame.

Another failure, sewn into Aurynth's tapestry.

She walked on like that toward the doors, a dozen stalls belonging to opposing members of the Quadren. Nearing them, Luscia saw the sky had darkened during her episode.

Too much time wasted.

When she crossed the last stall, something dark shot out and seized her arm, reeled her through the gate, and hurtled her around the divider. Luscia's back hit the planks, worsening her latent headache. Suddenly, a set of robust forearms were knocked against the wall, caging her to the side of the stall. It answered her question as to whom the multi-length stall belonged, for the haidren to Darakai was holding her hostage inside it.

Kasim didn't move and instead hovered his height over the slight vacancy between them. His long ropelike locs were half-bound. A golden-clad few dangled over the simple airy shirt he'd tucked carelessly into taut leather breeches. Its lacing untied, the pale linen was stark against the definition of his Southern chest, which glistened from a fresh sweat. Whatever he was up to, given his attire, he was off duty and alone.

Kasim's newly decorated brow compressed when he predatorially angled his mouth and stated, "We need to talk."

For a second, Luscia wondered if she were the *lycran* or the mare, given their similar familiarity. After unhooking the trigger's safety, she released Phalen's radials and pushed the fanned blades into the see-through material near his middle.

She was most definitely the *lycran*.

"Correction." Luscia enunciated, angry he'd caught her off-guard. "You need to back off."

Thrusting off the slats, she prodded the tiny luxiron fans threateningly, until they met the resistance of his hard muscle. He stilled there.

His stomach flinched at the Northern metal, yet his eyeline stayed true. With unrequited amusement, his broad lips smirked, and Kasim raised his hands in false surrender. Creeping forward, Luscia marched him in retreat against the opposite stall wall. Reversing their stances, she did not withdraw her weaponry.

Kasim sluggishly propped his hands behind his head, disregarding the minor bloom of scarlet staining his shirt. With a smug spark in his verdant eyes, his chin crooked downward. "For a creature who avoids close contact, you seem to savor mine." He nodded toward his gut, then past her shoulder. "Both of you, apparently."

Her head whipped around, toward where her enormous lycran loitered contently near the gate, his tongue swung over his serrated teeth. With a short snarl, Luscia sheathed her radials and solidified a considerable separation—feet away, leaned against the trough and crossed her arms, and feigning indifference.

"So talk."

Straightening, Kasim looped his thumbs into his thick belt and lowered his voice. "I propose a new deal. Continue teaching me the crescent wraiths, on an *expedited timetable*," he said contemptuously, "and in turn, I'll train you in hand combat."

Luscia scoffed, widening her stance. "That's done, Kasim. I made that clear a month ago."

Shrugging, he shoved off the wall and came closer. "Circumstances have changed," he said, crossing his arms as well. His expression took on a bitter shadow. "Wekesa, the alpha you met and, if I recall, fractured his fingers…" Kasim grinned, though fleetingly. "He plans to challenge me for alpha zà in Faraji. And he cannot win."

She remembered the alpha in question, a disdainful man roughly

Kasim's age, whose testament to violence had been chiseled into the side of his head. Luscia didn't care for Wekesa in the least, nor for Darakaian politics. But her aunt's caution chimed, reminding her to catalog opposing agendas, and then use them. "Pryde affairs have no bearing on Boreal," Luscia replied nonchalantly, genuinely interested in his response. There was a desperation in his tone she didn't yet understand.

He bit his full lip, perhaps calculating a rebuttal. His pause was disconcertingly uncharacteristic.

"Alpha zà is a title boasting two victories in one name," Kasim answered flatly. "Authority over the prydes, but more importantly, residence in the crown city. Should Wekesa succeed, my pryde must vacate the proper to make way for his. Would you prefer the streets of Bastiion under his thumb, over mine?"

Kasim waited. He was learning how to barter with her, what arguments would be heard over others, and she did not like it. For a second, he sounded like a peer, another haidren rather than a ruthless alpha. And where there was more to Kasim, there was more to distrust.

However, Marketown under Wekesa's governance would be an absolute bloodbath, the kind of oppression that took place outside the king's awareness, in the homes and pockets of the poor, the cross-caste, and the breakaways. From their limited interaction, Luscia knew Wekesa would tilt the city's resources in his favor, policing his own opposition instead of the threats to their people.

Yet Kasim could possibly defeat Wekesa without her involvement. It was an unfortunate risk, but after her previous association with Kasim had been revealed—when healing his young warrior—Luscia had promised her najjan she'd never privately partner with the Darakaians again. Fortunately, their dismantled deal regarding the wraiths and his training was still a secret, one she wished to keep that way.

Luscia could not afford to endanger the still-healing rapport with her five.

"Every gain has a loss, Maji'maia. It's time to reevaluate yours." Kasim prodded, enlisting his beta's Andwele nickname for her, meaning *Witchy Moon.* "Strengthen my vulnerabilities, and I will strengthen yours."

Luscia peered at Kasim. The image of him rocking an injured cross-caste boy on the docks was contested by the many more unsavory pictures of his nature, his malice, and his inherited brutality.

Marek's face, along with Declan's and the others, came to mind, proposing another way. "You've proven proficient in your circles, so you'll do it again. My najjan can refine my skill in hand combat. Besides…" Luscia stiffened her grip on either bicep and made toward the open gate. "You're the last person I want touching me."

She tried to release both radials as soon as she heard him dart through the hay, but Kasim caught her wrist right before she could trigger the second blade. Pinning it above her head, he dodged her swipe and snared the sleeve of her armed hand in his teeth. He locked his free arm around the small of her back, then pegged hers against the post and slipped the unsheathed radial off her knuckles.

"I know." He panted proudly. "Which makes me the perfect candidate to help you overcome your aversion." Kasim stepped on her upturned boot, keeping her from hooking it around his calf. Heat cloyed her thighs where their bodies intertwined against the stall. "Relying on your blades is making you sloppy, Maji'maia."

"As is your cockiness," she spat and rammed her free leg upward, between his legs.

Howling, he unhanded her and doubled over, clutching the softness all men harbored.

Huffily, Luscia snatched her brother's invention from the hay and snapped for her unhelpful *lycran* to follow. "You're losing your edge," she said, chastising Aksel as he yipped his farewell to the bruised haidren.

With a rasp, Kasim called after her, "I'm owed an answer!"

"I'll consider one!" she yelled.

Luscia threw her satchel across her body and left, thoroughly fed up with the entitlement of men.

Luscia slipped a finger over the embroidered collar of her riding jacket, peeling it off the clammy skin of her neck. It was an hour past dawn, and she was already sweating.

The clear morning light unveiled a spectator's buffet for the noble assemblage, grouped in pockets of buzz bordering the manicured green. A selected company of the royal regiment had already amassed on the lawn, the soldiers divided to bookend the king's touring party. The party was scheduled to leave at first light, yet the haidrens and their escort waited under a cloudless sun. What had started as excited chatter among the crowd for the king and Quadren's sendoff had quickly spun into scandalous rumor, as there were three haidrens present, not four.

The House of Pilar was unaccounted for, as Sayuri had not come.

Her absence did offer the Boreali one reprieve, at least. Luscia slid her gaze to Marek, unsmiling and straight shouldered to her right. Glinting triumphantly, a set of crescent wraiths crisscrossed his back like lethal wings of a mythical warrior. The red of his plaited hair reflected in the metal, casting a burnt halo about his severe composure. Misleadingly, aside from her father's kuerre, Luscia was naked of the coveted weaponry; her ability to wield them was a deadly skillset the Houses did not need to know she possessed. It was better to be underestimated by the vicious tempers of Orynthia's controlling powers than estimated accurately, for in knowledge there was advantage. Luscia planned to savor that advantage, despite Dmitri's loophole in their Unitarian legislation.

Behind her captaen's radiance, Creyvan was mounted on his gelding, wraiths sheathed, mirroring Declan and Noxolo on the opposite flank. Public outrage over their luxiron had lasted only moments, as the people had become more distracted by Pilar's prolonged absence.

Ahead, Ira swatted something buzzing the air. Without escort, relying on the royal regiment for security, Bastiion's haidren toured alone. Given his dependency for diversion and proclivity for all things lecherous, Luscia wondered how he'd adapt to life without his yancy comforts. Adhering to strict regulation on the weight of their gear, each haidren was permitted a single trunk, in addition to what they carried on their back, to journey more rapidly through the realm. With the crate of her aunt's tonics secured to her saddle, Luscia had shoved her essentials into the ballooned sacks behind each of her mare's legs.

The one exception was for their king, who, in front of Ira, was surrounded by his regiment and wagons of supplies.

Releasing a sound of annoyance, Ira swiveled in his saddle and yanked a pocket-dial from his overly embellished cream coat. He fiddled with the tiny gnomon, then propped it in his palm and stared intently, as if the little trinket would deliver him a revelation. Luscia stifled a smirk.

It would not, as he hadn't bothered to point it north.

"For the love of Rian and all its deplorable delights, will someone just pry her from that room already?" Ira tucked the misapplied sundial in his linens and leaned over his horse's rump toward Luscia. "That particular pitstop is serenading me to its door…" He cupped an ear and impishly waggled his brow. "We mustn't disappoint the citizens of this kingdom, especially Rian's free-spirited hosts!"

"I'm sure the town magistrate is doing just fine without you, Lord Bastiion," Luscia droned, inspiring Declan to snicker through his crooked nose. "Rian wants nothing with your nobility, and much with your coin. You should consider that when we meet their gate."

Ira propped his weight on an arm, atop the horse. "Which is exactly why we must make haste, my stern siren, so I can show you how to spend it when we get there!"

A growl emanated from Marek's throat, apparently displeased by the offer, but he refrained from comment, observing his station. He likely would have overlooked the observation in another setting, were they not on courtly display.

At the menacing rumble, Ira stroked his chest and shrugged. "Well, I suppose he can come too, if you insist."

Luscia envied the Darakaians, who'd opted for the rear of the precession due to the soldiers' doubled prominence toward the front. One lycran and five najjan were more deadly than a dozen Darakaians. Listening to Ira's incessant rubbish, she regretted not volunteering their own services instead. It seemed a communal opinion, as Noxolo uttered the same under his breath, earning a silent nod from Declan in her periphery.

Abruptly, the military throng before Ira broke apart, and Dmitri emerged atop his prized Andwele mare, gifted from Kasim. Her coloring was the inverse of her twin, and the bronze-and-indigo patterns of Dmitri's ceremonial regalia stood out commandingly against her steely sheen. Assuming his lengthy, embellished cape to be burdensome, Luscia imagined Dmitri nothing but eager to take it off, once outside the city. The same burly field marshal Alora had pointed out walked beside him on foot, headed steadily for the end of the lawn. An audible surge chimed through the gathered nobles as they shifted to see what had torn their king from his residence at the helm.

Ira too swung his outstretched body past Luscia with curiosity, only to flippantly toss his hands in the air. "Always one for a dramatic entrance," he sneered and settled back in his saddle. "Look at this crowd, wrapped around her naughty little finger. Why didn't I think of that?"

Luscia nudged her mare around and spied an oncoming wagon, driven by a palace attendant and a single Pilarese guard. Her head shook with disbelief. Stacked well beyond its capacity with trunks, rucksacks, and cases of all sizes wedged in between, their pretentious owner was completely disguised behind the ostentatious haul.

Dmitri called for their attention as he passed. "Lord Bastiion, Lady Boreal, if you could follow." Further along the line he added "Zaeth, you as well, please."

Thoroughly confused, they broke from the precession and pursued their king across the grass to meet the wagon. In an odd trio, the three haidrens formed a crescent about Dmitri and the field marshal, who did not seem partial to the nearness of his Darakaian nor Boreali guests.

The wagon was parked, accompanied by a concealed, haphazard scuffling. Dmitri paced his mare forward and cleared his throat. "Everyone, I'd like to introduce Hachiro Naborū-Zuo. Hachiro will be serv—" He interrupted himself and projected more loudly. "Um, Hachiro?"

Immediately the scuffling ceased, and a bushel of rolled parchment popped around the base of the wagon, hoisted in the slim arms of young Pilarese man, dressed modestly in the tailored ocher-colored robes of a shoto'shi scholar. His short erratic tufts of ebony hair poked overtop of the papers, suggesting he'd only recently awakened. Or, for that matter, had never slept.

"Present, Your Majesty," the shoto acolyte promptly stated over his bundle of scrolls.

"Relieved to see it." Dmitri pressed on. "As I was saying, due to Sayuri's present... limitations... her brother, Hachiro, will be serving as interim haidren to Pilar for the course of my coronation tour. Hachiro, I'd like you to meet the Quadren."

At Dmitri's motion, Sayuri's brother lowered his scrolls. He blinked superfluously before extending a brief Pilarese greeting.

"Hū meii." And instantly he returned to fondling his papers, ignoring the group.

"Are we sure they're actually related?" Ira mumbled out the side of his mouth, not discreetly in the least.

From her left, Kasim whispered accusingly, "Did you know about this?"

As he was always provoked by her quiet, Luscia stared squarely ahead and muttered in return, "I know many things. Unfortunately for Darakai, you do not."

Kasim's Andwele stallion reared its head back and forth, agitated by his master's unruly temper.

Oblivious, Ira said, "All I know is this library's not coming to Rian."

"Thank you, Lord Bastiion!" Dmitri exclaimed through a tense grin. "Hachiro, given our itinerary, you may select one trunk from your collection. The rest, I regret, must stay in Bastiion."

The Pilarese guard descended the wagon and began sifting through Hachiro's luggage. He reached in and retrieved a hefty, leather-bound book, its rough pages resembling a journal or ledger of sorts. Ditching the scrolls, Sayuri's brother ran toward his guard and crossly tore it out of the man's grasp.

Seizing some discarded documents, Hachiro blinked some more and then nodded toward the bigger man. "Be it a matter of weight, might I bring two trunks if I leave him instead?"

Dmitri's lips flattened, seemingly out of amusement rather than anger. "I must insist you bring only the one," he said, reiterating kindly. In an unfamiliar gesture, their king dipped his head side to side, perhaps mimicking some Pilarese custom, as he'd been known to appreciate some of Luscia's as well.

Hachiro drummed his wiry fingers atop the fat journal in thought. When the guard bent to reload one of the articles, Sayuri's brother wacked him with a scroll and seized the trunk protectively. With a laborious sigh, he faced their sovereign.

"Pyō jien, pyō chakrit. I accept this knowledge and affirm this wisdom, Your Majesty." The shoto'shi mirrored the gesture back toward Dmitri in a dual, oscillated bow.

Kasim's leathers creased when he grumbled, "I accept this bookkeeper is going to be a nuisance."

Heeding the field marshal's command, the towering Pilarese guard stepped aside to listen to Hachiro's extensive list of requirements. To a hissing backdrop of renewed rumor and speculation, Dmitri pulled his strained gaze from the crowd and longingly let it embrace the palace in the distance. Thinking of his mother, left alone with these scavengers, or maybe even Sayuri entombed in her apartments, he crinkled his nose as he stifled some emotion.

Turning toward his patchwork Quadren, Dmitri sat taller. "Time is of the essence. Are you with me?"

Kasim tightened his reigns. "Uni zà."

"Wem." Luscia confirmed wholeheartedly. "Se'lah Aurynth."

Dmitri looked to Ira, who, in an instant, paled. Clutching something hanging around his neck, he nodded wordlessly.

"Hachiro?"

The shoto'shi paused tallying his scrolls, patted the journal against his chest, and repeated the Pilarese bow. "My King."

"There is no going back. Only forward." Once he locked eyes with each of them, Dmitri's intensity finally fell upon Luscia. More emerald than brown, his eyes concealed both life and death. The blood of her fingertips pulsed in response. "Today begins the rest of the Stag Age. And it will take us all to defend it."

At Dmitri's brusque command, Harmonia reared and broke into a gallop after the southern gate. Not once did he look back home.

The coronation tour had begun.

CHAPTER SEVEN

Five nights the figure stalked them through the plains. And for five nights, memories taunted his tainted soul.

The royal caravan twinkled in the distance below, where they slowed to make camp. He knew the regiment's trek well, as if he'd charted it yesterday, rather than before the decades that had passed since he rode among them. It took his cursed legs, stronger than any mortal man's, mere hours to track their progress under the cover of darkness. As he was unfettered by the tolerable mists of the Boreali highlands, Southern travel under the merciless sun was unbearable for the figure in late summer. He'd stirred much too early that evening and was paying for it now; the singe of his fresh blistering only embittered the cause more.

The figure scorned his mistress for returning him to this ill-fated highway. But to his disgrace, he loved remembering her here, noble and daring... ignorant of the transgressions he would one day lay at her feet.

To that end, the figure popped a stubborn knuckle back into socket, sliding on his glove while he patiently watched from between the brush. There, the elevation bled into the foothills of the Andwele Mountains, providing him a new vantage from the emerging ridge-line. Heights the regiment would never scout unless provoked. These rising hills belonged to another breed, their transit concealed from king and Quadren, yet most certainly operated in mutual benefit. Trodden outside the governance of law and order, the dust of these crude byways hosted Orynthia's vilest porters: trafficking commodities too offensive for polite society. Their cargoes transported illicit goods, some the human variety, at the bidding of rich, lawless appetites. It was a dusty, obscured road like this where the figure had first laid eyes on Yannis, the slaver. But the elusive noble was not alone in smuggling the disadvantaged in shackles throughout the realm, many of whom were sold by their lenders when inflated debts came calling.

To spare another, some even sold themselves.

Rian, a trading outpost nestled in the crux of the Mirajii Forest and the Andwele foothills, was no different, though their denizens thought otherwise. A citadel to the breakaway, Rian was home to those of Unitarian, Darakaian, and Pilarese lineage alike, who'd denied their Houses, to risk an independence outside ancestral control. The figure hated Rian—even before. It took a particular spirit to abandon one's House for profit, only to chase aurus in the wind, typically toward their own demise. The reward of sordid coin was only temporary within Rian's walls, as were its inhabitants.

It was on such persons that slavers like the notorious Yannis preyed— and why the broken promise of Rian would always fill his ships.

At the thought of Yannis's trade, and his inability to thwart it, the figure ground his teeth, sore from another rotting. He'd have to pull it in the coming week, though it wouldn't matter. It was just one more illustration of his inhumanity, as he no longer required the sustenance of food.

He eyed his charge below, sighting the pale head of Alora's niece, golden among the rest as they constructed their tents by firelight. The bulk of the regiment encircled Korbin's son near the front, though the young king attempted to weave between the rigid groupings with a cane, speaking to each haidren. Were it Korbin in his place, by this time, wine would have been pouring with abandon. But here, the frail king appeared to check on each advisor, though from the intent of duty, it should have been the inverse.

The figure almost grinned, recognizing Lourissa walking in his skin, the humblest of them all.

Her and Korbin's successor found Alora's niece and privately ushered her into her improvised quarters while her najjan stood guard. The figure settled into his cloak, intrigued. Her men, though their ears would detect any trace of impropriety, did not seem disturbed by the exclusion. Instead, the titian-haired captaen gated the front of her tent protectively, as Emiere had always done for Alora.

Bile ascended the figure's scorched throat when a decades-old portrait of Emiere's stiffened back came to mind, from the night the captaen had escorted him, covered in blood, to Alora's confidence in secret.

That was the last time he'd ever spoken to the icy najjan—to anyone, except her and their beloved messenger.

Pained, the figure tore his eyeline from the redhead and, missing Amaranth, pulled the hawk's whistle from his pleats. She'd taken to the skies, searching for nourishment; something he would never find outside Alora's vials. Pressing the cool metal to his scabbed lips, the figure blew, summoning his companion. It was too pitched for even the najjan below, but the figure knew she would come.

Behind the Boreali cluster, he spotted the child of Masumi Naborū-Zuo, sister to the Pilarese sil'haidren, rummaging through a trundle of scrolls. Yet it was not her eldest daughter the figure spied but her son. Swathed in the ember hues of the shoto'shi sect, Masumi's child scribbled into a journal as he cataloged his artifacts. Warmth sparked within the figure's empty middle, though he could not define it, while observing the young man work. He appeared oblivious to the activity around him, engrossed in his literature. It had been an age since the figure carried a book, or piece of parchment for that matter, and meditated with it. He envied the shoto'shi, cross-legged on his unrolled mat, for in his untarnished hands he held the purest treasure within the cosmos.

Temper shattered the cloud cover when Amaranth's screech echoed over the plain, the hawk's cry fierce and troubled. Her sleek form glided over the caravan toward the base of the ridgeline. With a second screech, even shriller than the first, she dove beyond the regiment's outskirt patrol.

Instinctively, the figure sprung from his crouch and prowled through the brush, following her lead. She was a seasoned huntress, and he did not question Amaranth's hasty pursuit. Past the purview of the soldier's midnight watch, the figure fought through the dense foliage obscuring the dirt road, and he sprinted downslope. Catching his cloak, he soared over the rocks near the base, rolling into a run through the tall grasses.

In the moonlight, his enhanced sight caught a blackness move beneath Amaranth's descent. Yards ahead, the Eindrullagrass sporadically ebbed and flowed as something or someone darted from the hawk's chase, disturbing the lake of pasture.

The figure pushed the festering muscle of his limbs and in measure, welcomed the animalistic sting when his nature sprung forth. It lightened his footing, as if his weathered boot soles needn't touch the earth. Steering them in the opposite direction of the tour, the figure narrowed his sights on the tips of Amaranth's lilac wings, where the plain leveled and the grasses consumed him entirely.

Gaining speed, his mouth flooded with saliva and his canines throbbed when her talons protracted, and Amaranth plummeted in attack. Out of sight, he heard her struggle with their prey. The hawk screamed. She was thrust back into the air, favoring one of her wings from injury. Fury seared the figure's veins and enlivened him to a sharpened state.

A state ordinary men could not encounter, only the monsters that hunted them.

Nearing her mark, Amaranth rustled amid the undergrowth as he passed. Lunging through the wall of grass, the figure barreled into another form. The acrid stench of decomposition swamped his nostrils. With a hiss, he wrapped his arms about the opposing body. Impulse washed his senses, and his fangs anchored into flesh, prepared to rip apart the tendons and ligaments beneath his tongue.

But a cold, rotten slurry filled his mouth.

The figure violently spit the poison amid the mayhem. He spasmed fitfully when his opponent whirled and tore at his ribcage, slicing his skin beneath the rough fabric. The figure lurched back in horror, not at the blood pouring from his side but at the mirrored monstrosity before him.

An animated cadaver. What used to be a face had blackened with decay, fragments even hanging off the bone. Rags clothed it, swinging from arms of charred hide. Its irises were rimmed with scarlet, reflecting the moon in a sickening bloodlust that even war-taint could not trigger. Stooping on all fours, it twisted its head demonically and a grisly, gurgling growl came from a slimy abyss that had once served as a mouth. Long, yellowed canines, longer than the figure's, jutted out with its petrifying roar.

A wicked scent wafted off the creature, identical to what the figure had once tracked through Marketown. The scent was like his own and that of the cross-caste killer, Felix Ambrose—each of them an abomination, born not of nature but created by choice.

His choice.

Frozen, the figure gaped at his inhuman equal—his destiny, had Alora not intervened that terrible night.

It sprung, thrashing after him in a rabid hunger. The figure caught its momentum, careering them through the mud. The figure's jaws snapped, ripping a foul mass from the creature's arm as he fought off its relentless assault. Daggerlike nails ribboned his chest apart, and the figure roared in kind. As the putrid chasm angled for his throat, Amaranth sailed haphazardly from his right and carved the base of its neck. Rearing up, she doubled back with her hooked beak.

The creature released the figure, brutally struck Amaranth aside, and fled through the Eindrullagrass. In a terrible frenzy, the figure deserted his companion and took after it. Sending ripples through the prairie, he darted through the windswept land maze.

At the edge of the Eindrullagrass, the figure hurtled into a short-grass clearing where the heights receded. Ahead, the creature dropped and galloped on its fours like a wild, disjointed beast. Without delay, the figure pushed his endurance. Closing their gap, it glared over its rags, flapping in the breeze, and snarled. Only then the figure saw its objective: a murky line where a steep, narrow ravine divided the plain.

His legs seething in unholy anguish, the figure was just yards behind it. But before he could reach out, the creature surged for the lip of the ravine. In a blink, it vaulted and disappeared into the Depths from which it had surely come.

He spied over the rocky rim. Sharp outcroppings threatened the figure's plunge into the shadow. The fall would not kill him, but he could still feel, to an extent. For a moment, such penance seduced him, and he considered jumping. It'd be a retribution he surely deserved.

A flurry of wings knocked him onto his back, away from the ravine's emptiness. Amaranth hobbled toward his face, panting from her injuries, and croaked through her beak. In a wave of absolute sorrow, the figure wrapped his arms arm the hawk, steadied by her quickened heartbeat.

He'd warned Alora it was not mere war-taint that had been resurrected from in the past—but his own wickedness. Somehow the sins of one were becoming the sins of many, sins that were following Alora's niece to the brink of Darakai.

The diseased noble in Marketown had not been a mistake.

He was the beginning.

CHAPTER EIGHT
ZAETHAN

R ian stood out like a chipped piece of crupas against the golden grassland. As the sun set, Owàa's amber flare underscored the haphazard patchwork of the outpost's unending construction. A stronghold of discord in an otherwise peaceful plain, Rian was fortified like it were a fortress, rather than a breeding ground for renegade trade.

It was said that Rian's walls were intended to keep out the miscreants and thieves who preyed on the lowest class, but every Orynthian of every House knew it to be the exact opposite. From afar, an attempt to modernize dotted the old timber and daub of the outer walls, where segments of organized stonework framed the heights. Behind the defensive curtain, ancient, crooked towers rivaled newer buildings of bespeckled masonry, bridged by scaling scaffolds in between. Banners of disorderly plumage cluttered the pilasters and flapped in the breeze, like a rebellious welcome for their most recent king. A king for whom Rian harbored no fealty beyond the necessary acknowledgement of his crown.

Zaethan had come to the breakaway haven only once, well before his earning alpha *zà*, to assist in some local dispute involving the then magistrate's son. And after being dowsed in mead in his sleep, robbed at knifepoint, and forced to forfeit the clothes off his back, he'd absolutely no desire to return. Although truly, the mead had been Kumo's fault, not the whim of a pant-stealing bastard.

"Rian no place for the hillman, ano," Jabari announced to the pryde, riding the tail of the royal procession. His tight coils shook vigorously. "Breakaways everywhere, yeah? Picking pockets. Here hiding too many Pilarese trickers, far from watch of shoto masters—"

"Doru, Jabari," Zaethan snapped, shutting him up when in front of them, the Pilarese guard glared over his shoulder. Tersely, he ordered Jabari, "Keep it down, yeye qondai?"

The interim haidren paid them no mind. For a near week, Sayuri's brother had been studying his papers, scribbling in some and shredding others. But overall, Hachiro Naborū-Zuo ignored the existence of anything else, including Jabari's tongue-twisted commentary. Mopping sweat from his brow, Zaethan could not say the same.

If Wekesa's impending challenge wasn't to be the death of him, then Jabari's Yowekaon jabber would do the job. His half-Andwele, half-Unitarian slurry hadn't improved much—not enough for their communal liking. Even Zahra's patience was waning, proof by the blow dart she shot into his forearm.

The mountain cub unstuck the barb and shrugged, unperturbed.

"Always nose in book." Jabari motioned ahead at Sayuri's brother, where the reins of his horse were secured to his guard's so he could better focus on his ledgers. "Where a nose, there a book. Now he come to Rian. Bring a book, teach a tricker…"

"Depths, you don't even read!" Exasperated, Zahra knocked back her shaved skull and pleaded with the clouds. "And not everyone is a 'tricker'!"

"But you're definitely from the hills, Jabari." Kumo's hulking shoulders shuddered when he chuckled with Takoda. "Uni, you're all the way up in there."

"Dhalili can't meet us soon enough," Zaethan murmured, prodding Hellion.

He left his pryde to their banter and angled his stallion for Dmitri. He'd granted his friend space during the initial trek, honoring the widened disparity in their new stations. The escorting soldiers needed to revere Dmitri as their king, a deference Zaethan's multiple visits to the front would undermine. But it'd been a week, and he could only take the kakk of his warriors for so long before smacking more than one of them upside the head.

Zaethan trotted past Hachiro. His verdict on the odd shoto'shi had yet to settle, unsure if his budding aversion had more to do with the sound of crinkling parchment than the young Pilarese man carrying it. Distracted and disheveled, Hachiro was a reclusive little fellow, nothing like his well-groomed, insufferable sister. Perhaps the stark contrast was the most off-putting of all. Zaethan couldn't stand things he could not define, and he had one of those to contend with already.

Moving on, he came alongside the witch.

A snowfall of najjani eyes dusted Zaethan as he trotted past them, peering into their protective quadrant. The haidren to Boreal sat taller in her saddle, as if sensing his study, face forward. Her pastel braids rustled aside. The sharpened angles of her colorless face were emphasized by the steep sterling collar of her formal riding jacket. Dusted by the strange, platinum hairs that rivaled the rest of her tawny mane, her lips moved silently in witch-tongue. On her far side, the captaen of her guard responded in kind, mute and eerily, while his gaze darted toward Zaethan. For six days, Zaethan had watched the shining backs of her najjan carting their witchiron in the open. Were he honest, it wasn't offense Zaethan harbored against their unsheathed crescent wraiths, but sheer jealousy.

Jealousy and dread.

He needed an advantage like a wasteland needed water. If she didn't agree to resume training him in those lethal blades, Zaethan wasn't entirely sure he could claim victory over Wekesa again. In true *jwona* fashion, fate had not favored him as of late. The witch was Zaethan's last hope, though he would never let her see it. Nor her men.

If they even knew of his proposition in the first place.

Directly following Dmitri and the store wagons, Zaethan happened upon Ira in the precession. The yancy produced a flask from his coat and toasted the sky. "Do you see her, Zaeth?" Ira unscrewed the cap and took a long swig, then returned the flask to his pocket to point at the looming city gate. "There she is, my muse, at last!"

"You have to be an artist to have a muse, Ira."

Twirling the chained snuff canister around his finger, he quipped, "Zaethan, must I always remind you, what I do behind closed doors *is* art."

At that, Zaethan kicked Hellion and bypassed the yancy.

He drove the Andwele stallion's grand frame through the swarm of soldiers, spotting Hellion's twin, Harmonia, carrying Dmitri near the lead. Today, no royal cape descended his spine, Dmitri having opted for a humbler ensemble for their visit to Rian. Beside him, Bessus, field marshal to the attending regiment, rode closely by, gesturing at the disjointed city as they came into range. A few of the men nodded dutifully at Zaethan, granting him passage toward their king.

"At least one of us is thrilled for your kakka-shtàka sojourn," Zaethan muttered dryly, flanking Dmitri's left. "Ira won't shut up about it."

"Yes, he expressed his evening plans with me last night in great, unwanted detail." Dmitri eyed Zaethan crossly, recollecting Ira's particulars.

"At Rian's gate, stay close to me, uni? You're the first regent to enter their domain in a century," he said, discreetly warning Dmitri, "and you've dragged her shadowmen with you. We've no idea what kind of reception awaits us."

"My regiment is at the ready, Lord Haidren."

Bessus leaned over the horn of his saddle and pompously narrowed his beady gaze. Zaethan had never been a fan of the fleshy middle-aged marshal, whose sudden rise through the ranks garnered reasonable suspicion given his lowly services during the Shield Wars. With so much courtly coin in the pockets of whom it didn't belong, Zaethan didn't trust Dmitri's safety to a man whose first allegiance probably resided in the coin purse of a wealthy benefactor.

"The marshal assures me of the magistrate's welcome. It was

arranged weeks ago." Relaxing the reins, Dmitri braced his knuckles upon his slender thigh. "These are citizens of the realm, making Rian a fitting place to rest. Truthfully, I'm rather looking forward to a bed with legs." Reaching across, Dmitri squeezed his friend's shoulder. "It's just one night, Zaeth."

Bessus's back arrowed arrogantly, emboldened by Dmitri's confidence in the regiment and subsequent reports of the town. But there was good reason for kings to avoid Rian.

And that was the absolute anarchy within its walls.

Orynthia had allowed the rebel refuge near autonomy since its original establishment, over two hundred years ago, before the Mworran Wars. Self-governed by the maligned, the breakaway, and the cross-caste, Rian did not want a king. Yet the trade they facilitated, both legal and illicit, profited the regents they so openly despised. In exchange, Thoarne's descendants protected the settlement for a steep tax on Rian's curated commerce. Overlooking the defiant disdain for a price, the throne left them to their own corruption.

Zaethan couldn't comprehend Dmitri's decision to break that traditional segregation, chiefly due to the growing unrest among the lower classes in Bastiion proper. One would think a public decapitation during his friend's coronation parade would have dissuaded him from a destination like this. But when it came to the latest inner workings of Dmitri's mind, Zaethan understood him less than he thought.

At the royal procession's approach, the heavy gates, fashioned from a miscellany of iron and wood, screeched apart. In their gap stood a gathering of arbitrary individuals with a shared air of authority. Zaethan saw little similarity between them all, aside from the randomness of their attire. Each town official was clad in a comical combination of ruggedness and gaudy adornment. Feathers were stuffed into mended hats. Rags were adorned in mismatched trim. Polished gold buckles held up patched trousers.

But his personal favorite was the peg-legged buccaneer on the end, leaning on a stump encrusted in ladies' broaches.

Furling his lips, Zaethan suppressed a grin. At least Rian had dressed for the occasion.

"See, Zaeth? Nothing to worry about," Dmitri said through a toothy grin when an ensemble of fiddlers began playing from the jagged parapet atop the outer wall. Their off-kilter tune was joined by a bevy of instruments Zaethan could not place, but then again, Rian *was* Orynthia's catch-all for the unusual.

Zaethan's boots hit the dusty road when he dismounted before the others. He eyed the archers through the uniform slits in the wall exterior. If Bessus noticed the same, the field marshal gave no inkling when he too dismounted and instead escorted their king to make introductions with their renegade hosts. Tossing Hellion's reins to the nearest soldier, Zaethan mouthed mention of the bowmen and signaled for the regiment to be on guard. He marched to Dmitri's side, glaring at the back of Bessus's balding head for overlooking such an obvious threat.

From the middle of the assembled officials stepped a rotund man. Rian's magistrate, Zaethan presumed, from the ornate robe he dragged behind him. Nearing their cluster, Zaethan realized it was really a repurposed tapestry sewn to the epaulettes of his coat, tassels and all.

"Welcome, Your Majesty!" His ballooned arms extended in exaggerated hospitality as the magistrate projected over the crowd in Andwele as well as Pilarese. "Owàamo, and hū meii! Welcome all to the sanctuary…" He dipped a knee theatrically. "Of Rian."

When the townspeople did not follow in his descent, the magistrate barked over his shoulder in an array of languages, pointing his fingertips at the ground. With a nervous chuckle, he tilted his blended features toward Dmitri, Zaethan, and the marshal. His topaz eyes creased with his overstated and evidently forced reception. It was common knowledge that more than all other places for stowaways, Rian was home to an abundance of Pilarese-Darakaian cross-castes, but Zaethan had not realized they were led by one.

Aside from Salma, who'd managed her own tiny metropolis in the backstreets of Marketown, this man was the highest ranking cross-caste he'd ever met. For even Darakai, a House that had opened its border to their blended offspring, still restricted the land and titles a cross-caste held.

Which meant they held none at all.

"That is all too kind, Sir Magistrate," Dmitri replied, beckoning the citizens rise from their apprehensive half kneels. "It's an honor to share this short night in your company. But, as you can see"—he waved behind himself—"I've brought with me an outfit of weary travelers. My primary concern is their comfort and quarter. Then..." Looking beyond the magistrate, Dmitri scanned the various buildings, likely at those peering out their windows for a glimpse of the youthful king. "I should very much like to meet all of you."

Chatter buzzed among the ragtag line of leaders, half male, the other female, as the magistrate groaned himself upright and came to stand before their trio. Up close, Zaethan could appreciate the Southern strength of the man's puce coloring, though not the gluttonous grease that smeared his upper lip. Zaethan felt his appetite suddenly disappear.

The fatty streak spasmed when the magistrate sputtered, "Of course, of course! The haidrens will be housed, along with yourself, in the luxury of my manor." He flapped a golden palm at the winding tower in the distance. It stood out flashily by the unrolled banner that scaled its exterior, bearing a sort of weathered insignia of an axe and a wing.

Regardless of the attempted grandeur, Zaethan was not confident sleeping in that teetering steeple.

"The regiment and all the other attending parties will be hosted by the gracious members of the Free Council."

A wrinkled, well-muscled woman elbowed her peg-legged peer to stand at attention. Sucking her gold tooth, she interlocked her arms.

Gracious, all right. Zaethan crooked a brow.

"Absolutely wonderful." Dmitri's hands clapped together. "Let us relay lodgings to the haidrens and their escort—"

"As I expressed to the marshal…" The magistrate interrupted and nodded strictly toward Bessus. "While the haidren to Boreal may enter the inner city, her y'siti shadowmen are prohibited from coming any further. They must remain here, in the outer ward between walls."

Dmitri spun toward Bessus. Flustered by the news, there was an obvious bite in his voice when he said, "That was not reported to me, Marshal, and we *will* discuss my future expectations later. Sir Magistrate," Dmitri entreated. "Surely an exception can be made for her najjan, considering the occasion."

The plump, jovial qualities of the magistrate's face instantly hardened. "For no occasion will another shadowman step inside this city ever again," he stated harshly, the insurrection of Rian seeping into his friendly veneer when he added a curt "*Your Majesty.*"

This was why Zaethan had warned Dmitri to tread carefully, not into Rian but around it altogether. It was not for regents to concern themselves with regional resentments from wars long past. Even Zaethan could not blame the cross-caste magistrate for his refusal. For it was near the end of the Mworran Wars, two centuries before, when Rian had called for Boreal's aid and their najjani order did not respond.

As a result, Rian had fallen under siege by a crusade of Mworran militia aiming for command over the emerging rebel storehouse in the Eindrulla Plains. With the Darakaian prydes and Orynthian forces divided between the slaughter at Razôuel's border and the barricade at Port Khmer from Tavish invasion, the plains had been all but abandoned. It was then, in desperation, Rian had ultimately sent word to Boreal. But favoring their king at the front line in, not one shadowman came to the town's defense.

Instead, by the shields of a single pryde, the bows of a few mudmen, and the outright resilience of Rian, they scarcely survived the Mworran onslaught. Left in utter wreckage, the civilization of untouchables had been rebuilding ever since. And after the carnage, Rian vowed to never seek friendship from the Boreali again.

"Magistrate, my sincerest respects, but I insist—"

"We are accustomed to our bedrolls, Your Majesty."

A jolt went through each man at the witch's unexpected voice. Spinning on his heel, Zaethan only then registered she'd at one point joined their conversation. Cordially, he stepped aside so she might come between them, where he could better watch her movements.

It irked Zaethan when she didn't, opting to remain uncannily still.

"Lady Boreal, I'll not have your guard sleep on the ground while you in the warmth of the magistrate's home."

"*Niit.*" She blinked coolly. Her eyes darted toward Rian's leader and the nearly colorless iris of her right brightened. "I trained with the order on the Isle of Viridis. I too am najjan, Your Majesty, and therefore must make camp here, alongside my men."

Whispers crackled through the growing mob at the gate. An angry puff shot from Zaethan's nostrils as he glowered at her.

This was exactly what Dmitri needed... more rumors about his Quadren.

At Dmitri's protest, she entwined her arms and bowed reassuringly. "I bid you all good night. Tredae'Aurynth, Your Majesty, Sir Magistrate."

In turning, the witch peered at Zaethan. Nearly looking into him, she posed a challenge. It crispened her kohl-rimmed lash line, like she was sending a message, to him or the others, before their ultimate destination of Faraji.

She was haidren. She was najjan.

So much more, yet nothing less.

Zaethan observed her soundless stalk back to her najjani guard. In a ripple, the regiment split apart for her to pass, granting her a liberal breadth. The planes of her form-fitting slate jacket were firmly set, and her ashen plaits sailed in the warm breeze behind her like a band of trailing spirits. He found himself counting the silver threads of corseting along her spine, wondering what kind of opponent she'd make strapped into it.

"Zaeth," Dmitri stated, tearing Zaethan's attention back to the magistrate. "Let's get a good meal in you, brother."

He patted his back genially before walking on ahead with Bessus and the so-called Free Council.

Among the soldiers, Zaethan guided Hellion by the reins into Rian. Swaths of fabric sloped overhead as they charted the puzzling road system toward the magistrate's tower. Where Bastiion's infrastructure mirrored the spokes of a wheel, Rian's mirrored madness. Under multi-hued awnings, peddlers pushed exotic goods and cockamamie contraptions. Ill-strummed music poured from various buildings, and to their melodies, women shouted wicked vows to the regiment of lonely men.

There is a place called Rian, where the cross-caste and breakaway flee...
There's a place called Rian, where fate is rewritten by walking freely...

A revolutionary refrain whistled by Zaethan's ear when he lost track of Dmitri in the lively crowd. After climbing atop Hellion, he swung his stallion to locate Kumo and Zahra, who had been swallowed by the packed street of bronze and copper faces.

There is a place called Rian, where no man bends his knee...

Spinning in his saddle, he found an old woman swathed in silks, hoisted on a barrel and playing a sitar. At his interest, she sneered, revealing a mouth of missing teeth.

There is a place called Rian. Run away. Run away and see.

CHAPTER NINE
ZAETHAN

"No one else feels a bit off?" Kumo asked, dragging his thick bicep along the curling, stone stairwell.

Each age of its construction was marked by the noticeable tilt of the many fused additions to the magistrate's tower. The beta hugged the interior curve, which granted them an unbalanced chronicle of the structure's varied architects through history. It was a shame their efforts never seemed to line up with each other's, otherwise Kumo would've been able to climb the steps upright without threat of toppling over, given his weak stomach.

"Keep it in, yeah?" Zahra advised, smacking Kumo over his leathers when she bypassed him, dodging the line of fire.

Peering over, Zaethan watched Kumo's full swart cheeks drain, taking on a leafy tinge. He cursed. They had planned to spar that evening after most had fallen asleep. Zaethan's rival was wasting no time in preparing for their looming challenge. Even if the witch didn't come around soon... Zaethan should not waste it either.

It could be said he and Wekesa were evenly matched, but even that hinged on the weapon Wekesa would choose. It was the challenger's right. Zaethan needed to sharpen his defense against both the mace and the axe, two of Wekesa's favorite bloodletters.

But with Kumo hacking up with lunch, Zaethan was light on choices—literally, as Zahra was half his rival's size.

"Shtàka, cousin," Zaethan muttered, skipping steps toward the young woman who guided them to their lodgings. She was dressed in patterned textiles and nomadic accessory, like most of Rian's citizens, so he couldn't determine if she was a slave or another tenant in the magistrate's home. He figured it rude to ask and blustered irritably. "How much further?"

They'd shared their escort with Hachiro and his guard, both already deposited to his door. Neither were likely to have ever stepped foot outside Gakoshū, the City of Learning, before Dmitri's summons, so Takoda had valiantly rescued them from the labyrinth of Rian's market-place before the pryde had regrouped.

Hachiro's rooms had been a much shorter hike.

Unbothered by the spiraling asymmetry, the guide peeked around at Kumo, who'd slumped over and held his gut. Amusement puckered the bow of her freckled lips before she blew a sorrel dreadlock out of her sight. "Nearly there, Lord Haidren." Rolling her hooded eyes, the young woman resumed her untroubled ascent. "Your page has already arrived and waits in your chamber."

"Eh." Zahra whacked Zaethan's arm. "You make us run around when we have a page?"

"Apparently so…"

Providing no further detail, the woman directed them another floor higher, to a flat landing situated on an interior terrace. The railing and trim were both finished in gold flake, but bits were missing from the uneven plating around the mosaic door. It would be easy to remember the stoop, as none they had passed were tiled the same.

"Your rooms." Her beaded bands chinked when she folded her arms and nodded at the door indifferently. "I'll return later to retrieve you for the magistrate's feast."

His hand clenching the handle, Zaethan hollered after her as she descended the steps, "And His Majesty's rooms?"

Without a twist backward, she pointed a finger to the rising heights and disappeared around the bend of the sloped stairwell.

"Hmph." Zahra snorted contently and rocked on her heels next to Zaethan. "No nonsense. Rian is my kind of place."

"Yeah, well don't get any ideas, uni zà?" he barked to his third, gripping his kopar in one hand while he unlatched the handle with the other. Past Zahra, he called down to Kumo where Jabari helped him up the steps. "Rhaolé! Hurry up, swamp legs, so we can meet this page of mine."

Wedging the door ajar, they entered a room just as uncoordinated as the city. A medley of chandeliers, some brass and crystal, others wood, were hoisted from the ceiling as if the one would not suffice. Beneath their flicker dozed Zaethan's supposed page, wrapped in an oversized coat. Snoring, a battered old hat covered the owner's face. Beside the sprawl of five teeny fingers lay an unbuckled satchel of correspondences. The page's short legs, lost inside threadbare gunja pants, stretched not even halfway down the lumpy, velvet mattress.

Zaethan broke into a grin and slammed the door as loud as he could.

"To the Depths!" she bellowed, jolting upright, hat in hand. "Eh, owàamo, Alpha Zà! Was just warming it up with my beauty sleeps…"

"Dhalili!" Takoda and Jabari sang in unison, unloading their beta's weight when they both ran to sweep Dhalili up in their arms. They took turns, and her tiny feet didn't touch the ground.

"Gave yourself a promotion, I see." Zaethan's stance slumped questioningly as he tucked his thumbs into his belt. "Didn't know I was in need of a page, Dhalili."

"Uni, you are to get into Rian," she retorted with a wink before she bit Takoda's finger and escaped his embrace.

"Shtàka, you're worse than the grass-nasties!" He rubbed the mark, albeit playfully. "This is why we stash you away in the plains, yeye qondai? Feral little cub…"

To Takoda's sentiment, Dhalili swung gaily between the two warriors and chattered her teeth as if she gnawed an ear of maize. Granted, a bit unpolished, this was precisely Dhalili's value to Zaethan's pryde. Older than both Takoda and Jabari, the scout matured agelessly and was clever enough to impersonate an unascended cub of either gender.

And as such, she always gained access to the places his other warriors could not.

Zaethan knew she missed them immensely. Her affection was obvious, creasing her round, cherubic face. The cool sepia sheen of her cheeks, darkened further from cloudless days scouting for the pryde, betrayed her twenty-four years far more than her tiny stature or her boyish grin. Gobbled up by the gigantic coat knotted with cord about her waist, she could go begging in the streets and gain every mercy for it, as well as a bit more when no one was looking.

"How'd you fool the patrol?" Zahra skeptically asked, hiking his brow at the sack of papers.

"Swiped some wares to look the part." Dhalili shrugged. Landing on the tilted floor, she snagged a letter off the bed. "Saw this seal sticking out of a rich-runner's bag near the gate." Zaethan's scout flapped it high, flashing a waxen insignia of an axe and a wing. "So gave him a nap, meme na ràtomdai—claimed my rights—and here we are."

Zahra ran her palm along the inked runes on her scalp. "Dhalili! That is the magistrate's seal!"

Toying with one of her short, twisted knots, coiled tightly all over her head, Dhalili dropped the letter and, with the toe of her boot, scooted it under the bedframe. "He's not going to miss it…"

"Takoda, pick that up and bring it to dinner. Say we found it on the way," Zaethan instructed, trusting him not to steal anymore of Rian's artifacts, something which could not be said for his scout. "Dhalili, no more thieving, uni zà?"

"No more Rian." Kumo moaned near the doorframe, clutching a decorative bowl just in time to catch his expelled kakk. He shoved the bowl into Takoda, wiping his mouth. "Take that too."

With a grimace, Takoda grabbed the bowl as two blows pounded the door. Upon the second set of thumps, Zaethan swung it open and found Bessus. And three soldiers with him. The Unitarian marshal greeted them in a formal navy tunic and bronze sash, his few trivial medals pinned to his chest. One would think the magistrate's feast was in his honor, rather than Dmitri's.

Frantically, he poked his sweaty face through the threshold around

Zaethan. "Is he in there with you?" Bessus demanded and tapped Zaethan's chest.

Zaethan looked down at Bessus's stubby fingers against the braided Darakaian leather. Glaring up, he snatched Bessus's hand and used it to tap his own chest in turn. "Is *who* with us?"

Letting go, the field marshal tried to loosen his too-tight collar. "I'm to take His Majesty to the magistrate's feasting. Perhaps…" Bessus whirled in place. "Perhaps he's left with the haidren to Bastiion."

"Oh, ano." Jabari's long nose cleared Zaethan's periphery. "We see yancy haidren take a turn. Him seeking downside friendlies, but that short-time papyon bring a long-time scritch-scratch."

"Doru." Zaethan shoved Jabari aside and stepped onto the landing. Fuming, he backed Bessus into the rail, blood beating his temples. "Are you saying you've lost the king, after dark, in *Rian*!"

"Well, he goes where he pleases—"

"Get out of my way." Seizing his sash, Zaethan whipped Bessus into the stairwell and yelled for his pryde, "Search the city! Kumo, wake every soldier from his bed!"

Skidding the steps, Zaethan hustled down the twisted steeple, infuriated by the stupidity of Bessus—but more than anything, the foolishness of his friend.

It was the children who had betrayed his whereabouts.

Nothing spread faster than in the network of insignificants, no matter the city—least of all news about a king who forwent a grand feast to dine with commoners.

After an hour expended in pursuit of Dmitri, Zaethan led his pryde through the swarm of street cubs. They giggled in their moonlit race toward the outer wall. Cricking his neck, Zaethan trailed one boy in particular, a grubby thing in an old cap and mismatched boots. When the cross-caste cub waved him around the corner of a building near the city limit, Zaethan rebuked himself for not thinking of it sooner.

Of course, Dmitri had come here. It was the only place *she* could.

There, beyond the ring of civilians two or three bodies deep, the king of Orynthia leaned against a cart, deep in discussion with the captaen of her najjani guard. Taking turns, brave cubs scampered up and interrupted them, daring each other to greet their unusual king.

At Dmitri's instruction, the few soldiers he'd opted to bring tossed bread to the courageous few. Firelight danced over his so-often-fatigued features, now sparked in good spirits. Off to the side, the witch and the rest of her shadowmen ate, sprawled around a sizzling pot. Surprisingly, Sayuri's brother was eating with them. Next to her, he scrawled in his ledger, plate untouched, though his single guard happily gorged at his back. Zaethan pushed through the bodies. It was easily done, as the amassing crowd kept their distance, probably unsure what to make of it—a king who fancied the friendless.

At least, that was how Zaethan hoped Rian interpreted Dmitri's spectacle, as opposed to his blatant insult to their magistrate.

With a flick of his fingers, he motioned for his pryde to head toward the fire. Zaethan stalked toward the wagon, parked himself on Dmitri's right, and folded his arms, staring at the captaen. The blaze dyed his Northern pallor with auburn shadows as the shadowman raised his chin incrementally. Dmitri's statement trailed, sensing the standoff.

"Thank you for the discourse, Captaen Bailefore, but I owe a word to Lord Darakai."

With a stiff bow, the tall captaen scanned Zaethan and left, though even in the darkness, he caught a sputter at the edge of his mouth, the most fleeting of sneers. Zaethan reciprocated the expression as he imagined striking it off the other man.

The Boreali esteemed themselves victims of the realm, but it was they who were the most arrogant of all.

"You've caused a stir," Zaethan said to Dmitri and monitored the crowd. "*Sir Magistrate* is not going to be pleased, not to mention your incompetent field marshal."

"I didn't come for *Sir Magistrate*. I came for them," Dmitri unhurriedly replied and waved at a shy child hiding behind her grandmother at the edge of the onlookers. "Orynthia's most vulnerable should know the heart of their king. They can't do that if I'm trapped in a tower."

A cheer went up through a cluster of people when bottles appeared, hoisted high above their heads. Winding toward the clearing, Ira emerged. Bare chested beneath his brocade jacket, the yancy gave a shimmy and tossed a bottle in either direction, to the crowd's merriment.

Strutting by them, Ira ironed his hair behind his ears, which appeared wet for some reason, and pulled his trouser pockets inside out.

"Rian is a greedy b-broad!" He hiccupped. He sauntered to the fireside and, plopping down beside Hachiro, gave his bowed back an enthusiastic clap.

Zaethan eyed the people who pointed at the three haidrens eating and drinking together. Their murmurs grew louder when the witch's shadowman, the one with the ruddy beard, proffered a plate to Zahra and relinquished for her his seat on the bench.

Sloping back, Zaethan assessed Dmitri where he stood, vest unbuttoned, utterly at ease.

"You knew this would happen..." he said, piecing things together.

"You knew the shadowmen would be forced to camp outside the city and that she'd do so with them."

"The unity of Orynthia starts with this Quadren—here, tonight. Look at them, Zaeth." He scanned the butting buildings, where blended faces poked out into the night. "These people leave their Houses and join with Rian because they believe *that*"—Dmitri pointed his cane where Zaethan's fellow haidrens casually conversed—"would never occur on their behalf."

"Ano, Dmitri. When it's orchestrated, *that* isn't real." Zaethan's forehead crinkled at his friend, whom momentarily he did not recognize. "When did you become such a politician?"

Dmitri sighed, his chest deflating as he caught Zaethan's shoulder. "When did you forget we've been training for it our whole lives? And it *is* real. Each of you found your way here on your own, did you not?"

"That's a stretch—"

"That's a start, Zaeth. My father's generation fought for peace upon the battlefield, as did their ancestors before them. How dare we not preserve it with our every word and deed, or meal for that matter? Now, go on. We've one night. Let's not waste it. Ah, shtàka—" Dmitri started buttoning his vest. "You were right. *Sir Magistrate* doesn't seem pleased in the least. Duty calls, I'm afraid."

Hearing a hint of King Korbin in his parting, Zaethan couldn't repress his slight grin as Dmitri waltzed over to deal with the magistrate, whose scowl had become even greasier. Stomach growling, Zaethan rebound his heavy locs, and proceeded as his king had tasked.

At their simmering cauldron, or what smelt like it, the leanest shadowman, his long snowy braids curtaining either side of his lanky neck, pushed a steaming plate into Zaethan's hand.

"Horned thissleweed," he stated, as if that meant anything to anyone.

Suspicious of the slop, Zaethan stepped over the sleeping highlander wolx and into in the opening beside the witch, opting for her nearness over Ira's prattle, which he was spewing at Hachiro—literally, since he hadn't bothered to fully chew.

Zaethan angled his spoon at her beast and grumbled, "Don't let that war-tainted huwàa roam. Things that don't belong in the plains tend to die in the plains."

She did not respond. Under harsh brows, the witch's unnatural eyes surveyed him where he sat.

Zaethan pressed into her sphere and, seizing the opportunity, lowered his tone. "I've waited patiently for an answer to my proposition, Maji'maia. I think it's time you give me one."

She studied their audience, demonstrating caution among other witch ears.

"I think you're the least patient person I've ever met," the witch countered, her jaw tensed. "And mine is not an answer you'll soon receive. Do not ask again." She swirled on the bench toward Sayuri's brother.

Exasperated at her aloofness, Zaethan tore into the lumped mash that filled his plate. He wasn't sure what "thissleweed" was, but it tasted as strong as it smelt.

"Hachiro, how you are coping with your abrupt appointment to Pilar's seat?" the witch asked the shoto'shi. "Tell us, are you concerned for your sister?"

Without a stall to his scribbles, Hachiro adjusted the monocle apparatus situated over is left eye and answered indifferently, "Until I receive an unsatisfactory report regarding Sayuri's well-being, concern for her would be a pointless emotional expenditure."

"She won't come out of her apartments," Ira muffled through his food, which Hachiro promptly flicked off his pages upon which he wrote.

"That is common practice for my sister, as is the Orynthian tradition of interim haidrenship and therefore no reason for alarm." Swaddled in his shoto'shi robes, Hachiro rewet his quill as he continued. "An assumption of another's Quadrennal duties is normally brief and not the result of some calamity, like in the case of my uncle," he said bluntly to his journal, "or that of Lord Darakai's father—"

Zaethan spit his food out, his heart racing. "Shut up, Hachiro."

"Although, two out of four in one generation is a particularly high percentage—"

"I said, *shut up*."

The witch threw her hand back to hush Zaethan. "I don't understand. To what calamity are you referring?"

"My uncle, Tetsu Naborū, assumed the Pilarese haidrenship upon the death of his brother, Akito. I never knew him; I was not yet born. My uncle retained the seat as my mother was third in line behind him. It is a consternation you did not already know this, Lady Boreal. I must say... The king's Quadren is worryingly uneducated about their own history."

Zaethan snapped his spoon in half when Hachiro's inky script hastened.

"I ought to notify His Majesty of this collective shortcoming among his advisors."

"Wait, are you writing that down?" Ira exclaimed, attempting to rip the journal out from under the shoto'shi's quill. "Have you been writing about us this whole time!"

"Your delayed observations are paradoxical to your purposes, Lord Bastiion," Hachiro stated to Ira and shuffled through the tinted lenses of his monocle using a gear affixed to his ear.

"I don't know what that means, but I take ample offense!"

Bug-eyed, Hachiro's blinks were magnified behind a circlet of pale blue. "As you should."

"Well then... I'm better looking than you!"

Zaethan stood, having endured enough of Dmitri's foolhardy social experiment.

"Wait," said a husky voice. "What did he mean about your father?"

From the bench, the witch pinned Zaethan under her lustrous gaze. But he tore from it, pegging his shaking fists to his sides, and stalked past the fire.

"Your calculable symmetry is clear, Lord Bastiion, thus I'm inclined to agree," Hachiro stated in Zaethan's wake. "And to your question, Lady Boreal, the tribes voted their chief warlord adopt his wife's seat when she didn't survive the birth of their son. Otherwise, Lord Darakai's cousin would be sitting in his place—"

Zaethan pivoted in the dirt and hurled his plate at the feeble shoto'shi. "Don't ever speak about my mother!"

The witch shot her arm outward in front of Sayuri's brother, who twitched beneath his monocle like a frightened frog, and caught the wooden plate. Zaethan glowered at it in her pale clutch as the frigid landscape of her face softened, each peak weighted with pity.

Pity and confusion.

Nyack Kasim forbade all talk of his late wife, revealing what he cherished more than any love or loss. By the time of Zaethan's birth, his father had become his mother's superior in every way except one.

Haidrenship.

So upon her death, he took it—his father's greatest prize of all.

Zaethan edgily spun in place to discover all of Rian gaping with the Quadren. Their stunned expressions crowded the fireside. They were a generation shielded from the heroic legacy of Cyra Shà Kasim, a legacy his father demanded everyone forget, to inflate his own.

He was trapped in their circle. Suffocated. Cornered.

Zaethan found Kumo, his cousin and beta, in the abrupt silence. As Hachiro had disclosed, had the haidrenship passed to Zaethan's aunt, Léola, Kumo's path would have been so different today. Deliberately, the larger man brought his fist against his chest and bent his head in allegiance, despite what alternate histories had in store. Nodding at Kumo, Zaethan sucked his teeth, spying the spectators.

At the uproar—or perhaps the flying plate—Dmitri jogged toward the fire. Carting his cane, he flattened it against Zaethan's middle like they were co-conspirators in a game. "Takoda! I hear you are our best story giver," Dmitri announced, distracting the crowd from his outburst. "My Quadren and I must hear your favorite tale tonight!"

Breathing heavily, Zaethan was relieved when Zahra cupped her hands and yelled, "Tell Rian of Owàa and Àla'maia!"

Wedged between Jabari and the gruff, ginger shadowman, Takoda sprung and hopped to the center, where Zaethan stood awkwardly with Dmitri. Swinging his arms about, the warrior faced the masses, preparing to give them a show.

As Zaethan stepped out of the firelight with his king, Takoda fleetingly bumped his heart, like Kumo had, and whispered, "We follow you, Alpha Zà. Always."

Then Takoda stooped, changing his countenance to match his mysterious tenor. "Uni, come close, my friends, as I tell of the roaring sun and his lover moon. A tale of love, which ends in woe. A tale that paints dawn and sets evening aglow…"

Dmitri chuckled, nudging Zaethan's folded arms when the street cubs inched onto their knees to listen. Dhalili sat cross-legged as if she were one of them.

"Give them this to recount in the morning as substitute," Zaethan's friend said into his ear.

Zaethan squeezed the bridge of his nose. This was the last story he wanted to hear.

"In the day when hours were not yet old, and what was, was not yet new, the twelve Fates came together, wishing for a child. The sowers tilled the cosmos." Takoda plucked two burning sticks from the kindling and twirled them for the children's delight. "And in their eternal garden, planted each a piece of themselves. Our *jwona*, their seed of fate, was sewn into the soil and skies. But the world was dark and cold. Life could not bloom." After dunking the sticks into the steaming pot, Takoda clutched his arms in mock shiver. "The Fates searched for a light, powerful enough to warm their children forever. The brightest light of all! That's when they found it..." He kicked the embers, bursting them alive. "The love of *Owàa* and *Àlamaia*."

Zaethan's prickly stare wandered beyond Takoda to where the witch sat, fixated on the warrior. She perched forward, twisting her head to his Southern tale.

"Owàa, the sun king, reigned mighty and ablaze, his wings like the eagle stretched across the universe. Strength like a bear, roar like a thundering lion, Owàa was untamed... beholden only to one." Takoda skidded a finger across his lips and strolled around the circle. "Àlamaia... his beloved... his lover moon. Radiant and pure, her wisdom pierces the murkiest seas, for her splendor is supreme throughout the heavens. And within each other's presence, Owàa and Àlamaia burn for eternity."

Takoda retrieved another pair of sticks and crooked them at either end. "But the Fates needed to warm their children, for without light, the world would die. The sowers captured Àla'maia and bound her to a court in the clouds. Among the starry hosts, they imprisoned her beauty to an infinite terrace, knowing Owàa would surely come."

Raising one flame higher, Takoda blew it with glorious flare. The people's breath caught in his trance. Without cause, Zaethan again found the witch among them. Her spectral features were scrunched, unhappy by the story's turn.

"Brilliant and unashamed, Owàa arose to her rescue, but it was trap… for the twelve Fates were lying in wait."

The crowd sucked a gasp.

"With the blade of time, they clipped Owàa's wings and chained his ankles, anchoring him to the deep. The lovers were separated forever. But to warm us all, the Fates allow each their passing glimpses, peering over the earth both morning and night. See her now…" Takoda heralded the full moon above. "Awaiting Owàa's mighty return, trusting him to burst forth, streak his rage across the heavens, and douse her court in color. When Owàa will war with his shackles… Will tire his clipped wings… Just to see her shine and remind Àla'maia of his devotion once more. His ankles may mangle to the bone. His wings might shed every gilded feather.

"But the sun king will never accept defeat!" Takoda shouted triumphantly. "Will never stop coming for his lover's freedom! Until he can fly no more, the entire world… we children of jwona… will be warmed by Owàa's undying passion for Àla'maia ever more!"

Rian erupted in applause. A few women, kneeling with their children, wiped at their eyes as they clapped for Takoda.

Zaethan bat his palms together, though his heart did not mean it. He thought of his parents, of their much realer story.

After all, the story of Owàa and Àla'maia was only a tale for cubs. Soon, their little hearts would learn the truth, and that wishful myth would shatter, as it had in him.

Such love did not exist.

CHAPTER TEN
LUSCIA

A chill overtook her, flesh to bone.

Luscia's lashes stirred, caught within the lake between dreaming and waking. Disturbing her slumber, a million peaks and valleys formed along her naked arms, bristling her skin.

A harsh shiver raked her side. Drifting to consciousness, Luscia realized she was alone on the bed of furs. Aksel had not returned from his late hunt with Noxolo. She'd freed the *lycran* under supervision, heeding Kasim's warning. Prying her lids apart, the night was shockingly cold in the animal's absence.

Too cold.

Silently, Luscia sidled off the bedding onto her elbows. Her ears quirked, mining for sound among the tall grasses. It should have encompassed the chirping of insects and activity of Rian's outer wall, but she only heard a disturbing emptiness, as if the world had gone mute.

Her gaze skimmed the wall of the tent, seeking beyond the thick hide, but the sky cast no shadows against it. The moon had darkened; Aurynth's watchman, whom Darakaian fable called Àla'maia, had stepped away from his post.

In a disciplined, measured exhale, Luscia watched crystals form where her breath met the air, contesting summer's embrace. This frost was not of the south. Under her delicate, linsilk shift, fear crawled across her prickled members.

Then came the pain.

It throttled her skull with authority. Javelins of fire pierced her mind. Her temples aflame, a fresh sweat broke out over the chill, enwrapping her in a bitter inferno. Luscia clutched her head and thrashed against the bedding, ransacking her belongings until she felt Alora's modest crate. Her fingers found the stopper of a vial, but when she tugged it to her chest, a thundering chorus hissed through her hair.

Ambiguous whispers clamored over each other. The rush smothered Luscia's senses. The whispers harmonized to voices.

The voices were angry.

"Niit. Bolaeva, Aniell." She panted to the High One against their torment while her fingers struggled with the stopper. "Spare me this... Spare me."

A blast of light forced her onto her back, and a gust from the *Other* burst through the veil, blistering her cheeks. Luscia was lurched into the Sight. Against her will.

Tears escaped her widening eyes when she gaped up at the pitched hide. Lumin engulfed the tent. Stuffing every crevasse, light energy glittered about her trembling body in unwanted needlepoint. From the bottom of Luscia's vision, the most vivid, incandescent thread snaked into the open.

In the chasm between a makeshift ceiling and her nose, the harbinger thread twitched erratically, and the voices roared. The lumin angled sharply at her forehead and beamed.

"*Luscia...*"

Pained, she stole a look at the vial clenched in her fist. At Luscia's attention, a crowding of thinner threads sputtered about her closed hand. The lumin licked her fingertips agitatedly. Fresh panic overcame Luscia when she felt static in their touch.

She should not feel them at all.

"*Awaken, Luscia...*"

She squeezed the undrunk vile against her thumping heart as the choired syllables sharpened. Staring down the harbinger thread, Luscia had nearly removed the cork with her shaking fingers before its radiance sparked and frizzled. The thread lurched backward and sailed straight at Luscia, driving her head against the hard earth. Flickering, it wavered just above the tip of her nose.

It was then a cooler breeze swept in through the tent seams and the voices blended into a single vocalization, both harrowing and serene.

"*It has come for you.*"

Distressed, Luscia rammed her eyes shut and tipped her chin with the vial. Her aunt's acerbic remedy met her lips, and she welcomed the sour bite as the blessed herbs coated her throat. Luscia panted into the furs, lying back, and waited for the whispers and their agony to subside.

The shelter regained its quiet, and her arms slid to the ground in exhaustion. Though her ears pounded with remnant aches, she'd never been so grateful for stillness.

Behind her throbbing lids, Luscia replayed Alora's guarantees about her condition. Her panic was unfounded. She had not heard the threads, for they did not speak. Therefore, these aberrations were mere manifestations of stress, nothing more. Normalizing her breathing, Luscia ordered herself not to become a slave to absurdity. Rather, to sleep.

Unexpectedly, something hot and slimy dribbled down her neck, glazing her scar.

Not the first time, Aksel must have dredged his half-eaten prey into her quarters. A new heftiness pressed onto her legs and pelvis. Though Luscia was glad for the lycran's return, an acrid scent battered her nostrils. Akin to the rotten carcasses along butcher row, the stench caused her to trundle aside and dry heave over her shoulder.

Luscia froze in place.

It was not Aksel in her tent.

Beside her bared aspen shoulder, tissue and tendon protruded from what used to have been a hand. Fingers, which had once ended with nails, split into bloody talons, staking her loose tresses to the bedroll. In the darkness, Luscia discerned the scraps of dead flesh caught under the mutated cartilage. Another drop of soiled saliva splashed her jawline, and in the most precise movement, Luscia rotated her face upward through the musty air.

A messenger from the Depths was waiting from above.

The creature screwed its head beyond mortal limits as an abyss parted, revealing needlelike fangs. Disfigured by what could only be war-taint, the host was robbed wholly of humanity, the sickness having metamorphosed well past the case of Felix Ambrose. Where the infected noble had been recognizable at his death, this *thing* was a recognized nightmare.

With a snarl, it scented between her breasts, where fitfully, her blood pumped in horror. A long decomposing tongue, the surface cracked and splitting, wound out from its cavernous mouth and dragged a trail of mucus along her dampened skin. Luscia's stomach turned at the sensation. Unlike Ambrose's bloodshot eyes, two crimson orbs glowed in its face of blackened tissue, framing the cavity of its missing snout. With her trapped under its mass, the creature seemed to savor what was to come.

Luscia's lips trembled uncontrollably, and she broke into a soundless sob, no longer in her handstitched tent but somewhere else altogether. Beneath the creature's weight, her arms and legs hardened to stone. All instinct vanished, replaced by an onslaught of memories—memories that pinned her down and pressed a dagger to her throat while the unforgiveable ensued. And in that vile captivity, she could no longer move.

Again.

Just like before, Luscia, with watering eyes and sudden detachment, stared at the ceiling, making ready to die.

Less man than monster, the creature reared its talons and scraped the underside of the taut hide. A gurgling rattled from behind its barbed teeth, where spittle foamed and drooled over a hunk of shredded ligaments hanging off the bone.

At its heralding growl, the darkness seemed to swirl beyond the creature's shoulders. Then with a *whoosh*, something skidded into the foot of her tent. A black cloak swelled through the flap opening, like the Depths had come to devour them both. Its red glare fixated, the creature's talons sliced after Luscia, but a pair of gloves appeared around its emaciated ribcage, and with a ferocious inhuman snarl, the creature was ripped off Luscia, lurching her upright too.

With savagery and the gnashing of teeth, the creature grappled with another out through the flaps, just as the hood of the stranger's cloak fell back. The clouds parted, and the moonlight illuminated tufts of black hair atop a head of boils and blistering. Luscia, fear-stricken on her sweat-soaked bedroll, realized the snarl had not come from the creature but the cloaked figure who'd spared her. They were the same; the figure too was infected.

The echo of their feral struggle, driving farther and farther from her dwelling was replaced by a blood-curdling wail that bruised her eardrums. As the walls of her throat chafed, Luscia only then comprehended the noise was coming from her. She was screaming.

She'd never emitted such a sound before, not even when she'd been scarred by a luxiron dagger.

Luscia didn't know how long the screaming went on or precisely when Marek had appeared, but his frantic expression was set aglow by the dull cast of a lumilore stone. The shallow lines banking his lower lashes strained. His scarlet hair swung unbound as the captaen's hands mimed over her body in a frenzied investigation for injury. Untouching, he did not upset her skin. Sitting on his knees, Marek towered over her slighter frame. In a daze, she noticed he sat in his linsilk undergarments of all things, partially tucked into his unbelted breeches. Through the sheer Boreali fabrication, Luscia blankly counted the rivulets in his musculature.

It'd been his shift to sleep, as Declan's, she remembered.

"Ana'Sere... Ana—shtàka, where was Creyvan?" Marek scowled, articulating her own question aloud. Averting his eyes, he held up a spare fur between them, probably able to see through her undergarment as well. "Tell me what happened. Were you harmed? Was it one of *them*? If they dared enter your quarters..." The captaen swore threateningly, implying it was a citizen of Rian. "That pompous excuse for a leader, making you camp out here like some wandering vagrant—"

"Niit," Luscia said, cutting him off. "It was Ambrose—a creature like Ambrose—infected. Worse. Its eyes, Marek… They were scorched. And… and its face…" Her fingers shuddered over her nose and wiped the sweat that pooled beneath. "Was just *gone*. There were only teeth… Teeth and talon."

Immediately, Marek's nose flared as he took aromatic inventory of the tent. Bringing the fur near his mouth, he jerked backward from the unnatural traces left by the creature. Discarding it, the najjani captaen resumed his inspection, this time gently cupping Luscia's chin and searching for scrapes beneath her mane. His fingers skimmed her shoulder ever so slightly, and he elevated her arm to examine the underside for the same, then repeated with her opposite. Marek's lips parted and warmed the lumilore in exhale. With it relit, he blushed and quickly set it aside, obscuring the stone's brightness, apparently recalling why he'd covered her in the first place. Her buttery linsilk shift, stronger than traditional silks, had not torn in the attack, but it had slid low down her slickened chest. Quite low.

With a hard swallow, he scooped her hand with both of his. "And you destroyed it? I don't see any ashes. Was there after-dust, like the end to the war-tainted yancy?"

Luscia noted how delicately Marek had phrased her part in Ambrose's death. He alone had witnessed Luscia's struggle to accept her first kill, despite the crucial nature of its cause.

Her head hung, shaking as she shamefully replied, "I couldn't. I was just… frozen in time."

A tear was freed, and he was one of few who knew why.

"Captaen! Ana'Sere!" The flaps thrust apart when Declan, half-clothed and hairy chested, bashed into the tent. Looking about, her staunch najjan exclaimed, "Where in Aurynth is Creyvan?"

Marek grimaced. "We'll have to reprimand him later, brödre. We need to scour the area for another victim of war-taint, like she and I encountered in Bastiion the eve of the King Korbin's murder. This one attempted an attacked on Ana'Sere herself, and it's on the loose."

Declan let loose a fisherman's cast of Boreali curses. "Ock! Meh fyreon, Ana'Sere," he said, apologizing for the expletives, and nodded grimly at Marek. "Wem, I'll find Creyvan, the vanishing weasel, and start a search. By Aniell, I miss Böwen more by the day."

Trudging off, Declan disappeared into the inky gloom. Alone with her captaen, the lumilore dulled where it rested beside her thigh.

"Did you hear me, Marek?" Luscia croaked, undistracted by the interruption. "I said I froze... There are blades stashed everywhere in this tent, yet I did nothing... *nothing* to stop the assault." Shaken, she reached for his shoulder. Though her fingers could not fully encompass it, they dug in determinedly. "You need to train me in hand combat. Formally this time." Luscia begged, for he hadn't on the Isle.

Like the other najjani trainers, Marek had respected her with an untouched margin in the wake of her trauma, just as he did now.

"Bolaeva, Marek, you must. I am our people's haidren. I can't crumble from fear the next time I'm confined in close range. I know the whole guard has respected the issue of... my past... but this is a vulnerability now, Marek, and it cannot be avoided any longer. We must face it."

Marek's imperious brow buckled. Cautiously, he brought palm atop her mess of tangles. He held it there a while, and Luscia let him. As he lowered to her level, his eyes brimmed with a tender association of temperance and sadness. She'd not seen it swim there since they had first met, at Viridis.

The look was rooted in kindness, and Luscia scorned its resurgence.

"That is our sacred obligation, Ana'Sere." Marek bent forward. "To ensure you never *have* to face it. We gave our lives to become your weapons. To wear your scars as our own." Like disturbed mossy waters, his irises flicked toward the ugliness carved down her neck. "To make certain you are never touched again, unless you will it."

In frustration, Luscia denied herself more tears, acutely aware they would only underscore his argument. "And it is exactly *that* sort of coddling which has left me so weak." Her scar itched, but she rejected its demand. "I would have met my death tonight, Marek, had the second not fought it off."

"Ykah lö—the second what?"

"Another creature less infected," Luscia clarified. "Still in men's clothing, it swooped down, and just as those talons came for me, it hauled the first one off."

Easing away, Marek's countenance changed, flattening, and he warily moved the lumilore nearer her feet. When his chest puffed with a sharp intake, Luscia turned to see the empty vial overturned on the ground next to Alora's unopened dosages. She swiftly slammed the lid of the crate, covering the other vials. Unharmed on the surface, she knew how it looked, and the acrid smell—the single shred of evidence in her tent—was dissipating by the second.

Her men weren't informed of her episodes, but they were familiar with her mother's madness and her tragic end. Only the High One knew what Marek assumed, seeing the mysterious vials now.

"You don't believe me."

The captaen draped the spare fur around her condolingly. "I believe our demons delight in revisiting us on sleepless nights. And I believe you have met far too many in your short life." A tendon skittered below Marek's lean cheekbone as he moved to caress her head once more.

Luscia jerked out of reach. She didn't know if it was her face or the luxiron that heated, but the bow of her lip scorched under the solrahs. Jaw set, Luscia shook the fur off her back.

"Exit my quarters at once and track down your lost najjan," she directed in a low, absent tone. "And when you find him, you remind him of his *sacred obligation* to his haidren."

Marek's thin mouth stiffened, yet he did make to leave.

"I wish to be alone."

"Luscia—"

Simmering, she glared at Marek, parked stoically before her. "That was an explicit order, Captaen!"

Rigidly, he rose off his knees. "As you command, Ana'Sere."

The leather of his belt hung, still unfastened, where he lingered in the tent flap.

Luscia threw her chin aside and listened to his reluctant steps and their quiet departing swish through the Eindrulla grasses. Curling onto her hip, Luscia studied the drop of fluid left in the emptied vial, alighted by Marek's weakening lumilore, which he'd forgotten behind. In a mournful sigh, she reignited it. At Luscia's breath, the lumin-enriched stone lit up, shining more clearly than it had in his possession.

She'd permitted Marek into her world. She'd entrusted her failure to him.

And she'd never felt so alone.

A few days passed before Luscia spoke again.

She rode on, alone in her ruminations, aside from menial directives to her men and small quips to her lycran.

Luscia had forgotten how much she appreciated her own company, as she'd depended on it once, seasons ago. With a blanketed somberness befalling each man, her najjani guard didn't seem to mind. There was a time Luscia wouldn't have even noted their preference. Perhaps she had grown too familiar with their companionship.

Perhaps she'd just grown soft.

Aksel trotted cheerfully beside the dappled mare, ignorant of the tension among his acquired pack. Luscia adjusted in the saddle, her tailbone numb, and offered him a sardonic look when he yipped perkily. The miracle of his mixed genetics was apparent when his capacious vulpine tail swatted the horse's leg. Her mare was much less enthusiastic about the endless journeying than he.

With the tribulation of Rian far behind, she estimated Faraji to be close, as the royal caravan tirelessly ascended the base of the Andwele range. Foothills swelled taller, and cliffsides sprouted on either end of the sprawling valley through which the king's regiment navigated. At his demand for shorter nights and longer days, Dmitri was pressed to reach Darakaian soil, had they not already crossed onto it.

Luscia could sense Marek's stubborn attempts to catch her eye; however, she averted hers, unready to pretend he was forgiven. She would forgive him, eventually, but she would not forget that defining moment when he had dismissed her claim, even after he'd smelled it on her sheets. It would have cost her life, had forces beyond her understanding not intervened.

She was significantly less ready to explore the magnitude of those forces, for the harbinger thread had not only spoken, but its speaking had come to pass.

Marek's stallion edged closer, so Luscia opted to fall back between Noxolo and Creyvan. In an act of clemency, she'd granted Creyvan opportunity to lick his wounds, so to speak. Luscia could still smell the crude poultice he had since washed off the bruises Marek, or even Declan, had presumably gifted him for his insubordination. Naturally, his Boreali skin had since healed. She might have heard the account of his whereabouts that night, were she speaking to her own captaen. Alas, it fell to Luscia to seek out the information once she wanted to hear it.

"Do you wish to enlighten me where you were the other night?" she asked the golden-locked najjan, looking straight ahead.

Creyvan knew it was him she addressed, not Noxolo; over horse hooves crunching the trail, she'd heard him gulp nervously. Luscia did not rush his reply.

"A tavern at the edge of Rian's city limit didn't mind my *y'siti* coin, and I wanted a drink before I slept in the mire, like a dog." Creyvan's voice shook with disturbing vehemence. "Meh fyreon, Ana'Sere, they do not know who they put in the dirt… But they should."

Luscia revolved in her saddle. Creyvan's youthful features hardened under his sheet of blond stubble. It was a dangerous narrative, not for Boreal but rather the rest of the realm. Dangerous to those who did not fix, fight, or forge as they did. Many centuries ago, before the fortification of Aksel's Keep, commenced by her lycran's namesake, there was initial dissention among the clans as whether to shield the world from the Dönumn Lux or to weaponize it against them. It was Marek's same ancestor, Aksel Bailefore of Clan Ciann, who persuaded the early descendants of Tiergan the first to keep to the path of peace.

Their Gift of Light was not meant to harm but to heal. Any deviation from that calling was dangerous indeed.

"Boreal was wrong to deny Rian aid all those generations ago. Our victory at Orynthia's frontline against the Mworrans will always bear that stain, Creyvan," Luscia told him candidly. "It is our responsibility to bear the misjudgments of our Boreali forefathers as humbly and graciously we can, to honor the High One, who is merciful to our shortcomings. In your rejecting that charge,"—she squared her shoulders toward the najjan— "you put me at risk."

"Meh fyreon... Ana'Sere." Creyvan lowered his face, but his expression puckered defiantly. "Though, I'm sure Böwen would have felt the same."

"Creyvan!" Noxolo called from her right.

Luscia's hand stilled Noxolo's commentary, but just as she steeled herself to handle Creyvan's blatant bitterness, the haidren to Darakai galloped his Andwele stallion past their unit, whistling for his pryde to follow. At the atypical urgency in Kasim's sudden eruption from the rear of the procession, Luscia grimaced at Creyvan, anchoring his piercing, sapphire stare with her own.

"This conversation is not over," Luscia stated and kicked her mare, exploding through the protective boundary of the four najjan.

Luscia ran her horse alongside Kasim's third. Zahra, she'd heard her called. Beautifully, the warrior's sable skin danced under the sun, better suited for its wrath than Luscia's agitated pinked porcelain. Trailing her sprint toward the helm of the line, Luscia coveted how gratified the other woman appeared, the wind flapping her Darakaian sparring pants like homecoming flags.

She coveted the day the group instead climbed the brisk highlands of the north.

Bounding by Bastiion's excuse for a haidren, who had passed out in his saddle and was slumped, Luscia approached the men congregating around Dmitri. The regiment had stalled at the approach of three figures on horseback, racing out from the base of the mountain.

Weeding through the dense collection of soldiers, Luscia brought her mare next to Kasim's spirited stallion. He did not welcome her nearness. Nor did his rider.

"Get back with your shadowmen," Kasim scoffed and walked his stallion a few paces more, ahead of the field marshal.

Doing the same, she replied, "Niit."

A bluster of irritation emitted from Kasim as he sneered, "Then do us all a favor and keep your witchtongue to yourself."

She complied, only as the incoming riders drew near. At the center was Kasim's rival alpha, the one he'd mentioned in his revised proposition in the stables.

Wekesa, the lower alpha, had pounds on Kasim, she could easily see, as he was flanked between two lesser warriors. One was a man about Marek's size, with chicory cheeks and a half-exposed kopar. The other, a female, was even more striking than Kasim's third. Her rich voluminous curls were gathered in bulbs by a half dozen brass ties and descended to her waist. Reaching the royal party right before her alpha, her mountain mare stopped just shy of Kasim.

"Owàamo, Zaeth." She purred in an allusive alto, earning a snort from Kasim's third behind them. "Welcome home."

"Now, Kehari, is that a proper way to greet our alpha zà and his y'siti guest? Surely, ano." Wekesa trotted up alongside the woman. His pitch-colored eyes narrowed abrasively at Kasim. "Shamàli, you'll have to overlook my pryde's lacking manners. You've not been with Kehari in *so* long."

Luscia ascertained that the opposing alpha implied Kasim's absence from the territorial bounds of her bed, not a map. In her periphery, the Southern haidren clenched the reins in his grasp.

"Speak to your posting, Alpha," Kasim stated, his leathers creaking when he crossed his wrists over the horn of his saddle. "You're blocking the king's path."

Wekesa smirked. It was an unseemly thing that warped the scarring along his skull. "We are here to escort you into Faraji."

"Ano zà. As haidren to Darakai, I am the king's escort into Faraji."

Breaking from his trio, Wekesa stalked his horse closer to Kasim. Even Luscia recognized the satisfaction in each step. She couldn't stand Kasim, but he was right. She could stand Wekesa even less.

"Uni—an escort chosen by the king..." Wekesa's blocky teeth shone wide as he grinned fearlessly. "But not your father. From this point, you follow *me* to Faraji."

CHAPTER ELEVEN
ZAETHAN

The socket of his eye thrummed in protest. Zaethan didn't need a court physician to diagnose the cause of the ache; he was staring right at it. Beyond the pillar of dancing flames, Wekesa animated some outlandish story to Bessus and a huddle of the regiment. Zaethan counted the chunks of meat that flew from his fat mouth as he spoke.

Four. Five. Six.

For each fleck that landed in the dirt, he devised another method to end the combatant alpha. By the seventh, Zaethan decided a fork to Wekesa's jugular would send a nice, straightforward message to the prydes. It'd be poetic in its simplicity. But Zaethan merely cracked his knuckles instead, hoisted over his uneaten dinner. He'd lost his appetite, watching that entitled hog devour his rations.

"Ho'waladim…" Kumo elbowed him, offering a crude flask. "It's definitely due you, given the circumstances."

Zaethan snatched the flask from his beta. It'd been crafted from low-grade Yowekaon ore, by the speckling in the metal grain. He cleared his throat, swallowing the weakened sting of Kumo's diluted bwoloa.

"Zullee." Zaethan accepted it, keeping the flask low to the moss-covered log, out of sight. "That tastes like backwoods creek shtàka."

"Rainwater preserves the spirit." Kumo swished the watered-down liquor and tucked the flask into his hardy belting. "You're going to need it, yeah? Especially with Kehari warming Wekesa right next door." Folding his great arms, he grunted. "She always won playing both sides… but eh, what do I know of women? Meme ano'qondai, maybe some rivalries never die."

Through the fire, Zaethan spotted where she melted against Wekesa's side, her arm slung territorially over his shoulder. Kehari laughed at something he'd stated to Bessus, knocking her divine face backward toward Àla'maia as if they were heavenly friends. A hefty bronze-and-turquoise choker embellished her slender neck.

He could only scoff. She'd worn it on purpose, having received it from Zaethan when they were infatuated cubs, well before titles and pryde politics had deepened the ravine between him and his rival, whom Kehari adored. It was a bold move to parade in front of Zaethan now—the heirloom passed on from his aunt, Léola.

Coolly, Zaethan shrugged. "Kehari is like a duel-edged scythe. Embrace her, and either way you get stabbed in the back. When I claimed alpha zà, Wekesa claimed Kehari. In the end, she chose the bastard back."

Her eyes, sparkling from laughter, slipped toward Zaethan over the flames, echoing the blaze's vibrant hue into the night. He used to get lost in them, back when he still believed in enduring fables of love.

"Kàchà kocho. Kehari chose wrong."

"That's why Wekesa didn't strut into Bastiion with her at the start of the summer, ano?"

"It's likely."

A cane whacked Zaethan's bicep, and he spun around on the fallen timber.

Stooping, Dmitri's slender chin was balanced atop the byrnnzite handle of his walking stick. "My tent. One hour. We need to talk."

His friend's careful gaze wandered, then moored onto Zaethan again. The hollowness had returned beneath his fatigued eyes. Dmitri needed a decent night's rest before he faced Darakai's tribe chieftains. For a people who praised the fortitude of their flesh, they would interpret weakness in their new king's complexion. A few more sleepless midnights and he'd look just like the witch.

Dmitri rocked back and forth on his cane, like he wanted to stay, then stretched to stand. "One hour," he said again, leaving both Darakaians to traipse toward Sayuri's brother, who sat far away from the throng with his Pilarese guard.

"Ahoté." Kumo swatted Zaethan abruptly. "Look."

Across the kindling pyre, Zahra, cup in hand, strode by Wekesa's growing club, where others had assembled around him, Kehari, and the field marshal. In passing, Wekesa yanked Zahra by the wrist, stalling her in front of his audience. Zaethan couldn't make out his words, except for the infuriating snicker when he uttered them and the mirth that rippled through the nearby men. Zaethan's fork bit into his palm when he clenched it, watching Wekesa's derisive antics unfold. Not the type to roleplay the captive, Zahra made to break from the alpha's hold, but Wekesa wrenched the skilled, lithe warrior closer and mouthed into her ear.

That time, she did not pull away.

Zaethan fired himself upright, the fork and bowl rattling to his feet. Not a second later, Kumo joined him off the log.

Still whispering to Zaethan's third, Wekesa winked at Zaethan, yards away. The twinge returned in Zaethan's eye socket. He reached for his kopar and tightened his grip on the hilt at his rival's outright disrespect. Slowly he unsheathed the Southern sickle sword, and Wekesa unhanded his third's wrist, palm wide, and pointed it at Zaethan, her leader across the bonfire. With his motioning, Wekesa's lips shaped the higher-ranking title "alpha zà."

Zahra's sleek, tattooed head twisted around. Her eyes did not meet Zaethan's, but he didn't overlook the crumpled bridge of her nose, disturbed by whatever Wekesa had spewed into her ear. She chucked her cup into the embers and stalked off, not toward her pryde but alone, vanishing into a tide of murky grasses.

"Shtàka," Kumo bellowed. "I should have punched him earlier, yeah? For trying to get her attention all night long."

"He's striving to burrow under my skin," Zaethan replied, kneeling for the discarded bowl. "Wekesa won't declare his challenge here, in this field or another. He's too cocky. He wants a much bigger crowd than this. So he'll bite wherever he can in the meantime."

If Zaethan's instincts were right, his rival would wait until all his supporters were gathered in Faraji. There, Wekesa would declare his move publicly, confronting Zaethan into setting the time of the challenge. Yet set it too far off and he'd be named a coward.

Zaethan needed the witch's luxiron. And soon.

"Your third is an odd place to start his chewing."

"Wekesa has coveted Zahra's loyalty for years. But he'll never have it."

His beta hmphed, patting the coin purse under his leathers. "I bet two dromas our Zahra lobs off one of those stubby fingers the next time Wekesa tries that *kakka-shtàka*."

"Uni, let's hope," Zaethan echoed, not completely convinced. "Wekesa's emboldened kakk won't stop. It's only begun."

"What are you going to do about it?"

"Nothing. Yet." Zaethan scooped up a handful of reddish soil, instead of the fractured bowl. "By his action, my father declared support for Wekesa's impending challenge, sending him as a personal envoy like that. As of sundown, a new precedent took effect, yeye qondai? Things are different inside the chief warlord's dominion, cousin."

Zaethan ground the rich minerals and brought the soil to his face, relishing the bittersweet splendor he smelled. "We're in Darakai now."

Approaching Dmitri's regal pavilion, Zaethan sensed more unwanted company cloistered within the vaulted enclosure.

Explicitly, the company of Ira Hastings.

But as usual, the yancy's voice was merely the loudest and lewdest of the other haidrens, invited to what Zaethan presumed to be a privileged private meeting. It was becoming a habit of Dmitri's, advertising an event as one thing whenever Zaethan was doubtful to attend the thing it really was.

He was getting good at it too.

Swishing aside canvas and linen, he entered the vaulted tent, which was roomier than he'd imagined, with its circular design and generous height. Their regent's indigo lodgings were topped with a bulbous bronze finial, distinguished at the center of the camp, which imitated the cupolas of the monumental palace they'd left in Bastiion. Zaethan had opted to observe the wandering structure as a kingly sanctuary, thus it was his first visit inside Dmitri's regal dwelling.

Under suspended lanterns, his friend sat cross-legged on a cushion, clasping a small box. To Dmitri's right, Hachiro twiddled with a quill, which bowed from relentless use. On Dmitri's left, Ira lazed across a swell of pillows, all appearing to have been dragged off his king's bedding. Forming a circle, two empty cushions awaited their hosts.

Great, Zaethan thought sardonically. *It's going to be the whole gang.*

"Lord Darakai," Dmitri said, greeting him in Quadrennal address and gesturing toward either piece of upholstery. "Take a seat. We will get started shortly."

Stepping over the vacant cushions, Zaethan bent down and flicked Ira in the temple. "You're in my spot."

"Zaeth, really?" Dmitri chided in the haidren's defense.

"Ow!" Ira whined, massaging his scalp. "And here I thought you were finally starting to appreciate all I have to offer in a relationship. By the Fates, my friend, you've soured tonight." Ira toasted the air and took a long swig of wine as he scooted off the silky padding and plopped onto the next one. Rearranging himself, his mouth slackened and the yancy cocked his head, frowning at his pants.

"We're not friends—" When Ira used the goblet base to scratch near his genitals, Zaethan flicked his temple even harder. "Doru, stop that!"

"The Depths!" he cried. "We're practically brothers in arms, considering our similar taste in *veiled ladies*..." His brow hiked toward his hairline, like a splash of dark wine against his recently sun-soaked skin. "I'll scratch yours if you scratch mine."

"Our tastes could not be more dissimilar. Touch me, and your swollen pellets will be fed to that war-tainted wolx outside."

"No exchange of service, however rigorous, would do you good, Lord Bastiion." Hachiro piped up, examining the shaft of his quill. "Only abstinence can treat the communicable issue of your so-called… tastes."

The shoto'shi glanced up at Ira, blinked a few times, then hastily glanced back down.

From the corner of Zaethan's eye, Dmitri pressed his forehead into the trinket box, clearly exasperated with them all. Zaethan wished he could take that box and break it over Ira's head. He fleetingly considered the impulse. However, the Peerage were sure to throw a bit of a ruckus upon his returning to the crown city, and the nobility already had enough on their docket, overtaxing the poor and the like.

"The Fates bless you, Lady Boreal." Dmitri hailed the witch with relief when she slipped into his tent, her hybrid beast trailing her every step.

Inside, she fastened the flap toggles tightly behind them.

"Your steadying presence could not be timelier."

She dodged a tray at the entryway, crammed with dainty morsels and assorted refreshments. At the sight of the wolx hugging her hip, Ira placed his goblet aside and warily locked his arms around his lean legs. He eyed the animal while the witch descended onto the empty cushion and tucked her legs beneath herself neatly. The wolx, alerted to Ira's nervous watch, fixated on the yancy as it lay down and curled around her, engulfing the Northern haidren in his snowy tundra of dense fur.

"Looks like it's ready for a snack," Zaethan muttered to Ira when it yawned and flashed its lethal canines, longer than those of any wolf.

With a nervous giggle, an octave shriller than usual, Ira casually uncrossed his legs. He nestled a pillow under his beltline between them and cautiously eyed the wolx. Then, loosening the slack lacing of his costly shirt, he pulled out a chain and clutched the snuff canister hanging by it.

"I hope my delay was not detrimental to the agenda," the witch said cordially, folding her small hands together.

They were so demurely deceiving, those hands. She rested them where her riding skirt split apart and the silver embroidery near the top of her stocking stretched across a patch of uncovered thigh.

Zaethan decidedly looked away from the delicate stitching—and the pale skin beneath it.

"The best gifts are those for which we've waited," Dmitri replied, inching to the edge of his cushion. "I've gathered you here tonight because tomorrow, a new chapter in the Stag Age begins. The peace we adopted stains the very ground we sit upon. Given our rare opportunity to continue such peace, I wish to honor those sacrifices by commencing with our own."

A battered codex was laid at Dmitri's bare toes. He cracked the vellum pages apart and held up an old five-sided box. Studying the crinkled pages, he slid each faded pane out of socket. Etched with an ancient geometric pattern Zaethan had only seen in the catacombs, the lackluster wood locked into a strange shape. Dmitri placed the distorted box at the center of their circle, unfolded the sides away from the lid, and snapped them toward the floor.

He flattened his palms, and each pane glided away from its hinge, the box extending outward into five points. Returning to the weathered codex, Dmitri chewed his lip, nodded once, and with his fingertips, fanned each point wider, broadening it into a surface of reenforced reed. When he twisted the knob atop the lid, a mechanism unlocked with a *click*, and four spindles ejected from the closure. Again referencing the aged parchment, Dmitri elongated each spindle, not unlike a spyglass, and unleafed the reedy components into sizable darts. Inverting them into the hollow corners of the now-horizontal board, he slid the darts on hidden tracks and secured them in place.

Dmitri leaned back, and a profound dimple formed in his waned cheek when he grinned. There, in the middle of their formation, rested an antique makeshift pentagonal table.

Grabbing the spine, Dmitri skimmed the vellum, then abruptly plucked the knob off the lid.

"Nearly forgot…" His teeth entrapped his tongue while he pressed the knob onto the board in front of Zaethan. With tension, Dmitri twisted it against the reed slats. As he did, the discolored head of a panther spun into view on a secret panel.

Darakai's crest.

Ira bent beyond his protective pillow when Dmitri reached over and used the knob to rotate a circlet beside the Southern marker, exposing the head of a bear for Bastiion.

Zaethan couldn't name one Unitarian who embodied the nobility of the bear, save Dmitri. And while Unitarian in descent, he hardly counted, as their regent was to represent the royal House of Thoarne in balance to all the rest.

Moving around the board, Dmitri did the same for Boreal and Pilar, leaving the fifth and final side unmarked. "There," he said, satisfied. "I can confidently call this Quadren to session."

Hachiro collected Dmitri's codex and, turning it upside down, tried to make sense of the sketch in relation to the transformed pocket board. From the pleats of his ocher-colored robe, he produced his multipronged monocle. Choosing a mint lens, the shoto'shi snapped the apparatus onto his ear.

"It's a pleasant perplexity." Hunched to the ground, Hachiro leveled his magnified eye with the panes and blew a chunk of his black hair out of the way, blinking thrice. "When was it engineered?"

"There was an era when haidrens could not meet within the walls of a palace but rather deliberated the riddles of the realm by candlelight, under leaky canopies on waterlogged battlegrounds. Our ancestors designed the Quadrecipher to hide classified codes, maps... even wartime correspondences away from spies and opportunists," Dmitri explained, his finger gently tracing the trim of the artifact. "Mine is the first Quadren to be seated free of conflict, and though Orynthia's treaties remain intact, I imagined we could put this craftmanship to use while traveling together."

Under his dusky waves, Dmitri searched the circle, the marigold glint of his eyes giving way to a sleepy green. He paused and closed them. "Only together will we write a chronicle worth remembering. There is but one thing I long for this Quadren be remembered by..." His lashes parted wide in petition. "And that is the unification of a kingdom. Each of us are of a different House, a different line, but we are all *equally* Orynthian. It is under that single banner we must lead the many.

"The accords wane thin. House divisions have worsened, infecting the Ethnicam, breeding more dissension rather than collaboration. The disparity of the classes is literally bleeding out into the streets."

A tremble threatened Dmitri's voice, at the memory of his coronation parade, Zaethan presumed. "Tomorrow we enter Faraji. Tomorrow the real work begins. As Zaeth—Lord Darakai—can and has already attested, the Darakaians must see strength among our fledgling regime. We need the South's support to secure a more intimate arrangement with

Razôuel. The tribes have not yet voiced opposition to my betrothed, Bahira'Rasha, but they might, which Orynthia cannot afford."

Zaethan stared at his crest on the board, where from age, the outline of the panther's fangs faded into nothingness. It posed a fine line, voicing too much about his people.

The ways of Darakai belonged to the Darakaians. As haidren, he was to personify their best interest yet also the interest and security of his king.

In Dmitri's expectant pausing, Zaethan fought his instinct and eventually shared. "The chieftains will count every weakness. They will assess and measure, weighing each against my father's judgment." His lips pursed guardedly. He could not serve two masters, though the Ethnicam would have him try. Zaethan lowered his voice, disclosing another truth. "Here, Nyack Kasim is not commander of the Orynthian armies, something a child of Thoarne can take away."

Dmitri steepled his fingers, listening.

"Here, my father is the law. He is their judge and jury, their sword and shield. He is chief warlord. To Darakai…" Zaethan let out a troubled breath. "He *is* king."

The tent went quiet as Dmitri soberly thumbed his chin. It was a dice game, Zaethan divulging the scope of his father's might to the entire Quadren—yet even more precarious for his friend if he did not. The scarlet thread peeping out from under Dmitri's cuff bolstered Zaethan's resolve. He treasured Darakai, but the Fates help them if his people ever forced him to choose.

Because Zaethan would choose the man to his right every time.

"But… You're king." Ira raked his hair, bewildered. "Darakai can't have two."

Sayuri's brother congratulated Ira for the obvious, a tic sputtering his brow. "An invariant deduction, Lord Bastiion."

Through tightened lips, Zaethan's temper flared. "Read the room, Ira."

Over the Quadrecipher, he assessed the witch, who coolly pondered the information he'd presented. Reaching backward, she stroked the wolx's snout, her expression unreadable in the most irritating way.

Flatly, she stated to the board, "So in summary, our objective is to get along." Her mismatched irises flicked upward at Dmitri.

Zaethan squinted under the weak lanterns, swearing the light was pulsating within the strange, milky iridescence encircling her left pupil.

"A demanding task, I know," Dmitri wryly replied. "I cannot overstate the gravity of this tour or the Quadren's position with the Ethnicam. Our objective is to reinforce Darakai's fealty to the throne, without giving Nyack Kasim reason doubt Darakai's fealty to him. His sending a lesser alpha to monitor our party, under the guise of hospitality, was a sign he may already feel threatened."

"Ano." Zaethan glowered and glanced at his king. "That was personal to me, not you."

Handling his cane, Dmitri balanced it across his lap under either elbow. "Even still, we ought to treat it as such. A man rarely shows his nature until his roots are dug up for him." Lifting off his forearms, Dmitri propped onto the cane. "With that, I believe this late Quadrennal session has robbed you enough. Sleep deeply, so that when you wake, we shoulder tomorrow as one."

Disbanding, the three haidrens piled out of the draped pavilion.

"Zaeth," Dmitri said once they were alone, "be sure to look out for them."

Knowing to whom Dmitri referred, Zaethan gave a terse nod and lingered, hoping for a chance to confer with his friend despite the hour. But to Dmitri's adamant urging, he too was sent off to bed.

Meandering about the regiment shelters, he dodged a lively match of darts and dice, earning plenty of slurred cheers in the distance. His tent a few yards off, Zaethan ducked under the low branch of one of the few trees abutting the encampment.

A blade caressed his spine, the pressure through his simple threadbare tunic unassuming and light.

"To the other side of the trunk, out of sight."

At the velvet gravel of her instruction, he stepped over the gnarled roots underfoot.

The witch guided him to where even the moonlight was scarce beneath the cover of rustling leaves. Her blade skimmed his ribcage and wrapped round to his navel when his back met the bark. She looked so inferior. Her upturned boots were anchored hip-width apart, and nearly half her body was engulfed by lofty Eindrullagrass.

"I could have those confiscated in Faraji." Zaethan inclined his head toward the arced witchiron unleashed at her knuckles, a set of Boreali gadgets he'd come to scorn.

The angle of her pallid cheek crispened under the dappled moonbeams.

"Then you'd have to confiscate all our luxiron." With a snap, she retracted the blade, and it collapsed into jewelry once more. "Do that, and you'll never get what you want."

"You've so vexingly resisted what I want. Why take the risk?"

Boreal's haidren retreated a fraction, inviting a heap of grass to separate them, proving his point about her reflexive need for space.

"You'll be delighted to know I've reconsidered your proposed arrangement." She artfully crossed her arms, the breeze fluttering her filigree sleeves. "When shall we begin?"

Zaethan's scrutiny narrowed. Elation, however, swarmed his chest. If Wekesa's timeline had expedited under his father's endorsement, he needed the witch's upper hand sooner than later.

"Why the change?" He couldn't help but ask. "Your revered shadowmen can train you in close combat, as you so confidently contended. Why me, over them?"

She stiffened, and he saw where her nails dug into her biceps. He'd hit a nerve. Zaethan reclined into the trunk, propping his heel against the bark, but the corners of her curvaceous lips curled.

"You said it best. You're the last person I want touching me, being nothing like them." She scanned his taller form and stopped where his hands were casually interlaced. "Ought to make it a challenge, considering where those have been recently. How was it, sleeping in the den of a convicted traitor?"

The shores of The Wastes suddenly lapped his ears, as did Salma's screams. Zaethan pushed off the tree and towered over the witch. Without a trace of empathy, he stooped low, relishing the admission. "Ask your flaxen shadowman. I think he enjoyed it even more than I did."

Her ignorant smirk slipped.

Walking backward, Zaethan waded into the grasses and let Àla'maia's luster spill over him unabashedly. "Meet me at midnight in Faraji. You are going to learn, Maji'maia, just how right you are." His fingers rapped his own abdomen. "I am nothing like your men."

Turning his back on the witch, Zaethan smiled into the dark.

Kwihila rapiki mu jwona. By defiance and trickery, maybe Wekesa really was jwona rapiki, a fate writer.

But then again, so was Zaethan.

CHAPTER TWELVE

The blades danced in and out of focus as the figure crouched low in the breezy grasses. He monitored Cyra's son, haidren to Darakai, where he loomed over Alora's niece under the whistling crown of an ancient oak. The vision would have made Cyra happy, offered her some reprieve in the end, to have seen him inherit her seat as intended.

After all, it was she who'd predicted, before her last, that his haidrenship would be in jeopardy. Positions of power always were—though most perilously when within the reach of Nyack Kasim.

In the cocoon of heavy knotted limbs that lumbered toward the soil, the young diplomats spoke of an arrangement concerning some exchange of skill. In secret the two negotiated, despite the ever-widening divide of their Houses. One would have thought such recent appointment, their Seating amid the Ethnicam's distrust and disquiet, would have driven the pair further apart, right back to their respective factions. Yet here they were, nose to nose, forging another strained association.

Alora would not be pleased—unlike Cyra, who used to enjoy making deals.

But the crown had passed to Korbin's heir, and the actions of Alora's successor were no longer within her realm of control. That was... if Luscia's choices had ever been under her control to begin with.

As his arid eyes fastened onto the pair beneath the tree, the figure swatted away the gnats that swarmed his wounds. These muggy lowlands were full of the nasty things. He knew his fetid shoulder, mauled by the creature he'd wrenched off Alora's niece, would heal no further.

Running the abomination far into the plains outside Rian, the figure had ultimately eradicated it, but not without paying a significant portion of tissue to its hunger. Their struggle, lasting well into the raging sunrise, had only ceased when he'd ultimately torn off its head. The creature's remains, like those of Felix Ambrose—described to Alora in Bastiion—turned to dust and ash and was swept away over the grassland. There was nothing to prove the creature had ever existed, except for the grotesque cavity it'd left in the figure.

His parting gift from an alternate destiny.

Bothered by the pests, he tightened the filthy muslin wrapped about the damage. It needed to be cauterized soon, as the deadened flesh along the surface had begun to rot. He wouldn't feel the pain; the nerves had died days ago.

He resumed his observance. Alora's niece did not back down to the

opposite haidren's boasted dominance. Instead, Luscia quirked her head
ever so slightly when his lips bent near her ear. His whisper unheard
from the distance, it was clearly far from a lover's secret. Immediately,
her posture wilted like an oak's weighted branches. With a satisfied
bounce in his step, seemingly elated by her despondence, Cyra's son
plodded backward.

"You are going to learn," he called. "I am nothing like your men."

Amusement split a scab on the figure's mouth. There was a time
he too had considered himself on equal footing with a daughter of
Tiergan, only to grasp their intrinsic disparity far too late. Yet as Alora
had previously cautioned, the young man could never learn quite how
different he was, for his knowing could strike a match and ignite the
undoing of them all.

Retreating, the Southern haidren left Luscia, wading deeper into
the Eindrullagrass away from the old tree. The figure grimaced, unimpressed with the subject of Alora's warning. Cyra's son was starting to
exhibit a penchant for dramatic exits, a notable disposition he had not
inherited from his mother.

The figure watched her there, motionless in her presumed privacy.
As she looked up toward the heavens, Luscia's chin trembled, her cheeks
shimmering in the moonlight when tears fell. Her hands motioned at
her heart as she conversed with the star-stricken sky. Though hushed, it
sounded like an apology.

Intrigued by her lonesome outpouring, the figure crept forward.
Swathed under his battered cloak, his knee snagged and caught a twig,
snapping it. The noise jolted her attention at once. Alora's niece bent
into a defensive stance and circled, her scrutiny scanning the rolling
plain. When the breeze picked up, her nostrils flared, and with deadly
focus, Luscia unleashed her radials once again.

She smelled the reek, the decomposition of his shoulder.

Parting the grass, she glided toward his scent. When she hesitated just feet away, he peeked out the brim of his hood, staring into the underside of her fierce countenance. His breathing stopped, making him as lifeless as the pebbles, while she hovered over him, sniffing the air above the place where the figure lay in the dirt.

Just as her leg hitched, as she prepared to explore deeper into the plain, songs of inebriation chimed from the distance. One song loudened above the other ballads, heading their way.

Luscia withdrew and with a pivot glanced in the direction of the oak.

The figure heard her radials latch when she swiftly sheathed them. With a rush of relief, he shot upward, seeing her trudge back toward the camp.

A group of blundering soldiers ambled along the bordering row of tents, their cups sloshing with their merry chorus. Breaking from his company, a stout, rounded man stumbled after the tree, nearly tripping over its roots. He whistled while he propped against the trunk and fumbled with his buckle, keen to relieve himself.

"Marshal," Alora's niece stated in guarded greeting as she promptly strode on.

The figure glowered at the repulsive man General Lateef had elevated to field marshal over the king's regiment. The figure recalled Bessus, the yancy officer who had sacrificed nothing to the Shield Wars except his unwelcomed passions to a slew of unascended sufferers. Orynthia, or rather the commander of its armies, merely buried his crimes during the drafting of Korbin's progressive treaty with Razôuel, the reports of Bessus's young victims never to be investigated.

Bessus leered at Alora's niece when she bypassed him, her stride rigid.

His hand down his breeches, the field marshal jeered at her. "You thirsty, y'siti?" He wriggled his fist inside the material and snorted, grabbing himself. "Come back here and I'll give you a taste of Bastiion!"

She halted, then continued without comment. An unidentified brutality stirred within the figure, honing his fascination, when he saw Luscia raise her fingertips to touch the place she'd been scarred. As she turned, disappearing into the maze of tents, those same fingers wicked away moisture from her cheeks.

The figure's blistered lip curled. His ruthless glare twisted toward the drunken marshal, where he was urinating onto the bark.

Slinking through the grass, the figure melded into the darkness. He lingered behind Bessus as the yancy hummed, buckling his breeches. Saliva frothed the figure's tongue when it raked the tip of his canines. But it wasn't a depraved hunger that beckoned his anticipation forth. It was the pain due Bessus for his crimes, a pain the figure could so effortlessly deliver were he permitted.

The figure growled, his hot breath coating the neck of Bessus's filthy tunic.

"Shtàka, get off—" The field marshal staggered, spinning around, and stopped. Bessus reached wide, clinging to the bark at his back when the figure crept closer, until his cloak brushed the marshal's sweat-stained belly.

The figure removed his hood, and his blisters met the breeze. Bessus's jowls shuddered in horror as he absorbed the figure's grotesque disfigurement.

"Anything, Bessus, done to her or another…" Wrath rattled from his throat with every ounce of his monstrosity. "I will find and see done to you tenfold."

With dread shining from the whites of his bleary eyes, the figure shot his arm out, and with restraint, he seized Bessus by the hair and rammed his skull into the oak. Knocked out, the field marshal slid to the earth.

The figure looked at him there, bleeding into a crib of twisted rootage. Its age unfathomable, it was the kind of tree that remembered things. Unspeakable things.

But just as it was with names, some stories should be forgotten.

He returned the threadbare covering over his ravaged scalp and abandoned Bessus under the oak, darting through the grasses like a savage from a sorrowful memory—a memory Alora bled herself to preserve, no matter the cost.

CHAPTER THIRTEEN
LUSCIA

Dominance thundered over the steep ravine. The sheet of moss and vinery, encrusting the soaring russet cliff walls, trembled at each triumphal strike of the mammoth kettledrums, played from either lip of the narrow channel.

Darakaian rhythmists bordered the sprawling heights and drummed with fervor. Their imposing zeal added shade to the lush entryway, heralding the royal procession into the shrouded stronghold that lay beyond.

Well above their heads, children ran along the precarious ridge trails, keeping pace with the advancing soldiers. Vividly colored beads and copper bands decorated their sable arms and legs, jangling as the cubs flew streamers behind their advance. Atop her mare, Luscia's wary gaze followed the flock of eager children to where a shirtless young boy led the way. Sprightly in his momentum, he'd occasionally spin on his tiny legs to look back at them, down in the base of the rocky open. Thrusting a sharp, little spear in the air with a bushel of streamers knotted to the shaft, the boy would hop on the boulder jutting out from the cliffside and totter on the edge.

It gave Luscia a panic every time. His bones could not recover as hers would were he to slip.

Cupping his mouth, he let loose a whooping call, earning reciprocal cries from Kasim's pryde below—even, on occasion, from her Northern lycran, winning Aksel the delighted giggles of the other children before the boy bounded onward along the scant trail once more.

Their cries chimed throughout the canyon mouth, carried through an echo chamber to the beat of the kettledrums, as she attuned her ears to the crunch of grass and gravel at the rear. Hearing the cadence of her men's breathing, the grinding of their teeth, and even Noxolo swatting the air caused Luscia to chuckle inside. Whether the Darakaians were apprehensive about her accompanying najjan guarding her on horseback, they'd created an open-air bomaerod, unknowingly sharpening the already-superior senses of the Boreali.

Beside her, Marek's head tweaked ever so slightly as he experienced the same audible shift. A reinforced jacket of sterling linsilk, ornamented with the trim of elegant wheaten threadwork identical to her own, hugged his triangular frame. The najjan rode in unison, matching their haidren in dress and stature, along the bank of a gushing creek bed, its rigor flowing in the opposite direction down the vast gorge. When Luscia lengthened her spine and hardened her shoulders, she heard the material her men's meticulously crafted garb tauten as they all followed suit. In solidarity, a sheer silk trim sleeved their necks above their upright collars, as if they too were marred there. Though unlike Luscia, choosing to appear unassertive and unarmed, her najjan each had a crossed set of gleaming crescent wraiths strapped to their backs, the tips of their blades unsheathed in proclamation.

Meekness was not the same as weakness. And however meek, the Boreali were not to be trifled with.

Toward her right heel, Noxolo's boots creased when he twisted in his stirrups.

"Ykah lö?" he questioned breathily. "What in Aurynth do they think they're doing?"

Bordering the beaten path, Kasim progressed up the line, but when he came between Declan and the bank of the waters, the current increasing with each step, he slowed his stallion in tandem with Luscia's mare. Covertly tucking her chin, she saw his third, Zahra, come alongside Creyvan, and when she rotated, discovered his hulking beta attempting squeeze between Marek and the rock wall.

In frustration, Luscia braced a hand on her hip and revolved in her saddle completely. Takoda, the warrior she'd healed in Bastiion winged Noxolo, and the other two members of Kasim's pryde, the lanky one, with bobbing coils, and the small scout trailed her najjani guard, nearly blocking Hachiro Naborū-Zuo's scholarly robes from sight.

"They'd have you enter like a prisoner." Marek seethed in a tone unheard by their handlers.

Leashed resentment oozed off the captaen. She'd yet to reconcile with Marek. His doubts of her report, that there were more war-tainted creatures on the loose, pained her beyond reason. The severity of that pain frustrated Luscia more than the cause.

She'd not realized she'd sowed so much confidence in their budding relationship until it had shattered. While her anger was justified, a more fragile part of Luscia felt utterly foolish for having trusted him in the first place. And admittance of such fragility made her all the angrier, which was precisely why she could not *not* let it go.

Worse than Marek's dismissal was his refusal to fill the gaps in her training, forcing Luscia into another arrangement with Kasim, something Marek would neither understand nor ever endorse. However, the fact remained that Luscia was at risk in her own skin. To her disgrace, she needed someone to free her from its cage. If that someone was Kasim, so be it.

Otherwise, she would always be a prisoner to fear, and that reality, Luscia decided, was unacceptable.

Despite her festering rancor with the captaen, she wholeheartedly agreed with him now. The najjan may be on Darakaian soil but as a convoy to the Boreali haidren, not pryde detainees.

"Is this really necessary?" Luscia spitefully sniped at Kasim. "Your posturing suggests you intend to collect a bounty on our heads."

"Don't flatter yourself." The Darakaian haidren rolled his eyes, hitching the twin rings pierced through his brow. He dropped his reins and re-bound his ornamented locs in annoyance, the gilded cuffs flashing in the setting sunlight as he did. "We're merely following my superior's orders."

Spinning, Luscia caught Declan's strained grip turning red, although it might have been his Boreali skin succumbing to the oppressive temperatures. Gone was his creamy veneer, as the brawny najjan's freckling had tripled within the past weeks. Luscia caught his iron eyes. At her terse nod, he softened marginally and unfurled his fists, the tension through his cheeks smoothing beneath his braided titian beard.

Up ahead, a towering formation of eroded Andwelestone connected the opposing bluffs at the end of the gorge, where a massive burgundy bridge arced over the royal caravan. Leading the regiment, Dmitri and the field marshal passed under it at the lead. The little boy sprinting above them paused to call out to the pryde once again, and Kasim's beta, Kumo, returned for him a joyful howl, imitating a coyote's cry.

But not Kasim. His voice was absence among the rest.

"Your home awaits you, Alpha Zà," his third said to his back.

For some reason, Luscia looked over and observed the irregular swells of Kasim's chest. Buckled into formal Darakaian armor, it sped up and down between a set of scaled pauldrons, the sharp reptilian hide more menacing than the solo styles strapped across the right shoulders of his pryde. Fixed on the bridge ahead, his full lips rounded, and he released a slow, measured exhale.

Kasim was nervous.

Then she saw why.

The drumming hastened, rumbling louder as bellowing war horns shook the skies. Marching toward the bridge overhang, what Luscia had initially mistook as vertical striations in the red stone, she now distinguished as centuries of blood. Rivaling the cheerful overhanging flora, variegated veins of scarlet gruesomely stained the entire face of sediment, from where it had been poured over the edge and onto the path they trampled. Luscia's head hit the back of her linsilk jacket when they trotted under the magnificent yet harrowing archway, and her mouth slackened as she took in its enormity. With thanks to the High One, relief rushed over her.

The bridge was dry... for now.

On the other side of the archway, a crash of sound hammered their Boreali ears as the bomaerod effect dispelled and the constricted heights opened into a colossal basin. Cliffs of amber soared around them in every direction, heating under the setting sun where it painted the mountainous Andwelestone in a spectacular display of out-of-place tenderness. As her hearing adjusted, balancing to the explosion of cheers and percussion, Luscia then understood why the stream had been rushing against them, for waterfalls plummeted the varied altitudes, feeding into a lake and coloring it in a way Luscia had never seen. Mottling the water's surface in shifting shadows, the Darakaian rhythm erupted the birds from their perches in squalling flight patterns overhead.

Leading toward the astonishingly vibrant teal pool, thousands of citizens banked the roadways, where the caravan's horse hooves left dirt and touched down on smooth stamped rock. Luscia couldn't but gawk beyond their number.

Built into the encircling cliffsides, shaded under leafy slabs and overhanging bluffs, an entire city had been carved into the protective ruddy rockface, tallying well past thirty stories. Banners flew from several apertures in the homes, adorning the sanguine construction jubilantly. Pillars, chiseled into warriors, upheld a sprawling grid reinforced by stone buttresses engraved in foreign runes, like those marking the skull of Kasim's third. An intricate pulley system supplied the rising levels from promenades built into the first three, where no steps of any kind were present, except for the countless ladders that connected them. Ladders which could be removed, Luscia grasped, during an attack. Scanning the elaborate expanse, she felt her reticence melt, giving way to awe. The climbing network of Andwele dwellings wrapped around the entire basin, sculpted not on top of the earth but inside it.

The capitol of Darakai, Faraji, was not a fortress.

It was a canyon.

"By Aniell," Marek breathed, his oceanic eyes squinting back the glare. Perspiration beaded his stubble as the captaen crooked his neck. "I did not know such places exited under Aurynth."

"Niit," she responded, slack jawed. "Neither did I."

Fleetingly, a smile pricked Declan's lips. "Böwen's never going to believe us."

Overtaking the streets, the amassed Darakaians chanted in unison, timed with the resounding kettledrummers. When the masses saw Kasim near the back of the procession, their intensity doubled, drowning the canyon in a single invocation.

"Hewe hai Darakai! Hewe hai Darakai!"

Some called out to their haidren by name, and others, who donned militia garb, shouted praises as their alpha zà rode by. Handcrafted garlands of flower and bone were thrown over he and his pryde. Slightly ahead of Declan, Kasim plucked a garland off his stallion's ear and looped it around his forearm, over his studded bracers.

His men chanted with the crowd as the road rounded the massive pool. Together, they pounded over their hearts. Past Marek, Kasim's beta picked an animated young boy off his father's shoulders and let him ride in the saddle with him through the impassioned throng, but the exuberant reception was short-lived, once the crowd saw who accompanied Kasim's homecoming.

Without warning, their smiles warped into snarls as Andwele cursing rippled around them. A riotous explosion ejected from Luscia's left, where the mob turned angry and shouted after the "y'siti." Others screamed at the sight of her lycran, a beast most probably only heard of from frightening fables of sorcery and the occult. Riled by their shrieks, Aksel barked and menacingly snapped his serrated teeth at the onlookers. Her ears bombarded by the outrage, Luscia didn't hear the stone coming before it whizzed past her face and struck another Darakaian beyond Noxolo.

Enraged, Darakaians pressed into the road, blocking their path.

At Kasim's roar, his entire pryde drew their kopars and thrusted the weapons in warning toward the cloudless sky, shocking his kinsmen on the road. Their haidren marched his stallion at the blockade and reared his horse in an aggressive demonstration. His mare's hooves landing, he pointed his blade at one man who had impeded their progression. A rock was cupped in his hand. Ordering him sternly in Andwele, Kasim sheathed his sickle sword and gestured for the man to step aside.

Surprise jolted through her gut. His pryde hadn't been shielding the Darakaians from the Boreali, but rather she and her guard from the Darakaians.

Kasim saw her understanding sink in when he reined his stallion around and yelled, "You can thank him later!" His head whipped in the direction of an unmissable stone podium down the way, where Dmitri's mare climbed the reddish steps, rising out of the masses. Trailing his ascent, Ira's buckskin horse followed. "Rhaolé, hurry—the chieftains wait for us." He whistled to those in the back. "Jabari, escort Maji'maia and the haidren to Pilar up the line."

After some commotion from the rear, the trim warrior came forward with Sayuri's brother in tow, who, from his shellshocked expression, wished to be anywhere else in the realm. A small journal clutched to the breast of his robes, Hachiro held onto the horn of his saddle as Jabari hitched the frightened haidren's reins to Luscia's mount and led them both to Kasim. Against her attempts, Aksel would not stay.

"We will be fine," Luscia said to her najjan as she left their huddled defense. Sensing their ire toward the teeming Darakaians, she instructed quietly, "Don't retaliate."

The people filled every chasm, brimming the dense vegetation at the foot of the monolithic steps to glimpse the three haidrens. For a second, Kasim stalled their climb. Noticing Luscia's stare, he abruptly cleared his throat.

"Let's go."

As Kasim's ascent, renewed ovations swelled throughout the open assembly. Luscia tailed him, for the first time hoping his shadow would fall upon her. If anything, it would be for Hachiro's benefit, who hunkered timidly with his journal as if expecting someone to chuck a rock at him next.

Reaching the top, high above the sea of Darakaians, one face came into view, elevated before all others.

Flanked by his chieftains, Nyack Kasim loomed over his people from an octagonal pedestal at the center. His pockmarked cheeks were exaggerated in the unforgiving sunset. His harsh, tar-black eyes smoldered as he watched them trail his son across the podium. Plumes of alabaster yak hair cascaded his swart shoulders, and from under their exaggerated volume, a plaited cape of the same plunged to the stone. Standing erect, he anchored his war-torn hands to each hip, widening his stance where his windswept gunja pants billowed. Leather bands cut across his bare torso, unveiling the timeless vigor of the middle-aged warlord.

And atop his head rested a wreath of moss and bone, eerily like a crown.

Luscia considered Kasim's forewarning the night prior. Here, his father was not the sil'haidren. He was not the commander of Dmitri's armies. On red soil, the chief warlord was a king. And today, Nyack Kasim proved it.

Placing their backs toward the crowd, the next generation of haidrenship formed a semi-circle about Dmitri, whose head was free of any royal ornament. Five formidable men, clad in distinctive Darakaian armor and dressed in scars, flanked Nyack Kasim, the commanding brigade capped by a ruggedly fearsome female on either end. The force of his court's assessment fastened on Luscia all at once, as the twelve chieftains imperiously scanned the Quadren up and down. To the right hand of each chieftain, a beta warlord glared from behind their shoulder, just as General Lateef did behind the pedestal. The appraisal was intent and unrelenting, except for one, Luscia spotted.

Across the stone, a beta warlord with long graying locs beamed at the haidren beside her.

Peering over, Luscia found the younger Kasim staring back at the older man, and though his countenance did not untense, he gave him a fleeting nod.

The chief warlord raised his hands, spreading them over the multitudes as the drumming ceased. "Faraji!" He boomed to their clamor. "Today Orynthia knocks at our door! Your regent has traveled far and wide to witness the unparalleled might of Darakai! My warriors, let him hear you roar!" Nyack Kasim's teeth gleamed when the pebbles on the podium shuddered at the crowd's noise. "May he taste our eternal kwihila, burning his tongue! May he feel our jwona rattling his bones! The Quadren of Dmitri Korbin Thoarne has crossed under Zwaàlu Ghopar, the Kindred Bridge cloaked by our ancestors... Tonight, we show the Ethnicam whose blood has quenched it! We"—his arms stretched as if summoning a storm—"are Darakai! *Hewe hai Darakai!*"

The chieftains and their betas beat their breasts as the entire canyon resumed the chant.

Kicking his horse, Dmitri broke from his line of haidrens and turned to address the droning masses. His image, humbly buttoned into an embossed coat of navy and bronze that draped his thighs, seemed lackluster compared to their chief warlord's battle regalia. Conscious of Dmitri's disfavor for theatrics, Luscia ground her teeth.

Now was not the time to project humility. Her king needed to project his eminence, lest he forfeit it to another.

"It is an honor to be with you, Darakai!" Dmitri shouted, though his weaker lungs did him no justice. "For centuries we have fought alongside each other. We have shared in both tragedy and in triumph! Your place in this kingdom is not forgotten. I, your king, exalt your bravery, your relentless sacrifice, to the highest esteem.

"Today, I celebrate Darakai's heroism, for you are each unmatched in fortitude and valor! You are each prized! And you will each be remembered for it!" His fervent expression panned the canyon as meaning pinched his brows. "Shamàli, if you see fit, may we learn from each other this season, so that one day *all* Orynthians may know the taste of your victory and the force of your fate, not just this day, but for every generation to come!"

Luscia witnessed the palpable wave through the Darakaians, as their initial skepticism in Orynthia's king, being slight in stature but bold in heart, evolved in a dignified rush. They hollered, applauding his unexpected remarks. The horns blew and the kettledrums resumed their festivity when Dmitri encouraged his mare around to the gathered chieftains and dismounted. Attending them, he personally greeted each tribal leader and their beta.

King Korbin must not have been talented in the way of speeches, because Darakai's chief warlord seemed rather surprised by the impact of his heir. Luscia caught the scorn convulsing in the crook of Nyack Kasim's nose, his presence occupying his pedestal like a Darakaian ornament.

After dropping out of her stirrup, Luscia offered her hand to Hachiro to help the frazzled shoto'shi to the ground. His robes, sailing atop the podium, blended into the canyon's backdrop as the sun drenched the rock in shades of orange and saffron.

"I've often read that Darakaians are a... passionate people," he mentioned when his sandals met the ground, to himself more than Luscia. "Such accounts are criminally understated."

"You have no idea."

Luscia guided him to where the other haidrens joined Dmitri's introductions. Aksel hugged her hip as she and Hachiro nestled into a void between a few brawny men, roughly her grandfather's age. None greeted them, instead turning from the foreign haidrens to discuss the evening arrangements with another.

Having lowered himself to reunite with his countrymen, Nyack Kasim paraded authoritatively through their clustering behind his pedestal, scattering their footing in his wake. Angling for Luscia's counterparts who socialized on the far end of the podium, he stopped short of Dmitri, entrenched in a genial conversation with one of the female chieftains.

"The matriarchs will escort you into Làtoh Ché," the chief warlord asserted.

Drowning out their discussion, he gestured toward the sloped path leading off the backside of the expansive podium. Between identical statues of shield-brandished warriors, a train of elderly women, toting baskets of garland, were congregated near the top.

"Ah, here it is." Hachiro shuffled through pages of a squattier book he'd also been carting. "*Làtoh Ché...* The City Nest." His aurulent eyes, the singular genetic likeness to his self-absorbed sister, scaled the metropolis built into the cliff face. "Aptly named."

Dmitri respectfully excused himself from his interrupted audience with the chieftain. Smiling, he called Ira to his side and strode toward the expectant matriarchs and the slew of tribal officials attending in tow, while a couple betas collected the horses. Nyack Kasim's lips fluttered, wording something to General Lateef when he and a gruffer chieftain strutted by. In Andwele, Luscia could not ascertain what it entailed, and she discreetly peered over into Hachiro's pocket lexicon.

The chief warlord finally departed after his true king, the plaited cape regally sweeping the Andwelestone. But with his leave, he said not a word to his son, who stood a few feet away.

In no way was he acknowledged in the least.

The younger Kasim, presumably expecting some form of welcome, lingered beside the graying beta warlord. But as the immense ashen robing dusted the toe of his boot, he fluidly moved out of his father's way and lowered his eager gaze, like he was enacting steps in a decades-old dance.

The older beta gently reached up and squeezed Kasim's shoulder as their regard mutually pursued his father—as did Luscia's, only for her to sight Wekesa leaning against one of the statues, arrogance hooking his leathery mouth to one side. The hideous damage on the shaved side of his skull caught the last bit of light as the chief warlord threw his arm around the lesser alpha, and together, they disappeared up the sloped path.

Kasim shirked off the beta's hand of comfort. Rubbing his nape, he trudged down the wide steps alone, in the opposite direction. Luscia nudged Hachiro, commencing their lengthy walk into the City Nest, her lycran sniffing every sculpture along the way. Unexpectedly, she felt her own father's crushing embrace, as if they were back in the royal stables saying good-bye, instead of a thousand miles apart.

What it must be like, she contemplated, to never know the arms of someone who couldn't let go.

CHAPTER FOURTEEN
LUSCIA

L uscia and her four najjan followed the matriarch up the steep, craggy steps, at least a dozen stories from the base of the canyon. It was a wonder how she managed the significant climb without a drop of sweat barreling down her thoroughly age-ripened features. Nevertheless, the woman's knobby legs propelled her higher and higher.

It could have been sheer impatience fueling her rigor, Luscia supposed. The matriarch had grown quite perturbed, having been made to wait on the entire Boreali ensemble to convene.

At last, the elderly woman plateaued their hike. She led them along a slim promenade, enclosed by lit torches and dense curling vine. Luscia didn't peer over the steep, rocky ledge to see how high they'd risen, intuiting it was better not to know.

Stepping up to a larger platform, like the stoops down the row, the matriarch gradually squatted and grabbed hold of a bronze ring bolted to an octagonal wooden hatch. Like her wrinkled arms, it was covered in ornamental etchings. With a puff, her beaded neckpiece chattered when she heaved it open and gestured into the cavity at her gnarled sandaled toes.

"Byumbé," she said, ushering them underfoot into the hole.

"Wem." Noxolo scratched his hooked, ivory nose. "*Go into the dark pit*, she said… *It will be fine*, she said…"

Marek thrusted Luscia's locked apothecary against Noxolo's pelvis, unloaded his extra gear, and stepped in front of his haidren.

"Heh'ta. Let me go first." He tucked a few garnet strands behind his ear, and his fingertips scraped the hilt of his kuerre as he descended the steps into nothingness. After a few minutes, they heard him abruptly blow out, "Shores of Aurynth…"

Interpreting his go-ahead, Luscia snatched the Viridi chest from Noxolo's arms and snapped after Aksel to pad alongside her into the mysterious opening. With each step, her eyes adjusted to the cozy glow of the upcoming bend—as did her skin, for the air above had forfeited its abrasive heat to the nightfall. Rather than the humid assault of Darakai's notorious climate, dryness wicked her dampened flesh, offering a blessed reprieve.

When she turned at the bottom of the tight stairwell, her upturned boots met cool, packed earth. The walls widened and she entered a large room, its frame more octangular than round, matching the hatch. Reinforced by timber beaming, the walls and ceiling were daubed with red dirt, along with other deposits, creating a marbled splash throughout the dwelling.

Marek knelt, examining an unusually shaped hearth at the center, pinched toward the ceiling and bulbous at the base where a meager fire crackled. Slit windows horizontally lined the underside of the rafters, adding additional ventilation as well as a refreshing breeze. Where the backwall cut into the cliffside, a recessed bench lined the inground residence, buried under a heap of elaborate textiles. Luscia strolled through the interior, which was stocked in abundance with bushels of fruit, carafes of wine, and jugs of oil. Three rune-inscribed archways led into separate bedrooms, each lavishly groomed with plush bedding and extravagant rugs.

"Byumbé," the matriarch repeated, touching the ruddy stone that encircled her and the rest of Luscia's guard piling in from above. Lugging her basket, she drew out a garland of white blossoms and bone shale, and she shakily lifted it over Luscia's head. Breaking into a toothless chuckle, she patted Luscia's arm with the same gentleness she had the wall and bobbed her head of receding coils. "Shàla'maiamo."

They watched her hobble up the steps, retreating to the heights. When the hatch shut, Luscia reached for a prepared pitcher of water and located a bowl, pouring it out for her restless lycran.

"Double-bunk in those two rooms. I'll take the third. Search for any insecurities," she directed and hurried to dress, as she was due to join the Quadren for the chief warlord's feasting. "Declan," Luscia beckoned, calling him aside while the others inspected the perimeter. "I'm appointing you to first watch, starting tonight. There are things I must see to, things that don't require your approval, just your discretion. Can you make peace with that?"

Confusion quivered Declan's freckly forehead but momentarily. The eldest najjan folded his burly forearms and shrugged. "Wem, Ana'Sere. Where you must go, I go. Se'lah Aurynth."

"Waedfrel." Luscia inconspicuously handed him a scrap of parchment. "Find me after the feast. Bring these items. I'll inform Captaen Bailefore of the new rotation."

With the matter of her guardian settled, she riffled through her belongings resting near the hearth until she found an airy gown, appropriate for the evening's festivity. Luscia wished she'd known about Faraji's lower ladder system when selecting her limited wardrobe for Dmitri's tour, as fragilities now seemed absurd. Favoring lacework for the suffocating temperatures, Luscia fished out a copper-and-cream filigree dress, the sleeving and collar fitted but breathable, and made toward her chamber to re-dress.

She crossed Creyvan, where he crouched on the built-in bench, peering out a window at the twinkling canyon fortress.

Luscia halted halfway across the room when Creyvan cynically griped, "Why would He give them so much? How can the High One show favor to these barbarians?"

"Has Aniell not favored us, doubly so?" Luscia countered, yet again unsettled by the contemptuous bite in his latest sentiments. Worsening the unease was Kasim's word about her "flaxen shadowman" and the prospect that it might be true.

Her thoughts spiraled back to his piddling excursion in Rian, when Creyvan was meant to be on watch. For a man who so openly criticized the other Houses, he sure coveted their offerings. Such duplicity had no place among the najjani order, nor Luscia's elite.

Raising the garland around her neck by a single bloom, she answered, "The Darakaians permitted us into their home, something even our Houseless hosts in Rian could not reconcile. Boreal should be grateful, my brödre, for their effort of diplomacy."

Noxolo ducked out from under a doorframe, too tall for his snug bedroom. "They did try to stone you, Ana'Sere…"

"Our effort should lead theirs," Luscia replied, voicing Dmitri's request for harmony over division.

She could not blame another House if her own men were part of the problem, but even so, she prayed her quick thanks to Aniell that the distempered Darakaian's aim had faltered that day. Luscia would have healed from the stoning, but what a cumbersome phenomenon that'd have been to explain. Faraji's citizens already suspected her of sorcery.

Aksel's surprising growl resonated from the third chamber, from which Marek marched. The veins running up his throat protruded as his fist clamped around a lump of fabric. Without notice, the captaen reached for her fingers and thrust the rough-hewn object into her palm.

"Found that under your bedding." Furiously, he lashed out at it. "You might have spoken too soon about your Southern diplomats."

Luscia turned the bundle over. In her palm lay a figurine, a tuft of snowy animal hair sewn to the head. Her lips crushed and her nails bit into her palms, peering down. In its face of blanched burlap, two pale eyes were stitched.

And through the left, an arrowhead was stabbed.

Hot fragrant steam rallied her lungs, floating off the most colorful plate she'd ever beheld.

Luscia briefly pardoned whoever had sewn the hex doll, just to impale and wedge it beneath her bed, for similar hands had produced this meal. As the zesty unfamiliar spices mingled, her stomach, neglected from travel, grumbled eagerly, even for the grassy glob heaped on the edge of her dish. With great anticipation, she tasted it. Her mouth twisted sourly. With expert slight-of-hand, Luscia gifted the stodgy mash to Aksel under the huge table.

She wasn't all that ready to forgive the matter of the doll anyways.

"I saw that." Dmitri winked, a deep-seated dimple stressing his amusement. Acting the lookout, he too scraped some off his plate and passed it to the hungry hybrid, exhibiting his courtly finesse while the young king observed the entertainers performing their daring acts.

Encircled by basins of fire, the archers' routine was staged upon a vast terrace overlooking the canyon. A quartet moved into a compass formation, their backs toward each other. Four more launched knives at each bowman, in tempo with the accompanying percussionists. In tandem, they release their arrows and impeded the oncoming blades. When partnering knife-throwers emerged, the archers doubled their defense, freeing two arrows at a time. The drumming paused but picked back up when both groups rotated in rings, the archers in one direction, the blade-throwers another. Luscia joined Dmitri when he stood to his feet, applauding, genuinely impressed with their skill. She confessed the bow was not her personal strong suit, though it was undoubtedly one of Darakai's.

"How did you find your byumbé?" Clapping, he leaned over to ask, sensitive after her camping outside Rian. "Were the lodgings satisfactory? I made my wishes clear and known."

Luscia bent to sit, and Dmitri promptly slipped behind her chair, pushing it in. He returned to his own and shifted toward her earnestly. His lips rolled inward as he raptly awaited confirmation.

She dipped her head courteously, deciding not to mention the fiendish figurine. "Everything was very inviting." Luscia admitted truthfully, "There is even enough room to comfortably accommodate my men."

Pleased, Dmitri reclined, his hands spread on his thighs. He'd fore-gone a formal coat, instead adorned by a jade vest of silk, immaculately embellished in gilt frond. The stitched palms flashed when Dmitri reached for a hunk of mealy flatbread.

Ripping it in half, he inquired, "How are they acclimating, Captaen Bailefore and the others?"

Her response was judicious, for both Marek and Noxolo were stationed a stone's throw behind her king's table. "The Captaen is... focused, as always. The rest count the days until we are reunited with Böwen, Creyvan's twin, in Roüwen. I suspect they feel a bit homesick."

"As do you, I'd imagine." A dark-walnut wave fell forward when Dmitri gave a slight smile. "What a gift to watch your parent live on through your sibling."

Her heart tugged as Phalen came to mind, along with his sooty cheeks, skipping to show her his newest contraption. Their mother, Eoine, always shone in the way he'd light up at the wonder of his inventions. Empathetically, Luscia touched Dmitri's forearm. She was the only member of the Quadren he'd entrusted with the reality, not only of his deteriorating condition but the unborn brothers and sisters he'd lost along the way.

"They'll adjust." Ira's half-eaten drumstick lumbered over her shoulder when the yancy wrapped around, piping up from Luscia's left. "Never met most of my siblings—as they weren't allowed in the house—and I turned out just fine."

"Weren't allowed..." Hachiro plopped his journal onto the table, and the shoto'shi tilted past Kasim, squinting down the table. "Why ever not?"

"Well, Hachi..." Ira boosted the drumstick. "Would your mother approve such a thing?"

Dmitri pushed his plate off, sincerely intrigued. "Just how many siblings do you have?"

"My father is a great man, Your Majesty, and great men make a great impact wherever they go." Ira smirked proudly, praising Gregor's exhibitions.

"Depths." Kasim's chair screeched when he abruptly rose. "Excuse me."

He didn't go far, Luscia saw, just far enough to not have to listen to Ira babble on about his father's prowess. However, Kasim had been disagreeable all evening, even before Ira had opened his mouth.

Her eye tracked him easily through the crowd, standing out in his relaxed white gunja pants, more formal than those she'd seen on other Darakaian officials. A snug sleeveless buckskin tunic partnered the relaxed pants, displaying his well-toned arms. His terra-cotta skin had darkened in the past weeks, adopting a kiss of dusk, as he'd steadily worn more liberating garb like the other Southerners, representing himself as the highest ranking Darakaian alpha, rather than their stately advisor. Luscia wondered if that distinction was intentional now that they were in Faraji.

Finding his beta among the gathering, Kasim inclined by his side, cross-armed against a boulder. Studying his forced nonchalance, she noticed his sharp chartreuse stare never left the vicinity where Wekesa dined, near the chief warlord and his tribal leaders.

She understood then; Kasim wouldn't dare adorn a stitch of yancy clothing here, not when he could lose his earned agency to a home-grown usurper.

General Lateef surfaced as the archers cleared the center of the terrace.

"And now, the prydes bring the Quadren an orchestrated gaibai of our conquest and cunning. For it was a *Darakaian* who turned the tide of the Mworran Wars..."

Rallying cries went up among the hundreds invited to feast.

"A *Darakaian* who braved enemy lines... and a Darakaian, uni," Lateef clamored, his baritone resonating throughout the City Nest, "who slayed Mworra's most feared and ruthless general, the *Bone Eater!*"

Cheers erupted as men and women, dressed in ornate furs and skins, convened in front of the king's table.

"Oh, a story-dance!" Dmitri eagerly tucked his palms between his knees, perked at the premise. "They don't perform their gaibai outside Darakaian borders."

Before him, the pryde dancers swayed, separating into two groups when a daunting rhythm ricocheted off the Andwelestone and enveloped the revelry. Those bearing furs, beads, and bangles of copper spread out, pounding their chests and those of their neighbors as they stomped with the beat. Reeds and shards of bone wreathed the others, acting the Mworran incursion. In an enchanting pulsation, their fists pummeled the ground in time with their intimidating shrieks, somersaulting through the air in attack toward the fur-clad dancers.

Gourds shook and bells rattled, attending the battle anthem. Luscia traced a disturbance in the shadow, where the younger Kasim sauntered outside his dauntingly graceful warriors. Between their movements, one of them handed off a heavy pelt, and a swarm of dancers blocked him from view. Suddenly, at the blow of a horn, Kasim exploded through their arrangement.

He landed in a crouch, drumming the stone at his feet. When he released a heralding cry, the audience shouted passionately, imitating him. Lengthy bands of mottled yak hair draped his arms, and crowning his head was the headdress of a slaughtered panther. In slow, unwinding undulations, his hips rocked with the music, their circulation both heady and daunting. The ebony muzzle shaded the ferocity in his eyes, and the bulky pelt lapped his ankles with each lively stride.

Luscia swallowed though she'd not eaten, suddenly unseduced by her plate.

Kasim led the players in ripples of elegant, defensive kicks. Lunging into the open, he heaved his torso back and forth at their opponents. Luscia detected joy leaking through his combatant façade. There was nothing fraudulent in the grin he suppressed under his scowling, as if each step offered him a release, but of what she didn't know.

The corded muscle along his thick biceps threatened the constraints decorating him. The Mworran pretenders screamed in mock assault, emitting a carnal aggression as their tongues flailed diabolically. Kasim reeled back to his party of dancers, clutching the panther's skull in an undulated frenzy. As the Darakaians oscillated around him, they mirrored the movements of his arms, thrusting one after the other. Another horn blew, and all at once, they spun and flattened to the stone, forming an expectant human trench.

A dancer near the chief warlord's table leaped out with a mallet and struck one of the massive wooden statues nearby. The narrow slice down the front of the warrior's shield brought it to life, turning the carving into a slit gong that echoed for miles. The Mworrans broke apart, and a new dancer, clattering under heavy tiers of bone, turned around.

Wekesa.

Luscia's attention whirled to Kasim, who, low to the ground, grated his chin across the rock acrimoniously. With a spark to his bright-green eyes, he whooped, loud and brash. Kasim's entire troupe rotated onto their backs and, in a synchronized surge, threw their arms wide and backflipped off the ground. Coming down on one heel, they twisted into a hunkered circle. From the middle, Kasim's hands speared upright and splintered apart, pointing at the malevolent Mworrans.

The dancers encasing Wekesa swiveled in place. A wall of reeds abutted the lesser alpha, positioning his character in fabricated isolation. Wekesa dipped and bowed to the thrumming music, his braids stirring to the polyrhythmic clash. A pair of warriors whirled away from Kasim's group, Luscia's still healing patient, Takoda, one of them.

Rattles and shakers hastened as the duo slid into Wekesa's ring, slinking their steps dramatically. Another gong struck, and the music quelled. In unison, Kasim's group started to hum in a throaty, menacing tone. Takoda knelt at the hem of Wekesa's bone shawl, smacking the stone, but the alpha exposed a wooden blade. When he lifted it above himself, the second dancer jumped out from behind and mock-slid his own knife across Wekesa's throat.

Ovations boomed across the terrace when Wekesa theatrically collapsed, the instrumentation gaining for a victory encore. Again, Luscia met Dmitri on his feet. Yet when they rose from their chairs, Sayuri's brother did not.

"Hachiro." Dmitri glanced aside to the robed shoto'shi, who scrawled away. "Is something the matter?"

"The inaccuracies of this retelling are contemptible." His inky lashes fluttered as he rewet his quill. "The Bone Eater was assassinated by a pair of breakaways, deserters during the Mworran Wars who enlisted as agents for Razôuel. The House of Darakai has rewritten Zôueli history for its own glorification."

Forcing a smile, Dmitri spirited his clapping, masking anxiety over Hachiro's blunt disapproval and whoever might have observed it too. "The Scourge Age was an exceptionally long time ago. One can never entirely trust the record of our historians."

"I'm compelled to disagree, Your Majesty, that we most certainly can, because one of those breakaways…" Hachiro clasped his journal and wrapped the leather cord matter-of-factly "Was Pilarese."

Uneasy herself, Luscia guided Dmitri into his seat when with a shudder, he gripped the table's edge. Gratefully, the Darakaians were too distracted by, as Hachiro put it, "their own glorification" to note his momentary shake. While it could have been nerves, for the shoto'shi's abrasive comment could certainly upset the Quadren's cause, Luscia decided she ought to drop another batch of elixirs at Dmitri's byumbé before reconvening at midnight with Kasim.

The dancers dispelled, forcing Darakai's haidren to return to his place at Dmitri's right. Perspiration glistened Kasim's forehead as he plopped down and mopped his face, out of breath.

Without warning, great cattle horns were blown, signaling all eyes to their chief warlord. His extravagant cape drew like a shade as he strolled to the heart of the terrace, crossing one fist over the other.

"My people, my warriors." Nyack Kasim's warworn voice grated the air. "Tonight, I present the king of Orynthia with a gift… a coronation offering from Darakai to the throne."

There was a thrill within his boding countenance, a dark, dangerous excitement she sensed had little to do with Dmitri. An ominous pain pricked Luscia's temple.

And then she heard the screams.

Ira slunk lower into his chair, cradling his cylindrical snuff canister. "Why do Darakaians always have to ruin a nice party?"

General Lateef burst forth from the adjacent table of guests, hauling a near-naked prisoner by a set of canes. Abrasive chains, tethered to the canes, had already butchered his dusky abdomen and throat. His head was shaved, but it looked to have been done recently and without mercy, for bits of flesh were missing from his scalp. A reed bit had been jammed into his mouth and half his rounded Western features had swollen, one bloated eyelid melding into his cheek.

Nyack Kasim tilted his pocked face, speaking over the prisoner when he pushed him to kneel before the king.

"Scouts from Faraji have apprehended Tane Abwé, the notorious cross-caste smuggler whose black-market trade plagues the Andweles." The chief warlord switched to the prisoner's other side, hunching lower. His starless study assessed the gashes that tore the man's mixed ancestry apart. "A cross-caste who trafficked every pammu export out of Calluc, all the way to a night den in Bastiion…" He seized the chain and yanked the beaten smuggler by the neck. "Tonight, I give our king and Quadren the man who aided the infamous murderess, Salma Nabhu."

Next to Luscia, Dmitri went ashen, and without thought, she grasped his limp hand under the table. The other pulled Aksel against her leg, suddenly chill inside her lacy gown. The collection of chieftains and their betas took their cups and clanged them in unison.

Three archers lined behind their chief warlord as he prowled the perimeter toward General Lateef.

"Ours is a gift of restitution, uni… restitution for the assassination of King Korbin Aquila Thoarne," Nyack Kasim proclaimed.

The bowmen notched their arrows, taking aim. Hearing the strings stretch, the smuggler howled, his sob muffled by the reed bit.

"Treason is a betrayal of the heart."

The first arrow flew, tearing him through the chest.

"Of the body."

Another bow released and blood spurted through his abdomen.

"But most of all…" Darakai's leader tapped his forehead. "Of the mind."

Luscia sucked a breath when the third arrow soared between the smuggler's eyes and sprayed the thirsty Andwelestone. Hundreds of onlookers rejoiced when his corpse buckled forward. Without word, she felt Dmitri's fingers come alive, tightening hers.

This was Darakai.

This was the House of War.

CHAPTER FIFTEEN
ZAETHAN

"With me" was all Zaethan murmured to his third, briskly passing her under an archway as he turned from the gore across the terrace. Vivid fruit flowers and creeping vine spilled merrily over the runes etched into the Andwelestone, presenting a gateway to paradise rather than an execution.

Without comment, Zahra paced him through a cliffside colonnade of moss-laden buttresses. He needed to get out of earshot and the entirety of Làtoh Ché had awakened, rallying behind his father's demonstration. Because that was what it was, a demonstration of his sprawling reach, his judicial brutality, and his unquestioned authority to exercise it. The smuggler's massacre had rattled Dmitri. Zaethan could see it plainly in his friend's manner when he'd mutely risen from the table. A tremble had carried even through his walking cane. And if Zaethan had seen it in his friend, Faraji had seen it in their king.

His father had not apprehended Abwé as a gift.

Nyack Kasim did not give gifts. He only gifted violence—and provocation.

Tonight, Darakai's chief warlord had provoked skepticism among his council of chieftains. If it fell to their scouts to track down the associate of Salma Nabhu, tribal leadership would deduce that their Orynthian king had not been the one to pursue justice.

After all, a person sought vengeance on their own behalf with more ferocity than for that of another.

The tribes equated justice with equal retribution. And if it were their chief warlord who smiled in the moment of that retribution, not their king, the chieftains would conclude their contractual regent did not carry a stomach for true justice. That his Unitarian blood was too weak to beat for theirs.

Impassioned, Zaethan ripped the ceremonial livery off his forearms, chucking the yak wrappings into the open between the buttresses. He believed in true justice, but only after a *true* trial. It was an after-thought he knew haunted Dmitri to this day, for in his first act as king, he'd refused that very precursor from the woman convicted for King Korbin's assassination. The conviction had been championed by Zaethan's father—the same man who'd just ordered three arrows into her alleged accomplice.

That made two trials averted in connection to the same crime, but the tribes viewed it differently. And it would not be their haidren's voice they listened to in contest. The chief warlord had effectively seen to that, through his constant undermining of the Darakaian seat on the royal Quadren, asserting it nearly worthless under his son's occupancy.

Even Zaethan's uncle, the beta warlord from Holona, had witnessed his brother-in-law's total dismissal on the podium that day.

Zaethan hadn't been able to meet Yousif's sympathetic eye since.

His jaw clenched as he ducked under a fall of pod blossoms, trusting Zahra to follow. Should he lose alpha zà to Wekesa's challenge, the chieftains would surely vote to replace him as haidren too. His mother's legacy could only sustain their support for his succession for so long. The rest was up to him.

Zaethan couldn't bear being stripped his haidrenship. Nor could Dmitri.

He steered Zahra into a recess within the centuries-old construction rounding the precipice of the canyon. The red dust was free of footprints, making him confident they would not be interrupted anytime soon. Inside, the dangling foliage blocked Àla'maia's shine. Zaethan pivoted on his heel and prodded Zahra backward, until she stiffly thudded against the rockface. Though her body was unnaturally still, her velvet throat bobbed when she swallowed.

"I'm only going to ask once." Zaethan's arms pleated across his chest as he interrogated his third. "When Wekesa pulled you in last night, outside Faraji, did he tell you they arrested the pammu smuggler?"

The whites of her hooded eyes flashed, broadened by surprise. "Ano zà, Alpha Zà. I'd no idea they even hunted Abwé until… that happened to him."

"You've always come to me, yeah? Right away, with everything. But all day, ano. You've been tight-lipped and standoffish." His head cocked distrustfully at Zahra. "So, what did Wekesa say that rendered you so quiet ever since?"

Zahra's tongue tucked her teeth as she glimpsed aside. "He relayed there was a defection from our pryde. And that the defector opted to take up with his outfit instead, abandoning our brothers and sisters in Hagarh."

His arms uncrossed. Throwing them up, Zaethan hooked his hands behind his locs, and growled, "Who is the coward?"

She stooped.

"Nigan Hanovi. My cousin." Her downcast face shook before her chicory irises glanced up. "Shamàli, Alpha Zà. If you see fit, grant him clemency... Nigan told Wekesa the pryde is being picked off at the border—by the mudmen or something else. They disappear, they turn up dead. None live once they vanish." Zahra eased off the wall and ran her palm over her scalp. "But worse, General Lateef nor the chief warlord will report it. Meme ano'qondai. For some cause, your father's circle is keeping this information from us as well as the tribes."

"Shtàka!" Zaethan snarled and smacked the stone. "Of course Nigan wants to defect to Wekesa! My warriors are siphoned from me, get dumped in the wetlands, and are led to think I don't care for their security!" He let out a bitter laugh, rolling out his shoulders. "Depths, it's brilliant on my father's part. I can't deploy pryde reinforcement, and I'm not authorized to pull them out. He's strapped me to a piss pot, forcing me to watch *my* warriors run straight into the arms of my rival. That's why Wekesa confronted you." Zaethan knocked his head against the Andwelestone, opposite his svelte, capable third. Resting his eyelids, he grunted wryly, "Where one Hanovi goes, the other might follow."

He heard her boot scuff the dusty rock as she came closer. Opening his weary lids, Zaethan found Zahra inches away. A fist hoisted on her narrow hip, she reached out. Her grip tightened above his elbow.

"Where else would I go, Alpha Zà, but to your side?"

"Words are easier said than shown. Before we depart Darakai, you might be pushed to prove them."

Zahra's nose scrunched. "Then I can't wait to see the look on your ugly mug when I do," she said with a wink.

Zaethan grabbed the back of her slick skull and brought her forehead against his. Holding her there, he nodded, then let her go.

When he slid toward the lip of the recess, she teased him. "Eh, I hope it is your bed you seek, not Kumo and Jabari's late-night wagers. Ano zà, I won't spot them any more coin."

Knotting the belt of his traditional buckskin tunic, Zaethan looked back at Zahra. "I promised you in Bastiion that I'd be ready. Wekesa may have the benefit of a Darakaian weapons master." He brushed a couple pod blossoms aside, checking Àla'maia's posture in the night sky. "But what I have… he'll never see coming."

He'd forgotten how deafening the insects were this time of year, endlessly whirring and chirping.

A swarm of spark-fliers dotted the dense timberline where they glided, imitating the stars above. Zaethan used to catch them when he was a cub, up on these bluffs overlooking the canyon.

Faraji's splendor alighted from where it nestled below, its dangers seemingly far away. There was a time, during his youth, he'd come up here alone to watch the falls and cascades across the formation plummet to the depths. Even after being dispatched into Dmitri's service in

Bastiion, his life evolving into a dualistic struggle of House and home, he still considered this bluff the most tranquil place on earth.

The rush of water, married with the high-pitched trill of winged natives, nearly drowned out the Boreali advance. Only the jangle of incoming equipment foretold her arrival. The shadowmen might be able to traverse with unnatural hush, but wood and metal could not.

Zaethan rolled off the boulder he'd been sitting upon. Turning, he was surprised to see she'd not come on her own. Through the brush, the witch emerged not only with the highlander wolx but the bearded, barrel-chested shadowman. Shorter than the rest of her men, he was certainly the thickest—and possibly the meanest, given the hostility that dragged his entire expression toward the dirt as he carted her sack of supplies.

Ahead of them, the wolx trotted cheerfully, as if he and his mistress were taking a common stroll instead of having snuck off to train with a member of an opposing House.

The overgrown beast circled Zaethan, sniffing, before stalking back to the witch possessively. When she and the shadowman reached where grass ceded to the rocky overhang, she laced her arms, buttoned into a stiff black jerkin over men's breeches. No wonder she avoided close range… She'd hardly be able to move inside it. Zaethan would have to outfit her too, it seemed. Her attire would not do.

Catching him appraising her form, her shadowman snarled and unceremoniously dropped the sack. The man, flecked in fresh sunspots, threateningly wedged in front of his haidren. But when he smacked his own neck, his aggression redirected to a cloister of bugs.

"Only irritates them more," Zaethan advised frankly, having endured the onery blight his entire life.

"Tadöm, Declan." She sidestepped her kinsman, seizing the hauled equipment. "You may stand guard at the top of the trail, like we discussed. I will return in a few hours."

His square face whirled toward the tree line and back toward his impassive haidren. Buried under coarse brassy whiskers, his flattened lips stirred, though there came no sound. A brisk, silent debate broke out between them in witchtongue. She allowed her men to question her command more than Zaethan ever would his pryde—at least in public.

Kumo would be nursing a bruise by this point, were it his man instead of hers.

"As we discussed, brödre," she reiterated sharply, reverting to her normal, husky tone.

The shadowman balled his fists but lowered his head respectfully, backing away without taking his sleety eye off Zaethan. A few yards off, he eventually turned and marched into the horde of spark-fliers.

When his form vanished among the floating illuminations of the entangled timberline, the witch pivoted and intertwined her fingers. "How would you like to begin?"

Zaethan peered at the materials she'd brought, eager to begin where they'd left off in Bastiion. Wekesa grew bolder by the day. He hadn't been wasting any time preparing his challenge for alpha zà. Zaethan would have to train twice as hard to catch up with his rival's stride, and her sack housed the path to do so.

His gaze traveled back to the witch, standing arrogant as ever, and he decided they ought to begin with his side of the bargain. A show of good faith might secure their deal, which at present, he needed more than she did.

Besides, the witch's objective would take a lot more work than his.

He untied his tunic and pulled it off over his head, getting the stifling fabric out of the way. Hand combat centered around the body and little else. Already barefooted, he wore nothing but his Darakaian gunjas, swathed taut at the waist and strapped ankle to calf. She would need a sparring pair herself, to permit her legs a fuller range of motion. Perhaps Dhalili could donate, though charity was never her forte.

He reached behind the boulder and produced a rope made entirely from sleek Andwele mane. Winding over his shoulder, he walked back toward her. Zaethan sank a hand into his pocket, the other holding the lead in place.

"We'll start with close range training, the first hour dedicated to you…" Unraveling the lead rope, he stretched out his neck. "The second for me. Now, remove that oppressive footwear and whatever else you're willing to shed."

The witch's glare tapered, but she crouched and slid off her upturned boots. With measured care, she neatly placed them aside. She trailed her fingers along her body and popped short blades out from under her belting, unsheathed the curved dagger strapped to her thigh, slipped the gauntlets off her hands, and stuffed them all into her boots. Rising, she paused and stooped again to add a tiny knife, which had been buried in the crown of her pale braid of ash and fawn, to the collection.

"Eh, eh, doru—those too." He flapped the lead rope toward her bone rings.

With a huff, she rolled her spectral eyes, adding the lethal trinkets to the pile. Zaethan sighed when they jangled against the rest of her compact armory. He'd been at the other end of those triggered blades enough times to know she'd always rely on their defense. And without a set of his own, he was sick of the disadvantage.

She eyed Zaethan and the lead rope when he stepped closer with it.

"I don't see your stallion in the vicinity." She mock-scanned the area, squaring her posture. "So I'm not sure what you think you'll be doing with that."

With a smirk, Zaethan flung the rope around her back and caught the tail in his opposite hand. "I think I'll be making a point."

Once they were a couple feet apart, he gradually ran it over the witch, tugging the tails side to side, down her biceps. Zaethan gave the rope a shake, slapping it against her tense form. Under her caustic observation, he descended it lower.

"You're wasting both our time." She tossed her arms, letting them hang as she sneered, "I am not one of your horses, Kasim."

The rope glided along her right wrist, causing her to flinch. Promptly, she regained composure. Her dense brow curved dismissively. Swiping toward her thighs, the lead rope grazed her hip. Immediately she stepped back, putting tension on the cord. Something happened there, Zaethan catalogued with the issue at her wrist. The witch's rigidity intensified when the rope skidded even lower, along the backs of her legs and to the ground.

"Ano. You're not a horse, Maji'maia." Zaethan withdrew the lead, angling his head. "But you're scared like one."

The witch scoffed, as if the notion were ludicrous. "I'm not afraid of you."

"I've broken many Andweles, yeah?" he said. Closing their gap again, he crept nearer.

Instantly, she retreated, maintaining distance.

"Not one of those horses were ever afraid of me." Zaethan relaxed his posture and inched closer. "Just what I represented. Arms out."

He patiently waited for her to comply.

Reluctantly, she elevated her arms. Zaethan looped the lead around her abdomen, prudent to not graze her with his fingertips. It'd only spook her. Secured, he gave it a short tug, testing the knot. She fought the subtle momentum, arching her spine, and heatedly gaped up at him. Casually, he inclined, returning her stare. The skin around her Boreali eyes, nearly colorless in the moonlight, puckered with offense at the tactic. Zaethan hardly minded. Signs of offense were useful.

They meant his assumptions were right.

"Dominance is asserted when breaking a horse." She glowered at him, a luminescent spark sputtering through her right iris. "Is this your attempt to dominate me?"

Disturbed, Zaethan looked away from the living opalescence and snorted. "Hardly."

He held the end of the lead rope in his teeth while he tightened the leather binding his locs out of the way. Her face dropped a fraction, investigating his chest and the four rough ridges scarring the front of his bare torso. Catching her attention, the witch rubbed her wrist awkwardly and squinted into the distance.

"Then what is this, Kasim? What are we doing?"

Zaethan swung the free end of the rope around himself, tethering them together with a simple slipknot. "We're walking," he said and backed away, granting the lead over a yard of slack.

At first, the witch refused to budge—as expected. She threw her weight into one hip, anchoring her heel on the rock with the stubbornness of a bull.

Smirking, Zaethan edged forward, wound the slack around his forearm, and wheeled, lurching her flat on her face. Pure hatred distorted her angular, ashen features as she slammed her palms to the earth and pushed herself upright.

Treat a horse like it's been abused—coddling and fussing over it—the longer it takes to move beyond its fear.

Treat a woman like a horse... Well, Zaethan was playing that one by ear.

Back on her feet, she stretched out her ankle. With his consequences communicated, Zaethan exposed his hands, far from the lead, and walked backward, towing her by the makeshift harness. Her resistance constricted the roping, her refusal digging into his spine. His jaw clenched when he tried to conceal his discomfort, but from the haughty swagger in her dawdling gate, he knew the witch saw right through it.

At random, Zaethan switched and paced in her direction. She sputtered into withdrawal. He blew out a sigh. This was going to take a while.

Over the next half hour, he walked her in circles over the bluff, alternating his approach and retreat to her evident chagrin. With pretend disinterest, Zaethan kept his sights anywhere but ahead, on the witch. Her stress on the lead had relaxed, but not nearly enough. She'd been fighting him at every turn, not seeing the irony in the harness.

He too was fastened to her, an arrangement she could exploit at any time. It wasn't Zaethan's harness that made her operate like a captive. She was doing it to herself.

In his periphery, the witch ambled on, her arms weaved snugly together. Out of nowhere, she asserted bluntly, "There's a story down your chest."

"You mean like the one down your throat?" His scrutiny returned to her, his eyes focusing on the jagged line engraving her cadaverous flesh where it disappeared under her collar. "It was a bit of kakk when

Kumo and I were cubs. How's one more deal? I tell my story when you tell yours, Maji'maia."

She reached for her short collar and promptly drew it higher. "We found a hospitable little hex doll under my mattress today. Wouldn't happen to know anything about that, would you?"

Zaethan shifted to an advance. She fumbled backward.

"Ano. Likely just some cubs welcoming the Boreali to Faraji. Kàchà-kocho," Zaethan answered, transitioning into another retreat, tugging her along.

She tossed her hands. "And what child could I have provoked to make it?"

"Meme ano'qondai. How should I know?" Zaethan shrugged. "All of them, probably."

Her mouth dropped open, then closed resentfully as she struggled against his backward progression.

He truly hadn't known about the doll, but it hardly alarmed him. All Darakaian children heard terror-filled fables of the Boreali occultists, frightful tales spoken late at night when they lay their heads to sleep. What other explanation could parents give cubs for a Northerner's ability to meld with the shadow, except that they were born of its myth? Or how Boreali skins lose their spirit during mystic rites, for their coloring had been bled out?

Come to think of it, Zaethan was mildly shocked a single doll was all she had found in that byumbé.

The witch dallied willfully. Zaethan tugged the lead, clicking his tongue, which earned him a sour scowl. The kind that scrunched her dainty nose and rounded her severe cheekbones like a rabid woodland squirrel's. When her face smoothed out, he did it again, hoping to see it twice.

"That theory is totally absurd," Boreal's haidren said dismissively, shaking her head askance. Angrily, she flicked the rope binding them together. "As is this entire exercise. I agreed to a trade, expecting it to be of equal value and intentionality. If you intend to taunt me with bizarre games—"

Zaethan halted, pocketing his palms, and watched her march along, entirely consumed with her own monologue. Her sight was set on the horizon instead of her partner. She'd not noticed the slack in the lead, or that he was even standing still. Zaethan steadied himself, for a few minutes later, she collided straight into his middle. Bewildered, she braced against his biceps.

Clutching him in place.

He sucked his teeth, eyeing their lack of space. The witch scanned him up and down, astonishment wrenching her brow as she registered their sudden closeness.

And that it was *she* who had caused it.

"Absurd, you said?" Zaethan's mouth curved. When he lowered his jaw, it grazed the top of her forehead. "You can let go now, Maji'maia."

In a rush, her hands flew off his skin. She unknotted the lead and ripped it off her hips. It was difficult to see, but he almost spotted a flush climb her throat when she hurtled back.

He'd be embarrassed too, if he had been schooled like a mulish mare.

The witch stomped over to her wolx, pretending to check on him. Zaethan licked his lips, thoroughly entertained by her effort to recollect her wits. Because considering how loudly the war-tainted mongrel snored, her wolx was just fine.

Stroking the russet fur between his twitching ears, she called, "I think we've done quite enough walking for one night."

She squatted beside her sack and retrieved a recognizable set of curved sparring rods. Brashly, she chucked them at Zaethan's head. Catching them, he let the familiar weight settle into his palms, and widened his footing. But rather than join him, the witch went back to digging through her supplies.

"Allöh, beautiful," she cooed, snaking out a braided whip he knew all too well.

Zaethan's grin evaporated, and his toes curled against the cooled rock. "Ano zà. That was not part of our agreement..."

With loving regard, she let it slip through her fingers before she hoisted the coil over her neck and cocked her hip.

"It's my turn now, Kasim." Her voice darkened. "Time to evaluate how much you've slowed." She unfurled the whip and clicked her tongue, mimicking his earlier taunt. "I suggest you start spinning."

CHAPTER SIXTEEN
LUSCIA

D mitri's elegant nose disappeared among the thicket of spiraled herbs as the curious king took an audible breath, appreciating the bouquet of the Andwele terrain. Hachiro, following suit, bent his uncombed head into an identical bushel but reared back and violently sneezed across the steep promenade. Were it not teaming with local traffic amid the evening cool, Luscia might have worried the shoto'shi would propel himself over the edge, straight into the canyon.

The herb merchant, her rumpled skin about as craggy as the rock overhang shading her merchandise, was far from amused. She seemed like the type of woman who perpetually frowned, time having encased her in the very expression. Her cloudy, onyx stare crinkled as she resumed gnawing on a stalk of camilla. It was a bizarre gesture, considering she had very few teeth.

"And this one?" Dmitri queried, rolling back the cuffs of his linen shirt as he pointed at another basket. The plant in question was a pile of chubby, clipped leaves oozing a fragrant sap.

The plump shrew spat out a chunk of pulverized camilla and mumbled, "Shumabin."

Hachiro returned to Luscia's side, his hand shrouding his nostrils like he was about to burst. "Ah, *shumabin*, Your Majesty. That would be... paladin's aloe, as I thought." Flipping through his pocket lexicon, which Luscia noticed he carried with or without his sizeable journal, he read aloud studiously. "*Paladin's aloe, native to the high altitudes of Yowekao, is a time-old medicinal agent for deep gashes, wherein the sap is applied to seal the wound, protecting it from the elements.*"

"How very intriguing." Bending beyond Hachiro, Dmitri found Luscia inspecting the squishy red-and-green clipping. "Luscia, would you like to plant some in the royal gardens?"

"If it will grow. I'm sure we could find a use for it." She set the leaf aside as Hachiro assisted Dmitri to translate, requesting they purchase not the planting but the seed.

The merchant scratched her fissured cheek as they haggled over price, a transaction it appeared Dmitri enjoyed immensely. Luscia doubted he had ever bartered for anything in his life, much less with a stubborn old woman. Nor was his likely a request she regularly received, particularly from a botany-besotted king.

But then again, there was only one Dmitri Korbin Thoarne, a ruler who scrupulously counted seeds in his palm, whereas his predecessors would have counted coin.

Luscia twirled and leaned against the vendor counter, smoothing out her airy gown of crocheted linsilk where it had snagged on a basket weave. She clasped her hands, studying the civilians of Faraji passing by.

Along the busy walkway, her men were scattered, their purpose the same. Creyvan, and his mood dreadful as ever, watched the Darakaians from another shop down the way, his golden head disguised behind a garland of citrus blossoms. Similarly, Noxolo lingered between a shaded crevasse stocked with pallets of dried wheat, while the captaen, hooded under his olive cloak, hunkered discreetly within the adjacent vegetation. Against an ancient pillar in the open, Declan nonchalantly observed the merchant's sale.

Few looked for najjan in shadow when they were in plain sight.

A few rock-ribbed stalls down, members of Kasim's pryde assembled around an outdoor tavern. He and Ira had joined them there when the two haidrens had lost interest in Dmitri's herbaceous pursuit.

Kasim came around the front and placed an order past the slab serving as a bar top. As he loitered, Luscia saw him absently grind the heel of his boot overtop the other. She snickered softly. He deserved every one of those lashes for the harness-and-lead stunt he'd been pulling over the last week, as if she were an animal boarded in his stables. In principle, he deserved her reenlisting the feidierdanns, the najjani whip he'd met in Bastiion, because despite her derision for his methods, they were working—an accomplishment she was battling to accept.

As was her dignity.

Kasim's sage gaze flicked upright and narrowed coolly. Their contrast against his cinnamon face was bright and distinct, even from afar.

He widened his stance onto both heels. It was strange to see him this way, otherwise at ease, alongside his countrymen. There was little to distinguish him as their superior, except perhaps the quality of the trim sleeveless tunic fastened over his athletic frame. Blatantly, he assessed her in turn, feeding Luscia's resentment. His sights traveled to her middle, above the curve of her hip, as if he could tug an imaginary rope and lurch her forward whenever he pleased.

Kasim laughed at something yelled over the bar, though he did not turn toward the hilarity. Instead, he nodded toward his boots and quirked his brow in question.

Luscia's lips cracked apart, almost charmed. He wanted to know if she was done with the feidierdanns.

She considered extending his pain, momentarily, but her conscience caught up with her scheming. Kasim had upheld his end of the bargain, however much she detested it. Acquiescing, she bent her head subtly, communicating the end of the speed exercise—that tonight would be different. At her signal, Kasim knocked back his drink and slammed it to the slab, then vanished under the overhang to reconnect with his unit.

"I must admit, Hachiro, you're proving a valuable addition to the Quadren." Dmitri's voice neared as her companions exited the herb merchant's burrow. "Might I task you in illuminating us further on Darakaian custom? It might be prudent to discuss such nuances, given the upcoming festival."

"Festival?" Luscia asked, strolling down the promenade as her king explored every consecutive burrow and trade.

"The Holiday of Hands, as we would call it," Hachiro answered for him when Dmitri fell under the intrigue of a rattling gourd. "An annual affair in which the Darakaians renew their 'claim' to one another. It's said to bolster mutual fidelity among the tribes, but from what I've gathered, it's an altogether untidy sort of spectacle." Sayuri's brother brushed unseen grime off his shoto'shi robes, indicating he was not entirely thrilled about whatever impending mess the holiday entailed.

Exchanging his coin for the rattling gourd, Dmitri resituated himself at Luscia's side and continued down the cliff walkway. "Instruments you can grow. How marvelous. Just think... an entirely vegetable orchestra." An indulgent grin cheered his lackluster pallor in the setting sun. "Though, I would squander all noble support at the next courtly gala, no doubt."

"No doubt." Luscia laughed, envisioning Ira's vapid sister, Flourette Hastings, trying to waltz to a symphony of squashes.

"A peculiar experiment, Your Majesty, but I'll see it notated nonetheless," Hachiro said, jotting in the back of his journal and missing the jest.

Stifling a laugh, Dmitri led them into the next burrow, nearing the tavern. "I am most grateful for your diligence, Hachiro. Thank you."

Torches were lit along the packed promenade by various venders as the sun all but disappeared behind the ridgeline. A pair of chieftains sauntered past the fragment of Dmitri's Quadren, their examination cool as it swept their visiting regent, who rummaged through a series of baskets. It was too noticeable he'd never shopped in a common market. The chieftains would mistake Dmitri's enchantment for detachment.

She doubted they would ever respect the power of childlike wonder in a leader. Not when Darakai wielded their own power like a rod instead of a staff.

"The perfect place to begin our education, Sire, for Darakaians do not boast an equivalent to 'thank-you.'" The shoto'shi's deportment changed, adopting the straight-spined posture of a seasoned Pilarese tutor. "'Zullee,' being the closest comparable, is merely an honorable articulation of one's acceptance. Our Southern neighbors equate thanks to an admission of debt, which is why no clear translation exists."

"Likewise, with a customary 'please' or 'you're welcome,' I presume?"

Dmitri inquired, tapping a decorated wooden statuette to ascertain if it was hollow. "In all our years, I've never heard Zaeth use either, even when speaking in Unitarian."

"Precisely. 'Shamàli' respectfully propositions the recipient, under the terms the request ought to be fulfilled only *if they see fit.*" Hachiro paused, beholding Dmitri severely overpay for the delicate carving.

Grinning, the fledgling king dropped two silver dromas into the eager merchant's calloused hands.

"Conversely," the shoto'shi said, resuming his lesson. "A phrase like 'ho'waladim' is directed solely by tone. A gentle *as is do you,* communicates a deserved reward. Spoken forcefully, it looms a warning."

Luscia leaned toward Dmitri as they crossed to an adjacent burrow. "That statuette was not worth your dromas."

"Of course not," he replied, offering her his arm. "Why would I buy a mere statuette when I can buy a month of meals for that man's family?"

Luscia thought back, realizing he'd purchased a good from every vendor on his post-dinner excursion. Appraising her regent, she took hold of him. Kasim's midnight drills made the physical act far easier than it would have been a week prior.

"It is the poorest kings who feed only themselves, Luscia," Dmitri stated, patting her fingers over his rolled cuff. "Hachiro, explain for us the Darakaian refusal of apology. I cannot express how maddening this is to navigate in my personal life."

Hachiro produced the strange monocular device from his pocket. After securing it over one ear, he flipped through the magnifying lenses to better investigate an octagonal puzzler on sale, made from bone. "Darakaians do not believe in the notion of an apology," he muttered, attempting to solve the rotating cubes. Rubbing his shallow chin, he continued simultaneously. "They consider it cowardice to retract one's actions after the fact, rather than owning the consequence, positive or negative. It's a pride of theirs, really."

Dmitri tossed another dromas to bauble merchant, who scrambled to catch it, then the young king elbowed Hachiro. "Keep it. Some late-night recreation for you there."

They strolled before the tavern, and Luscia found herself searching for Kasim among the throng.

Hachiro's cultural insight whisked her back to her apartments in Bastiion, the night Kasim had brought Takoda, tattered and torn, to her door. She remembered how they'd spoken over the sleeping warrior. How after she'd broken off the initial bargain to train him in the wraiths, Kasim had danced around an apology for his abhorrent behavior.

It had been a well-earned apology for how he'd turned their sparring into something sordid, when he'd driven her hips into his, presuming she would cower and fold at his intimate touch.

Luscia hadn't understood then why he'd made such a point to *not* apologize, when days later, his own revulsion disturbed him still. But it made sense now.

In retrospect, by refusing Luscia an apology, Kasim was forcing himself to own what he'd done in that room—to own his actions, those that could not be undone. And over the broken body of his friend, Kasim had tried his best to make sure Luscia now grasped.

Her neck, sheathed in linsilk, twisted again toward the rowdy tavern.

What a conundrum you are, she thought, though he was no longer there.

"Ah, Kumo, Jabari!" Dmitri called to Kasim's beta, as he and a long-legged warrior stepped out onto the promenade. "Won't you join us? Hachiro, my interim haidren to Pilar, was just informing us on the ways of Darakai. Perhaps you both could weigh in, being the experts?"

The enormous beta shrugged when Dmitri gestured for them to accompany him.

"Hachiro, Kumo Shà is beta over the Proper Pryde, stationed in the crown city, and cousin to our own Zaethan Kasim."

"Uni." Kumo lumbered onward, slowing his massive stride to flatter Dmitri and his walking cane. "Our mhàddas are sisters. But I grew up free, in the hills of Halona, yeah?" His beefy forefinger twirled overhead. "Not in this bunker like Zaeth."

"I'm curious." Hachiro bustled between the beta and his comrade. "Why do you carry your mother's name and not your father's, like your cousin?" Intrusively, the shoto'shi blinked up at Kumo, whose belly rumbled at the query.

Tucking his bulky thumbs behind his buckle, he responded, "Darakai favors the highest-ranking mate. My mhàdda was third in her pryde, like Zahra, when she married a horse breeder. So, I took her name, and the king took my fhàdda's horse! Titles…" he chortled. "They're all kàchà kocho."

"Your mhàdda," Jabari said, interjecting. "She scary like Zahra too. One look wilt a man 'till he work no more."

Luscia heard pages flutter as Hachiro tried to make sense of the warrior's jumbled remarks. His research was interrupted when the shirtless haidren to Bastiion was ejected from the tavern, sending him sputtering onto the walkway. Buttoned askew, the pocket of Ira's flashy vest was turned inside out.

Dodging a passerby, he toyed with the fabric and glanced upward, swallowing cheekily at Dmitri. "Well, that went quick!" he exclaimed, ducking when his shirt was chucked out as well.

Recovering, he folded it neatly over his forearm. The haidren dawdled there, inelegantly scraping himself behind the material.

"See." Jabari tut-tutted at Ira in the street. "Yancy haidren caught the scritch-scratch from them downside friendlies…"

"That he did, Jabari." Dmitri leaned on his cane with a sigh. "That he did."

A scuttle of children scampered around Ira, knocking him off balance as they trailed their mother, who carted a hamper of produce down the congested lane. A young girl, running behind her siblings, bounced into Hachiro. He yanked back his hem, which she'd accidentally trampled. There was an audible intake among the Darakaians surrounding Dmitri and his guests.

When the mother looked back, her haggard demeanor hardened. Marching over, she averted her gaze and snatched the child's hand, prepared to move her daughter out of the king's way.

"Doru." Dmitri stopped her leaving and, using his cane, knelt to the girl.

Her tiny chest puffed bravely as his handsome, aristocratic face came to her level.

Dmitri presented the painted statuette he'd purchased and proffered it tenderly. "Ho'waladim, little one."

Many stopped in their tracks, gathering around the unexpected exchange. The woman, clearly fatigued from the day, opened her mouth to speak but said nothing. Setting the hamper aside, she crouched beside her daughter in the street and, nodding into her dark strands, whispered.

"Zullee." Shyly, the girl's fingertips swept her heart, grazed the dimple in her chin, and drifted openly toward him in some native gesture. "Accepted with honor," her timid voice enunciated in Unitarian.

The mother urged her again. Gulping, the child's sable lashes skirted her cherubin cheeks as she emitted the softest of declarations.

"*My King.*"

Luscia looked up at their multiplying audience. The Darakaians encircling them started to mutter. Then, those mutters rippled throughout the entire promenade, turning dark, radiant faces toward one another in the rows behind. Her Tiergan ears quaked as she regarded Dmitri, stooped humbly on his knee. In astonishment, she gaped at the people, deciphering fragments of their hushed Andwele words.

Words that spoke of an Orynthian king, one who bowed not to the mighty but the weak.

Luscia gripped Kasim's foot determinedly, holding it still.

She was beginning to lament her conscience, which had returned her to the herb merchant's burrow before departing with Declan on their lengthy hike to the bluff. Dmitri must have overpaid in his barter for those shumabin seedlings because the hag certainly drove a hard bargain for the fresh, aloe-bearing trim.

Perched on a boulder, Kasim's leg dangled into her care. Luscia unfolded the leaf of a waxy parcel, which carted the costly mixture she'd produced. Again, he jerked out of her grasp.

"If it's Darakaian-grown, then why is it *glowing*?"

Her lips pursed at the shimmering goo resting on the ground. Its faint light reflected off the pebbles and weeds, thanks to a crush of yolk yarrow and more than a few drops of nixberry oil. Both were lumin-enriched ingredients she'd added to the local aloe for his benefit, to better soothe his pain-ridden feet. To numb the sting, she'd even laced it with common Orynthian thissleweed—an effort that seemed gratuitous on her part, given his uncooperative attitude.

Luscia snatched his wayward ankle and pithily retorted, "Let's just say that homegrown has been improved." Her nails dug in when she smeared a liberal coating on his lacerations, some already having scabbed.

"Shtàka!" Kasim's toes buckled, dark atop her aspen forearm. "Spurned sorceress! You said this kakk is going to help—Oh, Depths... Depths, that works fast." Relief suspended his budding tantrum. His head tipped back as he released a heavy exhale. "Was this your apology for the mutilation you caused?"

Luscia let go of his foot, glazing the concoction over his second. Hachiro's lesson on Southern semantic came to mind, as did that morning in Bastiion when Kasim had acknowledged the indignity of his deed.

"Darakaians don't apologize" was all Luscia said, wiping the excess goo onto her pantleg.

He stirred atop the boulder. "Ano zà." Kasim's head angled downward as she refolded the parcel of leftover aloe. "No. We don't."

Luscia rose and handed it to him for his later use. Catching her eye, Kasim swallowed stiffly. He'd heard it, his quoted remark from that wearied morning.

Unhurried and purposeful, he blinked, and what she construed as regret furrowed his skin. The folded parcel was suspended, each of them holding onto it. His strong chin dropped with a stiff nod. Just as he'd done earlier that day, Kasim posed another question—a harder question. And while silent in asking, he was far from voiceless.

It still bothered him, Luscia grasped, what he'd done earlier that summer. And he wanted to know if it could stay there. If she could leave it in that forgotten training room.

She toggled between his intense jade irises, seeking a hint of duplicity. None was found. With a jerk, Luscia bent her head and let go of the leafing.

The past was the past, but the present was changing.

Consequently, so should she.

"Yeh'maelim," Luscia said in Boreali and motioned toward the aloe. "That is welcome to you."

"Zullee," he replied in his own tongue and set it aside, coming to stand. "I've something for you too. Here—these are Dhalili's." Kasim offered a set of clothes, the textiles distinctly Darakaian. "But don't mention I took them. She's not keen on sharing."

"I'm already wearing pants."

"Now take them off."

Kasim crossed his arms and pivoted, showing his back so she could undress.

In a surly fumble, Luscia shook out the fabric. Unlike her linsilks, the gunjas ballooned in the breeze. Curiosity won out, and stifling her prudishness, she removed her jerkin to unbuckle the trousers she sported. At the clatter, Kasim fidgeted but courteously stayed put. Sliding her thigh into his scout's clothing, she tucked her silken Boreali shift and secured the gunja strappings at the waist, wrapping the stays tightly up her abdomen while the dreamy fabric billowed everywhere else.

Squatting low, she stretched out her hips. Completely unencumbered, she felt practically nude.

"Ready."

Turning round, a smirk needled Kasim's ample lip as he examined the fit of his native attire, which, although generous, snatched Luscia in her smallest places.

"Better." He cleared his throat and proceeded to remove his tunic.

"Niit. Tonight, we begin with blades."

A spark of anticipation disrupted his cool demeanor when she cited iron instead of wood.

Luscia retreated to the equipment sack at the edge of the grass. "Heh'ta. Wait here and put that thing back on. Access to your skin will just be a distraction."

"A distraction for who, Maji'maia?"

Luscia twisted over her shoulder at his playful inflection. Four perpendicular scars pleated him, from his chest to the taut muscle of his torso. Claw marks, perhaps. She didn't want to think of what else might have created them in this place.

Kasim snorted, pompously misreading her inspection and likely proud he'd goaded her into it.

You're feeling plucky. She gnashed her teeth and resumed her rummage. She unsheathed a kuerre, longer than her own, and paced toward Kasim.

"That is not a crescent wraith." His tenor altered sorely, stating the obvious.

"Have you ever handled luxiron before?"

He declined to answer.

She persisted. "From the forge, this sacred element is distinct in every way. Its burden…" Luscia balanced the center of the living blade upon her fingertips. "Is lighter than a branch." Her opposite hand reached for his, guiding it over the pommel and around the hilt.

When he touched the metal, his eyes widened.

"Its warmth, a deceptive invitation. But its blade…" She pressed a withered root against the burnished edge. The root sizzled where it met the sword's deadly candescence. Pulling it away, the organic matter continued to crackle.

Kasim's mouth parted, bathed in the sword's luminosity.

"Its blade injures even after separation. This weapon is equally as dangerous to you as it is to your opponent, which is why we cannot begin with the wraiths." Striding to the rest of the weapons, she then retrieved a dagger and another kuerre. "It's also why you should wear a shirt."

She returned to him, and Kasim rotated the sword under a pocket of moonlight.

"Your entire nation carries this?"

The mysterious opaline sheen, much like her Tiergan eye, glinted as he lunged, testing how it sliced through the air.

"Wem, as you well know."

He blew out heavily, running his thumb along the inscribed fuller. "I wouldn't trade this with the Ethnicam either."

Luscia recalled when she'd held her first kuerre on the Isle of Viridis, how hot courage had hummed from the metal and into her bones, rousing her tormented heart to take up the najjani creed. That one memory overpowered the other, when luxiron had scorned her skin instead. By a single blade, Luscia had abandoned her aunt's education in the apothic arts and returned to Roüwen three years later, resilient and renewed.

She offered Kasim a dagger, urging it into his less dominant hand.

"The Order of the Najjan do not employ shields. Boreali luxsmiths do not even create them for trade. Our blades, with our momentum, shield us in synchronized attack." Luscia bent and grabbed her kuerre, gifted by her father, along with her mother's consort dagger. "When our strength is balanced, we wield our weapons interchangeably."

She tossed the blades, catching their hilts in either palm. After spinning the luxiron with her wrists, she swapped them once more.

A ravenous expression tugged Kasim like an undomesticated cat, observing her weapons switch back and forth. Luscia paused while he mirrored the exercise. His rhythm uncoordinated at first, he held the kuerre but missed catching the dagger. He barked when the luxiron nicked his palm, searing it, then snatched the dagger off the bluff and tried again. By the fifth attempt, Kasim found his cadence, alternating his weaponry with ease.

He broke into a victorious grin, filling out his sculpted cheeks, as he steered himself into various combat maneuvers. The stars showered his form as it glided into a hybrid elegance, blending his Darakaian footwork with the blade exchange of the najjan.

"Waedfrel." Luscia reservedly commended him, stunned he succeeded after a mere five tries. On the Isle, it'd taken her six. Disrupting his delight, she challenged, "Do you remember the third principle of the wraiths?"

Kasim bit his lower lip and sank into a crouch. He lifted his blades at the ready. "Sheer endurance."

"Then show me what you can endure."

Luscia raced for the bolder, sprinted up the side, and lunged for Kasim with the kuerre. A deep, liberating cry erupted from her as she hurtled through the air. The inky night shattered with a brilliant burst, and she was captured into the Sight. Threads of lumin sailed across the bluff behind the veil, casting a glistering web that Kasim could never witness.

Hitting the ground, luxiron sparked against luxiron. With a clash of spirit and spite, *Ferocity* shrieked heresy to her own House. Luscia raked her mother's dagger against his sword, evading the attack of her Darakaian adversary, his forbidden initiation one that could not be denied. Her dissent from the creed, her unfaithful irreverence, only fevered Kasim's determination, freeing and bolstering his dueling assault. Whispers from the *Other* stormed Luscia's ears, drowning out his Andwele curses.

Kasim lurched forward, slashing her borrowed attire when she blocked his strike. Whirling, Luscia showed him her teeth when the Sight's torment tore through her skull. Instead of surrendering, she gritted through it, diving for Kasim within the luminous net of cavorting threads. She reined in her blades, and a new fright enraptured her soul.

The freedom he felt... Luscia felt it too.

CHAPTER SEVENTEEN
ZAETHAN

A howl of exasperation tore from his lips. Zaethan, rankled by her bullheadedness, cracked his neck as the witch twirled away from him.

Just like she always did.

As every avoidance yet, she spun out as far as the rope would allow, stopping only when it commanded her to. The slack snapped taut in the space between their middles. Zaethan considered shortening the lead rope even more, as he'd already removed a yard's allowance, but any added confinement might intensify her thinly veiled compulsion to flee, which was irritating enough, after a near fortnight since coming to Faraji.

Zaethan's heel dug into the pebbles, and he diverted his stare. Chase a horse's hindquarters, and it will give its eyes. Chase a horse's eyes, it'll show its rear every time.

That was the theory at least, one his finicky subject was putting to the test. Zaethan was sick of seeing that lissome rump dodge each of his exercises. The muscle of his legs burned.

Because he'd been doing all the work.

Once more, he bolted after the witch. Zaethan skidded through the grass, swiping for her ankles. But she twisted her face away, lurching to the left, and threw her weight against the roping. Though substantially heavier than she was, Zaethan bowed his spine, and his upper body was wrenched away with her intensity, driving him into the earth.

Spitting out a clump of dirt, he seized the lead rope and gave it a brutal jerk. With a yelp, the witch's bare feet flew out from under her, and her errant rump hit the ground with a thud. Like a lethal little field mouse, she scurried to stand, spattered in soil. Zaethan kept his grip on the lead as he rocked off his knees and rose onto his toes.

"That was completely uncalled for," the witch spewed, swatting residual dirt from her backside. As if she were she a field mouse, Zaethan pictured whiskers quaking with her distinctly disgruntled pucker.

"Depths." He loosened the slipknot over his navel and stomped toward the witch. "You still won't turn into me! How many nights do you want to repeat this, hm? Turn in, not away. Face what you've been taught to avoid, or you'll never conquer it."

Her pale, heart-shaped face crisped. "I've bested you so many times now, Kasim, I don't need to be facing you to do it." With a lofty exhale, she rotated her spectral, scarred neck toward the trees and glared off at her dozing wolx. Her chin hovered there crossly.

Arrogant and stupid.

Zaethan lashed out, and his hand cupped her beneath the jaw. His other punched her in the hip. Displacing her footing, he lurched her by the knotted harness over her pelvis.

In one effortless swoop, Zaethan hoisted her entire body off the ground.

"Uni—That right there." He fumed, speaking straight into her panicked, mismatched eyes. "The fear you wield so confidently, yeah? The fear that keeps turning you away... *that* is what's going to get you killed."

Zaethan let go, dumping her on her soles.

The witch stumbled backward and clutched at her windpipe, rasping. She had bested him, over and over, but only at the end of a blade. Her luxiron spun lies about her resilience—armed her against every threat when the real threat was her own pride. The lies she told disguised resistance as independence, reluctance as restraint.

She was a walking falsehood, and he saw right through it.

The sincerest thing Zaethan could do was force her to see the truth. He'd always hated this point when breaking a stallion, the moment their own reality and their limitation set in. Even the toughest of creatures could be broken. Zaethan didn't intend to break her pride, but he'd committed his help, for hers in exchange. And for it, he'd do what he must.

Unrushed, he carefully closed in and placed his hand over her hip bone. "Relax this."

She flinched, snarling as he probed the tension in the tissue.

"Relax it," he repeated, rocking the curvature in place until she guardedly submitted it to his guidance. "You constantly lock your right hip. That's how I so easily destabilized it."

A puff emitted from her nostrils, and she tracked his fingers when they moved up her figure, analyzing the rest of her posture. Without the sparring jerkin, her bare arms were warm to the touch.

"Close combat is just another story-dance," Zaethan said and let go of her elbow, "like the gaibai we danced for Dmitri. You must engage and evade, over and over, while never losing sight of your partner."

"My opponent is *not* my partner," she snapped.

"They are until you're dead," Zaethan said, adding some give to the rope as he backed away a fair distance. "We need to reorient your instinct, Maji'maia. Get you to start using the thinking side of your brain, rather than the reactive."

She absolutely did not like that assessment. Her head bent askew at a predatory angle as she crouched.

"Good. Get angry, embrace that rage. Dictate it. Refine it." He baited her, priming his limbs. "And by Owàa, don't you dare drop your eyes from it."

Zaethan leveled his eyeline at the witch, tied to him across the clearing. A breeze coming off the bluff swept a lock of her moonlit hair over the savagery that pricked her nostrils and arrowed her strident, tawny brow. Free of warning, he ran for her. Wavering for but a moment, she held his ferocity and squared her frame. He reached around her ribs, about to tackle, but she clung onto his harness and, using his momentum, swung them both around.

Her fist struck his face like a thunderclap.

Cheek aching, Zaethan ducked under her shoulder and delivered a powerful blow to her side, severing her hold of his harness. Firing off what he assumed were the finest Boreali expletives, the witch barreled over, into the grass.

"I wish I could say you were a fast learner." He huffed, dabbing blood from his lip. "But eh, kàchà kocho, life is full of letdowns."

She hunched in the undergrowth. He didn't bother to stifle his snicker when she lobbed a rock at him.

Zaethan undid the knot and liberated himself from the harness. Glancing up, he spotted a newcomer prowling out from the timberline. Her ruffled plait hung over her witch ears, and sensing the approach, the Northern haidren sprung up. Instantly, she removed the roping.

"Niit, heh'ta!" She cradled her ribs, calling out to her henchman. "All is waedfrel, Ana'Brödre."

In the dark, his mass halted a way off. The brawny shadowman was indiscernible beneath the heavy cloud cover, as was his expression.

Matting down her disheveled tresses, she tidied herself. She refastened a scabbard against her thigh and snatched her kuerre and her weapon-filled upturned boots off the boulder, along with her original attire. Carting it off in a bulky bundle, she waltzed past Zaethan as if they'd just concluded a genteel game of cards.

"Tadöm. Until tomorrow, Lord Darakai."

Bending over, Zaethan grabbed the lead rope and recoiled it. The witch trudged through the grass toward her shadowman. When she joined her escort near the wall of trees, Zaethan regarded her as she paused and spoke to the grim fellow. After a few moments, the shadowman extended his arms for her gear. Placing it in his care, she continued, disappearing into the timberline.

The silhouette of the shadowman remained, pivoting toward where Zaethan stood, the lead looped over his shoulder.

Zaethan stretched his spine, not to be intimidated by the highlander's motionless watch. After a few breaths, the outline of his face tilted at his haidren's gear in his arms, then back toward Zaethan. Ever so briefly, he did it again in a nod.

Uneasily, Zaethan returned the gesture, and within a matter of paces, the shadowman was gone.

Like Bastiion, Faraji never slept—not entirely nor at once.

Unlike the crown city, the red-rocked fortress operated through the nights in a waking slumber. Percussive music played from the chiseled corners of Làtoh Ché, lulling the rowdiest citizens to sleep. And stirring others to rise.

The music never ceased here, be it the drums of battle or those about a fire. The heart of Faraji beat relentlessly for its people. Even now, Darakai's resilience echoed throughout the canyon, commanding Zaethan home.

He strolled the heights of the rugged labyrinth filled by the sound.

Home had become a fickle concept. For over the years, the heart of Faraji, as well as the entire House of Darakai, had started to beat for one man above all others—a distinctly un-Darakaian premise. Southern ears across the Andwele range were being shaped to fit their chief warlord's lips, devouring every word he uttered without question. And in devotion to the almighty Nyack Kasim, no one dared to question why he hated his son.

Is home where we want to be, Zaethan mused, *or where our being is wanted?*

He didn't often ponder such things. He usually begrudged the answers.

Zaethan ran his palm along the Andwelestone, welcoming the subtle vibrations from the drummers above, and descended another steep stairway. He'd lived his life in this stone… had charted every nook and cranny.

Crossing under the sweeping buttresses, bordered by sculptures swathed in greenery, Zaethan wondered if the stone remembered him too. If these shield-bearing statues recalled him hiding behind them during his youth. Or how he'd tracked and measured his height against theirs. He used to pretend these red warriors, leading the way to his father's compound, were his friends.

They had been his very own watchmen, like those of the great Thoarne. But these mighty, unmovable men had never saved Zaethan from brutality. And they certainly couldn't now.

He'd long moved out of his father's colossal byumbé, its towering altitude situated at the center of Làtoh Ché. Nyack Kasim preferred a more modest dwelling, concealed in the overgrowth of the secluded, torch-lined row. Zaethan nodded at the succession of seasoned guards who protected the archway into the skyrise compound. Decades of experience peppered their time-crusted skins, variegating each man like he were fashioned from coarse wenge-wood.

None said anything as Zaethan passed.

He circumvented the main structure, a notorious octagonal edifice protruding from the cliffside. Zaethan navigated the worker alleys that segregated the tight assemblage of adjoining byumbés. It was snug, back in the roofless passages. But Zaethan preferred onset claustrophobia to the midnight reception possibly awaiting him on the promenade.

"Alpha Zà," someone hissed from the shadow. "A moment, shamàli, my Lord Haidren."

A bedraggled relic of a man staggered into the torchlight. Above his snarly beard, a lone bloodshot eye, courtesy of his master Kasim, darted around to ensure they were alone.

"Machàkwe," Zaethan whispered, helping the old bondservant onto a barrel to sit. "You should be resting, old man."

"Your father entertains tonight." Machàkwe coughed, and his rickety forefinger pointed toward the largest byumbé. "There's some grain stacked under the window... yeye qondai?"

Zaethan appraised the elderly man, whose servitude, originally vowed to his mother, had transferred to his father with everything else after her death. A quartz post pierced the upper cartilage of Machàkwe's ear, designating him as such.

Digging into the pocket of his tunic, Zaethan felt for some coin. "Ho'waladim—for your loyalty," he said, pressing his last dromas against the man's chest.

"The son of Cyra will always have it." Machàkwe bowed on the barrel, taking the silver. "You were a Shà, uni, before he made you a Kasim."

Zaethan let out a sigh, recognizing the resentment in his inflection. "Go. Find your bedroll now, yeah?" he replied, leaving the pledged laborer to hopefully get his much-needed sleep.

Quietly, Zaethan hustled through the jagged, moss-laden alley and snuck around the backside of his father's home where it cut into the cliff. Like most byumbés, additional aeration encircled the height of the exterior in the form of slim, horizontal windows. The mortared slits in his father's byumbé were all blacked out, except for one, which flickered dimly.

Just as Machàkwe had assured, a pile of sacked grain had been stored beneath it. It wasn't the first time the old man had left Zaethan a perch for eavesdropping. He'd just been a lot smaller when he'd felt a need to employ it.

He climbed the grain, mindful of the meticulous crunch beneath his sandaled soles. Zaethan maintained few scruples about spying, for in his experience, the content matter was much worse than the offense.

Easing his weight onto a sack near the top, Zaethan reclined, relishing the chill that soothed his backbone. His nape pressed against the whittled red bedrock, and he tipped an ear into the light.

"*And brother are making great progress.*" General Lateef's voice was muffled through the window. "*He claims Wekesa is twice the warrior he was five years ago.*"

"*Is that so, Wekesa?*" Zaethan's father asked, a familiar warning laced in his gravelly timbre. "*Ni yeye ràtomdai, do you claim this too, that your kwihila will be able to write over his?*"

Zaethan held his breath at his rival's response. He'd always assumed his father was directly involved in Wekesa's preparation, but their exclusive conference confirmed it.

"*Uni zà, Chief Warlord,*" his rival asserted.

Zaethan's lip curled.

"*Bastiion has weakened Zaethan. Under my blade, he will crumble...*"

Bootheels clobbered the stone as someone walked around inside.

"*My investment in your advancement is not without its hazards,*" Zaethan's father stated. "*Bring me kwihila, or I will carve your next failure into the other side of your skull.*"

Contemptuously, Zaethan grinned.

At least he was not alone in receiving such threats. Were Wekesa wise, he'd heed it. Nyack Kasim was known to follow through.

Besides, it was true; Wekesa's first failure was irrefutable—and stamped into his head. Whatever twist of luck or favor of fate had dictated his opponent's misstep, when the rains had come during their initial challenge five years ago, it was Zaethan's knife that had landed the winning blow. And it was Zaethan's *kwihila*, his victory, that inhabited Wekesa's gruesome flesh now.

No matter what the future held, no matter who aided his cause, Wekesa could never wash him off.

"*Too soon a challenge could unsettle the masses, ano? Korbin's spawn seems to have made an impression on them,*" the general grated out.

"*Uni. Faraji fawns over a weakling while greatness slumbers in their blood. Our people forget who they are,*" he heard his father rumble, "*and it is up to us to remind them—*"

A pebble struck the wall beside Zaethan's face, tearing him away from the slit window as it bounced down the grain supply.

He scanned the rising levels of Làtoh Ché, high above the secluded row. Nothing but the drowsy traffic expected of the hour traversed the visible promenades overhead. Carefully, he scooted back into position, eager to hear the remainder of his father's vitriol and Dmitri's political success.

It'd equally surprised Zaethan, being so different than his royal predecessors.

Korbin had pacified the House of Darakai with his affluence, whereas Dmitri's grandfather, Aquilla, had riled them with conquest. But their heir was doing neither. Darakai's budding favor for Dmitri was not curried through campaign or bribe, strategies every Thoarne ruler had used to secure the South. Instead, Dmitri was counting on his altruism to speak louder than any drum.

The tactic worried Zaethan increasingly the more it accomplished. To Darakai, selflessness was the worst kind of liability. For what was offered would be taken.

Again, something smacked the Andwelestone, and it tumbled into his dreaded heap. Irritated, Zaethan felt for the nugget between the locs pulled over his crown. It was slick in his fingers, polished for such purposes. He searched the leafy foliage that shielded his father's compound.

There. Where a tree split from the cliffside, a set of jeweled toes dangled off a crooked branch.

Zaethan leaped off the sack pile and strode down the worker alley to stand directly beneath it. He should have checked the trees for listeners before he had joined them.

"All these years giving Wekesa papyon and you're kept outside the room?" he inquired, angling upward into the murky leaves. "You were never one to settle, Kehari."

Her ankle swayed. "Yeye ano'qondai, Zaeth. After all these years, I'm kept in the room that counts."

Zaethan grunted at that, imagining them together enough times to have grown numb to it. With a rustle, Kehari's leg swept low, and she sprung from the branch. Catching it in both hands, she hung there, a typical slingshot caught between her teeth. In a supple leap, she dropped onto the path before him. Kehari's lashes, darker than the gleam of her burnished skin, fluttered as her hands cupped her trim waist. It was smooth and bare where her tunic split beneath her breasts.

Zaethan's glanced up at the roots bursting through the rock. "Still climbing my trees?"

Pouting, Kehari sauntered nearer and pushed the prongs of her slingshot over his heart. "You don't let me climb anything else"—she sensuously dragged it past his navel—"anymore."

He gripped the branch she'd descended and loomed over her. Zaethan shoved his hips against her slingshot. "A yaya unsatisfied will climb anything she passes."

Kehari's mouth parted, and the lovely roundness twitched resentfully. "Uni... An unquenchable appetite you didn't used to mind."

"I minded when it was *him*." Zaethan's whisper hoarsened.

Five years ago, he would have picked Kehari up by the thighs and carried her down this alley until morning. She loved to climb, and he'd offered her a forest. Never jealous. Never controlling. But out of all the men in Darakai, she had to taste Wekesa.

And afterward, it was not Kehari whom she left unsatisfied, but he and his rival alike.

"It will be soon, Zaeth. His challenge." Kehari's seraphic face jerked toward the men gathered inside the byumbé. "He craves it, yeah? Whatever Wekesa craves, he takes. And keeps. Wekesa has become a true jwona rapiki, Zaeth. He is set on taking alpha zà, I've seen. Don't say I didn't warn you…"

Zaethan's fist swiped her slingshot, and he snapped it in two. "I well know how he keeps what he takes. Get off my property, Kehari." He fumed, chucking the shards. "And don't come back."

"I am Wekesa's guest!"

Zaethan caged his arms as she sashayed after the broken slingshot, and corrected, "Ano zà. You are his consolation prize."

Affronted, the puffed tail of Kehari's ringed mane whirled around when she spun. The copper neckbands decorating her throat clinked with her heated return.

"I saw you with her!" She charged Zaethan. Pointing at his chest, she uttered viciously, "Uni. I saw you meeting under that oak, outside camp in the foothills. You… and that filthy occultist. The son of our chief warlord caught in secret with his very own *consolation prize*. A revolting y'siti—"

"Don't speak to me with that shtàka on your tongue." He forcefully took hold of her chin. "On the Quadren sits your betters. And you're to consider the haidren to Boreal as such."

Her laughter turned rancid as she tossed her head, scanning his torso.

"A y'siti—my better!" Kehari crooked her nails into a claw and ran it along the scarring down his chest. "It's like I never knew you at all, Zaeth."

"Ano, yaya." Zaethan skimmed his nose along hers, like he used to. "You never knew what you wanted. I'll make it easy for you though. It wasn't me then, and it isn't me now. Go on, *rhaolé*." He fanned his palms. "Hurry to the room that counts. Wekesa's bed is getting cold."

Kehari's skin brushed his when she swerved away in anger and stormed off into the dark. He stood there until her pleasing contour was lost between the crowded structures.

Zaethan walked back to the massive byumbé and mounted the sacks of grain when a hawk cried out unexpectedly. As it dove across the passageway, its talons nearly scraped his nape as he dodged out of its path.

Feeling for blood, Zaethan crooked his neck up at the window where the bird had perched. In the dimness, the feathers of its belly reflected a bizarre lavender gleam as it compressed its wings and squeezed through the taut opening. Zaethan's gaze trailed it inside as he reverted to his post atop the grain pile.

That bird had traveled far and wide to get to the Andweles. The only messengers with feathers that peculiar flew from the west. And so did the missives they carried.

Affixing under the window, Zaethan strained to listen as someone unraveled a document.

"*My guests are on their way,*" his father stated, a horrible pledge in his pronouncement. "*And with them… our new kwihila.*"

Zaethan's exhales hastened as he huddled outside his childhood home. A new kwihila.

His father's new victory, he feared, meant to overwrite his king.

CHAPTER·EIGHTEEN
LUSCIA

Plumes of vermillion and ruby dusted their shoulders as Noxolo and Marek escorted Luscia under a willowing canopy. Luscia's arm tightened around the captaen, each Northerner wholly out of place amid the explosion of grisly splendor.

Raining from above, garlands of frothy blossoms had been strung across the base of the canyon. Together, she and her najjan descended the massive steps into a natural arena. Like grand banners unraveled over the cliffside, dueling waterfalls framed the colossal pit, the surge of both cascades rivaling the energetic orchestrations that drowned the garden of bodies. Their number stretched far beyond the breadth of Thoarne Hall, belittling Bastiion's picturesque masonry and majesty.

Under the flowering, scarlet cloud, Luscia reached up and toyed

234

with a bloom. The suspended clusters reminded her of herbs Alora might hang out to dry, had she dipped them in blood. It comforted Luscia when she dragged her dry fingertips away from the garland; its macabre pigmentation was natural, unlike the gore it resembled.

She peeked down at the gossamer layers of periwinkle that sheathed her figure. Instead of sleeves, *Bahira'*Rasha's gifted ensemble fanned over Luscia's shoulders, plunging to the stone with a cape that trailed her fitted, collared bodice. The opulent Zôueli garment, as costly as any adorning Rasha herself, flattered a pair of flowing pants, identical to those worn by such women across the burgundy beaches. It was the singular article of Luscia's presentation that somewhat resembled the twirling Darakaians throughout the festive arena, bearing a similarity in style to their gunja pant.

Yet unlike their conventional leathers and warworn raiment, the congregated Southerners circled their kinsmen sporting next to nothing at all.

In vivid contrast to the crimson strung overhead, the Darakaians were draped in the brightest ivory, emphasized by their talismans of tusk and bone. The men, bare-chested and unburdened, cavorted in their gunjas, as the women, wrapped in strips of alabaster linen and blanched buckskin, countered their rhythmic steps.

Their twirling limbs were brilliant as topaz and rich as obsidian. But what was uncovered soon became covered, camouflaged under a chronicle of handprints. Where the creamy paste had crusted over the arms of one, a milky sheen shone afresh on another.

In melodic oscillations, the Darakaians mingled throughout the congested expanse of the pit, pressing their palms into the skins of their neighbor.

And after letting go, they left there a mark of claiming.

Across the Andwele Mountains, Darakaians of every tribe were said to be doing the same. This annual act, this communal retelling of their belonging and that of their brethren, was *Fàkkadim'Chalim*.

The Holiday of Hands.

Marek led Luscia and Noxolo by one of the many clay-filled basins scattered throughout the pit, each bubbling, bronze bowl warmed over a bed of coals.

"By the Watchman, I did not expect this to be so—"

"Beautiful?" Luscia finished for the captaen, taken aback by the perplexing magnificence too.

Such magnificence didn't fit with what she knew about the House called Darakai.

Noxolo's hand hovered over the basin, comparing it to the tonality of the clay mixture. "This will make it easier to blend among them… for today."

"Ana'Sere, the king beckons." Marek's palm settled against the small of her back as he nodded at Dmitri, somewhere among the Darakaian thicket. He presented Luscia his arm, his sterling jacket identical to the one encasing Noxolo, the same Boreali uniform they'd donned upon entering Faraji. The auric embroidery accentuated his eyes, bluer than the Vasil, when he glanced downward, awaiting Luscia to take hold. "Shall I usher you to him?"

Her hesitancy had little to do with Marek's nearness and everything to do with the chilling ordeal outside Rian, however much she'd tried to forgive him for his skepticism.

Every day, Luscia doled her forgiveness in bits, whatever bits she could muster. His disbelief had said so much more about her than it ever would him. It spoke to her character, her intelligence. Her very sanity. And those implicit messages were now whittled between them, evident in the divide between her fingertips and his jacket sleeve.

But this season was not about Luscia, or Marek.

It was about a young king and his Quadren, a king who expected Luscia at his side.

Swallowing her reluctance, she reached for him. Marek's tendons tightened through the silken material beneath her hand. As he guided her past another simmering basin, Luscia anxiously twiddled with the collar of Bahira Rasha's frock.

"It is concealed," Marek whispered, too lowly for even Noxolo to hear, who trailed their path through the carousing Darakaians. An errant lock, like the feather of a cardinal, fell into her periphery as his lips dipped intimately while they walked. "You are resplendent, Luscia. I will stay near, should you wish, and ensure that is all they ever see."

"Bolaeva. I find myself wishing Mila were here with me, for matters of dress and other profound excuses." With a fleeting smile, Luscia released the fabric covering her scar and said formally, "Tadöm, Captaen Bailefore. We can only unveil our strength in this place."

"Se'lah Aurynth, until those hallowed shores, Luscia, I can be the shelter to your strength... if you'll only let me."

Halting, Luscia pivoted at Marek and his inopportune reference to courtship.

Over her shoulder, Noxolo scratched the back of his head uncomfortably, shifting himself away as if to look anywhere but at his captaen, who unabashedly buried her hand with his over the jacket. Stuffed into the cuff, his rejected kurtfieri enwrapped his porcelain wrist.

Luscia's face heated with the coal-rimmed basins in their vicinity. She stared at the leather bands, the beaded token of her father's approval, and commanded her complicated emotions into steely sensibleness.

It was neither the time nor the House to revisit the notion of courtship. And even if it were, that didn't mean Luscia was ready to do so, especially after Rian.

She swore to Aniell, men and their universal entitlement grew more taxing by the day.

About to voice her reprove for his ruining a perfectly fine stroll, a group of linen-swathed children scampered in all directions through the maze of dancers, giggling. Luscia pulled from Marek's grasp when a boy, no taller than her hip, ducked around her gleaming cape and peeked around either thigh at the young girl who hid in front of Luscia's knees. Without looking up, they played back and forth. Switching places with the girl, the boy peeped at his friend, snatching a fistful of Luscia's pantlegs. When he let go, a soggy white smudge plastered the gauzy fabric.

Luscia scooped a dallop of the clay with her finger, catching his attention as the boy noticed who they played beside. With a high-pitched wheeze, his little body, decorated in handprints, went stricken as he finally gazed up at the wicked haidren to Boreal.

"Zullee," she acknowledged in Andwele. Grinning, Luscia teasingly dabbed the excess mix onto the boy's nose.

His deep-brown eyes rounded excitedly, and he burst into laughter, gleefully taking off into the crowd with his playmate. Luscia watched them go, sighting the intermittent bob of Dmitri's rumpled hair where he mingled a few yards off.

"The king beckons," she stated, echoing Marek and heading that way on her own, free of his company.

A handful of tribesmen scurried back as Luscia weaved by, possibly afraid she'd leave her mark on them as well.

Regardless, she headed toward the Quadren, gathered near a particularly large basin before a string of musicians who lined the pit. Sayuri's brother was not with them. Instead, situated off a way, Hachiro counted the rows of percussionists that crowded the step-style cliffside risers.

His lone guard idled at the hem of his robes, an uninvited participant in the shoto'shi's calculation.

"Our Lady Boreal, at last!" Dmitri called, signaling for her to join his conversation with Ira, an elder chieftain, and the same middle-aged warrior whom she recognized from their first day atop the city's podium.

The man who'd tried to comfort Kasim.

"Gird your loins, lads, for my frigid gale blows," Ira said in warning to the two Southerners. He emitted a subsequent squawk, for Dmitri inconspicuously whacked him in the shin with his cane.

"Lady Boreal, allow me to introduce Chief Sefu of Holona, the central leader for all minor tribes throughout the foothills." Leaning onto the byrnnzite handle of his walking stick, Dmitri gestured toward Chief Sefu before he indicated the man with dreaded locs like Kasim, though his grayed all the way to his waist. "And his beta warlord, Yousif Shà, the uncle of Lord Darakai." With a chuckle, her king fixed his concentration on the masses, seeking the Southern haidren. "Wherever he is."

Their relation made sense. Kasim resembled this beta considerably more than his own father, sharing a parallel breadth to their cheekbones and eyeline, as well as the barest cleft in their chins. It also explained his experience in horse breeding. Holona was famed for its Andwele stallion trade. Across from Luscia, Yousif Shà's gaze was empty of the chronic malice seeded in the older Kasim's.

In its place, curiosity radiated from his woody eyes before they closed in greeting. "Owàamo."

His welcome was not wedded by the greeting of the senior chieftain, who with a gruff shake of his jowls, submitted a curt "Your Majesty" before blustering away from the Boreali in his midst.

"Shamàli, let me express that your occupancy in Faraji is a history in the making, Lady Haidren." Faint markings, both scarred and tattooed, stretched over the beta warlord's dark torso as he hooked his hands behind his back.

"Did not my aunt accompany the rest of King Korbin's Quadren during his own coronation tour?"

A slight smirk rucked his lips, reminding her very much of his nephew. "Uni, but your predecessor—as hers before her—was never as… visible… as you have made yourself to be."

"And a vision she is at that." Ira snaked his arm around Luscia's waist, an endeavor she quickly disarmed.

"I'm discovering that while a predecessor's footprints chart a path, it is we who obligate ourselves to retrace them," Dmitri diplomatically remarked.

Yousif Shà lifted his un-sandaled soles, exposing the dirt from the bedrock. "I tend to agree. A topic for our next encounter. Shàla'maiamo, Your Majesty." He brought his fist to his chest, then gave a scant bow to Luscia and Ira alike. "Lord and Lady Haidren."

The beta warlord excused himself, joining his fellow Southerners when the clamor swelled to a heightened revelry. Ira meandered away with it, pursuing a precession of belly-bared dancers.

"The patience you extend them is not in vain, Luscia. I promise." Dmitri adjusted his gilded, shell-stippled vest and looked out at the legion of jubilant Darakaians.

She mimicked his study. The people formed a lung, their recurrent steps a communal inhale and exhale under the canopy of bloodlike teardrops.

Standing with her king, Luscia felt a shiver in her temples.

Alora often said Luscia ought to pass in and out of the Sight continuously, however discreet. Luscia never chose to solicit her gift so cavalierly, for fear of the pain her Sight always caused. But here, witnessing mothers marking their children's cheeks, and the youth claiming their seniors in embrace, Luscia chose differently—not to sneak off for a taste of her aunt's sour tonic…

But to *see*.

For on this side of the partition, between the physical world and the one that upheld it, she'd never met a contradiction so arresting. The House of War—a house of devotion.

Calming herself, she bravely tested the bounds of her awareness. Luscia let her eyelids fall, initiating the tug to see beyond the veil.

When her lashes broke apart, she was rendered breathless beside her king.

Weaving among the garland overhead, she saw the threads convulsing with the dancing throng. Shuddering amid the Darakaians, so brilliantly—as if every thread as far as her Tiergan eye could see had coalesced for the fete—the lumin responded to their rhythm. Twisting threads of the *Other* swayed and shuddered throughout the whole arena, the unearthly illumination casting a kaleidoscopic glimmer over the sanguine flourishes above.

A thread wound around Luscia, radiant and ablaze. It continued to drift, merging with the cloister of lumin shrouding the people of Faraji. Luscia crumpled her brow, bemused.

There came no whispers. No ominous intonations. There was only light. And the bearers of that light, the porters and keepers of the *Other*… were pleased.

Lambent and alive, the lumin was pleased with Darakai.

"You are quite all right?"

Dmitri's voice jolted her out of the *Other* and back to the natural side of the veil.

"Wem." She blinked, her Sight dissipating as she answered his concern, "Oddly, I am."

Quizzically, Dmitri studied her a moment. "I could have sworn there was something in your eye... a trick of the light, I suppose," he stated and peered up at the rays of sunlight breaking through the canopy. "As I was saying, you're all so different, Luscia, but that's not a bad thing. Goodness comes in many forms. It is goodness that makes things foreign familiar to us all." Unexpectedly, he handed Luscia his dazzling cane. "And in that spirit, I think we ought to join the good the Darakaians are doing."

Dmitri undid his cuffs and folded them up his bronzed forearms. Unceremoniously, he then undid the top three buttons of his waistcoat, revealing a smooth pane of much lighter, Unitarian skin. A dimple depressed his cheek as he boyishly grinned, his lips smashed together.

Marching over to a basin, the clay bubbling, Dmitri dipped his palms into the thick, creamy balm. He brought them out thoroughly drenched, waltzed to Hachiro, and commanded the distracted shoto'shi to hold still. The Orynthian king cupped the westerner's face in both hands, plastered in place. Dmitri's mouth moved, gently voicing something to Pilar's interim haidren.

He released Hachiro, and a set of chalky handprints flanked his normally upturned nose, which erratically twitched. Across the basin, his wide-eyed stare flitted back and forth, horrified by the soggy mess he now sported. Dmitri grabbed Hachiro's hand, who'd barely moved, and transferred the extra clay onto the shoto'shi's palm. Chortling, he shepherded Hachiro to mark the exposed portion of his own arm in exchange.

"Now this is my kind of holiday." Ira leered over Luscia's shoulder, having returned from an unsuccessful galivant. "Everyone gets so handsy."

Tearing her attention from Dmitri's interaction with Hachiro, Luscia replied dryly, "Must you cheapen everything, Lord Bastiion?"

"Cheapen oneself." He came round, stroking his vest of plum-and-copper brocade. "But never one's attire." Ira stepped back, scanning her, and nodded appreciatingly. "A lesson I don't need to teach you, my tigress. I'm enjoying this exotic deviation of yours… one of Rasha's, I presume? Such diplomacy holds a lady captive by the seams. All she needs is a nimble master to unravel her confines—"

"These seams will remain intact, Lord Bastiion."

Circling the generous basin, Dmitri plunged his hands back into the smoldering mixture. Bending over the rim, he revealed a stupefied shoto'shi behind him. Hachiro really did despise untidiness. Beneath the drying clay crust, his features were pinched. Assured he was not Dmitri's next intended, Sayuri's brother guardedly unwrinkled his amber robes and recommended his writings.

The drumming deepened, and the music transitioned the Darakaians into a new dance step, wielding their limbs like wings. Their king angled for Ira, white clay dribbling to the floor of the pit the entire way. Dmitri indicated the haidren clear some space.

"Your turn, Lord Bastiion."

"Is this the part when we get to take off our clothes?" Ira asked.

With the patience of a thousand sighs, Dmitri unhurriedly said, "Within margin, Lord Bastiion."

Dramatizing his sulk, Ira unfastened his vest as well as the linen finery underneath, displaying an elegant belt. Dmitri plucked the chained canister off Ira's hairless sternum, lifting it levelly between them. The eastern haidren immediately sobered, focusing on it.

Luscia witnessed something like shame pass through his gaze, sapping his color, normally so much richer than his fellow Unitarian. But elevating the snuff higher, Dmitri pushed his other glazed palm over Ira's heart, where the canister normally hung. He dropped the thing, letting it fall over the backs of his knuckles. His opposite hand seized Ira's shoulder in the same embrace.

Fixed there, Luscia didn't entirely understand what his ardent expression conveyed. For though seemingly chaste, it was full of passion.

"There lies everything you need," Dmitri phrased curiously and retreated his hand. He repeated the act, swiping the leftover mixture onto Ira's fingers and guiding the yancy haidren to subsequently claim him in turn.

A bright handprint had been stamped under Ira's necklace, and in subdued silence, he gave no comment, no wanton quip, as he buttoned his clothing over the mark of his king.

Dmitri rewet his hands at the basin once more, then stepped toward Luscia. She noticed the subtle limp in his gait, but he denied the cane when she offered it back into his care.

"If you consent to it," he said softly, as he hadn't with the others, and hinted at her upper arm.

With little reluctance, Luscia worded her yes and rotated her bicep out from the sheer tiers. In one motion, Dmitri swooped up her left hand, drenching it in the slurry, as his other encircled her stiffened muscle. She sensed a tremor shoot through his hold, and she searched his steady regard, unshaken by his diminishing strength.

Dmitri's mossy irises, embrowned in a soulful ring, didn't falter when his fingers relaxed, and he repeated his earlier sentiment. "Goodness comes in many forms, Luscia... especially in those we least expect. We've only to seek it."

She followed those irises when they swung aside and dampened as he watched the people of Darakai, now nearly uniform in their collective painting.

"In the words of their tradition…" Dmitri focused his beaming on Luscia. "*Hewe ràtomdai na hewe.* We claim us."

Luscia peered at the already drying print below her shoulder. "Tadöm, Ana'Brödre. My King."

Dmitri led her dampened hand to his wrist. Turning it over, he showed the deep blue of his veins and forced his tendons upward into her palm.

Barely voicing it at all, he whispered, "Promise you will hold fast to each other when I am gone."

An exuberant beat thrummed throughout the arena; thousands stomped to it, shaking the floor underfoot as Luscia sniffed back an abrupt flow of feeling. Behind Dmitri's pregnant stare, she saw Hachiro squatting with his journal, sketching diagrams of the basin warmers. Feet from him, Ira loitered, his demeanor oddly somber and naïve, as if he were lost.

They were nothing without Dmitri. She was just as scared as he for the day her Tiergan blood could no longer sustain him. And he'd no idea that was from where his elixirs came.

"Wem. I promise you."

Comforted, her king retrieved his cane and let out a tranquil breath. "Now to find the man of the hour…" Dmitri revolved, narrowing his search for Kasim. "That is, if he can still be identified."

With a laugh, he plunged into the crowd, his cane rapping the stone as he hunted down his oldest friend.

Luscia flexed her fingers, cracking the thin, blanched crust forming there. If all goodness was authored in the same High place, perhaps it pleased Aniell no matter who recited it. She felt fresh tickle along her temples at the thought.

Luscia decidedly made her way to the same basin Hachiro was

sketching. Patterning Dmitri, she submerged her caked hands into the mixture, the viscous heat both comforting and bizarre. Keeping the slop from tarnishing Rasha's garment further, Luscia strode, her arms wide, to where Noxolo and Marek were positioned nearby.

She stopped before them, both so much taller than her. Noxolo's transparent eyebrows quirked at the concoction coating her fingers as she waved each najjan to her height. Complying, Luscia stretched her arms and scooped their pale faces up in either hand.

Noxolo's elegance filled her left, Marek's fortitude in her right.

"Nox." Luscia's pinky pushed a fall of his platinum hair out of the way and kissed his forehead, then Marek's, however more delicately. "Captaen." She drew back, his head inching after her lips. "Se'lah Aurynth, my brödre. Until the shores that do not end, we claim us."

When she released them, small handprints adorned her men, cheek to earlobe. Seeing the Darakaian clay on their highland features, she started to laugh. Noxolo broke into a toothy grin, soaring back to his lofty stature.

But Marek, with no mirth at all, anchored his stare onto Luscia as he tightly bound his hair, showcasing her mark with pride. "Se'lah Aurynth, Ana'Sere…"

She cleared her throat, which had not needed to be cleared, and excused herself to find the others, uncertain where Declan and Creyvan had settled among the activity.

After saturating her hands in another basin, she searched for their Boreali jackets among the spinning Southerners. Sidestepping their synchronized gestures, timed to the festive clamor, Luscia bypassed a cloister of the royal regiment. The rowdy sentries, most Unitarian in descent, relished the moat of emptied goblets littering their boots.

Among them lounged Bessus, whom she'd scarcely seen since his repugnant proposition outside their traveling camp that night before entering Faraji. His gluttonous chortle carried, nauseating to her ear. Luscia's skin crawled but she kept walking, just as she'd done that very evening, eager to get away from the field marshal's repulsive presence.

Luscia meandered toward the farthest side of the rumbling arena, tense, when a couple of soldiers bumbled out of nowhere. Suddenly, she tripped out of their way and straight into the arms of a Darakaian warrior.

Her soaked palms stopped her momentum, dousing his caked chest with the clay mix. Cemented there, her chin twisted toward the warm, broad hands swallowing her shoulders and the Zôueli material, soiling under the warrior's painted thumbs.

"You finally turned in to me."

His lungs expanded proudly beneath her touch. Unrushed, Luscia's neck arched upward, for withdrawing would only add to his satisfaction.

Beneath the backdrop of bloodlike blossoms, Kasim was a sculpture. He was buried in handprints, overlapped so much they'd become indistinguishable, which, she supposed, was the whole point of the tradition. The clay flaked off his clavicles and coated some of the locs hung over his chiseled face, distinct even under the accumulation.

"Apparently all it took was three weeks on a leash and a walk to the park."

At her bitter retort, Kasim leered more closely, causing his eyes, surrounded in flat alabaster, to sparkle. A rare gene, their vibrancy was so unlike that of the eyes of his brethren. His unvoiced laughter darted to her hands on his chest, marking him.

"Ni yeye ràtomdai na meme?"

He'd changed the phrasing, and Luscia swore she'd misheard it. Her ears knew better.

Her eyes did not.

CHAPTER NINETEEN
ZAETHAN

Amid the tangle of bodies, Zaethan recognized her touch before he ever glanced down. He didn't need to; it was in the way her wrists locked up. The way the pads of her fingertips froze the moment they met his clay-caked chest.

On this day, Fàkkadim'Chalim, hands were meant to proclaim. To be forceful and commanding. But gazing at the witch, her hands considered themselves, melded to his amply marked abdomen.

He clutched her shoulders authoritatively. After all, it was she who'd lumbered into him. She'd yet to identify the Darakaian she had inadvertently imprinted, too lost in the centuries-old mixture that bound them. Zaethan did not draw back, entertained by her ignorance. All this time he'd used a harness to guide her through her fear, when here she stood, to the beat of a hundred drums, willingly pressed up against him.

Clay cracked when his lips crooked at the irony. For a creature so maddeningly self-assured, she could really be obtuse. Were they alone on the bluff, he'd rub it in even more than he was about to.

Zaethan dragged out his words, low and slow. "You finally turned in to me."

His mouth twitched again when he saw her nostrils flare.

Assuming indifference, she languidly pulled her eyes up toward his. A surge of champagne waves spilled off her heart-shaped face, knit with raw stones and tortuous plaits. The platinum about her hairline, even brighter than her skin, accentuated the tenacity in her discolored stare. And unlike their previous encounters, it was not the cloudy iridescence of her right iris that left him dismantled.

Zaethan mastered a smirk, unnerved by the rosy flush that pranced along her cheeks. A result of the southern heat or her embarrassment. It didn't matter. But it did distract. The flush tinted her lips, normally so ghostly and muted, emphasizing their rigid curve. In such a regal garment, its textile foreign and its shade a melancholy sky, she did not look like a witch—a chilling figure of fable and lore. Nor did she resemble the ambassador her stately ensemble decreed.

Ano, here she looked like a woman. Nothing more and nothing less.

"Apparently," she said with pointed articulation, "all it took was three weeks on a leash and a walk to the park."

Depths. Zaethan bore down closer. *An insufferable woman at that.*

A ring of voyeurs started to congregate around them, the Darakaian alpha of alphas and the haidren to Boreal, but he hardly cared. *Let them watch.* They had his whole life. Zaethan foresaw how this would conclude anyways. Pride made people predictable, and she was nothing if not proud.

Zaethan's attention slipped to her hands, still stiffened against him.

"Ni yeye ràtomdai na meme?" he provokingly inquired.

Zaethan didn't know why he asked it. Or why it'd sounded as throaty as it had. She wouldn't understand the Andwele saying, but he'd developed a fondness for knocking her off-kilter these last weeks, and a question of her claiming him would do just that.

His eyes brazenly flitted back to the highlander in challenge. Engulfing her shoulders, his thumbs, crusted in white, grazed the lacy folds just above her collar. Subtly, temptingly, he inched them up either side of her scarred throat. As he stroked the rough flesh under his left thumb, she inhaled briskly and wrenched off his chest. Instantly, she cradled her hands to herself.

Zaethan grunted. She'd understood every word.

"Unhand me." Her voice crispened. "You have trespassed my skin. Release me. Now, Lord Darakai."

Behind her incensed visage, a blurred, scarlet blob emerged among the bystanders. Shifting focus, Zaethan saw that her captaen had located his haidren, who stood currently in the grips of a Darakaian. He'd never much considered the pair's interpersonal dynamic, the lead of her guard being an impassive sort of fellow. But the shadowman was far from impassive now; his unrestrained snarl shattered any illusion of a man's platonic disregard.

Beneath a dried, delicate handprint, the sheer fire in his reddened face wasn't platonic in the least.

Casting his palms, Zaethan let go of her neck. Leisurely, his thumbs hooked the waistline of his ivory gunjas, revealing a skim of dark, unpainted muscle. Despite her anger, she was fastened onto it.

"Uni, call me a trespasser," he said loud enough for their audience, "after manhandling me with such ease!" Zaethan's mouth hovered over her ear, though he didn't speak into it. "Besides, we wouldn't want to give your captaen the wrong impression of Orynthian diplomacy."

In her gauzy gown, she reeled around toward the enraged shadowman, his riled pigmentation the second consequence of Zaethan's gratuitous wit. With a vengeance, the Boreali haidren spun back toward Zaethan, furrows splicing her brow.

"That was wholly out of line!"

He smeared the solidified clay across his chest, dispersing her markings, and grinned. "Oh, but Maji'maia, it was wholly enjoyed."

She flashed her teeth, then stomped over to the captaen to argue in tones he couldn't hear. Their volume was irrelevant. The shadowman's unfettered glare, reserved for Zaethan, said it all. He winked at the Northern warrior in reply, which, to Zaethan's satisfaction, only roused their heated discourse further.

He turned in search of Kumo, whom he'd originally abandoned for refreshment. His well-earned smugness faded when he discovered Kehari watching from the circlet of dispersing Darakaians. Her scowl, masked in coats of claims, visibly shook with her balled fists. His former lover appraised him through the river of dancers in their rekindled celebration. Her sepia eyes narrowed.

Her scathing allegation trolled to mind. *It's like I never knew you…*

Unapologetically, Zaethan widened his posture at Kehari. Perhaps she hadn't known him after all, not really, except for what he gave her.

But Zaethan undoubtedly knew Kehari.

As she angrily twirled into the crowded dance, he tracked her splattered figure under the tiers of crimson willows. Zaethan was certain her spite would soon seed rumor where it didn't belong as retribution for whatever disloyalty she'd misread. For to his bittersweet recollection, Kehari was extraordinarily proficient at two trades, both employing her mouth.

A succession of horns blew out.

Instantaneously, the impassioned bodies spread beneath the canopy stilled. All drumming ceased mid-performance, though the pebbles continued their clatter, shaken across the base of the pit. Every citizen of Faraji went silent, gathering their cubs in hushed instruction as the leaders from each tribe mobilized from the varied corners of the paused celebration. Zaethan's fellow Darakaians beat their breasts to the horns in deafening chorus as the chieftains answered the beckoning call of their chief warlord—a call one should never hope to hear.

His father had summoned the War Council.

On this day.

Each Andwele leader had entered the arena as a chieftain but departed it now as a warlord of old.

Zaethan whirled in desperate search for his king among the hushed festivity. Scanning the crowd, the council carved their way toward the massive steps. There, trailing the chief of Yowekao, he spotted Bessus ushering Dmitri along with them.

Zaethan shoved through his neighbors, stalking the field marshal's advance. The Unitarian's role in his father's summons was disturbing at best. Zaethan caught flashes of amber shuffling after Dmitri, where the soldiers escorted both Ira and Hachiro. Zaethan's mouth felt like The Wastes as his king climbed the stair with the least protective members of the Quadren.

This was why Zaethan had argued Dmitri travel with a unit of Thoarne's Watchmen. The ways of the Houses were too unpredictable.

The outer territories abided their own governance. Here, precedent favored a regional regime, not that of Bastiion. But in his altruism, Dmitri had listened to Bessus's deranged assertion that the regiment would offer enough security on his tour. The field marshal had played on his eagerness to travel faster and lighter than most regents had before—the same man who was steering Dmitri into a historic bunker, conceivably against his will.

There wasn't enough time to both locate Zaethan's pryde and catch up to the others. Trusting Kumo and Zahra to remember protocol, he charged through a group of gong players and vaulted up the stair. Up ahead, a band of sentries lined the street leading toward the war chamber. Zaethan broke into a sweat, jogging past them around the bank of the Great Pool. Crossing the canyon, he saw where the backs of Dmitri and his haidrens disappeared behind the roaring waters. Behind one of the twin falls, they entered a system of tunnels in the cliffside.

Zaethan bounded up the rocky ledge. He'd been in that tunnel once: the dawn of his Ascension five years ago when he'd won alpha zà. But he still remembered the twists and turns to the secreted bunker, the room that had won a hundred battles and would a hundred more.

"Kasim!"

He glanced over his shoulder. Boreal's haidren and her captaen were close behind. Bypassing the narrow climb, they hurdled up a labyrinth of boulders. They reached the natural landing and mist spattered her side, matting the frothy material to the swell of her hip.

"Where have they taken the king?" she bellowed over the rushing cascade.

"The War Council has been summoned!" Zaethan shouted back and dipped toward her shadowman. "We need to hurry, but he can't accompany you past this point."

She mopped the moisture out of her lashes and put a hand over the mark on her protector's face, where the clay rinsed off. "We will return, brödre."

The shadowman's piercing gaze darted to Zaethan.

"Captaen—Bailefore, is it?" To his stoic veneer, Zaethan shouted his pledge, "With me, she is under my protection!"

Her unnatural, kohl-rimmed eyes rolled, and she sidestepped Zaethan. "Thank Aniell I am under *his* protection and not your ego."

Vanishing behind the overspill, she left him with the skeptical Captaen Bailefore.

"You have my word!" was all Zaethan yelled to the man and retreated behind the waterfall.

The torchlit tunnel illuminated the other haidren's progress, yards down the ancient passage. Zaethan sprinted ahead until he came to a hatch, etched in the runes that memorialized the descent into the ancient chamber. Crouching, he gripped the bolt and peered up at her gravely.

"Get behind me, and by Owàa, keep quiet."

"We are equals, Lord Darakai. You're not in a position give me orders."

"And you're not in a position to decipher centuries of Darakaian overtone." Zaethan jutted his chin at her, adopting her words. "Did you study *barbarian* on that isolated peninsula?"

At that, she knit her arms in a neat fold, displaying the bone bands across her knuckles. Unhappily, she tucked behind him.

Like the entry of a byumbé, the hatch opened to a stairwell and plunged into the earth. Voices echoed up the compressed walls as Zaethan led them lower into the chilled gloom. His footing sped toward the crude light at the bottom when he heard Dmitri among the council assembly, his brusque remarks muffled but on edge. As

Zaethan met the final steps, the muffle became clearer, and his heart raced at the sound.

"To be no proceeding absent of your own haidren... least of all, at the expense of an allied treaty."

"Not all matters concern the Quadren." His father asserted himself from the farthest hollow of the excavated chamber. "If the haidren to Darakai refused this summons, then it is for the council to rectify his seating, not a Unitarian agency—"

Zaethan knocked a few soldiers out of the way and charged into the open.

Torches alighted a horseshoe-shaped Andwelestone counter, hosting the ten major chieftains of the Andwele range, surrounding an unoccupied recess at the center. And behind them were a ring of soldiers.

"I am right here," Zaethan announced to the clay-plastered leaders, locking eyes with each warlord until his sights landed on Dmitri. He'd been seated at the counter's crescent, between Ira and Sayuri's worried brother. Zaethan's stance momentarily relaxed, and for his king's assurance, he crooked his chin over a shoulder at his highlander counterpart. "We both are."

She wedged forward, surprisingly observing Zaethan's request to follow his lead. More than a few chieftains whispered heatedly about her presence in their privileged chamber, but the rushed protests were stifled when their chief warlord stalked their chairbacks, coming into view.

Nyack Kasim was not a man to oppose, in any form, but especially in a form such as this.

Crowding the room, his leading lessers were daubed in the clay claims of their friends and familiars. Even their Unitarian king and the foreign ambassadors on his Quadren had observed Fàkkadim'Chalim.

Dmitri's prints smattered their varied skins. Yet coming to a foreboding halt exactly opposite his son, Zaethan's father dominated the room solely with his dark earthen flesh. Untied, a sleek, black tunic show-cased his robust torso, rippled despite his years.

A torso untouched, unpainted, and unclaimed.

His father's infinite stare swept Zaethan's frame, honored under countless layers of crackled clay. Instead of pride or even apathy, his nose buckled when a sadistic smirk upturned his flattened mouth. When he left his son, his glower melted toward his own waistline, like molten tar, and he fixated it on the chalky hand that gripped his other wrist. With the speed of an arrow, his eye darted back toward Zaethan, stressing the disparity between him and the successor of his haidrenship before the council of chieftains.

Zaethan answered to the House but belonged to the throne.

The chief warlord belonged to none, and all Darakai answered to him.

"Make way." His father instructed those blocking them from the seats reserved on either side of Ira and Hachiro. "Allow these haidrens to rejoin their Quadren, so we may hear out our visitors."

Between them, Dmitri's expression was shadowed, unnervingly anchored onto someone unseen.

"A series of developments have been uncovered in the west, posing a threat to our Darakaian kwihila, but above all, to our vulnerable Unitarian King."

Uneasy, Zaethan strode by Bessus and his assembled sentries. There came a smacking noise he couldn't quite place as he neared the slab counter.

"The only threat I wish to discuss has been seated across me at this very table." Dmitri steeled himself, bracing off his chairback as he laced his fingers measuredly. "Explain to me, concisely, why the commander of *my* armies would break a treaty he saw forged by *my* father without *my* dispensation. Tell me, Commander Kasim, why you would dare coerce your king into an audience with Mworra?"

The half-digested slop in Zaethan's stomach plunged toward his sandals when he shoved the final sentry aside.

In line with Dmitri's scorn, three bare-backed Mworrans gorged like lurid kings. Brazen and unrepressed, the enemy feasted before the ruler of the central kingdom. But on what or rather whom they dined, he would never know.

By the blood trickling down their sallow jaws, he did not wish to either.

Before the Mworran triad, a platter of raw meats pooled, a gift they devoured with primal greed. Sinew ripped and snapped against their teeth, which, true to rumor, were filed into sharp points, resembling the exact predators expected to plague the mines of Calluc.

The anterior of the southwestern range was a harsh maze of septic pools and toxic soil, driving the earliest inhabitants into the mountains since the Forgotten Wars. There they'd hunted each other to survive. As the terrain healed, restoring to Mworra pockets of harvest, it was said the practice endured.

Tearing at their meal, Zaethan saw that even their fingernails had been ground into barbs to better assault their prey. Wearing as little as Darakai's male warlords, the Mworrans bent their sunless hides over the platter. All three were withered leather. Thin jet strands dangled to their grayed shoulders like slick oil drippings. Rawboned beneath it, their fibrous musculature protruded disturbingly—a testament to their cannibalism.

Zaethan paused behind Ira, who without being asked, hastily rose for Zaethan to preside at Dmitri's right hand. The yancy haidren nearly tripped as he switched seats. An ivory, clay-pasted arm shot out, and the witch gracefully stabilized Ira as he scrambled into the other empty seat.

Before this day, Zaethan had never met a Mworran in the flesh. She hadn't either, by the tense microshift in her movements. They were becoming more noticeable after their close durations together. Orynthia's enmity with Mworra had renewed during the latter Shield Wars, thus this shocking encounter was likely a first for an entire generation inside the bunker, especially those seated on Dmitri's Quadren.

On the edge of his chair, Zaethan emulated his king. Clay molted from his fingers when they interlocked over the spherical counter. The witch patterned them both, flanking Hachiro, and her hands outstretched beyond his fat academic journal.

Zaethan's father strutted through a gap in the ringed stone, speaking from the inner recess to his council. "Ano zà. It was not *we* who broke the Shield Treaty, but our deceptive friend… Razôuel."

Grumbling broke out among the tribal leaders, quarrelling in disbelief, while others assented, unsurprised. Hidden behind the counter, Dmitri's knee knocked Zaethan's, signaling alarm. However, his thin chin stayed resolute to the room.

"Doru, doru." Their chief warlord spread his arms, quelling the rising dispute. "I too did not want to believe it when I initially learned of Razôuel's deceit. Our strongest ally… in league with the atrocities of Tane Abwé and the cross-caste murderess Salma Nabhu."

Steadying his friend, his leg pressed against Dmitri's while the bunker erupted. Boisterously, the leaders were drowned in vitriol at the mention of his convicted acquaintance and friend, Salma.

The lump in Zaethan's middle stirred again with nausea.

Suspiciously silent, General Lateef uncorked a bottle of pammu and refilled each of their visitor's goblets—the irony in the drink itself. Renowned in this place as the ranking beta warlord, Lateef rubbed the syrupy claret off his lip after taking an open swig of the contrabanded brew.

"We apprehended Abwé with the aid of Calluc," Lateef announced to the council, reclining in his seat. His outrageous report corralled interest. "Associates of the executed smuggler confirmed his runners routed the lethal shipment through his contacts in Jol'Nune. It was there that poison was added to the pammu that killed the *dear* King Korbin. Repackaged, it crossed the Orynthian border through the northmost foothills."

The bunker quieted, drinking in his summary.

"One such associate, a brewer from Calluc, was brought to us by these fine Mworran emissaries, and testified against Razôuel's part in the regicide."

Pages scuffled. Discreetly, Zaethan looked over as Hachiro scurried a quill across the parchment of his journal.

Suddenly, Darakai's warlords were shouting over each other. In the middle of the discord, his father turned about, observing their riled and overturned tempers. His pitted, torchlit cheeks smiled ever so faintly.

A muted signal from his youth which Zaethan knew to beware.

"I doubt anyone in this room speaks fluent Tar'tar; therefore, such allegations are a waste of my Quadren's time. They are senseless at best, but due to the nature of these remarks… treacherous at worst," Dmitri warned in a dark tone Zaethan had never heard.

"While not a warrior, our fledgling king is clever beyond his years!" His father exclaimed, earning a snicker around the bunker.

Dmitri's laced hands tensed atop the counter.

"For his safety, it is not only the House of Darakai that has snuffed out our ally's ruse, ano, but others in the Ethnicam! Others who *do* speak Tar'tar."

The council hushed when someone emerged from behind the field marshal and his fractured regiment.

"Oh, not him." Ira clutched his enchained snuff canister. "Anybody but him."

"What is he doing in Darakai?" Dmitri growled under his breath.

Wading in front of the torches was Tetsu Naborū, his voluminous shadow casted connivingly over the seated Mworrans.

Like the Pilarese pearls that often adorned his absent niece, the white sheen of his unspoiled robes looked bizarre in the rugged chamber. In the weeks since the coronation, the shoto prime's jaundice had worsened. Marrow yellowed his teeth and eyes in an even sicker contrast to the cannibals he hovered over.

"The chancellor of the Shoto Collective assisted in these debriefings—a shoto prime fluent in both the Mworran tongue as well as the Zôueli." Tetsu Naborū inclined his slicked, waxen hairline toward the council and their chief warlord.

Zaethan's father continued. "Through the chancellor, the Shoto Collective validates Abwé's ties to Nabhu, his smuggling route through Razôuel, and the queen's party to their scheme. Bahira'zol'Jaell has proven herself an enemy to the Orynthian throne and an enemy to Darakai! Her betrayal must be avenged! It must be obliterated!" Zaethan's father roared, garnering outcries from his assembled warlords. "My warriors, unleash your slumbering kopars, drown your blades, and seize our true kwihila! May Bahira'zol'Jaell be cut to the knees when we take her golden city and bleed her last tears as we conquer the queendom of Razôuel!"

Zaethan's respirations shallowed when the rare messenger hawk, from outside his father's byumbé, flew across his mind's eye.

These were his secreted guests. War was his new victory. And Tetsu Naborū, hooking his tapered beard with a gleaming silver nailpiece, was the sender.

Dmitri snatched his cane and sprung onto his feet. "There's a ruse at play in this room, gentlemen. These proceedings took event without my license nor my foreknowledge. Lest I remind you, Commander..." He aimed the handle of his cane at their chief warlord. "It is I who am king. And while you may propose such, it is I and *only* I, who shall declare war. You are granted three days to remove these men from Faraji. By my order, they are to leave Orynthian soil and return to the pits of Calluc."

Zaethan's father's face dropped, his scars catching the light. But his obsidian eyes raised in defining opposition.

"This soil is Darakaian, *Your Majesty*, and its loyalty is clear."

The bunker went stale, witnessing the unprecedented standoff. Dmitri's arm shook where he held out his glittering walking stick. In anger or apprehension, the waver would be viewed as the latter.

"You have three days, Commander Kasim." Dropping his arm, the king of Orynthia pushed back his chair. Without acknowledging any of his haidrens, Dmitri's cane clacked the floor. But in passing, he hastily muttered quietly to them, "They overlook Hachiro."

The sentries parted for his exit, and the warlords whispered as he went. The Quadren rose after his precipitous departure. Off his chair, Zaethan glimpsed the clay flecks scattered upon the ancient counter. And then, for only a second, he glimpsed his father at the center of the tribes.

Unmarked. Unclaimed. Unmatched.

Nyack Kasim was not a man to oppose, especially in a form like this.

Chapter Twenty
Zaethan

Dusk befell Faraji. And with it came a shadowed breeze, the cooled breath of an illusory scowl in the sky.

Concealed beneath a leafy overhang, Zaethan waited for the lone guard to plod along. The Darakaian warrior yawned as he did, likely nearing the end of his shift in keeping watch of the interim haidren to Pilar.

Dmitri had been right about the patrols. Faraji underestimated Hachiro Naborū-Zuo, the quirky shoto'shi more interested in scrolls than a sword. He was their blind spot, making him the perfect host for his king's secret congress.

Fittingly, Pilar's haidren was housed among the westmost byumbé village carved into the City Nest. Dmitri's generous lodgings, on the most opposite side, were under the constant surveillance of his father's compound—a shrewd tactic, affording the charade of luxury to keep him within arm's reach. Knowing Zaethan's father, it'd be the reach of a muzzle.

The western residencies were nothing like the more opulent dwellings that housed their king, or even Ira—no doubt pampered in his accommodations on the east bend of the canyon. Here, Zaethan having crossed two bridged waterfalls, the byumbés were fitted into modest rows and buried in shrubbery, like identical craggy pots lining the rockface.

It was an understated beauty.

Sayuri would have loathed it.

He slipped past the patroller and skirted the boulders along the vined promenade. He angled for the fourth dwelling, where a Pilarese guard leaned against a half-walled barrier, as if overlooking Àla'maia's mounting reflection over the Great Pool. It was a ruse of nonchalance, meant to pinpoint Hachiro's residence for the others.

Zaethan had exhibited the same, returning to his own byumbé to wash off after leaving the bunker, if just to establish his presence on the compound before sneaking off. The council, primarily his father and General Lateef, needed to believe the Quadren had dispersed for the night. Otherwise, their congregation would be spied upon. Or thwarted altogether.

The last thing impassioned warlords wanted right now was a level-headed regent who thought for himself, a regent who gleaned counsel not from Darakai's battle-starved bunker but a Quadren of outsiders.

When the patroller had not yet reached his pivot at the end of the row, Zaethan dodged around the structure and onto the compact steps toward Hachiro's rooftop hatch. The air was still. Halfway up, he heard the rasp of dueling winds.

Feeble, indiscernible gusts of witchtongue whistled up from a scant alleyway abutting the stair.

Carefully, he crooked his gaze beyond the shrub of entangled creepers. Below the spill of jasmine, the witch looked to be arguing with her captaen. Her small, alabaster hands gestured pointedly from under the foliage. Bailefore, her lead shadowman, was obstructed, except for the peak of his crimson crown and an elbow, fixed as firmly as any statue.

With astonishing zeal, she quietly broke from witchtongue.

"Niit, Marek. There is Phalen! If I am harmed, Boreal has my brother to see and to speak to. But the king has no such assurances. None but *us*. We are his assurance."

Most of his elbow disappeared when Bailefore moved closer to his Haidren. "Darakai plots against the Quadren, as you said. Bolaeva, Ana'Sere, let me take you to safety while there is still opportunity—"

"Allegiance to me costs a greater allegiance to your king." She'd cut him off, stepping into the torchlight. The tail of her wolx appeared, swatting her thigh. "As long as he stays in Darakai, here we will remain. Weh'dajjeni Lux. That is our charge, Marek, and that is the end of it."

When she headed for the stair, Zaethan hiked toward the top and seized the latch.

It befuddled him. Her fidelity to Dmitri sounded genuine, enough to negate her own welfare. It'd only been a short while since her

Ascension and their collective Seating, yet she'd expressed her loyalty almost as ferociously as Zaethan might describe his own. In the eye of the Ethnicam, the House of Boreal had always prioritized itself. The adamant refusal to her captaen's entreaty didn't make sense.

Then again, she was an obstinate little beastie, who didn't like being told what to do...

Zaethan retied his locs and descended into Hachiro's byumbé. At the base, a soothing warmth hugged his arms, free of his sleeveless tunic. At the center of the common room, the shoto'shi blew the quaint fire, coaxing smoke up the stucco chimney.

To the side, glasses clinked. Ira, clearly rattled, fumbled with the stopper of one of Hachiro's untouched liquors. Unlike his usual chatter, the yancy had left the bunker mute and jumpy, like his Pilarese counterpart. Ira tossed back a shot of green fluid—one of the local bitters—and, grimacing, poured himself another.

Cross-legged next to the flames, Sayuri's brother twiddled with his quill. Swathed in the acolyte robes of the Collective, Hachiro buried his head in his palm. His messy, raven tufts poked out between his knuckles as he'd repeatedly write a segment, then blot it out.

Beside the hearth, their king rested atop a modest burlap cushion. His elbows were perched on his knees.

Dmitri stared beyond his steepled fingers at the outspread Quadre-cipher on the floor, like it were an intricate game board rather than an old relic. Zaethan had seen that strained look on men in the dangerous ventures of back-alley chance—the look as if a man's next wager could be his last.

The witch came down the steps, though only he and Ira glanced her way. Accompanying her subdued stride, the Orallach hybrid pressed against her as she crossed the fire. Its ears quivered with the log's crackle and pop. They flattened when Ira offered its owner one of his twin goblets.

"Somehow I doubt that was intended for me." She eyed the drink, flush to the brim.

With a delicate scratch below the belt, he winked, clanking their cups. "A gentleman always shares his wares with a lady in need."

"Your wares are worn out, Lord Bastiion. You ought to stop."

She set his liquor aside and circled to Boreal's crest on the Quadrecipher.

Dmitri didn't flinch when Zaethan snatched an identical cushion and lowered to the rock before Darakai's crest, spun over the panel. The faded panther studied Zaethan. Taunted by the Southern crest, he mulled over Captaen Bailefore's line of thinking. Perhaps it wasn't the shadowmen who should be contemplating early departure for their haidren but Zaethan for his king.

To bypass a partisan storm, one involving Mworra, the coronation tour could proceed as planned, just sooner than scheduled. Relocating the king would stall any act on Darakai's behalf until Dmitri could deny the warlords from the strength of his throne in Bastiion. It wasn't ideal—but it might work.

Zaethan peered at his friend, whose forefingers tapped in thought.

Hushed, he leaned over. "Dmitri, we may want to consider—"

"The Quadren cannot leave."

Tone flat, Zaethan saw his friend's mind had already toiled ten steps ahead, just as it always had when they were boys, strategizing over Dmitri's checkered pads of pawn and ploy.

"If I leave under these terms, we lose Darakai," Dmitri said into his fingers. "Accords be damned. They will never follow a king who flees, and you know it."

Zaethan bit down, embittered by his father's snare. On Darakaian soil, the king of Orynthia held less power in the Southern House than accredited him through the Accords. Dmitri could deny the council but at substantial risk to his own reign. Yet leaving the territory under political pressure posed an even bigger threat: Darakai's fealty to Orynthia.

As the House of War, Darakai monopolized the bulk of the Orynthian forces. Hold hostage a kingdom's army, hold hostage its king. Dmitri's lips compressed rigidly. His friend well understood the peril of that proverbial noose.

And so did Nyack Kasim.

"This Quadren is now in session," Dmitri mirthlessly announced, beckoning the others to sit. "I can't express how precarious my position in Darakai is after today's events. It's critical we dissect the council's alarming allegation against Razôuel and discern for ourselves a united response. Unfortunately, much of these assertions rely on the endorsement of one man. Lord Pilar."

The shoto'shi shed his quill at their king's sudden attention.

"Can you testify to Tetsu Naborū's fluency in the Mworran tongue?"

Tics fired through Hachiro face, possibly nerves. Zaethan did not yet know how to read his quirky tells.

"My uncle speaks Tar'tar, Zôueli, and every other language spoken by the modern realms. His specialty lies with those of ancient origin. This is customary in his position as chancellor of the Shoto Collective to effectively govern both the philosophical and quantifiable pursuit of every field of study fostered in Gakoshū," Hachiro explained, blinking frantically. "It was my uncle's proficiency that inspired me into my own disciplines of dialectology and primitive linguistics."

Dmitri nodded, his pupils flitting across the Quadrecipher. "As I suspected."

"However…" The shoto'shi interjected apprehensively. "That is not to say what was professed in Tar'tar… was unreservedly true."

"Nor the translation professed by your uncle," the witch tersely stated, narrowing her eyes at Hachiro while she stroked the strip of burnished fur between her wolx's snow-white ears.

The apple of Hachiro's throat jumped. "I concur, the regrettable liability in translated testimony. Yet as none of us were privy to the Mworran deposition, I am unable to affirm or reject your suspicions, Lady Boreal."

The wolx yawned at the silenced room, displaying its deadly fangs. The witch slanted her head a fraction, analyzing Sayuri's scholarly sibling, who continued to perplex them all.

"Thank you, Lord Pilar," Dmitri murmured, "for your steadfast objectivity."

In Pilarese fashion, Hachiro bowed side to side and retrieved his runaway quill. "My King."

"Then this is not an issue of speaker credibility, be it the Mworran witness, the Pilarese interpreter, or the Darakaian advocate," she stated. Her sharp gaze withdrew from Hachiro, skirting over Zaethan when she straightened toward Dmitri. "Rather, the validity of their joint testimony. At least, the *probability* of it being valid."

"You propose a reconstruction of events, Lady Boreal?" Hachiro flipped to previous pages in his journal.

"Wem, of a sort."

Dmitri toyed with the blank panel before him, spinning the head of a bear over the reeds—Bastiion's crest.

"I've long suspected Salma Nabhu did not act alone. My father's assassination could not be the product of her lone machination. A scheme so treacherous demands support in high places, particularly those at court." Absently, Dmitri traced the outline of the bear in thought. "If my distrust in the Province of Agoston is well-founded, and the missing Unitarian lord, Felix Ambrose, was in fact Nabhu's key benefactor, then her involvement with Razôuel is incredibly far-fetched. Though, admittedly, my theory of Lord Ambrose is sheer conjecture…"

At Dmitri's mention of the dead noble, Zaethan's regard darted toward the witch, who was already watching him with grave focus.

Neither had discussed Ambrose's war-tainted condition, murders, and ultimate death since that night in Marketown. Both, however, *had* kept the noble's secret from their king. Safeguarding Dmitri's ignorance for his friend's sake, Zaethan retained his reasons but couldn't name hers, particularly since Ambrose's unascended victims were the half descendants of her own House.

The witch lifted her jaw, close-mouthed, and resumed petting her beast when Dmitri continued.

"The Province of Agoston had far more to gain from a removal of power than Razôuel. Ending the line of Thoarne gives false hope to some nobles that the regency would transfer to an elected member of the Peerage… a legislative body more likely to examine the fine print minted on their coin than what's written in the Accords." At that, Dmitri cocked a brow at Ira, who was checking the reflection of his teeth using his goblet. "But Bahira'zol'Jaell is not the type to overlook such detail in her daughter's marriage contract.

"The queen realizes, in the clearest understanding, that Bahira'Rasha would be barred from assuming the Orynthian throne and its rule over the Houses should I no longer occupy it. Hachiro—Lord Pilar…" Dmitri rubbed his forehead wearily. "Can attest as much from his thorough analysis of the signed duplicate."

Timidly, Hachiro twitched and rearranged himself on his cushion.

"The contractual language is unmistakably explicit, Your Majesty. I've failed to discover a loophole to your mortality clause."

Zaethan felt the room begin to shrink... Dmitri had a mortality clause. Most royal contracts entailed such articles, but hearing one specifically written about his closest friend made it all so... finite.

Spying to his right, the squat flames backlit Dmitri in an illusioned casket. Zaethan's throat tightened, imagining the loss. Great or small, no man was impervious to death.

Eventually, the soil reclaimed them all.

Resigned behind his tumbling waves, Dmitri looked at Zaethan, unacquainted with the wilt of his friend's crestfallen feature. A blaze spirited him to reach out. He grabbed Dmitri between his shoulder and neck. His friend patted his grip over the baroque vest with a morose smile.

Troubled, Zaethan gingerly let go.

"What if the Zôueli court hates reading just as much as ours?" Ira plunked onto his elbow. Popping a ripe pip from the striped huckle-buckle fruit he'd peeled apart, the yancy slurped back bright fuchsia nectar as he chewed. "I mean, a Unitarian noble doesn't know all the ins and outs of royal agreements. How could one of theirs?"

Dmitri slid one leg beneath the other. "A scheme within the queen's court then?"

"Nobles get bored on any coast." Ira shrugged. "Conspiring gives them something to do—ow!" He massaged his chest after the witch swatted him, her pale face shaking with stern reprove. Ira quickly recovered and simpered. "I prefer it harder next time, dear..."

"Lord Bastiion." Hachiro bookmarked his page, sitting forward concernedly. "That very attitude is what contracted the malady colonizing inside your trousers. I can't imagine why you'd attempt to molest it further—"

"No one expects you would, *Hachi*," Ira rebutted, "since all *your* blood flows above the shoulders, leaving nothing for that wee rudder below."

"What an uneducated fallacy. Surely, your tutors from Gakoshū—"

An ivory hand smacked the middle of the Quadrecipher.

"Heh'ta, stop squabbling! These events are bigger than this Quadren! Our discussions not only safeguard our king but our voiceless people." Crossly, the Boreali haidren flattened the front of her sleek linen jerkin. "The people of some Houses more than others, I might add."

It impressed Zaethan how her swift reprimand instantly tempered the room, as Ira put an extra inch between their cushions. Scooping up a handful of brambleberries, he eyed Hachiro as he ate them one by one. In a haughty hush, the shoto'shi tucked his journal against his belly without comment.

Zaethan saw Dmitri almost break into a grin, but he suppressed it with the other symbols of their youth.

"Right you are, Lady Boreal." Dmitri shoved back his hair and sighed. "Returning to the matter of Razôuel… Were the royal courts colluding, then perhaps Nabhu's smuggler *did* route the exports through the region of Jol'Nune before crossing the border? There, Abwe's shipment could be tampered without tracing back to conspirators in Bastiion. It is plausible."

Zaethan cricked his neck, wishing he could steer the conversation away from the convicted madam. Again, the wicked surf of that barren coastline crashed his memory, just like it had the rocky shoreline when he'd sailed away from her cries.

Reluctantly, Zaethan dislodged the lump in his throat. "Ano zà. It's not plausible."

Dmitri swiveled in place. "Lord Darakai, whatever do you mean?"

Kneading his brow, Zaethan grimaced at the ancient board, unfolded by his feet. "Salma Nabhu was deeply involved in bootleg trade, uni. But like any good businesswoman, she sampled every shipment upon arrival. Those bottles could not have been tampered with in Razôuel prior to Salma's receipt. What's more plausible is that the poison was administered after the handoff from her illegal depot in Marketown."

"How could you possibly know the protocol of her trafficking, Lord Darakai?" Hachiro inquired. Primed to write, he reopened his pages of parchment.

Risking a glance at Dmitri, whose cheeks had hardened in the firelight, Zaethan exhaled heavily. "Because I watched her test a bottle intended for King Korbin."

He didn't add that he'd also been assigned to sneak it into the palace, though the quiet highlander across the Quadrecipher must have speculated as much when she'd caught him with the crate. It was there, in the alley behind The Veiled Lady, where they'd both found the drained body of Wren, one of Salma's cross-caste night-callers, another unascended youth whose life had been stolen by Ambrose.

Shirking the image of the adolescent's corpse, Zaethan spoke before his friend could ask. "Salma smuggled specific imports for your father. Mworran pammu, one of many. A month or so before his murder, she sampled a shipment while I was in her office," Zaethan confessed to Dmitri, trying not to shrink from the hurt that rounded his lichen eyes. "But I can't say which shipment it was or how many followed, simply that Salma was adamant the contents passed her lips first."

Appalled, Dmitri's hand blanketed his mouth, and his shock bore into Zaethan, stinging him to the core. He felt that look score their friendship, creating a rift between trust and understanding, while the others watched on, gaping at the admission.

"How could you keep this from me?"

The vessels around Dmitri's eyelids protruded in anger.

"I tried—" Zaethan hammered his fingers against his heart, ignoring the other haidrens as if they were alone in the byumbé. "By Owàa, I tried to tell you. Afterwards, in private, yeah? It's why I urged you to grant her that trial, because I knew she probably didn't do it. I tried, Dmitri, I swear."

Recalling the memory, Dmitri's gawk darted back and forth. The color drained from his Unitarian face.

"Our talk in the garden… before you left for The Wastes…"

Relief swelled Zaethan's shoulders, and he nodded profusely. "Uni. Whoever arranged your father's murder," he said in a rush, "knew of Salma's contacts and her handoffs—in Bastiion."

"Then for what purpose accuse the Zôueli?" Huskily, the feminine voice scraped his ear, tearing him from Dmitri. "What does Darakai, or Pilar, have to benefit from a conflict?"

"There is rumor that the war council met before your coronation," Zaethan said, answering her questions to Dmitri. "My father and several chieftains disagreed with King Korbin's Shield Treaty and now, your betrothal to a Zôueli princess. I think… shtàka." He deflated, stunned he dared to express the theory aloud. "I think the council is using your father's assassination to justify rewriting the end of the Shield Wars. They want Razôuel. They always have."

She spoke again, like a buzzing bee he couldn't smack away. "Is it true Darakai secured the ships for it?"

Zaethan glared at her, polished and placid atop her cushion. How she'd learned of the addition to the navy fleet or that it extended beyond Korbin's order, he didn't know. Having always discredited Alora Tiergan's position on the last Quadren, her aunt's means of intel must have deeper roots than her fellow sil'haidrens realized. The trustworthiness of Boreali intelligence steeled her niece's challenge across the Quadrecipher.

"Your insight is as good as mine, Lady Boreal." He scoffed, dismissing her statement. "I heard of a naval expansion, that it was the biggest yet. But I've not seen it. Have you?"

"I have," Hachiro said candidly. "Quite impressive. I'd estimate another hundred vessels berthed in Lempeii during my last term at the coastal libraries."

Dmitri pivoted toward the shoto'shi. "That contract with Lempeii was for forty ships."

"Oh, there are more than that now," Hachiro stated, counting invisible vessels in the air. "Many, I assure you."

"No one told me about any boats," Ira grumbled and fondled his snuff canister. "I like boats... I have three."

"This is exactly what I've been talking about!" Vexed, Dmitri hobbled off his knees and onto his feet. His arms flailed about, startling the entire Quadren. "When all of you commit these minor deceits, they stack up to a mountain of lies! Keep something critical from each other, you injure one House or another. Keep something critical from *me*, your king!" he shouted, stalking their circle on the floor. "You injure the whole kingdom! *Our* kingdom—for generations! We must walk together, not in deed... but in mind too." Dmitri pinched his elegant nose, pausing beside the recessed bench built into the octagonal walls. "Perhaps I haven't earned your trust yet... And if not, the price is too great to wait any longer for it. Consider this your final chance to disclose any lingering intel, any shred of importance, before it's too late."

Zaethan scanned the snug room. Wide-eyed, Ira gazed at his king with nothing to hide but his smoking habit, and even that he wore about his neck in broad daylight.

By contrast, Hachiro's countenance scrunched up, like he was attempting to catalog every conversation from his entire lifetime. But across, the witch's ghostly, uneven pastel eyes tightened at Zaethan. Then intently, with the drop of one shoulder, her expression relented.

She wanted to speak.

Strictly, Zaethan jerked his jaw. Having carried out another betrayal in sailing off The Wastes, he knew more than anyone that there were things Dmitri never needed to know. Truths that would only bring him more heartbreak.

When her mouth parted, his posture arrowed. She was about to make everything worse.

"There is something we haven't divulged, Your Majesty." Without turning, she spoke to Dmitri, behind her, and stared resolutely at Zaethan. "Ambrose is dead."

"The earl from Agoston? Lord Felix Ambrose?" Dmitri reiterated, dropping onto the bench.

"Wem. The killer responsible for the Boreali cross-caste slayings throughout Bastiion *was* war-tainted, to a functioning degree. The disease drove him to hunt down those least valuable to the aristocracy. We believe the children became his easiest targets. That war-tainted killer and Felix Ambrose were one in the same. His sickness overtook him completely the evening of the solstice celebration. To secure the citizens from his crimes and contagion, he... died at my hand." Her focus plummeted to her palm, which she caressed with a thumb. Her hair swung forward, concealing her expression, save the tremble in her lower lip. "I hope you can find enough mercy to pardon my unsanctioned intervention."

"Pardon *us*," Zaethan amended, declaring himself like an utter blockhead.

Her face lifted at that. She was just as baffled by the act of solidarity as he. Those eerie eyes overtook his body, as if they could puzzle him out, but Zaethan shirked their weight, twisting toward his friend, who sat in a daze on the bench.

"Alerting you of his death—and our part in it—would only complicate your standing with the Peerage. The first day of your reign, you'd have been forced to either charge or pardon members of your Quadren." Zaethan justified their actions in earnest. "So… we chose your ignorance. If we were wrong, then I carry the blame. It was the pryde's duty to stop the cross-caste slayings from the start. We would have ended Ambrose sooner or later, bringing us into the same dilemma."

Wordlessly, Dmitri slunk against the rock wall. He folded into the bench where he processed their joint confession. After a bounty of silence, he went to speak but could not.

The fire burned to embers, shading the space as it started to sprinkle outside the byumbé. Droplets rattled the rain catchers affixed to the adjacent buildings. The whole row chanted drearily for Àla'maia.

And in that sputtering darkness, Dmitri laughed. Desperate and depleted. "You worked together. To save the city. *You two.*"

"That's the gist of it, uni," Zaethan awkwardly replied.

"But you hate each other!" Dmitri rummaged around, chuckling in bewilderment.

The logs were stoked, and the room brightened.

A tear trailed his friend's cheeks, from sorrow or elation or sheer delirium from everything in between. "Of course you're pardoned! You spared those children from the next horror, and the people from outbreak!" Dmitri swiped his under eyes. "This is why you come to me. Always."

"Since we're sharing secrets… I seem to have misplaced my coin purse… or it's misplaced me." Ira launched another brambleberry into his mouth. "So that scary gentlemen running the gambling pits—you know, with the messy eye—he expects one of you to saddle the bill. Oh, and there was a thing with your sister, a blindfold, and a hairbrush once…" he said to Hachiro through his chews. But as he readied to write it down, Ira tossed off his hand. "Never mind that, Hachi, we all lived."

The witch shook her head at the yancy in disgust. "The fact remains," she said, solemnly interjecting for Dmitri. "Ambrose did not assassinate your father. I don't think any of us believe Razôuel did either."

With a breath, Dmitri sank to his knees.

He seized Zaethan and Hachiro in either hand. Pushing, he motioned for them to follow suit. Tentatively, Zaethan rested his palm over Ira's shoulder while wrapping his other around his king.

Together, their arms encircled the Quadrecipher on the floor, bearing every crest of Orynthia.

"I've given Commander Kasim three days to deport his Mworran envoy. Until then, we move by fact, not fear." Dmitri locked his gaze onto them all. "The forces outside us may be many, they may be strong, they may hold a power all their own… but they will never hold this in their clutches."

A fresh vitality warmed the lilac blooms beneath his eyes. "For this is *ours*. And I will not let you go."

CHAPTER TWENTY ONE

The figure's bootheels dug into the sacked grain, his eyeline coasting the slit window of Nyack Kasim's industrious byumbé. Beneath his threadbare hood, he spied into the past, both sinister and still.

It was the charged rumblings of Faraji that'd brought the figure to this place, one he'd deliberately circumvented during his nocturnal patrols. Most of them had been devoted to scouring the ridge of the canyon for threats to Alora's niece, threats not of this world but those manifested outside it.

Threats like himself.

Only recently had the figure descended into the skyward rows of the City Nest, anxious another creature had bypassed his avid watch and stalked Luscia into Faraji. While he'd exterminated the monstrosity that had attacked her in the plains, his instinct nagged, raising alarm that more had to exist.

Abominations were unmade and reborn, just as he'd unmade himself.

His own cursed rebirth would consume him in the end. Until then, his mistress's blood stalled the torment in his veins. His unmaking would not result in the rebirth he'd calculated—his coveted change into something new, something more like *her*.

Now, this terrible transformation had been discovered by another, and somewhere, these unnatural facilities were being replicated. By whom, the figure only had theories, theories fabricated around a society and generation to which he no longer belonged. Yet the one willing to do such things, to conduct their beastly operation at the expense of cross-caste innocents, was far more dangerous than the creatures he feared were being drawn to Alora's niece.

All these were misgivings he owed in report to his mistress.

Bent, he looked back into the vined trees where Amaranth tidied her lavender feathers among the cliffside. The hawk, his friend who'd communed with them both, paused under his battered stare. His withered gut wrenched. Her next message to Alora would be his worst.

The world was darkening to a shade he knew well but could not define, the same way it'd darkened twenty years ago.

The figure twitched uncomfortably atop the opportune pile of provisions that scaled the enormous byumbé. Well before her husband had been named commander of Korbin's forces, Cyra had once defined her home with Nyack as a prison, and the figure understood why. Aside from the stake-walled barricades, the compound was less resplendent than it was imposing, fortified with as many spear-toting warriors as there were stone replicas decking the restricted row.

The figure trusted Amaranth to alert him if one of those guards meandered into the sleepy servant's alley. Exit options here were limited at best, even for his elusive talents. It was no wonder Cyra clung so intimately to Bastiion. It'd become her haven.

In some ways, it'd become his haven too.

He was too close to them here, the ghosts of his past life, before he'd unmade it. Unlike his assignments in Bastiion, segregated by its spiraling towers and elitist chambers, or even the unending horizon of the plains or port towns, here the figure was forced to reconcile his ghosts in the flesh—and worse, what ventures they'd devised in his absence.

Balancing upon the grain store, the figure settled his shaded, bloodshot gaze over the daubed sill, waiting for an overtly masculine discourse to come near his slim vantage under the window. As the minutes passed, he wondered if the rumor throughout the City Nest was nothing more than drunken gossip amid the holiday chatter or, in the case of Darakai, a warrior's wishful thinking.

Under his cape, the figure turned his mauled shoulder away from the cutout, preparing to leap off the heap.

But it was then he heard it, Tar'tar spoken within the byumbé. The guttural barking was so unlike the smooth, full-bodied expression of the Darakaians, or the lilted staccato of the Pilarese. Its sound had scourged the Ilias coast for centuries—preceded the blackening of fields and the savage death of all who toiled them.

It was the sound of Mworra meeting with Nyack Kasim.

The figure swiveled atop the lumpy burlap, and his gloved, blistered fingers anchored against the sill. His parched eyes shut and reopened, testing if it was a hallucination. The deterioration of his body would meet his brain eventually, slowly eating his mind to the stem.

He'd prefer hallucination over the reality. But the men conversing inside the home of Darakai's chief warlord were corporeal and not the apparitions of the figure's afflicted memory. As Nyack, Korbin's most trusted confidant, paced across the great room, he saw that the chief warlord was not alone with the Mworrans.

They trailed his mighty step inside the massive pit house. Behind the three emaciated cannibals—a trio festooned in patched leathers and whittled bone—the robes of a shoto prime glided across the Andwelestone. They weren't the robes of any prime, but those of the crispest white, those worn only by the chancellor of the Shoto Collective.

The figure whipped around and breathed heavily, though he didn't need such air like he used to. A scale of dead skin flapped off his nostrils as he processed the unthinkable and fastened onto Amaranth nestled among the lush, coiled branches.

To be here in Darakai, Tetsu Naborū had to abandon his prestigious post as chancellor, an inarguably more prestigious post than the adopted role of haidren after the passing of his brother. He'd chosen this room rather than the commemorated libraries of Gakoshū, the very chambers Tetsu had vowed to control once he finally led the Collective.

But he'd left all that—for this.

Fearing what it meant, the figure returned to the window. The pristine fall of Tetsu's robes could be seen from the back, as well as the jaundice of his neck that Alora had mentioned. Yet another symptom of his pipe marrow dependence. Gnawing a boil over his lip, the figure embraced the pain, so minor compared to the decay in his chest.

He hadn't set eyes on Tetsu in over a decade, not so proximate as this. And he didn't wish to now.

The Mworrans argued brusquely, though the figure's interpretation was hollow. He'd no need to speak Tar'tar since the Shield Wars, and knowledge unused was knowledge unguarded.

Nyack strode forward. The same old sneer engraved his pocked face, which the figure wanted to claw off as he scraped the sill—for Cyra's sake… maybe his own.

"Explain it to them again!" He growled at Tetsu, statuesque before their cannibalistic enemy. "We mobilize when I send word. No sooner. My war will be declared by the council, one way or another, and when it is, they will be signaled. Mworra waits on *Darakai*—with more restraint, I hope, than for their next meal."

Tetsu's raven hair cocked at the warlord. *"Your* war, Nyack?"

His voice was timeless, as slick and twisted as the oiled loop bobbing his nape. The figure recoiled irrationally when Tetsu pivoted from Nyack and translated his chilling statement in Tar'tar.

The Mworrans bickered among themselves, their bony frames prodding each other in fierce debate. Angled toward the window was the most dominant. A row of sharp, filed teeth snagged the torchlight. Disconcertingly, the figure was reminded of the inhuman creatures being spawned and mutilated somewhere within the depths of the earth.

Yet they were entirely human, and entirely in the business of mutilation.

When their argument hushed, the dominant Mworran pricked his finger with his tooth and dragged it up the bulging veins of his upturned forearm. The smell of iron hit the figure's senses as the thick gore was drawn onto the Mworran's grayish hide. His two comrades did the same, illustrating their agreement before Nyack.

"I believe, Chief Warlord, you've secured an ally in Mworra."

Tetsu swirled in place, combing his fine, pointed beard with the silver nailpiece that decorated his forefinger. Perplexed by it, the figure recalled an older shield, in pewter or bronze, few shoto primes wore for hazardous experiments and procedures. But Tetsu's model was more sharply hooked and embellished than those occupational shields.

As the leader spoke, Tetsu dropped it from the hairs of his jaw and interpreted the Mworran's final claim. "It seems they agree to Darakai's terms."

Like flint-stricken iron, a flame sparked Nyack's countenance as he was armed with enough might to burn countless cities to ash. Proudly, Darakai's chief warlord unfolded his forearms over his dark torso, came to the Mworran lead, struck the cave dweller elbow to wrist in accord.

"Convey Darakai's respect to my new allies," Nyack ordered Tetsu, who, tensing, translated in a gruff, throaty sibilance. "And tell them I've arranged a fine dinner. By midnight, prisoners will be delivered to their camp—a change in execution order."

To this, the Mworrans collectively licked their barbarous chops, more mongrel than men.

"Return the way you came so none follow. And wait for my call… It *will* come."

When the Mworrans filed out of the room, the figure pushed off the sill, seeking the best method to observe their departure. He stretched for the flat roof of the byumbé and hoisted himself over top. The figure crept along the mortared beams and peeked off the side. Below, the trio whispered in the unoccupied alley, out of sight from the main promenade. Yet only the enemy had exited the chief warlord's abode.

Tetsu was still inside.

The figure returned to where the grain was stacked, but little sound, aside from the spit and crackle of a dying hearth, laced through the window. They'd switched rooms within the byumbé.

Prowling the perimeter, he listened intently. When a hiss tore from one of the vented slits, the figure plunked to the rooftop. His hood drooped over the edge, and he peeked through the narrow opening upside down.

In a room lined with weaponry, Nyack's wrist was in the firm grasp of the Pilarese chancellor. Trapping him, Tetsu venomously crooked his nailpiece along the rich onyx flesh of his fellow sil'haidren. As he dragged it, discomfort creased Nyack's forehead, wrinkling his scars. The figure could not see the wound, or why he endured it.

"The oath we have taken, Nyack." Tetsu hissed, tapping the silver claw. "Is part of you now. He says to restrain your hubris, before it destroys everything at stake."

Ripping his arm free, Nyack clasped his wrist. "Get out of my city, Naborū." A snarl buckled his entire manner as he bent toward Tetsu contentiously. "While I let you walk inside it."

"Restrain yourself, Nyack," Tetsu replied with a cunning smirk. "We are no longer who we were." His robes backed out of sight, though his silky hypnotic voice carried. "You and I are becoming so much more…"

The figure slung himself upright just as Nyack roared, and weaponry clattered when an object was smashed against the wall.

On the rooftop, the figure scurried to where Tetsu joined the Mworran cabal in the alley through an atypical, discreet passage out the farthest wall. He'd be unable to drop behind them without being seen. Trailing their path up in the defensive pickets around the compound would be even harder. The figure's legs propelled him onward, despite the risk of being sighted, worried what he might find if he did.

In a split-second decision, he knotted the corners of his weathered cloak around his beaten body and vaulted for the first angled stake, plastered into the abutting palisade. He swung across the rungs after Tetsu, as he and the Mworrans needled through the craggy lane. Ahead, their illicit party paused in front of a thicket of vinery over the cliffside.

The figure paused, anxiously suspended from a pair of stakes like a nocturnal primate.

In a confident sweep, Tetsu parted the vines and, after some struggle, wriggled through a fissure in the rock. The three cannibals entered the hidden tunnel after him with a fluid ease, adept traversers of their own winding mines in Calluc. Once they were out of the alley, the figure plunged to the stone path. He hugged the wall and darted after them.

His gloved fingertips shuffled among the bountiful vinery, seeking the gap they'd accessed. When he felt a depression through the leafing, the figure thrashed it aside.

As he slipped into the tunnel, Amaranth cawed from her post atop the palisade. Her lilac feathering was radiant in the moonlight. She would not join him into the earth. The hawk couldn't bear to be constrained. And as her liberator, who had freed her from her cage into this bleak existence, he would not dare confine her again.

In the tunnel, his vision was empty, save the sparse flicker of the single torch carried yards farther, into the deep.

Tracking it, the figure pursued them down a flight of twists and turns until the thin shaft widened to a cavern inside the mountain. Above a steep drop-off, firelight crawled up the interior of a vast cavern. Murals of shadow and light shifted across the expansive Andwelestone canopy. Over the ledge, the projected sienna shapes were indeterminate.

Scents of iron and malice blasted his chafed nostrils. Boiled marrow and fermented sap wafted from the belly of the cavity. And from the center of his aching bones, the figure was chilled.

He wedged behind a rock formation when the Mworrans strutted into the glow and toward the rim of the natural shelf. Through the stalagmites, the figure watched the leader crouch and clutch the steep rim near his calloused feet.

Opening his throat, the gaunt Mworran released his tongue and shrieked. His companions squatted low, mimicking his rallying cry. Panicked, the figure seized the rock spires when deafening howls erupted from the unseen depths and ricocheted throughout the cavern.

At the harrowing sound, the chancellor of the Shoto Collective slithered forward, his immaculate robes fluttering like a cape. With an almost imperceptible sputter, a twist contorted his jaundiced visage. Serpentine and sinister, it spanned the decades that'd separated them. Even from afar, the figure could see Tetsu was pleased. Ever the achiever, he'd wasted his youth trying to master those nearly conquered tics, but his tells were unchanged, stored in the angles of what now resembled a waxen mask.

And in the shrunken places the figure had long buried, this single, horrible tell birthed true and honest fear.

Oh Tetsu, he lamented. *What have you done?*

The ruckus echoed, and the group descended an ancient, plummeting stair. Writhing between the formations, the figure rounded the drop-off until the enormity of the cavern sprawled below.

The little vigor in the figure's heart thudded strenuously, beating through his ribcage.

It was worse than any rumor.

Crude forges smelted bubbling ore. Metal screamed as iron was sharpened. Shields were pounded in salute. Crowding the base of the cavity, over a thousand Mworran warriors were camped, baying for the three rejoining their ranks. And soaring above their bone-laden caucus, a familiar Pilarese hawk dove for the shoulder of a shoto prime—an almost identical creature both he and his Amaranth had bid farewell decades before.

Tetsu was in Darakai. Mworra was in Darakai.

And not that far away, so was Luscia.

Chapter Twenty Two
Luscia

Sweat streamed her spine. Tucked into the borrowed gunjas, her linsilk shift stuck to her like the flora she had darted through, amassing the early morning dew.

Luscia mopped the perspiration from her hairline as she stared down Kasim. The harness, soaked from his own fatigue, slung low around his trim hips. The lead rope snapped tautly as they circled the grassy mound in a predator's dance, Kasim's sharp exhales joining the symphonic trill ringing from the trees.

It was well past midnight. Past what classified as night at all, and the lack of sleep was catching up to them both. Functioning on partial rest for days on end had taken a clear toll on their vastly different frames. As a child of Boreal, Luscia could manage such taxation for a season, though it was far from preferable. How Kasim did was beyond her. Along with the common sense to end their standoff and go to bed.

They'd exhausted the evening on his blade training before switching focus to hand combat. A strip of dawn teased the horizon, but Kasim's unyielding grit endured, prolonging the vigorous sparring drill.

He'd thwarted at least a dozen of her offensive maneuvers. The thump of her enhanced Tiergan lineage pulsed commandingly in her ears. Luscia's irritation seeped from her pores; irritated she'd not managed to overtake him, a beast so breakable. He was tired, obviously more tired than Luscia. Yet when his heel drove into the soil, she knew Kasim held no intention of conceding.

Neither did she.

Noting the angle of his toes, she lowered, priming for his forceful assault. When Kasim sprung, Luscia dove after his legs. Hooking his shin with her foot, she jerked it back, but in a smooth somersault, Kasim leaped out of her hold. After landing on his soles, he kicked her square in the ribs. With a gasp, Luscia rolled aside, dodging his downward strike.

His fist smacked the earth. She snatched his arm and hoisted herself onto his back like a rider. Fastening her ankles around his constricted abdominals, Luscia slid an arm under his throat, locking the other over his shoulder. Her smile savage, she squeezed against his windpipe.

Oddly, Kasim did not buck or claw at the suffocation. Instead, he rose them both off the ground and, using their combined weight, flung backward and smashed Luscia into the soggy dirt. Rancor rivaled the ache that throbbed through Luscia's entire skeleton, assuredly bruised.

He'd accomplished that brutish trick twice now.

Off-guard, Kasim gagged and rubbed his neck. Luscia flung onto her feet and, with unbridled intensity, barreled right into him. With the might of a bull, she drove them off the squat knoll and onto the rocky bluff, gaining more traction. Backpedaling, Kasim sped their momentum, loosening her grip, and whipped his hips in a semicircle.

Thrown off, Luscia speared a punch, which Kasim dodged. He smirked wickedly, the cusp of daybreak brightening his crinkled juniper eyes. Catching her missed strike, he twisted her forearm behind her head, under his bristly chin. Hurriedly, she slithered her calf around his, preparing a flip, but sensing the move, Kasim jabbed her thigh with his knee, dismantling it.

He encased her arms in his. Before she could thrust her elbow anywhere that hurt, her wrist was seized and pegged between them. Her back rocked against the heaving of his chest.

A hot breeze lapped her sticky cheeks where his tired breath puffed out. "I know your body, Maji'maia." Kasim's grip clenched as she battled it, heating the muggy air that scarcely split their skins. "I've memorized it, uni. How it moves… how it reacts. You can't surprise me anymore."

Unsuccessfully, Luscia tried to hitch his leg a second time. Growling, she wiggled against his larger frame, a frame that could be his downfall. Luscia huffed through her nose and smashed her heel into the bones of his foot. Heaving his upper body in an arched crouch, she slung him over like a sack of rocks.

But Kasim did not let go.

He never did.

Landing on the pad of one foot, Kasim swerved. Hauled by her upper arms, Luscia was lurched onto the stone expanse. Atop the bluff, she pummeled him in the side, but he persisted, as ever, flipping her by the neckline flat onto her backside once more. Pebbles dug into her shoulder blades when she wrestled to intertwine her thighs around his corded bicep. Disrupting the tactic, he scooped one of her legs over the other. The cusp of his hipbone crushed her thigh. Luscia swung for his determined grimace, yet in a harried sweep, Kasim captured her hands and bound them with the slack roping.

Shocked by his clever trap, Luscia wrestled with the braided mane, angered she'd not thought of it first. He was creative, she admitted, and impetuous. And equally as conceited.

Which was why she couldn't let him win.

"Just yield already." He hovered over her, winded. His dark hair tumbled aside in a curtain of locs, blocking them from the waking sun. "You are out of surprises."

"And you're just full of them, aren't you?" Luscia gritted her teeth.

Tauntingly, he flashed a bright grin and brought his face close. The rust of his skin melded with the Andwelestone he pinned her against, like Kasim too had been fashioned from it. "I told you, Maji'maia, I know you too well."

Unwilling to accept that pompous notion, Luscia scrutinized their position, only to find that she was thoroughly stuck.

Her focus traversed his upper body to where, with their panting, the swell of her breast fanned him aggravatedly. As it rose and fell, she concluded there was one move Kasim would never anticipate.

Determinedly, Luscia elongated her neck. Kasim's ringed brow, expressive and distinct, compressed as she arched her back off the bluff, holding his disconcerted stare.

Then, to his outright bewilderment, Luscia pushed her lips against his velvet mouth.

Every aspect of Kasim stiffened, and those velvet lips steeled to stone. The arm pegging Luscia's legs against his thigh became a rod of iron. Pinched and strained, Kasim didn't draw away. His static heat radiated into her.

Instead of combusting like she'd anticipated, he had stilled.

Suspended there awkwardly, Luscia second-guessed her ploy. Trapped between the bluff and Kasim, she computed an exit to the human knot she'd been tied in. Squirming, Luscia tested the tautness of the lead rope restraining her hands. There was much more leeway than before. With fresh slack in the line, she calculated her options as her lips parted farther… guided gently, warmly, inquiringly.

And it was then Luscia realized she was being kissed.

Properly kissed.

By a Darakaian.

Her lashes flapped open when Kasim's body slackened. Giving into gravity's lure, his palm coasted her outer thigh and slithered over her hip, finding where the gunja pants cinched at her waist.

Kasim's fingers dug in as his mouth glided over hers in eager exploration. His lips wielded the hungry reluctance of a starved man bound to table manners. Luscia ignored the way his breathy famine heated her core. Ignored how his unshaven bristle roughed her chin when he teased her lower lip dangerously with his tongue. She ignored it all.

This was her ploy, not his.

Making quick work to unbind her hands, crammed between their slick abdomens, Luscia reminded herself that his obvious finesse was hardly the point of the exercise. Glistened in sweat, she'd anticipated the flavor of salt and brine and was unready for his emboldened correction. Rather, Kasim tasted of camphor and smoldered oak. Woodsy and resonant, his voyage was brushed with a spiced sweetness—a taste so pleasingly problematic, Luscia nearly regretted putting it to a stop.

Because she'd not come to the bluff to kiss Zaethan Kasim; she came to prevail.

The lead undone, Luscia dragged her knee coaxingly along his side.

She broke the embrace, pulling back to look Kasim in the eyes. Panting, his pupils, ringed in clover, danced over her mouth like he'd never seen it before, then darted upward.

Offering him her most satisfying smirk, Luscia winked and uppercut him in the jaw.

Full of force, her left strike followed. She crammed her legs under the disoriented Kasim, planting her soles against his broad chest. As his head swung back to center, Luscia rammed it with her skull, and with all the might she could muster, she booted him into the air. Kasim rocketed across the cliffside, her untied harness flailing after him. Slamming into a rock, scuffing his athletic physique along the way, he trundled to a halt.

Luscia scurried to stand, seeing the other haidren was flat and motionless. Anxiously, she wiped the excess perspiration off her neck and ran toward him. Soon enough, Kasim roused, and his aggravated groans joined the deafening drone of wildlife waking for dawn.

Kasim braced onto all fours and smacked the stone. Luscia prepared for one of his heated explosions; he was a very poor loser, after all. He spit, and red spattered the bluff. He reached into his mouth, checking his teeth, and sat back on his calves. With shuddering shoulders, Kasim gazed up at the splintered sky and laughed.

And he sat there, licking the blood from his flushed lips, laughing for minutes on end.

Puzzled, Luscia idled where she stood. She was unsure what decorum dictated for hazardous kissing.

"Are you…" she asked clumsily. "Are you all right?"

"Shtàka, that hurts." He tested his mandible, assessing the alignment. Then he chuckled some more. "Depths, I needed that."

Luscia stared at him incredulously. "Which part?"

His head lolled over his shoulder. "I needed all of it." Grinning, his teeth showed pink when he chortled, "Didn't you?"

She had to admit it was a gratifying sight, his flabbergasted face when she'd catapulted him like a boulder. He really had looked ridiculous, right up until the point she worried he might have been dead. And soon, the troubled lump choking all her recent angst and anxiety melted in her belly... because Luscia started laughing too.

Lungs quaking, she stumbled back on the knoll and fell into a mat of damp grass. She couldn't recall the last time she'd laughed so hard. Neither could Kasim, she guessed, watching him snigger even as he spit up more blood and finally stretched to his feet. With a sly grin, he scooped up the lead rope and began to coil it.

"Can we agree I've officially graduated from that thing?" Luscia called out, resting her sore limbs onto her side.

"I can agree it's officially a kakka-shtàka working hazard..."

A snort burst from Luscia's nose, reaping another chuckle from her tattered trainer.

It was bizarre how relaxed she'd become in just a matter of weeks. They'd developed an odd familiarity on this overlook, one that bypassed shyness or reservation because it hinged on necessary. In truth, she'd been touched by this man more than her own najjan, the individuals meant to protect and prepare her, those who ought to have pushed her beyond her fear.

And for that, Kasim remained her private conundrum. He was doing what they could not.

His taut chest bulged with each rotation of the rope, protruding the four prominent scars that rippled toward his navel. Again, her curiosity was piqued at their origin. Studying the lines, Luscia quieted. She observed Kasim at the edge of the overgrowth.

"I want to hear it," she announced, despite the hour, and pointed at his upper body. "Tell me how those came to be."

Kasim hiked his brow as he finished coiling the rope. His locs swayed when he tossed it atop the rest of his gear. "Another trade then, my tale for yours?"

Luscia's neck itched under her clump of half-knotted hair. She turned away, her regard raking over the canyon toward the northern vista. He would learn the truth sooner or later—some version of it. They all would in the end.

Hardening, she twisted toward him. "Tell me your story, Kasim."

He looked at her a moment, tugging on his sleeveless tunic. Leaving the buckskin unfastened, he squinted southeast and pointed behind her.

"See that ridgeline there?"

Rotating, Luscia nodded at the higher altitudes beyond Faraji.

"There's a pass leading up the Andweles. Kumo, my cousin, and I used to hunt there every summer when we were cubs, yeah? Maybe a half a day's hike to our favorite spot. We'd trap rabbit. Shoot wild fowl. Kumo speared a boar once, though it bushwhacked him a time or two... and I tracked my first doe." Wistfully, Kasim tore himself away from the view and plopped down beside Luscia on the knoll. Leg outspread, he twiddled with a blade of grass. "One year, the hunting dried up. The animals shied from the streams, abandoned their hovels and dens... The game had vacated an entire strip of range."

"Others started coming back to Làtoh Ché empty-handed and talk spread of angry spirits cursing the mountain. Signs from the ancestors. Hillman nonsense. But when some Yowekaon tradesmen spotted a rabid predator prowling the pass, there were no more excuses. Ano zà, not in my father's estimation." Kasim ripped the blade in two and flicked it aside. "I'd brought him nothing for months. To him, a hand unstained is a hand unworthy. So my father handed me a spear and told me to either come back with its head," he said flatly, "or to not come back at all."

Luscia felt herself gawking and hurriedly controlled her expression as he continued, speaking to the open.

"Nearly a week later, I staggered home," he said, a smirk toying the edge of his lips. "My scrawny chest filleted, drenched in blood, I hauled the head of that savage cat with more pride than most men know in a lifetime. *Kwihila rapiki mu jwona...* That was the first time I wrote over my fate. And it's how I know I can do it again."

At a loss for words, Luscia twisted, hearing the turf crunch as her lycran trotted out from the thicket. Beyond Aksel's bobbing tail, she traced Declan, leaning cross-armed against the knobby trunk of a faraway tree. Even in the distance, she sensed his calm, unrushed despite the earliest beams alighting the clouds.

She patted the ground, summoning Aksel between her and Kasim. Yawning, the hybrid plunked down, as Declan's outline disappeared into the tree line. Needing sleep of his own, the najjan likely assumed she'd soon join him at the trailhead. But instead, Luscia shifted her weight onto a palm and contemplated Kasim's second, as well as his noticeable fondness for nicknames.

"Is that why your beta, your cousin, calls you 'Ahoté'?"

With a grimace, Kasim scooted over to grant Aksel ample space; however, with a dissenting yowl, the brute pawed at him to stay.

"Restless bobcat." He scoffed. "Kumo says I 'took its spirit' or that I still roam the mountain—whatever kakk cubs spout when they're nine years old."

"Your father expelled you into the wilderness, alone, when you were only nine years old?" Luscia questioned, appalled by such a heartless act, one her own father would never even consider.

"Being younger than Kumo, I was eight," Kasim answered matter-of-factly. With a shrug, he added "but I came back. I always do."

She scratched behind Aksel's ear, her very own *champion of peace*. Her father's gift nuzzled into her touch, a gifting so unlike the marks Nyack Kasim had encouraged be left on his son. It was astounding, their differences in upbringing, yet here they sat, two haidrens on either side of an Orallach wolx, each for the aid of the other.

"Meh fyreon, but that's a truly dreadful story..." Sitting up, Luscia shook her head.

Kasim snickered, wrapping his arms about his knees. "I'd like to hear how yours is better."

"It's not."

His amusement trailed off as Luscia fixated on the bluff where the earth's fortitude plunged into nothing, the way her world had fallen asunder, its jagged shards scattered like the puffs of dandi wafting over the edge. Her fingers skimmed Aksel's back, the only being she'd permitted into that dark, empty place, however infrequently she allowed herself to go there. But Luscia owed Kasim the truth now; he'd earned as much. As with all their dealings, he'd fulfilled his part of the bargain first.

Luscia credited him that.

Gathering her wits, she mined for where to begin, having never told it from the start. In Boreal, those who knew the story behind the grisly carving down their haidren's neck knew so from those who'd witnessed the events that followed—who'd seen how a single scar had broken a treaty as pitilessly as the young woman who carried it.

She reached up and drew her hair more tightly, covering the disfigured flesh spread ear to clavicle. "Do you know the reason Orynthia outlawed trade with Tevaár?" she asked.

Luscia sensed the confusion in his pause. "Ano."

"Well, you're looking at her." Luscia lifted her chin, concentrating on the sharpest point of the rock ledge. "Before the Tavish embargo, Boreal would trade with Tevaár when the trees sprouted their earliest leaves and again when the leaves changed form, right before the autumn equinox.

"This trade primarily occurred in Ödetha, our northmost clan and port village. But three years ago, Boreal extended an invitation to host the Tavish in Roüwen." Her voice grew bitter and gruff from a drying throat. "The firstborn son of King Harvak had come of age, and the clan elders, eager to secure long-term contracts for our exports, thought he might relish the... beauty... of our legendary citadel, defended among the stars."

She would never agree with their decision, however well intended. The Tavish were known for their ruthlessness, most notably the way they treated their women. No contract was worth risking Boreal's own.

And yet, the elders had still placed her beside him—asked her to welcome him at her father's table. They'd expected her to listen and nod, under the hope that his nature would not escape his being. Luscia could still remember the way he ate... the way he'd lick the grease off his fingers while leering at her as if through her clothing. And like a good girl, she'd swallowed her revulsion, her distrust, and smiled.

Luscia wasn't smiling now.

"As one expects, Prince Darcain was received with a regal feast after his voyage from Sovllim. His party was hosted among the highest families of Roüwen, a warm *courtesy* from the elders. And the prince..."

Luscia's nose flared, hating the way her mouth trembled. "Was hosted in mine. In fact, he was right down the hall."

Kasim was mute, making no attempt to interrupt, though Luscia probably wouldn't have noticed if he did. Absently, she wrung her wrists in her lap, rubbing off the rough memory of Darcain's calloused grip. Despite their terror, Luscia's demons didn't have red eyes or decaying corpses, as Marek had eluded outside Rian.

"On the third night, the prince entered my room. He covered my mouth and took my mother's blade from my bedside table." She ground her teeth, bracing her emotion. "And with *Ferocity* holding back my screams, he did what he'd come to do."

Unlike Marek, Luscia had learned that the vilest demons were completely human.

Acid scathed her throat, strained against her mother's blade. Luxiron sizzled. The smell of her own burning flesh engulfed her nostrils, covering the cloying reek of mead and urine. A new agony decayed her insides as her hair was sniffed, hiding the pain that thundered her hip where she'd been struck. Where she'd been fondled. Pressed. Prodded.

The weight was overpowering. Through tears, her vision blurred, gazing up at the rafters as her head thumped the headboard repeatedly. Numb. Everything was numb—

Enough. She stopped herself.

He'd had enough.

Luscia stilled and breathed deeply. She felt for Aksel's snout and caressed it like the day she'd first held him in her despondent arms.

"My brother heard the disturbance and shrieked for my father. I was newly fifteen. Phalen even younger."

Her heart turmoiled for him, having to carry that vision of her for the rest of his life. He'd saved her that night, her sooty-cheeked baby brother, but at the cost of his innocence. In many ways, his childhood had died with hers. Although, that was the scale of evil. It cut wide and spared none, leaving her father, the widowed Clann Darragh, to tend wounds he could never unsee.

"Harvak's heir was shipped back to Sovllim, his people banished from future trade with Boreal and therefore Orynthia, though not before paying some recompense for his crime." Luscia's posture unclenched incrementally, recounting Darcain's punishment. "My father gave him a thief's mercy and cut off his right hand—another courtesy of the elders, for he'd planned to remove a different extremity. Months later, with his blessing and my mother's consort daggers, I abandoned girlhood for the Isle of Viridis. And there I grew into a woman of the najjan."

Luscia heaved an exhale. Glancing over, she found Kasim staring at her intently.

Cradling one fist in the other, he slowly faced forward. A tendon flexed through his jawline as a flock took flight across the canyon, squawking to their heavy silence.

Finally, he murmured, "I'd take it back if I could—what happened in Bastiion."

His shoulders sank under her stunned scrutiny. Darakaians didn't take back their actions, and yet crossing that line disturbed him enough to wish he could. Luscia saw the guilt bowing Kasim's head forward, guilt she had never expected him to harbor.

"I meant what I said in my apartment. You were forgiven nonetheless."

"A benevolence of your part," he gingerly acknowledged. He

winced, and his tongue probed a cut on his lip. "Darakai view scars as the narrators of the soul, storytellers in our skin… some beautiful, some ugly."

Kasim flexed his hand.

Luscia wondered what else was written on his body, for the of worst hurts never saw the surface.

"My aunt used to tell me, '*Chombà ano'ruko yon namàa tswé.* The pot is not named by the tool that shapes it.'"

"Who knew Darakaians were so poetic," she said dryly.

"Our marks don't define us, Maji'maia, but good or bad, they bear meaning."

"Regardless of what it means, this scar is hideous," Luscia replied, fiddling with the ashen tendrils that framed it, "and it will remain that way until my end of days."

In her periphery, Kasim's head shook. "Kàchà kocho. Doesn't mean you should hide it. That scar is a symbol. A message to the world."

Affronted, Luscia wheeled her face aside. "A symbol that men can steal whatever they want?"

"A symbol that you cannot be stolen." Kasim met her eyes intensely. "Can't take what must be freely given." A quiet fury strained his words, and he did not look away. "Fates help the next man who tries."

"You don't believe in the Fates," Luscia stated.

"I do not."

Hesitantly, Kasim elevated off the knoll and balanced over Aksel. He carefully skirted the tangles back from her throat, skimming them down her shoulder with unaccustomed tenderness. And with stalled breath, Luscia let him. He held it off her neck like a curtain while his thumb delicately brushed the uneven tissue.

Neither moved, except for the stroke of his thumb and the mounting beat of her veins.

"It's not hideous," Kasim whispered, "for the record."

"Tadöm."

Unexpectedly, his hand withdrew, and he again said brusquely, "You shouldn't hide it."

Luscia blinked multiple times, angling back as Kasim readjusted agitatedly. The sun half breeched the distant ridge, dousing him in a citrus glow. His handsome features were pinched for some reason. However, he remained seated, beside she and the lycran.

Her eyes narrowed, rattled by how long it took for her pulse to normalize.

"You are not who you first seemed," she asserted.

Kasim responded to the dawn rather than Luscia. "The same could be said of you, Maji'maia."

"You no longer think I'm a witch?"

"Oh, uni, you're definitely a witch… but I'm starting to think you might not be my enemy."

"You made slow work of that revelation."

"My best work is slow." Kasim roguishly grinned. "So I'm told."

Luscia heard her pulse again, pesky thing, and looked instead at the sleeping wolx, focusing on how badly he needed a bath.

"Our time has run its course, Lord Darakai." She motioned toward the sky and rose. "We'll start with the blades tomorrow."

Kasim did not get up.

His mouth creased as he stated, "I learned Wekesa skipped the festival to train. He will announce his challenge any day now."

"You will defeat him," Luscia said in assurance, offering him an arm up. "I'll make sure of it."

His vibrant gaze, full of devilish determination, traveled up her pale outstretched arm, and without any indecision, he took it.

He hauled himself up gracefully. "Until tomorrow," he replied, releasing her.

Turning to gather his things, he suddenly pivoted backward. Stopping when their torsos were barely apart, he lowered his face toward Luscia's scar. Kasim's mouth skirted the tip of her ear, just above its origin, though there was no one to overhear his whisper.

The memory of toasted camphor prickled her lips when he drew away, leaving Luscia standing barefoot on the knoll.

Breathless, she watched Kasim's slim-hipped figure saunter off, while in her ears echoed the most arresting statement she'd ever been told.

"Luscia, even in hiding you cannot be unseen."

CHAPTER TWENTY THREE
LUSCIA

L uscia hauled her gear off with surly vigor, cursing the muggy Andwele drizzle as crossly as her own trifling thoughts.

The rain pecked her forehead. She ignored Kasim as she departed from him on the bluff, just like the lycran and najjani guard at the edge of the thicket. Distractedly, Luscia thrust the bundle of luxiron straight into Declan's barreled chest and trudged through the tangle of mossy trees by her lonesome.

Luscia rattled her head in walking, as if she could dislodge the sound of his voice where it still lingered provocatively in her ear.

The sun had risen and set, but Kasim's whisper remained. He'd said her name.

Hushed and unhurried, he'd permitted those willfully unspoken syllables to leave his barbarous tongue. It opposed the compilation of monikers the Darakaian haidren so often preferred, a rather tender anomaly she might have imagined, for Kasim hadn't said it since.

Thus, marching through the sodden muck, she was saddled with a more vexing anomaly altogether, felt in the heaviness of her limbs when she smacked aside the fat waterlogged leaves curtaining her path. The desire was so intrinsically preposterous, it defied every ounce of logic she harbored.

Hers was just a name. And Luscia longed to hear him say it again.

She traipsed down the slippery unmarked trail leading to the City Nest, irked that something as trivial as that could muddy her already questionable association with the haidren to Darakai. How uttered in his rich, smoky tenor, one name had summoned a taste that ought to have dissipated with the contest it won.

Even now, soaked in sweet rain, his remnant flavor tingled Luscia's lips with maddening ease. Well into their training that stormy morning, that lingering taste dragged Luscia's reflex and stalled her defense. This was the counterproductive consequence of her finally besting him, exhibited in the shredded seem of her borrowed gunjas where the fabric flapped miserably off her scraped thigh.

Submit emotion to reason. Luscia recited Alora's consistent advice. *Emotion is capricious, but reason secure.*

It was reason that cautioned Luscia to remember how precarious her ties to Kasim already were.

How scathingly the rest of her men would respond if they ever learned that she'd aligned with an agent of Darakai... She had jeopardized the integrity of their sacred luxiron to sharpen him for some territorial challenge. She'd leaned on him, confided in him... all to hone the deficient skillset fostered from her najjan's overprotection.

It was reason that declared a haidren's primary pursuit was the insurance of her people, not her emotion. The pursuit demanded her stridence, above any personal want, for the honor of Boreal.

For devotion to Aniell.

Besides, Luscia considered, grabbing onto the knobby branches in her slick descent, it was a fragment of personal wanting that had hindered her all evening. Were she to creak ajar the gate to these misplaced attractions, it was Luscia who would become the mediocre opponent, while Kasim evolved into a greatness all his own at her expense.

Luscia was called to be many things in her lifetime... but not a single one was mediocre.

Annoyed, she kicked the verdant scrub across the path with her upturned boot. Aksel bolted merrily through the downpour under the upshot of twigs and mildew, slamming Luscia against a throng of moss-covered rocks and landing her flat on her behind. She would have yelled at the wolx were it the first time she'd found herself in that position that night.

Luscia let the sludge soak into the material, with the rest of her failure staining her back.

Unhurriedly, Declan plodded down the trail, lugging the sack of weaponry over his shoulder. Her fingers smeared mud along her hairline, pushing it aside as she watched him approach. The eldest of her guard gracefully carved his way through the rainfall. Droplets collected on his coarse beard, its blazing color muted in the moonlight.

She expected Declan to amble on, as Luscia was more than content to berate herself upon the little stump a while longer.

But the sturdy najjan parked in front of her bent head and proffered his hand. She stared at its creases and calluses, at the abundant freckles of one she'd betrayed, in many ways, yet who stayed by her side regardless. A groan escaped her compressed lips when she accepted his help to stand. Luscia's hand in his, Declan steadied her resumed hike.

They advanced onward like that the entire way to Faraji's metropolis.

Eventually, Declan spoke, cutting through the shrill vibrato that buzzed through the dense canopy. "He's changed the way you move. Your impulse is not the same it once was."

Luscia's cheeks burned as her chin dropped toward her partly buttoned linsilk jerkin, wanting to duck behind the stiff navy collar.

Of course he, an elite warrior of the najjan, would detect the effects of Kasim's influence. She knew Declan broke from his post to survey them periodically. And what else did he ever see but his haidren, his *Great Sister*, entangled with Boreal's centuries-old adversary.

Perhaps he'd witnessed her humiliating setback today, triggered by her foolish doublemindedness. Luscia eyed Aksel at the base of the rugged path.

"Meh fyreon," she said, grimly apologizing to the seasoned warrior. "I know my choices have caused unmitigated disappointment—"

Her arm was tugged abruptly aside.

"Ock!" Declan cradled her hand against his studded leathers, over his heart. Then, elevating her fingers as they strolled, he inclined his rumpled forehead to their joined touch. "Ana'Sere, show me my disappointment. I cannot find it. Can you?"

Her eyes widened. Over the last half hour, she'd felt no inclination to recoil. While she'd been in the care of her trusted najjan, her mind had spun and soured, never once concerned about their prolonged contact. Just six months ago, prior to Kasim's unconventional intervention, Luscia would have withdrawn, shielding her skin from the barest of brushes, even from the supportive hand of her favorite protector.

Before Kasim, Luscia would have ordered Declan away.

"Niit, brödre," she replied, mystified. "I don't find it either."

They made it to her byumbé before the sparks of sunrise awoke the neighbors and, most importantly, the remainder of her guard.

Birds chirped along the otherwise quiet row, still in its slumber, as Luscia, Declan, and her lycran climbed the Andwelestone stair to the rooftop hatch. Atop the platform, built into the northmost face of the canyon, Faraji's crude elegance was screened beneath a hazy cloud. Fog from the recent rainstorm blanketed the massive bowl. Over the City Nest, a subtle crescent of colors arced, the natural prism casting a blessing on the roughhewn warrior nation.

Soaking in the view, Luscia paused, her attention arrowing on a lavender glint soaring through the mounting daylight. Immediately, she halted on the stoop.

"Take Aksel inside and wake Creyvan for his watch," Luscia instructed Declan evenly, her gaze fixed on the bird.

Not just any bird. A hawk.

Its feathering was foreign to this land, and to most others this side of the Ilias, but its duty was unmistakable. The rare messenger hawk flew with purpose, dressed in extraordinary hues she'd only ever seen dispatched by her aunt's right hand. Luscia stared intently as it dove into the fog and vanished.

Alora's contacts were rooted across the realm, covert in places and positions. She knew her aunt exchanged correspondence with informants from the farthest corners of Orynthia. And yet Luscia's temples stung forebodingly. Amid a torrential bounty of threats to her king and the Accords, a hawk just like Alora's occupied the same city as Darakai's conspiring chief warlord.

Troubled, Luscia folded her begrimed arms where she stood on the stair.

Were it Amaranth darting through the skies, then in her emeritus role as sil'haidren, Alora was concealing more than Luscia had already assumed. But if the hawk was sent by another, likely someone of substantial means and unmitigated influence, like a certain Pilarese chancellor, then Nyack Kasim's reach, and probable collusion, spanned wider than any of them had imagined.

Neither prospect calmed her anxious heartbeat, thudding inside her chest, for neither prospect was one she could change.

When Luscia turned toward the hatch entry, something scuffed the gravel around the chiseled side of the byumbé. Attuning her Tiergan ears, she heard their breathing, puffing in and out within the dusky gloom.

"This will go much faster once you reveal yourself," Luscia stated to the unseen.

After a strained pause, a shapely woman crept out from under a downy tumble of flowering vine and into the morning. Bountiful curls were knotted down either side of her teak face. It was supple with the radiance of Southern lineage, rather than an obsessive use of high-priced cremes, like those prized by Unitarian women at court. Either his comrade or courtesan, though probably both, Wekesa's woman prowled toward the base of the stairway.

Heavily lashed, her feline glare shone just as predatorily as it had during their first encounter in the foothills. It scavenged Luscia's sullied attire, and she screwed her plump mouth when she sighted the torn gunja pants.

"The city whispers about you... Uni, the terrifying witch of the mists," she said mockingly, snatching her taut midriff in either hand. "But all I see is a small, bloodless rodent, skittering about, pathetic and plain."

Luscia released an unfriendly chuckle, hardly amused, and measuredly descended the steps until their eyes were level.

"Is that all you've come to say?" she asked, hooking a brow.

The woman's lip curled toward her nose in an ugly sneer. "Stay away from Zaethan. These little trysts—your dirty *papyon kakk*—will doom his kwihila."

Inching forward, Luscia responded to Wekesa's consort. "For such limited information on the subject, you've a whole lot of opinion."

"It was me they fought over the first time. Me, yeah? Who spent the night with him before that challenge. *Me* who made him moan..." Her head swayed with serpentine smugness. "And *me*, meme qondai, who knows how it can play again, with you out of the way."

Her jaw clamped, Luscia told herself that criticality of Wekesa's impending loss had little to do with Kasim's personal history with the woman. And that a short-sighted ex-lover, with a fondness for very small shirts, wouldn't be able to understand how this challenge affected the poor, the maligned, and the cross-caste littering Bastiion proper.

It was they who mattered. Not the buxom twit on Luscia's doorstep.

"I think your allegiance is as confused as your bedsheets." Luscia indicated the promenade. "It's time you returned home to them."

In her periphery, Luscia caught someone approaching down the row, svelte and slick-skulled. She recognized the newcomer as Kasim's third, Zahra, toting a folded set of Darakaian textiles. Slowing, Zahra neared the heated exchange outside Luscia's assigned byumbé.

Unaware of Zahra, Wekesa's woman did not budge.

"Stay away from him!" Her ringed forefinger jabbed Luscia in the chest, which she looked down upon as the woman heaved with blooming anger. "Now they will smell your filth on Zaeth before he ever faces my jwona rapiki. The prydes will spit out an alpha who rolls in the mud with a y'siti hog over one of his own!" The stunning bronze choker about her tall neck caught the sun when she lurched even closer, clattering her bands of turquoise. "You should have minded my warning tucked under your bed!"

"You made the hex doll?"

In anger, Luscia's vision flickered with glimpses of the *Other*. Threads of lumin licked and crackled the edges of her scope, blending the veil between worlds, as, dubiously, the woman started to gape, stepping backward.

The reflection of an ageless Tiergan eye sparkled in the woman's dilating pupils when Luscia threatened her savagely. "I ought to show you how very little I'm like a mouse or a *hog…*"

The air bristled between their opposing faces, charged with a mysterious static.

Luscia barely noticed when Zahra jumped to intervene. Fabric tucked under an arm, she appeared behind Kasim's ex-lover, dispersing the static as if it'd never existed.

"Better if I do it, Maji'maia," Zahra said by way of greeting, clamping down on her sleek shoulder. "Owàamo, Kehari—"

Zahra reeled back and socked the woman right in the nose, snapping bone by the harsh *crack* that ricocheted down the vacant promenade. After a teetered stagger, Kehari fell to the ground. Her honey-brown eyes boiled when she cupped her nose in disbelief at Kasim's third.

Blood swam between her fingers, trickling over her prominent neckpiece. Bending, Zahra forcefully grabbed Kehari's slick chin in one hand, jerking her neck wide. She flicked one of the turquoise bands disdainfully, dabbed a thumb in the dripping carnage, and smeared the blood barbarically over Kehari's forehead.

The woman hissed, fighting Zahra's hold. "You'll soon pay for this."

Patting her puckishly on the cheek, Zahra let her go and shrugged. "Kàchà kocho."

Kehari scrabbled upright, pinching her broken nose. Her glare speared Zahra, then Luscia at the base of the stair. Showing her teeth, she spat on the walkway and started to retreat, only exposing her back when the abutting byumbés obstructed her from view.

"You didn't have to do that..." Luscia said while Zahra inspected her torn knuckles.

Some faded, a few fresh, the tattoos decorating her scalp turned in the light as Kasim's third shook her head.

"Females like Kehari are a plague to men but a cancer to women. Eh, it was a long time coming." Zahra grunted, but mirth coaxed her characteristically downcurved mouth. "Her pryde answers to mine—for now. So I seized my chance." She licked blood off her fist and, returning for the stair, dumped the cloth into Luscia's care as originally intended. "Dhalili says you owe her two pairs for the one, calls it interest."

Luscia squeezed the new pair of gunjas. "Fair enough. Zullee," she cordially added in Andwele.

Arms crossing, Zahra clutched her muscular biceps as she angled back, sizing up the riddle of dirt and grim staining Luscia's clothing. Her tongue prodded her cheek in thought.

"I will give you some local advice, yeah?" Zahra told her. Unpredictably, her dark fingers flitted over Luscia's brow. "Don't resort to that Boreali kakk here. Kehari is right... It will hurt his kwihila much more than yours. Shàla'maiamo, Maji'maia."

She held Dhalili's donated pants as Zahra left, the warrior plucking a hucklebuckle fruit from one of the trees as she strolled down the waking promenade.

Luscia needed another dose of Alora's tonic, and soon.

These involuntary breaches of the Sight were becoming more regular when the nature of its manifestation was anything but. Her aunt's modifications kept most of the pain at bay, and even some of the whispers. She'd not seen the harbinger thread since the creature had attacked her tent in Rian. However, Luscia couldn't help her eerie panic that the lumin was battling the tonic's defense, as if the *Other* itself meant to consume her entirely, body and soul. Otherwise…

I'm not going mad, Luscia thought fiercely. *I'm not like her.*

Distressed in more ways than one, she opened the hatch, to the protest of her exhausted limbs, and plunged into her byumbé. Another anxiety fluttered her middle as she lowered down the cramped stairwell. Alighted by the crack of daybreak above, an upturned boot was propped against the russet stone, blocking her descent.

His sheepskin breeches creased, and Marek tightened his folded forearms at her arrival. Half-tucked, a linsilk shirt spilled over his belt clumsily, like he'd dressed in a rush. Undone, his hair flanked his jaw, as hard and chiseled as the Southern dwelling they occupied.

"Declan tells me you were out walking till dawn." Marek glowered at the wall. "But what kind of walk requires a whole luxiron armory, Luscia?" Pointedly, the captaen brought a fisted lumilore to his lips, setting the stairwell aglow. He twisted, looking through his crimson locks at her disheveled display. "The kind of walks you used to take in Bastiion… behind our backs?"

Luscia bridled her resentment. She was not a child caught sneaking after hours, nor was Marek a parent—or her superior for that matter.

Below her septum, the luxiron solrahs heated and abated with her riled skin. "The kind that got us stuck in a rainstorm, Captaen."

"Well, maybe now you can take a *walk* to your room and address the man who's been passed out on your bed all night," Marek snapped, his voice low.

Luscia's brow scrunched. "Who—"

His leg dropped curtly, and he motioned for her to pass. "That would be the king."

Without pause, she whipped by Marek and into the common space. She'd have to confront his dictatorial comportment later, preferably before he stepped further out of line, for their history assured it would happen again. Despite Marek's repeated attempts to push her tolerance, he was not Luscia's priority.

And never would be.

Before the stucco hearth, Aksel gnawed happily on the carcass a defeathered fowl, which he must had pilfered from their bubbling breakfast pot. Steering around the lycran's gnarls, Luscia nearly skidded into her door, left slightly agape.

She listened through the crack at the subdued snores within. Gently, she creaked it open, inched inside, and slid the partition closed behind her.

Asleep on a mound of pillows, Dmitri was slumped over the arm of his long brocade coat. His sallow eyelids stirred, lashes fanning the vermillion and teal threading. As he was still in sitting position, his knee was tucked into his slender chest, indicating he'd not intended to be found that way. She wondered how long he'd dozed—if Marek exaggerated or if her king had putzed around her byumbé for hours awaiting her return, ultimately succumbing to his lethargy.

He must have been trapped in a dream. Dmitri's breath hitched while she stood there, and his hand fell off his knee. Lying in his loosened grasp was an empty vial. Its residue had long dried over the interior of the glass. He'd taken the elixir days ago.

He was taking it more often; Dmitri was worsening.

And he'd not told her.

Kneeling, Luscia wavered near his mouth, slanted open as Phalen had always slept, though Dmitri did not drool like her brother. She withheld her exhale, attuning to his docile wheeze. Most probably couldn't hear it. But there it was, a deep listlessness in his lungs.

Silently, as not to disturb him, Luscia rocked on her heels and moved to her apothecary, situated on a low table off the floor. She tucked her legs, and her fingers felt under the wood where she'd hidden the skeletal key. Prevented from concealing it beneath her clothing in Darakai, where temperatures required thinner, sheer textiles, she'd been forced to keep it off her person most days. Upon detecting the sharpened point, Luscia retrieved her aunt's key and inserted it into the bone lock of her Viridi chest.

The box opened with treasured scents of the highlands. Pulling clean vials, Luscia commenced her aunt's memorized routine. She plucked a barb of ennus and flattened the chalky thorn using a paring knife. She repressed a sneeze when with the antlered handle, she ground it into a cloud of pale powder. Next, she combined the powder and nixberry oil in a beaker over an adjacent candle, which was already lit. With precision, she swirled in the eüpharsis at a tempered pace, eyeing the gelatinous extract until it formed a beryl serum.

Luscia raised her fingertip and punctured it with the rust-hewn key.

Five drops of her blood. No more. No less.

"It smells like moldy stew in here."

Rousing, Dmitri blinked sleepily as Luscia squeezed the final droplet into his elixir. She heard him swallow—hard—witnessing the final ingredient mingle inside the beaker. Putting pressure on her minor injury, Luscia swished the mixture as it turned plum. He said nothing while she poured a set of fresh vials.

"I apologize." Dmitri slurred, rubbing his forehead. "I'd not meant to commandeer your quarters."

He attempted to rise, but Luscia pounced to her feet, bringing a dose of elixir to him on her bed. "Niit. I should have been here to receive you. Take this." Guiding the vial to his lips, she helped him drink the temporary remedy. Even drowsy, Dmitri shuddered at the flavor. "Where are your guards?" she asked.

"Guards," he said mockingly, stretching his face in disgust. "They are spies for Commander Kasim. I ordered them back to his compound after I ended up here. What better protection is there than the najjan?"

"Meh fyreon." She huffed, pressing the back of her hand against his forehead. It was too warm for her liking. "You needed this hours ago."

"Life is lived outside the Quadren, Luscia, not at my beck and call. This wasn't my initial destination tonight either. My actions were capricious. You couldn't have anticipated my coming."

Seated on the edge of the mattress, she smiled at the irony, given how her own evening had started.

"Alora believes capriciousness is the enemy of reason. And that too often," Luscia noted, clasping her hands, "I am its advocate."

"Ah," he said weakly into the pillow. "But was it not capriciousness that led me to what I needed all along?"

Sluggishly, Dmitri offered Luscia his emptied vial. She stared at the fluid rimming the base, unable to say what she really thought. What he needed still led to his demise. And unable to save him, she advocated it. The drawn-out death of perhaps Orynthia's sagest king—that was the real enemy of reason.

She searched his half-lidded eyes. Red vessels reached through his whites for the circles of gold, alighting the forest of his irises. Luscia's mouth flattened.

His consumption was spreading.

"You've been downplaying your symptoms," she stated plainly.

Dmitri sighed and jostled up off the bedding, bringing his shoulder against hers. "To myself more than anyone. There is such fatigue. I'm tired… all the time. I feel like my bones are slumbering in my skin, yet I'm terrified to sleep." His chest heaved, and again she heard the faint wheeze. "At first, the heat helped the chills, but now… There are times everything goes cold when I least expect it."

He flexed his fingers on his thigh. Luscia found them with hers.

"I will write to Alora. We will make adjustments," she said resolutely. "This is not the end. Not yet."

Sadness bowed his thin frame forward, tottering and unbalanced on the mattress. "It can't be the end when we've still so much to accomplish. I don't want to leave them this way."

Luscia wound her face aside so he would not see her tears. Gritting her teeth, she controlled her emotion. The realm was on the verge of a duplicitous, unsanctioned war. The nobility, turning into a den of thieves and connivers. The Houses, splintered and hungry for power.

She too could not be left this way.

"To accomplish much, you need much sleep," she ordered lightly.

Dmitri wriggled his fingers, encouraging more circulation. "Perhaps I could lie here a while longer."

Mutely, Luscia moved over, presenting plenty of room for him to recline.

As Phalen would when he was a little boy, Dmitri folded himself on his side and shyly rested his head in Luscia's lap. A weight seemed to slip off him as he did, sinking into the blankets without much of a fight. Entangled in his waves, she stroked them absently as her mother had once done through Luscia's.

"Luscia," Dmitri murmured, all but unconscious. "Make sure I wake up."

Her skull slunk back against the wall with her spine as he was swept into a peaceful rhythm. She was nearly asleep herself when he coughed, and the wheezing returned even louder.

Praying to Aniell, Luscia unclenched and let her tears come.

Chapter Twenty Four
Zaethan

Owàa scorched their backs. Zaethan kicked Hellion to surge ahead of his twin toward the canyon rim.

Dmitri had chosen the hottest day for a race across the ridgeline, and despite the sweltering oppression that soaked his buckskin tunic to his spine, Zaethan had no intention of letting the eager king prevail.

He never did, not even when they were competitive cubs racing his friend's ponies, confined to the royal lawns in Bastiion.

Dmitri rarely won those boyhood contests, always selecting a steed with his heart rather than his eyes. But Harmonia, his gifted Andwele mare, was neither slight nor senior, and in the power of her haunches, she tested Hellion's own.

Digging his weight into the left stirrup, Zaethan lurched around as Dmitri tore through the sun-soaked brush, gaining on them. Boosted off his saddle, he sprinted his steely mare at a full gallop. Dmitri's satin vest flapped wildly when he jumped Harmonia over a boulder, running her parallel with the stallion. Zaethan clenched his reins, fueled by his friend's unusual intensity.

He rocked with Hellion as they leaped across a stream that fed the falls. Hooves chucked the dirt when they both landed on the other side, and Zaethan glanced aside. Dmitri's teeth swallowed his bottom lip as he aimed Harmonia for the twisted fig tree overlooking the cliff edge.

"Rhaolé!" Zaethan yelled for Hellion to speed his stride as sweat dripped into his silvery mane. "Rhaolé ono!"

Dmitri's unrestrained laughter rang out when, beneath him, Harmonia would not relent to her brother. Zaethan had not heard the sound in so long, he'd nearly forgotten the depth of its fullness. Her legs picked up, unburdened by her lighter rider, and tore past Hellion, putting a gap between their gaits.

Dmitri's fingertips trailed the underside of the branches before Zaethan even could raise an arm.

Plump figs bumbled the top of his head as he trotted Hellion into the well-deserved shade. His twin Andwele cockily blew dark hairs off her gray muzzle, earning a proud pat from the victorious king as he grinned and looked out over the natural fortress.

"This was sorely overdue." Dmitri panted, rubbing her neck to withers. "As was the win."

Swabbing his hairline, Zaethan scoffed. "Well, that Andwele isn't one of your lumpy old ponies."

"Like me, it was the lumpy ones who had something to prove." Dmitri's cheek dimpled as he reached up and tore a fig, and he bit into the violet flesh. The saddle groaned when he sank back, contented.

At high noon, Owàa flew bright and ferocious against his shackles. Sunlight heated them through the wide leaves overhead, but Dmitri didn't seem to mind, not even when his thumb swiped the perspiration beneath his nose.

Zaethan didn't mind it either, as he desperately needed the distraction. Huffing, he stared across the canyon, from the opposite rim of the bluff that hosted his midnight drills with a certain witch. Their evenings were becoming unrecognizable, and so was she.

So were her stories.

Every night Zaethan hiked that same trail, anticipating what awaited him at the top, and every morning, he left it more guarded than when he arrived.

She was a thorn in his boot, he'd decided, a temporary nuisance to which he'd grown acutely aware. Zaethan had kissed many women and had kissed them well. One infuriating highlander couldn't be that different than the others, nor was it any tribute to her that he'd made it such an enjoyable experience for them both.

And yet…

His talented tongue toyed his lip in thought.

"Father would have loved to see all this again."

Zaethan clamped his mouth irritably and peered over as Dmitri's chewing slowed.

"He used to talk about these massive falls plunging into Faraji… dreamed about them, well after the war. The harder this gets… the more I can't stop missing him," he admitted with a loaded sigh and rested the half-eaten fig against the starry, petrified byrnnzite pommel. "And you. I miss you too, Zaeth."

Scratching his bristle, having not shaved in days, Zaethan cocked a brow at his friend. "I've been right here, by your side."

"I know you cared for him too. Since his passing, you've been... distant... to say the least. I can't help but think there's a reason that this"—Dmitri motioned toward their horses—"is so overdue. Just last night, I ambled like an absolute ninny around your byumbé just wanting to talk to my friend—to my brother. But you weren't there. You haven't been for a while."

It was difficult for Zaethan to take a full breath, looking into Dmitri's disheartened gaze. First with Ambrose, then his risky dealings with Boreal's haidren, he'd hidden so much after the solstice. He didn't realize the wedge it'd planted between them. Guilt pressed his lungs, as the vision of his own hand pounding a stake into dead-man sands came and left with the breeze. Zaethan's conscience bore things Dmitri would never accept or understand.

For the first time since Bastiion, Zaethan found himself wishing for one more night with Chenoa, the only one who made his memories disappear into pleasing oblivion. But with a quick shake of his head, he hoped Chenoa had reached the freedom of a new life in Port Tadeas. She deserved as much after her many trials.

Unlike him.

Hellion stomped impatiently, like the stallion was awaiting his answer. Zaethan rolled his shoulders and returned Dmitri's pointed stare. Some truth was better than none.

"I have been distracted. I know, meme qondai," Zaethan said, dipping his chin. "One of my alphas is about to challenge me. Few have attempted it over the years. Comes with the job of leading them. But this is not just any challenge. We have… history. And now, Wekesa comes with General Lateef's backing and, I'm certain, my father's." His nostril flared resentfully. "I've dedicated almost every waking moment this summer preparing to face him."

Dmitri's thin brows furled. "The same Wekesa you defeated five years ago?"

"Uni. The morning of my Ascension, I took alpha zà from Wekesa. He'd ascended first and only held it for six months. Now he wants it back. Before, he didn't have the support he has now. Pryde allegiance is volatile. They hear the chieftains, my own father, calling him jwona rapiki—a fate writer—and suddenly the prydes forget all of his abuses."

Cynically, Zaethan snorted at that. The militia would forget him too, the last five years of his leadership and the scars that had paid for it.

"Pryde preference has little sway though, right?" Dmitri picked at the fig, focusing on Zaethan's conundrum. "Unless my understanding is flawed, the challenge alone dictates who becomes alpha zà."

"In title, yeah… but if the prydes support Wekesa over me, a challenger will come again and again. From Zahra's reports, the Provincial Pryde is on the fence. They didn't mind Wekesa's misuse and sharing of Bastiion's luxuries earlier this year. We're usure of the Ikaika Pryde. I'm constantly battling its corruption, so close to Pilar.

"The Proper Pryde stands with me, and the Valley Pryde with him. Zahra assures I retain the Mirajii, Yachel, and Eindrulla prydes. But it's the Khan, Andwele, and Foothill Prydes we might be losing to Wekesa. Meaning," Zaethan said with a huff. "They need to see him fall—hard. I can't just defeat Wekesa. I have to obliterate him."

"I see… That would be distracting," Dmitri told him benevolently. It was his strength as much as his weakness, empathizing with those who've wronged him—Zaethan more than anyone. "Alas, a one-sided friendship isn't a friendship at all, Zaeth. Even grieving, I would have cared about this. Why didn't you share it with me sooner?"

"Angst. Shame," Zaethan answered bluntly, with more meaning than his friend possibly knew. "I barely beat Wekesa five years ago. I won because of *his* misstep. If I misstep... if I lose alpha zà—"

His voice cracked unexpectedly, unable to say it aloud. Overlooking the mouth of the canyon, his eyes, suddenly burning, fell on Zwaàlu Ghopar. The Kindred Bridge. Maroon streaked the russet monument like emptied veins, stained by the blood of his people—the blood of his mother. If Wekesa replaced him as alpha zà, Zaethan wouldn't only lose his pryde's occupation in Bastiion, he would lose one of his last ties to his mother's legacy.

The only tie he'd actually earned on his own.

"Do you recall that winter your father returned south and permitted you to sojourn with my family for the season?" his friend randomly asked. "Remember how I'd force you to play checklerule with me, every single night? How you hated that game... It was the only thing I could beat you at. Yet despite your loathing, and routine losses, you'd start each match like the others never mattered." Dmitri tugged the reins, adjusting Harmonia so he could stretch across and capture Zaethan's shoulder. "It is not to failure we cling but the sheer audacity to face tomorrow as if today was powerless against it. You taught me that, Zaeth," he professed, his round eyes ringed in gold. "*You* did."

Zaethan nodded beneath the undeserved praise but then twitched with a smirk. "Depths, I hate checklerule."

Dmitri snickered quietly. "Brothers by choice..." His fist extended, showcasing the distressed scarlet thread around his wrist.

Zaethan knocked it with his. "Not by blood."

"I need that reminder as much as you right now. As a man, I must live with the decisions I made in grief. But as a king, I must keep them from affecting the decisions I make now." Dmitri withdrew, falling back in his saddle. "Today is the third day."

Zaethan cursed himself. He'd lost count of the deadline. From the heights, he spotted his father's compound, established at the center of Làtoh Ché. Cold dread crawled over his neck as he looked at it. Alike his control of Darakai, the chief warlord's reach tightened around the sprawling City Nest from a fixed, unmovable position.

Exaltation was the source of his father's power, feeding a dominion Dmitri couldn't even imagine... braced with a tyranny he would never see coming.

"What will you do," Zaethan asked uneasily, "if he does not comply with the order?"

Dmitri's noble features crispened until he resembled the statue of a hardened king. "If Mworra does not leave this soil, there is only one thing I can do. It's been far too long since Darakai's chief warlord and the commander of the Orynthian armies were two different men. Warn your uncle," Dmitri stated resolutely. "He must be ready. As must we all."

Tipping his wooden cup on its side, Zaethan watched the promenade's crowd hustle by the cantina.

He thumbed a crack in the rim, timeworn like the chipped table he shared with Yousif and his pryde. However, with his stool tilted against the rock wall, he nursed his bwoloa alone. Zaethan's cautious view shifted between the street and his crew, whooping from across the covered watering hole where they faced off Kumo and his uncle in a lively game of darts and dice.

It was a less-than-even match by the look on Kumo's glum mug, as he tore the darts out of the painted hide and sourly rolled again. With a tricky grin, Dhalili stepped up. Clapping, Jabari counted in Andwele while she pretended to crank one of the many black knots on her scalp, like a squirrely wind-up doll, dramatically puffing her childlike cheeks as she brought the blowpipe to her mouth in stages.

Zaethan turned back toward the rockbound promenade, knowing she'd hit the mark.

Takoda and Jabari's cheers disturbed the neighboring tables when her dart landed. After all, the blowpipe was his scout's weapon of choice, and Kumo should have picked a better partner.

Tucked under an expansive shelf, the cantina was situated in a shallow cave, shadowing its patrons from those who passed by thin swaths of tangled vining that spilt overhead. Behind the greenery, Zaethan took another somber swig of the finest bwoloa he'd had in ages. Heat coated his tongue, flooding with hints of barrel and rind. It was the taste of home, and he savored it while he could, envying the ignorance of his pryde. They deserved this moment of innocence. Of normalcy.

And as it was the third pour he sipped, Zaethan was procrastinating his taking it from them.

He'd gathered them at the cantina for its limited visibility. Here, Zaethan could be seen enjoying a drink with his men, out in the open. People assumed collusion occurred in the crooked corners of a city, but more often than not, it was at tables just like these. His nonchalance would be imperative, as any tip-off would alarm his father of Dmitri's probable announcement.

Zaethan did not expect his father to remove the Mworrans, not when he considered himself the true king of Darakai. But while Zaethan knew the chief warlord, the chief warlord did not know Dmitri. To reduce the likelihood of revolt, it was best to keep it that way. Any hint of reassigning the commandership to a beta warlord like Yousif—before it left Dmitri's lips—and his father would have his brother-in-law arrested in seconds.

Dhalili scampered over, barreling into the table in a wide-toothed fit of laughter. Hopping on an adjacent stool, she perched crow-like. "I made Big Kumo sour like a pruney old hucklebuckle, Alpha Zà!"

"Careful," Zaethan replied, warning her over his bwoloa, "or *Big Kumo* will squash you like a pip."

Snickering, Takoda came around the stool and flicked a few crupas at Dhalili, presumably her cut from their betting. "Eh, he'd have to aim first, ano?"

Jabari plunked down, looping his arm around Dhalili's petite shoulder.

"Kumo aim at lookers more than board. Give them all a prickle-tickle." He poked Dhalili's arm playfully with the crude blowpipe and smiled wildly under his buoyant heap of carob coils. "Now, Big Kumo got to buy them sips, so there be no smacks. In darts and dice, Uncle Yousif better beta."

Jabari set the weapon on the table, swapping it for a hefty pint of mountain mead.

Made from palm reed, the blowpipe and board of tapestried hide was more rustic than the bronze-and-byrnnzite set collecting dust in Dmitri's royal apartments. Having played it enough times throughout their adolescence, Zaethan's own set soon succumbed to their competitive wear and tear. For his own Ascension, Dmitri had the Darakaian staple commissioned and installed in his quarters for them to play whenever Zaethan wished.

Something they hadn't done since King Korbin's assassination.

True to Jabari's kakka-shtàka jabber, Kumo loitered by the bar on the far side of the cantina, ordering a round of liquors for a table of grumpy men. They seemed to unfurl as they spoke to Yousif. By their mutual grays and hearty banter, Zaethan expected they'd perhaps fought together in the late Shield Wars. While he'd not garnered the infamy of his sister, Yousif Shà had a few stories of his own.

Some remembered in Darakaian households to this day, the stories that were still allowed to be shared.

A queasiness returned to Zaethan's gut as he surveyed the street once more. It was that hard-earned respect, remembered or forgotten, that would make or break Dmitri's decision to elevate Yousif as the commander supreme of his armed forces.

Once his appointment was announced, it would require good, honest men on the war council to voice their support against his father's ruthless and guaranteed criticism. Here, on red soil, the chieftains answered to their chief warlord, but were he no longer Orynthia's commander, their warriors could be called to arms, away from Darakai, by another.

Then it would be Yousif Shà who controlled the Orynthian legions, not Nyack Kasim. And in a sense, control of the chieftains too.

Which was precisely why Zaethan wanted to throw up.

The table shook when Kumo unloaded a pair of pints and briskly dragged a stool next to Zaethan. With a gulp of hops, his beta pointed at Dhalili, who across the table had one of his copper coins wedged between her teeth.

"Doru! You know I'm good for it, you smug little grifter! Acting like you'd never played, feeding me all that sad *kakk* so I'd put money down! *Always with horsies, Kumo. Never get to play with pryde, Kumo.*" Sneering, be buckled his square nose as he imitated Dhalili's genderless treble. "What a swindling load of shtàka!"

"Boast in your victory, says Alpha Zà, not before it," she replied through her greedy, coin-stuffed teeth.

"Ano zà, Ahoté. You don't deserve either of these!" Kumo glared at Zaethan and chugged the other pint. "Cost me my last crupas too."

"You sure you didn't spend it on your casualties?" Takoda's lean chicory face beamed, holding back his laughter when Yousif strolled back to their group.

His uncle skidded in against the wall, directly to Zaethan's right. Yousif patted his nephew's knee, as if their relationship was more than it was. Over the years, they'd shared limited encounters, but never long enough to foster the closeness he displayed with Kumo. As beta warlord, Yousif traveled between the tribes of Halona more than the occasional visit to Faraji. Sitting beside him now was probably the fifth or sixth time Zaethan had ever done so.

Yousif rested a shot of bwoloa before him. "*Ho'waladim*—from the warrior at the bar." He gestured across the way. "Third in the Eindrulla Pryde."

Over Jabari's head, Zaethan inclined the glass toward the man, who pounded his chest in response.

"You remind me of her." Yousif leaned in, his dappled locs swinging over his thigh. "Cyra had this confidence, yeah? No one gave it to her, but uni, everyone recognized it. People looked to her without her ever asking them to. After the war, he never understood why his titles couldn't replicate that... That was your mhàdda's real kwihila, the victory he couldn't steal. You have it too, Zaeth."

Mouth ironed, Zaethan tapped his finger against the fresh glass irritably. His uncle hardly knew him, certainly not well enough to randomly bring up his dead mother in a cantina.

"I didn't invite you here to reminisce," Zaethan stated firmly.

His glare ticked up as a warrior, younger than the third seated at the bar, strolled to their table and delivered another shot of bwoloa. He gave a clipped bow, beat his chest, and said a quick "Alpha Zà" before backpedaling to his group. Zaethan pushed it off to Kumo, who gladly threw it back.

Zaethan angled his chin toward his uncle. "I've invited you here on the king's order. He may need to make a pronouncement tonight, the kind you must be prepared to accept when he does."

"Meme ano'qondai." Yousif scratched his stubbled neck. "Prepare how?"

"By choosing your general," he answered, locking eyes with his mother's brother.

He wondered, for a moment, if hers had looked the same when she'd been surprised. His bright and vigilant eyes, pools of molten goldenrod, tensed as Yousif comprehended his meaning—and the dangers it conveyed. He cupped his creased forehead as drums seemed to beat for his coming trial.

"Ahoté, do you hear that?"

Kumo whacked his elbow. On the table, the varying columns of liquid shuttered in their glasses. The drumming was real. And it was heading their way.

Scattered throughout the cantina, a procession of warriors kept delivering bwoloa to the table. But Zaethan didn't acknowledge them, transported through time to when it'd been him who'd paraded a challenging cry through the streets. The rhythm was menacing, each percussive bellow growing louder from farther down the promenade. The sound was unmistakable; the people knew it well. Its echoes dispersed a flurry of citizens outside the rock-covered cantina, running to get out of the way. The challenge sang a dream to their bones, and a nightmare to his.

Measuredly, Zaethan's boots met the ground and he stood.

Waiting.

The first line of Wekesa's posse crossed the cave opening. Together, like one beast, they progressed perpendicularly through the street step by step to the kettledrums, carted by those in the flanks. Wekesa's profile rocked back and forth, stomping imposingly between the swooping horns and threatening chants.

At the shrill whistle of a single flute, the entire posse turned toward the cantina.

The drummers went silent. Men and women, dressed in traditional beaded hides and breezy gunjas, dropped into a collective crouch, leaving Wekesa high at the center. Gradually, tauntingly, he lifted his face. Painted scalp to snout, it was dark as the night, just as Zaethan had once painted his.

Wekesa led their brutal clap, puffing and huffing with it fiendishly. Some of his supporters lashed their tongues like serpents, while others clomped with him farther into the cantina, jabbing and flipping symbolled rods to their choral tempo.

Heat raked Zaethan's body with an ageless anger. Kehari clapped among them in a fierce sashay.

She'd not marched in Zaethan's posse the morning he'd turned eighteen. Loving them both, Kehari had said she couldn't clap for either man. But two opaque black lines, run throat to navel, marked her fidelity to Wekesa—even under Léola's neckpiece cinching her neck.

Zaethan heard his heavy breaths above the sound and kept them level. He would not flinch.

Not for them. Not for anyone.

Wekesa seethed, adorned as the challenger in black feathering and dyed-pitch buckskins. His painted pectorals heaved and swelled with the emerging chant. Dragged off the stool by Takoda, Dhalili growled like a small bear at the intoned words, as Wekesa's rod wielders steered him toward Zaethan's table.

Just feet away, the flute was blown again, and everything quieted except the ancient chant. The rods swung out at Zaethan, arrowing for his heart. He felt Kumo stir beside him, anticipating what came next.

Wekesa drew a hand blade from his belt and pointed it straight at their ultimate alpha. Through the thick, dark paint, his scar puckered with his snarl.

His posse hissed at his back until he roared the chanted challenge. "Ano'puwàa dim'hakku, yona alpha ni ràtomdai!"

Unworthy and wanting, an alpha's blood will be claimed.

Vehemently, Wekesa plunged the dagger deep into the wooden table. His tendons strained around the hilt, surely wishing to slash his opponent with it. The eyes of Zaethan's rival, as black as the paint they'd both worn, pierced his composure.

Mouth dry, Zaethan swallowed. Wekesa tracked the bob of his throat and grinned, ugly and excited.

"Face me at sundown."

CHAPTER TWENTY FIVE
ZAETHAN

The sky turned as red as the earth, draping the crowded pit in glaring sprays of saffron and scarlet.

Gone were the wistful garlands and vessels of belonging. Surrounding Zaethan, Darakaians cheered, packing the rising levels of the massive assembly. They were thirsty. Excited. Each craved the pit's original purpose. For soaked in test and telling, it wasn't a scene of celebration. It was an arena of death.

Here, blood would be spilt. And here, their thirst would be quenched.

Drumming fueled their demand. Fast and ferocious, the percussionists thundered through the canyon. Lining the sunken arena, gargantuan stone warriors were pounded with zeal, awakening the slit gongs to the slaughter. In one harrowing melody they called a storm, but there came no lightening, except the flash through Wekesa's darkened stare across the empty combat zone.

Behind the boundary line, Kehari kneaded his beefy neck. Wekesa cracked his knuckles, impatiently awaiting Kumo's signal. He nodded at General Lateef, who was gesturing with his hands, undoubtedly coaching his strategy under the challenger paint. Zaethan assessed the weight Wekesa had added to his already-larger build during the months he'd spent training with the general's brother. Striding toward them, the weapons master carried more grays but as much brawn as Lateef. He examined selections from his arsenal, then twirled a double-ended spear with finesse and handed it off to Wekesa. With a curt jerk, he shoved it back, just as he'd done with the bow and the chained flail.

Not the spear, Zaethan noted. *That leaves you the kopar, the club mace, or the axe.*

He would have preferred the spear.

The masses were growing restless, and so was Zaethan. Zahra had long finished tracing his face, arms, and torso in graphic ivory patterns, marking him as the champion challenged. Contrasting Wekesa's midnight guise, Zaethan's locs were decorated in white feathers and copper threading, a match to his blanched leather bracers and spotless gunjas, unmissable from afar. A thousand eyes were pinned on him, the unmoving alpha zà.

He heard his third hiss something to Jabari, who dithered in place, clutching a polished spiked shield. But Zaethan had no use for it. With his palms free of his Darakaian weaponry, his fingers twitched nervously.

She was late.

"Ahoté." Kumo's brow bulged in the torchlight. "Why are we stalling?"

Zaethan combed the crowd for the Boreali. Not a single pale head stood out among his kinsmen.

"You'll see," he replied, more prayer than promise.

"It's he who's stalling," Dmitri voiced over his shoulder. Arms folded, he ignored the sweaty soldier in the risers who was expecting to usher the young king to his seat. "Stripped of your Darakaian title, he thinks I'll be cowered into going to war."

Nyack Kasim thought just that, Zaethan gauged, risking a glance toward his father in the stands. Atop private stone steps, Darakai's chief warlord overlooked the spectacle from a superior vantage. Yak hair caped his back and pooled around his seat. The regalia was upstaged by the wreath of moss and bone gracing his pitted skull. He'd dressed as a victor, certain of Zaethan's failing before his son even crossed the boundary line. It lay beneath the fingers he casually swept over his mouth as Bessus, the field marshal, conversed in his ear... the controlled, satisfied half smile his father wore whenever he struck and Zaethan no longer got back up.

Embittered, Zaethan cricked his neck.

No matter the outcome, he'd never stay down again.

A line of expectant chieftains flanked their chief warlord. Being the offspring of two Darakaian heroes, Zaethan had always carried the pressure of their unimpressed eyes. Pinning him now, their watch was abrasive, chafing Zaethan's back when he bent to retrieve his canteen.

Whatever he could do to buy her more time—if she showed at all. After swishing the water, Zaethan spit into the reddish dirt as his father's ill-boding commission polluted his thoughts long after his Seating.

"Darakai's kwihila hangs off your back. My entire House looks on, waiting to see how long before you crumble beneath it."

The House of War looked on. All of them, crammed into this arena.

Darakaians loved a champion's ascent, but a fall even more. They would applaud Zaethan's victory, his upheld kwihila, over his rival's. Yet nothing, not his deeds or his name, would deter their deafening ovation if he dropped to Wekesa's feet.

Opposite Bessus and the vacant seat intended for Orynthia's king sat a pair of anxious haidrens. Gnawing on the chain of his snuff canister, Ira offered Zaethan a weak wave. The most violence a yancy ever met was at a seedy dogfight, where the butchery of animals emptied and lined their bored pocketbooks. Zaethan was glad Ira squirmed, forced to put a human face on the huwàa he would normally place a bet on. Maybe he'd realize the cost of his opulence and spend it more wisely.

Cautiously, Hachiro, swimming in ocher robes, peeped around Ira, hurriedly scribbling in bursts when Zaethan's father wasn't paying attention. Zaethan hoped, for the shoto'shi's sake, he'd tuck that kakka-shtàka journal away. If caught by the chief warlord, he'd find his fingers broken before his quill.

"Perhaps I missed it as well, Zaeth." In his periphery, Dmitri rubbed his chin. "What is it we're waiting for again?"

As he was about to answer, a ripple passed through the risers. Heads whirled toward the enormous steps that plunged into the pit. Chest swelling, Zaethan charted their focus to the top.

"For that."

Those clustering the stair parted with a gasp. In her highlander silks, the witch treaded past them. Her uncanny eyes were cloaked in kohl and shadow. Her wild tresses glided after her like ghostly scarves from a fabled otherworld. Two curved swords rode her hips, dipping with each movement of her descent. Torches illuminated the witchiron like swinging prisms, casting a brilliant medley across the Southern stone. And strapped to the haidren to Boreal's back—as the backs of both her shadowmen—glinted a legendary set of crescent wraiths.

A flight of phantoms, the Boreali arrowed for Zaethan and his crew.

"A king shouldn't show favoritism," he told Dmitri. "Go to Ira and Hachiro, before Lady Boreal comes to me."

Locked solely on her and the salvation she carried, he didn't watch Dmitri head for the soldier. Zaethan swatted off his beta's emerging questions and strode forward.

Luscia Darragh Tiergan had shown.

She'd shown for him.

Guardedly, her captaen shepherded her right, and between them stalked her Orallach beast. The stockier, bearded shadowman, who often escorted her to the bluff, walked backward at her left, shielding his haidren from the surrounding Darakaians. Discreetly, Zaethan scanned for the others who'd dispersed among the masses, lost and unseen, the trick of the shadowmen's creed.

Zaethan met the trio in the dimming void, a stone's throw from his pryde. Her pale lips shuddered and her captaen fell back—reluctantly.

"Where were you?" Zaethan asked, hovering over her.

Lithely, she angled her neck, regarding him through the smeared kohl. "Praying," she bluntly replied. "Yeh'maelim. You can thank me once you're comfortable doing so."

With a swift sneer, he extended his palm, open wide for her fabled iron. The drumming stopped, the air stale, brimming with whispers. The subtle buzz reminded him of their evenings on the bluff and the ceaseless trill of the trees. All of it had led them to this moment, this final test.

"Well? I don't have all night."

He didn't like the way her mouth pressed before it opened.

"You've only handled the wraiths once. You're not ready to use them in combat."

Zaethan's hand shook as he closed into a tight fist. They were watching. All of them.

"You promised me," he said forcefully through his lips, anger bubbling behind his teeth.

Delicately, her small alabastrine fingers cupped his fist, rattling between their middles. At his contact with the Boreali haidren, the Darakaian mutterings grew, riling to jeers and taunts from some in the stands.

Stoking his ire, his enemy-turned-tutor stated with aggravating calm, "I will not be the cause of your death this day, Kasim."

He felt as if he'd been slapped. She'd simply come to refuse him, after everything they'd worked toward. After everything they'd buried.

"I should have never trusted you, ano." Zaethan fumed, jutting his nose at hers. "And what do you suggest I do *this day*?"

"What you're best at." Her body unmoving, the prismatic lamps under her thick brows flashed to her hips and the weapons sheathed there. "Paired kuerre. You've taken to these blades, and they to you. Claim them in your grasp, Kasim... and you will win."

Rescinding her fingers from his clenched fist, her arms swept upward. In a sinuous arc, they laced overhead, baring for him each hilt at her either hip. Unable to draw her blades in the arena, he saw she'd fastened them in reverse—pointing rearward, for his taking. Unblinking under his fierce scrutiny, she nodded once.

Her faith laid in the kuerre. And so must his.

Mapping the curves of her face, Zaethan wrapped his forearms around the haidren to Boreal, crisscrossing his wrists over her lower back. Her cheek twitched with the arena's collective breath, its occupants sucking in the scandal as he took hold of either sword. The unnatural warmth pulsed through each hilt. Beyond her shoulder, the head of her guard stood appalled. Captaen Bailefore glowered contemptuously, as over her hair, the fragrance of juniper and rain delighted Zaethan's lungs.

Every gain had a loss. The cost of his gain, he realized, was one she would pay.

"Thank you," he quietly said into her crown, the syllables unrolling clumsily off his tongue.

Zaethan tightened his grip when her lashes shuttered shut, and she whispered in Boreali, "Tredae'Aurynth."

The crowd shrieked and howled when Zaethan retreated with the witchiron, each kuerre whining as he liberated them to the Darakaian battleground.

Lightweight and expertly balanced, they were like nothing from his homeland. He welcomed the deadly metal as old friends, kept apart. Rotating his wrists, Zaethan revolved the Northern blades while he marched toward the combat zone, emboldened and unafraid.

Light refracted over the compacted red soil. Sounds of awe echoed from the spectators, superseding their prior animosity. Stalking past his countrymen, Zaethan touted the heralds of myth: symbols of secrecy and superstition, the privileged weapons of the najjan.

Finally, a Darakaian had acquired what even his father never could. And for that his people rose their feet, erupting in cheers for Nyack's son.

Zaethan stretched taller, filled with pride. A dark tower ran up alongside his stride.

Before Kumo could speak, Zaethan ordered his bewildered beta, "Signal Lateef. Now I'm ready."

After a dumbfounded pause, Kumo hooted to Àla'maia, marking

her appearance above them. He gestured widely at the general, then beckoned the drummers to blast for their alpha zà. Thirty yards ahead, Wekesa hunched under the wears of adversary, the black paint emphasizing his stunned gawk at the approaching witchiron.

Zaethan had told Zahra he would never see it coming. And it showed.

His rival snarled, shoving off Kehari. Hoisting a serrated-edge shield, Wekesa tore a double-bit battle axe from the weapons master's arsenal and stampeded for the ring of torches.

General Lateef attended the challenger into the marked combat zone. But, grinding his jaw, Zaethan angled for one man. Enormous horns sounded as his marbled form, illustrated in white runes, crossed the boundary line.

Alone.

Closing the gap, Zaethan faced his rival. Both panted eagerly, seething with anticipation.

From the center of the ring, the general announced to the arena, "Darakai! *Ano'puwàa dim'hakku, yona alpha ni ràtomdai.*" His voice boomed, and the people began to strike the stone on which they sat. "For the challenged, kwihila or surrender!" General Lateef pointed at Zaethan, then to Wekesa. "For the challenger, kwihila or death! Hewe hai Darakai!"

The first horn sounded, and grinning hungrily, the general backed away.

"We won't follow a pretender, or your y'siti bitch!" Wekesa barked at the Northern kuerres.

At the second horn, adrenaline primed Zaethan's muscles. "Don't worry, jwona rapiki. You won't have to." Zaethan dug his heel into the dirt. "You'll be dead."

To the thump of a thousand fists, the third horn blared.

Wekesa lurched, wielding the axe of smoked Andwele ore. Zaethan dropped low, averting his initial strike. Above, Wekesa's huge axe swung again. Twisting on his soles, Zaethan parried his rival's passion with the kuerres. Screeching, the witchiron clashed the Southern metal, a sizzling grate raking against Wekesa's weapon. In a swift rotation, Zaethan withdrew a single kuerre and lashed the pitch fabric before him, dodging the serrated shield when it plunged for his neck.

He smelt first blood before it inked the earth. The crowd shouted when Wekesa staggered back. Snarling in pain and shock, he glared at where the witchiron had licked his flesh through the gunjas. Over his sturdy calf, his hickory flesh bubbled away from the wound, corroding into a pocket of pus.

She'd warned Zaethan what these blades could do. He'd heard the stories since birth. His gaze feasted on the putrid gash. Swapping the kuerres between his palms, Zaethan bent at the knees, gleaming at Wekesa.

It'd be the first of many.

He sprang for his dusky challenger with ferocity. A flicker of uncertainty stumbled Wekesa's footing before he whipped his axe overhead and rushed toward Zaethan's attack. Like a barreling bat, Wekesa hurled the sleek bit upward as they collided. Contorting his body, Zaethan took one kuerre, slammed the weapon into the shield, and rolled over Wekesa's spine, trailing the circulation with the second kuerre. It sliced his opponent laterally, across the ribs, earning him another angry bellow. The stench of burnt flesh bloomed from Wekesa's tinted torso. Blood dripped past his atrophying wound, splattering the dirt in a trail of carnage for the masses.

Zaethan bounced on his soles, shaking out the thrill. He exchanged his blades in the air, and their ovation flooded the risers. His people truly saw him.

Emboldened, he risked a look at his father atop his chiefly perch.

Biting his fist, Nyack Kasim was not entertained. There was hatred in his expression, hatred for his own child and, perhaps, the woman his son's existence had stolen from this world. It lived in the folds of his war-torn scowl. The deep depressions were visible from a distance. Dauntlessly, Zaethan took the famed witchiron and exalted it toward Zwaàlu Ghopar, the Kindred Bridge—to his mother's banner, sealed in Andwelestone.

The people started to chant, hailing her name. Valiant and vindicated, Zaethan huffed as her legacy resonated across the arena.

"Cyra! Cyra! Cyra!"

The fist of Darakai's chief warlord lowered, showcasing his revile. But then, like a shifting storm, his father's chin elevated, and his lip curled.

Agony ripped through Zaethan's shoulder blade. Pivoting, he evaded the hooked end of the axe, following in a downward combination. He fended off Wekesa's onslaught with a weakening sequence of parries, backing into the outer ring of the combat zone.

To cross the firelit boundary was to forfeit.

"You're weak, Zaeth. Kehari knew it too. Show Darakai the softness she sensed all along!" Advancing, Wekesa spewed spittle at Zaethan. "Uni, show them why your father chose me over his spineless son!"

His shoulder ached, assuring serious injury to his left range of motion. Blocked by the shield, his stronger, dominant arm was at a disadvantage.

"He chose wrong." Zaethan huffed. "Just like her."

Wekesa struck outward at Zaethan's chest. Pushing through the sting, Zaethan reeled the kuerre with his damaged side, shredding the inside of his rival's forearm, and angled the witchiron to flay his thigh with the right. But as the curved blade cut through the open, Wekesa

jerked away in agony. By the retreating axe heel, Zaethan's kuerre was
torn from his palm. Hurtling aside, it skidded in the dirt toward the
torches. Wekesa's shield thrust forward and bludgeoned Zaethan square
in the forehead.

As he slunk backward, his hearing became muffled and the sky
turned upside down. Àla'maia's court illuminated his sight scaling her
throne. Zaethan could almost hear her screaming from the clouds.

His neck slack, his cheek scuffed the dirt as it turned toward his
pryde and blinked. Zaethan moored onto a beacon of alabaster skin.
Frantic and impassioned, her mouth stretched wide, shaping with
Àla'maia's warbled demands. When the fog in his ears started to clear,
their voices joined as one.

"Kasim!" The witch's shrieks pierced his haze. "Start spinning!"

Start spinning, Zaethan echoed.

Trusting his tutor, he bowled aside just as Wekesa's axe rained down.
It clobbered the earth, chucking rock and soil into Zaethan's eyes. With
his spine flush to the ground, his feet punted the oncoming shield and
drove it upward into Wekesa's smug jaw. Zaethan overheard the crack
of his rival's mandible as he trundled once more, and he tossed up the
kuerre as he rolled. Catching it in his dominant hand, he used the
momentum to spring onto his heels.

Zaethan wiped the blood gushing from his brow and raced to
where the partner kuerre lay, covered in dust and gore. He retrieved
the witchiron blade and ran for Wekesa at full speed. Anticipating the
impact, his rival stooped and heaved his shield, tilting the toothed rim
at the last second—just as Zaethan had expected.

He vaulted onto the heavy disc. Leaping off it, Zaethan spun,
whirling in circles over Wekesa's mutilated scar. Feathers and decorated
locs lashed Zaethan's throat as he flew. In tandem, the kuerres plunged

like razored wings falling from the heavens. And in his descent, he carved twin gashes down the muscles of his challenger's back.

Zaethan landed with a thud, splaying the soaked highlander blades in the moonlight. Rocking, Wekesa sucked in an audible gasp.

The crowd's followed.

Zaethan walked toward his rival, who croaked inaudibly as his shield dropped from his care. He kicked Wekesa in the vertebrae, knocking him to his knees. Close up, the slashes fizzed and gurgled where his skin shriveled, endangering the deeper tissue. With a kuerre, he knocked the axe out of the way, then tossed it aside. Grabbing him by the braids, Zaethan yanked his head back, baring Wekesa's throat to the arena.

The fistful of coarse hairs grated his fingers as he panted to the thousands that packed the risers, and he basked in their thunderous cheers. Starting from the lower rows, fists started to pummel the red stone behind their mountain of legs—the Andwele range chanting for him alone. His grip stiffened intimately around the warmth of the kuerres' hilt as their kinsmen drummed a death song. Faraji hungered for it. They demanded this final blow. And as one, his people clamored for a show unlike any other.

Zaethan would not disappoint.

Kehari cried out from the sidelines. He swerved Wekesa in her direction, to see his lover tremble and weep between General Lateef and his sullen brother. His rival croaked when she collapsed to the excavated earth, drenching it with her sobs.

From the risers, the pounding loudened, drowning out Kehari's pleas where she threatened the perimeter on hands and knees. Zaethan turned them back toward its sound, the sound of Darakai lusting for blood.

Wekesa's blood. The chief warlord's chosen.

Not his.

"You're not the only fate writer here," Zaethan said to him. His wound sprinkled his rival's skull, marking him for the grave. "*Kwihila rapiki mu jwona.*"

Depleted, he flipped the backsword in hand and positioned it over Wekesa's gullet. Wekesa's thick gulps hissed against the witchiron, and the arena silenced hungrily as if they all could hear it too. Zaethan donned the tonnage of their eyes, stretching his back beneath its strain, knowing they each pinned him in this singular moment.

Above Wekesa's head, he released the breath he'd been holding for years.

This challenge had lasted half a decade. Here and now, Faraji would forever remember that it was *he* who ended it.

But a bloodcurdling screech broke out from the crowd. One by one, their heads veered, their attention no longer entranced by the final act in the combat zone as shrieks of alarm joined a woman's harrowing outburst. With Wekesa against the kuerre, Zaethan was losing their gluttonous witness to another feast. He chanced a glimpse of his father, who was coming to stand. Distracted, he too looked away from his son—the one person who mattered, who needed to be seen.

Yelling broke out through the stands. Frantic, Zaethan pivoted himself and his rival toward the commotion.

Dividing those atop the main steps was a rugged stallion.

It trotted into the pit, a lump slung over the saddle. Zaethan narrowed his gaze, making out an appendage dangling among the stirrups. His grip slackened on his defeated challenger when Zahra and Kumo abandoned their post, scurried to the horse, and pulled the man into the beta's arms. From inside the combat zone, Zaethan watched his third call for the haidren to Boreal. Her hands were wet with scarlet. Kumo scooped the man's head into the light.

The warrior was one of theirs, a member of the disjointed segment his father had dispatched the border of Hagarh.

Zaethan instantly dropped his handful of Wekesa's braids and sprinted past the torches without a second thought. Dread chapped his tongue as he skidded onto his knees beside Kumo.

"He barely has a pulse." The witch pressed her jacket against the maroon pooling his navel, where soiled rags were knotted and bound. "Kasim, he's losing too much."

Aghast, Zaethan cradled his warrior's gaunt cheeks, only then realizing his pryde hadn't eaten properly in months. "Omun!" He wailed his name, jostling him to wake. "You're home! Open your eyes, Omun!"

The warrior wheezed, creaking a lid. "Save us, Alpha Zà…"

"Save you from what, Omun?" Zaethan panicked, covering the haidren's hand over his wounds and adding pressure.

"War—" Omun rasped, his chest shuddering. "Taint."

In a ripple, they scuttled back, relinquishing the warrior. A tremor overtook his hands as Zaethan feverously rubbed the noxious gore onto his gunjas. Wide-eyed, he locked onto the only person who hadn't pulled away. Rocking the dying man, she spoke rapidly, either to Omun or her shadowmen. He couldn't understand her highlander words… except that they were panicked too.

In her Boreali arms, a dark pond formed around Zaethan's warrior instead of his challenger, whom General Lateef and his brother were dragging from the torchlit circle. Applause sprang up, the crowd forgetting the man at his feet, as if Omun's horror was just an extra act to their theater.

The wrong blood had been spilt. Looking up, Zaethan speared the crowd, wondering if theirs was a thirst that could never be quenched.

CHAPTER TWENTY SIX
LUSCIA

He lay motionless, growing cold in her embrace.

Pleading Aniell to welcome him on the High One's shores, Luscia had rushed her Boreali blessings while the Darakaian still heard her voice—anyone's voice—though he would never know her meaning. Not until Aurynth. She'd stroked his muddied braids as the tattered warrior took his departing breath, long before his chief warlord even deigned to depart the stands.

Darakai's leader took his time, even stopping periodically to address individuals along the way. The chief warlord held no urgency, except that suited his own purpose. His leisure disgusted her. She puckered her nose contemptuously as she witnessed his boot finally hit the base

346

of the arena and pivot, angling his stature not for the lifeless member of Kasim's pryde but toward his unconscious opponent.

Her head shook mutely, and she continued to pet the dead man's hair as if it would ease the days of pain he must have endured to survive the ride to Faraji. Tended by Jabari and a smaller boyish warrior, the stallion was yards off, where it had collapsed. Omun, as Kasim called him, had pushed the horse to its limit, competing for time against what bled from his middle.

Just to deliver that message to his alpha.

A heroic act on behalf of his endangered comrades abandoned in the Mirajii Forest. An act that garnered little expediency from Darakai's chief warlord yet, tellingly, much more from Orynthia's king.

Pacing back and forth along the edge of the pooled blood, Kasim squeezed his head between his dirt-dried palms. Luscia knew her Tiergan blood shielded her from the potential war-taint spilling from the warrior's entrails, after her wounds from Ambrose earlier that summer.

Kasim's pryde didn't question her refusal to let Omun go. Without discovering what manifested in her veins, his men had come to perceive that she was another breed altogether, set apart from her own najjani guard. Desperately, Kasim and his pryde stared at her. Their burning questions, and the answers she feared, were buried under this warrior's filthy, frayed wrappings. And it fell to Luscia to uncover them.

"He was one of mine," Kasim said over and over as Dmitri came up alongside him.

Clearly out of breath from his brief jog, their waning king clutched his cane and kept pace with his friend, rather than ordering him to still.

"Owàa knows I should have fought harder to get them out. Shtàka, I should have—"

"Brother," Dmitri said, grabbing his shoulder forcefully. "He rode to you out of trust, not disappointment. Hold fast to that, Zaeth. Whatever happened, we will forge a way for you to help the others."

At Dmitri's tender tone, Luscia cast her sights lower, offering them an illusion of privacy. Kasim muttered in return. She tried not to listen as he conveyed what had driven Omun to undertake such a dangerous dispatch. Steadily, her fingers peeled the ragged bandages off his abdomen, which was sorely infected. Luscia swallowed bile as putrefied tissue came away in strips, stuck to some of the dressings.

Kasim's beta could not boast the same, studying her intently beside the *lycran*. Hand to mouth, he promptly shuffled over Aksel and lurched aside. Kumo's uncontrolled retching was drowned out by the masses deserting the arena, impartial to the corpse they left behind.

An upturned boot scuffed the russet dirt, against her thigh. Luscia warily peered up at Marek. From below, his jaw resembled an ash wood carving, solemn and stern. She could nearly feel his resentment radiating through the Orallach leather encasing his feet.

In front of thousands, the captaen had finally uncovered why she'd made Declan take her on all those midnight walks. Why she'd carted their sacred, blessed luxiron through the dark, away from its keepers. What would his great family think, she pondered, removing the final bandages, when they learned Marek served the only haidren who'd ever shared such mystery with those outside Boreal's borders, outside Boreal's creed.

From a line of ancient protectors, a Bailefore would never commit such infidelity.

But Luscia was not a Bailefore, she was a Tiergan—a line of discerners, culled from the children of shadow and light, called to discern for others the gray.

There was nothing gray about Wekesa. For Boreal and all Orynthia, Luscia, in discerning conscience, could not allow him to prevail—a fact Marek must find a way to reconcile if he wanted to walk his life with his haidren, however difficult it was for a Bailefore to do.

Luscia's duplicity now shone like a lodestar. Naked and exposed, the luxiron gleamed from the center of the Darakaian combat zone where Kasim had discarded her kuerres to rush to his warrior. Reliving that heart-pounding moment, Luscia could hardly believe Kasim had let it go, his right to retribution. He'd allowed Wekesa, his vile challenger, to live in exchange for a few final seconds with Omun.

Inexpressibly, his sacrifice made Luscia all the more absolute in her decision to have helped him.

"Lady Boreal, I'm told you can explain what we are looking at?" Hachiro suddenly asked, causing Luscia to jump uncharacteristically.

She'd not paid attention to his and Ira's unassuming advent.

Beside her, Sayuri's brother perched forward. He polished the strange monocle apparatus and hooked it over his ear, under his raven clumps of unbrushed hair. With his robes tucked beneath his knees, the shoto'shi cracked his thick journal apart, prepared to write.

"Let us hope, Lord Pilar," Luscia somberly replied.

She rung out her linsilk jacket and carefully blotted the rest of the blood that bathed Omun's torso. Deep, gruesome lacerations flayed the flesh, nearly revealing his organs through tears in his musculature. She was unsure how far into the deadly forest his pryde had been stationed, but it was a miracle he'd outlasted any stretch of distance.

Sighting the mutilation, Kumo doubled over and resumed his vomiting.

"By the Fates…" Dmitri whispered. His royal eyes had seen more violence in one day than perhaps his entire life.

With a shudder, Luscia's hand coasted Omun's middle, wishing Alora, a more proficient healer, were examining the body in her place. "Animals don't rip their prey in this sweeping manner. Niit, these slashes here and here…" She signaled toward a set of long cuts, where the skin was ribboned neatly. "Display a sort of… whipping motion we'd see by the large talons on birds of prey, but these lacerations are too expansive for that explanation." Her eyes searched the disjointed group until they landed sympathetically on the one who'd gone green. "Omun's wounds are identical to those we found on Takoda early this summer."

Wedged behind Kumo and Kasim's third, the mended warrior hugged his side, staring into the other man's fileted gut. While Takoda's injuries had been significantly deeper, he was lucky his alpha had overcome his superstitions the night he was carted through her Boreali threshold. It was Boreal's lumin-enriched herbs that had spared Takoda in the end. There was a holy alchemy within the peculiar glowing jars that lined her aunt's apothecary, each filled with the same hallowed compound that nourished their seclusive lands. Through a web of warmed wellsprings and abundant aquifers, Boreal was fed by the living fountainhead sealed in Aksel's Keep, the guarded dwelling of their salvation.

The Dönumn Lux, their Gift of Light from beyond the veil.

By Aniell's providence, his drop of Aurynth flowed into their soil and into their veins. In the time of Tiergan, it had restored a desolate peninsula, devastated by the Forgotten Wars, into a highland of plenty and, upon that highland, restored a people to a glory not their own.

A people born in shadow, remade in light.

Remnants of the Gift had empowered Luscia to drive out Takoda's feverish sweat and knit his ordinary, fragile tissue back together. But even lumin, in its most potent forms, could only undermine human mortality past a permitted extent. And beyond that extent, the ethereal light energy would cause irreparable harm to anyone who dared hoard it. That was the High One's covenant, for unnatural blessing demanded natural boundary. And as the guardians of His covenant, Boreal dispensed its organic composites, these manifestations of lumin, with extreme reservation, be it one single incandescent leaf, fallen dull and stale.

Thus, if Kasim hadn't beseeched Luscia so quickly when his warrior had been caught in death's snare, if he had debated perhaps just an hour longer, Takoda would have shared his grave with Omun.

The cold reality had Takoda curling his arms about himself as he gaped at Luscia over the body.

"War-taint in the Mirajii. Depths, my pryde…" Scrubbing his face, Kasim fell into a crouch, as if his legs had given way. "This is what your cousin meant when he defected to Wekesa." He gestured toward Zahra, though his laden gaze seemed unable to follow. "You asked me to speak to Nigan, and I wrote him off as a coward."

"We all did, Alpha Zà," his third gravely replied, lowering her tattooed head. "Uni, even me. His kin."

Parchment flapped while Hachiro repositioned his journal and cocked his quill at the body. "Have you studied the symptoms of war-taint long, Lady Boreal?" he asked academically, unaffected by the Darakaians' mourning.

"Niit—no. There isn't much to study," Luscia stammered, startled by his question. The Shoto Collective monopolized archaic texts in Gakoshū. If anyone had access to those rare documents, it wasn't the Boreali. "Little was written about war-taint during the centuries people were trying to outlive it. But from his eventual disfigurement, deteriorating tissue, and primitive hunger… Ambrose fitted the narrative of the disease."

"Pyō jien, Lady Boreal. I accept this knowledge," Hachiro said absently into his pages. Clicking on a green lens of the monocular device, Sayuri's brother looked back up at Luscia, his eye exaggerated like that of a fish. "Although, given the inadequate paleopathology, there's a possibility you've encountered another equally-undocumented contagion altogether."

Luscia repressed a chill when he shrugged and resumed his sketch.

Stiffly, with the aid of his cane, their king lowered next to Hachiro, his regal brocade a bizarre juxtaposition to the low-class rags on the man they examined. Dmitri grimaced at the shoto'shi's macabre drawing of Omun's anatomy.

"Zaeth, you said that Lord Ambrose was cremated?"

"Uni zà," Kasim replied.

That's one way to put it. Luscia gulped, recalling the way the infected noble had disintegrated into dust.

Dmitri tapped his elegant chin. "If another contracted the contagion before his body was incinerated, we'd have seen a resurgence of killings in Bastiion, would we not? An outbreak of war-taint should have already occurred, at least in the proper."

Luscia's temples itched as she thought of Finnian, the boy who'd been murdered in the spring as north as Port Tadeas, then the traders Alora had mentioned, who'd been slain on the road to Port Niall well before her Ascension. The disturbing gash left in her own tent when she and her guard had camped in the lowlands during their escort to Bastiion…

The creature outside Rian, and the second that'd attacked it.

"Felix Ambrose wasn't the first," Luscia said numbly, dreading her own conclusion. "Simply the first in Bastiion. There were other victims this year. Not all cross-castes. Not all children. But all mutilated by the same savagery we see today. My aunt missed my reception tending a victim in Tadeas."

She became keenly aware of Marek's boot, flush with her thigh. It'd become stone.

"There was an attempted attack, on me, when I camped with my najjan outside Rian's walls." Nerves trembled her tone, as she was aware how implausible the untold story sounded. "Like Ambrose, it came in the night. His state of necrosis... the creature must have been war-tainted for far longer than Ambrose. But it was fought off by another less mutated, younger in its pollution. Ambrose couldn't have started an outbreak." Luscia shuddered as she said it aloud. "He was already part of one."

"Wait. You were attacked?" Dmitri wavered against his walking cane. Fright showcased the bloodshot whites cocooning his hazel irises. "Luscia, your safety is paramount to this Quadren! I disagree but understand your and Zaeth's desire to conceal Ambrose's death." He thumped his cane against the dirt. "But out of all the secrets you insist on keeping, your welfare is imperative to divulge!"

"That was over a month ago. There was plenty of opportunity to tell me—us—what happened!" Kasim sputtered. "Why the Depths would you withhold something so important?"

Luscia got up, planting space between she and her captaen.

She wrung her hands, buried the pain the whole ordeal had caused, and answered Kasim candidly, "I didn't expect you'd believe me."

My so-called protector didn't, she reasoned.

"Believe—" He sprung his arms overhead. The veins swelled in

Kasim's forehead while he erupted. "I was with you! I saw Ambrose! I even hauled my warrior to your door before we knew what Ambrose had become!" His hands flailed toward Takoda, then back at Luscia. "Tell me, Maji'maia, what kakka-shtàka reason did I have to *not* believe you!"

She suddenly comprehended. "None."

Kasim's angry logic expelled the smog of shame distancing Luscia from her lead najjan. Luscia's spine flattened. Rigidly, she twisted toward Marek.

"You're right," she replied for Kasim, but steel sharpened each of her words as it was spoken to her crimson-haired captaen. "You had every reason to believe me."

A swarm of emotion washed Marek's anguished gaze. His ginger lashes shuddered, his gaze flitting to the dead Darakaian's injuries and back to Luscia's blood-soaked palms, the carnage that drenched her ruined jacket, and the linsilk shift underneath. Marek's throat jumped, and she was glad. He should have believed his haidren. He had plenty more reasons to than Kasim.

Kasim might be boisterous. He might be brash. But he'd never suggested Luscia was touched by delusion. As the child of one who was, she'd rather be treated like a witch than a madwoman.

Marek's ordinarily smooth, ivory forehead wrinkled. "Meh fyreon, Ana'Sere—"

"I should have trust you sooner, Lord Darakai." Luscia turned to her Quadrennal counterpart before inclining toward the one who mattered most. "And you, My King."

Beneath his disappointed frown, her king's pallor lacked its warmth.

Unexpectedly, Ira cleared his throat. Dmitri flinched, evidently having forgotten his Unitarian haidren stood among them too.

"Tyrant incoming," Ira dramatically warned, then nudged Kasim. "No offense."

Hackles raised, Aksel circled Omun's lifeless legs, his muzzle bared at two Darakaians approaching from the opposing edge of the combat zone. In the darkened distance, Wekesa was gone, surely taken elsewhere to be tended. However, entering the ring of torches was Declan, striding swift yet soundless

In true najjani fashion, she'd not even sensed him leave her back.

The abandoned kuerres, she realized. The luxiron blades sparkled just paces from the last men the najjan wanted to access their weaponry. Luscia's heartrate sped as her eldest najjan embarked toward General Lateef and Darakai's chief warlord. When they were seconds from the blades, Declan sped up, coasted along the dirt, and glided like a falcon after its prey under a scavenger's ravenous watch, recovering both kuerres. His crescent wraiths mirrored the torchlight in a sharp flash when the brawny najjan spun, flipped the retrieved blades to shield them at his back, and in a fluid bow, gracefully withdrew from the combat zone without taking a silvery eye off the chief warlord.

Nyack Kasim's sneer followed the retreating najjan. His cape of long yak hair dusted the Andwelestone in his wake, the black-and-auburn vestment flaunting his support for the challenger over his son. His advance changed, becoming clipped and commanding. Ripping a burning stake from of the ground, the chief warlord carried the torch as he crossed the boundary line. It alighted the panes and hollows of a face piqued with fury. But fury at what, Luscia could not foresee.

His son led his pryde warriors in stepping aside and brought a fist to his chest in salute. "Chief Warlord." Kasim greeted his father with grim formality. "The pryde stationed in the Mirajii is under assault—"

"Another defection," he stated, callously interrupting. He gave no congratulations, no hint of concern for his son's injuries, but prodded Omun's bloodied cadaver with the end of the torch. "Tried to outrun his jwona. Gutless deserter. Lateef, see he's beheaded like one. His blood will never spill Zwaàlu'Ghopar."

General Lateef voiced his eager assent. "Uni zà, Chief Warlord."

Kasim's jaw quaked at the harsh penalty for Omun's desperate ride to Faraji. Beside him, his third held onto Kumo, calming the beta as his big brown eyes beat back moisture.

Luscia saw Kasim swallow immense feeling when his formality cracked. "Fhàdda, these circumstances are not of desertion. Wounded, Omun bravely traveled to report great danger to us all. War-taint has returned to these lands. It festers in the Mirajii Forest. Omun died a hero's death. Shamàli, let his family remember him as such."

"War-taint..." Darakai's chief warlord stared at the gruesome cadaver. Luscia's stomach churned when his lips momentarily ticked upward, enthused somehow, then flattened into a grim groove. "Then the days of old are upon us." He nearly crooned. "It seems a multitude of threats endanger the Orynthian realm."

"A multitude of threats indeed, Commander," Dmitri remarked, clenching his byrnnzite cane.

The chief warlord raised his head, tipping back the wreath of bone and moss that decorated his scars.

"Uni, too many for a kingling to battle." His condescending timbre resonated from his core, shocking Luscia by his open mockery of the young regent. "Lateef, sound the horns and call the war council to arms. Our assembly, our kwihila, cannot wait on anything, or anyone," he boldly ordered the general.

His boot lifted, readied to leave, then his gaze slunk toward his son.

Pressed against her thigh, Aksel growled.

Faster than his age should have permitted, Darakai's chief warlord unleashed the kopar from his hip and slashed the sickle sword through Omun's throat, severing it from his haggard corpse. Zahra screamed when her leader exhausted the torch in his sodden entrails and, with the whetted tip, speared his skull.

"Your pryde's weakness can't be allowed to stain my tribes more than it already does."

Kasim dropped to his knees, staring at what was left of his warrior. Luscia felt Marek's arm reach around her protectively. Ira's chest puffed erratically where he shook. Dmitri stood slack-jawed, and Hachiro folded himself, and his robes, around his journal by his king's feet.

Shocked into silence, they didn't speak as Kasim's father overturned the pike and carried Omun's head like a trophy through the arena.

He was Darakai.

He was cinder, and he was flame.

A fallen warrior was just kindling to his fire.

Chapter Twenty Seven
Zaethan

B ile and rage poached his throat. Zaethan glared at his beheaded warrior—not his body, which had been left in the pit like carrion, but the pike installed at the center of the crammed bunker.

It was a frightening portrait, stirring alarmed speculation murmured chieftain to beta.

Mounted atop the torch post, Omun's slack visage stared blankly at his alpha. Zaethan had known it for many years, but from the core of himself, he wished he didn't recognize it now.

Omun Yakaim. Second son of a buffalo herder. Skilled horseman. A fighting spirit, bred out of a minor tribe in the rolling hills.

Zaethan's sixth recruit, whom he'd gotten killed.

He was responsible for all of them, not merely those who crowded his back inside the bunker. It was Zaethan who'd chosen to send Omun when the majority of his pryde had been forcibly dispatched to the border. At the base of Zaethan's seat, Kumo's foot shifted uncomfortably. It could have easily been the beta on that pike.

Allotting five to remain at Zaethan's disposal in Bastiion, his father had preyed on his son's favoritism, jeopardizing those outside it, to cull his most loyal force—his personal militia. Zaethan balled his fists, hating the conflict he caged. He'd sent Omun to retain Kumo. Another to keep Zahra. Sacrificed fifteen honorable men, for Takoda, Jabari, and Dhalili. A storm raged inside, ripping him in half. For even now, soaked in the devastating aftermath of his choosing, Zaethan would not have selected his five differently.

The pryde was crammed shoulder to shoulder behind him, where he sat tensely beside his king. Quiet and watchful, Dmitri's posture was static. Noble patience exuded from his elegant fingers laced before him, directed at the council of warlords. But it was a false patience. Concealed beneath the boulder slab, Dmitri's knee jittered in his silk trousers, as it had whenever his tutors spent hours in flippant dialogue rather than getting to the point. The young king surveyed the room and its hushed comments with slow, controlled blinks.

He hid his offense—when he should have been shouting it.

Darakai wielded tongues of passion, speaking in the Andwele torrent of love and hatred. Ecstasy and enmity. Triumph and shame. If their king didn't show his anger soon, his words in this battle-worn bunker would fall on apathetic, unimpressed ears.

Zaethan cracked his knuckles, wedged between the stoics of east and north. The king sat rigid to his right, and Boreal's haidren sat unnaturally immobile on his left. A fair hand rested on her wolx's head, though not to stroke or comfort the beast. She was cut from highland ice, except for the melted quiver along her crisp cheekbone that moved with her ears.

She was listening.

Intently.

Her curvaceous lips fired a soundless flutter, uttering witchtongue to the pair of shadowmen angled at her back. Abutting the horseshoe counter, the tribal leaders shot uneasy glimpses at the shadowmen and the superior weaponry fastened to their ghostly frames.

The whites of many tensed eyes oscillated back and forth toward the chief warlord. Cross-armed, Zaethan's father whispered to General Lateef, seemingly unconcerned by the outsiders as the assembly waited for unknown cause.

"Kasim," she breathed, unturning. "Are my najjan not forbidden in this place? What has changed?"

The room was charged, for good reason. No shadowman had ever entered the bunker. It was hallowed rock, sanctified by centuries of teeth and toil. Darakaian blood stained the Andwelestone seats upon which they sat, where their forefathers had bled and fought for a war-torn people. Here, they'd left a crimson trail of their half-healed wounds, just as Zaethan's seeped from his shoulder, adding to their chronicle.

Shadowmen *were* forbidden, yet half her guard had been permitted to accompany her, witchiron and all.

"I cannot say, Maji'maia," Zaethan whispered back as a prickling scaled his spine.

His gaze skittered to his uncle, responding in low tones to Chief Sefu of Halona. When he noticed the attention, his peppered brows knit apprehensively. Yousif's golden eyes flitted toward the men still piling in from the tunnel. A few final soldiers filed in after Bessus, packing the ancient chamber with a brigade of Unitarian and Darakaian fighters.

Zaethan didn't understand how his kinsmen, the selected warriors from Faraji assigned to the royal regiment, could follow that self-serving worm. Beady-eyed, Bessus nodded at Darakai's chief warlord, who stepped into the recess surrounded by the circular stone counter. His father's mouth screwed unsettlingly, and the portly field marshal, drenched in his own sweat, ordered the mixed sentries to line the bunker. Zaethan trekked them over his shoulder edgily, not liking their unusual position at his back.

With a boom, the tunnel hatch was shut, sealing them inside.

At Ira's timid whine, Zaethan peered beyond Dmitri and saw the yancy inch closer to Hachiro's Pilarese protector. In the closeness, the guard managed to budge and discreetly reestablished that inch.

"My warriors! My chieftains!" His father thundered, strutting around the beheaded Darakaian and securing the notice of each warlord. "A new peril befalls us! War-taint has resurrected in the Mirajii Forest. It ravages the prydes, slaughtering our heroes while the cowards flee!"

Fuss and furor rippled through the gathered leaders at their chief warlord's lie. Cursing, one of the Yowekaons hurled a goblet at Omun's severed head, denting cartilage with its unmistakable squelch. Zaethan shook in place as the bloodied goblet rolled under the toe of his father's boot.

"But Darakai is not the House of cowards, ano zà. Hehe hai the House of *kwihila*! The House of war and valor! The House who must mobilize and cut down Orynthia's surmounting threats with a sharpened kopar." He hailed, thrusting his muscular arms in the air. "And a strengthened shield!"

Chieftains and their betas clamored in accord, beating the counter with their goblets. But Zaethan was fixated on the one splattered in Omun's blood. His fingers spread over the historic slab. Zahra's white runes still decorated Zaethan in geometric patterns, knuckle to neck and navel to nose. He felt his thighs rise off his seat without his agreeing to stand.

No one stood against the chief warlord. And he would be the only one who did.

Curving with the eyes of his council, his father twisted and faced him down. A wicked thrill crispened the onyx, pitiless pools he'd searched his whole life. They were bottomless, harboring a cruelty that fed itself. Under their weight, Zaethan stretched out his shoulder blades, biting back the freshened pain of his injuries.

He'd already stood. It was too late.

"The Proper Pryde, those left breathing, have endured this terror long enough." Zaethan beseeched the quieting council, breaking from his father's gnarled sneer. "Omun Yakaim is a hero. Uni zà! Without his courage, we would not know what prowls at our border. What lurks toward Rian. As alpha zà, I demand the right to recall my men to Faraji!" He pummeled the counter twice, indicating the soil beneath them. "Here, they can be tended and strengthened, then deploy with the rest of the militia to fight this pestilence before it spreads. Shamàli." Zaethan's stance widened. "I am alpha zà. I am their leader. Let me bring our brothers home."

The council muttered among themselves. Others nodded their consensus.

Lugging his bulky, imperial cape behind his heels, his father clapped dramatically, silencing them with each strike. Once. Twice. By the third, his calloused palms steepled and angled at Zaethan.

He intentionally tilted his skull into the torchlight, showcasing his decades of brutal warfare. The ugly, maimed retelling that marked him as an enemy captive…

His father commanded their revere in an instant, basking in the council's regard as he parted his hands and said, "Except that you are not alpha zà. Not anymore."

Zaethan's ears went hot, scalded by the outlandish assertion. He fastened onto his uncle, who looked equally baffled. In a micro gesture, Yousif propped a finger, mollifying Zaethan's angst by a fraction. Using the cane, Dmitri rose beside him with startling calm.

"Despite your opposition, Zaeth won," the slender king declared, girded and steady. "You son retains his title."

Instead of the scorn he so often oozed when addressed by his regent, Darakai's chief warlord slung his head like a pendulum as his grin returned—the cold grin of a conman who'd just duped his mark.

"He forfeited his title when he left his challenger alive in the combat zone." His black eyes glittered at Zaethan. "The true alpha zà recovers in the infirmary as we speak."

Zaethan's stomach plunged toward his kneecaps.

Reclining against the counter, General Lateef folded his thick arms and cocked a sparse brow. His looming voice reiterated his inaugural remarks from the arena.

"For the challenger, kwihila or *death*."

Zahra expelled a batch of Andwele curses as Kumo raised his fist and rumbled at them. "That's a kakka-shtàka technicality, yeye qondai! Everyone knows it is!"

"Muzzle your whelps, or I will knock out their teeth," his father snapped.

It wasn't a threat; it was a dare. He wanted to hurt them, Zaethan knew. He craved another example of what it meant to test his rule. To confront his grip on those who'd forged for him this plinth of power.

His wrist flicked.

At his directive, metal chinked, and the soldiers at their backs angled their weapons at Zaethan's pryde.

Huddled with their enormous beta, Takoda, Jabari, and Dhalili gawked at the lesser fighters. Huffily, Kumo knocked a sentry's blade aside, only to have it swung back closer than before. Sucking in a breath, Zahra snarled at the tip of the nearest Unitarian sword. His third's autumn eyes widened at Zaethan in outrage.

His had widened too.

Nyack Kasim was more than chief warlord. He was the commander of Orynthia's armies. And he'd just ordered the royal regiment to draw their weapons dangerously close to their king.

Weapons they'd drawn without hesitation.

Though a wall of bodies separated him from their swords, Zaethan sensed Dmitri's exhales becoming shallow. He was afraid. Pressure slid against them when the two shadowmen glided between them and his endangered pryde. Squeezing behind their king, both the tall and the barrel-chested highlanders seamlessly flanked Dmitri in a Northern curtain of iron and light. In a dazzling prism, the crescent wraiths teased the red rock where their witchiron towered off the shadowmen's backs toward the low, rugged ceiling.

Zaethan bared his empty palms at the council, who'd hardened uneasily at the highlanders and their curved, winged blades.

"I left Wekesa..." His speech soured on his rival's name. "To reach my warrior in his final moments. Sparing my challenger wasn't some *ràtomdai jwona*, some claim of fate, but hérumaa—a mercy—of necessity." Zaethan's accent thickened while he scoured the council in appeal. "Hérumaa. Nothing more, ano zà."

"Hérumaa." His father purred the word. Scanning his chieftains, he rapped his forefinger against his puckered lip. "Sefu, my friend, what is mercy to Darakai?"

Desperate for an ounce of vindication, Zaethan turned to the old Halonan beside his uncle. Chief Sefu petted his snowy beard, dreaded all the way to the leather belt strapped across his belly. It was tangled with totems. Surely one of them boasted a memory of Cyra Shà, the warrior who'd thrived from Halona. Who'd grown under his tutelage. Who'd fought with him during the Shield Wars. Who'd rescued the warlord he answered to now.

Beneath his wiry whiskers, Chief Sefu sucked his discolored teeth and leaned back. "Mercy is for the weak."

"Uni, for the weak," Darakai's chief warlord echoed. Bending toward Omun on the pike, he stooped as if to speak to the warrior's ghost. "And the weak shall not lead." He rotated, pinning Zaethan with derision, the kind he saved for his son, riddled with the excited gleam Zaethan learned to fear. "But the jwona rapiki can lead... and shall."

In one sentence, his father had denounced his victory, snuffed out his kwihila before the entire council. The sweat, the strain—it was all dust. It'd been for nothing.

Zaethan had been written over. Wekesa would take his men. His city. His title.

His rival would have it all.

"This is outrageous!" Dmitri shouted, slamming his cane on the slab. "That blackguard is barred from Bastiion. He will never police my streets!"

Zaethan felt faint as the council broke into arguing. His vision spun, ultimately latching onto hers. The haidren's discolored iris shone.

She rushed a whisper. "Get him out of here, Kasim."

Her expression contorted, like she was hurt, and her frame started to shudder. But her illuminated eyes brightened, dashing overhead at everything but Zaethan's face.

The opalescence about her pinpricked pupil swirled in an unearthly frenzy. Zaethan's heart raced at the inhuman light. He didn't know where it came from, that which was so bright and wrong, yet he couldn't let his kinsmen see the brilliance.

For they would snuff it out.

"Stop it," Zaethan hissed.

Her erratic gaze peeled from the heights and locked onto him.

"Your eyes. Make it stop, or by Owàa, they will slit your throat."

If she displayed any hint of the occult, the haidren to Boreal would never leave this room. No Darakaian would let her—Ethnicam Accords be damned. And stripped of his authority of alpha zà, the only title that had granted him military standing with the council, Zaethan wouldn't be able to stop them.

The witch's hand shot out and quivered around his wrist. "We need to leave. Something is happening." She blinked rapidly, diffusing the glow. "Something terrible."

"Beholden to the throne's governance…"

"Noble interference belongs in the Peerage!"

Leery of her fanatical intensity, Zaethan pulled the other haidren off himself before the council caught notice amid their argument, brewing around the slab counter.

Beside him, Dmitri stood his ground against the formidable Nyack Kasim. His aristocratic hands were fisted at his hips.

"The outer Houses are subservient to the Orynthian crown! As are their subjects, regardless of station!"

"And yet," Zaethan's father bellowed, "Darakaian politics are not subject to kingling debate!"

A slew of chieftains joined their chief warlord when he began to laugh, overt and unfettered, at the young regent.

Sobering, he petitioned his riled leaders. "You see, my friends, these vital missteps are why it falls to us—to Darakai, uni—to safeguard the realm in Bastiion's place! Our Orynthian borders face not only war-taint but foreign strikes, organized by our deceitful ally... One with resources to fight this plague before it consumes the entire Ethnicam!"

Zaethan's father rounded the central recess. His scarlet-smattered cape circled Omun's pike. "It falls to the warlords of the South to raise arms against Razôuel and finally take what they keep to their burgundy sands! We will avenge the Stag King's assassination and show the modern realms that we are Darakai! *Hewe hai Darakai!*"

The council exploded with a battle cry. Chieftains and their betas sprung to their feet, beating their breasts. Dmitri's cheeks bloomed a shade of hostility Zaethan didn't know existed in his genes. Zaethan's focus tore from his friend and shot to his uncle.

Yousif wasn't looking at his king, nor his chief warlord. Easing away from the table, he was cautiously fixated on the base of the stairs leading from the hatch into the bunker.

"I warned you, Commander Kasim, that is not your declaration to make—"

"But, *Your Majesty*..." The royal address spewed from his father's mouth like acid. "An heir of Thoarne should never forget, it is not Bastiion, but Darakai who wields Orynthia's armies."

He signaled toward the steps, and a billow of white sailed beyond the threshold.

A syrupy voice leaked through the veil of armed sentries. "And Pilar who tallies Orynthia's debts."

Gooseflesh coated Zaethan's arms as Tetsu Naborū snaked among the parting men, until he appeared at their chief warlord's right hand.

Zaethan couldn't explain the chilled draft that accompanied the chancellor of the Shoto Collective's slick movements—or how in the darkened bunker, the torch flames seemed to shrink from his nearness.

Sidling Zaethan's elbow, the Boreali haidren seized the edge of the counter. Her limbs were trembling, and she clutched her temple with a gasp. Zaethan looked up and saw that Tetsu Naborū was not staring at Dmitri, for whom he spoke, or even at his nephew, who was clutching his journal in fright. Instead, his head slanted, and he leered at the highlander intently, like she were the only one in the room.

Tetsu Naborū's gaze stretched with his reedy, jaundiced grin, and Zaethan realized that amid her quaking, her strange eye had resumed its glow.

He sidestepped, blocking her from the chancellor's obsessive view—and from those on the council. With a snobbery that reminded Zaethan of his niece, Sayuri's uncle clicked his tongue. Emerging from the bunker's stair, three gaunt bodies paraded at Tetsu's back. The glassy-eyed Mworrans flashed their filed yellow teeth, in greeting to Zaethan's father.

The chief warlord flashed his in return.

"Nyack Kasim!"

Heads swiveled from the Mworran agents to the king of Orynthia.

Leaning heavily on his walking cane, Dmitri's umbrous glower was overcast by his tousled waves. Zaethan's veins pounded as a metronome between his ears. This was it, the moment his king would see who really controlled his Southern subjects.

"Nyack Kasim," he said again, and the bunker clasped onto his every syllable, "sil'haidren and chief warlord to Darakai, you are hereby stripped of the Orynthian commandership."

Measuredly, Zaethan's father stalked forward and stopped just short on the opposite edge of the stone counter. His nose buckled as Dmitri continued, arrow-spined and unblinking.

"You have overreached the Ethnicam Accords. You have defied the throne. You have disgraced the name of my father, King Korbin Aquilla Thoarne, the man who appointed you to the position of power you've so blatantly abused." Dmitri leaned in and braced his cane against the rock. "Every plot of crown-ordained acreage and each piece of Unitarian antiquity, down to the very last crupas in the treasury at your disposal, will be seized, as I order you relinquish command of *my* armies and surrender to the authority of *my* appointed commander supreme, Yousif Shà."

His father's face petrified into a mask. With the slightest incline of his skull, his lips, twin planks of burnt bark, uttered the directive.

"Seize him."

Beyond their chief warlord, Yousif was wrenched from the ancient slab. A pair of chieftains, one from Faraji, another from the foothills, hauled him backward.

Their kopars were hooked over his throat.

"Uni, go ahead. Order what you wish, cub of Korbin." Zaethan's father scanned Dmitri, down to his cane. "They won't obey. You're in my court now." He elevated the wreath of bone and moss about his head. "And you are outnumbered."

"Arrest this man for sedition!" Dmitri yelled to Bessus, but swallowing, the squatty marshal didn't budge. Perspiration dribbled past Dmitri's jaw as he swirled within their tight confines and scoured the regiment beyond the shadowman's guard. "I said arrest Nyack Kasim this instant!"

Zaethan wheeled on his heel, catching the Boreali haidren in his arm. She panted into him with each convulsion, but he ripped his frightened gaze from her already-weak coloring and speared it along the sentries lining the bunker.

"Obey your king!" he warned them.

Kumo and Zahra recited his demand, howling vitriol at the armed soldiers. Nervous eyes and sweaty temples darted toward Bessus, though their bodies did not respond to the order.

The regiment was not complying.

"This Quadren reeks of weakness!" his father announced over the commotion. "And the weak *shall not lead*!"

In ambushed unison, the soldiers speared their swords and marched his pryde closer, trapping them with the Quadren against the counter. Zaethan caught hold of Dmitri's brocade cuff, yanked him nearer, and positioned himself as his king's shield.

But then Zaethan remembered he held no weapon. He'd deserted it in the arena.

Zahra yelped when a sentry lurched. She punched him before another grabbed her into custody, just as Dhalili and Jabari were apprehended. Kumo shouldered off a man, unsheathed his kopar, and raked it across the swords threatening Takoda. The Pilarese guard angled his back against the betas, protecting Hachiro and the yancy cowering in his shadow.

Just as a blade nicked his nape, Zaethan swung around to confront his only living parent.

A parent now enemy of the realm.

The two shadowmen freed their crescent wraiths, arching their gleaming witchiron around Dmitri as he shouted incredulously, demanding the council to intervene.

"This coup was never about war-taint or the Orynthian people! You dare stage a revolt against your king? You'd forsake your own haidren for a tyrant's delusion?"

"You are no more my king than that leech is my son."

Blades suspended, and the bunker fell silent. Or perhaps it was only Zaethan who did.

"Come, Nyack…" Tetsu Naborū crooned from the darkness.

At his cautioning, Zaethan's father grated the underside of his corded forearm with his nails, just above the leather bracer where the edge of a half-healed wound crested. An odd, circular wound Zaethan had never noticed before. But the material fell, concealing it again, as his father visibly shook off the warning, throwing his words back to the chancellor.

"He is *not* my son."

Zaethan's whisper was numbing. "What did you just say?"

The cape of yak blurred in Zaethan's sight when his father whipped around to the council and thrashed his finger toward him.

"I speak the truth, friends. Your haidren is an imposter!"

Shock sounded among the chieftains.

"I tried to hide Cyra's betrayal, after she spread her legs for Unitarian seed!"

Sickness bubbled up Zaethan's esophagus as his mother's name was murmured throughout the bunker.

"I meant to honor her legacy, the kwihila of our family before the tribes, but I cannot hide the weakness of that whore's son any longer!

Ano zà! He is nothing but her illegitimate cross-caste, a vulgar half-breed parading as a Darakaian hero!"

Zaethan's hands tingled, and the room spun around them. Beneath the faded runes, each finger was so much lighter than his father's. His head shook violently as his lashes blotted back a mist.

"How can you say these things about her?"

When he lifted his face, he was met by the hills and valleys he knew better than any in all of Darakai.

The obsidian veneer of Nyack Kasim's face split, plucking his pocked cheeks as Zaethan gaped at his father.

His tormenter. His teacher. His prison.

"Who do you think gave you those disgusting eyes? Now I'll finally get to pluck them out." He breathed, stealing the air from Zaethan's lungs. A vicious anticipation dragged his mouth to the side when he unfolded to his height and barked to the soldiers, "Arrest them all!"

Zaethan blinked back a burning flood as the chamber erupted in screams and snarls. Iron clashed. Canines snapped. Fur raked his leg. His mind was laid to waste, emptied, as his hollow limbs were carted aside with force.

He was nothing. He was no one. Cutting through the chaos, across the barren cavity of his soul, her cry met his ears.

Kasim.

But that was not his name. He no longer had one.

CHAPTER TWENTY·EIGHT
LUSCIA

Dmitri had begged them not to resist. He had ordered her najjan to stand down and lower their wraiths on his behalf—a betrayed king—pleading they not shed the blood of his betrayers.

Surrounded by traitorous swords, Luscia had been forced to let them tie and bind him. Just like her and the rest.

Prodded like cattle through the tunnels by his own soldiers, the king's regiment no longer answered to him but rather to Darakai—a House turned against both Quadren and throne. At the field marshal's directive, Luscia and her men had been driven from the bunker and into the dark.

An outed puppet for the chief warlord, Bessus was the worst kind of man. A spineless weasel who would turn on his sovereign for what-ever empty promise Darakai never intended to keep. His mousy eyes couldn't even look at Orynthia's king when he'd deposited them in the dank chamber, then fled their vengeful sight like a cornered rodent as soon as the marshal could scurry off.

By the tip of the sword, Luscia had counted three major turns since their exit from the bunker hatch, yet without a sliver of daylight from above, she'd lost all sense of the hour.

Trapped somewhere within low-lit passageways, the arrested had been divided between three ancient cells, each group secured behind time-rusted iron bars that upheld the depressed ceiling of the rock dungeon. The air was stale, muddied by vermin droppings, fermented piss, and aged gore. The scent exacerbated her drumming headache.

Though dulled, her episode was lasting longer than usual. Anxiety over the prolonged ache, and the thought of who might've witnessed it, rivaled her panic for the bars she'd been locked behind. Luscia's temples still twinged, as if she had been left partly in her Sight within the bunker, under a canopy of frustrated lumin. The memory of those fragmented light threads scratched her thoughts. It was all too strange, too tangible. Though she couldn't see the threads now, with her ankles crossed and planted on her rump in a dank dungeon, she felt them nearby. Each was a subtle, conflicting shift in the stale draft that tickled her neck.

The veil to the Other had not closed. It'd been left ajar.

Alora had once promised Luscia the ability to shift in and out of the Sight, but she had always alluded that the veil would seal behind her. Something was wrong, something more vast, more ancient than the treacherous acts that had dragged them into the dungeon.

Thumb tucked beneath her chin, Luscia stroked her forefinger along the solrahs through her septum. The warmed luxiron soothed her flesh as she vigilantly crept her gaze along the dirty floor of the dungeon, toward the lone guard who leaned against the heavy, metal-plated door, stationed inside with them. Only a fool would underestimate their watchers, for two dozen more soldiers surely lined the tunnel on the other side, just beyond the guard's sagging shoulder.

They'd been studying him for the past hour, she and her najjan, as he slowly gave way to his fatigue. It must be late, perhaps even the bleakest part of the morning. It was unwise of the Darakaian to doze in their presence, confident in the rusted chains that shackled each Boreali's wrists together. His eyelids fell, then shuddered awake before drooping toward his cheeks again. He thought the prisoners weapon-less, stripped and undefended.

But they were weapons, for her mind was sharper than any blade, like the blade she happened to retain in plain sight, hugging her three-ringed knuckles.

The shackles bit into the backs of Luscia's hands when she fiddled with her radials. Her feet bare, she'd at least retained their movement, unlike her two najjan. Beside her, Marek was crouched on his ankles, which were chained to a corroded weighted ball. He balanced on his middle finger in silence, listening to the man's deepening breaths. Flanking them both, Declan peeked over his laced forearms through ginger lashes at the sleepy guard with chilled patience.

Warming the small of her back lay Aksel, his hackles raised protectively.

The soldiers had tried to wrangle the lycran with elongated, roped poles, but the field marshal's failed attempts to contain the Orallach beast had only left him a limp—and a satisfying stain on Aksel's reddened muzzle. She smirked fleetingly at that. For the beast's own good, Luscia kept him close, even in imprisonment. The animal considered her his pack, and in many ways, she considered him the same.

Besides, she wasn't planning on staying there for long. The lodgings were terrible.

"Do you think they are safe?" Luscia asked Marek, her voice as muted as the rustle of her fabric.

"Creyvan and Noxolo will stay undetected until we emerge," the captaen whispered indirectly to his haidren, unable to hold her eyes since they had fallen on Omun's corpse.

Her account of the attack in Rian had finally been vindicated. Marek's shame, evident in the distinct faraway tilt of his jaw, solidified the invisible wall between them with every raw minute that had passed since.

"Najjan are trained to not endanger the advantage until it is crucial to do so," he added stoically. "We have every reason to expect they live, otherwise their bodies would have been paraded before us."

Luscia nodded with his estimation of her najjan's wellbeing, and Marek repositioned his hands on the ground. The chains jangled, garnering a small upstir from the guard before he drowsily resettled against the door. It was a sort of backhanded compliment, she supposed, that the old iron shackled the Boreali while the Quadren and others were merely bound by thick coiled roping.

The pryde, sequestered in the corner cell to their left, had eventually hushed after their barking an expletive torrent at the acting warden for hours on end. It had failed, to the vexation of their Boreali neighbors, as it only delayed the man's slumber.

Since, the Darakaians had scattered about their rocky containment in quiet clusters. Standing at the rear, Kumo rocked the base of his massive skull against the wall, while a muttered discussion continued between Zahra and Yousif Shà, the graying beta from Halona. She motioned with her knotted hands as she leaned closer, speaking into the ear of Dmitri's named commander. Paces away, Takoda lay across the floor, his braided crown settled in the lap of their tiny boyish scout, Dhalili. He swatted away the frayed strands tumbling onto his dusky forehead as she gnawed at her binds with the industrious intensity of a beaver. Jabari's coils cloaked her little shoulder where his face sank, surrendering to the same lure as the prison guard.

Unmoving in the corner sat their leader, their defamed haidren.

His limbs hung off his frame like a throwaway puppet. With despondent, listless blinks, he stared into an abyss, lost in a darkness not one of them could fathom. In a matter of moments, he'd been stripped of his entire being. The title of alpha zà had been offered to his defeated rival. The fate of the militia, of his own men, had been ripped from his grasp and handed to another like tossed coin.

But to then have the unthinkable taken within the witness of his brethren, to have his haidrenship denied by the accusation of illegit-imacy… Luscia would never forget the look that melted off his face when his father had disowned him. The way a few words had snuffed out that infuriating flame behind his ever-brightened eyes. Vivid, unruly green irises she'd always assumed were a lasting depiction of his mother, only to learn they were evidence of another lineage entirely.

The same eyes that were now set low with his rounded spine.

If what the chief warlord had said was false, then he'd become the unwanted son of a traitor. And if it were true, that his ancestry was split—that his mother had been entangled with a Unitarian—the House of Darakai would consider him lower than a breakaway, a speck of dirt on their bootheels. For even a breakaway, despite House aban-donment, bled from Darakaian veins.

If it was true that he was cross-caste, then he belonged nowhere and to no one at all.

His arm jutting through the tarnished bars, their king struggled against his constraints, reaching out for his friend. Dmitri's fingertips brushed the haidren's pantleg as his face earnestly pressed into the barrier. He spoke softly. Her king's thin cheeks were tear-stricken and not for his own welfare, she knew. From across the cell, she saw his wan lips flutter, trying to console him. But his ordinarily boisterous friend was unresponsive, except for the spasm through his busted, ornamented brow.

He had to be in physical pain as well. The gash along his shoulder blade needed to be cleaned and packed soon. Luscia already smelled an infection brewing.

She swallowed, unable to steer her regard from his downcast and defeated countenance, wondering if the man she'd come to both loath and appreciate was gone forever.

And at the oddest, most unexpected sensation of loss festering behind her sternum, she found herself praying to Aniell that this would not be the last way she encountered the one called Zaethan Kasim.

Beyond Dmitri, the Pilarese guard got up, stretched his legs, and paced behind his charge. Sharing the third cell with the young king, Hachiro Naborū-Zuo repeatedly tapped his knuckle in the air with steady rhythm. Curious by the shoto'shi's behavior, Luscia could only deduce that he must be keeping time. He had been separated from his notorious journal, and the monotonous act appeared to calm him when it would have maddened most.

Near Hachiro's knee, robed in citrine silks, lay Ira, sprawled on his back. In classic yancy fashion, one leg had been thrown over the other, and the noble held his enchained snuff canister between his bound palms and coasted it along his upper lip, presumably inhaling its powdered contents.

Stacked in a careless heap within the fourth cell rested their collective weaponry. She could almost hear her kuerre's call.

"He sleeps. Quickly now, Ana'Sere," Marek rushed under his breath.

The captaen outstretched his arms toward her, holding the old chain taught. He centered the weakest links between his grip, where rusting had discolored most of the iron. Herself bound, Luscia thumbed the secreted latch and unhinged Phalen's radials from her three-fingered rings. Though small and petite, the arced blades were as strong as any luxiron hatchet, to her brother's design. With a burst of strength, she swung the radials, busting through the ordinary ore.

The sudden chink startled the others, but Luscia's eyes flew to the guard. Restfully, the Darakaian smacked his lips a few times and resumed his congested snore.

Marek unscrewed the pins in his shackles while she made haste for his feet, repeating the gesture. As the second pair of chains broke apart, a couple members of the pryde crawled over to the bars that divided their cell from the Boreali.

Gawking, Dhalili spit a strand of roping from her teeth as she watched Luscia hand off her radials to her captaen. The loops too small for his knuckles, Marek hooked the pair in one hand and bashed through the metal links between Luscia's own shackles. Spinning toward the thickening line of Darakaians in the cell over, Luscia waved her forefinger over her lips, signaling their silence. She directed their interest to the napping guard. Behind the stout bars, Zahra cricked a brow, inclining it toward her tied wrists.

Luscia nodded back.

The pins removed, Luscia massaged her joints as Marek glided around Aksel to free Declan. Unimpressed, the stockier najjan snorted when his chains fell loose. At the final clank, untethering him from the anchoring ball, Dmitri rose too. Leaving the musty corner, their king came forward to find all three Boreali unencumbered.

How? he mouthed.

For his regent, Marek flashed her radials in the dim torchlight and returned them into Luscia's care. She swiftly slipped the rings back into position and padded to the cell barrier. Immediately, Zahra shot her knotted palms out expectantly. Without pause, Luscia grabbed the rope and began to saw, careful not to break her calloused skin. Hers were the hands of a warrior, evident in the healed layers of discipline and rigor. Luscia respected that she'd earned her place as third, and was doubtless that Zahra would make a fierce opponent were her allegiances different.

Wrist caught in her grasp, Luscia looked up at her intently. Zahra's lashes tensed, her sepia stare crisp.

She'd made a difficult choice, allying with her disgraced alpha and haidren over her own House. Luscia noted how the rest of the pryde admired Zahra, revered her even. She was an asset to Darakai and could have confidently aligned with the chief warlord instead, to her own gain, had she chosen it.

Letting go, Luscia moved onto the little being just beside Zahra. Beginning to slice through the devastated threads, she wondered if Dhalili's gums ached from her perseverance. It was starting to make sense why the petite scout been kept from Hagarh—she never gave up. In a huff, Dhalili wiggled out of the binds and punched the air, relishing her liberation.

Luscia handed Declan one of the radials to assist Kumo, Takoda, and Jabari as she transitioned to Yousif Shà. He examined her speedy work, spying the luxiron radial closely. When the rope was severed, the older man clutched her hand and turned over her knuckles.

"Is that luxsmith craftmanship?" Yousif murmured in wonderment.

"Wem," Marek said, answering for Luscia. Reaching past her shoulder, he pried off the new commander's touch.

Jaw tight, Luscia collapsed the radial and twisted on her heel. She seized the arm of Marek's linsilk jacket and steered him away from the bars. It was petulant to start bickering under such circumstances.

They'd needed the guard asleep to free themselves but would need to awaken him under the illusion they were still restrained. Then, once Luscia got him to walk along the cell, Declan would spring to hold him there, rendering him unconscious, as Marek retrieved the keys.

It was a perfect plan. Except that a dart just impaled the guard clean through his eye.

His dead body, along with the key, slumped to the ground well beyond their reach.

"Shtàka, Dhalili!"

Luscia and Marek swiveled, astonished to see the scout squatting low, a stout blowpipe in hand.

"Ho'waladim, tricky sapsucker!" she cried, proudly dusting off her palms.

"Where have you been hiding that?" Takoda asked incredulously and plucked the blowpipe from her.

Dhalili crossed her short arms and shrugged. "In my sneaky-sneak."

"Depths!" Zahra smacked it out of Takoda's hand, disgusted. "Do not put your mouth on that."

Declan pounded the bars in frustration, the echo jerking their attention to the angry najjan. "We needed the guard alive!" he yelled from behind his burnished whiskers. "He pocketed the key to our cells!"

"You stupid savage!" Marek shouted too, no longer wary of his volume. "Darakaians never give any thought to the havoc you all wreak!"

"Captaen," Luscia briskly warned.

They were, after all, still on Darakaian soil.

"Oh doru." Tossing up his hefty hands, Kumo hotly countered. "Like you planned to share your kakka-shtàka plan with us anyways!"

"Witchy-roachies you are, draining your cubs, yeah? Bleeding them dry…" Dhalili dragged her blowpipe up the underside of her deeply hued veining. "Y'siti are the savages!"

Luscia's skin heated at the slander. Against her hip, Aksel snarled.

Zahra whipped her arm around Dhalili's neck and clamped over her chattering mouth. "Ano zà. Alpha Zà said no more of that word."

"See, your prydes are lawless!" Marek raked his scarlet tresses, dangling out their lacing.

Luscia shoved against his chest, walking him backward. "Heh'ta. That is an order, Captaen."

"At least our law doesn't keep a cross-caste from entering their own House!" Kumo barked, his fist clamped. "Wewe qondai. We know how the Boreali treat your—"

"Just stop it!"

Dmitri gripped the cell bars, cradling the panes of his elegant face between his cinched palms. His bronzed brow rested against the iron. Exhaustion bowed his shoulders forward, and in his filthy finery, he seemed so frail.

"This fighting is not the way out of this dungeon. We can only withstand what we exude."

Turning back, Dmitri soaked in his crestfallen friend, as if waiting for him to eventually look up. But the Darakaian haidren did not. The young king recoiled, like he was stung, heaved a sigh, and faced the adjacent cells once more. Searchingly, his slender chin grated behind the bars.

"Unity is just diversity moving toward a common goal. You don't have to like each other, but I will require you to treat one another as equals. Now, without discriminating the connotations of such skill…" Dmitri swallowed thickly. "Does anyone have experience picking locks?"

Zahra uncovered her scout's mouth, and gradually, muttering commenced among the two groups. Lockpicking was not a forte of Luscia's, nor of her men, otherwise their scheme would have avoided use of the guard altogether. She held her lycran against her leg, observing Ira and Hachiro across the walkway. Neither had spoken, although the yancy had propped himself up, clearly interested in the commotion.

Luscia scoffed. *Even in crisis, nobility wished to be entertained.*

Hachiro's personal guard stepped around his interim haidren, counting on the floor. Without a word, the man ripped apart a seam in his modest, fabric-covered armor and removed one of the stays. It resembled a sliver of bone, from what Luscia could discern. After showing it to their king, he started fiddling with the lock on their cell.

At a loud boom, the Pilarese guard dropped the makeshift pick, then scrambled after it as another bang erupted outside the door. Marek put his body in front of Luscia, outstretching his arms. She backed into Declan and clutched Aksel's fur when a force slammed against the wood, and suddenly, the door shuddered off its bulky hinges. When it fell, it bludgeoned the rock, flooding the dungeon in a cloud of red dust.

As it cleared, two blond heads popped through the craggy tunnel opening.

"Ana'Sere!" Noxolo cried out, rushing toward her cell. "We worried we were too late!"

"The keys." Marek coughed in the settling cloud. "Check the guard's pocket."

Rounding the threshold, Creyvan approached the Darakaian guard, wraiths at the ready, only to realize he was already dead. Sheathing one of the weapons, he bent low and flicked the dart stuck in his eye socket. He rummaged through the folds of the man's gunja pants and produced a copper ring of timeworn keys.

"Nox!" Luscia couldn't help but smile her relief. She reached high to cup his cheek, then saw the crimson that soaked his linsilks. As it was not sweet, as his should be, she scented it did not belong to him.

Hurriedly, she instructed him, "Unbind the king and his haidrens while Creyvan unlocks the cells."

By the fifth try, Creyvan found the right match, freeing her and the najjan before the other haidrens. The najjan didn't even acknowledge them, Luscia noted uneasily. It was not the time to address her concern for Creyvan's brewing zealotry, but she expected it was coming later than it ought.

Declan ruffled his flaxen hair and briefly pulled him into a one-armed embrace. Passing them, Luscia gratefully brushed his back.

"Tadöm, Ana'Brödre. You could not have come sooner."

"You should have waited," she overheard Marek admonish as she crossed the walkway to assist her king.

Noxolo called to Creyvan to toss the keyring, having cut through the roping on everyone in Dmitri's cell. When he opened the gate, Luscia swooped in to assess her patient. A rash encircled his wrists, but otherwise, Dmitri appeared not to have been bruised, like some of the rest. Yet if it'd been too long since his last elixir, a bruise was the better alternative.

A puff of sweaty cologne invaded her study.

"When I proposed we get tied up during this tour," Ira muttered into her ear, "I want you to know, gosling, this is *not* what I had in mind…"

Luscia grimaced as he exited the cell.

"We need to move. Soon." Noxolo pointed at the blown-off door, into the tunnel. "Before the field marshal rotates the wardens."

With the fourth cell unlocked, her najjan retrieved their weaponry. She trailed the others toward the smashed doorframe, stepping into her upturned boots along the way. Overhead, Marek passed Luscia her father's gifted kuerre, as well as the spare she'd lent earlier that night. Belting the sheath onto her hips, the balanced weight of the luxiron felt right, as if she was whole again.

Buckling it, she glanced up. Yousif and the pryde of Darakaians stood at the helm of the tunnel, gaping, chins to their chests.

The rightful commander turned his head toward Noxolo. "But there were only two of you…"

Luscia marched through the entry and stopped in her tracks alongside them. A storm of pride and sorrow thundered through her heart.

Almost thirty soldiers lined the tunnel, every one of them slaughtered.

"They say one najjan is worth twenty men," Luscia stated.

"And another twenty," Noxolo replied," when his haidren is in need."

Heaviness befell on her shoulder. Marek warped her around to see Dmitri planted on his knees in the corner of the Darakaian cell. He was stooped like a beggar, instead of one who wore a crown.

"Time is running out, Ana'Sere."

Head low, Luscia brushed him off and reentered the dungeon alone.

Her boot scuffed the floor just short of Dmitri, who in rushed statements tried to rally his friend to rise. Gently, her fingers stirred the back of his ornate vest. "You must go with the captaen now, My King. We will be right behind you."

Dmitri palmed his mouth. Sniffing, he tore his watery gaze away from his friend. Nodding at her, he backed away, as if not wanting to miss a miracle. He only turned when Marek guided him into the tunnel, and the group disappeared from view.

Each minute precious for their escape, Luscia kicked her tutor's leg aside and crouched between his knees. His ivory gunjas were covered in russet dirt stains, his deflated chest and muscled torso smeared by the symbols his third had painted. He no longer resembled a champion.

And yet he was.

She propped up his clefted chin with her forefinger, leveling their faces. Luscia snapped twice before his deadened expression. Nothing.

Again, she snapped. "Kas—" She caught herself, for that was not his name. "Zaethan." She said it slowly, deliberately, though his pupils did not shift toward her voice. "He cannot survive this without you..." Luscia said blatantly, gripping his chin more forcefully. "And I don't want to try. So I'm going to do whatever it takes to get you off this floor."

At that, Luscia slapped him.

And then she slapped him even harder.

"Come back to me!" she growled, aiming for a third strike.

But her forearm was stalled, clamped inside his trembling fist. His shadowy, broad eyes seethed his jade wrath. Under his hunkered brows, they snapped toward hers and scored Luscia from the inside. She did not look away but grinned as viciously as the day he'd told her the same.

"There you are."

CHAPTER TWENTY NINE
ZAETHAN

Zaethan carted her kuerre over the wreckage as they ran. Blood was everywhere. It encased the rock walls, blurred in dark-red spindles. The sorrowful blend of Darakaian and Unitarian heritage, spilt to free them, splashed his bootheels. Mixed blood, he realized, that matched his own.

He was cross-caste.

In his veins, he carried a stranger, and for it, he'd been branded an imposter to his people.

But it was the man he'd called father who was the real imposter. Nyack Kasim, who was the liar. Darakai's chief warlord, the fraud.

That phony patriarch had beaten him for years. He'd been allowed to trample him with hatred and scorn, and in that allowance, had sent Zaethan into the scathing wilderness as a cub, just to later dump him onto the merciless streets of Bastiion. All while touting a smirk and barbarous gleam, because to Nyack Kasim, he wasn't a son, he was a plaything.

A leech. The memory rang hollow through Zaethan's thumping ears.

Molten rage consumed the bleak space that'd almost consumed him. Awakened from his shocked daze, the truth scorched his tongue, devoured his thoughts, and heated the witchiron hilt trapped in his hardened, unforgiving grip.

He was nameless. Title-less. Nobody… except the person he needed to be in this very moment: a friend to Dmitri Korbin Thoarne.

For his was the only name that *did* matter.

Sprinting ahead of Zaethan, the Boreali haidren leaped over the last of the bodies—the portions her shadowmen had left intact. The enormous wolx sprang after her, pairing her swift strides. Zaethan jumped, grinding his teeth when his shoulder blade lifted with his vault.

She decelerated at the end of the tunnel where it split into opposing directions. In a matter of breaths, she read the gruesome tracks and veered northward, selecting the passage that rounded with the canyon. Racing at her heel, Zaethan pushed his injured limbs to keep up, biting back the strain. Her sensitive ears must have heard his pants, but she surged forward mercilessly.

And he wanted her to. There was no time for weakness—not even his own.

At the next bend, the tunnels broke into thirds. The blood there had already dried, the tracks having faded behind them. There was scantly enough light to sight any if they tried.

Torchlight crackled as the haidren bent on her knee, rubbed the craggy, cool earth, and brought the dust to her pale nostrils. She sniffed and swished her head, wiping off her fingertips frustratedly. Twisting, she looked back over her shoulder. A question shone from her opaline, mismatched eyes. She expected Zaethan to answer it.

"Meme ano'qondai, Maji'maia. I've no clue where Yousif is taking them," he confessed. Scraping the stubble on his jaw, he glanced between the divergent passageways. "I was never permitted this far... Only the council knows where they lead."

With a curt nod, she cocked her blade. "Aksel," she said, beckoning the wolx.

Zaethan toed closer when abruptly, she sliced herself across the palm. Hovering her hand before the beast's snout, she blew over the cut into the shadowy tunnels.

"Weh'dajjeni Lux," she whispered to the animal. When she clicked her tongue, he took off, favoring the rightward route. The haidren stood and grinned. "Waedfrel."

Soundlessly, her feet were mist on the stone as she dashed after it. Yards away, Zaethan fastened onto her phantom plaits as her hair sailed around the next corner, plunging him into a tunnel barely as tall as it was wide.

He hunched low and his ankles tweaked, sensing the incline. The air swaddled his skin. Muggy and warm, the musty smell of moss predicated the sheet of dampness that slimed his biceps when the underpass narrowed, compressing his frame.

All of a sudden, they stormed into stagnant water.

"I hear them," she said, sending ripples over the inky surface, and she heaved the lone torch out of its rusty sconce.

The wolx splashed into the murky pool as it deepened to her waist. The waterline reached Zaethan's thighs. He didn't guess at what squished beneath his heels, never keen on realms he could not see nor the critters that ruled them.

Murmurs skated the algae-covered water. Together, they waded to the other side, where a rock shelf spread along the bank. The Boreali haidren handed Zaethan the torch as she hoisted out of the pool. But the wolx, shaking out his coat, doused its flame, and he trotted onward.

She emitted a soft growl in the abrupt blackness. Fabric squelched, and he heard her remove something from her soaked pockets.

At what sounded like a sigh, light was cast all around them, painting the slick crags in a pastel frost. Zaethan's mouth fell agape. Between her dainty fingers, she held out a smooth oval stone.

"What kind of spell—"

"It's just a lumilore." She waved the pebble in annoyance and started to walk. "As I've maintained, I'm not a witch."

Unconvinced, Zaethan followed her eerie beacon.

The glow unveiled a series of still-damp footprints heading toward a dead end. Yet as the muffled voices loudened, Zaethan saw they approached not a wall of Andwelestone but of dense greenery so thick, mere pinpricks of light were tearing through. She scanned the lumilore from where the tracks ended, over the fat vines, and to where the natural curtain had been broken. Wedging her hand inside the leaves, she peered up at him to do the same, and in unison they pulled the heaviness aside.

"Ahoté!"

"Ana'Sere!"

He was engulfed by a pair of swollen arms. Over Kumo's leathered shoulder, having somehow acquired his armor, Zaethan's sight adjusted to the shiest of dawns.

Under heliotrope skies, he beheld the bustle underway. The tunnel had opened to a secret ravine. It rose steeply above the assemblage of horses. Confused, Zaethan skittered his stare over the cluster of warriors and equipment until it fell onto the back of a slender, rumple-headed regent who, strapping his saddle onto Harmonia, had pivoted toward the commotion.

Dmitri's hopeful expression was blocked when Kumo finally let go, and Takoda bounced in his stead.

"Rhaolé, we have to rush, Alpha Zà." Takoda rambled past his cousin, shoving a braided breastplate into Zaethan's middle, along with his sheathed kopar.

Startled, Zaethan contorted as a bracer was buckled to his forearm from behind.

"Hellion is just there, yeah? With a shield and stash of your things," Zahra said, moving to fasten a pauldron harness around his bared chest. He jerked his neck, examining it. It was his battle armor, scaled in crocodile skin and studded with rings of bronze. She tugged it, patting the snug fit contently. "He is ready to run when you are, Alpha Zà."

Zaethan blinked at the title. Cross-castes couldn't enlist in the Darakaian prydes, and it was even more unfathomable they'd ever lead one of their own. He snatched Zahra's arm before she swung away, locking onto her spiced irises. Kumo would need her support in the changeover. As beta, the pryde was his now.

"I'll await Kumo's word," Zaethan stated weightily.

"Ano zà." Kumo interjected, swinging himself around to see the rest of their pryde stubbornly crowded behind his laced forearms. "We await yours, Alpha Zà, and yours alone."

Zaethan stared into the indigo web underscoring the skin of his wrists. He wasn't one of them anymore.

But Kumo—his beta, his cousin—boosted his bearded jaw defiantly and rammed his fist against his heart, leaving it there. With flattened lips, Takoda struck his own, then Jabari and Dhalili on theirs. Coming around him, Zahra backed into their group, her clenched fist dug into her chest.

He was their inferior. The House of Darakai had declared it.

But they didn't care. Instead, they pounded their hearts in wordless unison, the beat screaming with outlawed allegiance. It filled the hollow in his own heart. Zaethan's head hung. Eyes shut, he nodded to the rhythm, letting it brand him… allowing it to write something new, a fate not yet recorded. A fate that defied his last.

Kwihila rapiki mu jwona.

In a single decisive flash, Zaethan's face sprung up at them.

"Jabari, Takoda," he barked at the pair, "ensure the haidrens are prepared to depart. Zahra and Kumo, flank the king. At all times, yeah? Dhalili…"

She hopped delightedly at his command.

"Ride reverse with Jabari. Play the huwàa and sight attack from the rear." Zaethan didn't wait for their confirmation. Belting the kopar over his dirtied gunjas, he marched past Hachiro, who with an armful of scrolls, mumbled rapidly to his guard, and beelined for Dmitri. A hand on Harmonia's reins, he strode with her in line behind Yousif's Andwele stallion. But at Zaethan's approach, his friend discarded them and opened his arms.

"Zaeth, I was so worried—"

"My King." He sank to his knee, bowing before his sovereign. "I failed you back there… It will not happen twice."

"No, brother." Dmitri took to a knee of his own and palmed Zaethan's neck fiercely. "You're the one who was failed."

Brusquely, Zaethan sniffed. He broke from the pity wetting Dmitri's lashes and returned to his feet. Rising, he noticed the byrnnzite cane tied into a bundle on Harmonia's saddle, along with the Sword of Thoarne shining from Dmitri's scabbard. He'd not worn it into the bunker.

"How did all this get here?"

"You were wise to nominate your uncle," Dmitri said admiringly as he got up and pointed toward Yousif directing the assembled shadowmen. "A great leader always has a contingency plan."

But Zaethan's regard caught on someone else—hobbling alongside the haidren's mare, carting a small locked chest.

Machàkwe.

Dumbfounded, Zaethan rushed to the elderly bondservant's aid, just as he shakily handed off the item to its Northern owner.

"Was a crate retrieved as well?" the haidren anxiously asked Machàkwe. Zaethan sensed panic in her tone, despite the fearsome wraiths now winging her back.

"Ano, Lady Haidren. This and your weaponry were all my family could smuggle out of the byumbé."

Snatching his frail arm, Zaethan nervously exclaimed, "What are you doing here, old man? If the council discovers your aid…"

"We swore to serve, son of Cyra. To serve the line of Shà." Machàkwe's knotted beard trembled bitterly with his jowls. "Not Kasim."

Aghast, Zaethan shifted and stared at his uncle, who'd arranged it all. Sadness tempered Yousif's angular features as he nodded over the horsebacks. He knew the consequence.

"Machàkwe, the chief warlord will execute your entire family for this."

With the defiance of the sun, the hunched laborer narrowed his single eye, as if the other were still there, glaring through the stained cloth that covered it.

"Uni zà, my Lord Haidren." Machàkwe rasped. "And by Owàa, he will be repaid for it."

Zaethan kissed his palm and cupped the quartz post that pierced the bondservant's ear, treasuring him. It would be the last time he ever could.

For five days, their hooves beat the trails. From Faraji to the Yakov River, they'd stopped only at the point of exhaustion for an hour or two of rest. Never more.

On the second day, once Bessus and the regiment had left the canyon in hot pursuit, Yousif had circled back to the foothills under nightfall. Newly named, the council would never expect him to abandon the king's defense. And outside their periphery, his uncle raced for Halona instead.

Dmitri had no use for a new commander if there was no one left breathing to follow his command.

They'd agreed. Yousif would rouse Dmitri's supporters and discreetly escort them to temporary refuge in Rian. Then he was to rally the Eindrulla Pryde, send an emissary to the pryde along the Yachel, and ride himself to secure allegiance from those at Ikaika. From there, he and the alphas would sway the remainder of the prydes to repledge featly to the crown.

And to Zaethan.

By the third day, the Valley Pryde, led by Wekesa's beta, had caught up to the field marshal's chase, driving the king and his Quadren farther down the hills on the northside of the river. As they were outnumbered, sleep had reduced to a luxury, something tasted for a blink. Fatigue became another enemy, another arrow in the dark—perhaps the most dangerous enemy of all.

But on the fifth day, the pursuers' search evolved. The Quadren was being hunted. Not as kings. Not as men.

But as prey.

Zaethan booted Hellion faster as Ira bleated like a goat. He spit the yancy's sweaty hair out of his mouth, fixating his sight on the sprawling sinuous tree line in the distance. Twisting branches jutted from the woodland edge, as if the Mirajii Forest were a gnarled hag beckoning the Quadren inside her home. Alighted by the submerging sun, her impenetrable canopy hosted a deceptive shadow few dared to enter— one he'd get to sooner if Ira were able to cleave to his own horse.

Keeping up with Harmonia's twin, Dmitri galloped his horse directly behind Hellion, his quarters shielded by Kumo and Zahra. After them rode Hachiro Naborū-Zou with his Pilarese guard, much how Ira was encumbering Zaethan. Although mute in his fright, the robed shoto'shi was practically an oversized ornament compared to the yancy's barnyard bellowing.

In an arrow formation, the shadowman defended the flanks, their haidren and her wolx at the center. A modest pony in size, it bolted among the storm of hooves. Capping the rear was the rest of the pryde. Against Jabari rode Dhalili, backward at the offensive helm, her double bow engaged.

Gaining on them, the Valley Pryde blew a war horn. Zaethan

wrenched over his shoulder just in time to see the swarm of arrows descend.

"Shields!"

Zaethan hoisted his overhead, covering both himself and Ira as they cowered into Hellion's mane. Risking a glance, he ensured Dmitri had advanced under the shelter of both his beta's and third's shields. Over the glint of their rims, Zaethan watched as, unshielded, the stout shadowman swerved and lashed a crescent wraith through the shaft of an oncoming arrow—intended for his haidren.

"Shtàka!" Takoda shouted.

He ripped a rogue arrow out of his impaled bedroll, shooting feathers into their wake. Speeding up the line, he held it high enough for all to glimpse the triple-vaned arrowhead. Zaethan's gut sank. Atop each thorny ridge was a contrastingly coiled hook.

"They're shooting vulture-barbs! At their own people!"

"At their own king!" Zaethan roared, splintering Hellion from the lead to swing behind Dmitri.

An insidious keepsake from the Mworran Wars, vulture-barbs were designed to capture even the most elusive enemies. Spinning in descent, the arrowhead would enter the body at a sinuous curve. But it was the slim hooks that kept it there. Positioned conversely to the vanes, the victim would have to rip out his innards to remove it. Named for their purpose, an archer could rest easily, following the carrion birds for miles to where the enemy slowly bled out.

And if they were the prey in a vulture's chase, it meant the chief warlord had not ordered for them to be taken back to Faraji alive.

"Another wave!" Dhalili shouted, engaging her and Jabari's shields as one.

Having lifted his just in time, Zaethan's arm shuddered beneath the impact. Arrows bounced off the riveted bronze disc. Swiftly, he swung the shield's strapping over Ira's shoulders, careful of the iron spikes along the border. Hopping onto his heels, Zaethan dropped the reins into the yancy's lap.

"Hold these and aim for the tree line."

Ira fumbled them and gripped Hellion's mane even tighter. "I'm not trained for this madness, Zaeth! I'm usually the horse, not the rider!"

Grunting, Zaethan seized his bow and quiver. He stretched to stand, anchoring a heel in the saddle and the ball of his other foot against Hellion's haunches, like a towering mast upon the animal. Notching an arrow, he angled it with his eye. Not far off were a trio of Darakaians, spearheading the partnered pursuit. A string of renegade soldiers rode not too far behind.

"Maji'maia, protect the king!" he yelled, for her to switch in front of Hachiro.

As she complied, concentration laced her tawny brows as she surged her mare through the formation. The Pilarese guard ran aside, permitting Hellion to fall back with the others. Takoda stood reverse in his stirrups, facing the teaming horizon. Mirajii was not too far off, and in its entrapping, they might be able to lose them.

Zaethan whooped, and at his call, his pryde freed their arrows. The wind, on their side, carried them farther than the vulture-barbs. In the bobbing distance, a Darakaian and a soldier fell from their horses and were trampled underfoot.

He reached into his saddlebag. Then Zaethan tossed Dhalili a coiling of rope. "Stretch wide and set a knock-off when we get to the trees!"

"Uni zà, Alpha Zà!" she declared, stitching the rope to her next arrow. "Knock them kakka-jackals straight on their lickers!"

He and the others drew their bows. With another whoop, they

released their onslaught. The arrows battered their pursuers like unrelenting rainfall. Zaethan grinned when Wekesa's beta slumped forward—his arrow buried in his shoulder.

"Once we enter the Mirajii," Zaethan shouted to Kumo, unturning, "there's a gorge southeast of the river before the forest gives to the wetlands!"

"Third wave!"

Zaethan bent, stripping the shield off Ira, and ducked just as the sides of his vision blurred with vegetation. The forest hurtled by in Hellion's race. Roping whizzed at the rear, socketing a taut trap from one end of the woodland to the other. He hoped it'd hold strong enough to displace even a few.

There was no time to test it.

Forward facing, he stashed the quiver and swung the shield over his shoulder blade, the wound still packed with the Boreali poultice. The herbs had wetted, either by a break in the scab or his heavy perspiration. Zaethan swiped the saltiness off his lip and yanked the reins back from Ira, tearing through the shadowmen toward Dmitri. But a pained groan swung his head aside.

The Pilarese guard sagged backward, a vulture-barb lodged between his ribs.

"He's going to die either way. This would be hérumaa—mercy from his jwona."

"Murder is not mercy!" Dmitri snapped, rubbing his sallow cheek. He needed to eat. His complexion waned too similarly to the Boreali. "Enough men died in that tunnel, Zaeth. Need we add to their number?"

Dmitri cupped water from the stream, splashing his face when Zaethan rose. Across the gorge, stowed under a mass of fallen trunks, the Pilarese guard wheezed. He'd been spread on his side, over a sodden bedroll. Scarlet drenched the downy fabric beneath his ribs.

Moonlight was scarce in the earthen crevasse, as if Àla'maia shaded them from her own radiance just to grant a pause for the man bleeding out at Hachiro's feet. His journal was open, though the shoto'shi's quill did not budge.

The Boreali haidren blotted the man's forehead with cloth, offering him nothing but momentary comfort. Her wolx laid there too, watching over him somberly.

Rebinding his locs, Zaethan trudged through the stream past the drinking horses. Dmitri's cane clacked the stones a few paces behind.

He paused beside Kumo. His cousin sucked his teeth and whispered, "We can't stay here, Ahoté. It's been over an hour."

"Just do it, Darakaian." The guard boosted his head a fraction, coughing. Ruddy saliva spewed over the hem of Hachiro's robes, splattering the blank page. The westerner's haggard face was unwavering. His dark eyes tightened, as did his fist.

"No!" Pleading, Dmitri strained over his cane. "If we just give Lady Boreal enough time…"

He trailed off as her shoulders sank, and she shook her head sympathetically.

"The arrow is embedded in his intestines. Bolaeva, allow us to save him from a more painful death, Your Majesty."

Dmitri covered his mouth. His fingertips reached for the dying guard but dropped in defeat.

"Pyō jien, My King." The Westerner croaked, letting his lids fall. "Pyō chakrit."

Dmitri gaped at him. Zaethan stepped forward, around Hachiro, and knelt beside the guard. As he reached for the hilt of his kopar, a paler hand took his and pressed her dagger there instead. Her mother's, he recalled. She brushed the man's loose hairs off his neck, as if in caress. Curling his arms about himself, Dmitri nodded his concession and turned away.

Zaethan steadied his nerve and in a quick, clean jerk, ended the guard's life. His throat opened, flooding the bedroll.

They'd never even learned his name.

"We'll all end up like this," Zaethan said to Dmitri, staring at the corpse, "if we don't shirk them. They need to believe you've headed in a different direction."

"But if they're tracking us, how could we deceive them?"

Heaving a sigh, Zaethan returned the haidren's blade, his mind made up. "By actually sending some in a different direction…"

"Absolutely not, Zaeth."

"They know I wouldn't leave you." Standing, Zaethan cleaned his hands and retrieved Harmonia from the stream. He led her to Ira and gave him the reins. Next, he brought the haidren's mare to the tall shadowman, with long silvery tresses. "Neither would she. They recognize the horses better than our backsides. While you continue south of the river, we'll act as if we've broken off to escort our king," Zaethan said, indicating Ira as Dmitri's double, "home to Bastiion. We'll lose them in the Mirajii and reunite in Port Khmer."

Ira wafted the air proudly. "Mother always said I had a regality about me."

The Boreali haidren stepped aside, mouthing words to her men. Her captaen grimaced at the alabaster warrior when he let his hair loose at her instruction. With a stiff bow, he retreated from their frigid grouping, stepped into the stirrups, and threw a leg over the mare.

"I've not agreed to this." Dmitri wrenched Zaethan by the arm. "We're stronger together."

"Uni. Sometimes," he agreed. "But sometimes we're smarter apart. Do you trust me?"

His friend raked his waves in distress as Ira clumsily climbed into his kingly saddle and Zaethan's pryde started to assemble.

"Do you trust me, brother?" he asked one more time.

Dmitri hesitated before dragging Zaethan into a tense embrace. "Always." Squeezing, he said into his ear, "Protect Ira. He cannot die."

Then he let go.

Confused, Zaethan stumbled back as Dmitri briskly diverted his steps toward the yancy and uttered something to him atop Harmonia.

The pryde bundled around Zaethan when he stalked for Kumo. Disapproval in separating was written plainly across their warrior faces, but it was the best chance Dmitri had to survive. Under Nyack Kasim's command, the hunt would not stop here.

"Takoda, your Gulgou—is it what it once was?" With his confirmation, Zaethan unfurled his spine, confident in the strategy. "Uni. Cut through the wetlands. Barter with the mudmen for passage if you must, yeah? Kumo, Zahra, be the king's shadow. You eat, sleep, breathe at his heels. Jabari, Dhalili…" He brought their heads together conspiratorially. "Keep the other three alive."

Clapping Jabari on the back, Zaethan tore himself from them and splashed into the stream where the Boreali readied their mounts. He angled for their haidren, under the sharp scrutiny of her Captaen Bailefore. The redheaded shadowman ceased his task and charted Zaethan's steps like a wolf. He felt his glower burrowing into the wound she'd packed when he marched to where she affixed the locked chest onto a new horse. After buckling it in place, she massaged her temple. She stopped at his approach.

"Before I go," he said, presenting her kuerre.

A sprinkling of moonlight doused the witchiron core, illuminating the fullness of her upper lip. Zaethan cleared his throat, looking away from it and into her eyes.

"Niit. It is yours now, Kas—" She caught herself. "Zaethan."

She gently pushed the hilt against his middle.

Zaethan's fist constricted around the witchiron, holding it close. Observant, her shadowmen lingered in his periphery. He hurriedly sheathed the sword and braced his arm against her horse, blocking their view of them.

He stepped closer. The gelding stomped its leg as she melted into its body—her old habit reemerging in front of their audience.

"There's a rundown inn in Port Khmer. The Scaly Stowaway," he said hushedly. "Anything happens to Kumo, you find it. Hide there. And ask the barkeep to see Wren."

Her kaleidoscopic stare flitted carefully between his eyes. "The 'little songbird' in the alley…"

Banishing the awful vision of the dead girl they had once found wilted and drained, Zaethan leaned nearer. Pebbles crunched under his boot until their noses nearly touched.

"If we don't show within two days of your arrival… If I can't get back to you…" He swallowed harshly and scooped her chin in his grasp. She did not flinch in his hand. Nor did she breathe. "You keep him going, yeye qondai? You make a plan and force him to follow through without me. Swear to it."

Her focus dilated, consuming those spectral irises as her posture stiffened, and she elevated her face off his fingers resolutely. The tip of her nose brushed his in reply. "Wem. I swear."

Zaethan's thumb slid an inch. His middle finger skirted the peak of the scar beneath her ear. "Until Khmer, Domàa'maia."

Mouth dry, he dropped his hand from her skin. He pushed off the horse and marched away.

Gripping the horn, he swung into Hellion's saddle. Ira and the shadowman brought their horses alongside the Andwele stallion. Zaethan didn't look back. He couldn't. Instead, he surged Hellion onward before he changed his mind.

Together, Zaethan, the yancy, and the shadowman cantered past the dead guard for the mouth of the gorge.

There, Hachiro Naborū-Zuo still loitered by the corpse, his pages no longer blank but penned by the blood of his keeper.

CHAPTER THIRTY

The figure balanced upon a mossy branch, witnessing the funeral rites below.

It was a shallow grave. They'd not been afforded the time nor the shovels to dig much deeper. A risen mound was formed where the najjan had piled damp soil over the corpse of the *kiataki*. The short sword bequeathed by the Collective pierced the earth just above the guardian's crown.

On her knees, Alora's niece heaped dirt about the blade as her young king watched on with the joyless band of Darakaians. Together, they formed a sedate enclosure around the burial, despite the boot heel the massive beta drummed against the forest floor, eager to leave.

Their delay baffled the figure. Korbin would not have stalled for a burial, were he endangered and not his heir.

However, Korbin had not alone shaped the quiet boy who wore his crown. The figure had never known Lourissa well, not as endearingly as the others, but he recognized her steadfast tranquility now, assisting Luscia to rise with the aid of a byrnnzite cane.

Leaves shuffled overhead, and shrouded in his cloak, the figure let go of the branch to offer Amaranth her favorite roost. Her talons clamped around his inflamed arm with authority. He welcomed the sting in his sores, agitated by the hawk's constricted anchor, grateful he felt her there.

Grateful he felt anything at all.

Only when Luscia was free from danger would he part with the Pilarese hawk and send urgent word to his mistress. A bird of many talents, Amaranth's scouting and defensive tactics were too critical to surrender just yet. Alora would soon learn of Nyack's crimes and Tetsu's complicity in his Mworran scheme. It was not simply the king who was endangered by Darakai's machinations with Pilar but his mistress's entire House.

Any threat to the Orynthian throne set a parallel target on Boreal. The highlander peninsula had maintained their covenant with Thoarne's descendants, a life-altering covenant with Tiergan his heirs had forgotten. Yet in their forgetting, it was the bloodlines of the north who remembered, and they would defend that remembrance until every najjan had perished for the cause.

At once, the figure's lungs stilled, disregarding their contrived rhythm with the political winds. Beneath the netting of twig and vine,

Masumi's son bent over the mound. Under the hampered moonlight, the young shoto'shi resembled his mother with shocking pause. His youthful cheeks rounded the same way hers always had, protesting her adulthood. Not since her son's birth had the figure set his eyes on their rosy cheer. Nor would he ever again; to Masumi, the figure was nothing but a ghost.

With a grating inhale, the figure resettled into the shadows like one.

Stacking seven modest stones beside the man's entombed shoulders, the slim shoto'shi constructed a gate of knowledge and wisdom at the head of his *kiataki*—his sword-keeper. Blinking erratically, in sentiment or concentration, he dragged his robes toward the dead man's feet and built dueling pebble towers.

The pillars of discernment and fortitude.

At the center, the shoto'shi lingered, stacking them more considerately than the others. Positioning each stone with patience and care, he shaped the final tenet of the Collective's doctrine—that which was so often neglected.

The pillar of dignity.

Creasing his blistered lips, the figure wondered if anyone would have exhibited such care with his body, had they ever found it. He'd forfeited his dignity long ago, trading it for a horrible fiction and an everlasting penance in the dark.

Unlike the sword-keeper's tomb, the figure's darkness had no end. No destination or deliverance...

Not until Alora's hope withered to the dust he so desperately wanted to become.

Mutely, the shoto'shi waded toward the top of the burial mound behind the sword. Rounding his spine, he honored his kiataki in an undulated bow, inclining to either pillar at each shoulder. Stepping out from the onlookers, their king came to his side and, mirroring the Pilarese custom, did the same.

One by one, so did the rest.

"We fear we must leave this place before they find it," Korbin's son said in quiet gentleness.

From inside his frayed vest, he withdrew a journal, dusted it off, and offered it to the somber shoto'shi.

He wavered, staring at it. Then, with both hands, he reached out for its discolored pages. Masumi's child hugged the journal over his heart and uttered in the softest, most sensible whisper, "Pyō jien, pyō chakrit."

The night steeped further into darkness during onerous hours that passed.

He tailed them through the forest as their journey turned into toil. Furthering east, the ground, no longer a bed of dirt and decomposing brush, had morphed into a foretelling sludge. The Darakaians led the rest of the king's company to where the trees untwined, widening to spans of pooling muck.

Their ploy had worked. The field marshal and his regiment had diverted north, after Cyra's son instead of his regent. Thus, banded together, they slogged toward the border, escaping into the wetlands of Hagarh.

It was remarkably cunning, the figure was reticent to admit, albeit remarkably reckless. A small army against three men—two, if one didn't count the yancy. Cyra's bastard was proving more like the late haidren than Alora credited, as she had often dreaded it would be the child's father who appeared through his deeply cross-caste skin. In fairness to her, Cyra's defining traits were never those Alora herself exhibited, or exalted, thus their manifestation offered no comfort to her maneuverings. She'd long feared the boy and what his self-awareness would mean.

Perhaps his mistress was right to.

Ahead of the figure, the horses trudged through the deepening mire. Like a beaten pendulum, he released the slippery bark and swung between the branches at a distance from their muddied caravan. It wasn't Boreali ears that worried him but the lycran's. The Orallach hybrid had already circled back once. The figure couldn't risk being scented over the sulfuric, mineral-rich slop underfoot. One trace of the decay in his tissues, and the lycran would never let it go.

Seizing the next limb, the figure noticed the Darakaians at the front had come to an abrupt halt.

"No wonder Orynthia never invaded Hagarh," grumbled the sandy najjan carrying the rear, not yet realizing they'd stopped. "It reeks like a Tavish slop pot."

The barrel-chested najjan grunted and trotted on. "Always thinking everyone else's shite stinks worse than yours, Creyvan…"

"A Tavish brute isn't much worse than these Darakaian—"

"Heh'ta." The bearded ginger raised his fist, cutting off the other man.

Both their horses stalled in the murky slurry.

The figure clung to the tree trunk and melded into the sheet of lichen. Yanking his hood lower, he stretched around the girth of the trunk. Beyond the row of riders—their heads tilted back in silence—sprawled the sluggish waters that drowned Hagarh.

And erected above the brim of its swamp spread an archway of the dead.

Over a dozen cadavers had been strung in the treetops. Pulled like banners, the ravaged carcasses stretched wider than their nature ought to allow. The figure squinted, though his eyes were better than those of the pryde gaping directly beneath the bodies. Picked apart by scavengers, the remains had been dissected to the bone. Eye sockets scraped clean. Cartilage lost. Trenches of rotten tissue replaced every marker of humanity—except those left sagging in the form of buckskin shreds.

More than one of the victims were Darakaian.

"Shores of Aurynth..." murmured Luscia in her saddle. "What happened in this place?"

"Beg the Fates we don't find out," uttered the lean Darakaian at the lead.

Horrified, the figure soaked in the eerie image, recalling the rumors he'd delivered to his mistress earlier that summer, those reporting the missing men Orynthia's commander had dispatched to reinforce the border, here in the Mirajii.

When he'd met her in that cursed library, the figure had been convinced the disappearances were tied to territorial backlash. Having forfeited their forest to Orynthian dominion after the Mworran Wars, the mudmen's forced agreement had resulted in regional tensions ever since. Gulgons were not notorious for violence, but if provoked, a mud-encrusted spear did as much damage as a sword—when aimed to kill.

Yet scanning the cadavers and the vicious torment carved into their innards, the figure was not certain this had been committed by a sword or a spear. As he studied the flayed and flapping muscle, he suspected something far more brutal than any broken treaty.

Someone had created that bloodthirsty monstrosity in Rian.

And what evil invents... it does not restrain.

More existed, and here they hid. In the shriveled emptiness of his belly and the torment of his bones, the figure was certain. These water-logged lands were the perfect hunting ground.

"We should head north of the river," the leading warrior advised. The twin braids framing his long neck shivered alongside him. "Go back and find Alpha Zà."

"No." They all turned as their king said, "We're going to trust his intuition."

His shoulders curved forward, but with a gentle kick, Korbin's son urged his stallion on. Driving it between the Darakaian mounts, he passed under the gruesome archway and into the rippling waters. Afraid, the others hesitantly followed where the king of Orynthia led his protectors into Hagarh's midnight gloom.

The figure pursued them warily as they treaded more slowly through the black waters. Overhead, the canopy loosened, becoming a lacy portal to the stars. Dappled luster shone down on the runaway convoy, unable to penetrate the blanket of algae that concealed the depths, as well as what swam beneath.

Amaranth flitted between the treetops where she paced his advance. Then, over the sloshing of hooves, her screech splintered the night.

Just as the figure swung onto the next branch, an arrow tore through the drapery of moss and impaled the woolly cypress behind the najjani guards at the rear.

"Protect the king!"

With a squeal, the horses reared, spraying the others when a second set of arrows razored through the foliage. The large beta released an angry cry. Smacking where he'd been grazed on his bicep, he yelled for his pryde to encircle the young king and his unarmed shoto'shi. Arising in their stirrups, the Darakaians' shields formed a misshapen ring.

With fierce swiftness, Luscia and her najjan spread among the trees, preparing for ambush.

Hooking over the bough, the figure vaulted and soared through the mossy overhang. More arrows ripped by as he clutched each rung of bark, hurtling himself back toward the cadaver arch. A fresh vigor shot through his limbs, invigorating his speed. The outline of the ghoulish edifice sharpened across the wet expanse. On its other side was a Darakaian horde, bows drawn.

With a sweet pang, his incisors lengthened. The glands behind them pulsated expectantly, awakening the hunger he so tirelessly refused.

His mouth slavered after its prey. The sticky thirst cascaded the figure's chin as he closed the distance between them, hurling through the heights while their weapons sought the wrong enemy. Bursting the blisters, his lips curled.

Snarling, the figure dropped onto the pryde warrior at the center, snaking his legs around the Darakaian's middle as the impact slung them off the horse and into the mire. Arms and legs thrashed the mushy grass. The figure wrenched his prey's head aside and drilled his fangs into his throat.

Iron bathed his parched tongue, coursing over it pleasingly, and the figure, lost to its seduction, inhaled the detestable spice of his own depravity.

Something stabbed his thigh. With a jerk, he wrenched out the arrow and glared at the oncoming warrior. The sinew of his decimated leader dangled from the figure's jaws as the man flailed his kopar. Clamping hold of the warrior's abdomen, the figure snapped down on the soft tissue of his navel. Wrenching back, he took with him a mouthful of entrails.

The warrior screeched, trampling before his advancing cohorts.

Enlivened, the figure bolted and leapt into the saddle of an archer. Amaranth plunged from the clouds, her talons severing the spine of one of his nearby riders. Twisting the cloak about the archer's neck, the figure wrung it and dove onto the next. Exploiting the weight of his kinsmen's corpse, the rider was unseated and hauled into the marshy soils. Tumbling onto his stomach, the Darakaian stretched for his weapon in the grasses, but the figure smashed a knee into his arm, snapping it. In response to his shrieks, the figure yanked the bone and rolled him over to see Amaranth peck the eyes of the warrior coming to his defense.

Howling rang throughout the trees. The figure swiped the sickle sword from the dank earth and ran it through a warrior's ribs. Crouching over him, he withdrew it as the man's screams dulled to the frightened thump of his veins pouring into the earth. The hood fell from the figure's skull when it cocked unnaturally. Gurgling, bright whites ringed his prey's eyes as he brought the Southern kopar to his nostrils and breathed it in.

Spittle frothed from the figure's mouth, and his tongue lashed out to savor the taste upon the blade. But at an earsplitting screech, Amaranth swooped from above and tore the kopar from his grip. He snapped his fangs after it, ravenous and desperate, following the bird's ascent. Flapping her wings, the hawk doubled back and clobbered him onto his spine.

Uncovered, his head had wedged into the mud. The blotting in his periphery cleared and his unholy heartrate returned. It all faded, until the figure only heard a dying man's final gasps. Prying himself upright, he gaped across the sodden woodland.

Nausea washed his insides as he overlooked a field of bodies.

Listlessly, he removed his bloodied glove. Turning it inside out, the figure mopped his mask of carnage, relieved he could not see the remnant of the fractured man preserved beneath it.

That, his split nature, was the true penance for his wickedness—the splitting Alora could never accept, even as it devoured him alive. On bruised knees, she prayed to a divinity for what it should never bequeath.

Soaked in death, the figure knew what he was, and at Amaranth's call, he spun to face it.

His glands excreted their syrupy bane, the hunt unfinished. Barreling through the trees, a lone Darakaian escaped on horseback. Heading north, the warrior galloped straight for Bessus and the reinforcements that would destroy Luscia and her king. The figure growled eagerly.

He'd sworn never to maim unless he must.

But he never swore to not relish it when he did.

CHAPTER THIRTY ONE
ZAETHAN

Their hoofbeats were hailfall through the Mirajii Forest. Between the anchor of Zaethan's knees, Hellion rode like a storm, his gait torrential and smooth. Dirt and debris spit from the underbrush, casting a gravedigger's cloud on those trailing the aftermath.

The shadowman pushed his mount to keep up with the twin Andweles. His colorless hair flew past the crescent wraiths unsheathed at his back, echoing the moonlight with the same ghostly splendor his haidren's would were she there. The beak of his prominent nose dug into the mare's mane as he hunkered down to conceal his considerable height. Zaethan's gambit had fooled the regiment, along with each disguise. Not far behind, Bessus drove his soldiers after their supposed king—each a traitor to his crown.

Spiriting Hellion, Harmonia galloped between her twin and the haidren's dappled mare with a shrieking yancy strapped to her saddle.

Swaddled in the regal traveling cape he'd found folded in a saddle pack, Ira clenched the horn, white-knuckled, where Zaethan had bound his hands with the reins. His noble buttocks bounced off Harmonia— as did the stirrups—testing the strength of the knotting.

Prudently, Zaethan had tied his boots off too.

"I'm too pretty to die!" Ira wailed, cape flailing at his back. "Why couldn't I play Hachiro?" To his side, Ira's panicked face hopped up and down wildly. "I'll wear the dress, Zaeth, I swear! There's still time to turn—"

Over the crest of his shoulder, Zaethan eyed the regiment's nearing advance and shouted, "Do *not* turn around!"

He lashed out and snatched Ira by the cape when he did, in fact, turn around.

Ira sobbed into the saddle, tears streaking his cheeks. "Why was I the sheep to your slaughter!"

"They are closing in, Lord Haidren!" the shadowman yelled over Ira's cries. "We can't outrun them much longer!"

The highlander's gaze flicked to the sweat pouring down the mare's neck. By the air puffing from her snout, she was nearing collapse. They needed a place to stand their ground, and they needed to find it soon.

Desperate, Zaethan veered Hellion eastward to a break in the trees. Yards off, a recession cut through the forest floor, indicating a probable stream. Nearing it, their horses jumped over an uprooted trunk in tandem. The undergrowth sloped downward in a thicket of ferns toward the hopeful rippling of water.

At the mossy edge lay a deep-seated gully. Zaethan encouraged Hellion's hooves to slide into the divide rather than vaulting over it. He dismounted before they splashed into the stream, sliding off his shield in the process. Sprinting to Harmonia, he made quick work of Ira's restraints.

With his kopar, Zaethan sliced the rope from the yancy's fine boots, their costliness hidden under a layer of muck. He untied the reins and gallantly offered Ira his hand. Clasping it, Zaethan wrenched the yancy haidren down from the saddle and, with a turn, slapped both Andweles on their haunches.

The horses tore off downstream and out of sight. They wouldn't go far, not so fatigued, but he hoped far enough. If the regiment were smart, a means of escape would be a primary target, stranding the unlikely trio at the mercy of their swords.

The shadowman unhitched his longbow from the saddle and did the same, sending his mare in a frightened canter farther down the protective gully. Retreating toward the wall of rootage and rock, he unfastened the quiver belted to his thigh. He ducked under the overhang and shoved it, along with the longbow, into Ira's shaking arms. The yancy slunk against the soil when the shadowman crouched, rounded his spine, and freed his wraiths in a deadly sweep.

"Ano." Zaethan took the bow and impaled it into the dirt. "He's a terrible shot."

Crisp eyes, nearly as pale as the shadowman's skin, skated the witchiron blade and pinned Ira with cool skepticism.

He gulped loudly.

"Absolute filth, I'm afraid," Ira sheepishly replied and, with the quiver of arrows, inched the crescent wraith back a fraction.

Instantly, the stitched hide sizzled.

Ira gawked at it, pressed against the witchiron. Promptly, the shadowman snatched the quiver and stashed the arrows among the boulders. Out of habit, the haidren's spindly fingers sought the canister dangling about his neck, but Zaethan, grabbing his palm, stuffed it instead with the hilt of his kopar.

"Don't swing it at us" was all he said, unsheathing his kuerre.

As moonlight dowsed the rare metal, the shadowman's look was as sharp as the highlander blade.

"She was your teacher, my Ana'Sere?"

Zaethan nodded once, unapologetic.

"Then you might live after all," he commented dryly and sprung up to peek over the eroded shelf.

"I'm a fattened calf." Ira emitted a whimper and, curling around the kopar, blathered with dread as Zaethan joined the shadowman above. "A beautiful, well-fed calf…"

Their brows met at the top of the grass as they stared into the near-black timberline. Adrenaline surged through Zaethan. His quickened exhales swished the brush in front of his nose where he leaned to the earth beside the eerie highlander, who it appeared wasn't even breathing at all.

Overhead, an owl hooted ominously. The croaking of frogs and whizzing of insects accompanied its song before a choir of angry assault boomed through the darkened wood. Immediately, Zaethan recognized Bessus's nasally voice when it rang out brusque instruction to the regiment. It grew louder, as did the saddle groans of approaching men on horseback. The sentries were spreading out, their position concealed from the moon beneath the crowded lattice of leaves.

"A calf both juicy and sweet…"

"There," the shadowman said hushedly and pointed over the ground cover. Zaethan squinted, unable to see any movement.

"Bred on Wendyllean wine and cheeses…"

Zaethan grunted, booting Ira to seal his chatter trap before that sniveling kakk got them killed, and resumed his search through the brush. He heard the shadowman grind the dirt when his posture abruptly changed, as if preparing to spring. Widespread, his shoulders curled beneath his lengthy neck. The shadowman's brow lowered, skeletal in its near hairlessness, and leveled in the grass predatorially. Unnaturalness hooked the Northern warrior at the seams, defining his angles with unnerving grace. It puckered Zaethan's flesh.

It reminded him of her.

A stone's throw from the gully, twigs snapped. The head of a painted horse stepped into patch of light as Àla'maia parted the clouds.

Bessus marched it forward until the moonlight doused the field marshal's plump, pampered frame. A dozen soldiers emerged between the adjacent trunks, dotting the higher ground. Their renegade trio was more than outnumbered, as multitudes surely amassed beyond those in view.

Even if they crept along the gully unseen, the horses were still over-fatigued. Were they to climb in the trees, they had only the one bow.

"We have you surrounded, Your Majesty," Bessus called, his bloated jowls swinging in either direction. His soldiers too looked about— Zaethan's exact position still concealed. "Commander Kasim believes there has been a grave misunderstanding. Surrender yourself, and I give my assurance you'll leave unharmed."

"Tailored little calf, tender in all the right places…"

At the field marshal's call, Ira's babble grew shrill. Zaethan kicked him without reservation. The yancy howled, rivaling the owl's screech, and fearfully clamped a hand over his mouth when Zaethan glared down. A full-bellied chortle teased his ears, and he swerved back toward the field marshal. Bessus rode forward.

Two feet. Three feet. Four.

His eyes were dark pellets, eclipsed in his own shadow, but Zaethan could sense them smiling. Within the trees, there came the jangle of a tossed coin purse, followed by muffled laughter. Zaethan's teeth clenched.

The regiment had placed bets on locating their escaped king.

"If you do not surrender willingly," Bessus continued, "you compromise your own safety, Your Majesty, and condemn the criminals who've *abducted* you to execution. The cross-caste pretender nor that foul y'siti haidren will be spared."

Flanking Zaethan, a low growl hummed from the shadowman's throat. His teeth flashed when the field marshal smacked his lips and said crassly, "Not that we won't show her a good time before the commander has his way…"

Jeers swelled from the wood as the soldiers heckled the Boreali woman they believed hid in the gully with Dmitri. Sickened by their vile promises, Zaethan's mouth soured, and his grip chafed her gifted kuerre.

"This standoff is futile, King Dmitri… The army belongs to Darakai," the field marshal asserted, trotting closer. "The prydes belong to Darakai. There is no one left for your defense if you do not comply."

The pryde, Zaethan suddenly considered. Unlike Wekesa's, his own pryde was still loyal to the throne and, so he imagined, were those sequestered in the Mirajii.

Zaethan bellowed his bluff. "It is you who are surrounded, Marshal, by the prydes of the Mirajii and Bastiion proper."

The shadowman spied him quizzically in his periphery.

Metal rasped as Bessus glided his sword out of its scabbard. "A bastard pretender's wishful thinking. In fact…" He motioned with his weapon for another to join him. "We plan to pay them a visit, don't we, Hanovi?"

An Andwele stallion strutted into the spattered moonbeams, carrying Zahra's cousin—the same Nigan Hanovi who'd deserted his brethren and defected from Zaethan's pryde, fleeing to his rival.

Wekesa's poison had taken root, smug in the sneer that puffed Nigan's mouth. Zaethan's knuckles itched to deflate it.

"We won't leave any survivors, Zaeth," Nigan said in warning, like they were friends. "The chief warlord wants to send a message to the tribes, yeye qondai? Demonstrate his kwihila to come. It's either you—a muddy cross-caste—or them."

Trembling with a fury more tangible than his threat, Zaethan ruthlessly shouted, "Retreat the way you came, or I signal my men to fire! And by Owàa's blazing wing, to the tip of this witchiron sword, Bessus, it is your pack of gutless traitors who will not be spared!"

Hesitatingly, the field marshal planted a look at Zahra's cousin who, calling the bluff, shook his head and gripped his kopar. With a chuckle, Bessus raised his sword high in the air, about to wave the regiment's advance. But just as the blade started to descend, a bloodcurdling shriek sounded in the blackness from the south.

Bessus's arm froze overhead. Not a full minute later, there came a second—the outcry westbound.

Wavering, the field marshal's sword shook.

The shadowman leaned uneasily on his elbow. "Why didn't you say your pryde was here with reinforcements earlier?"

Zaethan's eyes were wide in response. "Because they're not."

In unison, their necks slowly turned toward a succession of screams. The pandemonium scattered as someone attacked from the outskirts. Rounding north, screeches popped off like invisible fire-

works, exploding with more fright than Zaethan knew existed. Above
the ground, soldiers twisted in their saddles, scouring the night as mud
squelched under running boots.

The noise stopped with a sharp yelp. A body slammed against a tree
trunk near the field marshal, staining the bark as it slid into the grass,
broken and limp.

Terror rippled through the row of men closest to Bessus, breaking
up their offensive formation.

"Hold the line!" he ordered and circled his horse.

Upslope, Nigan Hanovi edged into the defense of the clustering
soldiers. Zaethan felt his jaw dangle when between blinks, the man
nearest Zahra's cousin was wrenched from the saddle and into the
gloom. A piercing wail preceded the solitary leg that skidded through
the grass back into the open—the femur crushed where blood still
spurted from the arteries.

"Now's our chance to end it," the shadowman stated, backing
toward the stream as he prepared to leap.

"We should get out of this massacre while we still can!"
Zaethan yelled.

Whoever was up there, they could use the distraction to find the
horses and disappear to Port Khmer. Otherwise, they may not make
it at all.

"Lord Haidren, you and I have but one duty!" the shadowman
hollered over the mayhem. "To defend the king!"

In a nimble vault, he sprinted and soared over the rocky outcrop-
ping. A slurry of screaming greeted him in welcome.

"Depths!" Zaethan barked. He aimed his kuerre at Ira, who had
planted himself in the rootage like he was one of its sprouts. "Stay here
and stab anyone who gets close."

Ira nodded vigorously, cupping the kopar's hilt in both hands. At that, Zaethan hopped and hoisted himself out of the sunken gully.

Having landed in a bed of ferns, a squalling soldier bounded straight for Zaethan where he scrambled to his feet. The man outheld his weapon as he bumbled downslope, blood gushing from his eye socket. Knocking the sword aside with his shield, Zaethan ran his kuerre through his middle. Charring flesh stuffed his senses as the soldier sank off the witchiron and onto the ground.

Light was increasing with the hour, and a drab glow bathed the wound through the canopy. Zaethan bent over the deep scratches that crisscrossed the soldier's stolen eye. It was as if it'd been bored out by razors.

He raced uphill, his spine straightening under a sheet of ice, unready for the chaos that awaited him.

Men drowned in gore, most missing their limbs barreled out from the western trees. Blocking Zaethan, one loitered in the middle of the mayhem, clutching his butchered hand. The soldier raised it in front of his disbelieving, Unitarian face.

His fingers had been bitten off.

Suddenly, a pair of radiant arced blades appeared behind him, perched on either side, and in an instant, the soldier's head rolled forward. The fingerless hand with it.

In his place, the tall shadowman was splattered in scarlet, no longer a tower of alabaster but of ruin. His bright yet smokey eyes reflected the hazy predawn as he smirked at Zaethan and spun. The crescent wraiths haloed him in a frightening dance as he sliced two oncoming soldiers through their ribs. In a reverse spin, he hooked one by the leg with his boot toe, lurched him downward, and speared his chest, just as quickly as he swirled and, with the same wraith, carved the opposite sentry through the knees.

He glided across the underbrush like an unforgiving tempest. Zaethan had never seen anyone slaughter so fluidly. So seamlessly. The shadowman's haidren had bested their najjani captaen. If they all moved like this during battle, Zaethan couldn't even fathom what she was capable of...

She'd been holding back in their sparring. His tutor, able to slay him with ease.

Zaethan lifted the kuerre she'd given him. It warmed his stiff palm, comforting his rejected cross-caste skin. Accepting it as lord. Passionately, he flipped the hilt and roared at an advancing soldier, slashing the curved backsword across his thigh. Pivoting on his heel, Zaethan thrust it through his kidney.

He didn't stay to watch him fall.

Soldiers cloistered Bessus and Nigan on horseback, as most others darted on foot. Zaethan rushed toward the barricade. At his enraged approach, the field marshal ordered a coupling of soldiers to dismount. Zaethan's pulse quickened. The command had been shrill. Afraid. It rang like music through the whirring in his ears, drowning out everything except the coward's melody.

The initial soldier attacked like a fool. Sword hoisted over a shiny, unstained buckler, he cowered behind it and stormed him headfirst. Reeling out of the way, Zaethan turned, seized a fistful of greasy hair, and plunged his kuerre into the soldier's young heart, then tore it back from his spine. A wheeze escaped the soldier when he dropped, all but a cub. It couldn't have been but than a year since the boy's Ascension.

A second replaced him.

A calvary spearman, the soldier was Darakaian, decorated in scar-ified runes and beaded bandings. Despite the Orynthian uniform, his Yowekaon roots seeped from his pores. Standing as tall as the shad-owman, his legs were sturdy monoliths, each the breadth of Zaethan's hips, and the ground tremored beneath his incoming stomps.

Revolving the spear, the soldier bashed it against his buckler impos-ingly and let loose a throaty howl. He darted left. Zaethan ducked under his strike, drilling his spiked shield into the muscled meat of the soldier's thigh. He lumbered backward, but unfazed by the blood loss, he stampeded Zaethan with the strength of a wild ox. The spear was swung, and Zaethan moved with it, crooking his kuerre around the shaft. Locked there, he hinged his footing and yanked the weapon from the soldier's hold. He tossed it aside, right as the buckler blasted into Zaethan's face and the bronze rim descended overhead.

Suffocating, Zaethan's vision clouded, distorting the scene of terror-ized men tearing through the forest. His fingers went numb around the kuerre as the soldier's weaponless grip cut off the circulation to his sword arm. Sucking in what little air he could, Zaethan shirked his Darakaian shield and tossed the witchiron into his opposite hand. Overturning it, he rammed the corrosive blade into the soldier's gut.

Gasping, Zaethan wrenched away the buckler and, catching the Darakaian, forced the scarlet kuerre under his chin through his giant skull.

Droplets rained down, and Zaethan found Bessus beyond the bloody spray. The field marshal sputtered, and he squealed for their retreat. Kicking his horse, he wedged it out of the fray when a bird swooped from above. With a harrowing caw, protracted talons swiped one of the soldiers near Bessus and gouged an artery, misting him in another's gore. A lavender glint shone from its soiled feathers.

Zaethan decelerated mid-run.

The Pilarese hawk.

A crescent wraith severed the same soldier in half before the lofty shadowman landed in his saddle and simultaneously lunged the famed wraiths into either man on his flanks.

Zaethan raced as the soldiers guarding Bessus scattered like flies. Abandoned, the field marshal fled, his horse breaking into a canter. Climbing onto a riderless mount, Zaethan chased him. He balanced atop the galloping steed, and coming parallel with the frantic marshal, he jumped.

He hit the painted's hindquarters with a *thump*. Bessus swatted, feebly trying to displace Zaethan's footing, but swinging around his wide girth, Zaethan wheeled into his lap. He grabbed his sweaty head and, with an abrupt twist, shoved the pauldron spikes on his shoulder into Bessus's cheek. He reared back and punched him in the other. With a snarl, Zaethan locked his arms around the field marshal and jumped them both from the saddle.

They trundled to the earth and into a patch of fragrant clover. Bessus struggled against Zaethan's arms, but his for-hire hands were weak and slippery. Grappling him onto his back, Zaethan restrained his fleshy biceps under each kneecap and stretched across Bessus's strained belting.

Perspiration dripped off Zaethan's nose. With both hands, he elevated the brilliant kuerre and suspended it over the field marshal's heart.

Ammonia stung the perfume of clover. He'd pissed himself.

"Mercy!" Bessus cried into his butchered cheek. "You gave it to Wekesa, yes? I have coin, plenty of aurus to—"

The marshal gurgled when the kuerre speared his chest.

"You heard your master." Zaethan hissed over the hemorrhaging pool. "*Mercy is for the weak.*"

The field marshal choked on the blood pouring over his lips as he managed to whisper, "Then his w-work has already b-begun. You cannot s-stop him."

Zaethan jerked him by the collar of his military tunic. "Stop who? The chief warlord?" But only bubbles blew from Bessus's drowning snicker. "Answer me!"

At the scream, his beady eyes rolled aside to where his left hand twitched. "The Obscurer will s-set us f-free..."

The bubbling stopped. Zaethan followed his unclosed eyes toward his wrist. A familiar arch of scarification teased his thick, cobalt cuff. Cautiously, Zaethan eased off the corpse and unbuttoned it, pulling the fabric lower.

A strange symbol—a figure eight divided by a single line—disfigured the field marshal's flesh. A gust left Zaethan's middle. The symbol was unnervingly alike the mark he'd caught his fictitious father scratching inside the bunker, right before his act of treason.

Both were traitors. Both bore a brand, the brand of this *Obscurer*.

The underbrush crunched as someone neared from behind. Zaethan dropped the dead marshal's wrist, drew the kuerre from his chest cavity, and turned.

Soaked in red, the shadowman slowed to a stop. Huffing, he steered a wraith to the west.

"A few Darakaians—including the one who'd called out to you—managed to escape. I suspect they ride for Faraji."

Zahra's cousin had survived—and he was headed right back to the man Zaethan knew would always make good on a threat.

Whoever the "Obscurer" was, if Darakai's chief warlord was in league with a new adversary, one with enough influence to turn an entire House against the crown, then Dmitri needed every ally left at his disposal.

Especially those under the same peril as their king.

Zaethan spit, wiping his witchiron clean on the marshal's pants. "Grab the yancy. We have a stop to make before Port Khmer."

Amid the birdsong, the shadowman trudged with him through the awakening forest toward the gully. "What else could be so urgent as to warrant our delay?"

"You were wrong back there. I have two duties. And the other..." Zaethan snatched his Darakaian shield out of the grass with vigor. "Is saving my men."

CHAPTER THIRTY TWO
LUSCIA

L uscia anchored her sights on the back of Takoda's head as she sloshed through the black tea waters of Hagarh. For days he led them, caravanning amid the watchful taunts of an alien terrain. The wildlife jeered from their perches, their vocalizations haunting and malefic against a cricket ensemble. Day and night the swamp spoke to them; they were not welcome here.

Mere feet from Luscia, a banded snaked glided along the surface as if herding the trespassers. But in a splash, it was gone, taken by something hungrier. Luscia scanned the swaying lily pads. Freshwater crocodiles were said to lurk below the deceptive décor. Trusting Takoda's word, she stepped over the submerged roots that knitted the endless swamp together. The braided warrior had instructed a steady forge, that stagnant legs invited predators more than the steadfast moving in unison. Yet as her neck returned toward him at the front, she spotted a fanged snout peeking at her over the ripples.

Steeling herself, Luscia tugged the reins, directing the stallion into deeper waters behind her paddling lycran. Not that Aksel minded... when his next meal constantly swam beneath his muzzle.

The flooding entrapped her waist like an unwanted caress. Her linsilk jacket opened and skirted behind her, flowing against the horse's leg. They'd dismounted to better navigate the precarious footholds sprawled between the flooded trunks. Woolly cypress and ancient gum trees soared all around, reaching for the sunset as far as the eye could see, their enormous breadth boasting their thousand-year reign. Their contorted limbs cloaked in a primal mystique, veils of moss spilled from the heights, tickling Luscia's crown.

Reaching up, she spread the moss aside for her king to pass under, riding atop the stallion she steered. He alone remained on horseback, aside from Hachiro, whom Dmitri had permitted to scribble in the saddle with Zahra's escort. Luscia glanced back, unsurprised to see him examining a bit of fallen foliage in the orange light. The shoto'shi had taken the loss of his guard much harder than she would have expected, given his flagrant disregard for the man. Sparsely speaking, Hachiro hadn't even corrected the statements of anyone since, which for some reason felt just as eerie as the swamp.

"Takoda," Dmitri called to their guide, "because Gulgons are a migratory people, how do you plan to locate their village?"

"You don't find the mudmen, Your Majesty." Takoda's braids sashayed as his head shook in reply. "Ano, the mudmen find *you*."

It was not a promising plan, meandering through the wetlands on the sheer hope they were journeying in the right direction. Luscia couldn't tell one hollowed out stump from the next. How Takoda did so was a mystery, a mystery she'd started to suspect was a hoax.

The dull pang returned in Luscia's temples, needling her resolve as she mimicked Marek and waded around a floating log. Ebbing in and out, the ache had never fully dissipated after her episode in the bunker. Without Alora's tonics, abandoned in Luscia's ransacked byumbé, she sensed the pain would not lessen anytime soon. She had no desire to think about what that would mean—being deprived of her prescribed dosage—and thus ruminated on everything else during the silent hours they trekked.

She prayed for Noxolo's protection as he aided the two other haidrens in drawing the regiment north.

The cross-caste alpha she used to call Zaethan Kasim, and the blistering determination that'd heated his brusque parting in the gorge… Luscia didn't ruminate on that one particularly long, disconcerted by the way he'd told her good-bye. He'd worded her Andwele nickname differently, and whatever it had meant, it'd wheedled into her ears, taking a most vexing residence.

Thus instead, she thought on her gratitude to Aniell, that her apothic chest had been salvaged and buckled to the back of Dmitri's saddle. For some strange inclination, she'd felt to wear its bone key beneath her attire into the arena that day, with no premonition as to why.

Her thoughts churned, spurring a life of their own. Replaying the moment the captaen of her guard had seen Omun's corpse and realized she'd been telling the truth in Rian—and his look of disgrace when Marek finally understood he'd called his haidren a liar. She was not unhinged. She was not helpless.

She was right.

Luscia's hair licked her indignant scowl, despite the dryness of her upper body. The humidity was smothering, far worse than in the Andwele altitudes. Ahead, a river of sweat drenched Marek's spine through his thin shirt, having shirked the cumber of his jacket. Short, red curls pasted his nape beneath the drooping knot of his carmine-colored locks. Her eye trailed its trajectory toward the broad muscles bulging through the dirtied fabric with his every stride. It clung to his trilateral form, riling Luscia's resentment further. Though jaw clamped and fist clenched, Luscia found her anger descending his backbone, to where his shirt was shoved into his slackened belting.

It'd be easier to forgive him if he were ugly.

Ruddy stubble grazed Marek's shoulder when he looked aside, like he could feel her analysis of his trim backside. Golden twilight defined his sharp profile as he wetted his lips.

Luscia shot her chin upright, suddenly enthralled with the hanging mosses.

Beyond Marek, the lumbering beta smacked his throat irritably. The insects awoke overhead, their wings whirring in exploration. Boreal was not plagued by such pests, which here grew into brutes the size of her palm. That was the beauty of a highland winter; it purged the earth of the things that should never exist. Like her najjani brethren, she'd never missed the snow more.

Marek swatted the air, then swiped at it again. With a whizz, a dark glob tore by Luscia's lashes. The insect clasped to the captaen's back, a winged stain the length of her forefinger with feelers just as long. She gulped when it produced a bizarre click and its bulbous exoskeleton alighted like a match.

A few horses up, Kumo splashed out of line and into the lilies.

"Shtàka!" the beta howled, slapping his forearms frantically. "It's trippy-trancies!"

A shadow covered the party, blocking the final traces of sunlight. Luscia rolled her neck back, and her eyes stretched at the impenetrable blanket descending upon them. To her panic, the globular insects engulfed the open. One landed on Creyvan, covering a quarter of his face with a menacing click. The najjan screamed and whacked it off, sending his mare rearing into Marek. A torrent of wings swished through the canopy. Waves rocked her knees when the gangly Darakaian abruptly dove into the inky water, and a flurry of colossal bugs wafted off his armor.

"Doru, doru! Stop touching them!" Takoda's voice pierced the buzzing. At the helm, his entire side was caked in the neon critters. "The toxin is hallucinogenic, yeah? Trippy-trancies bite when threa—" He spit one out of his mouth. "Threatened. They light up once they feel safe!"

"Ain't no trippy spelling me in a kakka-shtàka trance!"

Up beside him, the petite scout immediately wrapped a scarf about her ears. Luscia quickly saw why when one crawled over Declan's earlobe, rousing him into a head-banging dance as the horde swarmed both him and Creyvan.

"The more proper term would be *venumnoctunae*," Hachiro mumbled from the rear.

Luscia ripped off her jacket and flung it over her king.

"There he is!" Dmitri cheered at the shoto'shi's commentary, hunching beneath her covering. "Welcome back to us, Lord Pilar!"

Not a moment later, an onyx mass thudded into her chest. Luscia peeked down as the insect creeped up her sweaty linsilk shift and onto her bosom, fanning its elongated feelers over her frightened gooseflesh. The feelers quivered, and with a deafening click, its entire body alighted like a fluorescent lantern.

At her whimper, a fresh horde camped up Luscia's arm, crawling and clacking over her itchy skin until her entire limb shone.

"They won't bite the horses," Takoda assured. Completely buried in trippy-trancies, the warrior's gestures were outlined in a venomous glow. "Just keep moving!"

Luscia checked on her king. A brilliant tortoise shell had formed over Dmitri's barreled spine, tucked inside her jacket. His eyes were closed, and his nose wiggled under the threat of an unlit insect. He held his breath until the thing chattered and began to glow.

Dmitri released a relieved gasp.

Arms spread wide, together the group resumed their expedition, bending as one lambent serpent between the woolly cypresses. Bugs were piled onto the *lycran's* fur-slicked coat, claiming Aksel as their feral ferryman. Night had not fully fallen, but covered in trippy-trancies, the group progressed further into Hagarh with trepidation, their yellow-green luster shining across the stirring waters.

When the trees parted, the group plodded into a reedbed. A warm breeze swept from behind. Whishing through the shoots, a tingle skittered up Luscia's nape.

And it wasn't the bugs.

"*Luscia...*"

Her stomach lurched when whispers joined the rustling. Threads from the *Other* flickered in the wind as, without her consent, her Sight flashed in and out of focus.

"*Look and see, Luscia...*"

Her aches sharpened, and the harmonic voices echoed through her skull. Afraid, she twisted, the water sloshing her thighs. Her eyes searched the ethereal flashes in the dark. With another gust, the reedbed flattened under its force, and Luscia froze.

Not all the reeds were moving.

"Surround the king!" she called to her najjan. Luscia reached for her kuerre. "We're not alone in this place!"

Marek waded to her side as Declan and Creyvan trudged to Dmitri's opposite. The entire caravan stopped, the Darakaians readying their bows. Declan unhitched his crescent wraiths and cursed. She heard him slap something, and he cursed again. It grew silent, except for the wind and the wildlife.

And it was then the stiffer reeds rose.

Surrounding them, mounds smothered in muck emerged from the soggy earth. Water and slime slipped to the surface as the muck heightened, exposing muddy skulls, torsos, and spears. Mud drooled down their covered faces, and Luscia counted twenty sets of eyes reflecting their caravan's insectile glow.

Takoda had spoken the truth. The mudmen found them first.

Reinforced reeds jutted from their smattered lips. Breathing apparatuses, Luscia then understood. His hands lifted high and unthreateningly, Takoda splashed through the reedbed, blowing phrases in a tongue she'd never heard. The airy syllables of Gulgou swished her ear, akin to the currents that whipped the Orallachs. He made gradual, sweeping gestures toward their group as the reeds divided, and two torch-bearing Gulgons approached. Takoda sucked in a breath, siphoning his speech, for each rode not a horse but a goliath, jaw-snapping reptile.

"The Collective believe the bohema croc to be extinct," Hachiro whispered in awe.

Both torchbearers snapped to the rapid scratching of his quill.

The enormous horned crocodile jerked its jagged jaws at Takoda. Jumping back, he sprayed them in trippy-trancies while they conversed uninterrupted. The toxic bugs zipped around but did not settle on either leader. In fact, Luscia assessed, the critters overpassed every mud-glazed Gulgon.

A torch waved, and one of the leaders jerked the braided sways coiled about the bohema croc's upper snout. Withdrawing, he vanished into the blackness while the other remained. The gathering of spears lifted, and in unison the Gulgons marched forward.

"Eh." Takoda retreated nervously. "So about those negotiations…"

Luscia tensed. Her fingernails gritted into her kuerre's luxiron hilt when a spearpoint was aimed toward her throat. But as she twerked her grip, the spear unexpectedly dropped, revealing a long, marshy visage. Seated in it was a set of bright-blue eyes, coming closer.

"Khoo-ah…" the man blew out, examining her features, then shouted to his fellows, "Khoo-ah-Lumee-sa!"

Words sailed through the reedbed, and their spears went upright in a rush. Surprisingly, the Gulgon proffered his slippery hand.

Luscia leaned past Marek to question Takoda.

Bewildered, the warrior spun and said, "Meme ano'qondai… I don't know what changed, but they've accepted us into their village. We are being taken to the high matriarch."

Bells and gourdes laced the branches, jangling in the gentle breeze with the group's arrival. The reception reminded Luscia of her own Boreali borders, strung with telltale chimes.

How she longed to hear that sound again.

The waters were shallower here, splashing their ankles as villagers ran out to greet them. Oil pans floated on the lily pads, alighting their path through the quagmire into the Gulgons' secreted borough. Clay domes populated the vicinity, from what Luscia could see over the heads of those who swaddled them.

Mud-crackled fingers reached for her cheeks, which too had been slathered in muck, courtesy of their spear-toting shepherds. "Khoo-ah," they kept repeating. Luscia brushed them off, glad it was hands, not poisonous insects, crowding her skin.

Declan could not say the same.

Marek hauled him through the swamp grass, the najjan's other arm pitched around Creyvan's neck. Swollen, greened veins ascended up his freckled throat and under his ginger beard. He'd been bitten at some point, likely when drawing his weaponry at the king's defense. The hallucinations were kicking in; he'd been singing for a while now, and at the cost of Marek's eardrum.

A lass so rare, her beauty bovine.
Of greater stature, no man can find.

In jolly spirits, Declan bellowed the ill-tuned sonnet at the captaen, dragging his boots behind his hulking mass.

One ride to Ödetha just to kiss her.
But close your eyes with Noxolo's sister.

Creyvan snorted at the reference to poor Dierdre Egon. Noxolo's sister had become a theme for her guards' jesting, ever since they had departed Roüwen in the spring, when they used to squabble over things like jerky and seasoning privileges.

Luscia's own chuckle stalled. The memory seemed so far away.

"Fancies himself a real bard when he's sloshed." Marek groused under the najjan's weight. Readjusting, he hollered to the front of their shuffling cluster. "Takoda, what is it they keep calling our haidren?"

The toned warrior strode alongside the torchbearer, his gaze locked on the fat-bellied bohema croc.

"Yeah it's, uh, 'cousin of something,'" Takoda anxiously shot back. "Whatever it means, just play into it, uni? Otherwise, the king could be this thing's dinner…"

Luscia twisted when Dmitri drolly interjected. "I'd more accurately be the appetizer to Kumo."

The beta's wide neck swerved round as she outstretched her arm protectively over her king's middle. It would never come to that—not with these people. She and the najjan still retained their weaponry, as did the Darakaians, but more violence was the last weapon Dmitri wanted to exert. And as the waterway brimmed with Gulgons, many of whom couldn't reach her chest, Luscia agreed. This multi-generational village was founded on family, and even in desperation, the Quadren meant them no harm.

She prayed to the High One the feeling was mutual.

They were brought before a large, bowed burrow, connected to a procession of minor mud huts along either wing. Smoke escaped the top in a spindly spire. The woven fabric over the entrance was thrust aside, and the other torchbearer appeared.

He gave an instruction to Takoda, who in turn scratched his braided rows uneasily.

"The high matriarch says she will speak to the king, Maji'maia, and myself," he conveyed, pointing toward the short ladder. "But our weapons are not permitted into her presence."

The warrior climbed the rungs and propped both his kopar and bow atop the stoop. Taking Dmitri by the hand, Luscia pushed past the captaen's grimace.

With her *lycran*, she lumbered after Takoda. She didn't want to set her luxiron aside either, but she was not unarmed. Phalen's radials shielded her knuckles, and coasting them, so did the darts stitched into his leather gauntlets.

Nearing the roughhewn structure, Luscia saw the Gulgou home did not reside in the water but was suspended just above it on a reedy platform, intricately hitched and secured to the surrounding trees. Though comprised of vine and wood, the complex arrangement of braces and bearings caught Luscia's fascination. She climbed the stout ladder slower, in disbelief.

The method was identical to that in the highlands.

Aksel pushed through the rugged doorway before Luscia and into a crude receiving hall. Muggy, the room smelled of tannins from the swamp. Gulgons lined the curved daub walls, their stalk-plaited clothing stitched with moss and lichen.

Luscia scanned the burrow guardedly. Muffled wails resonated through the packed siding, though on this side of it, not one Gulgon was crying.

Takoda and Dmitri flanked Luscia's either side before an elderly woman, seated among a ring of blazing urns. A quartet of ebony plaits, aged with silver, tumbled over her bench well past her knobby knees. The flames spotlighted her dark skin where it was not shrouded in the mineral-rich silt. But it was what lustered beneath her wrinkled deco-rated brow that made Luscia's mouth fall ajar.

Her right iris was the blue of an Orallach fjord; her left, that of living opal.

The high matriarch closed her wrinkled lids tiredly before pinning her inexplicable gaze on Luscia. A spasm shuddered Luscia's temple, and instantly, she was jolted into the Sight once more.

Threads of lumin dusted the ceiling of the burrow, twinkling above the old woman's crown. Her observation sluggishly drew upward and impossibly traced the glittering wisps with eyes like Luscia's own.

With the eyes of Tiergan.

Pursing her furrowed lips, the high matriarch sucked on a pipe as she watched the lumin with joyless reserve. Inside the *Other*, Luscia gawked at the woman sharing the Sight. She didn't know how it was possible. To Tiergan's descendants alone had Aniell bestowed the Higher Gifts.

Yet here they were on full display. In a mud hut. In Hagarh.

Luscia gasped when what felt like a knife pierced her forehead and the glimpse of the *Other* was gone. Plated in golden charms, the matriarch hooked her brow curiously, and smacked her lips.

"Khoo-ah-Lumee-sa..."

She puffed out the phrase in billows of tangy smoke. Tendrils escaped her nostrils and pooled to the floor. The pipe rocked between her stained teeth, and she mumbled another phrase around it to the torchbearer. Behind him, a Gulgon pulled a string of beads, upfolding a reeded tapestry.

Sobs and laments escaped the squat opening. Taking the torch, he disappeared into the adjacent hut.

Restlessly, Takoda shuffled toward the circle of fire and, lowering his stature to hers, addressed the high matriarch. Presenting their case in broken Gulgou, his hand angled at Dmitri, then waved like a fish. Bartering for their crossing, Takoda's palms flattened side to side, and he counted out all ten fingers, rapping his thumbs against his leather tunic, at himself.

Muttering, the matriarch took another drag of her pipe. Takoda shook his head and tried again, just as the reeds were drawn and the torchbearer returned. Murmurs cradled the room as another Gulgon exited the bewailing burrow too.

Their rumbling hushed when the matriarch began to speak. Luscia did not understand her words, but they were burdened with sorrow. Frowning, Takoda cocked his ear and listened intently.

"Erm, she says she won't grant us passage on the river—or provide skiffsweepers to travel it—in exchange for mere horses and supply." He translated, scrambling for the right jargon. "Her last remaining son lies empty in the bedroom beside us. He failed to defeat the… I don't know what this means… the *devoid*… and will ash the infinite waters with his brothers.

"The 'devoid' curses the blessed land of the Gulgons, tainting it with… cold death. It angers the Sacred Wind. When the Wind pointed to the trees, the Gulgons presented a warning, but the king of Orynthia did not listen, she says."

Luscia inhaled sharply. The desecrated bodies strung at the border of the Mirajii Forest were a caution, not a threat. A war-tainted creature, just like those she had faced in Rian, must plague the wetlands. To its monstrosity, to its massacre, the Gulgons were trapped as prisoners. And now, so were they.

She'd just paraded her king into a death zone.

The boards creaked under Dmitri's cane as he shifted his weight anxiously, yet not for his own welfare, she knew. Her king was thinking of his friend, the disowned haidren who'd steered away one threat just to encounter another.

Concluding her croaked remarks, the high matriarch tapped her pipe on the closest urn and, setting it back on her tongue, slanted it directly at Luscia.

Takoda pivoted too, his angular cheeks pinched with confusion.

"She will trade not with the Orynthian king," he stated awkwardly, tearing his gaze from Dmitri to stare at Luscia, "but with the 'cousin of... something'. She says, three skiffsweepers for the horses, if wielding the Jewel of the Great Ancestor, you can free their people and vanquish the 'devoid.'"

The torchbearer sidestepped, beckoning the other Gulgon into the center of the room. In his mud-crusted palms rested an ancient, carved spear. With one elegant, nimble sweep, he thrust it over the firelight, and a bouquet of prismatic radiance refracted across the domed ceiling. Beneath the luminescence, that same light twinkled within the old woman's eye as she gleamed at Luscia beyond the spear.

Its tip was made of luxiron.

Chapter Thirty Three
Zaethan

They chased the northern bank against the rippling rapids of the Yakov River. Atop solid ground, Zaethan stared across the vast divide toward the wetland realm—his friend and king journeying somewhere amid its sodden expanses.

The wind was picking up, whipping the current to an unfavorable churn. Squinting, he speared Owàa among the clouds, grimacing at the late-afternoon haze. Unless the sky cleared, his lover would be hidden tonight, and without Àla'maia's luster, these rapids were as lethal as whatever lurked below. Zaethan prompted Hellion onward, hoping Takoda already had Dmitri on a skiffsweeper upriver.

442

It was unclear where his warriors camped with the Mirajii Pryde, but it wouldn't be far from their patrols along the Yakov. Zaethan told the shadowman as much, though it did nothing to soothe his impatience. The longer he was delayed from reuniting with his haidren in Port Khmer, the more he grumbled in Boreali to the trees, as if the lush nature heard his plight—or cared. It should have been unnerving, yet accompanied by Ira's incessant prattling, it was just plain racket.

"Khmer hosts a bevy of diversion. I once woke up in a boatyard bungalow, wearing nothing but a half-eaten Uriel pie—"

Zaethan hated Uriel pie, almost as much as blathering, self-indulged yancies.

"Utterly melted, pastry crumbs in every cranny. You'd be amazed, my friend—"

"We're not friends."

Insulted, Ira pouted in his saddle, to which his legs were securely tied, in the event of more trouble. It seemed none of the noble's refined riding lessons had ever taught him to function under duress—like when being chased by assassins.

"Fine!" The Unitarian haidren tossed his chin-length hair. "Then I won't tell you about the buxom seafarer who fondly swabbed me up, or how she almost sold me to a touchy Tavish mercenary."

"Depths, I wish someone would."

Ahead, a heap of driftwood and debris dammed an intersecting stream, where the rapids raged against a mass of boulders. He trotted Hellion toward the pile, Harmonia and her yancy ward in tow. Decelerating, Zaethan strode along the streambank, scouring the sun-bleached articles among the fallen timber.

A knot unfurled behind his navel. No overlong oars and no skiffsweeper remnants were scattered among the wreckage. If Dmitri's group was on the river, they'd not crashed here.

A low garble sounded from the rear. Zaethan turned and found Ira massaging his beltline.

"Wouldn't happen to see a four-course spread down there, would you? Or a dusty, deserted bottle of Galina's finest?" he wistfully asked. "We can't go on like this, Zaeth, foraging like paupers—"

"Eat your berries," Zaethan snapped, steering the horses inland past the blockage. They'd cross it upstream.

The lead rope on Harmonia tightened, yanking Ira along as he scoffed. "You mean the berries that Bloody-Locks picked this morning? After my colorful ejection evening last, I'm half-certain he's trying to poison me!"

Paces off, the shadowman guided his mare over a tangle of roots. A wry smirk toyed the corner of his thin mouth. It disappeared as quickly as it showed, concealed behind his tangled fall of blood-stained tresses. They'd not wasted time bathing, aside from his splashing the carnage from his alabastrine features. Crimson discolored most of his Boreali garb, a grisly proclamation of his capabilities against the polish of his crescent wraiths, feathering his spine like an iron phantom from the beyond.

Thoroughly unblemished, the shadowman had made time to cleanse his blades rather than his person. His arced witchiron mirrored a leafy collage when the forest transformed into a congested, verdant maze. Zaethan navigated his stallion through the undergrowth where it pooled in thickets. It was baffling that the Gulgons would even fight for this place.

The Mirajii was a beguiling host to wanderers, enticing the ignorant with its fragrance and beauty only to ensnare them inside its puzzling contours. This forest was a living labyrinth where more than one man had lost his way—if not his mind. A sea of intertwined trees,

the Mirajii was riddled with chambers of darkness beneath an impenetrable canopy. Drapes of dense vine corralled travelers into meadows of
noxious flora and tarpits disguised by blossoming groundcover. Tread
too deeply into the forest, and one would not return from it.

Uneager to add to its number, Zaethan led them over a shallow
cascade in the stream and steered their return toward the timberline
along the security of the riverbank. But the shadowman circled his
mare. Ruddy tangles whipped his wide shoulders as he tensely searched
the brush.

His face swerved and he warned, "Archers."

At the word, an arrow impaled the trunk beside Zaethan. Hellion
reared as another flew past Ira and sank into the bark. Cords sailed
around them as a flock of arrows swarmed all sides. Within a matter of
seconds, they were fenced inside a rope pen.

Tugging a cord with his finger, Zaethan inspected the intricate
braid. He broke into a relieved grin.

"Owàamo!" Zaethan hollered into the treetops. "About time, yeah?
I was starting to think Kai went soft on patrols!"

Bow drawn, a muscled warrior dropped from the heights and
landed with a *thud*. But it was not Kai, alpha of the Mirajii Pryde.

It was his beta.

A row of ample, twisted knots lined his scraped scalp, towering over
the unamused scowl stamped into his square face. Stout and sturdy, the
beta rose from his squat. He'd yet to disarm the bow.

"We're spread a bit thin these days, Alpha Zà!" he brashly yelled
back. "So, uni. It's about time *you* showed up!"

Zaethan disregarded his impertinent tone. Though the beta did not
yet know it, he didn't owe him anything better—not anymore. That
choice would be theirs. He gingerly held up a hand, and using the

kopar in his other, he cut through the cabling, freeing Hellion from the restraints.

"Meme qondai, Chane. I know," Zaethan confessed to the beta, remembering his name, "which is why we have much to discuss. Where is Kai?"

"On a stretcher!" Chane barked.

Resentment pinched his stare, visible from the distance. Harmonia grazed Zaethan's boots when Ira jostled the reins and leaned over.

"Not the best conversationalist, is he?"

Zaethan smacked the yancy haidren off as more warriors leapt from overhanging boughs, plummeting to the earth. He lost count after fourteen, recognizing the pair of siblings rushing straight for him, Faraji natives. Their partnering smiles were stark and brilliant against the dappled shade of the abundant wood.

Sadik, the eldest of the two, sprinted ahead of his sister. He reached out and grabbed onto Zaethan's leg as if to ensure he was really there.

"Alpha Zà! Thank the Fates, it is you," Sadik cried. His ordinarily cheerful, bulbous cheeks were deflated and gaunt, deepening the creases from his grinning. "Our jwona has changed, Yhona! I told you he would come for us!"

Zaethan's heart sank at the warrior's confidence. They'd no idea how their House had turned on them all, how they'd become pawns in their chief warlord's grab for power.

No more than twenty, Yhona, his younger sister, ran up to the Andwele stallion and pressed her palms into his onyx coat. Zaethan eyed her woven buckskin vest, the patched holes and ripped trim. She was hardly in better condition. Her sable arms had leaned to the point of muscle loss. Just like her jawline, which could slice a hucklebuckle fruit in half, were she able to find one to eat.

Yhona tilted her malnourished face up at Zaethan and dusted her fingers down her forehead and over her unreserved smile. A gesture of jubilee, sealing her joy forever.

"We knew you would not abandon us, Alpha Zà," Yhona sang, tears spilling past the dusky lakes beneath her eyes.

His teeth ground as his anger reawakened, churning hotly inside his deflated chest. Zaethan didn't deserve her devotion. Her joy. He'd allowed Darakai to send her here. He'd let her starve.

Bending in the saddle, he gently cupped a handful of her twined braids. "Take me to Kai."

"Uni zà." She nodded vigorously. Worry pricked her bay eyes. "Rhaolé ono, Alpha Zà. Come fast."

An hour from the riverside, the pryde's camp was in tatters. Scattered around the fortification, if one could call it such, domed tents hung on their posts like rags. Every tent was worn to the threads. Most had been converted to strip hammocks, as their tatters served no other purpose. Constructed around high ground, the collapsing timber-laced ramparts were rotting at the joints, a consequence of the steamy humidity.

It didn't surprise Zaethan that the watchtowers were manned in the corners of the encampment but rather that they stood at all. However old the structures were, they'd not been sufficiently maintained.

Yhona and Sadik guided Zaethan, Ira, and the shadowman past the central firepit and beyond a queue of smoking racks. The rungs were sparse with game. Even the team of horses, hitched to the eastern palisade, looked better fed than the warriors dispersed to their duties. A man could not survive on grass like his steed, but as they passed an unwashed bowl, it struck Zaethan that was exactly what they'd been trying to do.

Word of his arrival spread as he rode through the camp. Six more warriors from the Proper Pryde joined their advance, parading with Zaethan on either side. Their shared elation weighted him, rounding his shoulders forward. The still-healing wound stung, but his coming would sting his warriors far worse. If their hearts had become as brittle as their frames, they would not be strong enough to handle his news, nor the decision each now faced.

Yhona stopped before the largest tent. The dome was sunken in sections, but it stood tall, capped by the skull of a tusked boar. Zaethan used to cap his own with that of a stag, to honor King Korbin and Dmitri whenever stationed outside Bastiion. A ribboned pennon, bearing Darakai's crest, fluttered in the wind above the alpha's lodgings. The weak firelight illuminated the embroidery of a panther.

Zaethan dismounted with a grimace. The symbol no longer held the same glory it once had. Nor was it his to claim.

Skirting the horses, Chane stepped in front of Yhona and seized the tent flap. Gripping it, the beta sucked his teeth and eyed the yancy haidren. The glance hardened to a glare when it coasted to the shadowman.

His chin jutted toward the makeshift stable. "Y'siti stays outside with the rest of the livestock."

Zaethan inflated his height as he marched toward the tent, bearing over Chane. "The haidren and shadowman walk where I do," he stated, clarifying for those in the vicinity.

In their bewilderment, most of the grins withered to glowers. The gathering warriors, their number multiplying by the second, gaped when Zaethan turned his back toward the beta, and, blocking the shadowman from Chane's warped snarl, motioned for him to duck inside the tent.

The shadowman wordlessly complied, but for Chane's sensibilities, he mimicked a horse's nicker as he dipped his skyward stature beneath the canvas folds. Zaethan harnessed his smirk and beckoned Ira to follow.

It reeked of mold. Mildew invaded the dank walls of the tent, blooming from a hole in the pitched dome. Zaethan covered his mouth, trailing the yancy haidren. Stepping around a broken chair and a modest meeting table, Zaethan crept toward the stretch-cot near the back, where the alpha in question dozed. A rough splint was bound to his leg, thigh to ankle. Cloth stays were soured in blood and pus. Worse, his visible flesh had taken on the same green as the tent.

Zaethan knelt beside the cot.

"Owàamo, Kai Wakhan," he said, embracing the alpha's thinned forearm.

Though in his mid-twenties, Kai's features had lived a decade beyond. Where his skin should have sheened like the amber yuckon syrups bottled in the mountains, it instead stretched dull and flat across his already exaggerated cheekbones. Underneath his short twisted locs, Kai's lashes edged apart.

His defining trait was bulging and overstated as ever, making him mostly eyes as they opened.

"I thought I'd dreamed your voice, Alpha Zà," he murmured. His sweeping lips smiled weakly, and his other hand stirred, coming to pat Zaethan's over his forearm. Kai quirked a brow at the men crowding his bedding. "Who have you dragged into my humble abode?"

"Ira Hastings, the haidren to Bastiion," Zaethan said, to Kai's surprise.

At his name, metal clattered and Ira spun, dropping a knife that did not belong to him. Tucking hair behind his ear, he offered the alpha a showy bow. All looked at the shadowman.

"Noxolo Egon, of Clan Ödetha," he proudly pronounced. His name was foreign to Zaethan too. "Personal guard to the haidren to Boreal."

"We're a far way from the Drystan Sea…" Kai's brow rose even higher at the shadowman, then toward Zaethan, expecting a story. "But eh, now that you're here, Alpha Zà, think you'd be able patch this shtàka back up?"

Bronze rimmed his unhopeful stare. Zaethan sighed.

"Ano, but I know someone who can—if we can get you to her in time. Depths, what happened here?"

"It used to just be the mudmen," the alpha said. "Stick and spear skirmishes, yeah? Sometimes stealing our supplies… But a couple months after your cadre of warriors showed up, the forest changed." Kai shivered under his sheet of sweat. "When Owàa slept, Mirajii rebelled. Meme qondai, I know it sounds like mudmen kakk."

"First, the big game disappeared. We've been surviving on squirrels and shrubs since. Then, our warriors started to disappear. And by the Fates, if we found them… Their husks were torn inside out. Some think it's war-taint. Some, resurgence from the wetlands."

Zaethan's flesh prickled at the account, recalling the regiment's screams in the wood just two days before—at all the horror his prydes must have endured amid this squalor. If the disease was spreading, it was being expressed through more primal behaviors than they had witnessed in Bastiion. Ambrose had drained his victims with meticulous precision before the war-taint had overtaken his system. But these were tales from a forgotten era, one they couldn't even imagine.

"There's a demon in these trees, Alpha Zà," Kai warned. "I've seen the fire in its eyes before I ran like a huwàa. That's how I broke it." He indicated his busted leg. "If the dawn hadn't come, uni, I would have been next."

"Death toll?" Zaethan asked, fearing the count.

"Four of mine, two of yours. But Nigan Hanovi deserted shortly after, and Omun—"

"Didn't make it," he finished brusquely. Zaethan rubbed his face. Including themselves, that left only thirty-eight warriors, plus his five traveling with the king. "And Nigan didn't desert. He defected. To Wekesa."

Kai spit in the grass, expressing his shared opinion for Zaethan's longtime rival. "So, our prydes are going home then? Shamàli, tell me we've been reassigned," Kai asked, straining against the cot where he propped himself up.

Scowling, Zaethan rose off his knee and pulled a stool to the alpha's bedside. Steepling his fingers, he said, "Kai, the home you remember doesn't exist."

Zaethan swallowed his reservations and launched into a summary of what had occurred in Faraji, ordering the events as he would any report, impersonal and to the point. Kai's forehead crumpled in haggard confusion, listening to how the chief warlord schemed with Pilar to frame their ally for King Korbin's assassination. How they'd tried to coerce Orynthia into war with Razôuel by intimidating the one who now wore his crown. He conveyed Wekesa's challenge, that he'd been hauled out of the arena just as Omun bled out his testimony...

Zaethan told him of Bessus, how the field marshal had sold his fealty to Darakai, then turned his entire regiment against the throne. Kai's wide jaw hung when he retold the moment Dmitri had stripped the chief warlord of his Orynthian commandership and appointed

Zaethan's uncle, Yousif Shà, instead. And then how he'd been arrested in the bunker before the war council... conveying that the chief warlord had ultimately imprisoned king and Quadren against their will, and were it not for the haidren to Boreal's shadowmen, they'd likely be locked there still.

But that was not what brought a lump to Zaethan's throat. He had to tell his alpha, his comrade in arms, the worst truth yet: that Zaethan Kasim had been declared illegitimate—that he was not a Kasim at all. He'd been cast out. Denigrated. Denied.

Because his veins were diluted. Darakai was not the only story swimming within them.

"Yousif rallies King Dmitri's supporters to shelter in Rian as we speak. But we will rendezvous with the king and his haidrens in Port Khmer. Defending the line of Thoarne, upholding the Ethnicam Accords—*that* is our kwihila, yeye qondai?"

Kai's fist bumped his chest passionately. "Uni zà, Alpha Zà."

Zaethan thought little of the title. It was probably habit for the men to use it. He scanned the alpha in the cot and stood, extending to him an arm.

"Can you ride? The decision is yours."

With a grim nod, Kai seized it. "Kàchà-kocho. I'll write over the pain. Be a jwona rapiki, like you."

Chane swooped under his alpha's opposite arm and handed him a pair of crude crutches. Helping Kai toward the tent opening, the beta peered out from under his hooded brow, scrutinizing Zaethan in his periphery.

"Eh, what of Wekesa?" Chane questioned unexpectedly.

The question earned a scoff from his leader, but Zaethan withheld nothing. "Last I heard, recovering in the infirmary with Faraji's best surgeons."

He caught the hint of contemplation in Chane's delay when they exited the dilapidated dwelling to address the many haggard faces that awaited them. Warriors pressed in, some already carting their packs and weaponry. They assumed he came to rescue.

When really, he came to commission.

Zaethan climbed atop a stump, hovering over them while Yhona and Sadik hurried to help Kai to stay upright. Crossing his thick arms, Chane backed up a fraction as it began to drizzle.

"On this cursed ground, each of you have a choice to make. The War Council has committed treason against the crown, mounting total insurrection against the reign of King Dmitri Korbin Thoarne."

Gasps were uttered all around, and heads shook in disbelief.

"Doru, doru." He hushed them. "He flees from Darakai's conspirators, even as a rebel regiment of the Orynthian army pursues at the chief warlord's order. The king needs your shield, uni. He needs your bow, and your kopar."

Rain smattered the lake of disconcerted eyes, collecting with their every blink. Few warriors nodded, aggrieved by his news; however, Zaethan predicted that once they heard who would lead them to Dmitri's aid, they would revolt too.

"When the Quadren discovered this betrayal, we learned another as well." He searched them, those he'd come to know so well—those he might lose. "I am not the person we believed me to be. Ano zà. I stand before you as no one—no one but Zaethan, the cross-caste bastard of a dead haidren... disqualified from any title except friend of the crown." Zaethan threw out his arms, bearing his rain-slicked abdomen clad in

Darakaian battle armor. "You owe me no allegiance, but if you follow me out of this forest…" He searched their desperate and conflicted faces. "You can proclaim that allegiance to your king."

The canopy swished with the incoming shower, adding to the whispers of the warriors below.

Soaking from the downpour, Zaethan's locs hung loose down his chest with the ridges of the wildcat scar. The heavy droplets chimed against his mother's gilded cuffs and the message her runes carried.

Courage. Strength. Victory. Honor. Heart. The quartet were common, but not the fifth. It was the value Darakaians seldom embodied, for which they so often fell short.

"I still follow you, Alpha Zà."

Zaethan rotated to where Kai leaned on his crutches. The warriors watched the alpha as he hobbled forward, swiped his hand over a dirt-smeared worktable, catching the rain in his grasp, and smushed it into a paste.

Caging his emotion, Zaethan's mouth trembled when Kai discarded a crutch and boldly pressed his palm against his cross-caste skin, claiming him before his kinsmen.

"*Meme ràtomdai na yeye.*"

Behind the stump, Yhona squatted, submerging both hands in the thickening mud. She scurried directly before him and marked his biceps.

"Meme ràtomdai na yeye."

His warrior stepped aside for her brother to take her place. Sadik wrapped his muddied fingers around Zaethan's ankles.

"I claim you too, Alpha Zà," he declared, rain dousing his grip. "Meme ràtomdai na yeye."

More surrounded him. Humbled, Zaethan's eyes squeezed shut as dozens of hands befell his body. Fingers dimpled his musculature and enveloped his bones, marking him as their own. Together, the neglected warriors enacted their own Holiday of Hands, speaking the same words of Fàkkadim'Chalim.

When they left his form, Zaethan gazed down at the muddy slop. And though it washed off within minutes, the impressions remained. They were a part of him, and he would carry each print with pride until the day he died.

Zaethan's shoulders broadened into a beam.

"Gather only what you need," he ordered the throng. "We're leaving now."

In a wave, their fists beat their chests, and the warriors dispersed. Zaethan descended the stump, turning to give further instruction to Kai, when they saw Chane atop his mount.

He'd not noticed him step away before… but he definitely noticed the supplies already strapped to his saddle.

"No self-respecting Darakaian would ever follow a half-breed! Ano zà!" the beta shouted at Zaethan, his lips screwing into a vehement knot. "The future favors Wekesa!"

Releasing a howl, Chane spurred his stallion into a gallop, and they hurtled over a palisade out of camp. Zaethan stared into the darkening forest as the chestnut dot disappeared. Chane presented another path, but he would become a traitor, just like the rest of his House. But they didn't have time for lost causes. The road to Port Khmer was winding and rough. And his king would be waiting.

It wasn't until Zaethan climbed into Hellion's saddle that he realized Chane rode for Faraji, armed with the most crucial weapon he had to offer.

The words "Port Khmer."

He'd been in the room when Zaethan told them to Kai.

Chapter Thirty-Four
Luscia

"Y ou shouldn't be doing this. You're clearly unwell."

Luscia snorted, continuing her impassioned trudge through the sloppy mire, despite the objection from the captaen of her guard. His last remark was a poignant summary of her unspoken quarrel with him. She massaged her temple, irritated both by Marek and the unending migraine, half convinced the two were related.

"I do what I must," she briskly stated, cinching her grip around the Gulgon spear.

Mud slung with each stomp of her upturned boots. Beyond Marek, her lycran plowed through the grasses where they ceded to the sluggish waters. Aksel's snowy fur, stained by the swampy tannins, blended into the russet streak along his spine. His ample tail sent ripples as it happily swatted the water's surface. It must be hot in his Northern coat. Luscia licked the sweat collecting over her lip, empathizing with the beast.

She too was burning up.

"Bolaeva, please," Marek pled in her periphery. Deadly blades sheathing his back, the captaen's face veered in her direction while his legs drove him in another. "You cradle your head as if it hurts. You're aflush and drowning in sweat. Ana'Sere, I can see the tremors in your hand!"

Luscia paused, her foot sinking deeper into the earth. Her focus drifted down to the luxiron-tipped spear. The ancient weapon shook with her shuddering wrist, inside Phalen's gauntlet. She'd been too perturbed to even notice.

"It's nothing." She plodded on, her chin upright.

"This is reckless. You are haidren to Boreal." Marek retorted like she'd forgotten, and he stooped, as if admonishing a small child.

Luscia's mouth pressed tight. His strides had paired with hers, which was dually aggravating. Without Alora's tonic, there was nothing to do but toil through the pain and fulfill the high matriarch's mission. Kill the creature, leave the wetlands. She could not allow Dmitri to get stuck in this place—an onset episode be damned. She was already in one.

No vials. No stopping.

Sacrifice for the whole. *That* was what it meant to be haidren to Boreal.

"The Clann Darragh will exile us all if anything happens to you. At least let us turn around and collect Declan."

"The najjan are the greatest warriors in the realm." Luscia steeled her spine. "So niit, Captaen Bailefore, I'll not siphon King Dmitri's defense simply to bolster my own."

She heard Marek sputter over the cricket song in the surrounding cypresses.

"Haven't you siphoned your guard enough?" he blurted, splashing her linsilk jacket with his heated gestures. "First, you sent Böwen to Roüwen as escort to some lowly attendant, and now Noxolo is lost to the Mirajii with a renounced Darakaian cross-caste—who plainly has become your backdoor ally! It's like you don't even want najjani protection!"

Incensed, Luscia stopped and yanked a curtain of woolly moss out of her way.

"Where was this need to protect me in Rian?" she snapped, spearing his seafarer eyes.

Marek's rusty lashes widened, in either surprise or offense, she didn't care.

"Where was it? Was it in your doubt?" Luscia demanded. "When you made me feel crazed even though I wasn't? Look where we are! Hunting the very creature that crawled into my bed!"

"The Watchman as my witness, Ana'Sere, I never meant to—"

The *Other* flickered behind him, haloing his glossy scarlet hair with hectic ribbons of light. Needles pierced her skull as she stepped toward his chest and looked up defiantly.

"Or was it when you chose to keep your haidren in bondage?" she asserted when a worse ache ignited in her heart. "Denying me the training I needed—"

"Bondage!" His arrow-straight nose buckled at the bridge. "Everything we do is to keep you from it! Shores of Aurynth, I would have given you anything—whatever you wished—if I knew that in your impatience, you'd recoil to *him* to give it to you instead!"

Luscia's jaw quivered irrepressibly as she stared into his pinched, azure irises. "He gave me what you couldn't... Not after the way you looked at me in that tent."

Aksel barked when around them, the lumin floated in the middle of the quiet swamp. Twinkling, the erratic threads blinked in and out of focus as the Sight fought to pull her entirely beyond the veil. Whispers cocooned her ears with the enveloping light energy, but she pinned her attention on the captaen's scorn when his hand cascaded the static-charged air along her figure, as if he couldn't feel it.

Marek's scowl shook. Genuine hurt rivaled the disgust in the crisp definition of his mouth. "So you invited a barbarian's hands onto your consecrated body… and gave him something almost as precious for the trouble."

Her cheeks flared when his regard shifted to the luxiron wraiths soaring over her shoulder, a metal that carried as much of the Dönumn as she did in her veins. She'd entrusted it to an outsider, for her House's sake as much as his. But under Marek's unbridled scrutiny, Luscia was too enraged to feel any shame. The High One saw her conviction, the case for her broken vow. It was Aniell's to absolve, not the captaen of her guard.

In Marek's unlit pupils, her Tiergan eye reflected a fit of luster, furious and aglow.

"You gave me your pity when I needed your belief." Luscia's voice shook. The torment between her temples worsened with every syllable. "That's all I wanted, Captaen. And you and I both know the reason you withheld it."

Hung like banners, a fresh wind swept through the mosses that encompassed them, and Aksel's growl rattled behind his canines.

"*Luscia…*"

Her face jerked, as if she could whisk the murmuration away, then returned, fastening onto Marek while he refused to answer. She hated the way her joints convulsed, quivering on display before him as the episode took hold, but she dug her heels into the sodden muck, even as her Sight consumed her vision.

Contorting threads sparkled and swarmed the breeze.

"Admit it," Luscia ordered the captaen through her teeth.

Marek gaped down at her, worry redrawing his ivory expression as her trembling increased. He reached out timidly.

"Listen, Luscia…"

Pressing her eyes, she shut out the light with the whispers, and shouted, "Admit it!"

"What happened to your mother can never happen to you!"

Her lids tore open. Marek stood in the moonlight, his hand bandaged over his mouth. But the damage was done. The truth released—finally.

As beautiful and eloquent and enchanting as Eoine Tiergan Darragh forever was, her people would only remember her ruin, that of a deranged taleteller who told her last to the wilds, never to be found again.

"Meh fyreon," Marek said through his fingers. "Forgive me, Ana'Sere, I didn't mean—"

Luscia slogged backward through the water. Anchored on the other side of the veil, a brilliant beam coasted between their noses. The more prominent thread curled, twisting its pulsating light just inches from her face. Dread seized her breath as she stared into the notorious specter.

The harbinger thread had followed her to Hagarh.

"Listen close, Luscia…"

The symphonic voices rattled her mind, then with a *pop*, they all dissipated. She twirled away from the harbinger thread, sloshing among the reeds at Aksel's low rumble, then shifted again toward the flooded stump on her left. But she heard only the shuffle of the leaves.

"Ana'Sere, I'm so—"

"Heh'ta." Luscia clamped her palm over his apology. "Did you hear that?"

With a nearly imperceptible twerk, the najjani captaen consulted the silence. The frogs had stopped croaking.

She retracted her hand when he stirred beneath it. "Where have the animals gone?"

Luscia craned her neck at the threads dancing throughout the vacant treetops.

She gasped in pain when with a disconcerting flash, the lumin writhed in unison and dispersed into the leaves. Her anguished, wide eyes pegged the captaen in fear. All of a sudden, a dark mass barreled into Marek and tore him right out from under her horrified gaze.

Luscia and the lycran ran through the shallow waters before she even saw where the captaen landed, thrashing against the creature of her nightmares. Scraps of cloth dangled from its emaciated frame like the flaps of its missing flesh. Brimmed its spiny fangs, sinew strained with the snapping of its dislocated jaws upon Marek. Water splashed, and his head vanished beneath the surface.

Dashing among the reeds, Luscia caught the creature's eyes, burning red and ravenous. It reared back its lethal talons.

Fitfully, its skull shook, and it released a chilling screech, launching off Marek. The creature charged Luscia on all fours in an inhumane gallop. Flittering threads of lumin shivered from its path as it carved a dark tunnel through the *Other*.

Luscia sped toward it, her hot breath crystalizing over the tip of her nose in the cooling air. Using her momentum, she thrust the base of the spear into the knee-deep water and catapulted over the creature. Twirling midjump, Luscia unsheathed her crescent wraiths, touched down, and, sliding across the muck, spun out as it double-backed.

Snarling, Aksel bit it by the ankle, pinning it in place. The creature howled when her sweeping luxiron hacked its ribcage, expelling bone and tissue into the reedbed. Its necrotic tissue sizzled and burned.

Yet it showed no distress. Beating her lycran aside, it tore part of its own calf muscle with him and barged for her with a gaping hole in its abdomen.

Waters sprayed when a tall body skidded between them. The captaen wielded his wraiths in the deadly dance of the najjan, slashing a curved blade through the creature's thigh as he glided onto his knee, whirled behind it, and swung the other wraith into its jagged spine.

A vile odor of brimstone and rot perfumed the swamp. Luscia moved to flank it, but another torturous screech pierced her ears, and before she could turn, a searing misery raked her lower back through the reinforced linsilk. In a silent scream, she gulped the bitter breeze, inhaling the taste of sulfur.

Streaks of brilliant illumination ruptured the lush canopy, and the harbinger thread soared into the open. It lashed at Luscia's face, forcing her to reel rightward when the second creature swiped its protracted talons. She ducked and, in tandem, swung both crescent wraiths to cut it through the thighs, halfway to the bone. Two claws clamped around the radiant luxiron blades. Disintegrating its own ligaments, the creature growled and wrenched the wraiths out of its putrefied muscle. It flailed its blackened tongue while, to Luscia's dread, it heaved the najjani weapons higher and with supernatural strength, stripped each wraith from her panicked grasp.

Luscia's long plait whipped her cheek as she scuttled backward through the reeds. Losing traction, her upturned boots slipped in the sludge. Her thumbs coasted the leather edge of Phalen's gauntlets, abruptly recalling the untested device. Backing into a log, she held her forearm steady and, with her middle finger, tugged the taut bowstring, praying her brother was the genius she suspected.

Luxiron darts flew from the panels and impaled the creature's gut. It slowed when its decaying flesh bubbled around the gleaming spines. Shrilling, the creature hooked its talons and scraped the darts out of its fetid entrails.

She couldn't prevent her scream.

It kept coming.

Like the creature in Rian, this monstrosity eclipsed Ambrose's symptoms. It wasn't near human. It wasn't even sick. But it was most certainly tainted. Whatever it was, whatever poison or wickedness that had brought this abomination into existence, it never stopped.

Aniell help me, for neither can I, Luscia prayed.

Luscia lifted the mechanism encasing her other wrist. Aiming higher, she fired at the creature's skeletal head. A dart skewered it in the eye, but unceasing in its strides, it yanked the organ from the socket with a nest of nerves before it sprung.

Water drowned her cry. Talons bore into her clavicles as she bucked, wedging her knees just enough to barricade her from the creature's fangs. Revoltingly, inky ooze slithered off its cavernous mandible, pooling in rotten welts. The creature drilled downward until her back hit the earth. Liquid glass overwhelmed her vision, and all she could see were a pair of bloated, bloodshot eyes, shining of scarlet.

And as if the waters had turned to canvas, Luscia found herself right back in that tent.

Holding her breath, she calmed her pounding heart, to think. Her thumbs unfanned the radials across her knuckles as a blurry light shimmered through the ripples. Brighter than any other, the harbinger thread plunged into the water with her.

Lumin floodlighted the roots of the cypresses.

"Push, Luscia…"

She tried, but the creature's weight was too great for her Tiergan bones. The glorious light swam beside her temple, sending an electric charge through the water as its harmonies assaulted her mind with haunting authority.

"Push through the seal, Luscia… PUSH IT NOW!"

Luscia ground her teeth and shoved with all her might.

Something tortuous ripped through her cranium, breaking her temples apart. Her eyes were shut, her remaining breath bellowed underwater. A kinetic current rushed through her limbs in excruciating euphoria. And like an inexplicable slingshot, Luscia's torso sprouted out of the mire.

She choked on the swampy silt, then stopped breathing altogether. The creature was no longer on top of her.

It was hoisted and bound in the air, entangled in a web of angry lumin.

The creature threshed against its dazzling confines where the harbinger thread strangled its rawhide throat. Dazed, Luscia got to her feet, her legs beckoned toward it. The tail of the harbinger thread fluttered irritably, highlighting a patch of disfigured flesh over the stripped muscle of the creature's neck. She leaned closer in disbelief. Stamped into the undead tissue was a symbol.

Two intertwining circles splintered by a vertical line.

She sensed its wrongness, freezing her soul like the frost of her shallow exhales. Without delay, Luscia planted her radials into either side of the creature's hairless head. The lumin retracted its binds, and in seconds, the thing withered to dust.

Cold darkness shadowed an ominous cavity within the *Other*, the same Ambrose's withering had left in the alley behind The Veiled Lady. And suddenly, Luscia understood the high matriarch's testimony; these creatures were devoid of everything…

On both sides of the veil.

A frantic snarl dashed her bewilderment. She reeled northward, searching the trees until she discovered Marek pressed against a cypress, holding the first creature at bay. One wraith missing, he was ramming his weapon against its navel while Aksel shredded its hindquarters with his serrated canines. The creature drilled itself into the najjani blade, expediting its own dismemberment. Luscia sprinted for them, seeing its fangs inch closer and closer to Marek's jugular.

The captaen dodged when the creature surged and sank its teeth into the bark. Emitting a lethal screech, it lunged for him again. She was still yards away.

"Niit!"

Luscia reached for him as she roared in fury. Her outstretched hands erupted like the sun, nearly blinding her as the harbinger thread sailed for the Gulgon spear, swathed it in light, and freed it from the earth. With a powerful wind, Luscia's body was hurled backward into the reeds, and the lumin tore the spear through the swaying mosses and straight into the creature's heart.

Dust showered the captaen. Afar, she heard Marek pant against the trunk in shock. But on her knees, as her Sight dispelled, returning her to the natural side of the veil, Luscia stared into her tremulous palms.

And began to cry.

No one heard the threads; never did they control them. Yet against ways of Tiergan, she'd just done both.

It was wrong.

And so was she.

Boot beats trampled the reeds, and her dampening cheeks were scooped into a set of warm hands.

"Ana'Sere, are you wounded?"

Marek examined her face, distress cracking his smooth tenor. The cuts across her lower back stung, but she said nothing of them. They would heal, unlike her defect. Her stain.

He reached for her fingertips, but she clutched them to her chest with her secret. Aksel's snout nudged her elbow, and his bushy tail wrapped around her folded form. Hidden behind her tawny mane, Luscia grazed the luxiron solrahs in her septum. Though no longer cold, she shivered against the sacred metal and its warmth, knowingly unworthy of it. Disgrace poured over her lashes.

"Was that... with the spear..." the captaen whispered. "Was that one of the Higher Gifts?"

Tears sprinkled Marek's forearm. Her head swung back and forth as she mouthed her confession, barely above a murmur.

"There's something broken inside me, Marek."

Propping her chin up with his knuckle, he swept back her matted snarls and met her unsteady gaze.

"Aniell's loom weaves infinite mystery." Under the moon, Marek's eyes glistened like ocean mist. "You, my Haidren, are one of his most precious tapestries. Whatever happened here, we will sort out the stitching. Together..." Unshaven, his stubble skimmed her cheekbone, and he pledged in a soothing timbre, "I'll never forsake you, Luscia."

She was exhausted. She was afraid. And unable to reply, she sank into his stable arms.

Strong and robust, they constricted around her like the branches of a Viridi giant. The flutter of his heartbeat, a Boreali chime in a strange land. Soaked from the marsh, his balmy skin still smelled of drösarra and pine through his armored tunic. A pang twinged within her breast. Marek radiated the highlands.

How desperately she longed to return.

He withdrew a fraction. Patient as the mist, his lips hovered next to hers, waiting.

Submitting, she twisted into them, their touch soft and discreet even though there was no one to watch. Marek's mouth yielded, ebbing with hers while she unfolded against him. The beads of her father's cuff dangled off his wrist, beside her earlobe. Even furious with her, after all her rejection, he still wore the courtship token openly. His calloused fingers tenderly combed through her hair, dampness dripping from his jilted kurtfierï and down her scar, before his grasp snaked behind her nape.

Luscia arched her neck in response, suspended inside his sturdy frame. She clenched the quilted linsilk covering his chest and pulled Marek lower, kissing him more deeply. Soothing waves flowed through her limbs as she sought the home she so dearly missed. But then he eased back, severing the sensation.

Walking his lips higher, Marek kissed the space between her brows. His smile dusted her skin. Somehow, Luscia felt herself smiling too.

Her headache was completely gone.

Hauling their tarnished weaponry back to the village, Luscia and Marek were received with cheers, but none so jubilant as those from their king, who'd demanded he settle at the community's edge, propped on his cane, until their reentry.

The fast-healing wounds on both Luscia and her captaen, along with their unwashed blades, bled a testament to their triumph. Although mysterious and masked in mud, the nomadic Gulgons proved honorable in their trade. Upon the return of her spear, the high matriarch wasted no time fulfilling her promise.

After relenting the horses and a few articles of gear, they were promptly provided the skiffsweepers Takoda had spoken of during negotiations.

Girded in braided vine, the reeds bowed like a boar's tusk at the prow of each skiffsweeper, better to pierce the waves and coast the roiling rapids with ease. For days they paddled upriver upon the gifted rafts, knelt between the lengthy bundled spars running either side. And just when Luscia could no longer feel her toes, the bordering flora widened, opening to the immense, sweeping inflow of the Yachel.

The river stretched for miles toward The Wastes, feeding life to one bank while withholding it from the other. Crammed between Dmitri and Hachiro, she paddled with Marek in line behind the Darakaians' skiffsweeper, hugging the shoreline where it bent north. Trees spired the vivid clouds as the terrain evolved into a barricade of emerald leaves. But beyond that towering horizon, outlined by a bejeweled splash of mulberry sky, were the jagged rooftops of a sleepy port town.

Before her, the tension in Dmitri's slender shoulders abated with a mollified sigh. "We're almost to each other again."

"Nox will keep the haidren safe, Your Majesty," Luscia reassured him.

Noxolo would indeed satisfy his duty to the Quadren; however, it was not Ira she had implied. Plum already fringed her king's worried eyes. He'd barely eaten since parting from his dearest friend, and being on the run from insurrectionists, scarcely more before that. Luscia prayed the others had beat them to Port Khmer.

She threw a cloak over Dmitri as Kumo's skiffsweeper steered them into the quiet harbor, then handed the same back to the shoto'shi. Like her najjani guard, she drew her cowled hood over her pale Northern features. While it was common for a Boreali merchant to occasionally dock Unitarian ports, it was supremely less common to see so many on one vessel.

They angled for a natural slipway on the outskirt of the half-occupied wharf. As the water shallowed, Luscia and Marek jumped from the skiffsweeper and onto dry land.

Disguised like the vagabonds who traipsed into towns like Khmer, the enormous beta made haste, weaving his way along the waterfront with the king. In prudent pairings, they spread out, following him down the cobbled rows of congested wattle-and-plaster structures. Finally, he slowed toward a rickety, lime-washed building overlooking the river. Above the door swung a dingy sign.

The Scaly Stowaway.

His hand pressed to Dmitri's back, Kumo ushered him under the capstone entryway. Luscia twisted toward Hachiro, who inspected a cockroach climbing a moldy barrel, and tugging his cloak strings, coerced his robe-covered legs after the beta. Hastily, she towed Hachiro inside. Under her breath, she instructed Marek and Declan to cover their backs.

The inn was deserted, aside from a pair of gray-haired sailors grumbling over their cards in the corner and the drunk salivating into his pint at the bar. Luscia scanned the interior: one visible exit on the main floor, three windows, and a stair—presumably to the lodgings.

Kumo leaned past a sticky, old spill, toward the thickset barkeep drying a still-dirty cup.

"We're here to see Wren," he stated in a muted baritone.

Meaning little songbird, the Boreali name struck Luscia just as it had months prior, in the backdoor office of a brothel.

The barkeep narrowed his eyes but, putting down the cup, retreated up the stairs. A bounty of minutes later, someone else appeared at the top. Unbelievably, Luscia's mouth parted. Her gaping stare swerved to Dmitri.

The king was completely ashen, for the woman could only be a ghost.

"The Fates are crowing—if they damned you to purgatory with me." A tart smirk splayed over her shapely lips when atop the landing, the woman knitted her cross-caste arms. "Now, where is my *Jaha?*"

Chapter Thirty Five

Zaethan

They made it. Yet with each cobblestone he strode, Zaethan's stomach knotted more sickeningly. It'd seemed a wise plan at the time, assembling in the rundown slum of Port Khmer, but now that the time had come, Zaethan found he was not ready to face what he had done.

That was, if Dmitri was even still there.

Though it was high noon, the docks were nearly vacant, except for a lone double-masted brig being unloaded by the barrel, and the few merchant stalls that lay beyond its cargo store, floating lazily on their mooring lines. Khmer wasn't a port of rigorous trade. If anything, it was a catchall for rogues and rapscallions who favored the freedom of the river over Rian's landlocked plain. The undulating expanse was stippled with fishing vessels. Some had even been converted to homes, anchored in wayfaring communities a mile off from the single wharf along the waterfront.

The back alleys Zaethan and the prydes traversed were even less occupied. Crooked, half-timbered walls corralled him toward his own incrimination. Sweat dribbled down Zaethan's back, and not because of the reinfected wound scorching his inflamed shoulder blade.

He'd sandwiched the yancy haidren between himself and the shadowman Noxolo Egon as they peered past the corner, spying the battered inn. Over an empty street, the sign for The Scaly Stowaway swung from one socket, the other rusted through. It wasn't the only inn in town… simply the worst.

"I've been here before!" Ira squawked, cowering under Noxolo's terse scowl, and dropped his voice covertly. "Remarkably springy mattress…"

At the yancy's waggling brow, Zaethan smacked him upside the head, disgusted when he gave his stones a relieved scratch.

The mattresses were probably just as diseased.

Catching Noxolo's regard, he angled toward the busted awning, then lurched Ira along. Zaethan planted himself against the entrance, lacquered in chipped red paint, and signaled for them to wait for his go-ahead. He eased the door ajar with his fingertips. Sheathed at his dominant hip, he gripped the kuerre.

The cheap inn was dark and dank, the windows all but shuttered to the riverbank, just as he'd instructed each remain when he'd bought it. While Zaethan had once dreamed of owning property of his own, a foul tinderbox in Khmer was far from an entrepreneurial prize. Though, it wasn't as if he'd had much time to secure anything better, nor was he the party who'd handled the purchase. And were the inn's conditions more inviting, it probably would have cost him exposure... not just his coin.

The dining hall was deserted. Chained to the pitted timber beams, cobwebs swathed the old candelabras where they alighted a room of mismatched chairs. The beefy barkeep glanced up disinterestedly at Zaethan in the doorway. But seeing the hold on his hilt, the man reached around his belt where a knife surely hid. Zaethan instantly tossed his hands up. The barkeep did not show his.

Glad to see he earns his keep, Zaethan thought. He'd spent enough dromas on good faith alone.

They were strangers to each other, having never actually met the mercenary he'd employed through Kumo. Using his leg, Zaethan shoved the door wider and waved the others inside. The barkeep brandished his knife while the warriors piled in, wading among the dusty tables. Kai, stumbling on his bloody splint, hung off Sadik and Yhona like a grain sack. The alpha needed to see her soon. Too much longer and he wouldn't make it.

Ira nestled alongside him. Zaethan elbowed him off and splayed his fingers over the bar.

"Owàamo." He eyed the edgy barkeep intensely as he said, "We share a songbird. Are the others in her cage?"

At the code, his mercenary gingerly stuffed the knife back into his belting and gave a brief nod. Zaethan's nerves shuddered his exhale.

"In that case, two shots of bwoloa."

Without comment, the phony barkeep poured the Southern liquor and slammed the smeared glasses onto the wood in front of him.

"Is this really an appropriate time for libation, Zaeth?" Ira questioned, turning against the bar and rubbing his throat apprehensively. "I mean, that's coming from me…"

Zaethan chucked the shot back, grunting at the throaty burn, and shoved the other at Ira. "You're going to need it." Then, bracing himself, he ordered the barkeep, "Take us to Wren."

The floorboards squeaked atop the third floor. Through the gap beneath a thick, unmarked door came muffled steps. Pacing steps.

Heart thumping, Zaethan sealed his eyes while the barkeep gave it a staggered knock. The pacing stopped, and someone strode to the door. On the other side, things would never be the same. His lids dragged apart when it screeched on its hinges.

A bundle flew into him with a thud.

"You're alive, Alpha Zà!" She nestled her tiny knots under his chin where Dhalili had jumped into his arms. "Jabari bet me two crupas you were dead, uni. Squashed like a mudpie, yeah!"

Her tiny arms crushed his middle. Zaethan found the leggy warrior crowding Zahra.

"Eh, you bet against me?" he indignantly asked.

Jabari shrugged guiltily and tossed Dhalili his copper coin. "Hillman tasty bait for Mirajii snap-trap."

His scout swung and caught it, flinging him around toward the others as the rest of his pryde shuffled into the tight, windowless apartment. Ira bolted straight for a tray table situated among the multi-hued throng, Darakaian and Boreali.

"Crumpets!" After wolfing the pastry, he stuck out his parched tongue, blowing bits into the shadowman's carroty beard. "Oh, that is *not* a crumpet."

"Shores of Aurynth!"

A husky voice rang out when Kai was hauled over the threshold. The haidren to Boreal sprouted through the wall of bodies, brushing into Zaethan in passing. Her spectral eyes flitted up to his as her steps seemed to slow, if just momentarily. Instead of a greeting, he felt her cool fingers discreetly wrap around his forearm. Squeezing it snugly, she let go, and rushed toward the injured alpha.

"Get this man into my quarters, now!"

He rotated, unsure what the touch meant, and watched her ghostly figure disappear into the shadowy hall as another hand clamped over his shoulder.

"It's not good, Ahoté," Kumo hastily warned in his ear before swinging him around, into the apartment.

Zaethan's crime loitered before him.

Unadorned cotton sleeves draped her russet shoulders as if she wore the richest velvet aurus could buy, coupled with a crude corset cinching her middle-aged curves. Under his examination, she tossed back her shiny voluminous curls, cropped below her chin, and chuckled darkly.

Donning her own invisible luxury, Salma Nabhu had not changed—even after he'd fashioned her into an outlaw.

The last time they'd spoken, Zaethan was tying her to a stake on the shore of The Wastes, binding Salma while he'd told her to scream like her life depended on it—because it had. Told her to give the illusion she was being left to die for the witnessing crew of the *Esafit Ramali*. Then he had sailed away, abandoning his prisoner to howl until nightfall, when he'd planned for Kumo to return and take her to safety across the Yachel.

The call had wrecked him… sequestered him into the comfort of Chenoa's bed for weeks on end. Anything to dull the conflict he hid in himself every day. But there was no escape from his deception.

There weren't even windows in this room.

"Owàamo, Jaha," Salma purred in Andwele. Her hips bowed as she leaned in, kissing him tenderly on either cheek. "If it brings a little *papyon*, I'm happy the past returned."

Salma smirked invitingly, and his throat tightened. Beyond her copious curls glowered Dmitri, parked erectly on a mangy, teal settee between two shadowmen.

He'd ordered her execution. Now he sat under her roof.

Red-knuckled, Dmitri's hands formed an angry fist atop the handle of his byrnnzite cane. Shaded under his chaotic waves, his haggard eyes were stripped of warmth.

To save a convicted cross-caste, to save both Salma and her executioner from that undeserved fate, Zaethan had defied his king. Outrightly and undisclosed. And in doing so, he might have lost his friendship forever.

Locked on Zaethan, Dmitri shakily rose and demanded through his teeth, "Everyone out."

He didn't project his voice, but the kingly command was as sharp as a scalpel.

Zaethan held his breath as the others, his pryde warriors and the shadowmen alike, quickly averted their eyeline and hustled out the entrance. Even Hachiro kept his posture lowered over his journal while the room cleared, tripping over his robes behind Ira into the hall. With a tremble, the door slammed closed, leaving him alone with his king.

He swallowed the mass in his throat. "Dmitri, I never—"

"No! You don't get to speak yet!"

He stepped back, astounded when Dmitri yelled across the space and wielded his cane. It wavered over the floorboards.

"I have spent my last waking hours sick over *your* welfare! Relying on the hope that you were okay, just to make it here, to this vault of deceit. Out of everyone I trusted, Zaeth!"

Zaethan winced at his friend's raw rancor and the wetness flooding his bloodshot eyes.

"Out of everyone, it was *you* who acted against me! Who undermined my opening judgement as king! You knew I would never question your obedience—that I would never doubt your loyalty—and using that, enacted your own version of justice over mine!"

"She was innocent, Dmitri. You realize that now." Zaethan pleaded, coming closer, but stopped when Dmitri lifted his cane higher.

The forced distance was more painful than the pang in his gait.

"I realize you orchestrated all this behind my back!" Dmitri shouted louder than ever, as moisture ran from his flushed nose. "You didn't even respect me enough to challenge the order to my face!"

"Shtàka, would you have even listened?" he asked passionately. "Just hours into your grief, could you really have been impartial to her?"

"I am a king!" His friend beat his breast. "I don't get to cower behind my grief, nor do *you* get to operate around it!"

"I asked you to grant a trial! There was no one to defend her—no House, nothing. Without fair prosecution, there would never be justice for your father *or* a cross-caste!"

"The cross-caste plight is not your concern!"

"Not my—Dmitri, I *am* cross-caste!" Zaethan flashed his mixed veins heatedly, hating the new truth almost as much as he hated the man who'd professed it. "You heard it as well as I did... She and I are the same, and so is our place in this realm."

Irate, his friend chucked his extravagant cane at the plaster wall. "You are nothing like that woman, Zaeth! And you never will be!"

Zaethan's palms scaled his temples, and he gripped the ropey locs over his scalp.

"I was never working against you," he promised defeatedly. "I was working *for* you, to protect—"

"You abused my love for you!" Dmitri bellowed, tears spilling his cheeks as he threw up his wrist, and the threadbare scarlet cord around it. "My *chosen* brother... You were supposed to be different than everyone else!"

The wind was knocked from Zaethan with disbelief, where the accusation harpooned him deep in the trenches of his soul. His eyes burned. Through blurred vision, he moved toward his friend, his king, but Dmitri held up his hand, weeping alone into his plain, knitted sateen vest.

Zaethan seized a ruby pillow from the chair and ripped off a tassel.

Holding out threads, he swore, "I *am* your brother. And because of that, I couldn't let you execute an innocent woman. Its why I couldn't turn you into a murderer!" Zaethan's tenor cracked ardently. "Is that the kind of king you wanted to be, Dmitri? A murderer?"

Dmitri's head flew upright. His brows contorted with a misery too lonely for Zaethan to even fathom. Without warning, he released an anguished cry and stormed at him.

Though slender and off-balance, he hit Zaethan with force, propelling him back a step. His friend's arms constricted around him. Tears bathed his bruised shoulder while Dmitri pounded his fist against Zaethan's back.

He sobbed as his frame weakly gave way.

"Thank you, brother."

Supporting him, Zaethan reached under his embrace and swiped his own soaked lashes. "I am so… sorry… that I misled you… It was tearing me apart."

Dmitri stilled at the apologetic phrase he'd not once heard Zaethan say aloud. The young king's spine straightened with his legs, yet he still clung to Zaethan in the center of the apartment. "I don't know how to do any of this without him," he whispered of his father in a shivering sigh.

"Ano. Me neither." Zaethan laughed dejectedly and held his friend tight. "But I do know Kumo will make a decent haidren for you. He does as he's told, unlike me."

Instantly, Dmitri separated from him. "Whatever do you mean?"

"Well, I'm ineligible." Zaethan sniffed gruffly, reaching up to rebind his locs. "Without another Kasim heir, the seat should lawfully be inherited by my oldest cousin, on my mother's side."

Defiantly, Dmitri's head shook.

"Darakai had lost its way." Gripping him by the nape, his friend's eyes, rimmed in lilac, bored into Zaethan. "You are the best thing to ever come out of that House, Zaeth. Hear me when I say, your blood is exactly where it's meant to be." He regally elevated his crisp, moist cheeks, unashamed by their stain. "And that's right here on the Quadren. With me."

Zaethan stood slack when Dmitri patted him over his heart. Hesitantly, he retreated toward his discarded cane, beneath the fresh dent in the plaster. Crooking down, he recovered it off the dirty floor.

He studied it for a long second, then dried his face with a shirtsleeve and nodded to himself. As if nothing had occurred, as if the betrayal had been nothing but a dream, Dmitri passed Zaethan toward the door. He thrust it open, entered the hall, and summoned everyone inside.

Though Zaethan had never asked for one, Dmitri had just given him a second chance.

Between his fingers, Zaethan stroked the ruby thread with care, as if it were the most precious artifact in the world. Swiftly, he knotted the replacement around his wrist. He'd lost it before.

He would never lose it again.

With his boot hitched against the squat serving table, Zaethan toyed with Darakai's panel on the Quadrecipher, shifting the panther illustration side to side in thought. He was reclined on the floor, his back pressed into one of the dusty sofas in Salma's apartment. His closest warriors piled atop it behind him.

They'd all taken to the floor, the entire Quadren. Across the archaic puzzle board, Boreal's haidren sat cross-legged, just like the adjacent shoto'shi. In her lap, the wolx's massive ears poked over the tabletop, revolving when someone else made a decent point regarding Port Tadeas as an evasive route back to Bastiion.

Despite the subdued conversation, she stared at Zaethan beyond their conflicting crests. Cool and impassive.

It used to unnerve him when she did that, how her irregular eyes would shutter gradually, measuredly, making him squirm in his seat. Now he found it distracting. He'd only caught half the sentences Kumo had said.

Her hair was gathered slackly, the netting of waves tumbling over her shoulder like a bushel of spelt. The palest, snowy tendrils dusted her clavicle, creeping beyond the embroidered detail of the tunic she'd donned. The lacing was loose at the front, her milky skin peeping through. Oversized, it likely belonged to one of the shadowmen, who cast an imposing shade from where most of them stood behind a pair of wingback chairs. Salma lounged in one, and the Boreali captaen perched forward in the other.

Sedately, the witch maintained her stare, and a tendon twitched in Zaethan's jaw. Abruptly he glanced aside, at literally anything else.

Cracking apart the pages of his stiff journal, Hachiro slid something fuchsia and fuzzy under the table to Ira, who'd comfortably sprawled out over the mountain of pillows between them. The shoto'shi bent toward him discreetly, while Zahra made mention of a trader's guild who might be able to provide a vessel.

"Elderwool. I clipped it for you in the wetlands," Hachiro murmured, indicating the bizarre, furry vine Ira began to play with. "The Gulgons reserve it for the most stubborn contaminants. Steeps a very tangy tea. This should help with your... well, your transmittables."

Blinking multiple times, Hachiro scholarly outlined the diseased bulge below the yancy's belt with his quill. Ira sniffed the clipping. Choking on the scent, he clapped Sayuri's jumpy sibling on the back.

"See, that's friendship, Zaeth," he whispered hoarsely, aiming the vine at him before shoving it into his pants. "You've never once considered my *transmittables*."

Steering his focus back toward Dmitri, Zaethan spotted the Northern haidren repressing a coy bend on her pale lips. Normally so reserved, the shaping was very unlike them. The pleasing curve grew under Zaethan's study.

Alluring. Full.

Unable to curb it, his began to smirk as well.

"Lord Darakai...? Zaeth, your thoughts?"

To his right, Dmitri waited for an answer. Zaethan cricked his neck, agitated he was not more clearheaded.

Port Tadeas. Trader Guild. Bastiion.

"We shouldn't return you to Bastiion. Not yet," he stated.

Dmitri leaned back, elbow on his propped knee. "I must return. I need to leverage the throne, the Peerage, everything I can to remove Nyack Kasim from power and force the House of Darakai back in line with the Ethnicam Accords."

"In the woods…" Zaethan tapped the thin slats of the Quadre-cipher. "Bessus mentioned a name before he died. The Obscurer. A symbol, this kakk with two unending circles cut through the center, was branded on his body. And I'm pretty certain it branded my fath—the chief warlord too."

"I've seen that symbol," the Boreali haidren stated, boosting herself taller. She swung toward her Captaen Bailefore and clutched his knee. She held onto it, and he did not mind. "Wem. On the creature that I…" Her words trailed. "There were two in Hagarh like Ambrose. The Gulgons call them the devoid. Infected or otherwise, that's precisely what these things are. They're devoid of all humanity."

"Hold on." Dmitri cradled his brow. "You're saying there is some heinous cabal, led by this person—this Obscurer—purposely producing and releasing these lethal creatures throughout Orynthia?"

"Uni. I think that's exactly what I'm saying." Zaethan chewed the inside of his cheek thoughtfully. "And since the Obscurer doesn't infect every follower, there's no telling who else is involved in his scheme. Or if it's linked to Darakai's conspiracy against our ally. Your father's assassination. Everything.

"The House of War is already opposed to you. How much of the broader army in Bastiion is aligned with this secret sect? How many councilmen? Palace attendants? Shtàka, even the sentinels posted outside your door. Thoarne's Watchmen could be his agents. It'd be Faraji all over again…"

Aghast, Dmitri's slim fingers fenced his mouth. "By the Fates, where are we to go?"

Zaethan slunk into the sofa as reality sank in. The cushioning rocked his spine when his warriors adjusted on it nervously, and a deafening quiet blanketed the assembly of runaways.

They couldn't trust anyone.

"W-well..." Ira sputtered, scrambling upright toward Hachiro. "Can we continue the tour west? I like beaches. A bit sticky, but in the right context—"

"My uncle clearly supported the chief warlord's coup to overthrow His Majesty," the shoto'shi told him, his nerves showcased by his erratic tics. "As chancellor of the Shoto Collective, there is not a grain of sand his eye will not uncover." Hachiro's sun-kissed nose crinkled ruefully, and he shook his disheveled head at Dmitri. "You cannot hide in Pilar, My King."

"Razôuel then?" Dmitri asked, raking his carob hair. "Send word to Rasha and Bahira'zol'Jaell. The Zôueli are obligated to grant me sovereign asylum in the marriage contract..."

"Somehow get to the Khan River and sail by Àla'maia's light to Jol'Nune," Zaethan's third said in agreement. Kumo grunted his consensus.

"Niit." The highlander captaen objected before Zaethan could. Hinging on the chair, Bailefore's bootleg nestled against his haidren where she ruminated. Brows knit, she didn't push him off. "Allied with Mworra and aided by Pilar, the House of Darakai could easily invade Razôuel. I fear it'd be stronger justification to conquer them."

Zaethan's sight fell on her, latching onto those unworldly irises. The left flashed like her witchiron when he said it decisively. "There's only one place Darakai would never venture—The House of Boreal."

Biting her lip, she turned toward Dmitri. To him alone, she bizarrely added, "Boreal is brisk in autumn, Your Majesty, but unforgivingly cold in winter."

Her concern for something so trivial surprised Zaethan, given her uptightness about most endeavors. However, Dmitri held her gaze, in another conversation of their own.

Swallowing harshly, their king responded to her. "Then I better bring a coat. Now, how do we get there?"

"My nephew can take you," Salma casually interjected to the quiet. "His ship is due in port any day now. He'll get you to the ghost coast."

They all swiveled toward her, where she inspected her nails in an armchair.

"You would do that?" Dmitri asked suspiciously.

Zaethan didn't blame him.

"Consider us even, Your Majesty..." Her smile was full of scorn. "For my reluctant pardon."

Dmitri's mouth flattened tensely. Steering the discussion, Zaethan crooked his head backward and knocked his scout's little knee, nestled against his nape. "Dhalili, we'll need you infiltrate the palace and get Queen Lourissa to a safehouse."

"The Hastings estate in Arune, I should think," his king said.

Zaethan muttered to Dmitri, "Gregor Hastings is still minister of the Peerage. He could be part of—"

"Do you really think so low of my family?" Ira perched onto his knees, affronted. His forehead crumpled. "My father was loyal to King Korbin and remains so to this day. He may be a drunk, but he would give his drunken life for this kingdom." Crossing his arms, encased in linen brocade, the yancy haidren skewered Zaethan vehemently with his gaze. "And I think I know my own father more than you know yours—whoever you believe he is."

"Lord Bastiion, not another word!"

Dmitri's fierce reprove cut off as Zaethan bitterly pushed onto his feet, and he walked to an empty part of the room where there wasn't anything to throw. Still on the floor, Ira's sophisticated features shuddered hotly, flaring his rich Unitarian cheeks.

"Fine." Zaethan crisply addressed his scout on the sofa. "Dhalili, you're to depart immediately. Smuggle the queen to the minister's estate in Arune. Then, hightail it north. She'll need a letter, Dmitri. Maybe your ring too."

"My maid, Tallulah. Bolaeva, please take her as well!" the Boreali haidren exclaimed, rising.

"And my sister," the shoto'shi said faintly into his pages. "If... if Sayuri will come."

Dhalili nodded at them, then at Zaethan and hit her childlike fist against her chest. "Uni zà. I'll get them out. Take queenie to yancy country."

The apartment turned somber, so many driven from their homes, trapped within those bleak, ramshackle walls. With his cane, Dmitri hoisted himself up and took a deep sobering breath.

"We should all get our rest while we can," he ordered the room. Moving toward the tiny desk in the corner, Dmitri tugged off his father's ring. "Lady Boreal," he said to a piece of parchment, dipping a quill in the ink, "see to that shoulder of Zaeth's."

One by one, they filtered into the snug hallway, dispersing into the various nooks along either side.

She fell in step beside him, their nearness both familiar and foreign. Her hand accidentally brushed his as she led him to tending in her quarters. Against his best effort, Zaethan's regard skirted lower, drawn to her unforgettable, ivory face.

Orynthia's hope was in the highlands now.

Chapter Thirty Six
Zaethan

The room was cramped. She'd moved the washbasin to the trunk, stowed between the dressing table and the splintered doorframe. Her fragrant case of shimmering jars occupied its dust-ringed place. Threadbare, the drapes were drawn over the porthole window above her narrow bed, blocking the light within, for there was none outside.

Zaethan fidgeted impatiently, tottering the rickety bench over the floorboards as the Boreali haidren ground a handful of herbs beneath her pestle. Her hips swayed with the rigor of her arms. The navy sleeves of her baggy tunic were rolled tightly toward the strength of her biceps, much like the embossed belt snatched about her waist. An arm's reach from his shirtless perch against the wall, the contour of her strong, shapely physique was not lost under the borrowed clothes.

It made Zaethan despise the fresh set folded beside him, wondering if the leather breeches and quilted olive jacket had come from the saddle bag of her attentive Captaen Bailefore—made him despise how the same question applied to the clothing she wore now.

But the captaen was not here.

The door had been shut to the hall, as leaving it open crowded her workspace more. They'd been sealed inside—alone.

Idle and eager to leave, Zaethan wrung his hands where they grew clammy.

Mutely, she shifted from the table. The mortar in one hand and a damp cloth slung over the other, she scooted her Boreali apparel aside and settled on the bench there instead. Zaethan coiled his locs into a high knot and pivoted where he sat, presenting his back before she could tell him to turn. Anything to make the suffocating minutes go by faster.

It wasn't like sparring in the openness of a canyon bluff or over the musty mats of a training room. There was no training equipment here—no barking of orders or bouts of rivalry. The bedroom was too quiet. Too close. Too private for the man who'd taught her how to move on a battlefield.

They were far from a battlefield now... and yet he was just as frightened.

He loathed the way his breath shortened when the cloth, cool and damp, stroked his rounded shoulder blade. Gooseflesh raced down his forearms, a hideous sight, where they braced atop his knees. Methodically, she cleaned debris out of the deep gash, and he relished how it stung… clung to the normality of it. Zaethan could comprehend pain, could control his response to the biting twinge when she plucked a shard of shrubbery from the infected tissue and tossed it onto the floor.

It was everything else that didn't make sense.

"It will hurt less if you stabilize your breathing," she said patronizingly and smeared poultice into his raw wound.

Zaethan wanted to rip those hands from his back. But at the thought of seizing her, he huffily readjusted his seat on the bench, suddenly feeling pinched.

Angry at his own body, he gripped the edge of the wood and changed the subject.

"How many days?" Zaethan tersely asked.

The spread of the soothing goop slowed, then mechanically resumed. "Four."

"Depths, Maji'maia," he bit out. "I told you to stay here no more than forty-eight hours."

Her touch withdrew, and the cloth brushed his spine as she cleaned her hand. "Well, you are not king. As you suspected, he refused to leave."

She pushed off the bench and stood before him. Zaethan promptly joined her. The door was but three steps away.

"Sit. We're not done." Her thick brow quirked, and she indicated the mess of cuts underneath his shredded gunja pants. "Don't treat it today—we'll be right back here tomorrow."

Zaethan sucked his teeth, blowing off her concern, and proceeded to slide around the other haidren. But catching him off balance, she pushed him down, knocking him against the plaster with a thud.

"I said to sit," she repeated, flat and stern, then lithely lowered to her knees, thumping the mortar on the floorboards next to his boot.

Zaethan lurched back when she thrust his legs apart commandingly. Wedging between them, she tore the filthy fabric, exposing his bare thigh, and inspected the abrasions more closely.

He became a statue, unmoving beneath her care. Just another powerless article in the room.

"I would have waited even longer," she murmured to his leg. "Had it come to that."

"For your shadowman," Zaethan clarified. Tense.

Steadily, her wet rag dragged across his shallow wounds. He didn't feel them.

"For you."

Her whisper was matter-of-fact. Of course she wouldn't have fought Dmitri, had he held out an entire week for Zaethan's return.

He didn't know what he sought in her tone, only that it was a pity he searched it at all.

A tremor skittered across his muscle as her fingers scanned his heating skin. She leaned over his thigh. A platinum tendril, lighter than the rest, dangled into her closed-off study. Zaethan watched her blow it aside, tracking the wisp's rebellion when it swung right back toward the cliff of her cheek. Testily, she did it again, and he was transfixed.

His throat constricted cruelly as she bent her crisp profile to retrieve more poultice from the mortar and coated it onto his thigh.

Zaethan hissed and tore his gaze away.

"Meh fyreon," she muttered. The pressure lessened. "I'll be gentler."

With his fists clamped to the wood, he stared at a mildew stain in the ceiling and ground his crown against the plaster. "It's an agony to look at you sometimes," Zaethan confessed to the timber framing.

The pressure of her palm left, and he heard the mortar clumsily scrape the floor.

With a curt sigh came her stoic reply. "I regret my image is such a burden to you."

Titling his head downward, he squeezed his skull between his fingertips. It was no longer his—but occupied by another.

"Each time I do, my eyes betray me..." Zaethan said, continuing as if she'd never even spoken. "When I start to look, I can't stop. But is that what you want, Luscia?"

His hand dropped with her name—that bewitching, evocative name. He'd only used it once, on the bluff. Frigid and poised, she stilled within the cage of his legs. Uncertain, Zaethan inched off the wall.

Pulling the stray tendril out of her eyes, he held it off her face and asked raggedly, "Do you want me to stop looking at you?"

Candlelight flickered, bathing the savage beauty at his feet. She was forbidden. An incantation from the north.

And for once, he didn't care.

Her tawny-brown lashes, naked of kohl, fanned her cheeks. In silence, her pearly jaw leapt though no sound rolled off her tongue. Then abruptly, her eyes snapped toward his and he was seized, lost in their unnatural incandescence. His hand hovered beside them, and Zaethan stopped breathing altogether.

She swallowed. Unblinking.

"My eyes betray me too."

The air left him. Brazenly, Zaethan seized her by the nape and drilled his lips against hers.

In a reckless chase, his fingertips charted the panes of her face, the tingle deluding his senses. Her mouth opened to him freely. But it was no trick, or rivalry of sport. No ploy to win a match that never mattered.

This was slick. This was irresistible.

Fire licked his thighs when her nails dug in. Her upper body drove off her knees and into his hold. He reached around her, the woman he'd confined in his arms more times than he could count. Detaining the base of her head, he locked her there, confirming she was real and not a highland mist—not a dream like so many troubled nights before.

Trapped in his hold, she bit his bottom lip. Zaethan growled into the kiss, consuming her mouth, and slid his arms lower, seizing the curves of her.

In one sweep, he hauled her off the floor.

The bench battered the wall when he brought them back down. Solid and powerful, her legs entrapped his hips. He panted beneath the pressure of her palms while she grappled the brawn of his chest, exploring it… defining its expanse before they deftly skated along his shoulders, and entwining her arms, she cradled his head in her forceful hands, shooting a chill along his spine. A dam broke behind her kiss, her lips chasing his as if being unshackled. Zaethan met her in kind, thrusting his support under the daunting rhythm of her hips. And in waves turbulent and untamed, her body wrestled closer than ever.

Hammering, his heart sprinted even as it sank.

Cupping her backside, his grip constricted over the leather. Full. Firm. His other hand snaked toward the lacing in her hair. Zaethan skimmed it off her throat, exposing what she so often hid, and skillfully wound her wild tresses about his forearm. Bound to her, he tugged her backward and broke from her lips. In a ravenous path, his tongue cascaded her hot skin where the tunic slipped.

An unknown creature escaped her frame. Swelling, then sinking, her chest unrolled against his thundering pulse. Zaethan breathed her in, delirious and heady. He'd never wanted anyone more than he wanted this mystery, who moaned under the scrape of his teeth.

Luscia gasped when he panted her name into the hollow above her collarbone. Zaethan dragged his nose back up the bend of her neck, grating the uneven flesh as he said it again and again, like a plea.

"Heh'ta." She exhaled heavily toward the ceiling, her breast brushing his chin.

At her voice, his mouth skidded over hers and drowned her murmur as he kissed her more deeply. More languidly.

Suddenly, his chin was captured, and Zaethan was shoved into the wall.

"Stop it!"

In a gust, she scooted off the bench and clambered into the dressing table across the snug space. Unexpectedly, she sheltered her chest, covering herself with her overlong sleeves. And ducking behind the Boreali weave, Luscia wiped her mouth clean.

The action slashed him more than any blade could.

Flushed, her fingers shielded her swollen lips as she huskily rasped. "We can't do this, Zaeth."

He gaped at her.

Under his disoriented stare, she cinched the tunic embroidery modestly over her scar, grabbed the borrowed clothing off the bench, and presented it to him awkwardly. "I think you should leave."

Rising, Zaethan tore the apparel from her grasp. Stealing the door-handle, he nodded bitterly and swung around to her.

"You mean you can't do this with *me*," he scathingly accused.

"Niit." Luscia barely met his eye when her head shook ashamedly. "That I cannot."

He yanked the door open, making her flinch when it crashed into the plaster. Outside, her freckled henchman loitered in the hall. Wide-eyed, the shadowman stared down his beaded beard and at his boots when Zaethan stormed through the threshold.

Meeting the staircase, Zaethan punched the wall, incensed at his own stupidity. His weakness. His desire.

Raw and torn, Zaethan's knuckles split open—like himself—overwhelmed by the torment of his entire collapsing world.

His life was a wreckage. And so was he.

A roach scrabbled across the sticky bar top. Zaethan's chin bit into the cushion of his forearm as he watched the bug enviously, thinking it unfair that even vermin knew their purpose while he'd been dispossessed of his. His identity was a myth, a story of woe that Darakaians would tell their purebred cubs for generations.

The tale of the cross-caste pretender, who hadn't known he was pretending.

Dmitri was a fool to imagine otherwise. The haidrenship belonged to Kumo now. Until their imperiled king accepted that, the House of Darakai would only see an imposter in his cousin's place on the Quadren.

The matter was far from settled, considering they'd debated well into the night. He'd no clue of the hour. Both men had long retired to their beds, rendering Zaethan the final patron left in The Scaly Stowaway's dingy dining hall. And a poor patron at that. With a sobering puff, Zaethan blew the roach away from his untouched bwoloa, poured roughly two hours earlier. Behind the golden liquor, the critter disappeared, continuing its trek toward moldier pastures.

"Little good it does in the glass, Jaha."

Sluggishly, Zaethan's scowl slid to the stowaway herself when she popped up from behind the bar. Salma boosted a crate of jugs and dropped it pointedly on the counter. A filthy dishtowel was tucked into her apron. He found it odd, seeing her in anything other than Bastiion's finest. She ruffled her Southern curls off the newly noticeable creases on her forehead and, hitching a hand on her hip, leaned against the crate expectantly.

"I buy. You pour, yeah?" Zaethan grumbled grimly. "What I do afterward is my business."

Snapping the towel from her waist, Salma snorted. "You sound just like her," she said, wiping down the jugs. "Cyra spouted much the same when we first met."

"Wait." Zaethan straightened off his arm. "You knew her?"

"*Jaha...*" Salma's brow arched sardonically. "You are not the only lovely in Bastiion. Out of so many to choose, why else would Madam Salma keep inviting such a cheap customer back to The Veiled Lady, if not to keep watch of him, eh?"

Zaethan sat up on the stool, baffled. In comparison to most men, sentry, yancy, or otherwise, he'd spent very little at the night den over the years. Cumulatively, hardly an entire dromas on all his drink and never on anything else. Well, not until Chenoa.

He *was* a cheap customer.

Scratching his bristle beneath the collar of the Boreali jacket, he answered bluntly, "I guess I was operating under the impression you thought I was the prettiest of them all."

"Cocky." Rolling her hooded eyes, Salma wiggled the towel at Zaethan. "You get that from her too. She didn't show it much, ano... but it was there. Oh, it was always there."

One of his boots touched down on the foot rail, lured into the way her smile tilted crookedly at some memory of the mother he'd never meet. He'd spent his whole life repressing the questions he was forbidden from raising, having been told countless times how it was his breath that took her last.

Muzzle a child long enough, eventually he'll stop asking questions. But blame a child, he'll forget they ever had the right to.

Yet another effective tactic of Nyack Kasim.

Hardening, Zaethan crossed his arms. "Why would you hide that from me all this time?"

"Because of the promise I made to your mhàdda, twenty-two years ago." Salma twisted the fabric in her grasp as sadness dragged across her blended features. "But after that kakka-shtàka ordeal in Faraji, I've come to learn the need for secrecy no longer applies."

"I went against my orders to save your hide, Salma." Gratingly, he eyed her across the bar. "You owe me the truth."

"Uni zà," she agreed and plucked a bottle, along with another glass, off the shelf. Spying the top of the empty stair, Salma came round and climbed onto the worn stool opposite Zaethan. "However, this is a truth you deserved to hear long before that, Jaha."

Sinuously, she glided one leg over the other as she measured out a fresh shot of bwoloa. Taking his neglected glass, she swapped them, pushing the more aromatic serving into his hold. Something pinched the older woman's brow when she swiveled toward him. Wavering, she kicked back the older pour, set it down, and braced her elbow on the bar.

"I met Cyra shortly after I purchased The Veiled Lady from its prior overseer, a whoremonger with foul breath. Acquiring enough coin and enough blackmail..." Salma simpered to the side. "I bought my freedom as well as his livelihood. In the early years, I stayed at the front of the house, yeah? Keeping watch of over drunks and thieves when every crupas counted most. And it was on one such night"—her hazel gaze floated upward—"that your stubborn, demanding mhàdda walked into my life."

Reminiscing, Salma stroked her bottom lip as she continued. "I didn't even know who she was when she plunked down, ordered something strong, and stared into it just like you do. One of my haidrens, if I could name a House, right there, wasting my best stock. She let loose the title at some point, ordering me about like her huwàa." Pausing, Salma's head quirked. "Or perhaps I was ordering her... meme ano'qondai, there's no telling."

She shrugged, quietly amused, though her expression lines smoothed out somberly. "She never explained why she was there—in the lowly dump it used to be. But the next time, ano, she didn't have to."

On the bar top, Salma scooted the bwoloa closer to Zaethan's fingers and pointedly tapped the glass. He took a sip, not liking the bereaved depression in her sultry pose.

"A few months later, Cyra visited wearing a bruise. And a month after that... she returned with a necklace of them."

Zaethan's hand constricted around the glass as Salma's touch lowered to her throat. He blinked at it, imaging a garden of black and blue. His nose flared. Resentment simmered beneath its buckling. He thought his mother was the exception to her husband's violence, not a beneficiary of it—like Zaethan.

He thought she'd been loved.

"It went on like that for a year. Maybe more. My brothel became the perfect refuge for Cyra. No one would ever expect a woman of her stature to be in the friendship of a madam," Salma said, pouring herself another shot. "I started hiding her upstairs, yeah? In the office, overnight. A haidren couldn't be recognized like that, ano zà. The rumors, yeye qondai? Because Nyack"—her teeth appeared with his name—"was gaining popularity. Fast. Everything worsened when the tribes exalted him to chief warlord. Within Darakai, Cyra was not the senior member of the union. Not anymore. And her husband, well... he wielded that.

"Nyack left Bastiion armed with his new supremacy, but as haidren, your mhàdda chose to stay with the Quadren—safer in courtier walls than her own in Faraji. It was another solstice and equinox before I saw her again. And I can never unsee the fear she carried when I finally did." She looked away and tipped back the glass, swallowing hard.

"That was the very first time I met you, Jaha." Salma's inhale shuddered as she tenderly tapped her stomach, securing her hand there like a shield. "You were about to be in the world, and she was so scared of what Nyack would do... if he discovered that you were not his. Your mhàdda was confident he did not yet suspect, but it seems that somehow, somewhen, he ultimately discerned the truth."

Salma's regard strained sympathetically. Twisting toward the bar, Zaethan swabbed his face as the information leveled his already-weighted shoulders.

"Do you know who he is?" Zaethan locked his eyes shut. "My real father?"

"Ano zà," Salma confessed, dashing any fragile hope for a conclusion to his nightmare. "All Cyra revealed that final night was that he was a Unitarian in Bastiion, but as to his station or province, she refused to say."

A cavern burrowed in Zaethan's middle, like the pang one gets after not eating for days. Though he could not dam them, Zaethan hated the frail words that leaked from his childish heart.

"Does he know I exist?"

"I am not sure, Jaha."

Lifting his head, he stared directly ahead, into the splotchy glass behind the bar.

There, imprisoned by warped shelves and busted paneling, lay the distorted image of a cross-caste bastard in Boreali clothes—more confused than ever. Sourly, he shook his head at the irony.

"I thought I was so much better than you, when I finally followed the sentries into your place. Just an unascended, fifteen-year-old cub. Smug as ever," Zaethan admitted to Salma and grimaced at the man occupying his reflection. "You let me talk down to you. All the while, you knew exactly what I was."

In the mirror, Salma—a boss diminished to a barmaid—reached across the gap and tilted his chin toward her melancholy smirk.

"Uni. I knew. But it's not these extraordinary eyes..." Stroking his brow, the back of her roughened hand caressed the length of his cheek. "Or the depth of this skin that makes you so lovely, Jaha. It's Cyra's thumbprint on your soul. And she would agree that you and I..." Salma raised her chin triumphantly, despite the dirt stains on her cross-caste jaw. "We're not less than anybody."

Zaethan covered her fingers, holding them against himself with a sigh. "As our Unitarian fathers might say, I ought to thank you—"

He grabbed Salma when a wine cask crashed through the shutters, sheltering her from the shower of rubble as shards pelted his back.

Through the shattered window, shouting and chaos boomed from the street.

Zaethan sprinted off the stool. Burgundy juices bathed the boards of the dining hall, slipping his boots underfoot. He slid into the wall, gripping the framing to get a better vantage of the unnaturally orange light across the wharf.

A pillar of fire engulfed the midnight sky where along the docks, a newly moored merchant vessel was up in flames. Yelling, men sprinted past the inn, lugging buckets. Zaethan swung out of sight and unsheathed his kuerre just as Salma scuffled it to his side.

"Shtàka, Rafe!" she cried, reaching through the busted glass at a rogue barking orders to a crew of frenzied scallywags. "That's my nephew!"

Zaethan held her back from the window as more men bolted by, sloshing water inside. But it was a disturbance in the dark beyond their pandemonium that pricked his attention.

He squinted down the wharf at a salvaged stack of barrels, illuminated by the fire. A ripple shifted their shadow. Something like black moss swung around one of the casks. In the scorching light, the moss sharpened to braids, and the brutal flames alighted the scarred head that followed. Blood thumping, Zaethan lurched away from the broken pane in shock—It was impossible. He feared they would come. But the wrong man was leading the charge.

"That's Wekesa!" he spat.

At a deafening boom, they ducked. Creeping over the frame, he saw the hull of the merchant vessel had exploded into the Yachel.

Salma clutched Zaethan by the quilted jacket. "And that, Jaha, was your ship!"

CHAPTER THIRTY SEVEN

Across the valley of thatched roofs, a few drowsy deckhands passed the shuttered inn without pause, seeking lodging elsewhere down the waterfront. It was bolted and shut. Barely a sliver of life peeked through the crack under the chipped door, nor behind the blackened windows scattered above it.

The Scaly Stowaway gave no summons to Khmer's wanderers. Below the figure's vantage, a different duo putzed by the darkened establishment, oblivious that the king of Orynthia was tucked inside.

And Luscia, tucked somewhere with him.

He flattened against the roof of the smithy when the sailors paused, poking around in search of the drunken blacksmith who'd retired his forge for the evening. The stiff water reeds poked through the figure's cloak, grating the sores spread up his abdomen. Shifting quietly, he spewed the mouthful of chewed elderwool onto his gloved fingertips and reached under his tattered shirt to dab the crude salve over the worst of the lesions on his stomach.

His flesh stinging, the figure grimaced. The furry vine puffed his pocket, what was left of it, from his scavenge through the Mirajii Forest. It was an uncommon find as he'd tracked the Darakaian haidren from the carnage of traitors and into a reckless detour to retrieve his pryde.

Cyra's son had wasted it—squandered the advantage, the additional time, the figure had given him to reroute the regiment and rush to their ramshackle rallying point in Khmer. Every hour here was a danger to Luscia and her king. If he had let the cross-caste heir perish in the wood, perhaps Alora's niece would have fled without him. Perhaps they'd already be safe on an unmarked vessel, missed on Lake Vasil.

But the boy, now a young man, was too great a complication to die just yet, for his birth had set a disturbance in motion, a divergence to history. And his death would prove the same.

Even Alora had recognized that much when she'd put her quill to that paramount piece of parchment and signed her name as Cyra's witness—next to his own.

As astringent and acrid as the memory, the elderwool left a vinegared aftertaste on his dried tongue. The figure spit his sour drool into the thatching. Beneath his nostrils, the musty roof reeked of rodent droppings—to Amaranth's fancy—plaguing every unkempt structure that dotted the neglected port town.

Khmer was a citadel of vermin, and Amaranth, just another midnight marauder of its wares.

The hawk's feathers shuffled as she shoved her beak into the reed thatches near his blistered toes. The figure wriggled them against the hole in his boot. He'd have to scour the alleys later for a new pair. With the influx of sailors and a tavern touting cheap ale down the cobbles, one man was bound to pass out soon.

Bending his neck, the figure scanned the traffic across the docks, where the flock of newcomers had originated.

Splashed in moonshine, a three-masted galleon ebbed on its lines, freshly moored to the docks. A muster of sailors offloaded their cargo down the gangway off the visiting ship, an imposing neighbor to the sleepy brig many vacant slips over. Barrels and crates cluttered the walk where members of the crew embarked onto shore. It was risky to deliver goods at night but in these less-regulated waters, even riskier to wait till dawn. Carting bins, the team of vagabonds did not match the grandeur of their ship. By the look of their contradictory features and gypsy raiment, the sailors did not belong to any House, nor did the ship originally belong to them.

Abruptly, Amaranth cawed, and abandoning her half-eaten mouse, she launched off the rooftop toward the other end of the waterfront. Afar, the figure saw the crew members scrabbling back the way they had come from the docks, with their cargo in tow. He tugged his hood taut, intrigued and alert. His elbows sank into the reeds as he stretched beyond the rough trim.

Single file, men crept along the adjacent buildings. The figure hissed low. In line, they inched closer toward the inn, fencing access to the riverbank. Each wore a dark Unitarian tunic.

Military stock.

Springing into a crouch, the figure's cloak skirted the thatching as he prowled higher, up the incline of the slats. He exposed his scourged ears and swerved to the right, his eyes sifting the foliage that bordered the tail of the wharf. There, mingled with the leaves, a slew of Southern warriors filtered out of the brush and into the streets of Khmer. Over a dozen were migrating into the crooked alleyways. Like locusts, they leaped onto the gutter pipes and shimmied up the gables, bows flapping at their nimble backs.

Survivors of the regiment had come for the Quadren—and they were far from alone.

The figure hopped over the pitch and dropped behind it when a hand clamped onto the reeds and a warrior rolled over the framing. Fixated, the figure's vision sharpened as he stalked the Darakaian down the creaking slats, matching the man's steps where at the end of the structure, he knelt in an archer's pose. The figure crept into his blind spot. Bow resting at his side, the warrior reached for an arrow from his quiver, but not before the figure seized the weapon first. In a second, the bowstring was around his neck. The Darakaian convulsed as the figure cranked the grip, twisting the line into the man's throat until his struggling ceased.

He dragged the limp corpse to hide it in the shadow of the chimney while the surrounding rooftops were swarmed by bowman. Snarling, the figure reached around the stone lip and leaned away from the plaster, ready to drop.

A piece of fruit rolled down the cobblestones.

Straw and reed fluttered into the street when the figure curled against the wall, his gloves clenching the wattled timber. Heated, hectic whispers foretold the footfalls of those who followed.

He peered through the frayed threads of his hood. Two stories below, a third band of warriors slunk into the alley. The Darakaians spread across the filthy backstreet, tucking under ragged awnings and out of the sparse lanternlight peppering the adjoining edifices. The figure immediately identified the squadron as pryde militia, armored in reptilian hide over their buckskin leathers and traditional gunjas.

Though the militia had turned against its king.

They scrabbled in after their leader. A lengthy set of hideous slashes scoured him, shoulder to hip. Severely damaged, his swart tissue was blackened around the thick sutures, just like the rest of the wounds marring his broad-backed, muscular build. Pain did not impair his gruff, robust movements. The figure speculated as to what Andwele concoction could possibly be overriding the torture of his taut flesh.

Then again, the House of Darakai revered war as well as the price of its pain.

The warriors halted their procession when at the front, the leader's fist struck out, wavering before a fork in the alleyway.

"Which is it, Chane?"

"M-meme ano'qondai," stammered his warrior.

Instantly, the leader whipped around and snatched him by the throat. A rumble brewed from the figure when he placed that inklike stare. Recalled the gruesome patchwork over his disfigured skull, and the braids that hung from one side, baring the malice on the other.

He was the alpha from Nyack's byumbé, the one he and Lateef were honing to overthrow Cyra's son.

The one whom Cyra's son had defeated... but had allowed to live.

Scornfully, the figure sneered at her heir's foolishness once again. Cyra had been bold, not benevolent. That seed of mercy was from the boy's Unitarian father, and it was about to get the entire Quadren killed.

The mutilated alpha seethed, reeling the warrior to the rumpled bridge of his nose. "You told me outside the Mirajii you knew where they would be, uni? *Choose carefully, huwàa.* If they escape before I find them, it is you we will drag back to the chief warlord to feed to the Mworrans."

"Uni zà, Alpha Zà." The warrior wheezed the stolen title, combing his windpipe when the alpha released him. Like a dog, his backside tucked, and he dipped left, guiding the Darakaians in the opposite direction of the inn.

The figure pulled his limbs after them, but tonguing his sharp incisor, he clung to reason beyond the eagerness gushing through his veins. He could wipe them out, but the rest of the warriors and soldiers infiltrating Khmer would already be turning the town upside down in their partnered search. If the chief warlord's hunting party was unsure of Luscia's exact hideout, then there was still time to warn her of the incursion while driving it away from the inn. To get out, she'd need a window of distraction. But remaining unseen, unheard and unknown, he couldn't provide it alone.

He kicked up a leg and trundled overtop the roof of the smithy. His message would have to be big, loud, and fast. The figure examined the cluttered skyline, fixating on the merchant vessel and the innumerous casks coming off it.

His message would have to be unmissable.

With a growl, the figure rushed across the thatching, his boots barely grazing the reeds in his momentum. He leaped off the edge where it leaned into the neighboring structure and bounded onto the warped truss of an unfinished building. Grappling the posts, he flung himself across the narrow expanse and onto the gutter of The Scaly Stowaway. Like the Darakaians had, he mounted the pipework and clambered to the top of the gambrel slope, where a bowman stooped, arrow drawn at the ready.

Stealthily, the figure lowered onto his fours, shrinking his silhouette from the eyes of those who combed the rooftops. He crawled behind the bowman and, anchoring a glove over his mouth, snapped his neck. The warrior collapsed, and the figure moved onto the subsequent building in his cutthroat crusade toward the wharf.

Bow skewering viscera, the figure left the next warrior gurgling in his wake. The following soldier, unable to gurgle at all.

He launched off a rafter tail, projecting from the bustling tavern and into the trees. A nest of twigs and leaves raked his already-blighted arms as he swung between the branches, decelerating when he met the riverbank. Beneath his weathered boots flowed the waters of the Yachel.

And not too far downstream bobbed an unsuspecting ship.

The figure let go and plunged into the cool current. His cloak billowed around him, blocking the moonbeams that pierced the waves. Submerged, his feet touched down in the weed bed. Whacking away the aquatic spindles, he pushed off against the waterflow and embarked through the murky deep.

He didn't need to breathe, though the desire to had never left. Gliding, he snaked toward the haul of the vessel, akin to the eels he felt slithering against him. When he neared, his fingers skated the lacquered wood as he kicked to the surface. Droplets poured over his lashless lids as he searched for the buoy barrel floating over the swells. He dipped back under, identifying where one of the bower anchors was tethered to the earth.

The figure scaled the corded cabling out of the waters where it stretched to a hawser hole along the deck. Clinging to the exterior, the figure listened for footsteps, and once assured it was clear, he swung over the railing.

He melted against the walls of the forward deck. Wood creaked against wood as sailors rolled more barrels onto the gangway. Locating a hatchway beyond the main mast, the figure snuck through the pools of shadow and descended the ladder into the lower decks. Inside, the vessel groaned its naïve welcome.

Crossing to another hatchway, he careened into the galley when a sailor, stinking of mead, blocked his path. Unmoving, the man leaned against a beam and began to peel an apple. The figure looked around, stole a dingy, cast-iron pot off the counter, and slammed it into his head with a *clang*. Then, stepping over the unconscious body, he found his way into the cargo hold.

Lanterns swung from the rafters. The figure retrieved one, shining it upon the merchant store. Wine casks were stacked against the bulkhead, along with pots of oil and lard, lining the provision pile. All standard materials, but they'd burn the same.

Losing no time, he dumped them over, basting the wood in a tide of grease toward the foot of the ladder. About to toss the lantern, he paused, whiffing a metallic bite in the stale air. Quickly, the figure knocked the lid off the nearest bin and dipped his gloves into a vat of black silt. He brought it to his nostrils and sneezed at the abrasive hit of sulfur.

His scabbed lips split when he grinned at what he'd been hoping to find. Like many in rogue waters, the ship was smuggling gust powder from Razôuel. Hiking up the ladder, the figure hurled the lantern into the lake of oil and ran.

Like the Accords, everything was about to go *boom*.

Chapter Thirty-Eight
Luscia

She slipped the empty vial from her king's slackened grasp. He was finally asleep. His fingers unfurled, as if asking the High One for a cure to his affliction. Luscia lamented his pallor, how sallow Dmitri's Unitarian cheeks were in the candlelight, resembling the dusty alder bedframe more than the rich vitality of his own people.

He would only worsen in Boreal. Woefully, she rubbed the pinprick, already healed, on her forefinger. Tiergan blood was meant to sustain him, yet Tiergan's homeland would snuff him out.

The billows of his chest had soothed to a breezy lull as the herbs did their work, sloughing the congestion from his lungs. Disturbing Aksel, she scooted the chair back, sliding her upturned boot from under the lycran's hefty snout.

Luscia left Dmitri's side and gathered the fresh batch of elixirs into a discreet pouch. Hushedly, she stashed the jars of nixberry and eüpharsis into her portable apothecary. Luscia picked up a glass cylinder, eyeing the scant barbs of ennus thorn she had left. As his consumption intensified, so did her rate of production. Her king required they reach Boreali shores more than he even knew. For while the air was biting and the winters fierce, the grounds were a wellspring, and her apothic fount was quickly drying up.

She locked the Viridi chest with a *click* before tucking the bone key beneath the neckline of Declan's loaned tunic. A sigh escaped her as she peered around at the grimy plaster walls. The warped rafters above. The moth-eaten quilt that swaddled Dmitri's slender legs below.

None of it was worthy of a king.

Nevertheless, she preferred his room to hers, vowing not to leave until he woke. Luscia held no desire to return her chamber, for it would only be to lie in bed and stare at the slim bench across from it, reliving the acts that had occurred there hours before—acts Luscia could never allow to occur again.

She'd forgotten herself on that bench.

Enraptured by his smolder.

Fevered by the ravenous impulse he incited with every conflicted shudder through his tensed limbs, like his entire body had been bracing for a gale and she were the storm.

He'd undone her in that moment, Zaethan had. Tempted her by the nakedness of his wanting.

Shocked her by it, really.

She could not want him back, the very man she'd reviled, then come to respect. He was just a heady lie, an illicit deviation from the inescapable.

Luscia was haidren to Boreal, a daughter of Tiergan and time.

Such moments carried a weight he would never understand. Each were spoken for, sealed, dedicated to a calling far more fundamental than mortal wanting. Not one moment in this skin was hers to steal.

Penitent, she dipped a rag into the washbasin to scrub the beryl stain from her hands, whirling when a riotous pounding drilled at the door, threatening to bust it off its hinges.

Luscia thumbed the latch on her rings, engaging her radials. Arcs unleashed, she unlocked the door and yanked it ajar, to a pair of bright, sage-green eyes.

And an urgency of cerulean right beside them.

Her gaze scurried between the opposing men.

"Ykah lö?" Luscia blurted in question to Marek when she saw the captaen held her crescent wraiths. His own sheathed his spine.

Zaethan answered for him, wedging past her to Dmitri's bedside. "We have to move. Fast." Kneeling, he gently slid his arm beneath their king's head and lifted him as he blinked to consciousness. "Dmitri." His voice softened. "You got to go. Wekesa is here in Khmer, a militia with him—"

"How—"

"Doesn't matter right now, yeah? The shadowmen are going to shield you, Ira, and Hachiro from the inn to the docks, while my prydes keep the traitors off the wharf. Salma and the mercenary are already out in the fray with her nephew. I think they sabotaged his ship, but one way or another, we're getting you on that river."

Hoisting Dmitri to his feet, Zaethan found his cane and forced it into his rumbled vest. Dmitri snatched his arm when he stepped away.

"Wait—what about you?"

Luscia didn't miss the flicker of emotion Zaethan staved as he grasped their king in a brotherly embrace.

A tendon snapped along his jaw, and he stated firmly, "Get on the boat, Dmitri."

His hold dropped. Luscia's stomach tightened as he came toward her for the door. Arm to arm, Zaethan paused before the hallway. Boldly, she looked up at him over her shoulder, not entirely sure what she wanted to find in his hardened features. For a mere instant, Zaethan met her eyes before his regard darted toward the najjani captaen behind her.

"Salma's nephew, Rafe—look for the hat. You can't miss it."

Fleetingly, his cool departure brushed her elbow as he marched into the hall and commanded his warriors to evacuate the building.

Without delay, Luscia hooked her arms though the sheath harness Marek outheld, and she belted on her kuerre. Then she traded him the apothecary for her crescent wraiths, clenching the hilt of each Northern blade. Fully armed, she nodded at Dmitri, who cleaved his byrnnzite cane like a bat.

She fastened onto the captaen. "Let's go."

Her najjan flanked the hallway. Jammed between Declan's brawn and Noxolo's stature were both haidrens, apparently having been wrenched straight from their beds. Antsy, Creyvan shook out his wrists at the far end of the line, his luxiron glittering at his every agitated movement.

Luscia crossed the threshold after her king, to find Hachiro anxiously blinking at her behind the floppy fall of his matching ocher-colored nightcap. He hugged the pages of his prized possession, along with her apothecary that Marek had stacked atop it, burdening the shoto'shi's robe-swathed custody. Meanwhile, Ira hurriedly buttoned his shirt and stuffed it into his trousers, winking as he did.

Aksel's tail beat her thigh, alert, hackles erect. Indicating Dmitri follow her lead, Luscia strode them past Ira's inane simper to the top of the staircase after Marek. As they descended, the yancy's sloppy whispers to Hachiro plagued all their ears.

"It just tickles me when she's all business..."

Frowning, Luscia and her najjani guard crept down the steps. The rough plaster scraped her back as they transitioned floors. By the landing, shouts from the exterior loudened exponentially. Metal clashed in combat. Property smashed into the siding. Horse hooves beat the cobbles.

She strained her hearing, attempting to filter the layers and discern if they were alone on the second story.

"She growled at me in Bastiion once. I liked it very much—"

"Silence, Ira!" Luscia barked through her teeth, to him up the staircase.

The boards creaked when Marek shifted, deeming it safe to round the landing and proceed lower. In front of her, his athletic frame caught the cobwebs, but the captaen didn't blow them off his bulging brow. Adjusting his balance, he floated down the wood soundlessly toward the final landing, overlooking the dining hall.

"See, Hachi, when a woman tells you how she wants it, always execute—"

Luscia swerved violently and impaled Ira with her glare. Wordlessly, he slunk away from the twitching shoto'shi and offered her a compliant bow. When he came up, calloused knuckles clapped over his trap. Wide-eyed, Ira shrunk under Declan's bewhiskered scowl, who without reservation, had also angled a dagger at the yancy ambassador's throat—for good measure.

To the eye, the hall was empty. But mirroring Marek's statuesque stance, Luscia stiffened upon the last steps, listening intently over the insurrection clamoring through a shattered window along the waterfront wall.

Glass clinked behind the bar.

Like the feathers of a falcon, Marek wheeled his wraith around the corner. Blood sprayed the grimy tables just as higher up the staircase, Creyvan dove off the landing and, rolling onto the bar slab, swung both kuerres into the concealed shelving. At a maimed yelp, bottles trundled and clanked, and the luxiron whipped back over Creyvan's shoulders, dripping crimson down the seams of his linsilk jacket.

She mimed for Dmitri to remain quiet on the stair while Luscia and her men spread out among the barren tables. Streaks smeared the wall where Marek had laid siege, the dead soldier's innards draining into a sanguine pool where he slumped against the floorboards.

"Clear. Waedfrel, Creyvan," the captaen commended the flaxen najjan hopping off the bar. Merging with his half-knotted hair, gore peppered Marek's face, as if painted in a gruesome rendering of Declan's innumerous freckles. Lithely, he crept alongside the busted shutters, scrutinizing the street. "Out the door, form an Aurynth star about the king. I'll charge at apex. Declan, second spur. Ana'Sere." He instructed Luscia deliberately. "You'll take third, keeping in my periphery. Without a nadir, Nox and Creyvan will pan each spur at the rear. We'll steer them past the loading platform on the wharf, then cut northeast to the far dock. Se'lah Aurynth…"

"Rul'Aniell," she and the najjan said together, finishing the proverb in agreement.

In an unspoken harmony, they arranged after Marek's primed position behind the rusty handle. Claws clacked the unlevel boards as her lycran herded the others toward the middle of their armored convoy. Carting an ornate, sheathed sword, Noxolo bowed his height before Dmitri.

"Pardon, Your Majesty," he said and reached around to buckle the Sword of Thoarne onto the slim hips of their king. He tugged at the ornamental belting, securing the fit.

Gulping, Dmitri stuffed his cane through the stamped, leather looping, and his elegant fingers encased the hilt, guarded by a basket of gilded antlers. Luscia rotated her thigh for Noxolo to retrieve her mother's consort dagger from where it was strapped. The pastel najjan slid it out reverently.

"Lose that, and you really are a dead man," he said in warning, giving the dagger to Ira.

The yancy haidren blanched as Noxolo took to his position at fourth spur, rearward and adjacent to Luscia. Readying herself, she looked across the cradle to Declan. His slate eyes jutted to the vacant position of zenith, the central crest between them and Marek at the front, where Bowen should have been.

Instead, she found Sayuri's brother—shaking.

The Viridi chest rattled against his skinny arms. Beneath a nervous sheen, the ligaments of his golden cheeks twitched uncontrollably. Buried in the Mirajii Forest, his guardian was lost, and she was sure Hachiro had never felt more afraid.

Dmitri unsheathed his historic luxiron short sword. Variegated light showered the shoto'shi as Dmitri wrapped his free arm tightly around Hachiro. Woodsy waves sheltered the fear in their weary king's eyes when his chin raised valiantly. "At the ready, Captaen Bailefore."

A wraith sheltered Marek's broad back, its twin shining across his sheepskin breeches. Marek gripped the doorhandle. Screams echoed though the old wood when something thudded against it from the other side.

The captaen cautioned one last time, "Stay inside our formation," and burst it ajar.

Mayhem choked the life from Khmer.

Townspeople shrieked as soldiers and pryde warriors cut each other to the ground. Barely into the street, a mass dropped onto Marek from the rooftops, over his second wraith still pinned in its harness. Luscia spun, sinking her blade into the Darakaian's ribs where he adhered to the captaen like a leech. With a lurch, she wrenched him to the ground, splattering the hem of Hachiro's robes on the doorstep as she severed the warrior's spine. Under his breath, Marek uttered his hasty thanks, and after scouring the heights, he surged into the cobbled valley of fighters.

Luscia planted her back to the king, and a soldier attacked her from the mouth of the alley. Aksel snarled and sprung at the man, snapping his ferocious jaws just when a second soldier replaced him. In full turn, she sliced his throat open with one wraith as fast as she reversed and caught his falling form beneath the shoulder blades by both weapons. Hooked into his frame, blood flowed down Phalen's gauntlets over her forearms. At an oncoming kopar, she used the limp torso as a barricade. The sickle sword was plunged into the meat of the corpse's belly, and kicking it off her crescent wraiths, Luscia flipped over its collapse. Midair, she punted the warrior's chest with her bootheels, knocking back his footing, and once she landed on her toes, she twirled, her blades razoring him through his kneecaps. Charging with Marek's advance, she left him there howling.

That warrior would never walk again. Nor did he deserve to.

Between her and Declan, the lycran guarded Dmitri and the two haidrens in defensive circles. Within her periphery, the hedge of battered buildings receded as the wharf came into view. The flames of a raging fire consumed the night beyond it, backlighting the human moat of cutting and chaos.

To his word, Zaethan's partnered prydes held most of the onslaught off the access to the riverfront. Ahead of Marek's flashing wraiths, tearing through the trunk of a soldier were Zahra and Takoda. Together they shared a shield as their kopars beat back their own brethren. Hacking with fury, a barrier of Zaethan's warriors stretched out alongside their butchery, where warriors cloistered the very loading platform for which Marek aimed.

Luscia and Declan instinctively closed in, shrinking the gap that housed the trio within the Aurynth star. As lethal windmills, they spun in synchronized fervor, their arced blades carving a path through the onrushing melee.

At her battle cry, iron splattered her tongue. Her vision was bathed in a fiery film when they neared the blaze across the docks. Luscia's body shaped the wind with otherworldly momentum. The solrahs through her septum heated as her speed increased, her senses sharpening to an acute awareness of her every step—and of those around her. To each tiny gust, their weapons disturbed the air.

Weapons belonging to the enemies of Tiergan and Thoarne.

Their number thickened. Flashing her teeth, Luscia struck a warrior through his chest, and letting go of the wraith, she vaulted off the planks. Rolling across his back, she landed in a crouch, then ripped the blade from his skeleton to thrust it straight into the groin of his comrade. Wetness spattered Luscia's scar. Heart pumping, she swung her opposite wraith, cleaving the warrior behind the thighs. She hurtled upright, dragging him under the merciless trample.

A foreign resilience soared through her bones. It was lightening her spine and fevering her assault when suddenly her Sight flickered amid the frenzy.

With a soundless spark, the cloudless sky burst into lake of lumin.

Luscia swiveled and stared into the brilliance of the harbinger thread. Soaring in front of her nose, it brightened and crackled fitfully.

Indiscernible symphonic whispers reverberated through Luscia's ears over her lycran's barking.

Overhead, the lumin flickered like lightening from the *Other*, illuminating the wharf in an angry cloud. She backpedaled over the bodies toward the najjani formation in terror, the harbinger thread flying right toward her.

In unison, the voices screamed. *"Cover them!"*

Affrighted, she turned away from it, her arm knocking Ira aside just as an arrow whizzed by, the sharp fletching clipping her cheek. Luscia shoved all three out of the way when another chased it.

She threw herself over her king.

"Shtàka! Watchman on high!" Declan roared.

Creyvan rushed toward him, scanning the slaughter across waterfront as Noxolo defended the rear. The tip of a vulture barb protruded from Declan's calf.

"Niit," he barked, punching the arrowhead all the way through the muscle before snapping off the fletching and pulling the arrow out the other side. Panting into his beard, Declan's forefinger shot backward at the bordering gables. "He's *literally* on high!"

Luscia's neck snapped upward, and she spotted an archer atop the thatched roofing of a cooper's storehouse. Threads of lumin cavorted above, surrounding the sightless Darakaian amid the *Other* as he drew his next arrow and angled his bow right for Luscia.

Reflexively, she sheltered her king with her outstretched wraith, but radiant and sparkling, the harbinger thread coiled around Luscia's hand and the central hilt.

Static nipped her skin.

"Luscia, seize the light!" the whispers wailed, their chorus drumming her tendons.

Her vision doubled when the lumin spun together in a lustrous netting and bridged overtop the heads of warriors. It stretched from the rooftop all the way to the harbinger thread wound about her fist.

"Seize it now!"

Luscia recoiled her hand when the lumin sputtered with an energetic jolt. Alighting the *Other*, the netted threads flung in with the direction of her withdrawn arm.

And so did the archer.

Luscia shrieked when the Darakaian's body was swept off the thatching and met the cobblestone with a splat. On his injury, Declan whirled. His ginger whiskers framed his gaping mouth. Noxolo and Creyvan gawked at each other, then at Luscia.

Her men couldn't see the threads, but they believed in them, and they had most certainly seen the unnatural havoc those threads had just caused.

Upturned boots skidded closer to where she and her wraiths hunched over the members of the Quadren. Noxolo's pastel brow furrowed in awe and confusion. "Ana'Sere?"

She tore from his worried inspection, checking on the welfare of the others. On his hands, Ira scrambled back on the planks, startled by what he'd encountered. Luscia peered down at her blood-soaked braid, then at Hachiro, who didn't seem capable of blinking at all. Her stomach constricted in panic, and at last, she sought Dmitri's face. Hovering, the lumin cast gaunt caverns beneath his cheekbones. His stare rounded, mesmerized by the eerie glow reflected from her unearthly iris.

Her king reached out to touch it. "By the Fates, Luscia, your eye…"

Blood spurted across his regal nose when a crescent wraith revolved overhead, shredding an enemy warrior in half. Marek swooped down

and lifted Dmitri off the ground. "Not far now, My King." Huffing, the
captaen ordered the broken formation. "Reposition. Don't stop!"

Between neighboring combat, Hachiro and Ira scrambled to their
feet. Rejoining as one, the najjan pushed through the battery, driving
their spurred assault through the pryde barricade and around the
protection of the loading platform.

Floating over the waters, the lumin glittered the waves, rivaling
the glare of the billowing inferno just a couple of docks off where a
lofty galleon exploded. Another gaping hole in its stern, blown strips of
wooden wares drifted beneath the boardwalk as took water.

Brandishing their luxiron, the group scurried after Marek as he
drove them toward the two-masted brig swaying for eager departure.
Up the gangway, Luscia saw their horses being guided below decks, the
king's steely Andwele mare the last to vanish beyond the railing.

The assault pressed in behind them as they neared the ship, Zaethan's
prydes pulling back in order to escape with them once Dmitri was
safely aboard. Running, she tried not to look back.

Failing, for only a second, Luscia did. To her alarm, she couldn't
pinpoint Zaethan among the approaching forces.

She faced forward, focusing on her own duty.

Dead sailors littered the outermost dock. Some hung off the dock
posts, bobbing in the river's current. Lighting the path, shimmering
threads of lumin skittered up the gangway. At the base of it awaited a
man packed in a plum, brass-buttoned coat and a heavily feathered,
tricorn hat. Yellow-toothed ruffians were stationed at his either elbow.

Relief washed Luscia, recalling Zaethan's remark; this was Salma's
nephew. Meaning they were just a sprint away from freedom.

Suddenly, a hand clamped around Luscia's ankle from the depths,
tripping her down to the planks. A tide of warriors erupted from the

waters, mounting the dock from either side. Men screamed at the taste of luxiron and the sizzling of their flesh, to the refrain of Aksel's savage assault.

Luscia's chin throbbed where it split. She rolled aside as a kopar hacked the timber beside her skull, and rolling back, she sank her luxiron into the Darakaian's kidney. Back to the planks, Luscia lobbed both wraiths over her shoulders, anchoring them into the wood, and booted herself backward, somersaulting to stand.

She stamped her radial into a warrior's jugular and thrashed him into the river. In turning, she found a rebel kopar kissing Dmitri's throat.

His Sword of Thoarne swung lifelessly in his grasp, though the luxiron was stroked in scarlet. Declan's and Noxolo's blades lifted threateningly, but the sickle sword only pressed harder against Dmitri's uneasy swallow.

Unarmed, Luscia held out her hands for their blades to lower. When the najjan complied, the warrior sneered, his beaded braids smacking his hostage when he took a step back.

"Stupid y'siti swine!" the warrior called, taunting her across the splintered slats.

The harbinger thread snaked from behind him, picking up a lock of Dmitri's hair as if it were just another breeze. It shuddered and wound toward her brother's gauntlets.

Luscia's wrist moved, aiming with the tail of the harbinger thread where it targeted the warrior's brow. She'd only recovered a single dart after the battle in the wetlands. With her right eye behind the veil, the left before it, Luscia had but one shot.

"Don't move," she whispered for Dmitri, and her middle finger drew the hidden trigger.

The kopar clanked to the docks. Dmitri blew out a blustery exhale when the warrior fell into the waves, a dart stuck between his brows.

Without pause, Noxolo hauled their king, still in shock, down the dock and up the steep gangway. Declan limped after them, pushing Hachiro toward the ship in similar fashion. Hurriedly, she waved Ira and Creyvan to board next.

With her lycran, Luscia gripped the roping but abruptly paused at the clutter of corpses bumping against the hull.

With a sharp turn, she questioned Salma's nephew. "Who are all these men?"

"Previous management." The stranger's swart mustache twitched, as coolly, he glanced past her at the oncoming ambush.

She swerved toward Marek. "We can't trust the king to a pirate!"

"Privateer. Rafe Nabhu, breakaway at your service." He proudly tut-tutted and hastily uncoiled the mooring from a cleat. "Up you go, Lady Haidren."

Luscia and her Orallach beast hiked after the captaen, jumping when the line lapped her across the buttocks. Appalled, she twisted at the top, in time to see the cheeky grin the pirate sported as he and his counterparts hoisted the gangway and drove the ship off the docks. Instantly, a succession of rope ladders swung over the railings, just as the flimsy promenade splashed into the water. Luscia hugged the balusters, out of the sailors' way as they rushed the rigging.

A new wind swelled from the heavens, a cyclone of lumin churning the brightening skies. The gusts favorable, the sails ballooned in response as Rafe Nabhu and his brutes leaped into the Yachel after the brig.

They scaled the knotted ladders with skill. Drenched, the pirate joined them on the main deck.

"We can't just leave them!" Dmitri screamed. "Zaeth!"

Restrained by Marek and Declan, the king of Orynthia pressed against the railing as below, Zaethan's warriors flooded the end of the dock. Some even dove after the brig, though the waves separated them by the minute. Even farther than that desperate mob were two warriors battling over the wharf, their clashing blades lost in an arena of their own.

Luscia captured the railing, so hard the wood chafed her palms. There was no need for ivory and onyx markings; the spectators spread across the ship already knew each contender well.

Their challenge had unfolded once before.

"He won't make it across in time, Ana'Sere," Noxolo said to Luscia.

His gaze was strained by the same concern when, looking down, they beheld the prydes swimming against the current.

"Nor will they."

Rafe Nabhu sauntered behind them toward the ship's helm. "You shadowmen think you put on a decent show?" At his piercing whistle, a brigade of archers raced portside, forcing themselves between Luscia and her najjan. "Watch mine."

CHAPTER THIRTY NINE
ZAETHAN

Drenched in sweat, his spine merged with Kumo's as together they whirled in place, completely outnumbered.

Warriors pressed in from either end of the poorly lit alley. The gash along his shoulder blade stung, pressed inside the quilted Boreali jacket. Zaethan knew what their disloyal kinsmen saw—the image that incited their nerve and emboldened their advance down the uneven cobblestones. To them, he was no longer alpha zà of the Darakaian militia.

Ano, their defamed leader was worse than any other unwanted cross-caste.

He was a bastard of the South—sheathed like a shadowman.

Hatred sparkled through their eyes when Zaethan spun the Northern kuerre. The witchiron refracted a lustrous medley onto the predatory horde as they pushed closer, trapped between plaster siding, stories high.

"Hope you're feeling lucky, Ahoté," Kumo said, the muscles of Kumo's back rumbling. "This pack of kakka-jackals wouldn't recognize true Darakaian blood if they swallowed it, and they don't deserve a lick of ours!"

In his opposite hand, Zaethan's grip constricted around his kopar. His scrutiny darted from one warrior to the next, their boots inching forward. "Our luck was wasted when we were cubs, cousin!"

Zaethan braced against his monolithic beta. Directly across his outstretched kuerre, one of Wekesa's warriors snarled into the blade's spectral sheen and, with blatant acrimony, hawked a wad of spit onto the foreign metal. Zaethan pointedly titled the kuerre, letting the saliva dribble off the edge, before leveling it higher at the traitor. He didn't want to kill his kinsmen, but to save his king, he would kill them all.

Enraged, the warrior released a brutal rallying cry and charged.

Whipping his kuerre, Zaethan deflected the onrushing axe, and with the hooked end of his kopar, he snared the spiked shield and slammed it into the face of a different attacker. He ducked when another's sword lashed from the left, and he sank his witchiron into the warrior's middle. The Darakaian screeched in horror, flaying back into the throng as his swarthy flesh sizzled, deteriorating from his mutilated navel.

Zaethan shifted with Kumo as he sidestepped, rotating them within the tunnel of aggressors. Warriors rushed them from both sides.

Instantly, he swung out and plunged either blade into the blockade of chests. Bones cracked under the corrosive witchiron. After letting go of each hilt, Zaethan reached up, gripped his beta's thick corded neck, and jumped off the ground. His ankles crooked around the beaded neckband of a stocky warrior before him. And with a rapid snap, the man collapsed.

His bootheels thudded against the cobbles. Zaethan wrenched both kuerre and kopar from the sternums of the two men, and a curtain of blood shuttered between them.

"What's your count?" he shouted to Kumo.

"Meme ano'qondai—a dozen?" the beta yelled back with his next strike. "Maybe two… or three… They keep popping up like thissleweed!"

Zaethan grimaced and, parrying the blitz of a blade, headbutted a warrior as his Boreali backsword cleaved into another. In flashes, he glimpsed the slanted heights that caged them within the crooked alley. A stone's throw beyond the warriors caging Zaethan was a heap of pallets, stacked nearly to the second-story window of a tilted, timber-beamed storehouse. If they could just hack their way through the herd—

A chair smashed through the windowpane, and glass showered the street as a dark procession leaped out after it.

Warriors rolled from the alley, disappearing behind the river of rebels. Shrieks ruptured at the back of the cluster, turning the tide in the opposite direction toward the newcomers. Using the distraction, Zaethan surged his blades forward in a frenzy. Spinning out, he slashed the spines of those closest to him, and with a thump, he replanted his own against Kumo's once again.

"What's all that kakk?" his beta asked, his shoulders knocking Zaethan's skull with each punchy maneuver.

But before he could formulate a guess, a pair of bodies dropped to their knees, revealing a lanky warrior and a toothy grin.

"We fly on time, Alpha Zà!" Jabari proudly announced, his bushel of coils bouncing with his huffing. "Swoop like birdies, uni. Come a peck them huwàa trickers to the Depths!"

Jabari emphasized his mountain jabber by swinging his hobnailed Yowekaon shield into an assailant's nose. A kopar was protruded through the same warrior's gut. With a shrill whoop, the body was punted from the sickle sword, uncovering its owner under the scarlet spray. Mopping the gore from her sable forehead, Yhona winked at Zaethan across the shrinking wall of bodies, and with a passion that defied her withered frame, his warrior let out a murderous cry and thrashed her blade through a coupling of rebel torsos. Her brother surfaced from the fray, thwarting a dual-edged hatchet soaring straight for Yhona.

Clockwise, Zaethan swerved with Kumo while their disjointed pryde fought toward the onslaught his beta fended off. The enemy warriors were easily doubled down that end of the alley. But the sum didn't add up…

For mobility, a militia outfit was no more than twenty to thirty, so these weren't just members of the Valley Pryde. Wekesa must have brought recruits with him from Faraji. And for any chance at taking them out, Zaethan needed to get to the alley's other side.

Crossing his blades, he tore through tissue and bone, clearing the tight space between himself and the pitted plaster wall.

His heel gritted into the bumpy stones underfoot and he bellowed, "Jabari, rhaolé ono! Swap out!"

Trusting the Yowekaon to take his place against Kumo, Zaethan sprinted at the wall. As he vaulted, his boot caught enough friction to run up the side before he pushed off a torch sconce and propelled his body over encroaching warriors. Somersaulting through the air, Zaethan buried blades, forged of North and South, into the very men he'd once called his.

Greif tore through his spirit with every swing of iron, as if his past were being cut down with his fallen brethren. Unstopping, Zaethan shred through their assembly. Tossing the hilts, he traded hands and used the kopar to grapple a warrior by the calf when his shield stormed from the right, flattening him to the ground. Zaethan hopped on the bronze disc, crunching his ribs, and instantly stooped beneath the swipe of a sickle sword. Mercilessly, he staked the kuerre through the wielder's beltline. The whites of the warrior's eyes ringed his stunned gawk as crimson trickled from his half-open mouth.

Wekesa's recruits might remember how Zaethan had first won his title.

But they'd forgotten how he'd kept it.

The female archer behind him backpaddled, her arrow aimed at Zaethan when he stepped off the shield and wheeled his kuerre menacingly. A spire blocked the torchlight as Kumo fell into step at his side. Slowly, the warrior's panicked gaze lurched about as Zaethan's pryde circled the street of cadavers. Perspiration doused the tight curls pasted to her shuddering brow.

The warrior was the last one standing.

"*Y'siti lover!*" the archer spewed at Zaethan's borrowed, highlander garb. Quaking, she lifted her bow with her voice. "Dirty cross-caste fraud, you will never be one of us! Hewe ano'ràtomdai na yeye!"

We don't claim you.

"Uni zà," Zaethan replied, blinking eyes he knew did not belong among theirs. "They say every gain has a loss. You can't claim me, or your king, ano… so claim your death instead."

The archer's face curled just as a kopar spurted through her throat.

"Looky, looky, blinded birdie," Jabari whispered into her hair and yanked his blade back, dispatching the archer to the cobbles with her comrades.

He snatched the quiver of arrows and tossed it to Sadik, the last of Zaethan's best archers, who'd already stripped the double bow from the corpse. Zaethan had ordered the rest of the pryde's most skilled shots to reenforce the wharf with his third.

Zaethan panted, scanning the half dozen warriors who'd joined them in the alley. "Where's Takoda?"

"With Zahra and the rest, Alpha Zà," Sadik answered as he strapped on the quiver, likely having broken from the same standoff to rescue them. "The Mirajii Pryde defends the bank while ours blockades the southeastern dock to the ship."

"And their alpha, Kai?"

"On a cot, already aboard—as you instructed, Alpha Zà," Yhona replied, her countless slinky braids jostling with her nod.

Zaethan steered that way, under the indigo drapery of Ala'maia's court, and trudged over the carnage without a glance down. The moon speared through the clouds overhead, her light hazy compared to the smoldering galleon still ablaze in the distance across the wharf. In a fatal marigold bouquet, the flames backlit the mouth of the alley where it spilt to the waterfront main.

He jutted his chin at Kumo. "Lead them to Zahra, yeah? Then locate the king and keep the ambush out of the shadowmen's path to the docks. You make sure they get on that ship!"

"Uni zà!" His beta pummeled a fit to his chest. "But Ahoté, where will you go?"

Hungrily, Zaethan combed his gaze across Khmer's battlefield, charting the wharf toward the timberline, then back up to the gables overhead.

He'd need a better vantage.

"To find Wekesa." His grip gnawed each hilt. "This ends tonight."

Zaethan pinpointed his rival not by the scar on his scalp but the one sutured down his back.

It was a free-for-all below the dilapidated, thatch-covered balcony. He saw Wekesa's thick shade cut through the brawl toward the waterfront, an avalanche discharging from the end of his blade as he flattened the bravery of Kai's warriors with single swipes of his axe.

In his bloodlust, Wekesa's slaughter snared the unlucky soldiers who stumbled into his stampede, headed right for the loading platform—the same platform the shadowmen would have to bypass to deliver Dmitri onto the brig.

Zaethan searched the frenzy. They weren't too far from it. Inescapably, his eyes locked on Luscia—and her fatal dance among the lake of her enemies. The moon illumed her tawny plait, swinging with her ravaging wraiths, and the precision of their massacre. Her agility was unyielding.

She was a devastation. A phantom to the living. A sentence to the dead.

Luscia Darragh Tiergan was unmistakable, and in a matter of moments, Wekesa would see it too. Zaethan immediately let go of the awning post and hurtled into the street, though not out of fear for Luscia.

When Wekesa beheld her, he'd behold their king in her shadow.

The impact with the stone stunned his bones, but freeing his blades, Zaethan ran at the wharf with all the speed his mortal legs could muster. At a flood of adrenaline, his heartbeat pulsed through his ears, muffling the cries of those he passed, dropping like brittle leaves in his periphery.

At Zaethan's approach, renegade soldiers ruptured from the mayhem, barging sword-first. He pivoted, stabbing his kuerre through a man's thigh, and continuing the spin, he hooked another with the kopar and torqued his abdomen into the Boreali backsword. Under his weight, Zaethan withdrew the kuerre from the other soldier and spilled the entrails of the second. He smeared the blade's taint across the navy threads of the imperial uniform both men had betrayed.

The soldier crumpled to his knees. Beyond his matted, Unitarian head raged the ringleader of their mutiny. Furious flames silhouetted the two-sided axe as he thrust high into the night.

"Wekesa!"

His rival's onyx head swung round like a giant defaced capstone. Locating Zaethan in the crowd, Wekesa dragged a grin, laying bare his blocky teeth outlined in fresh claret. The fire glared off his weapon when he swung it low.

Friend or foe, Wekesa didn't even glimpse his next victim.

Blowing through his lips, Zaethan measured his breathing as the warriors parted for his usurper. Wekesa's corded chicory muscle rippled with each wolfish step. Zaethan didn't blink. The entire wharf seemed to burn away, turning to ash behind Wekesa's nearing. A decade of hatred narrowed between them. Zaethan swallowed, malice scorching the walls of his throat.

Wekesa's fat braids battered the side of his square jaw when he skill-fully revolved his axe. The move was fluid, defying the twin gouges that Zaethan had chiseled into his spine, like he'd never even been injured in that arena.

"I butchered your back," Zaethan said, his voice hoarse over the elevated kuerre. "You should be a maggot, crawling where you walk."

But Wekesa rolled his shoulders nimbly.

"You have your sorcerer." His tongue swabbed the blood from his teeth. "Now Darakai has ours."

In sync, they began to circle. Alert, Zaethan combed over the smaller stitches dappling Wekesa's calves and arms. The faint markings had nearly healed. Darakai rarely called on medicine men from the deep mountain—the kakk-spitters from Yowekao—healers who could never achieve such rapid recovery for wounds as Wekesa's, even if they *had* been summoned to his bedside.

Beneath his inspection, Wekesa sniggered. Something was very off, and he cradled it like a secret within his swollen sneer—the expression uglier than ever before.

"I'm the real alpha zà, Zaeth." Wekesa's pitch eyes flashed with his axe, but Zaethan repelled it with the kopar as they orbited each other. "It's my *jwona*, yeah? To do the things you never could. Uni, me—I'm the son the chief warlord never had!" He hammered the butt against his beefy, leather-bound chest. "The son who's willing to do whatever it takes, no matter the assignment. No matter the pammu-drunken Unitarian slug Orynthia sits on a throne and calls our king!"

Ice crystallized in Zaethan's belly, almost causing him to miss the bit of Wekesa's axe when it hurtled forward.

He sidestepped, his hips screwing aside just as the weapon pierced the air he'd occupied. Zaethan retreated in shock, the revelation heavying his heels. Nyack Kasim had vehemently accused Razôuel of regicide, but he was the agent who'd coordinated the transport of King Korbin's shipments from The Veiled Lady—from Salma herself—the same Nyack Kasim who was rallying for a war his king never wanted. Nyack Kasim had campaigned to conquer the hard-earned ally King Korbin had fought with his life to secure. He wanted a war of broken treaties, its start only made possible once their peacekeeper was eliminated.

Nyack Kasim had Darakai.

He had the Orynthian armies.

He only needed to enlist another bastard, one even more desperate to please him than Zaethan, to execute his bidding. And his crime.

"It was *you*?" He heard himself shout. "You poisoned the king!"

Wekesa's shield hammered Zaethan's kuerre when he struck, his reflexes somehow even sharper than during his challenge in the arena. "Darakai's kwihila isn't to submit to an oppressor, ano zà!" Wekesa bellowed, bludgeoning his axe with power. "It's to become the oppressor!"

Swiftly, Zaethan dodged his opponent's next swing, though it plucked the hem of the Boreali jacket. Wekesa's glare glittered as he dramatically puffed the spruce fabric off the heel of his blade. Keeping their distance, Zaethan walked backward onto the planks, closer to the loading platform, yet no warriors impeded his steps.

They were no longer there.

Unable to turn, Zaethan aligned his footing with the border of the planks, where wood met the cobbles. "You're a traitor to the realm," he stated deliberately, stalling until he met the structure.

Amusement warped Wekesa's snarl.

"Not to the chief warlord. He's the *real* jwona rapiki. He claims what he wants, becomes what he wants, and accepts it with honor!" A scar stretched over his protruding brow as it arched sardonically. "Did you really think this was his first time?"

Zaethan smacked against a pillar of the platform, unable to tear his gaze from the terrible glee that taunted from Wekesa's eyes. Black and pitiless, they trickled over Zaethan's long dreaded locs and fixed on the gilded cuffs beading them.

His mother's cuffs.

"Uni, go on. Think, Zaeth…"

His jaw clamped taut as he suddenly rolled, and Wekesa's axe bashed into the log pillar. It lodged there, like Zaethan had planned, and he jumped, trundling across his rival's shield. He rammed the crook of his kopar between Wekesa's ribs, ready to pull, but the bronze shield spanked his skull. Zaethan staggered, only to witness Wekesa wheedle the sickle sword from his own side and flip it hilt to hand. Scraps of bone, entangled in sinew, hung there, like the ghoulish garland strung at Fàkkadim'Chalim.

He showed no pain.

Brashly, Wekesa chucked the shield aside and balanced their arms— the same cocky mistake he'd made in their first challenge five years ago.

Zaethan lunged. His knees skidded the weathered wood, tearing the sheepskin breeches as the kuerre slashed his rival over the hip. Wekesa did not slow, not even when his skin bubbled and blackened beneath his Southern gunjas. Instead he swiveled, and in a robust roundhouse, he expelled Zaethan across the docking.

His vision shimmered with the stars. Agony fired up Zaethan's neck as he slid toward the edge, hovering just above the churn of the midnight waters. He felt thunderous vibrations when Wekesa sprinted down the planks. Trundling onto his stomach, Zaethan pushed himself upright and whirled the kuerre. It clashed against his own kopar.

The opposing metals cavorted in a variegated luster of embers and witchiron, as from the fiery galleon, smoke blustered onto the docks with a gusted breeze. His eyes burning, Zaethan squinted back tears. Their swords broke apart unexpectedly, and Wekesa vanished into the waist-deep smog, crouching beneath it somewhere in the smoldering darkness.

With the kuerre, Zaethan ringed his hidden legs. Abruptly, the sword was torn from his grasp, and an acrid wall clamped over both his mouth and nose. Suffocating agony bloomed over his abdominals when the kopar fastened across his beltline and hooked him sideward.

Wekesa flung them around to face the brig as it sailed out of port. Straining to breathe, Zaethan blinked through the wetness at his warriors, those who were left, swarming the end of dock. Their screams for it to turn back battered his undeserving heart. He'd led them to their deaths.

He'd led them to his own.

From afar, he heard a series of shrill whistles spear the night. From the brig, a shower of rope-tied arrows penetrated the clouds, raining lifelines from the ship into the Yachel.

At the sight, Wekesa's palm constricted over Zaethan's lips. He leaned closer, intimately, when Zaethan started to wheeze.

"I will never understand why he didn't smother you." Wekesa's breath chafed his ear. "Just like he did that bitch the moment you were born."

Nyack Kasim had murdered his mother.

And her memory. For spite.

The shrinking ship in Zaethan's eyeline hued red as rage exploded through his entire being. He roared behind Wekesa's rough fingers until he'd no more breath to banish. Unarmed, his bare palms clamped around the rim of the kopar, and discrediting the sting, he tore the blade off his bleeding abdomen.

Wekesa only laughed, dark and rasped. "You can't beat me, Zaeth, ano zà. Not anymore."

Contending for the sickle sword, Zaethan lodged his boot around his captor's ankle. His left hand released the kopar to elbow Wekesa in the face, and jerking his calf forward, Zaethan drew Wekesa off his less-dominant foot. Wheeling around, he kneed the hilt out of his rival's clutch and caught it in both ravaged hands, then twisted and nailed it into his throat.

The flames alighted the inky blood that gushed down Wekesa's chest. Zaethan huffed, his tortured gaze plundering the disfigurement of his rival's skull toward the kopar wedged into his windpipe. But it was then Zaethan froze, his angry glare halting just below the Andwele iron.

Branded into Wekesa's severed neck were two unending circles, divided by one harrowing line.

Zaethan eyes bored into his rival's as he shouted vehemently, "Who did this to you! Who is the Obscurer!"

Wekesa's mouth parted, showcasing a tongue half pink, half black. Murky sputum dribbled from his lips as he gurgled against the kopar. "He is more powerful than any king."

On the last word, Wekesa's arm came down, breaking Zaethan's grip on the hilt just as his heavy frame toppled into the water. Zaethan dove to the end of the planks and splashed the foam that rose to the surface.

Wekesa was gone.

And so were his secrets.

Head spinning, Zaethan sidled onto his soles and stood. Blanketed in bodies, the wharf was vacant, all of Khmer tucked under an atrocity. A foggy glow caught his eye where the smoke had cleared. He bolted to his kuerre, rescued the witchiron from the soiled wood, and ran for the last dock on the waterfront.

Corpses cluttered the water, lapping the pilings on either side. Most were Darakaian, some Unitarian, and fewer a mix of the two... just like him. Zaethan saw himself among the dead as he stood there in the moonlight at the end of the boardwalk. Too far to swim, the brig rode the Yachel, hurrying to the refuge of the ghost coast.

Zaethan emitted a relieved sob. Dmitri—his king, his friend, his chosen brother—was safe from the deception of Nyack Kasim, and with him on that runaway ship, so was everyone else he'd ever loved. His chin shuddered as he watched it sail off.

He was utterly alone.

Lost to himself, to the truth and those still to uncover. Lost to a name that was never his to claim. Lost to Àla'maia and a host of haunted thoughts.

For a disowned cross-caste, losing was all he had left.

Zaethan listened to the galleon crackle and flare, the ship's charred skeleton shriveling under the flames. Startingly, a chorus of whooping rattled the quiet despondence.

Out of the nothing, an arrow spliced the planks at his feet. Tethered to its fletching was a corded lifeline—meant for Zaethan. Through the dark, he looked out at the ship as moisture rolled down his cheek.

Swallowing his gratitude, Zaethan wound the roping about his forearm and, with the unearthly kuerre, cut himself free.

Perhaps he was not lost after all.

CHAPTER FOURTY
LUSCIA

L uscia greeted daybreak like a forgotten friend. Beneath the shroud of darkness, colors of maize and mandarin crowned the waves where hope split the horizon. In the privacy of her thoughts, she felt it splitting her too.

Wrapping her arms about herself, Luscia rested against the starboard railing and watched the miles of wasteland drift by. Endless dunes blushed under the kiss of the sun. She found a strange peace staring into the starkness. Nothing grew that far east, and so there was nothing to destroy it… nothing to betray or to deceive. The Wastes simply were and forever would be.

To her right, Declan said little, except to occasionally grunt at the sundry crew of sailors scuttling behind them. Their garish captain, Rafe

Nabhu, barked orders from his grip at the helm. Mutely, Luscia peered over her shoulder.

Upon the quarterdeck, the copious plumage of the pirate's hat was as bloated as the sails, not unlike Aksel's tail, which carelessly wafted over her upturned boots. The lycran emulated her melancholy demeanor, his snowy snout wedged between the bulbous balusters. She combed the russet streak between his piqued ears and turned back toward the water, listening to it crash against the hull as her elbow nudged one of the decorative, golden finials atop the rail. Though smaller than Rafe Nabhu's lost galleon, the commandeered brig was unduly ornate. Which, perhaps, was why the pirate had so merrily taken it.

Hovering them over the frothy, churning waters, Luscia scraped the blood beneath her nails.

A spread of pryde warriors were laid out at her back. Cots cluttered the deck, foremast to mainmast, sheltered in the expansive shadow of the gaff sail. She'd already tended to those present, and the worst had sequestered to recovery in the sick bay. Though the ship was over-crowded, they had taken significant losses, the Mirajii Pryde suffering most of the casualties, due to their already-weakened state. And considering the extent of the injuries just a few decks lower, she suspected those would not be the last.

Scarlet trenches framed her fingertips. Luscia had scrubbed them until they went raw, but despite her struggle, some things did not so easily fade.

"Don't let what stains your hands stain your spirit, Ana'Sere," Declan murmured somberly.

Luscia dropped her picking as he folded his stocky arms and resettled his interest on the distance. The motion scraped the crusted gore caked to Declan's hide bracers, mirroring the braided armor over his woven linsilk tunic. Like her, he'd not yet changed.

Luscia tucked her chin as she gently replied, "I fear that in this life, both stains are the same, brödre."

A rumble of agreement resonated from the najjan's scruffy throat.

They stood there quietly, dressed as death bringers cloaked in a blood to which they did not belong. Every drop of it was vindicated. Necessary. She'd played her role, defended her king, but no morsel of logic nor depth of sagacity or moral justification could slough the tarnish from Luscia's soul. It was there to stay and with it, the memory of every wayward man who'd perished by her hand.

War came in many forms, but every version ended with a grave, one fed by the bones of the vanquished and the humanity of the victor.

"I can't help but question why Aniell would permit me the joy of sailing home after leaving Khmer a port of the dead," Luscia said to the warming humid air. Her voice thickened with guilt. "Why grant me solace, when everyone else lies in misery?"

As they coasted the Yachel, the misgiving hung unanswered between them.

She sensed his weight shift with his thoughts. Declan's stance uncrossed, and his roughened palms splayed over the railing.

"Maybe home isn't where we find solace for our sins but for the atrocities that weren't."

"It takes immense faith to discern the difference between the two."

"Wem. Yet, for what it is worth," Declan stated to the river, "you fought with unwavering grace—a breathtaking testament to our najjani order. It was my honor to battle alongside you today. And se'lah Aurynth, until those infinite shores, Ana'Sere, an honor it will remain."

Luscia's lids collapsed. Her lashes fluttered in the wind as she caged the billow of feeling behind them.

Her path to the najjan, to her training on the Isle of Viridis, had been a hard one—a journey appointed by her father, which her aunt had never affirmed, not even once. Even now, Luscia considered herself more najjan than haidren, more at ease with a blade than her birthright beyond the veil. It posed a walking dichotomy that Alora would never accept in a successor. And Luscia couldn't ask her to accept it… not yet.

Not until Luscia knew what was wrong with her Higher Gifts—because something was. And it was very wrong indeed.

"Tadöm, Declan." Gripping the handrail, Luscia turned toward him, meeting his steady gaze. "It means a great deal. More than you'll ever know."

Narrowing, his slate irises bounced to beyond Luscia, then returned. Declan twisted a bead in his copper beard pensively. "Your skill, your instinct and ingenuity, have all surpassed your inherent talent for combat. You've grown, *Ana'Sere*," he commended. Declan angled his crooked nose at the opposite end of the ship. "You grew because of him."

Luscia scorned the heat flushing beneath her cheeks when she twisted and followed his eyeline toward the bow.

On a bench, braced against the ladder to the forecastle rested her unlikely ally. The breeze whipped his dark locs as Zaethan stared into a darker horizon on the other side.

Propped on his knee, his split palms were bound by rags. She'd thought they'd lost him to Khmer. But Rafe, the breakaway pirate, had spoken true. He had put on an unforgettable show, its climax when he'd snatched the Darakaian double bow from one of the warriors and shot that last line to the docking himself. It was by a team of grit, headed by Kumo, the mountainous beta, that Zaethan had been hauled through the current to the brig. And directly behind Kumo's efforts, championing the call, had been Dmitri.

Drained from the ordeal, their king had retired somewhere below decks, having nearly passed out once his friend had finally been pulled over the rail, gasping like a hooked fish.

She'd tried to help him—Zaethan—when she spotted the gashes across his hands. But with weary, expressionless regard, he'd brushed her off.

Luscia found it difficult to look away from him now, at the down-turn of his maddening mouth, the haunted depression of his never-flattened brow…

Zaethan didn't want her help. From afar, she watched as he absently flexed his fists, almost as if he wanted the pain instead.

"My father is a master luxsmith in Roüwen. I apprenticed him a bit as a lad, until I learned how much I enjoy stabbing things… So it wasn't until Khmer that I understood why you maneuvered around us in Bastiion, and Faraji, as you did, Ana'Sere."

Declan's deep baritone compelled Luscia to turn around, and she was taken aback by the apologetic tilt to his bearded jaw. "The Southern haidren—the alpha—he is an unknown iron." The najjan's consideration darted back to Zaethan's position near the forecastle. "You could not test the strength of your own against the standard you knew. And so, you were quenched and tempered. And opposed to his anvil, you discovered your strength. I see now that his was a crucible we could not provide."

To Luscia's surprise, Declan bent his rumpled head, a lock of ginger falling from its tether over his reverential bow. "Meh fyreon, My Haidren, for doubting the forge you so wisely chose for yourself."

Stunned, Luscia's lips parted without a sufficient word to speak. Under Boreali law, she'd broken a vow, trading their luxiron for gain.

Luscia did not condone hypocrisy and did not consider herself above it. Therefore, Declan's forgiveness, and his support for her offence, knowingly abetted that brokenness too.

To Luscia, there was no semantic more profound.

"Let us forgive each other, Ana'Brödre," she said, tenderly uplifting his chin. "I've been a frustration to you all, in many arenas. The captaen most of all. I hope that one day the rest of the guard will see my conviction the same way you do. Regrettably, I suspect it might take many more Port Khmers to broaden their lens of me." Luscia's fingertips dropped to her waist, and she knitted them together. "Until then, I will endeavor to regain their trust and become someone they can be proud of, Marek's most of all."

Through his buckled nose, Declan blew out a sigh and leveled his height to hers. "Ana'Sere…" he whispered, planting his ruddy palm over his heart.

She anchored her stare onto his freckle-rimmed eyes as his head shook.

"What is the opinion of men to a woman anointed?" An enduring grin stretched under his whiskers.

Her lashes moistened unexpectedly, and she blinked to clear her vision, to behold the kind of devoted expression that made her want to stand taller, yet she found herself pinned, humbled beneath the weight of it.

Unmoving, Declan's awareness flicked upward. Still stooped, his forefinger playfully batted the underside of his septum, indicating where her solrahs was pierced, and he winked. Then, lifting himself straight, he brusquely nodded at someone over her shoulder. "Captaen."

Her ears focused behind her. Marek's footfalls approached with a sober calm, sounding neither rushed nor delayed. An abrupt nervousness settled behind Luscia's sternum, unsure if he'd overheard her and Declan's exchange above the creak and moan of the ship's enterprise.

Regardfully, Declan stepped around her as his captaen neared. Her sullied torso swung along the railing after the najjan's exodus, wishing he would stay.

In turning, Luscia saw Marek's trim hip had settled against the balusters on her other side. A spotless white linen shirt, unlaced at the top and only half-tucked into his belting, hung off his broad shoulders. His tan breeches too were free of blemish, though the leather drooped where it was often taut over his thighs. It had likely been loaned by one of the sailors below. Luscia awkwardly rubbed her arm, keenly aware of their disparity in dress. While irrational, she couldn't help but feel they were on uneven footing. Thus, recognizing her irrationality made it all the worse.

Her eye discreetly followed Declan's path through the cluster of cots toward the hatchway. As his first boot stepped down, onto the ladder, the najjan stared across to the wounded Darakaians, turned toward Luscia, and deliberately brought his fist to his chest, imitating their salute for her. With a confident nod, Declan descended out of sight.

A heavy exhale escaped her as she rotated beside Marek, perching her elbow a few inches from his upon the railing. Aksel yawned between them and, in a bumbling ordeal, eventually laid his hybrid belly over her feet, crushing her toes.

Sly brute's just keeping me from bolting, Luscia privately griped.

Overlooking the Yachel, the sun loomed above the ocean of sand, defining the crests and valleys that made up The Wastes wading in her periphery. Marek stood alit. Unbound, his crimson hair dusted off his shoulders with each gust, its striking hue a glorious crown beneath the morning rays. Like Declan, he did not pressure her to speak, although unlike his shorter counterpart, he appeared under pressure himself.

Marek's hands gestured sporadically over the emptiness, as if preparing to relay something before clamping his lips together again. By the third instance, Luscia charitably interjected instead.

"Creyvan and Noxolo, did they find somewhere to sleep?"

"Wem," he replied, relief in his timbre. "Strung up a couple hammocks on the orlop."

"Waedfrel. For that I'm glad."

Marek massaged his palm. "I think Creyvan has half a mind to sleep the entire voyage to Boreal, with the hope he'll see Böwen once he wakes."

Luscia mulled over the sentiment, and that which he'd accused her of in the swamp. The memory still stung.

No matter their ardency, apologies didn't erase the opinions that caused them.

But glancing to the vacancy on her right, she heard Declan's words replaying louder.

Solemnly, Luscia replied, "Böwen is a missed man. After all this sorrow, the unending chaos, it will soothe each of us to be reunited with him again. And with my friend," she said, unashamed of her decision to send her. "Mila."

The palace attendant's name rode with the ship's wake, replaced by their mute reticence once again. Marek did not voice his critique, if he still harbored one. Rather, his belt scraped the black lacquer as he pivoted to face her.

Unshaven, he scratched the titian prickling over his jaw. "Bolaeva,

Ana'Sere… Luscia…" He carefully continued. "Are you willing to tell me what happened with that archer, off the roof in Khmer?"

Luscia's toes wiggled under Aksel's numbing weight, and she scooted back a fraction.

"Niit," she said honestly, softening the defensive tightness in her throat. "Not until I'm sure what there is to tell you."

Her focus fled overboard and into the waters.

She didn't know what to say. Her Sight was out of control, like she was enslaved to the *Other*. Every time she convened with the lumin, she was left in both terror and awe. Whispers had turned to choirs, choirs to single melodies that frightened Luscia more than she could admit. The threads were not supposed to speak. Not one record—not one psalm—stated otherwise. But the more she heard them… the more they tormented her ears and commanded her members, the less plausible her own insanity seemed.

And if it was real—the power as much as the curse—Luscia had no idea what it meant. The only thing she knew for certain was the most disturbing factor of all.

Luscia had not taken her aunt's tonic since Faraji, where her crate of vials had been abandoned. Without it, she'd encountered the bizarre and taken part in it too. But her episodes were not the same. They'd evolved, because her head…

Her head no longer hurt.

"I'm able to wait," Marek said, interrupting her uneasy ruminations. Her neck arched back toward him, noting where her father's beaded cuff dangled off his wrist. Absently, Marek tapped the rail. "I'll be here to listen whenever you're ready."

Her eyes pinned on the cuff, Luscia puffed through her nose. "You're good at that… Waiting."

Conviction tugged her by the navel, and she knew another decision soon needed to be made. She was not a little girl anymore, not her father's "*lu'Lycran*" who could run from the realities of this life and bury herself with her treasures in a corner of the wood.

Luscia was a woman. The daughter of the Clann Darragh. The haidren to Boreal.

Her entire being was a manifested duty. To the House of Boreal, she was a lantern.

To the Quadren, a voice.

And to her king, a promise.

There was one duty every other haidren owed to the crown, but from Luscia to Dmitri, it was so much more: an heir who could safeguard his own.

She needed an heir of Tiergan, born of pure Boreali descent, whose veins were blessed by lumin, and for the coming generation would shelter the lineage of Thoarne.

To her chagrin, Luscia's glance traveled to the forecastle, taking in the restless man saddling the bench. From under his rolled sleeves, a captive fury coiled the definition of his forearms. Kumo was right; Zaethan was the unsettled mountain cat for which he'd been named. She allowed her eye to linger, if just for a moment, at the smudge smeared across his chiseled cheekbone and the pensive furrows through his cinnamon brow. Out of time, Luscia heard their breaths rushing, like contentious gales thrusting her into a dusty room from another day and hour. Tingling, the hairs of her nape lifted in remembrance. It was deafening.

It was futile.

Sharply, Luscia broke away from the sight of him—of what she could never let be—and stared instead at Marek's rejected kurtfierï.

She considered it fairly, not out of desire but of hope. A verdict such as this could not hinge on the turbulence of desire, the very influence that had once maimed Luscia. Desire couldn't be trusted, no matter to whom it belonged. For better or worse, that force was the beast of mankind, wreaking havoc wherever untamed. Luscia stifled the caged pang in her chest, stilled its trepidation, and sculpted her spirit into order.

If desire was a beast, then she was intended to conquer it.

Reaching over, Luscia untied the banding on the cuff. His exhale froze at her touch. Careful of its drop, she gradually slithered it off Marek under his unwavering watch. The leather was old and pliable and full of heat when she slid the courtship token onto her wrist.

"Ask me again."

Marek's copper lashes spread wide, his highlander irises so much brighter and bluer than the silty river below. Without a look down, his fingers started to move with the utmost tenderness across her skin, each movement diligent, like him, as to not expose an open hand during the restated ritual.

"My eyes to steal, my body to hold," Marek declared lowly and tied the first knot, then glided over the silver beads onto the second. "My heart to seal, my soul to mold." He secured the third and fourth. Palms downward to the deck, he skated a hand beneath and another above her own. "Enjjen anar, Luscia Darragh Tiergan, to *none other* do these things I offer."

The apple of his throat hitched when, intently, Luscia's free hand turned his over, atop the kurtfierï.

She melded her palm against it in acceptance.

Brilliant as the sunrise, a joyous grin broke across his alabaster cheeks, transforming the captaen's entire countenance. Biting her lip, Luscia's fingers squeezed those of her recognized suitor.

"Marek?"

"Wem, Luscia?"

She charted the spindles of stardust shining from his Northern stare. There, hers reflected, and in their gleam, Luscia glimpsed the Dönumn Lux and searched it for what was to come. The realm of Orynthia was in tatters, and the House of Boreal, her refuge. Hidden in Aksel's Keep, Luscia felt the Dönumn's call, commissioning her people to arise from their shadow and embody the light.

Marek Bailefore was good, but one day, he would become great. So too then must she.

Luscia clasped onto his steadfast gaze and the highlands within. There was no turning back. "Take us home."

CHAPTER FOURTY ONE
ZAETHAN

The last time Zaethan rode this river, it had been under a ruse. He recalled the anguish he'd endured, deserting Salma on those shores only to arrange for her rescue, and knowingly mislead Dmitri for it later. Here again, the irony was richer than the fields of Galina, the honey of Agoston, and the marble of Arune combined, how both king and convicted sailed the Yachel with Zaethan now, stowed below the very bench upon which he stewed.

Plucking at the tattered gauze that girded his palms, Zaethan peered past it, down the decking at Jabari. It was the mountain cub's first voyage by ship, and evading sleep, he was exploring its every bauble, to the agitation of the crew. Beneath the shade of the main mast, Jabari shook out a coiling of line with curious vigor, only to squabble with the one-eyed sailor who'd slapped it out of his grasp. Under Zaethan's heavy lids, he watched Takoda rush to translate Jabari's kakk soup, considering it an improvement.

At least he'd stopped testing if the brig would continue to float. The incessant rabbit hops were really getting old.

"Permission to knock out the cub and stash him on a cot?" The bench groaned when Zahra plopped beside Zaethan. Wide-legged, his third slouched against the lip of the forecastle and tapped the bulb of her nose. "Swift and square, yeah? Make him snooze day to night. Just say the word."

Stiffly, Zaethan rolled his sore neck to the side, not in the mood for company. "Why are none of you asleep?"

She crossed her lithe, robust arms and said with a curt sniff, "We sleep when you sleep, Alpha Zà."

"Noble." He snorted sourly. "But I'm the ineligible cross-caste, if you haven't heard. So, really, I'm doing you all favor—weakening myself so one of you yancies can rise in challenge and make it official. Ho'waladim."

Zahra socked him in the arm, knocking it off his propped knee.

"What the Depths!"

"Ano zà!" Swiveled on the bench, his third pointed her forefinger imperiously at Zaethan. "Don't you even speak of it!"

"Shtàka, that's a left hook..." He kneaded the soon-to-be bruise. Impressed and slightly scared, he scooted against the varnished ladder, backing from her tawny glare. "Listen, get stripped of your identity and we'll see what bitter little quips come out of your trap, uni?"

"You weren't stripped of your identity, Alpha Zà." Zahra's tattooed head shook vigorously. "Just the grime that coated it."

Beneath her bristle of growth, his gaze scoured the runes that adorned her normally sleek, carob scalp. Each mark was a declaration to her House. Her personhood. Her belonging.

Despite the slosh of water that stretched beyond the railing, Zaethan's tongue felt like gravel. "Careful," he said in warning through his clenched jaw, screwing it aside. "There's a litany of things you don't know anything about, Zahra."

Portside, Zaethan fixated on the bow wake surging from behind them. It cut across the river, chasing the verdant, Orynthian coastline in the distance. Mantled in trees, low-jutting cliffs contested the barren nothing to the east. Yet in either world, Zaethan was now a stranger.

Rustling his thigh, Zahra's leg hitched over the splintered wood. "Maybe so, Alpha Zà. But I do know who *you* are."

He glanced back as she clutched her ankle, swathed in her blood-smattered gunjas, and leaned closer.

"You were never a Kasim. Ano zà. You have always been your mother's, Zaethan Shà. Son of the mighty Cyra."

Zahra's face lit up at the mention of the woman, the haidren… the myth who lived in Darakaian whisper. "Zaethan Shà is who your pryde believed you to be. Now, with your *real* name," his third stated, "you can make it so."

Her words crashed into Zaethan like the battering waves against the hull.

Overturned, his entire life had been lived within the shadow of a monster. Always found wanting. Always a failure—a blemish in another's face. All those years, he'd poured himself out for a scrap of love from a man he hated, one he'd tried so hard not to emulate yet to please at the same time. Zaethan had suffocated in those dueling nooses for longer than he could remember, almost forgetting how to come up for air. He'd forfeited it to Nyack Kasim instead.

If every gain had a loss, maybe the inverse was just as true.

Zaethan was not the son of Nyack Kasim—but he could be hers.

He could punish the monster by choosing to live for her name, the one Darakai's chief warlord couldn't snuff out like he had her breath. She was gone, but Cyra's essence stained Zwaàlu Ghopar forever. Spilt over their ancestors, his mother's blood had soaked the Kindred Bridge, and though Zaethan's cross-caste offering could never join it in death…

Maybe he could try to in life.

"Even being a Shà," he stated, more to himself than to Zahra, "Darakai has spit me out. It won't ever be as it once was."

"Ano, it won't be the same. It can't because of you, me, all of us…" She answered with passion. The backs of Zahra's long fingers smacked his chest and then her own, over her leather-cased heart. *"Hewe hai Darakai."* She waved toward the wounded pryde warriors, sprawled between the masts. "We are our House, Alpha Zà—not him."

Backlit, the rising sun glinted off the resilience of her Southern skin. Unburdening a sigh through his nose, Zaethan gripped Zahra by the nape and brought their foreheads together in solidarity.

Keeping her there, he dryly retorted. "This doesn't excuse your punching me."

Zahra pushed him off with a wry smirk. His spine thudded into the ladder as his eyes, pinched in much-needed humor, absently settled across the main deck toward the railing on the opposite side.

The corners of his mouth slackened, and he stared like a captive fool. Escaped from her bedraggled plait, pale hairs flew in the wind, lapping the uncanny angles of Luscia's face. Battle rags hugged her strong, shapely figure. Zaethan's lungs strained under the heaviness of a boulder. He scorned the feeling, unable to blink.

Silhouetted by dawn, she was the most arresting eclipse he'd ever seen.

Her outline stepped nearer to her Captaen Bailefore, with whom she spoke. Zaethan squinted as the shadowman tied something to her wrist, but rather than moving away, the man closed in, hedging his hands around hers. Suddenly, the boulder pressing Zaethan's chest became a rockfall, slamming into him when he observed Luscia flip the captaen's hand over and join them together. Though he did not know what it meant, in his gut, he knew it was significant.

And he cursed himself for even caring.

"We heard what you called her in the gorge..."

Zaethan jerked his chin aside, toward Jabari's unsuccessful attempts to climb the rigging, and scoffed at Zahra. "I called her Maji'maia, like Kumo and the rest."

"Usually, uni, but that is not what you said."

"Slip of the tongue," he answered gratingly, burying the unforgettable fusion of trust and fear Luscia had cradled in her irregular eyes that night—when they'd shone just for him.

"Our oldest story is a heartache," Zahra delicately said to his rigid posture. "But it's not Owàa's shackle or his clipped wing that prevents him from being with his moon... Jwona is cruel, Zaeth. It's the fate of the world that will always keep them apart."

With flared cheeks, he swung toward her on the bench. His third never dropped titles. Concern laced her thin brows in the most angering way.

Bitingly, Zaethan said from the pit in his throat, "I said it was a *slip of the tongue*, yeye qondai?"

Zahra searched him and, submitting, nodded. "Uni zà, Alpha Zà."

"Go to bed, Zahra. That's an order."

He shoved off the crude seat. Zaethan directed his focus toward the hatchway, not allowing it to waver and slide portside to the Boreali haidren or her captaen.

Looking at her was his shackle. And he'd seen enough.

It was stuffy, wedging between the crammed hammocks strung about the orlop. All of them occupied, they teetered like chimes in the ship's commanding sway. He scanned the sleepers, having not spied Kumo for hours, but figured that was probably due to his notoriously weak stomach. Zaethan didn't try to find him either. He'd no desire to swim in his beta's breakfast.

The planks seemed to roll beneath him. He tripped on a discarded boot, disrupting an ensemble of snores. The beams overhead groused under the pendulous stress of seamen and warriors alike. Exhaustion was an equalizer of men, and Zaethan's weary legs were succumbing to it with every aftward step across the pasture of bedding, to the dim passageway where he'd been told Dmitri had retired.

After ducking under the screaky lanternlight, Zaethan paused when he got there. In the corner of the deck, huddled against the bulkhead, were a pair of drained haidrens. Out the higher hammock, Hachiro's empty palm dangled past the slung linen toward Ira below.

Zaethan bent to the floorboards and picked up his fallen journal. Rising from the crouch, he hesitated. Knees curled into his rumpled vest, Ira hugged the enchained snuff canister with both hands, like it were a talisman protecting him from the darkness.

They didn't belong on this boat, hidden in filth and hardship. The yancy nor Sayuri's brother were prepared for any of this.

Neither was Zaethan.

He dusted off Hachiro's journal and, as not to disturb him, meticulously tucked it back into the shoto'shi's unconscious care.

Entering the passageway, he located the door to the snug cabin Takoda had mentioned. Zaethan unhooked one of the rusty lamps and gingerly let himself inside. A sliver of day peeked through a rip in the drape, drawn over the porthole. The beam shot through the dusty particles and descended on a slumbering king, sprawled across one of two built-in bunks.

Dmitri's cane trundled back and forth under the bedframe. Hushedly, Zaethan hung the creaky oil lamp on a peg and caught the byrnnzite walking stick and buttressed it against a cluttered shelf with a dry grin, unsure why his friend cherished the gaudy thing so much. Perhaps that the was the real miracle—it too had survived Khmer.

He slipped off his boots with painstaking slowness and crawled into the empty bunk. The mattress was lumpy, but with a groan, Zaethan's body sank into it nonetheless. Finally, he let his lids fall.

"You gave me a real fright back there, you know."

As if lugging a carcass, Zaethan's head weakly twisted on the hard pillow. Across the narrow gap, Dmitri blinked sluggishly behind his disheveled hair.

"I didn't mean to wake you," he said to him meekly.

Zaethan's ruined breeches creased when he rolled onto his side, having only been able to find an unsoiled shirt when rummaging through the sick bay. His friend's watch narrowed, limp but quizzical.

"Is that Boreali sheepskin you're wearing?"

"To my regret," Zaethan grumbled.

"Comfortable?"

"Impeccably."

"That's something to look to forward to then, I suppose," Dmitri replied in a hoarse chuckle. On his back, he cleared his throat, but it ended with a cough.

Zaethan studied Dmitri's haggard pallor, mashed into the weave of the scraggy blanketing. The dark circles, the lean features... Those were characteristic to the young king, as he rarely slept and, in possession of a compelling stack of papers, often forgot to eat as well. However, the past fortnight had taken its toll, deepening the hollow where Dmitri's dimple should have emerged.

"You look like that smothered shtàka they sell on a stick in Marke-town," Zaethan said bluntly. "Do you feel all right?"

"I'm fine." His friend's listless eyes rolled when he skeptically arched a brow. "Really, Zaeth. There're far more pressing matters to fret over than me."

"Never," Zaethan answered, though he understood the attitude, having learned what he had during those final hours in Khmer. He blew out a hesitant gust. "Dmitri. I need to tell you something about your father. Wekesa..." He faltered, uncertain how to phrase such a horrible revelation. "Wekesa admitted he was the one who poisoned Salma's shipment—at the chief warlord's command."

Dmitri pinned his lips together and, sniffing, nodded into the dingy pillow. "Thank you, brother, for putting the question out of my mind once and for all."

In the dim lighting, a single tear trailed past the bridge of Dmitri's aristocratic nose. Zaethan glanced down at the straw poking out of his mattress where he fiddled with it.

"That wasn't all the bastard shared before he died," he said, damming a flood of clashing emotions. "My mother didn't pass in labor... Nyack Kasim killed her too."

Dmitri's head lifted abruptly. "Zaeth, that's—"

"I get what he stole from her, but why keep me?" His voiced cracked in raw honesty. "Why did he let me live, and under the guise as his own? It wasn't for love, *ano zà*..." Zaethan laughed darkly and harsh. "So what was it for then?"

Zaethan chucked a hunk of straw on the floor and rubbed his forehead gruffly. He listened to Dmitri adjust on the bunk, and he peered up through the fringe of his locs when his friend eventually replied.

"I'd think it rather obvious," his friend stated ruefully. "Nothing manipulates the masses like a child. Your aunt would have inherited her sister's haidrenship, so Nyack needed her son to sit at the one table he couldn't." Lethargically, Dmitri's knuckles slid under his jaw. "The chieftains gave him that seat because of you, Zaeth—not for who he pretended you were but for who you really are."

At that, Zaethan lowered back onto the mattress. His tired stare bored into the rafters above. There was so much power in a lie.

But even more when it hinged on the truth.

"We're not the men we imagined we'd become, are we?"

He looked over in Dmitri's silence, discovering a sorrowful smile sloping his cracked lips, and without a sound, they reluctantly mouthed *no*.

What fools they had once been. Now they were grown and crammed in a musty cabin, fleeing to Boreal on a stolen ship. This life was nothing like they'd dreamed. Dmitri's reign had nearly destroyed him when it'd only just begun. King and cross-caste, they stared at each other as if they were mere boys, hiding beneath a royal tapestry from Eugenio's wrath.

Perhaps in the ways that mattered, they still were.

Zaethan heard his friend gulp against the bedding. "Whoever you decide to become, I will champion that man," Dmitri whispered, "just as you've always championed me."

Drowsily and with hardly any strength, he reached toward Zaethan across the grimy chasm. His wrist fell into the faint sunbeam. Faded and timeworn, a red string stared up at Zaethan expectantly.

Dmitri's lids faltered when Zaethan stretched out and took hold of his friend's slim forearm. Yet even surrendering to his fear of sleep, the young king's fingertips tightened around the much brighter, newer threading tied about Zaethan's wrist. In seconds, his eyes closed too, and he followed Dmitri into oblivion.

Behind the blackness, he finally sensed his friend's grip giving out.

But his never did. And it never would.

EPILOGUE

Concealed, the figure crept beneath the loading platform. His mangled shoulder skated the raw bark of a log pillar, plucking his tattered cloak as he spied across the rippling expanse toward the brig and the young man being towed through its churn to safety.

With a shriek, Amaranth dove from her circle in the skies as he watched the stolen ship bob in the starlight under its new command. Instinctively and without pause, he offered her his perch. The hawk's talons wrapped around the arm of his ratty coat, one he did need but hadn't for some time. The figure no longer suffered the chill of winter, nor midsummer's blister. But even now, he sensed the wiry fibers of the coat scratching his scabs, and in that human sensation, he clung to the want to wear it still.

The figure waited beneath the platform patiently, despite the threat of a looming dawn, until Cyra's son was finally hauled aboard and heaved out of sight. A wave of sails unfurled over his rescuers as the ship captured the wind and harnessed its push down the Yachel, an entire generation of ascendancy smuggled in its belly like any other illicit good.

Unlike the cross-caste heir, he'd been prevented from securing a way onto the brig, unable to journey alongside Alora's niece from the shadows toward the refuge she surely sought. After the regiment's insurgence, the figure doubted the fledgling Quadren would return to Bastiion in response to a collaborated revolt with the House of Darakai. Their king had but one choice across Lake Vasil: northward, to the highland sanctuary of things unseen.

It was a sanctuary that might accept a king, but it would reject his keepers, for the light of Boreal was not a gift to all but only to some.

It was that lesson the figure had burned into his decaying flesh, the history that haunted his bones... the blood of another that sustained the half life he never should be living.

The Quadren of Dmitri Korbin Thoarne would soon discover a lesson of their own, the moment they stepped off that ship and onto an awakened land. A land that contradicted every other.

Not all mysteries were invisible. And in a matter of weeks, their ordinary eyes would be tormented for it.

From the isolation of his hood, the figure scrutinized the sparse vessels moored to the docks. None were large enough to board in secret—or at least to remain that way until the following nightfall. He'd have to wait for sunset to secure a viable ship he could take as far as Port Tadeas, as no one went farther, then trek the rest of the way by foot to Alora's niece. The Orynthian realm was being unraveled, stitch by stitch, at its seams. Even within the shelter of that fortified brig, the Quadren was not out of peril yet.

As his mistress often said, the game of politics was a masquerade. No player could be trusted.

With his pursuit thwarted, the figure adjusted beneath his weathered shroud. Amaranth ruffled her Pilarese feathers, their gloss mauver than lilac amid the gloom. Pulling the pool of fabric around his scraped-up legs, the figure turned back toward Khmer and the unburied graveyard on her doorstep.

Dozens of bodies were strewn across the wharf, forming a moat of refuse between the row of blacked-out windows and the waterfront. The air was soundless and fragrant of iron. At the scent, the figure wiped the fresh stickiness off his crusted chin, reopening a sore with the effort, as he recalled his role in their many deaths all too well.

There came a splash at his back—too big for any fish.

Ripping the worn wool, Amaranth tore from the figure's forearm, and he whirled in place. Orbiting above, she cawed at a disturbance within the slapping waves, just beyond the edge of the abandoned dock. Hesitant, he slunk forward, halting when a whiff of rot arrested his chapped nostrils, scenting the wrongness before he sighted it.

Out of the deep, an onyx hand blasted from the waters and slammed onto the planks.

The figure lowered into a predatory crouch, watching when the other came down and sprawled beside it.

A boulder of muscle hoisted onto itself in sinister resurrection. First came a head, crooked at an unnatural angle, dripping water from its thick, swollen braids. Then the river gushed off the broad shelf of its shoulders and streamed down the trough of a mangled torso, draining onto the wood. With a guttural snarl, a sodden boot came next. As a darkened tide, the thing erected onto its feet and raised its warped head as if it were still a man, yet it wasn't and would never be again.

Gloved, the figure's fingertips strained against the cobblestone as the creature pinned him through the darkness. Ever so faint but just as furious, an unmistakable ruddy glow emitted from its depraved eyes.

An anticipatory ache shot through the figure's gums, and he sprung.

Not far into its transformation, the creature caught him by nails, not claws, when the figure barreled into a puddle of its butchered tissue, driving it by its injured abdomen down the dock. The wounds were fresh, contending the sourness of the black blood oozing over the band of its Darakaian garb. Tainted plasma squelched his brow; this creature had only begun to decompose.

It was newly from its maker.

The figure sank his incisors into its brawny thigh, snapping the sinew, and in a savage leap, he grappled onto the slab of its back. Bucking under his hold, the creature lashed at him in a feral dance. It was then the figure recognized the snakelike sutures between his legs, winding toward its shoulders. This was the alpha who'd betrayed them all.

Ankles hooked, he ruthlessly seized it over the ears. Saliva gushed over the figure's lips when in a gargled growl, the mutated traitor attempted to speak. But it couldn't. Its vocal cords had been severed, and within an inch, so had its vertebrae.

Adrenaline ruptured through his extremities. Roaring, the figure squeezed the scarred skull and, in a single merciless screw, snapped it from the spine.

He descended the Darakaian's frame as it buckled onto the planks.

Fueled by a fury both mortal and monstrous, the figure flipped the head over in his gloved palms. When he did, his thumb coasted a mark of manmade ridges branded right below the ear.

Evil frosted his spine as he stared into the symbol stamped into the Darakaian's hide, a symbol he'd not seen for twenty years.

Trembling, the figure dropped the skull to the ground, but it flaked into cinders before it ever hit the wood. His hood fell backward when his knees plummeted to the planks where the flameless ash sifted into the night, as if it'd never been.

Pounding, the figure heard the dust beat from his own ageless heart.

Not voicing it in over a decade, he croaked in his native tongue as a fresh horror rattled the shards of his soul, as he pled against the inconceivable. That symbol was damned, and so were the hands from which it came. Etched in the dangers of desperation, that symbol should have died with him.

For it was he who had first drawn it.

And now, someone else was drawing it too.

The figure hardly felt Amaranth roost on his shoulder, her touch forgiving and constant. Torment betrayed his lashless eyes as he winced at the dawn, ready to let it burn him up—to exhaust the wickedness that had hunted him till morning.

But if he were to waste away, there would be no one left to face the cataclysm his transgressions had birthed. The figure looked out at the ship disappearing into the splintering of sun, knowing he could not follow it.

Alora's promise was a cruel fiction. It was far too late for him. Monsters did not hope for redemption. Because that's who he really was—the monster in their story. It was an ardent and wicked unending tale, which had scourged the past but was plaguing the future.

The figure did not deserve to hope.

But *she* did.

Perhaps redemption was still possible—for her—the one he loved beyond undeath.

Dread and shame tortured his legs when slowly, he stood. His withered flesh stung, and under dawn's threat, the figure tugged his hood over the patches of hair, where it belonged. Taking a pained step, he touched Amaranth's feet, readying her to fly.

Not to Boreal. Not to Alora. The figure recoiled from the dock, and already condemned, he braved the unthinkable and headed west.

He slunk farther into his shadows, back to where it all began.

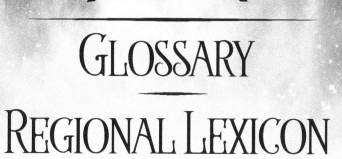

Glossary

Regional Lexicon

Visit **www.TheHaidrenLegacy.com/Glossary** to access digital references on your mobile device.

For a comprehensive list of terms, please consult the Master List succeeding this Regional Lexicon.

SCAN ME

ORYNTHIA
⫸ UNIVERSAL ⫷

al'Haidren: /al-Hay-dren/ The next representative in line to sit on the royal heir's Quadren, typically the closest blood relative from the generation behind the current haidren

Breakaway: Member of the outer Houses who chooses to live in Unitarian lands, typically in Bastiion proper

Cross-caste: One of split lineage; an individual born of two separate Houses

Ethnicam: The assembly or association of all four Orynthian Houses

Forgotten Wars: The unknown events that led to the old world's destruction

Hagarh: /HAY-gar/ Wetlands opposite the Mirajii Forest, inhabited by nomadic peoples

Haidren: /HAY-dren/ A legal, judicial, and social representative on behalf of his or her corresponding House, seated on the current ruler's Quadren

House: The collection of a people and their preserved, self-governed territory within Orynthian borders, though still beholden to the throne

Interim Haidren: The next familial relation to the Haidren, though sometimes elected by the House, put in place when the rightful Haidren is deceased or incapacitated

Orynthia: /OR-in-thee-Uh/ Central kingdom comprised of four Houses; governed by the royal line of Thoarne and the Ethnicam

Outer Houses: Self-governed Houses on the outskirts of the Unitarian lands

Quadren: The committee of advisors encircling each Orynthian ruler, consisting of one haidren from each House

The Wastes: A barren, uninhabitable wasteland on the eastern side of the Yachel River

War-taint: Residual, toxic poisoning as a result of the Forgotten Wars

War-tainted: An individual, animal, or land harboring the symptoms of war-taint

Witchiron: Najjani weaponry (slang)

HOUSE OF BASTIION
⫸LOWLANDS & PLAINS⫷

Aurus: /AUHR-ruhs/ Gold coin of Bastiion origin; adopted by all Houses

Bastiion: /BAHS-tee-on/ Crown city of Orynthia

Byrnnzite: /BERN-zite/ An organic composite of petrified ash, wood, and Old-World metallics

Crupas: /CROO-pahs/ Copper coin of Bastiion origin; adopted by all Houses

Drifting Bazaar: Merchant market of floating stalls along the bank of the Thoarne Bay

Dromas: /DROH-mahs/ Silver coin of Bastiion origin; adopted by all Houses

Inner Proper: Walled and fortified inner city of Bastiion encompassing the palace, Marketown, upper and lower-class districts

Marketown: Mass market within the streets of Bastiion's inner proper

Outer Proper: Royal land encircled by the noble provinces; the outskirts of the city of Bastiion

Pipe Marrow: A highly pungent opiate often smoked in the tents of Marketown

Province: Land bestowed to the heads of the nobility and their heirs

Vàssa Ship: /Vaah-sa/ Leisure vessel

The Veiled Lady: Popular tavern and night den in Marketown owned by Salma Nabhu

Unitarian: Primary language spoken in the House of Bastiion and the Unitarian lands; general mixture of ancient languages, refined over time

Unitarians: Orynthian bloodline comprised from a blended ancestry from centuries past

Yancy: /Yan-see/ Universal slang for any wealthy Unitarians; the nobility

UNITARIAN

Shtàka: /ShTAH-kuh/ Shit (slang)

Y'siti: /Yuh-ZEE-tee/ Filthy ice-witch (derogatory slang)

HOUSE OF BOREAL
⇛HIGHLAND PENINSULA⇚

Aniell: /AHn-ee-eL/ High One; sole deity of Boreal

Bomaerod: /BOH-may-rahD/ Vented staff utilized by the najjan; typically made of bone and/or wood; used to created audible reference points in a space while training

Boreali: /Boar-eell-ee/ Primary language spoken in the House of Boreal; term for the people of Boreal

Clann: Ruling leader of the clans inhabiting the Boreal peninsula

Clann Darragh: /Klan Dahw-rah/ High leader of the Boreali clans; named as Boreal's governing mighty oak

Clan Elder: Elected leader of a Boreali clan

Consort Daggers: A set of short, curved luxiron daggers; ornate in design

Crescent Wraiths: A set of long, arced luxiron blades used in unison; gripped at the center; serrated or scooped at the ends

Feidierdanns: /Fee-DYER-dons/ A braided whip used to increase the agility of footwork in najjani training

Isle of Viridis: /eyeL of Ver-EE-dees/ A remote island off the coast of Boreal; fortress where najjani train

Klödjen: /klode-Gen/ A wooden globe surrounded by a horizontal ring wide enough to hold a man; used in elementary training by the najjan

Kuerre: /Koo-AIR/ Luxiron backsword; curved blade

Kurtfierï: /Kert-FYE-ree/ Courtship token; an article of the father's clothing or dress, typically worn by the suited

Linsilk: Boreali fabric made of silk harvested from spiders around the banks of the Dönumn

Lumin: /Loo-men/ Sacred light energy native to the Boreali highlands

Lumilore: /Loo-meh-Lore/ Lux-stone; lumin-infused stone gathered near the banks of the Dönumn

Luxiron: Specialized najjani iron, forged in undiluted lumin; warm to the touch, prismatic in color, corrosive in nature, and lightweight; trade restricted

Luxsmith: A najjani smithy, dedicated to the creation of Luxiron (i.e., luxcrafting)

Lycran: /LIE-kran/ Orallach fox-wolf (wolx) hybrid; genes enhanced by war-taint

Najjan: /Nah-zhahn/ Elusive sect of the warrior faction; elite Boreali warrior(s)

Orallach Mountains: /Orr-uh-laK/ Range of frigid mountains; uninhabited

Radials: Hidden luxiron blades; worn as three-fingered rings; fans open when triggered

Roüwen: /Roe-OO-wen/ The village-fortress; capital of Boreal

Solrahs: /SOL-rahs/ Half-moon shaped septum piece made of luxiron; worn by the haidrens to Boreal

Tiergan: /TARE-ghan/ Sacred bloodline of the haidrens to Boreal; direct descendants of Tiergan

Wreath of Wisdom: The ceremonial headdress passed from predecessor to successor during the haidren's Seating ceremony

BOREALI

Allöh: /AH-loe/ *May peace convene with you* (informal greeting)

Allöh'jomn'yeh: /AH-loe zhoM-yay/ *May peace convene with you* (formal greeting)

Ana'Brödre: /Ahna-Broe-DRuh/ *Great Brother(s)*

Ana'Innöx: /Ahna-ee-NOCKS/ *Great Harvest*

Ana'Mere: /Ahna-Mare/ *Great Mother*

Ana'Sere: /Ahna-Sare/ *Great Sister(s)*

Aurynth: /Aur-rinth/ *Eternal resting place; heaven*

Bolaeva: /Bo-LAY-vah/ *Please*

Dönumn Lux: /Doe-nuM Lux/ *Gift of Light*

Eiide Corün: /Eye-dee-kor-OOn/ *Wreath of Wisdom*

Enjjen anar: /En-zhen ah-nar/ *To none other*

Fappa: /Fah-puh/ *Daddy*

Heh'ta: /HEH-tuh/ *Stay; halt*

Lu'Lycran: /Loo LIE-cran/ *Little Lycran* (nickname)

Mamu: /Mah-Moo/ *Mommy; Mama*

Meh fyreon: /Meh Feer-ee-on/ *I'm sorry; I apologize*

Meh'dajjeni Dönumn, weh'dajjeni Lux: /Meh Dah-zhen-ee Doe-nuM, weh Dah-zhen-ee Lux/ *My strength in the Gift, our strength for the Light*

Niit: /Neet/ *No*

Rul'Aniell: /Rool-AHn-ee-eL/ *In and to Aniell*

Rul'Lothadim Aniell: /Rool-Loth-uh-dim AHn-ee-eL/ *All Glory in and to Aniell* (formal declaration)

Se'lah Aurynth: /se-Lah Aur-rinth/ *Until the shores of Aurynth*

Tadöm: /tah-Dome/ *Thank you*

Tredae'Aurynth: /Tred-AYE Aur-rinth/ *Walk in Aurynth* (parting)

Waedfrel: /Wade-frell/ *Good; great; exemplary*

Wem: /whem/ *Yes*

Yeh'maelim: /Yeh-may-lim/ *Welcome to you*

Ykah lö: /Eye-kuh Loe/ *What; huh; come again*

HOUSE OF DARAKAI
⟫⟫SOUTHERN MOUNTAINS & LOWLANDS⟪⟪

Alpha: Leader of a regional pryde of militia

Alpha Zà: Leader of the militia prydes

Andwele: /An-DWEE-lee/ Native language of Darakai

Andwele Mountains: Mountain range forming the western border of Darakai, separating it from Razôuel and Mworra

Arrowball: Darakaian field game consisting of three baskets, two archers, and ladle-like sticks

Beta: Second to the pryde alpha

Beta Warlord: Official second to the chief warlord; second to a Darakaian tribal chieftain

Bwoloa: /Beh-WOE-lo-ah/ Golden liqueur imported from Darakai; made of fermented grain and citrus blossoms

Byumbé: /Beh-YOOM-bay/ Octagonal daub and rock dwellings built into the City Nest

City Nest: Soaring city carved into the towering, rounded cliffsides of the Faraji canyon

Chief Warlord: House leader of all native tribes and minor chiefs, appointed by the Darakaian War Council

Commander of the Orynthian Armies: Supreme military leader over the united Orynthian realm, of Darakaian descent, appointed by the king

Cub: kid (slang)

Darts and Dice: A Darakaian game coupling a set of dice, a hung board, and a blowpipe; adopted by gambling houses in Bastiion

Faraji: /Fah-rah-zhee/ Capital of Darakai; fortified mountain city; location of War Council and tribal leaders

Gunjas: /Goon-Juh/ Loose-fitting pants; wrapped at the waist and ankles; worn for drills and combat

Halona: /Hah-LOE-nuh/ Major tribe in the foothills of the Andwele Mountains

Holiday of Hands: Annual Darakaian holiday wherein tribes claim one another with their handprints

Kindred Bridge: Historic natural stone bridge stained by the blood of ancestors past

Kopar: /Koh-PAR/ Sickle sword carried by the Darakaian military

Mantle of the Fallen: Historic cape constructed of ancient, bloodstained arrowheads; typically worn by the haidren to Darakai or the chief warlord

Pammu: /PAH-moo/ Fermented pam sap; brewed with beetles in the base of the bottle

Pryde: Localized group of Darakaian militia

Yowekao: /Yow-uh-KAY-oh/ Remote mountain tribe within the Andwele Mountains

ANDWELE

Ahoté: /Ah-HO-tay/ *Restless Bobcat* (nickname)

Àla'maia: /Ah-lah MY-ah/ *The Moon* (name)

Ano: /Ah-noe/ *No*

Ano'puwàa dim'hakku, yona alpha ni ràtomdai: /ah-noe-POO-ah dim-hah-koo YOHN-uh Al-fuh nee rah-tohm-dye/ *Unworthy and wanting, an alpha's blood will be claimed*

Ano zà: /Ah-noe Zah/ *No* (final; absolute)

Chombà ano'ruko yon namàa tswé: /Chom-buh ah-noe-roo-koh yohn nah-MAH tet-sway/ *The pot is not named by the tool that shapes it*

Doru: /DOH-roo/ *Stop; wait; pause*

Fàkkadim'Chalim: /Fah-kuh-dim-Chah-lim/ *Holiday of Hands*

Fhàdda: /Fah-duh/ *Dad* (informal)

Gaibai: /Guy-buy/ *Story-dance*

Hérumaa: /Hare-oo-mah/ *Mercy*

Hewe hai Darakai: /Hay-way hi Dare-uh-kye/ *We are Darakai*

Hewe ràtomdai na hewe: /Hay-way rah-tohm-dye nah hay-way/ *We claim us*

Ho'waladim: /Hoe-wall-a-dim/ *As is due to you* (in place of "you're welcome")

Jaha: /Jah-Hah/ *Pretty thing*

Jwona rapiki: /Jeh-wahn-uh rah-pee-kee/ *Fate writer*

Kàchà kocho: /Kah-chah Koe-cho/ *This or that; so-so; either*

Kakk: /Kak/ *Babble; ramblings; nonsense*

Kakka-shtàka: /Kak-uh ShTAH-kuh/ *Dumb; shitty thing; useless* (slang)

Kwihila rapiki mu jwona: /Kwih-hee-luh rah-pee-kee moo Jeh-wahn-uh/ *Victory writes over fate*

Làtoh Ché: /la-TOH Chay/ *The City Nest*

Maji'maia: /Mah-zhee MY-ah/ *Witchy-Moon* (nickname); full moon

Mhàdda: /Mah-duh/ *Mom* (informal)

Motumbha: /Moh-TUM-buh/ *Arrowball*

Na huwàa tàkom lai na huwàa: /Nah hoo-ah tah-KOM lie nah hoo-ah/ *It takes a hound to hunt a hound*

Ni yeye ràtomdai na wewe: /Nee yay-yay rah-tohm-dye nah way-way/ *Do you claim rights to him/her/them/it*

Owàa: /Oh-WAH/ *The Sun* (name)

Owàamo: /Oh-WAH-moe/ *The Sun greets you* (greeting)

Papyon: /Pap-ee-on/ *Love; sex* (slang)

Qondai: /Kon-Die/ *To understand; to know*

Rhàana ne'Etswégo: /RAH-na neh-et-SWAY-go/ *Mantle of the Fallen*

Rhaolé: /Ray-OH-lay/ *Hurry; speed up*

Rhaolé ono: /Ray-OH-lay OH-no/ *Hurry faster*

Shàla'maiamo: /Sha-lah my-AH-moe/ *The Moon watch you* (farewell)

Shamàli: /Sha-mah-lee/ *If you see fit* (in place of "please")

Shumabin: /SHOO-muh-bin/ *Paladin's aloe*

Uni: /Oo-nee/ *Yes*

Uni zà: /Oo-nee Zah/ *Yes* (final; absolute)

Yaya: /Yah-Yah/ *Honey; an attractive woman* (slang)

Zullee: /Zool-lee/ *Accepted with honor* (in place of "thank you")

Zwaàlu Ghopar: /Zwah-loo goh-PAR/ *Kindred Bridge*

HOUSE OF PILAR
⟫⟫EASTERN COAST⟪⟪

Chancellor: Head of the Pilarese Shoto Collective

Gakoshū: /Gah-koh-shoo/ City of Learning

Lempeii: /Lem-PAY/ Port city; station of the Orynthian navy

Shoto: /ShOH-toe/ A philosopher or scholar; statesman dedicated to the pursuit of learning

Shoto'shi: /ShOH-toe-shee/ A shoto acolyte; training in the ways of the Collective

Shoto Collective: Pilarese congress of scholars and politicians

Shoto Prime: Senior leader within the Shoto Collective

PILARESE

Kiataki: /Kee-uh-ta-kee/ *Sword-keeper*

Pyō chakrit: /Pie-oh cha-KREET/ *Wisdom affirmed* (statement of accord)

Pyō jien: /Pie-oh JYEN/ *Knowledge accepted* (statement of accord)

GLOSSARY

MASTER LIST OF TERMS

Ahoté *Darakai-Andwele* /Ah-HO-tay/ Restless Bobcat (nickname)

Àla'maia *Darakai-Andwele* /Ah-lah MY-ah/ The Moon (name)

al'Haidren *Orynthia-Unitarian* /al-Hay-dren/ The next representative in line to sit on the royal heir's Quadren, typically the closest blood relative from the generation behind the current haidren

Allöh *Boreal-Boreali* /AH-loe/ May peace convene with you (informal greeting)

Allöh'jomn'yeh *Boreal-Boreali* /AH-loe zhoM-yay/ May peace convene with you (formal greeting)

Alpha *Darakai-Andwele* Leader of a regional pryde of militia

Alpha Zà *Darakai-Andwele* Leader of the militia prydes

Ana'Brödre *Boreal-Boreali* /Ahna-Broe-DRuh/ Great Brother(s)

Ana'Innöx: *Boreal-Boreali* /Ahna-ee-NOCKS/ Great Harvest

Ana'Mere: *Boreal-Boreali* /Ahna-Mare/ Great Mother

Ana'Sere: *Boreal-Boreali* /Ahna-Sare/ Great Sister(s)

Andwele *Darakai* /An-DWEE-lee/ Native language of Darakai

Andwele Mountains *Darakai* Mountain range forming the western border of Darakai, separating it from Razôuel and Mworra

Aniell *Boreal-Boreali* /AHn-ee-eL/ High One; sole deity of Boreal

Ano *Darakai-Andwele* /Ah-noe/ No

Ano'puwàa dim'hakku, yona alpha ni ràtomdai *Darakai-Andwele* / ah-noe-POO-ah dim-hah-koo YOHN-uh Al-fuh nee rah-tohm-dye/ Unworthy and wanting, an alpha's blood will be claimed

Ano zà *Darakai-Andwele* /Ah-noe Zah/ No (final; absolute)

Arrowball *Darakai* Darakaian field game consisting of three baskets, two archers, and ladle-like sticks

Aurus *Bastiion-Unitarian* /AUHR-ruhs/ Gold coin of Bastiion origin; adopted by all Houses

Aurynth *Boreal-Boreali* /Aur-rinth/ Eternal resting place; heaven

Bastiion *Bastiion* /BAHS-tee-on/ Crown city of Orynthia

Beta *Darakai* Second to the pryde alpha

Beta Warlord *Darakai* Official second to the chief warlord; second to a Darakaian tribal chieftain

Bolaeva *Boreal-Boreali* /Bo-LAY-vah/ Please

Bomaerod *Boreal-Boreali* /BOH-may-rahD/ Vented staff utilized by the najjan; typically made of bone and/or wood; used to created audible reference points in a space while training

Boreali *Boreal* /Boar-eell-ee/ Primary language spoken in the House of Boreal; term for the people of Boreal

Breakaway *Orynthia* Member of the outer Houses who chooses to live in Unitarian lands, typically in Bastiion proper

Bwoloa *Darakai-Andwele* /Beh-WOE-lo-ah/ Golden liqueur imported from Darakai; made of fermented grain and citrus blossoms

Byrnnzite *Bastiion-Unitarian* /BERN-zite/ An organic composite of petrified ash, wood, and Old-World metallics

Byumbé *Darakai-Andwele* /Beh-YOOM-bay/ Octagonal daub and rock dwellings built into the City Nest

Clann *Boreal* Ruling leader of the clans inhabiting the Boreal peninsula

Clann Darragh *Boreal-Boreali* /Klan Dahw-rah/ High leader of the Boreali clans; named as Boreal's governing mighty oak

Clan Elder *Boreal* Elected leader of a Boreali clan

Chancellor *Pilar* Head of the Pilarese Shoto Collective

Chief Warlord *Darakai* House leader of all native tribes and minor chiefs, appointed by the Darakaian War Council

City Nest *Darakai* Soaring city carved into the towering, rounded cliffsides of the Faraji canyon

Commander of the Orynthian Armies *Darakai* Supreme military leader over the united Orynthian realm, of Darakaian descent, appointed by the king

Consort Daggers *Boreal* A set of short, curved luxiron daggers; ornate in design

Cross-caste *Orynthia* One of split lineage; an individual born of two separate Houses

Crupas *Bastiion-Unitarian* /CROO-pahs/ Copper coin of Bastiion origin; adopted by all Houses

Crescent Wraiths *Boreal* A set of long, arced luxiron blades used in unison; gripped at the center; serrated or scooped at the ends

Cub *Darakai* kid (slang)

Darts and Dice *Darakai* A Darakaian game coupling a set of dice, a hung board, and a blowpipe; adopted by gambling houses in Bastiion

Dönumn Lux *Boreal-Boreali* /Doe-nuM Lux/ Gift of Light

Doru *Darakai-Andwele* /DOH-roo/ Stop; wait; pause

Drifting Bazaar *Bastiion* Merchant market of floating stalls along the bank of the Thoarne Bay

Dromas *Bastiion-Unitarian* /DROH-mahs/ Silver coin of Bastiion origin; adopted by all Houses

Eiide Corün *Boreal-Boreali* /Eye-dee-kor-OOn/ Wreath of Wisdom

Enjjen anar *Boreal-Boreali* /En-zhen ah-nar/ To none other

Ethnicam *Orynthia* The term used when referring to the assembly or association of all four Orynthian Houses

Fàkkadim'Chalim *Darakai-Andwele* /Fah-kuh-dim-Chah-lim/ Holiday of Hands

Fappa *Boreal-Boreali* /Fah-puh/ Daddy

Faraji *Darakai* /Fah-rah-zhee/ Capital of Darakai; fortified mountain city; location of War Council and tribal leaders

Feidierdanns *Boreal-Boreali* /Fee-DYER-dons/ A braided whip used to increase the agility of footwork in najjani training

Fhàdda *Darakai-Andwele* /Fah-duh/ Dad (informal)

Forgotten Wars *Orynthia* The unknown events that led to the old world's destruction

Gakoshū *Pilar-Pilarese* /Gah-koh-shoo/ City of Learning

Gaibai *Darakai-Andwele* /Guy-buy/ Story-dance

Gunjas *Darakai* /Goon-Juh/ Loose-fitting pants; wrapped at the waist and ankles; worn for drills and combat

Halona *Darakai* /Hah-LOE-nuh/ Major tribe in the foothills of the Andwele Mountains

Hagarh *Orynthia* /HAY-gar/ Wetlands opposite the Mirajii Forest, inhabited by nomadic peoples

Haidren *Orynthia-Unitarian* /HAY-dren/ A legal, judicial, and social representative on behalf of his or her corresponding House, seated on the current ruler's Quadren

Heh'ta *Boreal-Boreali* /HEH-tuh/ Stay; halt

Hérumaa *Darakai-Andwele* /Hare-oo-mah/ Mercy

Hewe hai Darakai *Darakai-Andwele* /Hay-way hi Dare-uh-kye/ We are Darakai

Hewe ràtomdai na hewe *Darakai-Andwele* /Hay-way rah-tohm-dye nah hay-way/ We claim us

Holiday of Hands *Darakai* Annual Darakaian holiday wherein tribes claim one another with their handprints

House *Orynthia* The collection of a people and their preserved, self-governed territory within Orynthian borders, though still beholden to the throne

Ho'waladim *Darakai-Andwele* /Hoe-wall-a-dim/ As is due to you (in place of "you're welcome")

Inner Proper *Bastiion* Walled and fortified inner city of Bastiion encompassing the palace, Marketown, upper and lower-class districts

Interim Haidren *Orynthia* The next familial relation to the Haidren, though sometimes elected by the House, put in place when the rightful Haidren is deceased or incapacitated

Isle of Viridis *Boreal* /eyeL of Ver-EE-dees/ A remote island off the coast of Boreal; fortress where najjan train

Jaha *Darakai-Andwele* /Jah-Hah/ Pretty thing

Jwona rapiki *Darakai-Andwele* /Jeh-wahn-uh rah-pee-kee/ Fate writer

Kàchà kocho *Darakai-Andwele* /Kah-chah Koe-cho/ This or that; so-so; either

Kakk *Darakai-Andwele* /Kak/ Babble; ramblings; nonsense

Kakka-shtàka *Darakai-Andwele* /Kak-uh ShTAH-kuh/ Dumb; shitty thing; useless (slang)

Kiataki *Pilar-Pilarese* /Kee-uh-ta-kee/ Sword-keeper

Kindred Bridge *Darakai* Historic natural stone bridge stained by the blood of ancestors past

Klödjen *Boreal-Boreali* /klode-Gen/ A wooden globe surrounded by a horizontal ring wide enough to hold a man; used in elementary training by the najjan

Kopar *Darakai* /Koh-PAR/ Sickle sword carried by the Darakaian military

Kuerre *Boreal-Boreali* /Koo-AIR/ Luxiron backsword; curved blade

Kurtfierï *Boreal-Boreali* /Kert-FYE-ree/ Courtship token; an article of the father's clothing or dress, typically worn by the suited

Kwihila rapiki mu jwona *Darakai-Andwele* /Kwih-hee-luh rah-pee-kee moo Jeh-wahn-uh/ Victory writes over fate

Làtoh Ché *Darakai-Andwele* /la-TOH Chay/ The City Nest

Lempeii *Pilar* /Lem-PAY/ Port city; station of the Orynthian navy

Linsilk *Boreal* Boreali fabric made of silk harvested from spiders around the banks of the Dönumn

Lu'Lycran *Boreal-Boreali* /Loo LIE-cran/ Little Lycran (nickname)

Lumin *Boreal* /Loo-men/ Sacred light energy native to the Boreali highlands

Lumilore *Boreal* /Loo-meh-Lore/ Lux-stone; lumin-infused stone gathered near the banks of the Dönumn

Luxiron *Boreal* Specialized najjani iron, forged in undiluted lumin; warm to the touch, prismatic in color, corrosive in nature, and lightweight; trade restricted

Luxsmith *Boreal* A najjani smithy, dedicated to the creation of Luxiron

Lycran *Boreal-Boreali* /LIE-kran/ Orallach fox-wolf (wolx) hybrid; genes enhanced by war-taint

Maji'maia *Darakai-Andwele* /Mah-zhee MY-ah/ Witchy-Moon (nickname); full moon

Mamu *Boreal-Boreali* /Mah-Moo/ Mommy; Mama

Mantle of the Fallen *Darakai* Historic cape constructed of ancient, bloodstained arrowheads; typically worn by the haidren to Darakai or the chief warlord

Mhàdda *Darakai-Andwele* /Mah-duh/ Mom (informal)

Marketown *Bastiion* Mass market within the streets of Bastiion's inner proper

Meh fyreon *Boreal-Boreali* /Meh Feer-ee-on/ I'm sorry; I apologize

Meh'dajjeni Dönumn, weh'dajjeni Lux *Boreal-Boreali* /Meh Dah-zhen-ee Doe-nuM, weh Dah-zhen-ee Lux/ My strength in the Gift, our strength for the Light

Motumbha *Darakai-Andwele* /Moh-TUM-buh/ Arrowball

Na huwàa tàkom lai na huwàa *Darakai-Andwele* /Nah hoo-ah tah-KOM lie nah hoo-ah/ It takes a hound to hunt a hound

Najjan *Boreal-Boreali* /Nah-zhahn/ Elusive sect of the warrior faction; elite Boreali warrior(s)

Ni yeye ràtomdai na wewe *Darakai-Andwele* /Nee yay-yay rah-tohm-dye nah way-way/ Do you claim rights to him/her/them/it

Niit *Boreal-Boreali* /Neet/ No

Orallach Mountains *Boreal* /Orr-uh-laK/ Range of frigid mountains; uninhabited

Orynthia /OR-in-thee-Uh/ Central kingdom comprised of four Houses; governed by the royal line of Thoarne and the Ethnicam

Outer Houses *Orynthia* Self-governed Houses on the outskirts of the Unitarian lands

Outer Proper *Bastiion* Royal land encircled by the noble provinces; the outskirts of the city of Bastiion

Owàa *Darakai-Andwele* /Oh-WAH/ The Sun (name)

Owàamo *Darakai-Andwele* /Oh-WAH-moe/ The Sun greets you (greeting)

Pammu *Darakai* /PAH-moo/ Fermented pam sap; brewed with beetles in the base of the bottle

Papyon *Darakai-Andwele* /Pap-ee-on/ Love; sex (slang)

Pipe Marrow *Bastiion* A highly pungent opiate often smoked in the tents of Marketown

Province *Bastiion* Land bestowed to the heads of the nobility and their heirs

Pryde *Darakai* Localized group of Darakaian militia

Pyō chakrit *Pilar-Pilarese* /Pie-oh cha-KREET/ Wisdom affirmed (statement of accord)

Pyō jien *Pilar-Pilarese* /Pie-oh JYEN/ Knowledge accepted (statement of accord)

Qondai *Darakai-Andwele* /Kon-Die/ To understand; to know

Quadren *Orynthia* The committee of advisors encircling each Orynthian ruler, consisting of one haidren from each House

Radials *Boreal* Hidden luxiron blades; worn as three-fingered rings; fan open when triggered

Rhàana ne'Etswégo *Darakai-Andwele* /RAH-na neh-et-SWAY-go/ Mantle of the Fallen

Rhaolé *Darakai-Andwele* /Ray-OH-lay/ Hurry; speed up

Rhaolé ono *Darakai-Andwele* /Ray-OH-lay OH-no/ Hurry faster

Roüwen *Boreal-Boreali* /Roe-OO-wen/ The village-fortress; capital of Boreal

Rul'Aniell *Boreal-Boreali* /Rool-AHn-ee-eL/ In and to Aniell

Rul'Lothadim Aniell *Boreal-Boreali* /Rool-Loth-uh-dim AHn-ee-eL/ All Glory in and to Aniell (formal declaration)

Se'lah Aurynth *Boreal-Boreali* /se-Lah Aur-rinth/ Until the shores of Aurynth

Shàla'maiamo *Darakai-Andwele* /Sha-lah my-AH-moe/ The Moon watch you (farewell)

Shamàli *Darakai-Andwele* /Sha-mah-lee/ If you see fit (in place of "please")

Shoto *Pilar-Pilarese* /ShOH-toe/ A philosopher or scholar; statesman dedicated to the pursuit of learning

Shoto'shi *Pilar-Pilarese* /ShOH-toe-shee/ A shoto acolyte; training in the ways of the Collective

Shoto Collective *Pilar-Pilarese* Pilarese congress of scholars and politicians

Shoto Prime *Pilar-Pilarese* Senior leader within the Shoto Collective

Shtàka *Bastiion-Unitarian* /ShTAH-kuh/ Shit (slang)

Shumabin *Darakai-Andwele* /SHOO-muh-bin/ Paladin's aloe

Solrahs *Boreal* /SOL-rahs/ Half-moon shaped septum piece made of luxiron; worn by the haidrens to Boreal

Tadöm *Boreal-Boreali* /tah-Dome/ Thank you

Tiergan *Boreal* /TARE-ghan/ Sacred bloodline of the haidrens to Boreal; direct descendants of Tiergan

Tredae'Aurynth *Boreal-Boreali* /Tred-AYE Aur-rinth/ Walk in Aurynth (parting)

Uni *Darakai-Andwele* /Oo-nee/ Yes

Uni zà *Darakai-Andwele* /Oo-nee Zah/ Yes (final; absolute)

Unitarian *Bastiion* Primary language spoken in the House of Bastiion and the Unitarian lands; general mixture of ancient languages, refined over time

Unitarians *Bastiion* Orynthian bloodline comprised from a blended ancestry from centuries past

Vàssa Ship *Bastiion-Unitarian* /Vaah-sa/ Leisure vessel

The Veiled Lady *Bastiion* Popular tavern and night den in Marketown owned by Salma Nabhu

Waedfrel *Boreal-Boreali* /Wade-frell/ Good; great; exemplary

War-taint *Orynthia* Residual, toxic poisoning as a result of the Forgotten Wars

War-tainted *Orynthia* An individual, animal, or land harboring the symptoms of war-taint

The Wastes *Orynthia* A barren, uninhabitable wasteland on the eastern side of the Yachel River

Wem *Boreal-Boreali* /whem/ Yes

Witchiron *Orynthia* Najjani weaponry (slang)

Wreath of Wisdom *Boreal* The ceremonial headdress passed from predecessor to successor during the haidren's Seating ceremony

Yancy *Bastiion-Unitarian* /Yan-see/ Universal slang for any wealthy Unitarians; the nobility

Yaya *Darakai-Andwele* /Yah-Yah/ Honey; an attractive woman (slang)

Yeh'maelim *Boreal-Boreali* /Yeh-may-lim/ Welcome to you

Ykah lö *Boreal-Boreali* /Eye-kuh Loe/ What; huh; come again

Yowekao *Darakai* /Yow-uh-KAY-oh/ Remote mountain tribe within the Andwele Mountains

Y'siti *Bastiion-Unitarian* /Yuh-ZEE-tee/ Filthy ice-witch (derogatory slang)

Zullee *Darakai-Andwele* /Zool-lee/ Accepted with honor (in place of "thank you")

Zwaàlu Ghopar *Darakai-Andwele* /Zwah-loo goh-PAR/ Kindred Bridge

THE HAIDREN LEGACY

MEH DAJJENI DÖNUMN, WEH DAJJENI LUX

TeamHaidren

For exclusive THL giveaways, events, and insider updates on Luscia, Zaethan, and Dmitri's adventures, subscribe to Orynthian missives by joining the #TeamHaidren Newsletter!

www.thehaidrenlegacy.com/contact

ACKNOWLEDGEMENTS

It will never cease to amaze me how something intangible, something completely and utterly imagined, holds the power to turn the tangible upside down.

Releasing *House of Bastiion* did just that. The year following summoned a wave of change I never saw coming, a wave that, too many times to admit, knocked me flat on my face. You see, commitment requires sacrifice. Not a one-time tax or exchange, but an ongoing outpour of one's best—the "special stuff"—buried deep inside. Authors bleed themselves onto their pages and often, from their bank accounts to do it. Since the inception of The Haidren Legacy, *House of Bastiion* taught me that creating has a cost—demanding time, emotional store, and perhaps the occasional chiropractic bill.

But it was *House of Darakai,* that taught me this cost is irrevocably worthwhile.

Over the course of the last twelve months, I've transported myself into a fabricated world of make-believe canvas, painting my fantastical imaginings onto every plane soaring around me. One of my key aims for *House of Darakai* was to create an almost 3-dimensional experience for the reader; to compose each string of words in such a way that you'd get lost in another land, with cultures, and politics, and a herbology nearly as vivid as those outside your window. At the end of it all, I didn't want to travel there alone. I wanted to bare every last drop of my expression and describe this world with the richest detail I possibly muster. To drape our story with excellence, granting it a fragrance that doesn't touch the nose. A melody that beats between lettering, not the ear. A motion picture that never meets the eye…

It's a tall feat, indeed. One I will never accomplish, not entirely. But as the insightful musician, Ryan O'Neal, from the band Sleeping At Last, proclaims in the song *One*, "I'm not saying perfect exists in this life, but we'll only know for certain if we try", I would never know how real Darakai could become unless I tried with every ounce of my fallible soul.

And from the depths of it, I hope that it shows.

House of Darakai is my proudest work to date. Not because it's my most recently published, but more frankly because this book is infused with my deepest joys. My boldest sorrows. And my bravest hopes for not only the world inside my head… but the one stirring it into motion.

There is one individual who ensured that stirring never ceased, and it is why the entire book is dedicated to her alone. Rory Gilson, the most steadfast fangirl and even dearer friend, picked up my banner years ago, never letting it touch the ground since. Even when it's heavy. When it's flawed. For whatever reason, Rory spends her bravery on me, donating it when my confidence dips. And oh, how it dips. Meeting me for margaritas, she reminds me that common sense ought to steer confidence, not the other way around. Like her dedication reads, Rory believed in what only I saw unfolding in my head. Her belief propels me still. It strengthens my resolve and sharpens my discernment. There is no denying that *House of Darakai* might never have coming into being, were it not for her many smiles over salted rims.

The cover encasing this book is barely mine for which to take credit. Fiona Jayde, our central artist, deserves a standing ovation. She has single-handedly gifted the THL universe with a recognizable and unforgettable brand. With her uncanny ability to weave my patchwork concepts into a masterpiece, I'm habitually blown away by her genius. Fiona is possibly the most integral member of my team, as most tend to pick up my books simply because of *her* work, not mine. Her artistry challenges me to be better, to be worthy of her investment. Fiona has prioritized me time and time again, well beyond my what my accreditations may or may not deserve. We, myself and this entire series, are blessed because she chose us, and despite her high demand, does still.

Beyond her unparalleled talents, another real credit goes to the people who inspired each textured bend and bow of the Darakaian mask on the cover of our book. The tribes and nations whose beautiful, under-celebrated, resilient cultures shaped nearly every aspect of my drafting:

From the Navajo to the Cherokee, the Sioux to the Seminole, and Anasazi to the Uros.

From the Bassa to the Bantu, the Yoruba to the Himba, and the Karo to the Zulu.

From my home of Detroit to the lessons of how glorious it is when people unabashedly come together...

Thank you for living a life more meaningful than artwork. And thank you for inspiring us to make it in your stunning shadow none-theless. May we never stop.

While Fiona's work continued to enthuse me deeper into my mind-scape, I could only travel there because Madeleine Booth-Smits was there to help. Hiring a PA so early in my career was quite possibly one of the best decisions I ever made. In accepting my troublesome inability to be social and productive at the same time, Madz protects me from the outside world. She shields my writing, and my recovery hours, from being wasted on excessive social media and networking endeavors. Things that are critical for publishing today, but are of little use when an author is too busy to actually publish. Like a yin yang, she has molded to my quirks and grants room for me to be myself. The process oversight and tasks Madz performs, allow me to stay where I thrive—tucked inside my dungeon-troll-of-an-office in the woods, away from literally everyone. And it's in that place, that *House of Darakai* came to be.

As an author, there are two recurring fears I face when publishing: the fear of never finishing a manuscript... and the even realer fear when I eventually do. It's then the story, no longer trapped in my mind, is presented naked and bare, full of its lovely shortcoming, for others to begin to critique. This is the reason writing is so terrifying—even my best needs polishing. It's a humbling, frustrating, yet reassuring paradox. No matter what I do, I need someone else's eye.

The first set of eyes to sweep these pages were my Betas. A huge thanks to each and every one of them. It's my Beta group who flag the special bits, the sacred unique things I need to safeguard from edits, be they my own or those of another. Betas carve out their time and mental energy, and invest it in a place which isn't real, for *me*, while getting nothing in return except that initial step into my realm. It's mind boggling, really. My Betas are imperative tools in my arsenal. They remind me what to love and what to release. This book and I both would be less without them.

Joining Team Haidren this year was our editor, Angie Wade. I'll admit, changing editors mid-series is pretty stressful… especially when it's unplanned. But Angie stepped in with ease and excellence. She adopted my intricate, possibly overcomplicated world, and embraced it like her own. I'll never forget that. She didn't try to undo it, or me for that matter. She just made all of us better. Because that's what it's like now, an entire troupe of bickering phantoms in my head, living at the mercy of my professional entanglements. Angie challenged me to take what was already working and showcase it better. She spent weeks chipping the unnecessary off our masterpiece so that readers like you could see it shine. Thank you, Angie, for accepting me the way I came—gigantic glossary and all. For becoming a fixture in my world, for putting your thumbprint wherever it needed to be, and holding it back wherever it did not. This series is stronger now, and so am I.

When a book is completed, it gratefully falls into the reliable hands of Brent Spears, my ever-patient formatter who performs miracles whilst owing me none. Appropriately dubbed "The Patron Saint of Interior Revisions", Brent is an imperative player on my publishing assembly line. His expertise, careful handling, and routine commitment to package my manuscripts with precision, have elevated my books beyond what anyone would ever expect from a no-name novice like me. The truth is... I'd be an absolute mess without Brent. Those are the facts.

During the drafting of *House of Darakai*, so many other members of Team Haidren were hard at work. Major thanks to Mary Toth for illustrating every deadly article of our new armory on the THL website, as well as more additions to the Apothic Catalog. To my character artists, Ana Damar, Steffani Christensen, and Nóra Ádámszki, thank you for your impassioned artistry in bringing fictional souls to bodily form. Your work is exquisite. I am continually blown away by the contracted and collaborative talent within the THL universe. It's not just my world anymore—it's ours.

This goes without saying, but I'll shout it from the rooftops anyways: Joseph Jacobson is a straight-up boss. While the book trailer for *House of Bastiion* exceeded every single person's expectation... *Darakai's* is on a whole different level. A level I could never achieve, or reach for myself, without Joseph showing me the way. As a cinematographer, he presented this book in the most epic light, but as a producer, gave the trailer a punch which truly sets it apart. Joseph has never considered THL a mere book series, but a vivid experience. He and his gifting prove that every time his video plays. I don't deserve him, or his labors, but he hears none of that, and instead continues to shower me with a praise not yet earned. Countless thanks to Joseph Jacobson Films for expressing his talent simply to showcase mine, just like Fleurie and Tommee Profitt, who granted us the rights to feature their track *Onward & Upward* in our trailer.

Outside of my own performance, and performance in collaboration with others, stands a tribe of confidantes. My unexpected friends who've scooped me up despite my inexperience and who wrapped me in their professional arms, blanketed me in their wisdom, their learnings, their advice... Thank you to the greats, who've sprinkled their greatness onto me: Sarah M. Cradit, Rebecca Garcia, Casey L. Bond, Angelina J. Steffort, and so many more. I need you guys. I really, really do.

As mentioned, I made some big changes this year. To pursue this adventure, this giant leap into hope and nothingness, I ended up walking away from a successful career in the corporate sector. And then when my part-time alternative still did not offer me the essential hours needed to complete my manuscript with diligence and distinction, I walked away from that too.

It was nerve-wracking.

It was unprecedented.

And it changed everything.

The people who convinced me to ultimately make that gut-wrenching decision were my parents—the two individuals who shaped me into the analytical creature I am today. Leaving my full-time position went against every principle for which I prided myself and preached to those under my influence. Why leave a prosperous career for a hobby? For six years, that's what I considered writing—a hobby. At best, it's a dream come true. At worst, an unfulfilling gamble. In publishing, the metrics don't always align right away. Success isn't as measurable as it is by traditional means. And boy, do I love metrics. I love how finite they are. I can count them. I can multiply them however I please to forecast the future. Hobbies, however, are not so controllable, or as guaranteed. And so, I kept this passion stifled under a label that made me feel safer, because then I couldn't really fail. All the while the hours kept compounding later into the night. Sleep got shorter. And days grew strained. Something had to go, for we can't have everything at once, and hobbies sit at the top of the chopping block. I knew what I had to do—what I might have to give up to restore a healthy balance. But life took a turn when my father, my pillar of reason, told me during one defining, tear-stricken phone call, "out of all your options, neglecting this book is not one of them".

Those words were branded on my heart that night, and it is from their etching that I will continue to write to the best of my ability. Because what I do is not a hobby. Not anymore.

It's a charge.

Finally, we come to the person I owe most of all. I've said on more than one occasion that I am the most blessed of women, but this year I've never meant it more. When positioned with the scary decision to leave my dependable day-job for something completely opposite, my husband, my very best friend, reached across the couch and holding my hand with unreserved resolve, said that we were meant to jump. And that his job, his *joy*, was to help me leap off an edge I couldn't let go of on my own. In that moment, and in all those that followed, Aaron bent his knee to my dream and called it his. There is nothing I can do, no ounce of willpower I can exhaust, that will earn that kind of unwarranted commitment.

Because that's love. It isn't earned. It's given freely and undeserved.

My words will forever fall short in describing this man. He is too big for the thickest thesaurus. Too real, too perfectly imperfect to define. This book may not be Aaron's creation, but the entire time it was coming to be, he was creating the environment of support I needed to see it through. There's a required selflessness to support... In that knowingly, he has intentionally evolved, made himself malleable, just so that I could stretch and grow. Just so that I might become more.

Thank you, Aaron. I love you more than anything—in this world or the imagined.

Lastly, I want to extend my sincerest gratitude to every unnamed cheerleader. And to you, for reading this very book. Years ago, you too were a figment of my imagination, yet here you are.

Never underestimate the intangible.

It has the power to turn the tangible upside down, if only we get out of the way and let it.

Throughout her life, K.L. Kolarich never expected to become a New-Adult epic fantasy author, nor one based out of Nashville, TN. But growing up in Metro Detroit, Kolarich developed a deep love for eclectic variety as well as the underappreciated. Both themes readily present throughout her series, The Haidren Legacy. An individual plagued by sarcasm, conviction, and an ever-present distraction of fable and lore, K.L. Kolarich dreams in the day and writes through the night. Often hearing her characters argue in the background, Kolarich stifles the daily temptation to abandon reality and lose herself in the realm of Orynthia. When fully present in the real world rather than another, Kolarich explores local waterfalls, habitually frequents the same Thai restaurant, adds to her ever-growing spice collection, and maintains a thoroughly messy kitchen for the sake of colorful vegan feasts. With too many cats and not nearly enough wine, Kolarich resides in the woods away from the noise, happily married.

CPSIA information can be obtained
at www.ICGtesting.com
Printed in the USA
JSHW050458250222
23276JS00001B/8

9 781735 460659